Dashiell Hammett

FIVE COMPLETE NOVELS

Dashiell Hammett

FIVE COMPLETE NOVELS

Red Harvest

The Dain Curse

The Maltese Falcon

The Glass Key

The Thin Man

AVENEL BOOKS · NEW YORK

This edition was previously published as
The Novels of Dashiell Hammett.

Copyright MCMXXVIII, MCMXXIX, MCMXXX, MCMXXXIII,
MCMXXXIV,
© MCMLXV by Alfred A. Knopf, Inc. Copyright Renewed MCMLVII,
MCMLVIII, MCMLIX, MCMLX, MCMLXI, MCMLXII by Dashiell Hammett

This edition is published by Avenel Books,
distributed by Crown Publishers, Inc.,
by arrangement with Alfred A. Knopf, Inc.
        e f g h
1980 EDITION

Manufactured in the United States of America

Library of Congress Cataloging in Publication Data

Hammett, Dashiell, 1894–1961

    Dashiell Hammett : five complete novels.

    Reprint of the ed. published by Knopf, New York,
under title: The novels of Dashiell Hammet.
    CONTENTS: Red harvest.—The Dain curse.—The Maltese
falcon.—[etc.]
    1. Detective and mystery stories, American.
[PS3515.A4347A6 1980]   813'.52   80-39931
ISBN 0-517-33841-6
ISBN 0-517-33628-6 (lib. bdg.)

CONTENTS

Dashiell Hammett was born in St. Mary's County, Maryland, on May 27, 1894. He died in Lenox Hill Hospital, New York City, in the early morning of January 10, 1961. We had met in 1930, but I was to see the writing of only one novel—*The Thin Man*. I have, and will perhaps someday publish, a part of a novel on which he had been working long before his death. I have been asked many times over the years why he did not write another novel after *The Thin Man*. I do not know. I think, but I only think, I know a few of the reasons: he wanted to do new kind of work; he was sick for many of those years and getting sicker. But he was a man who kept his work, and his plans for work, in angry privacy and even I would not have been answered if I had ever asked, and maybe because I never asked is why I was with him until the last day of his life. But five novels is no small amount to leave behind and I hope he would have been pleased that they are all together again.

Lillian Hellman

APRIL 1, 1965

Dashiell Hammett

FIVE COMPLETE NOVELS

RED HARVEST

TO JOSEPH THOMPSON SHAW

RED HARVEST

I · A Woman in Green and a Man in Gray

I first heard Personville called Poisonville by a red-haired mucker named Hickey Dewey in the Big Ship in Butte. He also called his shirt a shoit. I didn't think anything of what he had done to the city's name. Later I heard men who could manage their r's give it the same pronunciation. I still didn't see anything in it but the meaningless sort of humor that used to make richardsnary the thieves' word for dictionary. A few years later I went to Personville and learned better.

Using one of the phones in the station, I called the *Herald*, asked for Donald Willsson, and told him I had arrived.

"Will you come out to my house at ten this evening?" He had a pleasantly crisp voice. "It's 2101 Mountain Boulevard. Take a Broadway car, get off at Laurel Avenue, and walk two blocks west."

I promised to do that. Then I rode up to the Great Western Hotel, dumped my bags, and went out to look at the city.

The city wasn't pretty. Most of its builders had gone in for gaudiness. Maybe they had been successful at first. Since then the smelters whose brick stacks stuck up tall against a gloomy mountain to the south had yellow-smoked everything into uniform dinginess. The result was an ugly city of forty thousand people, set in an ugly notch between two ugly mountains that had been all dirtied up by mining. Spread over this was a grimy sky that looked as if it had come out of the smelters' stacks.

The first policeman I saw needed a shave. The second had a couple of buttons off his shabby uniform. The third stood in the center of the city's main intersection—Broadway and Union Street—directing traffic, with a cigar in one corner of his mouth. After that I stopped checking them up.

At nine-thirty I caught a Broadway car and followed the directions Donald Willsson had given me. They brought me to a house set in a hedged grassplot on a corner.

The maid who opened the door told me Mr. Willsson was not home. While I was explaining that I had an appointment with him a slender blonde woman of something less than thirty in green crêpe came to the door. When she smiled her blue eyes didn't lose their stoniness. I repeated my explanation to her.

"My husband isn't in now." A barely noticeable accent slurred her s's. "But if he's expecting you he'll probably be home shortly."

She took me upstairs to a room on the Laurel Avenue side of the house, a brown and red room with a lot of books in it. We sat in leather chairs, half facing each other, half facing a burning coal grate, and she set about learning my business with her husband.

"Do you live in Personville?" she asked first.

"No. San Francisco."

"But this isn't your first visit?"

"Yes."

"Really? How do you like our city?"

"I haven't seen enough of it to know." That was a lie. I had. "I got in only this afternoon."

Her shiny eyes stopped prying while she said:

"You'll find it a dreary place." She returned to her digging with: "I suppose all mining towns are like this. Are you engaged in mining?"

"Not just now."

She looked at the clock on the mantel and said:

"It's inconsiderate of Donald to bring you out here and then keep you waiting, at this time of night, long after business hours."

I said that was all right.

"Though perhaps it isn't a business matter," she suggested.

I didn't say anything.

She laughed—a short laugh with something sharp in it.

"I'm really not ordinarily so much of a busybody as you probably think," she said gaily. "But you're so excessively secretive that I can't help being curious. You aren't a bootlegger, are you? Donald changes them so often."

I let her get whatever she could out of a grin.

A telephone bell rang downstairs. Mrs. Willsson stretched her green-slippered feet out toward the burning coal and pretended she hadn't heard the bell. I didn't know why she thought that necessary.

She began: "I'm afraid I'll ha—" and stopped to look at the maid in the doorway.

The maid said Mrs. Willsson was wanted at the phone. She excused herself and followed the maid out. She didn't go downstairs, but spoke over an extension within earshot.

I heard: "Mrs. Willsson speaking. . . . Yes. . . . I beg your pardon? . . . Who? . . . Can't you speak a little louder? . . . *What?* . . . Yes. . . . Yes. . . . Who is this? . . . Hello! Hello!"

The telephone hook rattled. Her steps sounded down the hallway—rapid steps.

I set fire to a cigarette and stared at it until I heard her going down the steps. Then I went to a window, lifted an edge of the blind, and looked out at Laurel Avenue, and at the square white garage that stood in the rear of the house on that side.

Presently a slender woman in dark coat and hat came into sight hurrying from house to garage. It was Mrs. Willsson. She drove away in a Buick coupé. I went back to my chair and waited.

Three-quarters of an hour went by. At five minutes after eleven, automobile brakes screeched outside. Two minutes later Mrs. Willsson came into the room. She had taken off hat and coat. Her face was white, her eyes almost black.

"I'm awfully sorry," she said, her tight-lipped mouth moving jerkily, "but you've had all this waiting for nothing. My husband won't be home tonight."

I said I would get in touch with him at the *Herald* in the morning.

I went away wondering why the green toe of her left slipper was dark and damp with something that could have been blood.

∴

I walked over to Broadway and caught a street car. Three blocks north of my hotel I got off to see what the crowd was doing around a side entrance of the City Hall.

Thirty or forty men and a sprinkling of women stood on the sidewalk looking at a door marked *Police Department*. There were men from mines and smelters still in their working clothes, gaudy boys from pool rooms and dance halls, sleek men with slick pale faces, men with the dull look of respectable husbands, a few just as respectable and dull women, and some ladies of the night.

On the edge of this congregation I stopped beside a square-set man in rumpled gray clothes. His face was grayish too, even the thick lips, though he wasn't much older than thirty. His face was broad, thick-featured and intelligent. For color he depended on a red windsor tie that blossomed over his gray flannel shirt.

"What's the rumpus?" I asked him.

He looked at me carefully before he replied, as if he wanted to be sure that the information was going into safe hands. His eyes were gray as his clothes, but not so soft.

"Don Willsson's gone to sit on the right hand of God, if God don't mind looking at bullet holes."

"Who shot him?" I asked.

The gray man scratched the back of his neck and said:

"Somebody with a gun."

I wanted information, not wit. I would have tried my luck with some other member of the crowd if the red tie hadn't interested me. I said:

"I'm a stranger in town. Hang the Punch and Judy on me. That's what strangers are for."

"Donald Willsson, Esquire, publisher of the *Morning* and *Evening Heralds*, was found in Hurricane Street a little while ago, shot very dead by parties unknown," he recited in a rapid singsong. "Does that keep your feelings from being hurt?"

"Thanks." I put out a finger and touched a loose end of his tie. "Mean anything? Or just wearing it?"

"I'm Bill Quint."

"The hell you are!" I exclaimed, trying to place the name. "By God, I'm glad to meet you!"

I dug out my card case and ran through the collection of credentials I had picked up here and there by one means or another. The red card was the one I wanted. It identified me as Henry F. Neill, A. B. seaman, member in good standing of the Industrial Workers of the World. There wasn't a word of truth in it.

I passed this card to Bill Quint. He read it carefully, front and back, returned it to my hand, and looked me over from hat to shoes, not trustfully.

"He's not going to die any more," he said. "Which way you going?"

"Any."

We walked down the street together, turned a corner, aimlessly as far as I knew.

"What brought you in here, if you're a sailor?" he asked casually.

"Where'd you get that idea?"

"There's the card."

"I got another that proves I'm a timber beast," I said. "If you want me to be a miner I'll get one for that tomorrow."

"You won't. I run 'em here."

"Suppose you got a wire from Chi?" I asked.

"Hell with Chi! I run 'em here." He nodded at a restaurant door and asked: "Drink?"

"Only when I can get it."

We went through the restaurant, up a flight of steps, and into a narrow second-story room with a long bar and a row of tables. Bill Quint nodded and said, "Hullo!" to some of the boys and girls at tables and bar, and steered me into one of the green-curtained booths that lined the wall opposite the bar.

We spent the next two hours drinking whiskey and talking.

The gray man didn't think I had any right to the card I had showed him, nor to the other one I had mentioned. He didn't think I was a good wobbly. As chief muckademuck of the I. W. W. in Personville, he considered it his duty to get the low-down on me, and to not let himself be pumped about radical affairs while he was doing it.

That was all right with me. I was interested in Personville affairs. He didn't mind discussing them between casual pokings into my business with the red cards.

What I got out of him amounted to this:

For forty years old Elihu Willsson—father of the man who had been killed this night—had owned Personville, heart, soul, skin and guts. He was president and majority stockholder of the Personville Mining Corporation, ditto of the First National Bank, owner of the *Morning Herald* and *Evening Herald*, the city's only newspapers, and at least part owner of nearly every other enterprise of any importance. Along with these pieces of property he owned a United States senator, a couple of representatives, the governor, the mayor, and most of the state legislature. Elihu Willsson was Personville, and he was almost the whole state.

Back in the war days the I. W. W.—in full bloom then throughout the West—had lined up the Personville Mining Corporation's help. The help hadn't been exactly pampered. They used their new strength to demand the things they wanted. Old Elihu gave them what he had to give them, and bided his time.

In 1921 it came. Business was rotten. Old Elihu didn't care whether he shut down for a while or not. He tore up the agreements he had made with his men and began kicking them back into their pre-war circumstances.

Of course the help yelled for help. Bill Quint was sent out from I. W. W. headquarters in Chicago to give them some action. He was against a strike, an open walk-out. He advised the old sabotage racket, staying on the job and gumming things up from the inside. But that wasn't active enough for the Personville crew. They wanted to put themselves on the map, make labor history.

They struck.

The strike lasted eight months. Both sides bled plenty. The wobblies had to do their own bleeding. Old Elihu hired gunmen, strike-breakers, national guardsmen and even parts of the regular army, to do his. When the last skull had been cracked, the last rib kicked in, organized labor in Personville was a used firecracker.

But, said Bill Quint, old Elihu didn't know his Italian history. He won the strike, but he lost his hold on the city and the state. To beat the miners he had to let his hired thugs run wild. When the fight was over he couldn't get rid of them. He had given his city to them and he wasn't strong enough to take it away from them. Personville looked good to them and they took it over. They had won his strike for him and they took the city for their spoils. He couldn't openly break with them. They had too much on him. He was responsible for all they had done during the strike.

Bill Quint and I were both fairly mellow by the time we had got this far. He emptied his glass again, pushed his hair out of his eyes and brought his history up to date:

"The strongest of 'em now is probably Pete the Finn. This stuff we're drinking's his. Then there's Lew Yard. He's got a loan shop down on Parker Street, does a lot of bail bond business, handles most of the burg's hot stuff, so they tell me, and is pretty thick with Noonan, the chief of police. This kid Max Thaler—Whisper—has got a lot of friends too. A little slick dark guy with something wrong with his throat. Can't talk. Gambler. Those three, with Noonan, just about help Elihu run his city—help him more than he wants. But he's got to play with 'em or else—"

"This fellow who was knocked off tonight—Elihu's son—where did he stand?" I asked.

"Where papa put him, and he's where papa put him now."

"You mean the old man had him—?"

"Maybe, but that's not my guess. This Don just came home and began running the papers for the old man. It wasn't like the old devil, even if he was getting close to the grave, to let anybody cop anything from him without hitting back. But he had to be cagey with these guys. He brought the boy and his French wife home from Paris and used him for his monkey—a damned nice fatherly trick. Don starts a reform campaign in the papers. Clear the burg of vice and corruption—which means clear it of Pete and Lew and Whisper, if it goes far enough. Get it? The old man's using the boy to shake 'em loose. I guess they got tired of being shook."

"There seems to be a few things wrong with that guess," I said.

"There's more than a few things wrong with everything in this lousy burg. Had enough of this paint?"

I said I had. We went down to the street. Bill Quint told me he was living in the Miners' Hotel in Forest Street. His way home ran past my hotel, so we walked down together. In front of my hotel a beefy fellow with the look of a plain-clothes man stood on the curb and talked to the occupant of a Stutz touring car.

"That's Whisper in the car," Bill Quint told me.

I looked past the beefy man and saw Thaler's profile. It was young, dark and small, with pretty features as regular as if they had been cut by a die.

"He's cute," I said.

"Uh-huh," the gray man agreed, "and so's dynamite."

II · *The Czar of Poisonville*

THE *Morning Herald* gave two pages to Donald Willsson and his death. His picture showed a pleasant intelligent face with curly hair, smiling eyes and mouth, a cleft chin and a striped necktie.

The story of his death was simple. At ten-forty the previous night he had been shot four times in stomach, chest and back, dying immediately. The shooting had taken place in the eleven-hundred block of Hurricane Street. Residents of that block who looked out after hearing the shots saw the dead man lying on the sidewalk. A man and a woman were bending over him. The street was too dark for anyone to see anybody or anything clearly. The man and woman had disappeared before anybody else reached the street. Nobody knew what they looked like. Nobody had seen them go away.

Six shots had been fired at Willsson from a .32 calibre pistol. Two of them had missed him, going into the front wall of a house. Tracing the course of these two bullets, the police had learned that the shooting had been done from a narrow alley across the street. That was all anybody knew.

Editorially the *Morning Herald* gave a summary of the dead man's short career as a civic reformer and expressed a belief that he had been killed by some of the people who didn't want Personville cleaned up. The *Herald* said the chief of police could best show his own lack of complicity by speedily catching and convicting the murderer or murderers. The editorial was blunt and bitter.

I finished it with my second cup of coffee, jumped a Broadway car, dropped off at Laurel Avenue, and turned down toward the dead man's house.

I was half a block from it when something changed my mind and my destination.

A smallish young man in three shades of brown crossed the street ahead of me. His dark profile was pretty. He was Max Thaler, alias Whisper. I reached the corner of Mountain Boulevard in time to catch the flash of his brown-covered rear leg vanishing into the late Donald Willsson's doorway.

I went back to Broadway, found a drug store with a phone booth in it, searched the directory for Elihu Willsson's residence number, called it, told somebody who claimed to be the old man's secretary that I had been brought from San Francisco by Donald Willsson, that I knew something about his death, and that I wanted to see his father.

When I made it emphatic enough I got an invitation to call.

The czar of Poisonville was propped up in bed when his secretary—a noiseless slim sharp-eyed man of forty—brought me into the bedroom.

The old man's head was small and almost perfectly round under its close-cut crop of white hair. His ears were too small and plastered too flat to the sides of his head to spoil the spherical effect. His nose also was small, carrying down the curve of his bony forehead. Mouth and chin were straight lines chopping the sphere off. Below them a short thick neck ran down into white pajamas between square meaty shoulders. One of his arms was outside the covers, a short compact arm that ended in a thick-fingered blunt hand. His eyes were round, blue, small and watery. They looked as if they were hiding behind the watery film and under the bushy white brows only until the time came to jump out and grab something. He wasn't the sort of man whose pocket you'd try to pick unless you had a lot of confidence in your fingers.

He ordered me into a bedside chair with a two-inch jerk of his round head, chased the secretary away with another, and asked:

"What's this about my son?"

His voice was harsh. His chest had too much and his mouth too little to do with his words for them to be very clear.

"I'm a Continental Detective Agency operative, San Francisco branch," I told him. "A couple of days ago we got a check from your son and a letter asking that a man be sent here to do some work for him. I'm the man. He told me to come out to his house last night. I did, but he didn't show up. When I got downtown I learned he had been killed."

Elihu Willsson peered suspiciously at me and asked:

"Well, what of it?"

"While I was waiting your daughter-in-law got a phone message, went out, came back with what looked like blood on her shoe, and told me her husband wouldn't be home. He was shot at ten-forty. She went out at ten-twenty, came back at eleven-five."

The old man sat straight up in bed and called young Mrs. Willsson a flock of things. When he ran out of words of that sort he still had some breath left. He used it to shout at me:

"Is she in jail?"

I said I didn't think so.

He didn't like her not being in jail. He was nasty about it. He bawled a lot of things I didn't like, winding up with:

"What the hell are you waiting for?"

He was too old and too sick to be smacked. I laughed and said:

"For evidence."

"Evidence? What do you need? You've—"

"Don't be a chump," I interrupted his bawling. "Why should she kill him?"

"Because she's a French hussy! Because she—"

The secretary's frightened face appeared at the door.

"Get out of here!" the old man roared at it, and the face went.

"She jealous?" I asked before he could go on with his shouting. "And if you don't yell maybe I'll be able to hear you anyway. My deafness is a lot better since I've been eating yeast."

He put a fist on top of each hump his thighs made in the covers and pushed his square chin at me.

"Old as I am and sick as I am," he said very deliberately, "I've a great mind to get up and kick your behind."

I paid no attention to that, repeating:

"Was she jealous?"

"She was," he said, not yelling now, "and domineering, and spoiled, and suspicious, and greedy, and mean, and unscrupulous, and deceitful, and selfish, and damned bad—altogether damned bad!"

"Any reason for her jealousy?"

"I hope so," he said bitterly. "I'd hate to think a son of mine would be faithful to her. Though likely enough he was. He'd do things like that."

"But you don't know any reason why she should have killed him?"

"Don't know any reason?" He was bellowing again. "Haven't I been telling you that—"

"Yeah. But none of that means anything. It's kind of childish."

The old man flung the covers back from his legs and started to get out of bed. Then he thought better of it, raised his red face and roared:

"Stanley!"

The door opened to let the secretary glide in.

"Throw this bastard out!" his master ordered, waving a fist at me.

The secretary turned to me. I shook my head and suggested:

"Better get help."

He frowned. We were about the same age. He was weedy, nearly a head taller than I, but fifty pounds lighter. Some of my hundred and ninety pounds were fat, but not all of them. The secretary fidgeted, smiled apologetically, and went away.

"What I was about to say," I told the old man: "I intended talking to your son's wife this morning. But I saw Max Thaler go into the house, so I postponed my visit."

Elihu Willsson carefully pulled the covers up over his legs again, leaned his head back on the pillows, screwed his eyes up at the ceiling, and said:

"Hm-m-m, so that's the way it is, is it?"

"Mean anything?"

"She killed him," he said certainly. "That's what it means."

Feet made noises in the hall, huskier feet than the secretary's. When they were just outside the door I began a sentence:

"You were using your son to run a—"

"Get out of here!" the old man yelled at those in the doorway. "And keep that door closed." He glowered at me and demanded: "What was I using my son for?"

"To put the knife in Thaler, Yard and the Finn."

"You're a liar."

"I didn't invent the story. It's all over Personville."

"It's a lie. I gave him the papers. He did what he wanted with them."

"You ought to explain that to your playmates. They'd believe you."

"What they believe be damned! What I'm telling you is so."

"What of it? Your son won't come back to life just because he was killed by mistake—if he was."

"That woman killed him."

"Maybe."

"Damn you and your maybes! She did."

"Maybe. But the other angle has got to be looked into too—the political end. You can tell me—"

"I can tell you that that French hussy killed him, and I can tell you that any other damned numbskull notions you've got are way off the lode."

"But they've got to be looked into," I insisted. "And you know the inside of Personville politics better than anyone else I'm likely to find. He was your son. The least you can do is—"

"The least I can do," he bellowed, "is tell you to get to hell back to Frisco, you and your numbskull—"

I got up and said unpleasantly:

"I'm at the Great Western Hotel. Don't bother me unless you want to talk sense for a change."

I went out of the bedroom and down the stairs. The secretary hovered around the bottom step, smiling apologetically.

"A fine old rowdy," I growled.

"A remarkably vital personality," he murmured.

∴

At the office of the *Herald*, I hunted up the murdered man's secretary. She was a small girl of nineteen or twenty with wide chestnut eyes, light brown hair and a pale pretty face. Her name was Lewis.

She said she hadn't known anything about my being called to Personville by her employer.

"But then," she explained, "Mr. Willsson always liked to keep everything to himself as long as he could. It was— I don't think he trusted anybody here, completely."

"Not you?"

She flushed and said:

"No. But of course he had been here such a short while and didn't know any of us very well."

"There must have been more to it than that."

"Well," she bit her lip and made a row of forefinger prints down the polished edge of the dead man's desk, "his father wasn't—wasn't in sympathy with what he was doing. Since his father really owned the papers, I suppose it was natural for Mr. Donald to think some of the employes might be more loyal to Mr. Elihu than to him."

"The old man wasn't in favor of the reform campaign? Why did he stand for it, if the papers were his?"

She bent her head to study the finger prints she had made. Her voice was low.

"It's not easy to understand unless you know— The last time Mr. Elihu was taken sick he sent for Donald—Mr. Donald. Mr. Donald had lived in Europe most of his life, you know. Dr. Pride told Mr. Elihu that he'd have to give up the management of his affairs, so he cabled his son to come home. But when Mr. Donald got here Mr. Elihu couldn't make up his mind to let go of everything. But he wanted Mr. Donald to stay here, so he gave him the newspapers—that is, made him publisher. Mr. Donald liked that. He had been interested in journalism in Paris. When he found out how terrible everything was here—in civic affairs and so on—he started that reform campaign. He didn't know—he had been away since he was a boy—he didn't know—"

"He didn't know his father was in it as deep as anybody else," I helped her along.

She squirmed a little over her examination of the finger prints, didn't contradict me, and went on:

"Mr. Elihu and he had a quarrel. Mr. Elihu told him to stop stirring things up, but he wouldn't stop. Maybe he would have stopped if he had known—all there was to know. But I don't suppose it would ever have occurred to him that his father was really seriously implicated. And his father wouldn't tell him. I suppose it would be hard for a father to tell a son a thing like that. He threatened to take the papers away from Mr. Donald. I don't know whether he intended to or not. But he was taken sick again, and everything went along as it did."

"Donald Willsson didn't confide in you?" I asked.

"No." It was almost a whisper.

"Then you learned all this where?"

"I'm trying—trying to help you learn who murdered him," she said earnestly. "You've no right to—"

"You'll help me most just now by telling me where you learned all this," I insisted.

She stared at the desk, chewing her lower lip. I waited. Presently she said:

"My father is Mr. Willsson's secretary."

"Thanks."

"But you mustn't think that we—"

"It's nothing to me," I assured her. "What was Willsson doing in Hurricane Street last night when he had a date with me at his house?"

She said she didn't know. I asked her if she had heard him tell me, over the phone, to come to his house at ten o'clock. She said she had.

"What did he do after that? Try to remember every least thing that was said and done from then until you left at the end of the day."

She leaned back in her chair, shut her eyes and wrinkled her forehead.

"You called up—if it was you he told to come to his house—at about two o'clock. After that Mr. Donald dictated some letters, one to a paper mill, one to Senator Keefer about some changes in post office regulations, and— Oh, yes! He went out for about twenty minutes, a little before three. And before he went he wrote out a check."

"Who for?"

"I don't know, but I saw him writing it."

"Where's his check book? Carry it with him?"

"It's here." She jumped up, went around to the front of his desk, and tried the top drawer. "Locked."

I joined her, straightened out a wire clip, and with that and a blade of my knife fiddled the drawer open.

The girl took out a thin, flat First National Bank check book. The last used stub was marked $5,000. Nothing else. No name. No explanation.

"He went out with this check," I said, "and was gone twenty minutes? Long enough to get to the bank and back?"

"It wouldn't have taken him more than five minutes to get there."

"Didn't anything else happen before he wrote out the check? Think. Any messages? Letters? Phone calls?"

"Let's see." She shut her eyes again. "He was dictating some mail and— Oh, how stupid of me! He did have a phone call. He said: 'Yes, I can be there at ten, but I shall have to hurry away.' Then again he said: 'Very well, at ten.' That was all he said except, 'Yes, yes,' several times."

"Talking to a man or a woman?"

"I didn't know."

"Think. There'd be a difference in his voice."

She thought and said:

"Then it was a woman."

"Which of you—you or he—left first in the evening?"

"I did. He— I told you my father is Mr. Elihu's secretary. He and Mr. Donald had an engagement for the early part of the evening—something about the paper's finances. Father came in a little after five. They were going to dinner together, I think."

That was all the Lewis girl could give me. She knew nothing that would explain Willsson's presence in the eleven-hundred block of Hurricane Street, she said. She admitted knowing nothing about Mrs. Willsson.

We frisked the dead man's desk, and dug up nothing in any way informative. I went up against the girls at the switchboard, and learned nothing. I put in an hour's work on messengers, city editors, and the like, and my pumping brought up nothing. The dead man, as his secretary said, had been a good hand at keeping his affairs to himself.

III · *Dinah Brand*

AT the First National Bank I got hold of an assistant cashier named Albury, a nice-looking blond youngster of twenty-five or so.

"I certified the check for Willsson," he said after I had explained what I was up to. "It was drawn to the order of Dinah Brand—$5,000."

"Know who she is?"

"Oh, yes! I know her."

"Mind telling me what you know about her?"

"Not at all. I'd be glad to, but I'm already eight minutes overdue at a meeting with—"

"Can you have dinner with me this evening and give it to me then?"

"That'll be fine," he said.

"Seven o'clock at the Great Western?"

"Righto."

"I'll run along and let you get to your meeting, but tell me, has she an account here?"

"Yes, and she deposited the check this morning. The police have it."

"Yeah? And where does she live?"

"1232 Hurricane Street."

I said: "Well, well!" and, "See you tonight," and went away.

My next stop was in the office of the chief of police, in the City Hall. Noonan, the chief, was a fat man with twinkling greenish eyes set in a round jovial face. When I told him what I was doing in his city he seemed glad of it. He gave me a hand-shake, a cigar and a chair.

"Now," he said when we were settled, "tell me who turned the trick."

"The secret's safe with me."

"You and me both," he said cheerfully through smoke. "But what do you guess?"

"I'm no good at guessing, especially when I haven't got the facts."

" 'Twon't take long to give you all the facts there is," he said. "Wills-son got a five-grand check in Dinah Brand's name certified yesterday just before bank closing. Last night he was killed by slugs from a .32 less than a block from her house. People that heard the shooting saw a man and a woman bending over the remains. Bright and early this morning the said Dinah Brand deposits the said check in the said bank. Well?"

"Who is this Dinah Brand?"

The chief dumped the ash off his cigar in the center of his desk, flourished the cigar in his fat hand, and said:

"A soiled dove, as the fellow says, a de luxe hustler, a big-league gold-digger."

"Gone up against her yet?"

"No. There's a couple of slants to be taken care of first. We're keep-ing an eye on her and waiting. This I've told you is under the hat."

"Yeah. Now listen to this," and I told him what I had seen and heard while waiting in Donald Willsson's house the previous night.

When I had finished the chief bunched his fat mouth, whistled softly, and exclaimed:

"Man, that's an interesting thing you've been telling me! So it was blood on her slipper? And she said her husband wouldn't be home?"

"That's what I took it for," I said to the first question, and, "Yeah," to the second.

"Have you done any talking to her since then?" he asked.

"No. I was up that way this morning, but a young fellow named Thaler went into the house ahead of me, so I put off my visit."

"Grease us twice!" His greenish eyes glittered happily. "Are you tell-ing me the Whisper was there?"

"Yeah."

He threw his cigar on the floor, stood up, planted his fat hands on the desk top, and leaned over them toward me, oozing delight from every pore.

"Man, you've done something," he purred. "Dinah Brand is this Whisper's woman. Let's me and you just go out and kind of talk to the widow."

∴

We climbed out of the chief's car in front of Mrs. Willsson's residence. The chief stopped for a second with one foot on the bottom step to look at the black crêpe hanging over the bell. Then he said, "Well, what's got to be done has got to be done," and we went up the steps.

Mrs. Willsson wasn't anxious to see us, but people usually see the chief of police if he insists. This one did. We were taken upstairs to where Donald Willsson's widow sat in the library. She was in black. Her blue eyes had frost in them.

Noonan and I took turns mumbling condolences and then he began:

"We just wanted to ask you a couple of questions. For instance, like where'd you go last night?"

She looked disagreeably at me, then back to the chief, frowned, and spoke haughtily:

"May I ask why I am being questioned in this manner?"

I wondered how many times I had heard that question, word for word and tone for tone, while the chief, disregarding it, went on amiably:

"And then there was something about one of your shoes being stained. The right one, or maybe the left. Anyways it was one or the other."

A muscle began twitching in her upper lip.

"Was that all?" the chief asked me. Before I could answer he made a clucking noise with his tongue and turned his genial face to the woman again. "I almost forgot. There was a matter of how you knew your husband wouldn't be home."

She got up, unsteadily, holding the back of her chair with one white hand.

"I'm sure you'll excuse—"

"'S all right." The chief made a big-hearted gesture with one beefy paw. "We don't want to bother you. Just where you went, and about the shoe, and how you knew he wasn't coming back. And, come to think of it, there's another— What Thaler wanted here this morning."

Mrs. Willsson sat down again, very rigidly. The chief looked at her. A smile that tried to be tender made funny lines and humps in his fat face. After a little while her shoulders began to relax, her chin went lower, a curve came in her back.

I put a chair facing her and sat on it.

"You'll have to tell us, Mrs. Willsson," I said, making it as sympathetic as I could. "These things have got to be explained."

"Do you think I have anything to hide?" she asked defiantly, sitting up straight and stiff again, turning each word out very precisely, except that the s's were a bit slurred. "I did go out. The stain was blood. I knew my husband was dead. Thaler came to see me about my husband's death. Are your questions answered now?"

"We knew all that," I said. "We're asking you to explain them."

She stood up again, said angrily:

"I dislike your manner. I refuse to submit to—"

Noonan said:

"That's perfectly all right, Mrs. Willsson, only we'll have to ask you to go down to the Hall with us."

She turned her back to him, took a deep breath and threw words at me:

"While we were waiting here for Donald I had a telephone call. It was a man who wouldn't give his name. He said Donald had gone to the home of a woman named Dinah Brand with a check for five thousand dollars.

He gave me her address. Then I drove out there and waited down the street in the car until Donald came out.

"While I was waiting there I saw Max Thaler, whom I knew by sight. He went to the woman's house, but didn't go in. He went away. Then Donald came out and walked down the street. He didn't see me. I didn't want him to. I intended to drive home—get here before he came. I had just started the engine when I heard the shots, and I saw Donald fall. I got out of the car and ran over to him. He was dead. I was frantic. Then Thaler came. He said if I were found there they would say I had killed him. He made me run back to the car and drive home."

Tears were in her eyes. Through the water her eyes studied my face, apparently trying to learn how I took the story. I didn't say anything. She asked:

"Is that what you wanted?"

"Practically," Noonan said. He had walked around to one side. "What did Thaler say this afternoon?"

"He urged me to keep quiet." Her voice had become small and flat. "He said either or both of us would be suspected if anyone learned we were there, because Donald had been killed coming from the woman's house after giving her money."

"Where did the shots come from?" the chief asked.

"I don't know. I didn't see anything—except—when I looked up—Donald falling."

"Did Thaler fire them?"

"No," she said quickly. Then her mouth and eyes spread. She put a hand to her breast. "I don't know. I didn't think so, and he said he didn't. I don't know where he was. I don't know why I never thought he might have."

"What do you think now?" Noonan asked.

"He—he may have."

The chief winked at me, an athletic wink in which all his facial muscles took part, and cast a little farther back:

"And you don't know who called you up?"

"He wouldn't tell me his name."

"Didn't recognize his voice?"

"No."

"What kind of voice was it?"

"He talked in an undertone, as if afraid of being overheard. I had difficulty understanding him."

"He whispered?" The chief's mouth hung open as the last sound left it. His greenish eyes sparkled greedily between their pads of fat.

"Yes, a hoarse whisper."

The chief shut his mouth with a click, opened it again to say persuasively:

"You've heard Thaler talk. . . ."

The woman started and stared big-eyed from the chief to me.

"It was he," she cried. "It was he."

∴

Robert Albury, the young assistant cashier of the First National Bank, was sitting in the lobby when I returned to the Great Western Hotel. We went up to my room, had some ice-water brought, used its ice to put chill in Scotch, lemon juice, and grenadine, and then went down to the dining room.

"Now tell me about the lady," I said when we were working on the soup.

"Have you seen her yet?" he asked.

"Not yet."

"But you've heard something about her?"

"Only that she's an expert in her line."

"She is," he agreed. "I suppose you'll see her. You'll be disappointed at first. Then, without being able to say how or when it happened, you'll find you've forgotten your disappointment, and the first thing you know you'll be telling her your life's history, and all your troubles and hopes." He laughed with boyish shyness. "And then you're caught, absolutely caught."

"Thanks for the warning. How'd you come by the information?"

He grinned shamefacedly across his suspended soup spoon and confessed:

"I bought it."

"Then I suppose it cost you plenty. I hear she likes *dinero*."

"She's money-mad, all right, but somehow you don't mind it. She's so thoroughly mercenary, so frankly greedy, that there's nothing disagreeable about it. You'll understand what I mean when you know her."

"Maybe. Mind telling me how you happened to part with her?"

"No, I don't mind. I spent it all, that's how."

"Cold-blooded like that?"

His face flushed a little. He nodded.

"You seem to have taken it well," I said.

"There was nothing else to do." The flush in his pleasant young face deepened and he spoke hesitantly. "It happens I owe her something for it. She—I'm going to tell you this. I want you to see this side of her. I had a little money. After that was gone— You must remember I was young and head over heels. After my money was gone there was the bank's. I had— You don't care whether I had actually done anything or was simply thinking about it. Anyway, she found it out. I never could hide anything from her. And that was the end."

"She broke off with you?"

"Yes, thank God! If it hadn't been for her you might be looking for me now—for embezzlement. I owe her that!" He wrinkled his forehead earnestly. "You won't say anything about this—you know what I mean. But I wanted you to know she has her good side too. You'll hear enough about the other."

"Maybe she has. Or maybe it was just that she didn't think she'd get enough to pay for the risk of being caught in a jam."

He turned this over in his mind and then shook his head.

"That may have had something to do with it, but not all."

"I gathered she was strictly pay-as-you-enter."

"How about Dan Rolff?" he asked.

"Who's he?"

"He's supposed to be her brother, or half-brother, or something of the sort. He isn't. He's a down-and-outer—t. b. He lives with her. She keeps him. She's not in love with him or anything. She simply found him somewhere and took him in."

"Any more?"

"There was that radical chap she used to run around with. It's not likely she got much money out of him."

"What radical chap?"

"He came here back during the strike—Quint is his name."

"So he was on her list?"

"That's supposed to be the reason he stayed here after the strike was over."

"So he's still on her list?"

"No. She told me she was afraid of him. He had threatened to kill her."

"She seems to have had everybody on her string at one time or another," I said.

"Everybody she wanted," he said, and he said it seriously.

"Donald Willsson was the latest?" I asked.

"I don't know," he said. "I had never heard anything about them, had never seen anything. The chief of police had us try to find any checks he may have issued to her before yesterday, but we found nothing. Nobody could remember ever having seen any."

"Who was her last customer, so far as you know?"

"Lately I've seen her around town quite often with a chap named Thaler—he runs a couple of gambling houses here. They call him Whisper. You've probably heard of him."

∴

At eight-thirty I left young Albury and set out for the Miner's Hotel in Forest Street. Half a block from the hotel I met Bill Quint.

"Hello!" I hailed him. "I was on my way down to see you."

He stopped in front of me, looked me up and down, growled:
"So you're a gum-shoe."

"That's the bunk," I complained. "I come all the way down here to
rope you, and you're smarted up."

"What do you want to know now?" he asked.

"About Donald Willsson. You knew him, didn't you?"

"I knew him."

"Very well?"

"No."

"What did you think of him?"

He pursed his gray lips, by forcing breath between them made a noise
like a rag tearing, and said:

"A lousy liberal."

"You know Dinah Brand?" I asked.

"I know her." His neck was shorter and thicker than it had been.

"Think she killed Willsson?"

"Sure. It's a kick in the pants."

"Then you didn't?"

"Hell, yes," he said, "the pair of us together. Got any more questions?"

"Yeah, but I'll save my breath. You'd only lie to me."

I walked back to Broadway, found a taxi, and told the driver to take
me to 1232 Hurricane Street.

IV · *Hurricane Street*

My destination was a gray frame cottage. When I rang the
bell the door was opened by a thin man with a tired face that had no
color in it except a red spot the size of a half-dollar high on each cheek.
This, I thought, is the lunger Dan Rolff.

"I'd like to see Miss Brand," I told him.

"What name shall I tell her?" His voice was a sick man's and an educated man's.

"It wouldn't mean anything to her. I want to see her about Willsson's
death."

He looked at me with level tired dark eyes and said:

"Yes?"

"I'm from the San Francisco office of the Continental Detective
Agency. We're interested in the murder."

"That's nice of you," he said ironically. "Come in."

I went in, into a ground-floor room where a young woman sat at a table that had a lot of papers on it. Some of the papers were financial service bulletins, stock and bond market forecasts. One was a racing chart.

The room was disorderly, cluttered up. There were too many pieces of furniture in it, and none of them seemed to be in its proper place.

"Dinah," the lunger introduced me, "this gentleman has come from San Francisco on behalf of the Continental Detective Agency to inquire into Mr. Donald Willsson's demise."

The young woman got up, kicked a couple of newspapers out of her way, and came to me with one hand out.

She was an inch or two taller than I, which made her about five feet eight. She had a broad-shouldered, full-breasted, round-hipped body and big muscular legs. The hand she gave me was soft, warm, strong. Her face was the face of a girl of twenty-five already showing signs of wear. Little lines crossed the corners of her big ripe mouth. Fainter lines were beginning to make nets around her thick-lashed eyes. They were large eyes, blue and a bit blood-shot.

Her coarse hair—brown—needed trimming and was parted crookedly. One side of her upper lip had been rouged higher than the other. Her dress was of a particularly unbecoming wine color, and it gaped here and there down one side, where she had neglected to snap the fasteners or they had popped open. There was a run down the front of her left stocking.

This was the Dinah Brand who took her pick of Poisonville's men, according to what I had been told.

"His father sent for you, of course," she said while she moved a pair of lizard-skin slippers and a cup and saucer off a chair to make room for me.

Her voice was soft, lazy.

I told her the truth:

"Donald Willsson sent for me. I was waiting to see him while he was being killed."

"Don't go away, Dan," she called to Rolff.

He came back into the room. She returned to her place at the table. He sat on the opposite side, leaning his thin face on a thin hand, looking at me without interest.

She drew her brows together, making two creases between them, and asked:

"You mean he knew someone meant to kill him?"

"I don't know. He didn't say what he wanted. Maybe just help in the reform campaign."

"But do you—?"

I made a complaint:

"It's no fun being a sleuth when somebody steals your stuff, does all the questioning."

"I like to find out what's going on," she said, a little laugh gurgling down in her throat.

"I'm that way too. For instance, I'd like to know why you made him have the check certified."

Very casually, Dan Rolff shifted in his chair, leaning back, lowering his thin hands out of sight below the table's edge.

"So you found out about that?" Dinah Brand asked. She crossed left leg over right and looked down. Her eyes focussed on the run in her stocking. "Honest to God, I'm going to stop wearing them!" she complained. "I'm going barefooted. I paid five bucks for these socks yesterday. Now look at the damned things. Every day—runs, runs, runs!"

"It's no secret," I said. "I mean the check, not the runs. Noonan's got it."

She looked at Rolff, who stopped watching me long enough to nod once.

"If you talked my language," she drawled, looking narrow-eyed at me, "I might be able to give you some help."

"Maybe if I knew what it was."

"Money," she explained, "the more the better. I like it."

I became proverbial:

"Money saved is money earned. I can save you money and grief."

"That doesn't mean anything to me," she said, "though it sounds like it's meant to."

"The police haven't asked you anything about the check?"

She shook her head, no.

I said:

"Noonan's figuring on hanging the rap on you as well as on Whisper."

"Don't scare me," she lisped. "I'm only a child."

"Noonan knows that Thaler knew about the check. He knows that Thaler came here while Willsson was here, but didn't get in. He knows that Thaler was hanging around the neighborhood when Willsson was shot. He knows that Thaler and a woman were seen bending over the dead man."

The girl picked up a pencil from the table and thoughtfully scratched her cheek with it. The pencil made little curly black lines over the rouge.

Rolff's eyes had lost their weariness. They were bright, feverish, fixed on mine. He leaned forward, but kept his hands out of sight below the table.

"Those things," he said, "concern Thaler, not Miss Brand."

"Thaler and Miss Brand aren't strangers," I said. "Willsson brought a five-thousand-dollar check here, and was killed leaving. That way, Miss Brand might have had trouble cashing it—if Willsson hadn't been thoughtful enough to get it certified."

"My God!" the girl protested, "if I'd been going to kill him I'd have done it in here where nobody could have seen it, or waited until he got out of sight of the house. What kind of a dumb onion do you take me for?"

"I'm not sure you killed him," I said. "I'm just sure that the fat chief means to hang it on you."

"What are you trying to do?" she asked.

"Learn who killed him. Not who could have or might have, but who did."

"I could give you some help," she said, "but there'd have to be something in it for me."

"Safety," I reminded her, but she shook her head.

"I mean it would have to get me something in a financial way. It'd be worth something to you, and you ought to pay something, even if not a fortune."

"Can't be done." I grinned at her. "Forget the bank roll and go in for charity. Pretend I'm Bill Quint."

Dan Rolff started up from his chair, lips white as the rest of his face. He sat down again when the girl laughed—a lazy, good-natured laugh.

"He thinks I didn't make any profit out of Bill, Dan." She leaned over and put a hand on my knee. "Suppose you knew far enough ahead that a company's employes were going to strike, and when, and then far enough ahead when they were going to call the strike off. Could you take that info and some capital to the stock market and do yourself some good playing with the company's stock? You bet you could!" she wound up triumphantly. "So don't go around thinking that Bill didn't pay his way."

"You've been spoiled," I said.

"What in the name of God's the use of being so tight?" she demanded. "It's not like it had to come out of your pocket. You've got an expense account, haven't you?"

I didn't say anything. She frowned at me, at the run in her stocking, and at Rolff. Then she said to him:

"Maybe he'd loosen up if he had a drink."

The thin man got up and went out of the room.

She pouted at me, prodded my shin with her toe, and said:

"It's not so much the money. It's the principle of the thing. If a girl's got something that's worth something to somebody, she's a boob if she doesn't collect."

I grinned.

"Why don't you be a good guy?" she begged.

Dan Rolff came in with a siphon, a bottle of gin, some lemons, and a bowl of cracked ice. We had a drink apiece. The lunger went away. The girl and I wrangled over the money question while we had more drinks. I kept trying to keep the conversation on Thaler and Willsson. She kept switching it to the money she deserved. It went on that way until the gin bottle was empty. My watch said one-fifteen.

She chewed a piece of lemon peel and said for the thirtieth or forti-eth time:

"It won't come out of your pocket. What do you care?"

"It's not the money," I said, "it's the principle of the thing."

She made a face at me and put her glass where she thought the table was. She was eight inches wrong. I don't remember if the glass broke when it hit the floor, or what happened to it. I do remember that I was encouraged by her missing the table.

"Another thing," I opened up a new argumentative line, "I'm not sure I really need whatever you can tell me. If I have to get along without it, I think I can."

"It'll be nice if you can, but don't forget I'm the last person who saw him alive, except whoever killed him."

"Wrong," I said. "His wife saw him come out, walk away, and fall."

"His wife!"

"Yeah. She was sitting in a coupé down the street."

"How did she know he was here?"

"She says Thaler phoned her that her husband had come here with the check."

"You're trying to kid me," the girl said. "Max couldn't have known it."

"I'm telling you what Mrs. Willsson told Noonan and me."

The girl spit what was left of the lemon peel out on the floor, further disarranged her hair by running her fingers through it, wiped her mouth with the back of her hand, and slapped the table.

"All right, Mr. Knowitall," she said, "I'm going to play with you. You can think it's not going to cost you anything, but I'll get mine before we're through. You think I won't?" she challenged me, peering at me as if I were a block away.

This was no time to revive the money argument, so I said: "I hope you do." I think I said it three or four times, quite earnestly.

"I will. Now listen to me. You're drunk, and I'm drunk, and I'm just exactly drunk enough to tell you anything you want to know. That's the kind of girl I am. If I like a person I'll tell them anything they want to know. Just ask me. Go ahead, ask me."

I did:

"What did Willsson give you five thousand dollars for?"

"For fun." She leaned back to laugh. Then: "Listen. He was hunting for scandal. I had some of it, some affidavits and things that I thought might be good for a piece of change some day. I'm a girl that likes to pick up a little jack when she can. So I had put these things away. When Donald began going after scalps I let him know that I had these things, and that they were for sale. I gave him enough of a peep at them to let him know they were good. And they were good. Then we talked how much. He wasn't as tight as you—nobody ever was—but he was a little bit close. So the bargain hung fire, till yesterday.

"Then I gave him the rush, phoned him and told him I had another customer for the stuff and that if he wanted it he'd have to show up that night with either five thousand smacks in cash or a certified check. That was hooey, but he hadn't been around much, so he fell for it."

"Why ten o'clock?" I asked.

"Why not? That's as good a time as any other. The main thing on a deal like that is to give them a definite time. Now you want to know why it had to be cash or a certified check? All right, I'll tell you. I'll tell you anything you want to know. That's the kind of girl I am. Always was."

She went on that way for five minutes, telling me in detail just which and what sort of a girl she was, and always had been, and why. I yes-yes'd her until I got a chance to cut in with:

"All right, now why did it have to be a certified check?"

She shut one eye, waggled a forefinger at me, and said:

"So he couldn't stop payment. Because he couldn't have used the stuff I sold him. It was good, all right. It was too good. It would have put his old man in jail with the rest of them. It would have nailed Papa Elihu tighter than anyone else."

I laughed with her while I tried to keep my head above the gin I had guzzled.

"Who else would it nail?" I asked.

"The whole damned lot of them." She waved a hand. "Max, Lew Yard, Pete, Noonan, and Elihu Willsson—the whole damned lot of them."

"Did Max Thaler know what you were doing?"

"Of course not—nobody but Donald Willsson."

"Sure of that?"

"Sure I'm sure. You don't think I was going around bragging about it ahead of time, do you?"

"Who do you think knows about it now?"

"I don't care," she said. "It was only a joke on him. He couldn't have used the stuff."

"Do you think the birds whose secrets you sold will see anything funny in it? Noonan's trying to hang the killing on you and Thaler. That means he found the stuff in Donald Willsson's pocket. They all thought old Elihu was using his son to break them, didn't they?"

"Yes, sir," she said, "and I'm one who thinks the same thing."

"You're probably wrong, but that doesn't matter. If Noonan found the things you sold Donald Willsson in his pocket, and learned you had sold them to him, why shouldn't he add that up to mean that you and your friend Thaler had gone over to old Elihu's side?"

"He can see that old Elihu would be hurt as much as anybody else."

"What was this junk you sold him?"

"They built a new City Hall three years ago," she said, "and none of them lost any money on it. If Noonan got the papers he'll pretty soon find out that they tied as much on old Elihu, or more, than on anybody else."

"That doesn't make any difference. He'll take it for granted that the old man had found an out for himself. Take my word for it, sister, Noonan and his friends think you and Thaler and Elihu are double-crossing them."

"I don't give a damn what they think," she said obstinately. "It was only a joke. That's all I meant it for. That's all it was."

"That's good," I growled. "You can go to the gallows with a clear conscience. Have you seen Thaler since the murder?"

"No, but Max didn't kill him, if that's what you think, even if he was around."

"Why?"

"Lots of reasons. First place, Max wouldn't have done it himself. He'd have had somebody else do it, and he'd have been way off with an alibi nobody could shake. Second place, Max carries a .38, and anybody he sent to do the job would have had that much gun or more. What kind of a gunman would use a .32?"

"Then who did it?"

"I've told you all I know," she said. "I've told you too much."

I stood up and said:

"No, you've told me just exactly enough."

"You mean you think you know who killed him?"

"Yeah, though there's a couple of things I'll have to cover before I make the pinch."

"Who? Who?" She stood up, suddenly almost sober, tugging at my lapels. "Tell me who did it."

"Not now."

"Be a good guy."

"Not now."

She let go my lapels, put her hands behind her, and laughed in my face.

"All right. Keep it to yourself—and try to figure out which part of what I told you is the truth."

I said:

"Thanks for the part that is, anyhow, and for the gin. And if Max Thaler means anything to you, you ought to pass him the word that Noonan's trying to rib him."

V · *Old Elihu Talks Sense*

It was close to two-thirty in the morning when I reached the hotel. With my key the night clerk gave me a memorandum that asked me to call Poplar 605. I knew the number. It was Elihu Willsson's.

"When did this come?" I asked the clerk.

"A little after one."

That sounded urgent. I went back to a booth and put in the call. The old man's secretary answered, asking me to come out at once. I promised to hurry, asked the clerk to get me a taxi, and went up to my room for a shot of Scotch.

I would rather have been cold sober, but I wasn't. If the night held more work for me I didn't want to go to it with alcohol dying in me. The snifter revived me a lot. I poured more of the King George into a flask, pocketed it, and went down to the taxi.

Elihu Willsson's house was lighted from top to bottom. The secretary opened the front door before I could get my finger on the button. His thin body was shivering in pale blue pajamas and dark blue bathrobe. His thin face was full of excitement.

"Hurry!" he said. "Mr. Willsson is waiting. And, please, will you try to persuade him to let us have the body removed?"

I promised and followed him up to the old man's bedroom.

Old Elihu was in bed as before, but now a black automatic pistol lay on the covers close to one of his pink hands.

As soon as I appeared he took his head off the pillows, sat upright and barked at me:

"Have you got as much guts as you've got gall?"

His face was an unhealthy dark red. The film was gone from his eyes. They were hard and hot.

I let his question wait while I looked at the corpse on the floor between door and bed.

A short thick-set man in brown lay on his back with dead eyes staring at the ceiling from under the visor of a gray cap. A piece of his jaw had been knocked off. His chin was tilted to show where another bullet had gone through tie and collar to make a hole in his neck. One arm was bent under him. The other hand held a blackjack as big as a milk bottle. There was a lot of blood.

I looked up from this mess to the old man. His grin was vicious and idiotic.

"You're a great talker," he said. "I know that. A two-fisted, you-be-damned man with your words. But have you got anything else? Have you got the guts to match your gall? Or is it just the language you've got?"

There was no use in trying to get along with the old boy. I scowled and reminded him:

"Didn't I tell you not to bother me unless you wanted to talk sense for a change?"

"You did, my lad." There was a foolish sort of triumph in his voice. "And I'll talk you your sense. I want a man to clean this pig-sty of a Poisonville for me, to smoke out the rats, little and big. It's a man's job. Are you a man?"

"What's the use of getting poetic about it?" I growled. "If you've got a fairly honest piece of work to be done in my line, and you want to pay a decent price, maybe I'll take it on. But a lot of foolishness about smoking rats and pig-pens doesn't mean anything to me."

"All right. I want Personville emptied of its crooks and grafters. Is that plain enough language for you?"

"You didn't want it this morning," I said. "Why do you want it now?"

The explanation was profane and lengthy and given to me in a loud and blustering voice. The substance of it was that he had built Personville brick by brick with his own hands and he was going to keep it or wipe it off the side of the hill. Nobody could threaten him in his own city, no matter who they were. He had let them alone, but when they started telling him, Elihu Willsson, what he had to do and what he couldn't do, he would show them who was who. He brought the speech to an end by pointing at the corpse and boasting:

"That'll show them there's still a sting in the old man."

I wished I were sober. His clowning puzzled me. I couldn't put my finger on the something behind it.

"Your playmates sent him?" I asked, nodding at the dead man.

"I only talked to him with this," he said, patting the automatic on the bed, "but I reckon they did."

"How did it happen?"

"It happened simple enough. I heard the door opening, and I switched on the light, and there he was, and I shot him, and there he is."

"What time?"

"It was about one o'clock."

"And you've let him lie there all this time?"

"That I have." The old man laughed savagely and began blustering again: "Does the sight of a dead man turn your stomach? Or is it his spirit you're afraid of?"

I laughed at him. Now I had it. The old boy was scared stiff. Fright was the something behind his clowning. That was why he blustered, and why he wouldn't let them take the body away. He wanted it there to look at, to keep panic away, visible proof of his ability to defend himself. I knew where I stood.

"You really want the town cleaned up?" I asked.

"I said I did and I do."

"I'd have to have a free hand—no favors to anybody—run the job as I pleased. And I'd have to have a ten-thousand-dollar retainer."

"Ten thousand dollars! Why in hell should I give that much to a man I don't know from Adam? A man who's done nothing I know of but talk?"

"Be serious. When I say *me*, I mean the Continental. You know them."

"I do. And they know me. And they ought to know I'm good for—"

"That's not the idea. These people you want taken to the cleaners were friends of yours yesterday. Maybe they will be friends again next week. I don't care about that. But I'm not playing politics for you. I'm not hiring out to help you kick them back in line—with the job being called off then. If you want the job done you'll plank down enough money to pay for a complete job. Any that's left over will be returned to you. But you're going to get a complete job or nothing. That's the way it'll have to be. Take it or leave it."

"I'll damned well leave it," he bawled.

He let me get half-way down the stairs before he called me back.

"I'm an old man," he grumbled. "If I was ten years younger—" He glared at me and worked his lips together. "I'll give you your damned check."

"And authority to go through with it in my own way?"

"Yes."

"We'll get it done now. Where's your secretary?"

Willsson pushed a button on his bedside table and the silent secretary appeared from wherever he had been hiding. I told him:

"Mr. Willsson wants to issue a ten-thousand-dollar check to the Continental Detective Agency, and he wants to write the Agency—San Francisco branch—a letter authorizing the Agency to use the ten thousand dollars investigating crime and political corruption in Personville. The letter is to state clearly that the Agency is to conduct the investigation as it sees fit."

The secretary looked questioningly at the old man, who frowned and ducked his round white head.

"But first," I told the secretary as he glided toward the door, "you'd better phone the police that we've got a dead burglar here. Then call Mr. Willsson's doctor."

The old man declared he didn't want any damned doctors.

"You're going to have a nice shot in the arm so you can sleep," I promised him, stepping over the corpse to take the black gun from the bed. "I'm going to stay here tonight and we'll spend most of tomorrow sifting Poisonville affairs."

The old man was tired. His voice, when he profanely and somewhat long-windedly told me what he thought of my impudence in deciding what was best for him, barely shook the windows.

I took off the dead man's cap for a better look at his face. It didn't mean anything to me. I put the cap back in place.

When I straightened up the old man asked, moderately:

"Are you getting anywhere in your hunt for Donald's murderer?"

"I think so. Another day ought to see it finished."

"Who?" he asked.

The secretary came in with the letter and the check. I gave them to the old man instead of an answer to his question. He put a shaky signature on each, and I had them folded in my pocket when the police arrived.

.·.

The first copper into the room was the chief himself, fat Noonan. He nodded amiably at Willsson, shook hands with me, and looked with twinkling greenish eyes at the dead man.

"Well, well," he said. "It's a good job he did, whoever did it. Yakima Shorty. And will you look at the sap he's toting?" He kicked the blackjack out of the dead man's hand. "Big enough to sink a battleship. You drop him?" he asked me.

"Mr. Willsson."

"Well, that certainly is fine," he congratulated the old man. "You saved a lot of people a lot of troubles, including me. Pack him out, boys," he said to the four men behind him.

The two in uniform picked Yakima Shorty up by legs and arm-pits and went away with him, while one of the others gathered up the blackjack and a flashlight that had been under the body.

"If everybody did that to their prowlers, it would certainly be fine," the chief babbled on. He brought three cigars out of a pocket, threw one over on the bed, stuck one at me, and put the other in his mouth. "I was just wondering where I could get hold of you," he told me as we lighted up. "I got a little job ahead that I thought you'd like to be in on. That's how I happened to be on tap when the rumble came." He put his mouth close to my ear and whispered: "Going to pick up Whisper. Want to go along?"

"Yeah."

"I thought you would. Hello, Doc!"

He shook hands with a man who had just come in, a little plump man with a tired oval face and gray eyes that still had sleep in them.

The doctor went to the bed, where one of Noonan's men was asking Willsson about the shooting. I followed the secretary into the hall and asked him:

"Any men in the house besides you?"

"Yes, the chauffeur, the Chinese cook."

"Let the chauffeur stay in the old man's room tonight. I'm going out with Noonan. I'll get back as soon as I can. I don't think there'll be any more excitement here, but no matter what happens don't leave the old man alone. And don't leave him alone with Noonan or any of Noonan's crew."

The secretary's mouth and eyes popped wide.

"What time did you leave Donald Willsson last night?" I asked.

"You mean night before last, the night he was killed?"

"Yeah."

"At precisely half-past nine."

"You were with him from five o'clock till then?"

"From a quarter after five. We went over some statements and that sort of thing in his office until nearly eight o'clock. Then we went to Bayard's and finished our business over our dinners. He left at half-past nine, saying he had an engagement."

"What else did he say about this engagement?"

"Nothing else."

"Didn't give you any hint of where he was going, who he was going to meet?"

"He merely said he had an engagement."

"And you didn't know anything about it?"

"No. Why? Did you think I did?"

"I thought he might have said something." I switched back to tonight's doings: "What visitors did Willsson have today, not counting the one he shot?"

"You'll have to pardon me," the secretary said, smiling apologetically, "I can't tell you that without Mr. Willsson's permission. I'm sorry."

"Weren't some of the local powers here? Say Lew Yard, or—"

The secretary shook his head, repeating:

"I'm sorry."

"We won't fight over it," I said, giving it up and starting back toward the bedroom door.

The doctor came out, buttoning his overcoat.

"He will sleep now," he said hurriedly. "Someone should stay with him. I shall be in in the morning." He ran downstairs.

I went into the bedroom. The chief and the man who had questioned Willsson were standing by the bed. The chief grinned as if he were glad to see me. The other man scowled. Willsson was lying on his back, staring at the ceiling.

"That's about all there is here," Noonan said. "What say we mosey along?"

I agreed and said, "Good-night," to the old man. He said, "Good-night," without looking at me. The secretary came in with the chauffeur, a tall sunburned young husky.

The chief, the other sleuth—a police lieutenant named McGraw—and I went downstairs and got into the chief's car. McGraw sat beside the driver. The chief and I sat in back.

"We'll make the pinch along about daylight," Noonan explained as we rode. "Whisper's got a joint over on King Street. He generally leaves there along about daylight. We could crash the place, but that'd mean gun-play, and it's just as well to take it easy. We'll pick him up when he leaves."

I wondered if he meant pick him up or pick him off. I asked:

"Got enough on him to make the rap stick?"

"Enough?" He laughed good-naturedly. "If what the Willsson dame give us ain't enough to stretch him I'm a pickpocket."

I thought of a couple of wisecrack answers to that. I kept them to myself.

VI · Whisper's Joint

OUR ride ended under a line of trees in a dark street not far from the center of town. We got out of the car and walked down to the corner.

A burly man in a gray overcoat, with a gray hat pulled down over his eyes, came to meet us.

"Whisper's hep," the burly man told the chief. "He phoned Donohoe that he's going to stay in his joint. If you think you can pull him out, try it, he says."

Noonan chuckled, scratched an ear, and asked pleasantly:

"How many would you say was in there with him?"

"Fifty, anyhow."

"Aw, now! There wouldn't be that many, not at this time of morning."

"The hell there wouldn't," the burly man snarled. "They been drifting in since midnight."

"Is that so? A leak somewheres. Maybe you oughtn't to have let them in."

"Maybe I oughtn't." The burly man was angry. "But I did what you told me. You said let anybody go in or out that wanted to, but when Whisper showed to—"

"To pinch him," the chief said.

"Well, yes," the burly man agreed, looking savagely at me.

More men joined us and we held a talk-fest. Everybody was in a bad humor except the chief. He seemed to enjoy it all. I didn't know why.

Whisper's joint was a three-story brick building in the middle of the block, between two two-story buildings. The ground floor of his joint was occupied by a cigar store that served as entrance and cover for the gambling establishment upstairs. Inside, if the burly man's information was to be depended on, Whisper had collected half a hundred friends, loaded for a fight. Outside, Noonan's force was spread around the building, in the street in front, in the alley in back, and on the adjoining roofs.

"Well, boys," the chief said amiably after everybody had had his say, "I don't reckon Whisper wants trouble any more than we do, or he'd have tried to shoot his way out before this, if he's got that many with him, though I don't mind saying I don't think he has—not that many."

The burly man said: "The hell he ain't."

"So if he don't want trouble," Noonan went on, "maybe talking might do some good. You run over, Nick, and see if you can't argue him into being peaceable."

The burly man said: "The hell I will."

"Phone him, then," the chief suggested.

The burly man growled: "That's more like it," and went away.

When he came back he looked completely satisfied.

"He says," he reported, " 'Go to hell.' "

"Get the rest of the boys down here," Noonan said cheerfully. "We'll knock it over as soon as it gets light."

The burly Nick and I went around with the chief while he made sure his men were properly placed. I didn't think much of them—a shabby, shifty-eyed crew without enthusiasm for the job ahead of them.

The sky became a faded gray. The chief, Nick, and I stopped in a plumber's doorway diagonally across the street from our target.

Whisper's joint was dark, the upper windows blank, blinds down over cigar store windows and door.

"I hate to start this without giving Whisper a chance," Noonan said. "He's not a bad kid. But there's no use me trying to talk to him. He never did like me much."

He looked at me. I said nothing.

"You wouldn't want to make a stab at it?" he asked.

"Yeah, I'll try it."

"That's fine of you. I'll certainly appreciate it if you will. You just see if you can talk him into coming along without any fuss. You know what to say—for his own good and all that, like it is."

"Yeah," I said and walked across to the cigar store, taking pains to let my hands be seen swinging empty at my sides.

Day was still a little way off. The street was the color of smoke. My feet made a lot of noise on the pavement.

I stopped in front of the door and knocked the glass with a knuckle, not heavily. The green blind down inside the door made a mirror of the glass. In it I saw two men moving up the other side of the street.

No sound came from inside. I knocked harder, then slid my hand down to rattle the knob.

Advice came from indoors:

"Get away from there while you're able."

It was a muffled voice, but not a whisper, so probably not Whisper's.

"I want to talk to Thaler," I said.

"Go talk to the lard-can that sent you."

"I'm not talking for Noonan. Is Thaler where he can hear me?"

A pause. Then the muffled voice said: "Yes."

"I'm the Continental op who tipped Dinah Brand off that Noonan was framing you," I said. "I want five minutes' talk with you. I've got nothing to do with Noonan except to queer his racket. I'm alone. I'll drop my rod in the street if you say so. Let me in."

I waited. It depended on whether the girl had got to him with the story of my interview with her. I waited what seemed a long time.

The muffled voice said:

"When we open, come in quick. And no stunts."

"All set."

The latch clicked. I plunged in with the door.

Across the street a dozen guns emptied themselves. Glass shot from door and windows tinkled around us.

Somebody tripped me. Fear gave me three brains and half a dozen eyes. I was in a tough spot. Noonan had slipped me a pretty dose. These birds couldn't help thinking I was playing his game.

I tumbled down, twisting around to face the door. My gun was in my hand by the time I hit the floor.

Across the street, burly Nick had stepped out of a doorway to pump slugs at us with both hands.

I steadied my gun-arm on the floor. Nick's body showed over the front sight. I squeezed the gun. Nick stopped shooting. He crossed his guns on his chest and went down in a pile on the sidewalk.

Hands on my ankles dragged me back. The floor scraped pieces off my chin. The door slammed shut. Some comedian said:

"Uh-huh, people don't like you."

I sat up and shouted through the racket:

"I wasn't in on this."

The shooting dwindled, stopped. Door and window blinds were dotted with gray holes. A husky whisper said in the darkness:

"Tod, you and Slats keep an eye on things down here. The rest of us might as well go upstairs."

We went through a room behind the store, into a passageway, up a flight of carpeted steps, and into a second-story room that held a green table banked for crap-shooting. It was a small room, had no windows, and the lights were on.

There were five of us. Thaler sat down and lit a cigarette, a small dark young man with a face that was pretty in a chorusman way until you took another look at the thin hard mouth. An angular blond kid of no more than twenty in tweeds sprawled on his back on a couch and blew cigarette smoke at the ceiling. Another boy, as blond and as young, but not so angular, was busy straightening his scarlet tie, smoothing his yellow hair. A thin-faced man of thirty with little or no chin under a wide loose mouth wandered up and down the room looking bored and humming *Rosy Cheeks*.

I sat in a chair two or three feet from Thaler's.

"How long is Noonan going to keep this up?" he asked. There was no emotion in his hoarse whispering voice, only a shade of annoyance.

"He's after you this trip," I said. "I think he's going through with it."

The gambler smiled a thin, contemptuous smile.

"He ought to know what a swell chance he's got of hanging a one-legged rap like that on me."

"He's not figuring on proving anything in court," I said.

"No?"

"You're to be knocked off resisting arrest, or trying to make a get-away. He won't need much of a case after that."

"He's getting tough in his old age." The thin lips curved in another smile. He didn't seem to think much of the fat chief's deadliness. "Any time he rubs me out I deserve rubbing. What's he got against you?"

"He's guessed I'm going to make a nuisance of myself."

"Too bad. Dinah told me you were a pretty good guy, except kind of Scotch with the roll."

"I had a nice visit. Will you tell me what you know about Donald Willsson's killing?"

"His wife plugged him."

"You saw her?"

"I saw her the next second—with the gat in her hand."

"That's no good to either of us," I said. "I don't know how far you've got it cooked. Rigged right, you could make it stick in court, maybe, but you'll not get a chance to make your play there. If Noonan takes you at all he'll take you stiff. Give me the straight of it. I only need that to pop the job."

He dropped his cigarette on the floor. mashed it under his foot, and asked:

"You that hot?"

"Give me your slant on it and I'm ready to make the pinch—if I can get out of here."

He lit another cigarette and asked:

"Mrs. Willsson said it was me that phoned her?"

"Yeah—after Noonan had persuaded her. She believes it now—maybe."

"You dropped Big Nick," he said. "I'll take a chance on you. A man phoned me that night. I don't know him, don't know who he was. He said Willsson had gone to Dinah's with a check for five grand. What the hell did I care? But, see, it was funny somebody I didn't know cracked it to me. So I went around. Dan stalled me away from the door. That was all right. But still it was funny as hell that guy phoned me.

"I went up the street and took a plant in a vestibule. I saw Mrs. Willsson's heap standing in the street, but I didn't know then that it was hers or that she was in it. He came out pretty soon and walked down the street. I didn't see the shots. I heard them. Then this woman jumps out of the heap and runs over to him. I knew she hadn't done the shooting. I ought to have beat it. But it was all funny as hell, so when I saw the woman was Willsson's wife I went over to them, trying to find out what it was all about. That was a break, see? So I had to make an out for myself, in case something slipped. I strung the woman. That's the whole damned works—on the level."

"Thanks," I said. "That's what I came for. Now the trick is to get out of here without being mowed down."

"No trick at all," Thaler assured me. "We go any time we want to."

"I want to now. If I were you, I'd go too. You've got Noonan pegged as a false-alarm, but why take a chance? Make the sneak and keep under cover till noon, and his frame-up will be a wash-out."

Thaler put his hand in his pants pocket and brought out a fat roll of paper money. He counted off a hundred or two, some fifties, twenties, tens, and held them out to the chinless man, saying:

"Buy us a get-away, Jerry, and you don't have to give anybody any more dough than he's used to."

Jerry took the money, picked up a hat from the table, and strolled out. Half an hour later he returned and gave some of the bills back to Thaler, saying casually:

"We wait in the kitchen till we get the office."

We went down to the kitchen. It was dark there. More men joined us.

Presently something hit the door.

Jerry opened the door and we went down three steps into the back yard. It was almost full daylight. There were ten of us in the party.

"This all?" I asked Thaler.

He nodded.

"Nick said there were fifty of you."

"Fifty of us to stand off that crummy force!" he sneered.

A uniformed copper held the back gate open, muttering nervously: "Hurry it up, boys, please."

I was willing to hurry, but nobody else paid any attention to him.

We crossed an alley, were beckoned through another gate by a big man in brown, passed through a house, out into the next street, and climbed into a black automobile that stood at the curb.

One of the blond boys drove. He knew what speed was.

I said I wanted to be dropped off somewhere in the neighborhood of the Great Western Hotel. The driver looked at Whisper, who nodded. Five minutes later I got out in front of my hotel.

"See you later," the gambler whispered, and the car slid away.

The last I saw of it was its police department license plate vanishing around a corner.

VII · *That's Why I Sewed You Up*

It was half-past five. I walked around a few blocks until I came to an unlighted electric sign that said *Hotel Crawford*, climbed a flight of steps to the second-floor office, registered, left a call for ten o'clock, was shown into a shabby room, moved some of the Scotch from my flask to my stomach, and took old Elihu's ten-thousand-dollar check and my gun to bed with me.

At ten I dressed, went up to the First National Bank, found young Albury, and asked him to certify Willsson's check for me. He kept me waiting a while. I suppose he phoned the old man's residence to find out if the check was on the up-and-up. Finally he brought it back to me, properly scribbled on.

I sponged an envelope, put the old man's letter and check in it, addressed it to the Agency in San Francisco, stuck a stamp on it, and went out and dropped it in the mail-box on the corner.

Then I returned to the bank and said to the boy:

"Now tell me why you killed him."

He smiled and asked:

"Cock Robin or President Lincoln?"

"You're not going to admit off-hand that you killed Donald Willsson?"

"I don't want to be disagreeable," he said, still smiling, "but I'd rather not."

"That's going to make it bad," I complained. "We can't stand here and argue very long without being interrupted. Who's the stout party with cheaters coming this way?"

The boy's face pinkened. He said:

"Mr. Dritton, the cashier."

"Introduce me."

The boy looked uncomfortable, but he called the cashier's name. Dritton—a large man with a smooth pink face, a fringe of white hair around an otherwise bald pink head, and rimless nose glasses—came over to us.

The assistant cashier mumbled the introductions. I shook Dritton's hand without losing sight of the boy.

"I was just saying," I addressed Dritton, "that we ought to have a more private place to talk in. He probably won't confess till I've worked on him a while, and I don't want everybody in the bank to hear me yelling at him."

"Confess?" The cashier's tongue showed between his lips.

"Sure." I kept my face, voice and manner bland, mimicking Noonan. "Didn't you know that Albury is the fellow who killed Donald Willsson?"

A polite smile at what he thought an asinine joke started behind the cashier's glasses, and changed to puzzlement when he looked at his assistant. The boy was rouge-red and the grin he was forcing his mouth to wear was a terrible thing.

Dritton cleared his throat and said heartily:

"It's a splendid morning. We've been having splendid weather."

"But isn't there a private room where we can talk?" I insisted.

Dritton jumped nervously and questioned the boy:

"What—what is this?"

Young Albury said something nobody could have understood.

I said: "If there isn't I'll have to take him down to the City Hall."

Dritton caught his glasses as they slid down his nose, jammed them back in place and said:

"Come back here."

We followed him down the length of the lobby, through a gate, and into an office whose door was labeled *President*—old Elihu's office. Nobody was in it.

I motioned Albury into one chair and picked another for myself. The cashier fidgeted with his back against the desk, facing both of us.

"Now, sir, will you explain this," he said.

"We'll get around to that," I told him and turned to the boy. "You're an ex-boy-friend of Dinah's who was given the air. You're the only one who knew her intimately who could have known about the certified check in time to phone Mrs. Willsson and Thaler. Willsson was shot with a .32. Banks like that caliber. Maybe the gun you used wasn't a bank gun, but I think it was. Maybe you didn't put it back. Then there'll be one missing. Anyway I'm going to have a gun expert put his microscopes and micrometers on the bullets that killed Willsson and bullets fired from all the bank guns."

The boy looked calmly at me and said nothing. He had himself under control again. That wouldn't do. I had to be nasty. I said:

"You were cuckoo over the girl. You confessed to me that it was only because she wouldn't stand for it that you didn't—"

"Don't—please don't," he gasped. His face was red again.

I made myself sneer at him until his eyes went down. Then I said:

"You talked too much, son. You were too damned anxious to make your life an open book for me. That's a way you amateur criminals have. You've always got to overdo the frank and open business."

He was watching his hands. I let him have the other barrel:

"You know you killed him. You know if you used a bank gun, and if you put it back. If you did you're nailed now, without an out. The gun-sharks will take care of that. If you didn't, I'm going to nail you anyhow. All right. I don't have to tell you whether you've got a chance or not. You know.

"Noonan is framing Whisper Thaler for the job. He can't convict him, but the frame-up is tight enough that if Thaler's killed resisting arrest, the chief will be in the clear. That's what he means to do—kill Thaler. Thaler stood off the police all night in his King Street joint. He's still standing them off—unless they've got to him. The first copper that gets to him—exit Thaler.

"If you figure you've got a chance to beat your rap, and you want to let another man be killed on your account, that's your business. But if you know you haven't got a chance—and you haven't if the gun can be found—for God's sake give Thaler one by clearing him."

"I'd like," Albury's voice was an old man's. He looked up from his hands, saw Dritton, said, "I'd like," again and stopped.

"Where is the gun?" I asked.

"In Harper's cage," the boy said.

I scowled at the cashier and asked him:

"Will you get it?"

He went out as if he were glad to go.

"I didn't mean to kill him," the youngster said. "I don't think I meant to."

I nodded encouragingly, trying to look solemnly sympathetic.

"I don't think I meant to kill him," he repeated, "though I took the gun with me. You were right about my being cuckoo over Dinah—then. It was worse some days than others. The day Willsson brought the check in was one of the bad ones. All I could think about was that I had lost her because I had no more money, and he was taking five thousand dollars to her. It was the check. Can you understand that? I had known that she and Thaler were—you know. If I had learned that Willsson and she were too, without seeing the check, I wouldn't have done anything. I'm sure of it. It was seeing the check—and knowing I'd lost her because my money was gone.

"I watched her house that night and saw him go in. I was afraid of what I might do, because it was one of the bad days, and I had the gun in my pocket. Honestly I didn't want to do anything. I was afraid. I couldn't think of anything but the check, and why I had lost her. I knew Willsson's wife was jealous. Everybody knew that. I thought if I called her up and told her— I don't know exactly what I thought, but I went to a store around the corner and phoned her. Then I phoned Thaler. I wanted them there. If I could have thought of anyone else who had anything to do with either Dinah or Willsson I'd have called them too.

"Then I went back and watched Dinah's house again. Mrs. Willsson came, and then Thaler, and both of them stayed there, watching the house. I was glad of that. With them there I wasn't so afraid of what I might do. After a while Willsson came out and walked down the street. I looked up at Mrs. Willsson's car and at the doorway where I knew Thaler was. Neither of them did anything, and Willsson was walking away. I knew then why I had wanted them there. I had hoped they would do something—and I wouldn't have to. But they didn't, and he was walking away. If one of them had gone over and said something to him, or even followed him, I wouldn't have done anything.

"But they didn't. I remember taking the gun out of my pocket. Everything was blurred in front of my eyes, like I was crying. Maybe I was. I don't remember shooting—I mean I don't remember deliberately aiming and pulling the trigger—but I can remember the sound the shots made, and that I knew the noise was coming from the gun in my hand. I don't remember how Willsson looked, if he fell before I turned and ran up the alley, or not. When I got home I cleaned and reloaded the pistol, and put it back in the paying teller's cage the next morning."

∴

On the way down to the City Hall with the boy and the gun I apologized for the village cut-up stuff I had put in the early part of the shake-down, explaining:

"I had to get under your skin, and that was the best way I knew. The way you'd talked about the girl showed me you were too good an actor to be broken down by straight hammering."

He winced, and said slowly:

"That wasn't acting, altogether. When I was in danger, facing the gallows, she didn't—didn't seem so important to me. I couldn't—I can't now—quite understand—fully—why I did what I did. Do you know what I mean? That somehow makes the whole thing—and me—cheap. I mean, the whole thing from the beginning."

I couldn't find anything to say except something meaningless, like: "Things happen that way."

In the chief's office we found one of the men who had been on the storming party the night before—a red-faced official named Biddle. He goggled at me with curious gray eyes, but asked no questions about the King Street doings.

Biddle called in a young lawyer named Dart from the prosecuting attorney's office. Albury was repeating his story to Biddle, Dart and a stenographer, when the chief of police, looking as if he had just crawled out of bed, arrived.

"Well, it certainly is fine to see you," Noonan said, pumping my hand up and down while patting my back. "By God! you had a narrow one last night—the rats! I was dead sure they'd got you till we kicked in the doors and found the joint empty. Tell me how those son-of-a-guns got out of there."

"A couple of your men let them out the back door, took them through the house in back, and sent them away in a department car. They took me along so I couldn't tip you off."

"A couple of my men did that?" he asked, with no appearance of surprise. "Well, well! What kind of looking men were they?"

I described them.

"Shore and Riordan," he said. "I might of known it. Now what's all this?" nodding his fat face at Albury.

I told him briefly while the boy went on dictating his statement.

The chief chuckled and said:

"Well, well, I did Whisper an injustice. I'll have to hunt him up and square myself. So you landed the boy? That certainly is fine. Congratulations and thanks." He shook my hand again. "You'll not be leaving our city now, will you?"

"Not just yet."

"That's fine," he assured me.

I went out for breakfast-and-lunch. Then I treated myself to a shave and hair-cut, sent a telegram to the Agency asking to have Dick Foley and Mickey Linehan shipped to Personville, stopped in my room for a change of clothes, and set out for my client's house.

Old Elihu was wrapped in blankets in an armchair at a sunny window. He gave me a stubby hand and thanked me for catching his son's murderer.

I made some more or less appropriate reply. I didn't ask him how he had got the news.

"The check I gave you last night," he said, "is only fair pay for the work you have done."

"Your son's check more than covered that."

"Then call mine a bonus."

"The Continental's got rules against taking bonuses or rewards," I said.

His face began to redden.

"Well, damn it—"

"You haven't forgotten that your check was to cover the cost of investigating crime and corruption in Personville, have you?" I asked.

"That was nonsense," he snorted. "We were excited last night. That's called off."

"Not with me."

He threw a lot of profanity around. Then:

"It's my money and I won't have it wasted on a lot of damn-foolery. If you won't take it for what you've done, give it back to me."

"Stop yelling at me," I said. "I'll give you nothing except a good job of city-cleaning. That's what you bargained for, and that's what you're going to get. You know now that your son was killed by young Albury, and not by your playmates. They know now that Thaler wasn't helping you double-cross them. With your son dead, you've been able to promise them that the newspapers won't dig up any more dirt. All's lovely and peaceful again.

"I told you I expected something like that. That's why I sewed you up. And you are sewed up. The check has been certified, so you can't stop payment. The letter of authority may not be as good as a contract, but you'll have to go into court to prove that it isn't. If you want that much of that kind of publicity, go ahead. I'll see that you get plenty.

"Your fat chief of police tried to assassinate me last night. I don't like that. I'm just mean enough to want to ruin him for it. Now I'm going to have my fun. I've got ten thousand dollars of your money to play with. I'm going to use it opening Poisonville up from Adam's apple to ankles. I'll see that you get my reports as regularly as possible. I hope you enjoy them."

And I went out of the house with his curses sizzling around my head.

VIII · A Tip on Kid Cooper

I spent most of the afternoon writing my three days' reports on the Donald Willsson operation. Then I sat around, burned Fatimas, and thought about the Elihu Willsson operation until dinner time.

I went down to the hotel dining room and had just decided in favor of pounded rump steak with mushrooms when I heard myself being paged.

The boy took me to one of the lobby booths. Dinah Brand's lazy voice came out of the receiver:

"Max wants to see you. Can you drop in tonight?"

"Your place?"

"Yes."

I promised to drop in and returned to the dining room and my meal. When I had finished eating I went up to my room, fifth floor front. I unlocked the door and went in, snapping on the light.

A bullet kissed a hole in the door-frame close to my noodle.

More bullets made more holes in door, door-frame and wall, but by that time I had carried my noodle into a safe corner, one out of line with the window.

Across the street, I knew, was a four-story office building with a roof a little above the level of my window. The roof would be dark. My light was on. There was no percentage in trying to peep out under those conditions.

I looked around for something to chuck at the light globe, found a Gideon Bible, and chucked it. The bulb popped apart, giving me darkness.

The shooting had stopped.

I crept to the window, kneeling with an eye to one of its lower corners. The roof across the street was dark and too high for me to see beyond its rim. Ten minutes of this one-eyed spying got me nothing except a kink in my neck.

I went to the phone and asked the girl to send the house copper up.

He was a portly, white-mustached man with the round undeveloped forehead of a child. He wore a too-small hat on the back of his head to show the forehead. His name was Keever. He got too excited over the shooting.

The hotel manager came in, a plump man with carefully controlled face, voice and manner. He didn't get excited at all. He took the this-is-unheard-of-but-not-really-serious-of-course attitude of a street fakir whose mechanical dingus flops during a demonstration.

We risked light, getting a new globe, and added up the bullet-holes. There were ten of them.

Policemen came, went, and returned to report no luck in picking up whatever trail there might have been. Noonan called up. He talked to the sergeant in charge of the police detail, and then to me.

"I just this minute heard about the shooting," he said. "Now who do you reckon would be after you like that?"

"I couldn't guess," I lied.

"None of them touched you?"

"No."

"Well, that certainly is fine," he said heartily. "And we'll nail that baby, whoever he was, you can bet your life on that. Would you like me to leave a couple of the boys with you, just to see nothing else happens?"

"No, thanks."

"You can have them if you want them," he insisted.

"No, thanks."

He made me promise to call on him the first chance I got, told me the Personville police department was at my disposal, gave me to understand that if anything happened to me his whole life would be ruined, and I finally got rid of him.

The police went away. I had my stuff moved into another room, one into which bullets couldn't be so easily funneled. Then I changed my clothes and set out for Hurricane Street, to keep my date with the whispering gambler.

∴

Dinah Brand opened the door for me. Her big ripe mouth was rouged evenly this evening, but her brown hair still needed trimming, was parted haphazardly, and there were spots down the front of her orange silk dress.

"So you're still alive," she said. "I suppose nothing can be done about it. Come on in."

We went into her cluttered-up living room. Dan Rolff and Max Thaler were playing pinochle there. Rolff nodded to me. Thaler got up to shake hands.

His hoarse whispering voice said:

"I hear you've declared war on Poisonville."

"Don't blame me. I've got a client who wants the place ventilated."

"Wanted, not wants," he corrected me as we sat down. "Why don't you chuck it?"

I made a speech:

"No. I don't like the way Poisonville has treated me. I've got my chance now, and I'm going to even up. I take it you're back in the club again, all brothers together, let bygones be bygones. You want to be let alone. There was a time when I wanted to be let alone. If I had been, maybe now I'd be riding back to San Francisco. But I wasn't. Especially I wasn't let alone by that fat Noonan. He's had two tries at my scalp in two days. That's plenty. Now it's my turn to run him ragged, and that's exactly what I'm going to do. Poisonville is ripe for the harvest. It's a job I like, and I'm going to it."

"While you last," the gambler said.

"Yeah," I agreed. "I was reading in the paper this morning about a fellow choking to death eating a chocolate eclair in bed."

"That may be good," said Dinah Brand, her big body sprawled in an arm-chair, "but it wasn't in this morning's paper."

She lit a cigarette and threw the match out of sight under the Chesterfield. The lunger had gathered up the cards and was shuffling them over and over, purposelessly.

Thaler frowned at me and said:

"Willsson's willing for you to keep the ten grand. Let it go at that."

"I've got a mean disposition. Attempted assassinations make me mad."

"That won't get you anything but a box. I'm for you. You kept Noonan from framing me. That's why I'm telling you, forget it and go back to Frisco."

"I'm for you," I said. "That's why I'm telling you, split with them. They crossed you up once. It'll happen again. Anyway, they're slated for the chutes. Get out while the getting's good."

"I'm sitting too pretty," he said. "And I'm able to take care of myself."

"Maybe. But you know the racket's too good to last. You've had the cream of the pickings. Now it's get-away day."

He shook his little dark head and told me:

"I think you're pretty good, but I'm damned if I think you're good enough to crack this camp. It's too tight. If I thought you could swing it, I'd be with you. You know how I stand with Noonan. But you'll never make it. Chuck it."

"No. I'm in it to the last nickel of Elihu's ten thousand."

"I told you he was too damned pig-headed to listen to reason," Dinah Brand said, yawning. "Isn't there anything to drink in the dump, Dan?"

The lunger got up from the table and went out of the room.

Thaler shrugged, said:

"Have it your way. You're supposed to know what you're doing. Going to the fights tomorrow night?"

I said I thought I would. Dan Rolff came in with gin and trimmings. We had a couple of drinks apiece. We talked about the fights. Nothing more was said about me versus Poisonville. The gambler apparently had washed his hands of me, but he didn't seem to hold my stubbornness against me. He even gave me what seemed to be a straight tip on the fights—telling me any bet on the main event would be good if its maker remembered that Kid Cooper would probably knock Ike Bush out in the sixth round. He seemed to know what he was talking about, and it didn't seem to be news to the others.

I left a little after eleven, returning to the hotel without anything happening.

IX · *A Black Knife*

I woke next morning with an idea in my skull. Personville had only some forty thousand inhabitants. It shouldn't be hard to spread news. Ten o'clock found me out spreading it.

I did my spreading in pool rooms, cigar stores, speakeasies, soft drink joints, and on street corners—wherever I found a man or two loafing. My spreading technique was something like this:

"Got a match? . . . Thanks. . . . Going to the fights tonight? . . . I hear Ike Bush takes a dive in the sixth. . . . It ought to be straight: I got it from Whisper. . . . Yeah, they all are."

People like inside stuff, and anything that had Thaler's name to it was very inside in Personville. The news spread nicely. Half the men I gave it to worked almost as hard as I did spreading it, just to show they knew what was what.

When I started out, seven to four was being offered that Ike Bush would win, and two to three that he would win by a knock-out. By two o'clock none of the joints taking bets were offering anything better than even money, and by half-past three Kid Cooper was a two-to-one favorite.

I made my last stop a lunch counter, where I tossed the news out to a waiter and a couple of customers while eating a hot beef sandwich.

When I went out I found a man waiting by the door for me. He had bowed legs and a long sharp jaw, like a hog's. He nodded and walked down the street beside me, chewing a toothpick and squinting sidewise into my face. At the corner he said:

"I know for a fact that ain't so."

"What?" I asked.

"About Ike Bush flopping. I know for a fact that ain't so."

"Then it oughtn't bother you any. But the wise money's going two to one on Cooper, and he's not that good unless Bush lets him be."

The hog jaw spit out the mangled toothpick and snapped yellow teeth at me.

"He told me his own self that Cooper was a set-up for him, last night, and he wouldn't do nothing like that—not to me."

"Friend of yours?"

"Not exactly, but he knows I— Hey, listen! Did Whisper give you that, on the level?"

"On the level."

He cursed bitterly. "And I put my last thirty-five bucks in the world on that rat on his say-so. Me, that could send him over for—" He broke off and looked down the street.

"Could send him over for what?" I asked.

"Plenty," he said. "Nothing."

I had a suggestion:

"If you've got something on him, maybe we ought to talk it over. I wouldn't mind seeing Bush win, myself. If what you've got is any good, what's the matter with putting it up to him?"

He looked at me, at the sidewalk, fumbled in his vest pocket for another toothpick, put it in his mouth, and mumbled:

"Who are you?"

I gave him a name, something like Hunter or Hunt or Huntington, and asked him his. He said his name was MacSwain, Bob MacSwain, and I could ask anybody in town if it wasn't right.

I said I believed him and asked:

"What do you say? Will we put the squeeze to Bush?"

Little hard lights came into his eyes and died.

"No," he gulped. "I ain't that kind of fellow. I never—"

"You never did anything but let people gyp you. You don't have to go up against him, MacSwain. Give me the dope, and I'll make the play —if it's any good."

He thought that over, licking his lips, letting the toothpick fall down to stick on his coat front.

"You wouldn't let on about me having any part in it?" he asked. "I belong here, and I wouldn't stand a chance if it got out. And you won't turn him up? You'll just use it to make him fight?"

"Right."

He took my hand excitedly and demanded:

"Honest to God?"

"Honest to God."

"His real monacker is Al Kennedy. He was in on the Keystone Trust knock-over in Philly two years ago, when Scissors Haggerty's mob croaked two messengers. Al didn't do the killing, but he was in on the caper. He used to scrap around Philly. The rest of them got copped, but he made the sneak. That's why he's sticking out here in the bushes. That's why he won't never let them put his mug in the papers or on any cards. That's why he's a pork-and-beaner when he's as good as the best. See? This Ike Bush is Al Kennedy that the Philly bulls want for the Keystone trick. See? He was in on the—"

"I see I see," I stopped the merry-go-round. "The next thing is to get to see him. How do we do that?"

"He flops at the Maxwell, on Union Street. I guess maybe he'd be there now, resting up for the mill."

"Resting for what? He doesn't know he's going to fight. We'll give it a try, though."

"We! We! Where do you get that *we* at? You said—you swore you'd keep me covered."

"Yeah," I said, "I remember that now. What does he look like?"

"A black-headed kid, kind of slim, with one tin ear and eyebrows that run straight across. I don't know if you can make him like it."

"Leave that to me. Where'll I find you afterwards?"

"I'll be hanging around Murry's. Mind you don't tip my mitt. You promised."

∴

The Maxwell was one of a dozen hotels along Union Street with narrow front doors between stores, and shabby stairs leading up to second-story offices. The Maxwell's office was simply a wide place in the hall, with a key- and mail-rack behind a wooden counter that needed paint just as badly. A brass bell and a dirty day-book register were on the counter. Nobody was there.

I had to run back eight pages before I found *Ike Bush, Salt Lake City, 214*, written in the book. The pigeon-hole that had that number was empty. I climbed more steps and knocked on a door that had it. Nothing came of that. I tried it two or three times more and then turned back to the stairs.

Somebody was coming up. I stood at the top, waiting for a look at him. There was just light enough to see by.

He was a slim muscular lad in army shirt, blue suit, gray cap. Black eyebrows made a straight line above his eyes.

I said: "Hello."

He nodded without stopping or saying anything.

"Win tonight?" I asked.

"Hope so," he said shortly, passing me.

I let him take four steps toward his room before I told him:

"So do I. I'd hate to have to ship you back to Philly, Al."

He took another step, turned around very slowly, rested a shoulder against the wall, let his eyes get sleepy, and grunted:

"Huh?"

"If you were smacked down in the sixth or any other round by a palooka like Kid Cooper, it'd make me peevish," I said. "Don't do it, Al. You don't want to go back to Philly."

The youngster put his chin down in his neck and came back to me. When he was within arm's reach, he stopped, letting his left side turn a bit to the front. His hands were hanging loose. Mine were in my overcoat pockets.

He said, "Huh?" again.

I said:

"Try to remember that—if Ike Bush doesn't turn in a win tonight, Al Kennedy will be riding east in the morning."

He lifted his left shoulder an inch. I moved the gun around in my pocket, enough. He grumbled:

"Where do you get that stuff about me not winning?"

"Just something I heard. I didn't think there was anything in it, except maybe a ducat back to Philly."

"I oughta bust your jaw, you fat crook."

"Now's the time to do it," I advised him. "If you win tonight you're not likely to see me again. If you lose, you'll see me, but your hands won't be loose."

I found MacSwain in Murry's, a Broadway pool room.

"Did you get to him?" he asked.

"Yeah. It's all fixed—if he doesn't blow town, or say something to his backers, or just pay no attention to me, or—"

MacSwain developed a lot of nervousness.

"You better damn sight be careful," he warned me. "They might try to put you out the way. He— I got to see a fellow down the street," and he deserted me.

. .

Poisonville's prize fighting was done in a big wooden ex-casino in what had once been an amusement park on the edge of town. When I got there at eight-thirty, most of the population seemed to be on hand, packed tight in close rows of folding chairs on the main floor, packed tighter on benches in two dinky balconies.

Smoke. Stink. Heat. Noise.

My seat was in the third row, ringside. Moving down to it, I discovered Dan Rolff in an aisle seat not far away, with Dinah Brand beside him. She had had her hair trimmed at last, and marcelled, and looked like a lot of money in a big gray fur coat.

"Get down on Cooper?" she asked after we had swapped hellos.

"No. You playing him heavy?"

"Not as heavy as I'd like. We held off, thinking the odds would get better, but they went to hell."

"Everybody in town seems to know Bush is going to dive," I said. "I saw a hundred put on Cooper at four to one a few minutes ago." I leaned past Rolff and put my mouth close to where the gray fur collar hid the girl's ear, whispering: "The dive is off. Better copper your bets while there's time."

Her big bloodshot eyes went wide and dark with anxiety, greed, curiosity, suspicion.

"You mean it?" she asked huskily.

"Yeah."

She chewed her reddened lips, frowned, asked:

"Where'd you get it?"

I wouldn't say. She chewed her mouth some more and asked:

"Is Max on?"

"I haven't seen him. Is he here?"

"I suppose so," she said absent-mindedly, a distant look in her eyes. Her lips moved as if she were counting to herself.

I said: "Take it or leave it, but it's a gut."

She leaned forward to look sharply into my eyes, clicked her teeth together, opened her bag, and dragged out a roll of bills the size of a coffee can. Part of the roll she pushed at Rolff.

"Here, Dan, get it down on Bush. You've got an hour anyway to look over the odds."

Rolff took the money and went off on his errand. I took his seat. She put a hand on my forearm and said:

"Christ help you if you've made me drop that dough."

I pretended the idea was ridiculous.

The preliminary bouts got going, four-round affairs between assorted hams. I kept looking for Thaler, but couldn't see him. The girl squirmed beside me, paying little attention to the fighting, dividing her time between asking me where I had got my information and threatening me with hell-fire and damnation if it turned out to be a bust.

The semi-final was on when Rolff came back and gave the girl a handful of tickets. She was straining her eyes over them when I left for my own seat. Without looking up she called to me:

"Wait outside for us when it's over."

Kid Cooper climbed into the ring while I was squeezing through to my seat. He was a ruddy straw-haired solid-built boy with a dented face and too much meat around the top of his lavender trunks. Ike Bush, alias Al Kennedy, came through the ropes in the opposite corner. His body looked better—slim, nicely ridged, snaky—but his face was pale, worried.

They were introduced, went to the center of the ring for the usual instructions, returned to their corners, shed bathrobes, stretched on the ropes, the gong rang, and the scrap was on.

Cooper was a clumsy bum. He had a pair of wide swings that might have hurt when they landed, but anybody with two feet could have kept away from them. Bush had class—nimble legs, a smooth fast left hand, and a right that got away quick. It would have been murder to put Cooper in the ring with the slim boy if he had been trying. But he wasn't. That is, he wasn't trying to win. He was trying not to, and had his hands full doing it.

Cooper waddled flat-footed around the ring, throwing his wide swings at everything from the lights to the corner posts. His system was simply to turn them loose and let them take their chances. Bush moved in and out, putting a glove on the ruddy boy whenever he wanted to, but not putting anything in the glove.

The customers were booing before the first round was over. The second round was just as sour. I didn't feel so good. Bush didn't seem to have been much influenced by our little conversation. Out of the corner of my eye I could see Dinah Brand trying to catch my attention. She looked hot. I took care not to have my attention caught.

The room-mate act in the ring was continued in the third round to the tune of yelled Throw-em-outs, Why-don't-you-kiss-hims and Make-em-fights from the seats. The pugs' waltz brought them around to the corner nearest me just as the booing broke off for a moment.

I made a megaphone of my hands and bawled:

"Back to Philly, Al."

Bush's back was to me. He wrestled Cooper around, shoving him into the ropes, so he—Bush—faced my way.

From somewhere far back in another part of the house another yelling voice came:

"Back to Philly, Al."

MacSwain, I supposed.

A drunk off to one side lifted his puffy face and bawled the same thing, laughing as if it were a swell joke. Others took up the cry for no reason at all except that it seemed to disturb Bush.

His eyes jerked from side to side under the black bar of his eyebrows.

One of Cooper's wild mitts clouted the slim boy on the side of the jaw.

Ike Bush piled down at the referee's feet.

The referee counted five in two seconds, but the gong cut him off.

I looked over at Dinah Brand and laughed. There wasn't anything else to do. She looked at me and didn't laugh. Her face was sick as Dan Rolff's, but angrier.

Bush's handlers dragged him into his corner and rubbed him up, not working very hard at it. He opened his eyes and watched his feet. The gong was tapped.

Kid Cooper paddled out hitching up his trunks. Bush waited until the bum was in the center of the ring, and then came to him, fast.

Bush's left glove went down, out—practically out of sight in Cooper's belly. Cooper said, "Ugh," and backed away, folding up.

Bush straightened him with a right-hand poke in the mouth, and sank the left again. Cooper said, "Ugh," again and had trouble with his knees.

Bush cuffed him once on each side of the head, cocked his right, carefully pushed Cooper's face into position with a long left, and threw his right hand straight from under his jaw to Cooper's.

Everybody in the house felt the punch.

Cooper hit the floor, bounced, and settled there. It took the referee half a minute to count ten seconds. It would have been just the same if he had taken half an hour. Kid Cooper was out.

When the referee had finally stalled through the count, he raised Bush's hand. Neither of them looked happy.

A high twinkle of light caught my eye. A short silvery streak slanted down from one of the small balconies.

A woman screamed.

The silvery streak ended its flashing slant in the ring, with a sound that was partly a thud, partly a snap.

Ike Bush took his arm out of the referee's hand and pitched down on top of Kid Cooper. A black knife-handle stuck out of the nape of Bush's neck.

X · *Crime Wanted—Male or Female*

HALF an hour later, when I left the building, Dinah Brand was sitting at the wheel of a pale blue little Marmon, talking to Max Thaler, who stood in the road.

The girl's square chin was tilted up. Her big red mouth was brutal around the words it shaped, and the lines crossing its ends were deep, hard.

The gambler looked as unpleasant as she. His pretty face was yellow and tough as oak. When he talked his lips were paper-thin.

It seemed to be a nice family party. I wouldn't have joined it if the girl hadn't seen me and called:

"My God, I thought you were never coming."

I went over to the car. Thaler looked across the hood at me with no friendliness at all.

"Last night I advised you to go back to Frisco." His whisper was harsher than anybody's shout could have been. "Now I'm telling you."

"Thanks just the same," I said as I got in beside the girl.

While she was stirring the engine up he said to her:

"This isn't the first time you've sold me out. It's the last."

She put the car in motion, turned her head back over her shoulder, and sang to him:

"To hell, my love, with you!"

We rode into town rapidly.

"Is Bush dead?" she asked as she twisted the car into Broadway.

"Decidedly. When they turned him over the point of the knife was sticking out in front."

"He ought to have known better than to double-cross them. Let's get something to eat. I'm almost eleven hundred ahead on the night's doings, so if the boy friend doesn't like it, it's just too bad. How'd you come out?"

"Didn't bet. So your Max doesn't like it?"

"Didn't bet?" she cried. "What kind of an ass are you? Whoever heard of anybody not betting when they had a thing like that sewed up?"

"I wasn't sure it was sewed up. So Max didn't like the way things turned out?"

"You guessed it. He dropped plenty. And then he gets sore with me because I had sense enough to switch over and get in on the win." She stopped the car violently in front of a Chinese restaurant. "The hell with him, the little tin-horn runt!"

Her eyes were shiny because they were wet. She jabbed a handkerchief into them as we got out of the car.

"My God, I'm hungry," she said, dragging me across the sidewalk. "Will you buy me a ton of *chow mein?*"

She didn't eat a ton of it, but she did pretty well, putting away a piled-up dish of her own and half of mine. Then we got back into the Marmon and rode out to her house.

Dan Rolff was in the dining room. A water glass and a brown bottle with no label stood on the table in front of him. He sat straight up in his chair, staring at the bottle. The room smelled of laudanum.

Dinah Brand slid her fur coat off, letting it fall half on a chair and half on the floor, and snapped her fingers at the lunger, saying impatiently:

"Did you collect?"

Without looking up from the bottle, he took a pad of paper money out of his inside coat pocket and dropped it on the table. The girl grabbed it, counted the bills twice, smacked her lips, and stuffed the money in her bag.

She went out to the kitchen and began chopping ice. I sat down and lit a cigarette. Rolff stared at his bottle. He and I never seemed to have much to say to one another. Presently the girl brought in some gin, lemon juice, seltzer and ice.

We drank and she told Rolff:

"Max is sore as hell. He heard you'd been running around putting last-minute money on Bush, and the little monkey thinks I double-crossed him. What did I have to do with it? All I did was what any sensible person would have done—get in on the win. I didn't have any more to do with it than a baby, did I?" she asked me.

"No."

"Of course not. What's the matter with Max is he's afraid the others will think he was in on it too, that Dan was putting his dough down as well as mine. Well, that's his hard luck. He can go climb trees for all I care, the lousy little runt. Another drink would go good."

She poured another for herself and for me. Rolff hadn't touched his first one. He said, still staring at the brown bottle:

"You can hardly expect him to be hilarious about it."

The girl scowled and said disagreeably:

"I can expect anything I want. And he's got no right to talk to me that way. He doesn't own me. Maybe he thinks he does, but I'll show him different." She emptied her glass, banged it on the table, and twisted around in her chair to face me. "Is that on the level about your having ten thousand dollars of Elihu Willsson's money to use cleaning up the city?"

"Yeah."

Her bloodshot eyes glistened hungrily.

"And if I help you will I get some of the ten—?"

"You can't do that, Dinah." Rolff's voice was thick, but gently firm, as if he were talking to a child. "That would be utterly filthy."

The girl turned her face slowly toward him. Her mouth took on the look it had worn while talking to Thaler.

"I am going to do it," she said. "That makes me utterly filthy, does it?"

He didn't say anything, didn't look up from the bottle. Her face got red, hard, cruel. Her voice was soft, cooing:

"It's just too bad that a gentleman of your purity, even if he is a bit consumptive, has to associate with a filthy bum like me."

"That can be remedied," he said slowly, getting up. He was laudanumed to the scalp.

Dinah Brand jumped out of her chair and ran around the table to him. He looked at her with blank dopey eyes. She put her face close to his and demanded:

"So I'm too utterly filthy for you now, am I?"

He said evenly:

"I said to betray your friends to this chap would be utterly filthy, and it would."

She caught one of his thin wrists and twisted it until he was on his knees. Her other hand, open, beat his hollow-cheeked face, half a dozen times on each side, rocking his head from side to side. He could have put his free arm up to protect his face, but didn't.

She let go his wrist, turned her back on him, and reached for gin and seltzer. She was smiling. I didn't like the smile.

He got up, blinking. His wrist was red where she had held it, his face bruised. He steadied himself upright and looked at me with dull eyes.

With no change in the blankness of his face and eyes, he put a hand under his coat, brought out a black automatic pistol, and fired at me.

But he was too shaky for either speed or accuracy. I had time to toss a glass at him. The glass hit his shoulder. His bullet went somewhere overhead.

I jumped before he got the next one out—jumped at him—was close enough to knock the gun down. The second slug went into the floor.

I socked his jaw. He fell away from me and lay where he fell.

I turned around.

Dinah Brand was getting ready to bat me over the head with the seltzer bottle, a heavy glass siphon that would have made pulp of my skull.

"Don't," I yelped.

"You didn't have to bust him like that," she snarled.

"Well, it's done. You'd better get him straightened out."

She put down the siphon and I helped her carry him up to his bedroom. When he began moving his eyes, I left her to finish the work and went down to the dining room again. She joined me there fifteen minutes later.

"He's all right," she said. "But you could have handled him without that."

"Yeah, but I did that for him. Know why he took the shot at me?"

"So I'd have nobody to sell Max out to?"

"No. Because I'd seen you maul him around."

"That doesn't make sense to me," she said. "I was the one who did it."

"He's in love with you, and this isn't the first time you've done it. He acted like he had learned there was no use matching muscle with you. But you can't expect him to enjoy having another man see you slap his face."

"I used to think I knew men," she complained, "but, by God! I don't. They're lunatics, all of them."

"So I poked him to give him back some of his self-respect. You know, treated him as I would a man instead of a down-and-outer who could be slapped around by girls."

"Anything you say," she sighed. "I give up. We ought to have a drink."

We had the drink, and I said:

"You were saying you'd work with me if there was a cut of the Willsson money in it for you. There is."

"How much?"

"Whatever you earn. Whatever what you do is worth."

"That's uncertain."

"So's your help, so far as I know."

"Is it? I can give you the stuff, brother, loads of it, and don't think I can't. I'm a girl who knows her Poisonville." She looked down at her gray-stockinged knees, waved one leg at me, and exclaimed indignantly: "Look at that. Another run. Did you ever see anything to beat it? Honest to God! I'm going barefoot."

"Your legs are too big," I told her. "They put too much strain on the material."

"That'll do out of you. What's your idea of how to go about purifying our village?"

"If I haven't been lied to, Thaler, Pete the Finn, Lew Yard and Noonan are the men who've made Poisonville the sweet-smelling mess it is. Old Elihu comes in for his share of the blame, too, but it's not all his fault, maybe. Besides, he's my client, even if he doesn't want to be, so I'd like to go easy on him.

"The closest I've got to an idea is to dig up any and all the dirty work I can that might implicate the others, and run it out. Maybe I'll advertise—*Crime Wanted—Male or Female*. If they're as crooked as I think they are I shouldn't have a lot of trouble finding a job or two that I can hang on them."

"Is that what you were up to when you uncooked the fight?"

"That was only an experiment—just to see what would happen."

"So that's the way you scientific detectives work. My God! for a fat, middle-aged, hard-boiled, pig-headed guy, you've got the vaguest way of doing things I ever heard of."

"Plans are all right sometimes," I said. "And sometimes just stirring things up is all right—if you're tough enough to survive, and keep your eyes open so you'll see what you want when it comes to the top."

"That ought to be good for another drink," she said.

XI · *The Swell Spoon*

WE had another drink.

She put her glass down, licked her lips, and said:

"If stirring things up is your system, I've got a swell spoon for you. Did you ever hear of Noonan's brother Tim, the one who committed suicide out at Mock Lake a couple of years ago?"

"No."

"You wouldn't have heard much good. Anyway, he didn't commit suicide. Max killed him."

"Yeah?"

"For God's sake wake up. This I'm giving you is real. Noonan was like a father to Tim. Take the proof to him and he'll be after Max like nobody's business. That's what you want, isn't it?"

"We've got proof?"

"Two people got to Tim before he died, and he told them Max had done it. They're both still in town, though one won't live a lot longer. How's that?"

She looked as if she were telling the truth, though with women, especially blue-eyed women, that doesn't always mean anything.

"Let's listen to the rest of it," I said. "I like details and things."

"You'll get them. You ever been out to Mock Lake? Well, it's our summer resort, thirty miles up the canyon road. It's a dump, but it's cool in summer, so it gets a good play. This was summer a year ago, the last week-end in August. I was out there with a fellow named Holly. He's back in England now, but you don't care anything about that, because he's got nothing to do with it. He was a funny sort of old woman—used to wear white silk socks turned inside out so the loose threads wouldn't hurt his feet. I got a letter from him last week. It's around here somewhere, but that doesn't make any difference.

"We were up there, and Max was up there with a girl he used to play around with—Myrtle Jennison. She's in the hospital now—City—dying of Bright's disease or something. She was a classy looking kid then, a slender blonde. I always liked her, except that a few drinks made her too noisy. Tim Noonan was crazy about her, but she couldn't see anybody but Max that summer.

"Tim wouldn't let her alone. He was a big good-looking Irishman, but a sap and a cheap crook who only got by because his brother was chief of police. Wherever Myrtle went, he'd pop up sooner or later. She didn't like to say anything to Max about it, not wanting Max to do anything to put him in wrong with Tim's brother, the chief.

"So of course Tim showed up at Mock Lake this Saturday. Myrtle and Max were just by themselves. Holly and I were with a bunch, but I saw Myrtle to talk to and she told me she had got a note from Tim, asking her to meet him for a few minutes that night, in one of the little arbor things on the hotel grounds. He said if she didn't he would kill himself. That was a laugh for us—the big false alarm. I tried to talk Myrtle out of going, but she had just enough booze in her to feel gay and she said she was going to give him an earful.

"We were all dancing in the hotel that night. Max was there for a while, and then I didn't see him any more. Myrtle was dancing with a fellow named Rutgers, a lawyer here in town. After a while she left him and went out one of the side doors. She winked at me when she passed, so I knew she was going down to see Tim. She had just got out when I heard the shot. Nobody else paid any attention to it. I suppose I wouldn't have noticed it either if I hadn't known about Myrtle and Tim.

"I told Holly I wanted to see Myrtle, and went out after her, by myself. I must have been about five minutes behind her in getting out. When I got outside I saw lights down by one of the summer houses, and people. I went down there, and— This talking is thirsty work."

I poured out a couple of hookers of gin. She went into the kitchen for another siphon and more ice. We mixed them up, drank, and she settled down to her tale again:

"There was Tim Noonan, dead, with a hole in his temple and his gun lying beside him. Perhaps a dozen people were standing around, hotel people, visitors, one of Noonan's men, a dick named MacSwain. As soon as Myrtle saw me she took me away from the crowd, back in the shade of some trees.

" 'Max killed him,' she said. 'What'll I do?'

"I asked her about it. She told me she had seen the flash of the gun and at first she thought Tim had killed himself after all. She was too far away and it was too dark for her to see anything else. When she ran down to him, he was rolling around, moaning, 'He didn't have to kill me over her. I'd have—' She couldn't make out the rest of it. He was rolling around, bleeding from the hole in his temple.

"Myrtle was afraid Max had done it, but she had to be sure, so she knelt down and tried to pick up Tim's head, asking: 'Who did it, Tim?'

"He was almost gone, but before he passed out he got enough strength to tell her, 'Max!'

"She kept asking me, 'What'll I do?' I asked her if anybody else had heard Tim, and she said the dick had. He came running up while she was trying to lift Tim's head. She didn't think anybody else had been near enough to hear, but the dick had.

"I didn't want Max to get in a jam over killing a mutt like Tim Noonan. Max didn't mean anything to me then, except that I liked him, and I didn't like any of the Noonans. I knew the dick—MacSwain. I used to know his wife. He had been a pretty good guy, straight as ace-deuce-trey-four-five, till he got on the force. Then he went the way of the rest of them. His wife stood as much of it as she could and then left him.

"Knowing this dick, I told Myrtle I thought we could fix things. A little jack would ruin MacSwain's memory, or, if he didn't like that, Max could have him knocked off. She had Tim's note threatening suicide. If the dick would play along, the hole in Tim's head from his own gun and the note would smooth everything over pretty.

"I left Myrtle under the trees and went out to hunt for Max. He wasn't around. There weren't many people there, and I could hear the hotel orchestra still playing dance music. I couldn't find Max, so I went back to Myrtle. She was all worked up over another idea. She didn't want Max to know that she had found out that he had killed Tim. She was afraid of him.

"See what I mean? She was afraid that if she and Max ever broke off he'd put her out of the way if he knew she had enough on him to swing him. I know how she felt. I got the same notion later, and kept just as quiet as she did. So we figured that if it could be fixed up without his knowing about it, so much the better. I didn't want to show in it either.

"Myrtle went back alone to the group around Tim and got hold of MacSwain. She took him off a little way and made the deal with him. She had some dough on her. She gave him two hundred and a diamond ring that had cost a fellow named Boyle a thousand. I thought he'd be back for more later, but he didn't. He shot square with her. With the help of the letter he put over the suicide story.

"Noonan knew there was something fishy about the lay-out, but he could never peg it. I think he suspected Max of having something to do with it. But Max had an air-tight alibi—trust him for that—and I think even Noonan finally counted him out. But Noonan never believed it happened the way it was made to look. He broke MacSwain—kicked him off the force.

"Max and Myrtle slid apart a little while after that. No row or anything—they just slid apart. I don't think she ever felt easy around him again, though so far as I know he never suspected her of knowing anything. She's sick now, as I told you, and hasn't got long to live. I think she'd not so much mind telling the truth if she were asked. MacSwain's still hanging around town. He'd talk if there was something in it for him. Those two have got the stuff on Max—and wouldn't Noonan eat it up! Is that good enough to give your stirring-up a start?"

"Couldn't it have been suicide?" I asked. "With Tim Noonan getting a last-minute bright idea to stick it on Max?"

"That four-flusher shoot himself? Not a chance."

"Could Myrtle have shot him?"

"Noonan didn't overlook that one. But she couldn't have been a third of the distance down the slope when the shot was fired. Tim had powder-marks on his head, and hadn't been shot and rolled down the slope. Myrtle's out."

"But Max had an alibi?"

"Yes, indeed. He always has. He was in the hotel bar, on the other side of the building, all the time. Four men said so. As I remember it, they said it openly and often, long before anybody asked them. There were other men in the bar who didn't remember whether Max had been there or not, but those four remembered. They'd remember anything Max wanted remembered."

Her eyes got large and then narrowed to black-fringed slits. She leaned toward me, upsetting her glass with an elbow.

"Peak Murry was one of the four. He and Max are on the outs now. Peak might tell it straight now. He's got a pool room on Broadway."

"This MacSwain, does he happen to be named Bob?" I asked. "A bow-legged man with a long jaw like a hog's?"

"Yes. You know him?"

"By sight. What does he do now?"

"A small-time grifter. What do you think of the stack-up?"

"Not bad. Maybe I can use it."

"Then let's talk scratch."

I grinned at the greed in her eyes and said:

"Not just yet, sister. We'll have to see how it works out before we start scattering pennies around."

She called me a damned nickel-nurser and reached for the gin.

"No more for me, thanks," I told her, looking at my watch. "It's getting along toward five a. m. and I've got a busy day ahead."

She decided she was hungry again. That reminded me that I was. It took half an hour or more to get waffles, ham and coffee off the stove. It took some more time to get them into our stomachs and to smoke some cigarettes over extra cups of coffee. It was quite a bit after six when I got ready to leave.

∴

I went back to my hotel and got into a tub of cold water. It braced me a lot, and I needed bracing. At forty I could get along on gin as a substitute for sleep, but not comfortably.

When I had dressed I sat down and composed a document:

Just before he died, Tim Noonan told me he had been shot by Max Thaler. Detective Bob MacSwain heard him tell me. I gave Detective MacSwain $200 and a diamond ring worth $1,000 to keep quiet and make it look like suicide.

With this document in my pocket I went downstairs, had another breakfast that was mostly coffee, and went up to the City Hospital.

Visiting hours were in the afternoon, but by flourishing my Continental Detective Agency credentials and giving everybody to understand that an hour's delay might cause thousands of deaths, or words to that effect, I got to see Myrtle Jennison.

She was in a ward on the third floor, alone. The other four beds were empty. She could have been a girl of twenty-five or a woman of fifty-five. Her face was a bloated spotty mask. Lifeless yellow hair in two stringy braids lay on the pillow beside her.

I waited until the nurse who had brought me up left. Then I held my document out to the invalid and said:

"Will you sign this, please, Miss Jennison?"

She looked at me with ugly eyes that were shaded into no particular dark color by the pads of flesh around them, then at the document, and finally brought a shapeless fat hand from under the covers to take it.

She pretended it took her nearly five minutes to read the forty-two words I had written. She let the document fall down on the covers and asked:

"Where'd you get that?" Her voice was tinny, irritable.

"Dinah Brand sent me to you."

She asked eagerly:

"Has she broken off with Max?"

"Not that I know of," I lied. "I imagine she just wants to have this on hand in case it should come in handy."

"And get her fool throat slit. Give me a pencil."

I gave her my fountain pen and held my notebook under the document, to stiffen it while she scribbled her signature at the bottom, and to have it in my hands as soon as she had finished. While I fanned the paper dry she said:

"If that's what she wants it's all right with me. What do I care what anybody does now? I'm done. Hell with them all!" She sniggered and suddenly threw the bedclothes down to her knees, showing me a horrible swollen body in a coarse white nightgown. "How do you like me? See, I'm done."

I pulled the covers up over her again and said:

"Thanks for this, Miss Jennison."

"That's all right. It's nothing to me any more. Only"—her puffy chin quivered—"it's hell to die ugly as this."

XII · A New Deal

I went out to hunt for MacSwain. Neither city directory nor telephone book told me anything. I did the pool rooms, cigar stores, speakeasies, looking around first, then asking cautious questions. That got me nothing. I walked the streets, looking for bowed legs. That got me nothing. I decided to go back to my hotel, grab a nap, and resume the hunting at night.

In a far corner of the lobby a man stopped hiding behind a newspaper and came out to meet me. He had bowed legs, a hog jaw, and was MacSwain.

I nodded carelessly at him and walked on toward the elevators. He followed me, mumbling:

"Hey, you got a minute?"

"Yeah, just about." I stopped, pretending indifference.

"Let's get out of sight," he said nervously.

I took him up to my room. He straddled a chair and put a match in his mouth. I sat on the side of the bed and waited for him to say something. He chewed his match a while and began:

"I'm going to come clean with you, brother. I'm—"

"You mean you're going to tell me you knew me when you braced me yesterday?" I asked. "And you're going to tell me Bush hadn't told you to bet on him? And you didn't until afterwards? And you knew about his record because you used to be a bull? And you thought if you could get me to put it to him you could clean up a little dough playing him?"

"I'll be damned if I was going to come through with that much," he said, "but since it's been said I'll put a yes to it."

"Did you clean up?"

"I win myself six hundred iron men." He pushed his hat back and scratched his forehead with the chewed end of his match. "And then I lose myself that and my own two hundred and some in a crap game. What do you think of that? I pick up six hundred berries like shooting fish, and have to bum four bits for breakfast."

I said it was a tough break but that was the kind of a world we lived in.

He said, "Uh-huh," put the match back in his mouth, ground it some more, and added: "That's why I thought I'd come to see you. I used to be in the racket myself and—"

"What did Noonan put the skids under you for?"

"Skids? What skids? I quit. I come into a piece of change when the wife got killed in an automobile accident—insurance—and I quit."

"I heard he kicked you out the time his brother shot himself."

"Well, then you heard wrong. It was just after that, but you can ask him if I didn't quit."

"It's not that much to me. Go on telling me why you came to see me."

"I'm busted, flat. I know you're a Continental op, and I got a pretty good hunch what you're up to here. I'm close to a lot that's going on on both sides of things in this burg. There's things I could do for you, being an ex-dick, knowing the ropes both ways."

"You want to stool-pigeon for me?"

He looked me straight in the eye and said evenly:

"There's no sense in a man picking out the worst name he can find for everything."

"I'll give you something to do, MacSwain." I took out Myrtle Jennison's document and passed it to him. "Tell me about that."

He read it through carefully, his lips framing the words, the match wavering up and down in his mouth. He got up, put the paper on the bed beside me, and scowled down at it.

"There's something I'll have to find out about first," he said, very solemnly. "I'll be back in a little while and give you the whole story."

I laughed and told him:

"Don't be silly. You know I'm not going to let you walk out on me."

"I don't know that." He shook his head, still solemn. "Neither do you. All you know is whether you're going to try to stop me."

"The answer's yeah," I said while I considered that he was fairly hard and strong, six or seven years younger than I, and twenty or thirty pounds lighter.

He stood at the foot of the bed and looked at me with solemn eyes. I sat on the side of the bed and looked at him with whatever kind of eyes I had at the time. We did this for nearly three minutes.

I used part of the time measuring the distance between us, figuring out how, by throwing my body back on the bed and turning on my hip, I could get my heels in his face if he jumped me. He was too close for me to pull the gun. I had just finished this mental map-making when he spoke:

"That lousy ring wasn't worth no grand. I did swell to get two centuries for it."

"Sit down and tell me about it."

He shook his head again and said:

"First I want to know what you're meaning to do about it."

"Cop Whisper."

"I don't mean that. I mean with me."

"You'll have to go over to the Hall with me."

"I won't."

"Why not? You're only a witness."

"I'm only a witness that Noonan can hang a bribe-taking, or an accomplice after the act rap on, or both. And he'd be tickled simple to have the chance."

This jaw-wagging didn't seem to be leading anywhere. I said:

"That's too bad. But you're going to see him."

"Try and take me."

I sat up straighter and slid my right hand back to my hip.

He grabbed for me. I threw my body back on the bed, did the hip-spin, swung my feet at him. It was a good trick, only it didn't work. In his hurry to get at me he bumped the bed aside just enough to spill me off on the floor.

I landed all sprawled out on my back. I kept dragging at my gun while I tried to roll under the bed.

Missing me, his lunge carried him over the low footboard, over the side of the bed. He came down beside me, on the back of his neck, his body somersaulting over.

I put the muzzle of my gun in his left eye and said:

"You're making a fine pair of clowns of us. Be still while I get up or I'll make an opening in your head for brains to leak in."

I got up, found and pocketed my document, and let him get up.

"Knock the dents out of your hat and put your necktie in front, so you won't disgrace me going through the streets," I ordered after I had run a hand over his clothes and found nothing that felt like a weapon. "You can suit yourself about remembering that this gat is going to be in my overcoat pocket, with a hand on it."

He straightened his hat and tie and said:

"Hey, listen: I'm in this, I guess, and cutting up won't get me nothing. Suppose I be good. Could you forget about the tussle? See— maybe it'd be smoother for me if they thought I come along without being dragged."

"O. K."

"Thanks, brother."

∴

Noonan was out eating. We had to wait half an hour in his outer office. When he came in he greeted me with the usual *How are you? . . . That certainly is fine . . .* and the rest of it. He didn't say anything to Mac-Swain—simply eyed him sourly.

We went into the chief's private office. He pulled a chair over to his desk for me and then sat in his own, ignoring the ex-dick.

I gave Noonan the sick girl's document.

He gave it one glance, bounced out of his chair, and smashed a fist the size of a cantaloup into MacSwain's face.

The punch carried MacSwain across the room until a wall stopped him. The wall creaked under the strain, and a framed photograph of Noonan and other city dignitaries welcoming somebody in spats dropped down to the floor with the hit man.

The fat chief waddled over, picked up the picture and beat it to splinters on MacSwain's head and shoulders.

Noonan came back to his desk, puffing, smiling, saying cheerfully to me:

"That fellow's a rat if there ever was one."

MacSwain sat up and looked around, bleeding from nose, mouth and head.

Noonan roared at him:

"Come here, you."

MacSwain said, "Yes, chief," scrambled up and ran over to the desk.

Noonan said: "Come through or I'll kill you."

MacSwain said:

"Yes, chief. It was like she said, only that rock wasn't worth no grand. But she give me it and the two hundred to keep my mouth shut, because

I got there just when she asks him, 'Who did it, Tim?' and he says, 'Max!' He says it kind of loud and sharp, like he wanted to get it out before he died, because he died right then, almost before he'd got it out. That's the way it was, chief, but the rock wasn't worth no—"

"Damn the rock," Noonan barked. "And stop bleeding on my rug."

MacSwain hunted in his pocket for a dirty handkerchief, mopped his nose and mouth with it, and jabbered on:

"That's the way it was, chief. Everything else was like I said at the time, only I didn't say anything about hearing him say Max done it. I know I hadn't ought to—"

"Shut up," Noonan said, and pressed one of the buttons on his desk.

A uniformed copper came in. The chief jerked a thumb at MacSwain and said:

"Take this baby down cellar and let the wrecking crew work on him before you lock him up."

MacSwain started a desperate plea, "Aw, chief!" but the copper took him away before he could get any farther.

Noonan stuck a cigar at me, tapped the document with another and asked:

"Where's this broad?"

"In the City Hospital, dying. You'll have the 'cuter get a stiff out of her? That one's not so good legally—I framed it for effect. Another thing—I hear that Peak Murry and Whisper aren't playmates any more. Wasn't Murry one of his alibis?"

The chief said, "He was," picked up one of his phones, said, "McGraw," and then: "Get hold of Peak Murry and ask him to drop in. And have Tony Agosti picked up for that knife-throwing."

He put the phone down, stood up, made a lot of cigar smoke, and said through it:

"I haven't always been on the up-and-up with you."

I thought that was putting it mildly, but I didn't say anything while he went on:

"You know your way around. You know what these jobs are. There's this one and that one that's got to be listened to. Just because a man's chief of police doesn't mean he's chief. Maybe you're a lot of trouble to somebody that can be a lot of trouble to me. Don't make any difference if I think you're a right guy. I got to play with them that play with me. See what I mean?"

I wagged my head to show I did.

"That's the way it was," he said. "But no more. This is something else, a new deal. When the old woman kicked off Tim was just a lad. She said to me, 'Take care of him, John,' and I promised I would. And then Whisper murders him on account of that tramp." He reached down and took my hand. "See what I'm getting at? That's a year and a half ago, and you give me my first chance to hang it on him. I'm telling you there's no man in Personville that's got a voice big enough to talk you down. Not after today."

That pleased me and I said so. We purred at each other until a lanky man with an extremely up-turned nose in the middle of a round and freckled face was ushered in. It was Peak Murry.

"We were just wondering about the time when Tim died," the chief said when Murry had been given a chair and a cigar, "where Whisper was. You were out to the Lake that night, weren't you?"

"Yep," Murry said and the end of his nose got sharper.

"With Whisper?"

"I wasn't with him all the time."

"Were you with him at the time of the shooting?"

"Nope."

The chief's greenish eyes got smaller and brighter. He asked softly:

"You know where he was?"

"Nope."

The chief sighed in a thoroughly satisfied way and leaned back in his chair.

"Damn it, Peak," he said, "you told us before that you were with him at the bar."

"Yep, I did," the lanky man admitted. "But that don't mean nothing except that he asked me to and I didn't mind helping out a friend."

"Meaning you don't mind standing a perjury rap?"

"Don't kid me." Murry spit vigorously at the cuspidor. "I didn't say nothing in no court rooms."

"How about Jerry and George Kelly and O'Brien?" the chief asked. "Did they say they were with him just because he asked them to?"

"O'Brien did. I don't know nothing about the others. I was going out of the bar when I run into Whisper, Jerry and Kelly, and went back to have a shot with them. Kelly told me Tim had been knocked off. Then Whisper says, 'It never hurts anybody to have an alibi. We were here all the time, weren't we?' and he looks at O'Brien, who's behind the bar. O'Brien says, 'Sure you was,' and when Whisper looks at me I say the same thing. But I don't know no reasons why I've got to cover him up nowadays."

"And Kelly said Tim had been knocked off? Didn't say he had been found dead?"

" 'Knocked off' was the words he used."

The chief said:

"Thanks, Peak. You oughtn't to have done like you did, but what's done is done. How are the kids?"

Murry said they were doing fine, only the baby wasn't as fat as he'd like to have him. Noonan phoned the prosecuting attorney's office and had Dart and a stenographer take Peak's story before he left.

Noonan, Dart and the stenographer set out for the City Hospital to get a complete statement from Myrtle Jennison. I didn't go along. I decided I needed sleep, told the chief I would see him later, and returned to the hotel.

XIII · —$200.10—

I had my vest unbuttoned when the telephone bell rang.

It was Dinah Brand, complaining that she had been trying to get me since ten o'clock.

"Have you done anything on what I told you?" she asked.

"I've been looking it over. It seems pretty good. I think maybe I'll crack it this afternoon."

"Don't. Hold it till I see you. Can you come up now?"

I looked at the vacant white bed and said, "Yes," without much enthusiasm.

Another tub of cold water did me so little good that I almost fell asleep in it.

Dan Rolff let me in when I rang the girl's bell. He looked and acted as if nothing out of the ordinary had happened the night before. Dinah Brand came into the hall to help me off with my overcoat. She had on a tan woolen dress with a two-inch rip in one shoulder seam.

She took me into the living room. She sat on the Chesterfield beside me and said:

"I'm going to ask you to do something for me. You like me enough, don't you?"

I admitted that. She counted the knuckles of my left hand with a warm forefinger and explained:

"I want you to not do anything more about what I told you last night. Now wait a minute. Wait till I get through. Dan was right. I oughtn't sell Max out like that. It would be utterly filthy. Besides, it's Noonan you chiefly want, isn't it? Well, if you'll be a nice darling and lay off Max this time, I'll give you enough on Noonan to nail him forever. You'd like that better, wouldn't you? And you like me too much to want to take advantage of me by using information I gave you when I was mad at what Max had said, don't you?"

"What is the dirt on Noonan?" I asked.

She kneaded my biceps and murmured: "You promise?"

"Not yet."

She pouted at me and said:

"I'm off Max for life, on the level. You've got no right to make me turn rat."

"What about Noonan?"

"Promise first."

"No."

She dug fingers into my arm and asked sharply:

"You've already gone to Noonan?"

"Yeah."

She let go my arm, frowned, shrugged, and said gloomily:

"Well, how can I help it?"

I stood up and a voice said:

"Sit down."

It was a hoarse whispering voice—Thaler's.

I turned to see him standing in the dining room doorway, a big gun in one of his little hands. A red-faced man with a scarred cheek stood behind him.

The other doorway—opening to the hall—filled as I sat down. The loose-mouthed chinless man I had heard Whisper call Jerry came a step through it. He had a couple of guns. The more angular one of the blond kids who had been in the King Street joint looked over his shoulder.

Dinah Brand got up from the Chesterfield, put her back to Thaler, and addressed me. Her voice was husky with rage.

"This is none of my doing. He came here by himself, said he was sorry for what he had said, and showed me how we could make a lot of coin by turning Noonan up for you. The whole thing was a plant, but I fell for it. Honest to Christ! He was to wait upstairs while I put it to you. I didn't know anything about the others. I didn't—"

Jerry's casual voice drawled:

"If I shoot a pin from under her, she'll sure sit down, and maybe shut up. O. K.?"

I couldn't see Whisper. The girl was between us. He said:

"Not now. Where's Dan?"

The angular blond youngster said:

"Up on the bathroom floor. I had to sap him."

Dinah Brand turned around to face Thaler. Stocking seams made s's up the ample backs of her legs. She said:

"Max Thaler, you're a lousy little—"

He whispered, very deliberately:

"Shut up and get out of the way."

She surprised me by doing both, and she kept quiet while he spoke to me:

"So you and Noonan are trying to paste his brother's death on me?"

"It doesn't need pasting. It's a natural."

He curved his thin lips at me and said:

"You're as crooked as he is."

I said:

"You know better. I played your side when he tried to frame you. This time he's got you copped to rights."

Dinah Brand flared up again, waving her arms in the center of the room, storming:

"Get out of here, the whole lot of you. Why should I give a God-damn about your troubles? Get out."

The blond kid who had sapped Rolff squeezed past Jerry and came grinning into the room. He caught one of the girl's flourished arms and bent it behind her.

She twisted toward him, socked him in the belly with her other fist. It was a very respectable wallop—man-size. It broke his grip on her arm, sent him back a couple of steps.

The kid gulped a wide mouthful of air, whisked a blackjack from his hip, and stepped in again. His grin was gone.

Jerry laughed what little chin he had out of sight.

Thaler whispered harshly: "Lay off!"

The kid didn't hear him. He was snarling at the girl.

She watched him with a face hard as a silver dollar. She was standing with most of her weight on her left foot. I guessed blondy was going to stop a kick when he closed in.

The kid feinted a grab with his empty left hand, started the black-jack at her face.

Thaler whispered, "Lay off," again, and fired.

The bullet smacked blondy under the right eye, spun him around, and dropped him backwards into Dinah Brand's arms.

This looked like the time, if there was to be any.

In the excitement I had got my hand to my hip. Now I yanked the gun out and snapped a cap at Thaler, trying for his shoulder.

That was wrong. If I had tried for a bulls-eye I would have winged him. Chinless Jerry hadn't laughed himself blind. He beat me to the shot. His shot burnt my wrist, throwing me off the target. But, missing Thaler, my slug crumpled the red-faced man behind him.

Not knowing how badly my wrist was nicked, I switched the gun to my left hand.

Jerry had another try at me. The girl spoiled it by heaving the corpse at him. The dead yellow head banged into his knees. I jumped for him while he was off-balance.

The jump took me out of the path of Thaler's bullet. It also tumbled me and Jerry out into the hall, all tangled up together.

Jerry wasn't tough to handle, but I had to work quick. There was Thaler behind me. I socked Jerry twice, kicked him, butted him at least once, and was hunting for a place to bite when he went limp under me. I poked him again where his chin should have been—just to make sure he wasn't faking—and went away on hands and knees, down the hall a bit, out of line with the door.

I sat on my heels against the wall, held my gun level at Thaler's part of the premises, and waited. I couldn't hear anything for the moment except blood singing in my head.

Dinah Brand stepped out of the door I had tumbled through, looked at Jerry, then at me. She smiled with her tongue between her teeth, beckoned with a jerk of her head, and returned to the living room. I followed her cautiously.

Whisper stood in the center of the floor. His hands were empty and so was his face. Except for his vicious little mouth he looked like something displaying suits in a clothing store window.

Dan Rolff stood behind him, with a gun-muzzle tilted to the little gambler's left kidney. Rolff's face was mostly blood. The blond kid—now dead on the floor between Rolff and me—had sapped him plenty.

I grinned at Thaler and said, "Well, this is nice," before I saw that Rolff had another gun, centered on my chubby middle. That wasn't so nice. But my gun was reasonably level in my hand. I didn't have much worse than an even break.

Rolff said:

"Put down your pistol."

I looked at Dinah, looked puzzled, I suppose. She shrugged and told me:

"It seems to be Dan's party."

"Yeah? Somebody ought to tell him I don't like to play this way."

Rolff repeated: "Put down your pistol."

I said disagreeably:

"I'm damned if I will. I've shed twenty pounds trying to nab this bird, and I can spare twenty more for the same purpose."

Rolff said:

"I'm not interested in what is between you two, and I have no intention of giving either of you—"

Dinah Brand had wandered across the room. When she was behind Rolff, I interrupted his speech by telling her:

"If you upset him now you're sure of making two friends—Noonan and me. You can't trust Thaler any more, so there's no use helping him."

She laughed and said:

"Talk money, darling."

"Dinah!" Rolff protested. He was caught. She was behind him and she was strong enough to handle him. It wasn't likely that he would shoot her, and it wasn't likely that anything else would keep her from doing whatever she decided to do.

"A hundred dollars," I bid.

"My God!" she exclaimed, "I've actually got a cash offer out of you. But not enough."

"Two hundred."

"You're getting reckless. But I still can't hear you."

"Try," I said. "It's worth that to me not to have to shoot Rolff's gun out of his hand, but no more than that."

"You got a good start. Don't weaken. One more bid, anyway."

"Two hundred dollars and ten cents and that's all."

"You big bum," she said, "I won't do it."

"Suit yourself." I made a face at Thaler and cautioned him: "When what happens happens be damned sure you keep still."

Dinah cried:

"Wait! Are you really going to start something?"

"I'm going to take Thaler out with me, regardless."

"Two hundred and a dime?"

"Yeah."

"Dinah," Rolff called without turning his face from me, "you won't—"

But she laughed, came close to his back, and wound her strong arms around him, pulling his arms down, pinning them to his sides.

I shoved Thaler out of the way with my right arm, and kept my gun on him while I yanked Rolff's weapons out of his hands. Dinah turned the lunger loose.

He took two steps toward the dining room door, said wearily, "There is no—" and collapsed on the floor.

Dinah ran to him. I pushed Thaler through the hall door, past the still sleeping Jerry, and to the alcove beneath the front stairs, where I had seen a phone.

I called Noonan, told him I had Thaler, and where.

"Mother of God!" he said. "Don't kill him till I get there."

XIV · Max

THE news of Whisper's capture spread quickly. When Noonan, the coppers he had brought along, and I took the gambler and the now conscious Jerry into the City Hall there were at least a hundred people standing around watching us.

All of them didn't look pleased. Noonan's coppers—a shabby lot at best—moved around with whitish strained faces. But Noonan was the most triumphant guy west of the Mississippi. Even the bad luck he had trying to third-degree Whisper couldn't spoil his happiness.

Whisper stood up under all they could give him. He would talk to his lawyer, he said, and to nobody else, and he stuck to it. And, as much as Noonan hated the gambler, here was a prisoner he didn't give the works, didn't turn over to the wrecking crew. Whisper had killed the chief's brother, and the chief hated his guts, but Whisper was still too much somebody in Poisonville to be roughed around.

Noonan finally got tired of playing with his prisoner, and sent him up —the prison was on the City Hall's top floor—to be stowed away. I lit another of the chief's cigars and read the detailed statement he had got from the woman in the hospital. There was nothing in it that I hadn't learned from Dinah and MacSwain.

The chief wanted me to come out to his house for dinner, but I lied out of it, pretending that my wrist—now in a bandage—was bothering me. It was really little more than a burn.

While we were talking about it, a pair of plain-clothes men brought in the red-faced bird who had stopped the slug I had missed Whisper with. It had broken a rib for him, and he had taken a back-door sneak while the rest of us were busy. Noonan's men had picked him up in a doctor's office. The chief failed to get any information out of him, and sent him off to the hospital.

I got up and prepared to leave, saying:

"The Brand girl gave me the tip-off on this. That's why I asked you to keep her and Rolff out of it."

The chief took hold of my left hand for the fifth or sixth time in the past couple of hours.

"If you want her taken care of, that's enough for me," he assured me. "But if she had a hand in turning that bastard up, you can tell her for me that any time she wants anything, all she's got to do is name it."

I said I'd tell her that, and went over to my hotel, thinking about that neat white bed. But it was nearly eight o'clock, and my stomach needed attention. I went into the hotel dining room and had that fixed up.

Then a leather chair tempted me into stopping in the lobby while I burnt a cigar. That led to conversation with a traveling railroad auditor from Denver, who knew a man I knew in St. Louis. Then there was a lot of shooting in the street.

We went to the door and decided that the shooting was in the vicinity of the City Hall. I shook the auditor and moved up that way.

I had done two-thirds of the distance when an automobile came down the street toward me, moving fast, leaking gun-fire from the rear.

I backed into an alley entrance and slid my gun loose. The car came abreast. An arc-light brightened two faces in the front of the car. The driver's meant nothing to me. The upper part of the other's was hidden by a pulled-down hat. The lower part was Whisper's.

Across the street was the entrance to another block of my alley, lighted at the far end. Between the light and me, somebody moved just as Whisper's car roared past. The somebody had dodged from behind one shadow that might have been an ash-can to another.

What made me forget Whisper was that the somebody's legs had a bowed look.

A load of coppers buzzed past, throwing lead at the first car.

I skipped across the street, into the section of alley that held a man who might have bowed legs.

If he was my man, it was a fair bet he wasn't armed. I played it that way, moving straight up the slimy middle of the alley, looking into shadows with eyes, ears and nose.

Three-quarters of a block of this, and a shadow broke away from another shadow—a man going pell-mell away from me.

"Stop!" I bawled, pounding my feet after him. "Stop, or I'll plug you, MacSwain."

He ran half a dozen strides farther and stopped, turning.

"Oh, it's you," he said, as if it made any difference who took him back to the hoosegow.

"Yeah," I confessed. "What are all you people doing wandering around loose?"

"I don't know nothing about it. Somebody dynamited the floor out of the can. I dropped through the hole with the rest of them. There was some mugs standing off the bulls. I made the back-trotters with one bunch. Then we split, and I was figuring on cutting over and making the hills. I didn't have nothing to do with it. I just went along when she blew open."

"Whisper was pinched this evening," I told him.

"Hell! Then that's it. Noonan had ought to know he'd never keep that guy screwed up—not in this burg."

We were standing still in the alley where MacSwain had stopped running.

"You know what he was pinched for?" I asked.

"Uh-huh, for killing Tim."

"You know who killed Tim?"

"Huh? Sure, he did."

"You did."

"Huh? What's the matter? You simple?"

"There's a gun in my left hand," I warned him.

"But look here—didn't he tell the broad that Whisper done it? What's the matter with you?"

"He didn't say Whisper. I've heard women call Thaler Max, but I've never heard a man here call him anything but Whisper. Tim didn't say Max. He said MacS—the first part of MacSwain—and died before he could finish it. Don't forget about the gun."

"What would I have killed him for? He was after Whisper's—"

"I haven't got around to that yet," I admitted, "but let's see: You and your wife had busted up. Tim was a ladies' man, wasn't he? Maybe there's something there. I'll have to look it up. What started me thinking about you was that you never tried to get any more money out of the girl."

"Cut it out," he begged. "You know there ain't any sense to it. What would I have hung around afterwards for? I'd have been out getting an alibi, like Whisper."

"Why? You were a dick then. Close by was the spot for you—to see that everything went right—handle it yourself."

"You know damned well it don't hang together, don't make sense. Cut it out, for God's sake."

"I don't mind how goofy it is," I said. "It's something to put to Noonan when we get back. He's likely all broken up over Whisper's crush-out. This will take his mind off it."

MacSwain got down on his knees in the muddy alley and cried:

"Oh, Christ, no! He'd croak me with his hands."

"Get up and stop yelling," I growled. "Now will you give it to me straight?"

He whined: "He'd croak me with his hands."

"Suit yourself. If you won't talk, I will, to Noonan. If you'll come through to me, I'll do what I can for you."

"What can you do?" he asked hopelessly, and started sniveling again. "How do I know you'll try to do anything?"

I risked a little truth on him:

"You said you had a hunch what I'm up to here in Poisonville. Then you ought to know that it's my play to keep Noonan and Whisper split. Letting Noonan think Whisper killed Tim will keep them split. But if you don't want to play with me, come on, we'll play with Noonan."

"You mean you won't tell him?" he asked eagerly. "You promise?"

"I promise you nothing," I said. "Why should I? I've got you with your pants down. Talk to me or Noonan. And make up your mind quick. I'm not going to stand here all night."

He made up his mind to talk to me.

"I don't know how much you know, but it was like you said, my wife fell for Tim. That's what put me on the tramp. You can ask anybody if I wasn't a good guy before that. I was this way: what she wanted I wanted her to have. Mostly what she wanted was tough on me. But I couldn't be any other way. We'd have been a damned sight better off if I could. So I let her move out and put in divorce papers, so she could marry him, thinking he meant to.

"Pretty soon I begin to hear he's chasing this Myrtle Jennison. I couldn't go that. I'd given him his chance with Helen, fair and square. Now he was giving her the air for this Myrtle. I wasn't going to stand for that. Helen wasn't no hanky-panky. It was accidental, though, running into him at the Lake that night. When I saw him go down to them summer houses I went after him. That looked like a good quiet place to have it out.

"I guess we'd both had a little something to drink. Anyway, we had it hot and heavy. When it got too hot for him, he pulled the gun. He was yellow. I grabbed it, and in the tussle it went off. I swear to God I didn't shoot him except like that. It went off while the both of us had our hands on it. I beat it back in some bushes. But when I got in the bushes I could hear him moaning and talking. There was people coming—a girl running down from the hotel, that Myrtle Jennison.

"I wanted to go back and hear what Tim was saying, so I'd know where I stood, but I was leary of being the first one there. So I had to wait till the girl got to him, listening all the time to his squawking, but too far away to make it out. When she got to him, I ran over and got there just as he died trying to say my name.

"I didn't think about that being Whisper's name till she propositioned me with the suicide letter, the two hundred, and the rock. I'd just been stalling around, pretending to get the job lined up—being on the force then—and trying to find out where I stood. Then she makes the play and I know I'm sitting pretty. And that's the way it went till you started digging it up again."

He slopped his feet up and down in the mud and added:

"Next week my wife got killed—an accident. Uh-huh, an accident. She drove the Ford square in front of No. 6 where it comes down the long grade from Tanner and stopped it there."

"Is Mock Lake in this county?" I asked.

"No, Boulder County."

"That's out of Noonan's territory. Suppose I take you over there and hand you to the sheriff?"

"No. He's Senator Keefer's son-in-law—Tom Cook. I might as well be here. Noonan could get to me through Keefer."

"If it happened the way you say, you've got at least an even chance of beating the rap in court."

"They won't give me a chance. I'd have stood it if there'd been a chance in the world of getting an even break—but not with them."

"We're going back to the Hall," I said. "Keep your mouth shut."

∴

Noonan was waddling up and down the floor, cursing the half a dozen bulls who stood around wishing they were somewhere else.

"Here's something I found roaming around," I said, pushing Mac-Swain forward.

Noonan knocked the ex-detective down, kicked him, and told one of the coppers to take him away.

Somebody called Noonan on the phone. I slipped out without saying, "Good-night," and walked back to the hotel.

Off to the north some guns popped.

A group of three men passed me, shifty-eyed, walking pigeon-toed.

A little farther along, another man moved all the way over to the curb to give me plenty of room to pass. I didn't know him and didn't suppose he knew me.

A lone shot sounded not far away.

As I reached the hotel, a battered black touring car went down the street, hitting fifty at least, crammed to the curtains with men.

I grinned after it. Poisonville was beginning to boil out under the lid, and I felt so much like a native that even the memory of my very un-nice part in the boiling didn't keep me from getting twelve solid end-to-end hours of sleep.

XV · Cedar Hill Inn

MICKEY LINEHAN used the telephone to wake me a little after noon.

"We're here," he told me. "Where's the reception committee?"

"Probably stopped to get a rope. Check your bags and come up to the hotel. Room 537. Don't advertise your visit."

I was dressed when they arrived.

Mickey Linehan was a big slob with sagging shoulders and a shapeless body that seemed to be coming apart at all its joints. His ears stood out like red wings, and his round red face usually wore the meaningless smirk of a half-wit. He looked like a comedian and was.

Dick Foley was a boy-sized Canadian with a sharp irritable face. He wore high heels to increase his height, perfumed his handkerchiefs and saved all the words he could.

They were both good operatives.

"What did the Old Man tell you about the job?" I asked when we had settled into seats. The Old Man was the manager of the Continental's San Francisco branch. He was also known as Pontius Pilate, because he smiled pleasantly when he sent us out to be crucified on suicidal jobs. He was a gentle, polite, elderly person with no more warmth in him than a hangman's rope. The Agency wits said he could spit icicles in July.

"He didn't seem to know much what it was all about," Mickey said, "except that you had wired for help. He said he hadn't got any reports from you for a couple of days."

"The chances are he'll wait a couple more. Know anything about this Personville?"

Dick shook his head. Mickey said:

"Only that I've heard parties call it Poisonville like they meant it."

I told them what I knew and what I had done. The telephone bell interrupted my tale in the last quarter.

Dinah Brand's lazy voice:

"Hello! How's the wrist?"

"Only a burn. What do you think of the crush-out?"

"It's not my fault," she said. "I did my part. If Noonan couldn't hold him, that's just too bad. I'm coming downtown to buy a hat this afternoon. I thought I'd drop in and see you for a couple of minutes if you're going to be there."

"What time?"

"Oh, around three."

"Right, I'll expect you, and I'll have that two hundred and a dime I owe you."

"Do," she said. "That's what I'm coming in for. Ta-ta."

I went back to my seat and my story.

When I had finished, Mickey Linehan whistled and said:

"No wonder you're scared to send in any reports. The Old Man wouldn't do much if he knew what you've been up to, would he?"

"If it works out the way I want it to, I won't have to report all the distressing details," I said. "It's right enough for the Agency to have rules and regulations, but when you're out on a job you've got to do it the best way you can. And anybody that brings any ethics to Poisonville is going to get them all rusty. A report is no place for the dirty details, anyway, and I don't want you birds to send any writing back to San Francisco without letting me see it first."

"What kind of crimes have you got for us to pull?" Mickey asked.

"I want you to take Pete the Finn. Dick will take Lew Yard. You'll have to play it the way I've been playing—do what you can when you can. I've an idea that the pair of them will try to make Noonan let Whisper alone. I don't know what he'll do. He's shifty as hell and he does want to even up his brother's killing."

"After I take this Finnish gent," Mickey said, "what do I do with him? I don't want to brag about how dumb I am, but this job is plain as astronomy to me. I understand everything about it except what you have done and why, and what you're trying to do and how."

"You can start off by shadowing him. I've got to have a wedge that can be put between Pete and Yard, Yard and Noonan, Pete and Noonan, Pete and Thaler, or Yard and Thaler. If we can smash things up enough—break the combination—they'll have their knives in each other's backs, doing our work for us. The break between Thaler and Noonan is a starter. But it'll sag on us if we don't help it along.

"I could buy more dope on the whole lot from Dinah Brand. But there's no use taking anybody into court, no matter what you've got on them. They own the courts, and, besides, the courts are too slow for us now. I've got myself tangled up in something and as soon as the Old Man smells it—and San Francisco isn't far enough away to fool his nose—he's going to be sitting on the wire, asking for explanations. I've got to have results to hide the details under. So evidence won't do. What we've got to have is dynamite."

"What about our respected client, Mr. Elihu Willsson?" Mickey asked. "What are you planning to do with or to him?"

"Maybe ruin him, maybe club him into backing us up. I don't care which. You'd better stay at the Hotel Person, Mickey, and Dick can go to the National. Keep apart, and, if you want to keep me from being fired, burn the job up before the Old Man tumbles. Better write these down."

I gave them names, descriptions, and addresses when I had them, of Elihu Willsson; Stanley Lewis, his secretary; Dinah Brand; Dan Rolff; Noonan; Max Thaler, alias Whisper; his right-hand man, the chinless Jerry; Mrs. Donald Willsson; Lewis' daughter, who had been Donald Willsson's secretary; and Bill Quint, Dinah's radical ex-boy-friend.

"Now hop to it," I said. "And don't kid yourselves that there's any law in Poisonville except what you make for yourself."

Mickey said I'd be surprised how many laws he could get along without. Dick said: "So long," and they departed.

∴

After breakfast I went over to the City Hall.

Noonan's greenish eyes were bleary, as if they hadn't been sleeping, and his face had lost some of its color. He pumped my hand up and down as enthusiastically as ever, and the customary amount of cordiality was in his voice and manner.

"Any line on Whisper?" I asked when we had finished the glad-handing.

"I think I've got something." He looked at the clock on the wall and then at his phone. "I'm expecting word any minute. Sit down."

"Who else got away?"

"Jerry Hooper and Tony Agosti are the only other ones still out. We picked up the rest. Jerry is Whisper's man-Friday, and the wop's one of his mob. He's the bozo that put the knife in Ike Bush the night of the fight."

"Any more of Whisper's mob in?"

"No. We just had the three of them, except Buck Wallace, the fellow you potted. He's in the hospital."

The chief looked at the wall clock again, and at his watch. It was exactly two o'clock. He turned to the phone. It rang. He grabbed it, said:

"Noonan talking. . . . Yes. . . . Yes. . . . Yes. . . . Right."

He pushed the phone aside and played a tune on the row of pearl buttons on his desk. The office filled up with coppers.

"Cedar Hill Inn," he said. "You follow me out with your detail, Bates. Terry, shoot out Broadway and hit the dump from behind. Pick up the boys on traffic duty as you go along. It's likely we'll need everybody we can get. Duffy, take yours out Union Street and around by the old mine road. McGraw will hold headquarters down. Get hold of everybody you can and send them after us. Jump!"

He grabbed his hat and went after them, calling over his thick shoulder to me:

"Come on, man, this is the kill."

I followed him down to the department garage, where the engines of half a dozen cars were roaring. The chief sat beside his driver. I sat in back with four detectives.

Men scrambled into the other cars. Machine-guns were unwrapped. Arm-loads of rifles and riot-guns were distributed, and packages of ammunition.

The chief's car got away first, off with a jump that hammered our teeth together. We missed the garage door by half an inch, chased a couple of pedestrians diagonally across the sidewalk, bounced off the curb into the roadway, missed a truck as narrowly as we had missed the door, and dashed out King Street with our siren wide open.

Panicky automobiles darted right and left, regardless of traffic rules, to let us through. It was a lot of fun.

I looked back, saw another police car following us, a third turning into Broadway. Noonan chewed a cold cigar and told the driver:

"Give her a bit more, Pat."

Pat twisted us around a frightened woman's coupé, put us through a slot between street car and laundry wagon—a narrow slot that we couldn't have slipped through if our car hadn't been so smoothly enameled—and said:

"All right, but the brakes ain't no good."

"That's nice," the gray-mustached sleuth on my left said. He didn't sound sincere.

Out of the center of the city there wasn't much traffic to bother us, but the paving was rougher. It was a nice half-hour's ride, with everybody getting a chance to sit in everybody else's lap. The last ten minutes of it was over an uneven road that had hills enough to keep us from forgetting what Pat had said about the brakes.

We wound up at a gate topped by a shabby electric sign that had said *Cedar Hill Inn* before it lost its globes. The roadhouse, twenty feet behind the gate, was a squat wooden building painted a moldy green and chiefly surrounded by rubbish. Front door and windows were closed, blank.

We followed Noonan out of the car. The machine that had been trailing us came into sight around a bend in the road, slid to rest beside ours, and unloaded its cargo of men and weapons.

Noonan ordered this and that.

A trio of coppers went around each side of the building. Three others, including a machine-gunner, remained by the gate. The rest of us walked through tin cans, bottles, and ancient newspaper to the front of the house.

The gray-mustached detective who had sat beside me in the car carried a red ax. We stepped up on the porch.

Noise and fire came out under a window sill.

The gray-mustached detective fell down, hiding the ax under his corpse.

The rest of us ran away.

I ran with Noonan. We hid in the ditch on the Inn side of the road. It was deep enough, and banked high enough, to let us stand almost erect without being targets.

The chief was excited.

"What luck!" he said happily. "He's here, by God, he's here!"

"That shot came from under the sill," I said. "Not a bad trick."

"We'll spoil it, though," he said cheerfully. "We'll sieve the dump. Duffy ought to be pulling up on the other road by now, and Terry Shane won't be many minutes behind him. Hey, Donner!" he called to a man who was peeping around a boulder. "Swing around back and tell Duffy and Shane to start closing in as soon as they come, letting fly with all they got. Where's Kimble?"

The peeper jerked a thumb toward a tree beyond him. We could see only the upper part of it from our ditch.

"Tell him to set up his mill and start grinding," Noonan ordered. "Low, across the front, ought to do it like cutting cheese."

The peeper disappeared.

Noonan went up and down the ditch, risking his noodle over the top now and then for a look around, once in a while calling or gesturing to his men.

He came back, sat on his heels beside me, gave me a cigar, and lit one for himself.

"It'll do," he said complacently. "Whisper won't have a chance. He's done."

The machine-gun by the tree fired, haltingly, experimentally, eight or ten shots. Noonan grinned and let a smoke ring float out of his mouth. The machine-gun settled down to business, grinding out metal like the busy little death factory it was. Noonan blew another smoke ring and said:

"That's exactly what'll do it."

I agreed that it ought to. We leaned against the clay bank and smoked while, farther away, another machine-gun got going, and then a third. Irregularly, rifles, pistols, shot-guns joined in. Noonan nodded approvingly and said:

"Five minutes of that will let him know there's a hell."

When the five minutes were up I suggested a look at the remains. I gave him a boost up the bank and scrambled up after him.

The roadhouse was as bleak and empty-looking as before, but more battered. No shots came from it. Plenty were going into it.

"What do you think?" Noonan asked.

"If there's a cellar there might be a mouse alive in it."

"Well, we could finish him afterwards."

He took a whistle out of his pocket and made a lot of noise. He waved his fat arms, and the gun-fire began dwindling. We had to wait for the word to go all the way around.

Then we crashed the door.

The first floor was ankle-deep with booze that was still gurgling from bullet holes in the stacked-up cases and barrels that filled most of the house.

Dizzy with the fumes of spilled hooch, we waded around until we had found four dead bodies and no live ones. The four were swarthy foreign-looking men in laborers' clothes. Two of them were practically shot to pieces.

Noonan said:

"Leave them here and get out."

His voice was cheerful, but in a flashlight's glow his eyes showed white-ringed with fear.

We went out gladly, though I did hesitate long enough to pocket an unbroken bottle labeled *Dewar*.

A khaki-dressed copper was tumbling off a motorcycle at the gate. He yelled at us:

"The First National's been stuck up."

Noonan cursed savagely, bawled:

"He's foxed us, damn him! Back to town, everybody."

Everybody except us who had ridden with the chief beat it for the machines. Two of them took the dead detective with them.

Noonan looked at me out of his eye-corners and said:

"This is a tough one, no fooling."

I said, "Well," shrugged, and sauntered over to his car, where the driver was sitting at the wheel. I stood with my back to the house, talking to Pat. I don't remember what we talked about. Presently Noonan and the other sleuths joined us.

Only a little flame showed through the open roadhouse door before **we** passed out of sight around the bend in the road.

XVI · *Exit Jerry*

THERE was a mob around the First National Bank. We pushed through it to the door, where we found sour-faced McGraw.

"Was six of them, masked," he reported to the chief as we went inside. "They hit it about two-thirty. Five of them got away clean with the jack. The watchman here dropped one of them, Jerry Hooper. He's over on the bench, cold. We got the roads blocked, and I wired around, if it ain't too late. Last seen of them was when they made the turn into King Street, in a black Lincoln."

We went over to look at the dead Jerry, lying on one of the lobby benches with a brown robe over him. The bullet had gone in under his left shoulder blade.

The bank watchman, a harmless looking old duffer, pushed up his chest and told us about it:

"There wasn't no chance to do nothing at first. They were in 'fore anybody knew anything. And maybe they didn't work fast. Right down the line, scooping it up. No chance to do anything then. But I says to myself, 'All righty, young fellows, you've got it all your own way now, but wait till you try to leave.'

"And I was as good as my word, you bet you. I runs right to the door after them and cut loose with the old firearm. I got that fellow just as he was stepping into the car. I bet you I'd of got more of them if I'd of had more cartridges, because it's kind of hard shooting down like that, standing in the—"

Noonan stopped the monologue by patting the old duffer's back till his lungs were empty, telling him, "That certainly is fine. That certainly is fine."

McGraw pulled the robe up over the dead man again and growled:

"Nobody can identify anybody. But with Jerry on it, it's a cinch it was Whisper's caper."

The chief nodded happily and said:

"I'll leave it in your hands, Mac. Going to poke around here, or going back to the Hall with me?" he asked me.

"Neither. I've got a date, and I want to get into dry shoes."

∴

Dinah Brand's little Marmon was standing in front of the hotel. I didn't see her. I went up to my room, leaving the door unlocked. I had got my hat and coat off when she came in without knocking.

"My God, you keep a boozy smelling room," she said.

"It's my shoes. Noonan took me wading in rum."

She crossed to the window, opened it, sat on the sill, and asked:

"What was that for?"

"He thought he was going to find your Max out in a dump called Cedar Hill Inn. So we went out there, shot the joint silly, murdered some dagoes, spilled gallons of liquor, and left the place burning."

"Cedar Hill Inn? I thought it had been closed up for a year or more."

"It looked it, but it was somebody's warehouse."

"But you didn't find Max there?" she asked.

"While we were there he seems to have been knocking over Elihu's First National Bank."

"I saw that," she said. "I had just come out of Bengren's, the store two doors away. I had just got in my car when I saw a big boy backing out of the bank, carrying a sack and a gun, with a black handkerchief over his face."

"Was Max with them?"

"No, he wouldn't be. He'd send Jerry and the boys. That's what he has them for. Jerry was there. I knew him as soon as he got out of the car, in spite of the black handkerchief. They all had black ones. Four of them came out of the bank, running down to the car at the curb. Jerry and another fellow were in the car. When the four came across the sidewalk, Jerry jumped out and went to meet them. That's when the shooting started and Jerry dropped. The others jumped in the bus and lit out. How about that dough you owe me?"

I counted out ten twenty-dollar bills and a dime. She left the window to come for them.

"That's for pulling Dan off, so you could cop Max," she said when she had stowed the money away in her bag. "Now how about what I was to get for showing you where you could turn up the dope on his killing Tim Noonan?"

"You'll have to wait till he's indicted. How do I know the dope's any good?"

She frowned and asked:

"What do you do with all the money you don't spend?" Her face brightened. "You know where Max is now?"

"No."

"What's it worth to know?"

"Nothing."

"I'll tell you for a hundred bucks."

"I wouldn't want to take advantage of you that way."

"I'll tell you for fifty bucks."

I shook my head.

"Twenty-five."

"I don't want him," I said. "I don't care where he is. Why don't you peddle the news to Noonan?"

"Yes, and try to collect. Do you only perfume yourself with booze, or is there any for drinking purposes?"

"Here's a bottle of so-called Dewar that I picked up at Cedar Hill this afternoon. There's a bottle of King George in my bag. What's your choice?"

She voted for King George. We had a drink apiece, straight, and I said:

"Sit down and play with it while I change clothes."

When I came out of the bathroom twenty-five minutes later she was sitting at the secretary, smoking a cigarette and studying a memoranda book that had been in a side pocket of my gladstone bag.

"I guess these are the expenses you've charged up on other cases," she said without looking up. "I'm damned if I can see why you can't be more liberal with me. Look, here's a six-hundred-dollar item marked *Inf.* That's information you bought from somebody, isn't it? And here's a hundred and fifty below it—*Top*—whatever that is. And here's another day when you spent nearly a thousand dollars."

"They must be telephone numbers," I said, taking the book from her. "Where were you raised? Fanning my baggage!"

"I was raised in a convent," she told me. "I won the good behavior prize every year I was there. I thought little girls who put extra spoons of sugar in their chocolate went to hell for gluttony. I didn't even know there was such a thing as profanity until I was eighteen. The first time I heard any I damned near fainted." She spit on the rug in front of her, tilted her chair back, put her crossed feet on my bed, and asked: "What do you think of that?"

I pushed her feet off the bed and said:

"I was raised in a water-front saloon. Keep your saliva off my floor or I'll toss you out on your neck."

"Let's have another drink first. Listen, what'll you give me for the inside story of how the boys didn't lose anything building the City Hall—the story that was in the papers I sold Donald Willsson?"

"That doesn't click with me. Try another."

"How about why the first Mrs. Lew Yard was sent to the insane asylum?"

"No."

"King, our sheriff, eight thousand dollars in debt four years ago, now the owner of as nice a collection of downtown business blocks as you'd want to see. I can't give you all of it, but I can show you where to get it."

"Keep trying," I encouraged her.

"No. You don't want to buy anything. You're just hoping you'll pick up something for nothing. This isn't bad Scotch. Where'd you get it?"

"Brought it from San Francisco with me."

"What's the idea of not wanting any of this information I'm offering? Think you can get it cheaper?"

"Information of that kind's not much good to me now. I've got to move quick. I need dynamite—something to blow them apart."

She laughed and jumped up, her big eyes sparkling.

"I've got one of Lew Yard's cards. Suppose we sent the bottle of Dewar you copped to Pete with the card. Wouldn't he take it as a declaration of war? If Cedar Hill was a liquor cache, it was Pete's. Wouldn't the bottle and Lew's card make him think Noonan had knocked the place over under orders?"

I considered it and said:

"Too crude. It wouldn't fool him. Besides, I'd just as leave have Pete and Lew both against the chief at this stage."

She pouted and said:

"You think you know everything. You're just hard to get along with. Take me out tonight? I've got a new outfit that'll knock them cockeyed."

"Yeah."

"Come up for me around eight."

She patted my cheek with a warm hand, said, "Ta-ta," and went out as the telephone bell began jingling.

∴

"My chinch and Dick's are together at your client's joint," Mickey Linehan reported over the wire. "Mine's been generally busier than a hustler with two bunks, though I don't know what the score is yet. Anything new?"

I said there wasn't and went into conference with myself across the bed, trying to guess what would come of Noonan's attack on Cedar Hill Inn and Whisper's on the First National Bank. I would have given something for ability to hear what was being said up at old Elihu's house by him, Pete the Finn, and Lew Yard. But I hadn't that ability, and I was never much good at guessing, so after half an hour I stopped tormenting my brain and took a nap.

It was nearly seven o'clock when I came out of the nap. I washed, dressed, loaded my pockets with a gun and a pint flask of Scotch, and went up to Dinah's.

XVII · Reno

SHE took me into her living room, backed away from me, revolved, and asked me how I liked the new dress. I said I liked it. She explained that the color was rose beige and that the dinguses on the side were something or other, winding up:

"And you really think I look good in it?"

"You always look good," I said. "Lew Yard and Pete the Finn went calling on old Elihu this afternoon."

She made a face at me and said:

"You don't give a damn about my dress. What did they do there?"

"A pow-wow, I suppose."

She looked at me through her lashes and asked:

"Don't you really know where Max is?"

Then I did. There was no use admitting I hadn't known all along. I said:

"At Willsson's, probably, but I haven't been interested enough to make sure."

"That's goofy of you. He's got reasons for not liking you and me. Take mama's advice and nail him quick, if you like living and like having mama live too."

I laughed and said:

"You don't know the worst of it. Max didn't kill Noonan's brother. Tim didn't say *Max*. He tried to say *MacSwain*, and died before he could finish."

She grabbed my shoulders and tried to shake my hundred and ninety pounds. She was almost strong enough to do it.

"God damn you!" Her breath was hot in my face. Her face was white as her teeth. Rouge stood out sharply like red labels pasted on her mouth and cheeks. "If you've framed him and made me frame him, you've got to kill him—now."

I don't like being manhandled, even by young women who look like something out of mythology when they're steamed up. I took her hands off my shoulders, and said:

"Stop bellyaching. You're still alive."

"Yes, still. But I know Max better than you do. I know how much chance anybody that frames him has got of staying alive long. It would be bad enough if we had got him right, but—"

"Don't make so much fuss over it. I've framed my millions and nothing's happened to me. Get your hat and coat and we'll feed. You'll feel better then."

"You're crazy if you think I'm going out. Not with that—"

"Stop it, sister. If he's that dangerous he's just as likely to get you here as anywhere. So what difference does it make?"

"It makes a— You know what you're going to do? You're going to stay here until Max is put out of the way. It's your fault and you've got to look out for me. I haven't even got Dan. He's in the hospital."

"I can't," I said. "I've got work to do. You're all burnt up over nothing. Max has probably forgotten all about you by now. Get your hat and coat. I'm starving."

She put her face close to mine again, and her eyes looked as if they had found something horrible in mine.

"Oh, you're rotten!" she said. "You don't give a damn what happens to me. You're using me as you use the others—that dynamite you wanted. I trusted you."

"You're dynamite, all right, but the rest of it's kind of foolish. You look a lot better when you're happy. Your features are heavy. Anger makes them downright brutal. I'm starving, sister."

"You'll eat here," she said. "You're not going to get me out after dark."

She meant it. She swapped the rose beige dress for an apron, and took inventory of the ice box. There were potatoes, lettuce, canned soup and half a fruit cake. I went out and got a couple of steaks, rolls, asparagus, and tomatoes.

When I came back she was mixing gin, vermouth and orange bitters in a quart shaker, not leaving a lot of space for them to move around in.

"Did you see anything?" she asked.

I sneered at her in a friendly way. We carried the cocktails into the dining room and played bottoms-up while the meal cooked. The drinks cheered her a lot. By the time we sat down to the food she had almost forgotten her fright. She wasn't a very good cook, but we ate as if she were.

We put a couple of gin-gingerales in on top the dinner.

She decided she wanted to go places and do things. No lousy little runt could keep her cooped up, because she had been as square with him as anybody could be until he got nasty over nothing, and if he didn't like what she did he could go climb trees or jump in lakes, and we'd go out to the Silver Arrow where she had meant to take me, because she had promised Reno she'd show up at his party, and by God she would, and anybody who thought she wouldn't was crazy as a pet cuckoo, and what did I think of that?

"Who's Reno?" I asked while she tied herself tighter in the apron by pulling the strings the wrong way.

"Reno Starkey. You'll like him. He's a right guy. I promised him I'd show at his celebration and that's just what I'll do."

"What's he celebrating?"

"What the hell's the matter with this lousy apron? He was sprung this afternoon."

"Turn around and I'll unwind you. What was he in for? Stand still."

"Blowing a safe six or seven months ago—Turlock's, the jeweler. Reno, Put Collings, Blackie Whalen, Hank O'Marra, and a little lame guy called Step-and-a-Half. They had plenty of cover—Lew Yard—but the jewelers' association dicks tied the job to them last week. So Noonan had to go through the motions. It doesn't mean anything. They got out on bail at five o'clock this afternoon, and that's the last anybody will ever hear about it. Reno's used to it. He was already out on bail for three other capers. Suppose you mix another little drink while I'm inserting myself in the dress."

∴

The Silver Arrow was half-way between Personville and Mock Lake.

"It's not a bad dump," Dinah told me as her little Marmon carried us toward it. "Polly De Voto is a good scout and anything she sells you is good, except maybe the Bourbon. That always tastes a little bit like it had been drained off a corpse. You'll like her. You can get away with anything out here so long as you don't get noisy. She won't stand for noise. There it is. See the red and blue lights through the trees?"

We rode out of the woods into full view of the roadhouse, a very electric-lighted imitation castle set close to the road.

"What do you mean she won't stand for noise?" I asked, listening to the chorus of pistols singing *Bang-bang-bang*.

"Something up," the girl muttered, stopping the car.

Two men dragging a woman between them ran out of the roadhouse's front door, ran away into the darkness. A man sprinted out a side door, away. The guns sang on. I didn't see any flashes.

Another man broke out and vanished around the back.

A man leaned far out a front second-story window, a black gun in his hand.

Dinah blew her breath out sharply.

From a hedge by the road, a flash of orange pointed briefly up at the man in the window. His gun flashed downward. He leaned farther out. No second flash came from the hedge.

The man in the window put a leg over the sill, bent, hung by his hands, dropped.

Our car jerked forward. Dinah's lower lip was between her teeth.

The man who had dropped from the window was gathering himself up on hands and knees.

Dinah put her face in front of mine and screamed:

"Reno!"

The man jumped up, his face to us. He made the road in three leaps, as we got to him.

Dinah had the little Marmon wide open before Reno's feet were on the running board beside me. I wrapped my arms around him, and damned near dislocated them holding him on. He made it as tough as he could for me by leaning out to try for a shot at the guns that were tossing lead all around us.

Then it was all over. We were out of range, sight and sound of the Silver Arrow, speeding away from Personville.

Reno turned around and did his own holding on. I took my arms in and found that all the joints still worked. Dinah was busy with the car.

Reno said:

"Thanks, kid. I needed pulling out."

"That's all right," she told him. "So that's the kind of parties you throw?"

"We had guests that wasn't invited. You know the Tanner Road?"

"Yes."

"Take it. It'll put us over to Mountain Boulevard, and we can get back to town that-a-way."

The girl nodded, slowed up a little, and asked:

"Who were the uninvited guests?"

"Some plugs that don't know enough to leave me alone."

"Do I know them?" she asked, too casually, as she turned the car into a narrower and rougher road.

"Let it alone, kid," Reno said. "Better get as much out of the heap as it's got."

She prodded another fifteen miles an hour out of the Marmon. She had plenty to do now holding the car to the road, and Reno had plenty holding himself to the car. Neither of them made any more conversation until the road brought us into one that had more and better paving.

Then he asked:

"So you paid Whisper off?"

"Um-hmm."

"They're saying you turned rat on him."

"They would. What do you think?"

"Ditching him was all right. But throwing in with a dick and cracking the works to him is kind of sour. Damned sour, if you ask me."

He looked at me while he said it. He was a man of thirty-four or -five, fairly tall, broad and heavy without fat. His eyes were large, brown, dull, and set far apart in a long, slightly sallow horse face. It was a humorless face, stolid, but somehow not unpleasant. I looked at him and said nothing.

The girl said: "If that's the way you feel about it, you can—"

"Look out," Reno grunted.

We had swung around a curve. A long black car was straight across the road ahead of us—a barricade.

Bullets flew around us. Reno and I threw bullets around while the girl made a polo pony of the little Marmon.

She shoved it over to the left of the road, let the left wheels ride the bank high, crossed the road again with Reno's and my weight on the inside, got the right bank under the left wheels just as our side of the car began to lift in spite of our weight, slid us down in the road with our backs to the enemy, and took us out of the neighborhood by the time we had emptied our guns.

A lot of people had done a lot of shooting, but so far as we could tell nobody's bullets had hurt anybody.

Reno, holding to the door with his elbows while he pushed another clip into his automatic, said:

"Nice work, kid. You handle the bus like you meant it."

Dinah asked: "Where now?"

"Far away first. Just follow the road. We'll have to figure it out. Looks like they got the burg closed up on us. Keep your dog on it."

We put ten or twelve more miles between Personville and us. We passed a few cars, saw nothing to show we were being chased. A short bridge rumbled under us. Reno said:

"Take the right turn at the top of the hill."

We took it, into a dirt road that wound between trees down the side of a rock-ridged hill. Ten miles an hour was fast going here. After five minutes of creeping along Reno ordered a halt. We heard nothing, saw nothing, during the half-hour we sat in darkness. Then Reno said:

"There's an empty shack a mile down the way. We'll camp there, huh? There's no sense trying to crash the city line again tonight."

Dinah said she would prefer anything to being shot at again. I said it was all right with me, though I would rather have tried to find some path back to the city.

We followed the dirt track cautiously until our headlights settled on a small clapboard building that badly needed the paint it had never got.

"Is this it?" Dinah asked Reno.

"Uh-huh. Stay here till I look it over."

He left us, appearing soon in the beam of our lights at the shack door. He fumbled with keys at the padlock, got it off, opened the door, and went in. Presently he came to the door and called:

"All right. Come in and make yourselves to home."

Dinah cut off the engine and got out of the car.

"Is there a flashlight in the car?" I asked.

She said, "Yes," gave it to me, yawned, "My God, I'm tired. I hope there's something to drink in the hole."

I told her I had a flask of Scotch. The news cheered her up.

The shack was a one-room affair that held an army cot covered with brown blankets, a deal table with a deck of cards and some gummy poker chips on it, a brown iron stove, four chairs, an oil lamp, dishes, pots, pans and buckets, three shelves with canned food on them, a pile of firewood and a wheelbarrow.

Reno was lighting the lamp when we came in. He said:

"Not so tough. I'll hide the heap and then we'll be all set till day-light."

Dinah went over to the cot, turned back the covers, and reported:

"Maybe there's things in it, but anyway it's not alive with them. Now let's have that drink."

I unscrewed the flask and passed it to her while Reno went out to hide the car. When she had finished, I took a shot.

The purr of the Marmon's engine got fainter. I opened the door and looked out. Downhill, through trees and bushes, I could see broken chunks of white light going away. When I lost them for good I returned indoors and asked the girl:

"Have you ever had to walk home before?"

"What?"

"Reno's gone with the car."

"The lousy tramp! Thank God he left us where there's a bed, any-way."

"That'll get you nothing."

"No?"

"No. Reno had a key to this dump. Ten to one the birds after him know about it. That's why he ditched us here. We're supposed to argue with them, hold them off his trail a while."

She got up wearily from the cot, cursed Reno, me, all men from Adam on, and said disagreeably:

"You know everything. What do we do next?"

"We find a comfortable spot in the great open spaces, not too far away, and wait to see what happens."

"I'm going to take the blankets."

"Maybe one won't be missed, but you'll tip our mitts if you take more than that."

"Damn your mitts," she grumbled, but she took only one blanket.

I blew out the lamp, padlocked the door behind us, and with the help of the flashlight picked a way through the undergrowth.

On the hillside above we found a little hollow from which road and shack could be not too dimly seen through foliage thick enough to hide us unless we showed a light.

I spread the blanket there and we settled down.

The girl leaned against me and complained that the ground was damp, that she was cold in spite of her fur coat, that she had a cramp in her leg, and that she wanted a cigarette.

I gave her another drink from the flask. That bought me ten minutes of peace.

Then she said:

"I'm catching cold. By the time anybody comes, if they ever do, I'll be sneezing and coughing loud enough to be heard in the city."

"Just once," I told her. "Then you'll be all strangled."

"There's a mouse or something crawling under the blanket."

"Probably only a snake."

"Are you married?"

"Don't start that."

"Then you are?"

"No."

"I'll bet your wife's glad of it."

I was trying to find a suitable come-back to that wise-crack when a distant light gleamed up the road. It disappeared as I sh-sh'd the girl.

"What is it?" she asked.

"A light. It's gone now. Our visitors have left their car and are finishing the trip afoot."

A lot of time went by. The girl shivered with her cheek warm against mine. We heard footsteps, saw dark figures moving on the road and around the shack, without being sure whether we did or didn't.

A flashlight ended our doubt by putting a bright circle on the shack's door. A heavy voice said:

"We'll let the broad come out."

There was a half-minute of silence while they waited for a reply from indoors. Then the same heavy voice asked: "Coming?" Then more silence.

Gun-fire, a familiar sound tonight, broke the silence. Something hammered boards.

"Come on," I whispered to the girl. "We'll have a try at their car while they're making a racket."

"Let them alone," she said, pulling my arm down as I started up. "I've had enough of it for one night. We're all right here."

"Come on," I insisted.

She said, "I won't," and she wouldn't, and presently, while we argued, it was too late. The boys below had kicked in the door, found the hut empty, and were bellowing for their car.

It came, took eight men aboard, and followed Reno's track downhill.

"We might as well move in again," I said. "It's not likely they'll be back this way tonight."

"I hope to God there's some Scotch left in that flask," she said as I helped her stand up.

XVIII · *Painter Street*

THE shack's supply of canned goods didn't include anything that tempted us for breakfast. We made the meal of coffee cooked in very stale water from a galvanized pail.

A mile of walking brought us to a farmhouse where there was a boy who didn't mind earning a few dollars by driving us to town in the family Ford. He had a lot of questions, to which we gave him phoney answers or none. He set us down in front of a little restaurant in upper King Street, where we ate quantities of buckwheat cakes and bacon.

A taxi put us at Dinah's door a little before nine o'clock. I searched the place for her, from roof to cellar, and found no signs of visitors.

"When will you be back?" she asked as she followed me to the door.

"I'll try to pop in between now and midnight, if only for a few minutes. Where does Lew Yard live?"

"1622 Painter Street. Painter's three blocks over. 1622's four blocks up. What are you going to do there?" Before I could answer, she put her hands on my arm and begged: "Get Max, will you? I'm afraid of him."

"Maybe I'll sic Noonan on him a little later. It depends on how things work out."

She called me a damned double-crossing something or other who didn't care what happened to her as long as his dirty work got done.

I went over to Painter Street. 1622 was a red brick house with a garage under the front porch.

A block up the street I found Dick Foley in a hired drive-yourself Buick. I got in beside him, asking:

"What's doing?"

"Spot two. Out three-thirty, office to Willsson's. Mickey. Five. Home. Busy. Kept plant. Off three, seven. Nothing yet."

That was supposed to inform me that he had picked up Lew Yard at two the previous afternoon; had shadowed him to Willsson's at three-thirty, where Mickey had tailed Pete; had followed Yard away at five, to his residence; had seen people going in and out of the house, but had not shadowed any of them; had watched the house until three this morning, and had returned to the job at seven; and since then had seen nobody go in or out.

"You'll have to drop this and take a plant on Willsson's," I said. "I hear Whisper Thaler's holing-up there, and I'd like an eye kept on him till I make up my mind whether to turn him up for Noonan or not."

Dick nodded and started the engine grinding. I got out and returned to the hotel.

There was a telegram from the Old Man:

SEND BY FIRST MAIL FULL EXPLANATION OF PRESENT OPERATION AND CIRCUMSTANCES UNDER WHICH YOU ACCEPTED IT WITH DAILY REPORTS TO DATE

I put the telegram in my pocket and hoped things would keep on breaking fast. To have sent him the dope he wanted at that time would have been the same as sending in my resignation.

I bent a fresh collar around my neck and trotted over to the City Hall.

"Hello," Noonan greeted me. "I was hoping you'd show up. Tried to get you at your hotel but they told me you hadn't been in."

He wasn't looking well this morning, but under his glad-handing he seemed, for a change, genuinely glad to see me.

As I sat down one of his phones rang. He put the receiver to his ear, said, "Yes?" listened for a moment, said, "You better go out there yourself, Mac," and had to make two attempts to get the receiver back on its prong before he succeeded. His face had gone a little doughy, but his voice was almost normal as he told me:

"Lew Yard's been knocked off—shot coming down his front steps just now."

"Any details?" I asked while I cursed myself for having pulled Dick Foley away from Painter Street an hour too soon. That was a tough break.

Noonan shook his head, staring at his lap.

"Shall we go out and look at the remains?" I suggested, getting up.

He neither got up nor looked up.

"No," he said wearily to his lap. "To tell the truth, I don't want to. I don't know as I could stand it just now. I'm getting sick of this killing. It's getting to me—on my nerves, I mean."

I sat down again, considered his low spirits, and asked:

"Who do you guess killed him?"

"God knows," he mumbled. "Everybody's killing everybody. Where's it going to end?"

"Think Reno did it?"

Noonan winced, started to look up at me, changed his mind, and repeated:

"God knows."

I went at him from another angle:

"Anybody knocked off in the battle at the Silver Arrow last night?"

"Only three."

"Who were they?"

"A pair of Johnson-brothers named Blackie Whalen and Put Collings that only got out on bail around five yesterday, and Dutch Jake Wahl, a guerrilla."

"What was it all about?"

"Just a roughhouse, I guess. It seems that Put and Blackie and the others that got out with them were celebrating with a lot of friends, and it wound up in smoke."

"All of them Lew Yard's men?"

"I don't know anything about that," he said.

I got up, said, "Oh, all right," and started for the door.

"Wait," he called. "Don't run off like that. I guess they were."

I came back to my chair. Noonan watched the top of his desk. His face was gray, flabby, damp, like fresh putty.

"Whisper's staying at Willsson's," I told him.

He jerked his head up. His eyes darkened. Then his mouth twitched, and he let his head sag again. His eyes faded.

"I can't go through with it," he mumbled. "I'm sick of this butchering. I can't stand any more of it."

"Sick enough to give up the idea of evening the score for Tim's killing, if it'll make peace?" I asked.

"I am."

"That's what started it," I reminded him. "If you're willing to call it off, it ought to be possible to stop it."

He raised his face and looked at me with eyes that were like a dog's looking at a bone.

"The others ought to be as sick of it as you are," I went on. "Tell them how you feel about it. Have a get-together and make peace."

"They'd think I was up to some kind of a trick," he objected miserably.

"Have the meeting at Willsson's. Whisper's camping there. You'd be the one risking tricks going there. Are you afraid of that?"

He frowned and asked:

"Will you go with me?"

"If you want me."

"Thanks," he said. "I—I'll try it."

XIX · *The Peace Conference*

ALL the other delegates to the peace conference were on hand when Noonan and I arrived at Willsson's home at the appointed time, nine o'clock that night. Everybody nodded to us, but the greetings didn't go any further than that.

Pete the Finn was the only one I hadn't met before. The bootlegger was a big-boned man of fifty with a completely bald head. His forehead was small, his jaws enormous—wide, heavy, bulging with muscle.

We sat around Willsson's library table.

Old Elihu sat at the head. The short-clipped hair on his round pink skull was like silver in the light. His round blue eyes were hard, domineering, under their bushy white brows. His mouth and chin were horizontal lines.

On his right Pete the Finn sat watching everybody with tiny black eyes that never moved. Reno Starkey sat next to the bootlegger. Reno's sallow horse face was as stolidly dull as his eyes.

Max Thaler was tilted back in a chair on Willsson's left. The little gambler's carefully pressed pants legs were carelessly crossed. A cigarette hung from one corner of his tight-lipped mouth.

I sat next to Thaler. Noonan sat on my other side.

Elihu Willsson opened the meeting.

He said things couldn't go on the way they were going. We were all sensible men, reasonable men, grown men who had seen enough of the world to know that a man couldn't have everything his own way, no matter who he was. Compromises were things everybody had to make sometimes. To get what he wanted, a man had to give other people what they wanted. He said he was sure that what we all most wanted now was to stop this insane killing. He said he was sure that everything could be frankly discussed and settled in an hour without turning Personville into a slaughter-house.

It wasn't a bad oration.

When it was over there was a moment of silence. Thaler looked past me, at Noonan, as if he expected something of him. The rest of us followed his example, looking at the chief of police.

Noonan's face turned red and he spoke huskily:

"Whisper, I'll forget you killed Tim." He stood up and held out a beefy paw. "Here's my hand on it."

Thaler's thin mouth curved into a vicious smile.

"Your bastard of a brother needed killing, but I didn't kill him," he whispered coldly.

Red became purple in the chief's face.

I said loudly:

"Wait, Noonan. We're going at this wrong. We won't get anywhere unless everybody comes clean. Otherwise we'll all be worse off than before. MacSwain killed Tim, and you know it."

He started at me with dumbfounded eyes. He gaped. He couldn't understand what I had done to him.

I looked at the others, tried to look virtuous as hell, asked:

"That's settled, isn't it? Let's get the rest of the kicks squared." I addressed Pete the Finn: "How do you feel about yesterday's accident to your warehouse and the four men?"

"One hell of an accident," he rumbled.

I explained:

"Noonan didn't know you were using the joint. He went there thinking it empty, just to clear the way for a job in town. Your men shot first, and then he really thought he had stumbled into Thaler's hideout. When he found he'd been stepping in your puddle he lost his head and touched the place off."

Thaler was watching me with a hard small smile in eyes and mouth. Reno was all dull stolidity. Elihu Willsson was leaning toward me, his old eyes sharp and wary. I don't know what Noonan was doing. I couldn't afford to look at him. I was in a good spot if I played my hand right, and in a terrible one if I didn't.

"The men, they get paid for taking chances," Pete the Finn said. "For the other, twenty-five grand will make it right."

Noonan spoke quickly, eagerly:

"All right, Pete, all right, I'll give it to you."

I pushed my lips together to keep from laughing at the panic in his voice.

I could look at him safely now. He was licked, broken, willing to do anything to save his fat neck, or to try to. I looked at him.

He wouldn't look at me. He sat down and looked at nobody. He was busy trying to look as if he didn't expect to be carved apart before he got away from these wolves to whom I had handed him.

I went on with the work, turning to Elihu Willsson:

"Do you want to squawk about your bank being knocked over, or do you like it?"

Max Thaler touched my arm and suggested:

"We could tell better maybe who's entitled to beef if you'd give us what you've got first."

I was glad to.

"Noonan wanted to nail you," I told him, "but he either got word, or expected to get word, from Yard and Willsson here to let you alone. So he thought if he had the bank looted and framed you for it, your backers would ditch you, and let him go after you right. Yard, I understand, was supposed to put his O. K. on all the capers in town. You'd be cutting into his territory, and gyping Willsson. That's how it would look. And that was supposed to make them hot enough that they'd help Noonan cop you. He didn't know you were here.

"Reno and his mob were in the can. Reno was Yard's pup, but he didn't mind crossing up his headman. He already had the idea that he was about ready to take the burg away from Lew." I turned to Reno and asked: "Isn't that it?"

He looked at me woodenly and said:

"You're telling it."

I continued telling it:

"Noonan fakes a tip that you're at Cedar Hill, and takes all the coppers he can't trust out there with him, even cleaning the traffic detail out of Broadway, so Reno would have a clear road. McGraw and the bulls that are in on the play let Reno and his mob sneak out of the hoosegow, pull the job, and duck back in. Nice thing in alibis. Then they got sprung on bail a couple of hours later.

"It looks as if Lew Yard tumbled. He sent Dutch Jake Wahl and some other boys out to the Silver Arrow last night to teach Reno and his pals not to take things in their own hands like that. But Reno got away, and got back to the city. It was either him or Lew then. He made sure which it would be by being in front of Lew's house with a gun when Lew came out this morning. Reno seems to have had the right dope, because I notice that right now he's holding down a chair that would have been Lew Yard's if Lew hadn't been put on ice."

Everybody was sitting very still, as if to call attention to how still they were sitting. Nobody could count on having any friends among those present. It was no time for careless motions on anybody's part.

If what I had said meant anything one way or the other to Reno he didn't show it.

Thaler whispered softly:

"Didn't you skip some of it?"

"You mean the part about Jerry?" I kept on being the life of the party: "I was coming back to that. I don't know whether he got away from the can when you crushed out, and was caught later, or whether he didn't get away, or why. And I don't know how willingly he went along on the bank caper. But he did go along, and he was dropped and left in front of the bank because he was your right bower, and his being killed there would pin the trick to you. He was kept in the car till the get-away was on. Then he was pushed out, and was shot in the back. He was facing the bank, with his back to the car, when he got his."

Thaler looked at Reno and whispered:

"Well?"

Reno looked with dull eyes at Thaler and asked calmly:

"What of it?"

Thaler stood up, said, "Deal me out," and walked to the door.

Pete the Finn stood up, leaning on the table with big bony hands, speaking from deep in his chest:

"Whisper." And when Thaler had stopped and turned to face him: "I'm telling you this. You, Whisper, and all of you. That damn gun-work is out. All of you understand it. You've got no brains to know what is best for yourselves. So I'll tell you. This busting the town open is no good for business. I won't have it any more. You be nice boys or I'll make you.

"I got one army of young fellows that know what to do on any end of a gun. I got to have them in my racket. If I got to use them on you I'll use them on you. You want to play with gunpowder and dynamite? I'll show you what playing is. You like to fight? I'll give you fighting. Mind what I tell you. That's all."

Pete the Finn sat down.

Thaler looked thoughtful for a moment, and went away without saying or showing what he had thought.

His going made the others impatient. None wanted to remain until anybody else had time to accumulate a few guns in the neighborhood.

In a very few minutes Elihu Willsson and I had the library to ourselves.

We sat and looked at one another.

Presently he said:

"How would you like to be chief of police?"

"No. I'm a rotten errand boy."

"I don't mean with this bunch. After we've got rid of them."

"And got another just like them."

"Damn you," he said, "it wouldn't hurt to take a nicer tone to a man old enough to be your father."

"Who curses me and hides behind his age."

Anger brought a vein out blue in his forehead. Then he laughed.

"You're a nasty talking lad," he said, "but I can't say you haven't done what I paid you to do."

"A swell lot of help I've got from you."

"Did you need wet-nursing? I gave you the money and a free hand. That's what you asked for. What more did you want?"

"You old pirate," I said, "I blackmailed you into it, and you played against me all the way till now, when even you can see that they're hell-bent on gobbling each other up. Now you talk about what you did for me."

"Old pirate," he repeated. "Son, if I hadn't been a pirate I'd still be working for the Anaconda for wages, and there'd be no Personville Mining Corporation. You're a damned little woolly lamb yourself, I suppose. I was had, son, where the hair was short. There were things I didn't like— worse things that I didn't know about until tonight—but I was caught and had to bide my time. Why since that Whisper Thaler has been here I've been a prisoner in my own home, a damned hostage!"

"Tough. Where do you stand now?" I demanded. "Are you behind me?"

"If you win."

I got up and said:

"I hope to Christ you get caught with them."

He said:

"I reckon you do, but I won't." He squinted his eyes merrily at me. "I'm financing you. That shows I mean well, don't it? Don't be too hard on me, son, I'm kind of—"

I said, "Go to hell," and walked out.

XX · *Laudanum*

DICK FOLEY in his hired car was at the next corner. I had him drive me over to within a block of Dinah Brand's house, and walked the rest of the way.

"You look tired," she said when I had followed her into the living room. "Been working?"

"Attending a peace conference out of which at least a dozen killings ought to grow."

The telephone rang. She answered it and called me.

Reno Starkey's voice:

"I thought maybe you'd like to hear about Noonan being shot to hell and gone when he got out of his heap in front of his house. You never saw anybody that was deader. Must have had thirty pills pumped in him."

"Thanks."

Dinah's big blue eyes asked questions.

"First fruits of the peace conference, plucked by Whisper Thaler," I told her. "Where's the gin?"

"Reno talking, wasn't it?"

"Yeah. He thought I'd like to hear about Poisonville being all out of police chiefs."

"You mean—?"

"Noonan went down tonight, according to Reno. Haven't you got any gin? Or do you like making me ask for it?"

"You know where it is. Been up to some of your cute tricks?"

I went back into the kitchen, opened the top of the refrigerator, and attacked the ice with an ice pick that had a six-inch awl-sharp blade set in a round blue and white handle. The girl stood in the doorway and asked questions. I didn't answer them while I put ice, gin, lemon juice and seltzer together in two glasses.

"What have you been doing?" she demanded as we carried our drinks into the dining room. "You look ghastly."

I put my glass on the table, sat down facing it, and complained:

"This damned burg's getting me. If I don't get away soon I'll be going blood-simple like the natives. There's been what? A dozen and a half murders since I've been here. Donald Willsson; Ike Bush; the four wops and the dick at Cedar Hill; Jerry; Lew Yard; Dutch Jake, Blackie Whalen and Put Collings at the Silver Arrow; Big Nick, the copper I potted; the blond kid Whisper dropped here; Yakima Shorty, old Elihu's prowler; and now Noonan. That's sixteen of them in less than a week, and more coming up."

She frowned at me and said sharply:

"Don't look like that."

I laughed and went on:

"I've arranged a killing or two in my time, when they were necessary. But this is the first time I've ever got the fever. It's this damned burg. You can't go straight here. I got myself tangled at the beginning. When old Elihu ran out on me there was nothing I could do but try to set the boys against each other. I had to swing the job the best way I could. How could I help it if the best way was bound to lead to a lot of killing? The job couldn't be handled any other way without Elihu's backing."

"Well, if you couldn't help it, what's the use of making a lot of fuss over it? Drink your drink."

I drank half of it and felt the urge to talk some more.

"Play with murder enough and it gets you one of two ways. It makes you sick, or you get to like it. It got Noonan the first way. He was green around the gills after Yard was knocked off, all the stomach gone out of him, willing to do anything to make peace. I took him in, suggested that he and the other survivors get together and patch up their differences.

"We had the meeting at Willsson's tonight. It was a nice party. Pretending I was trying to clear away everybody's misunderstandings by coming clean all around, I stripped Noonan naked and threw him to them— him and Reno. That broke up the meeting. Whisper declared himself out. Pete told everybody where they stood. He said battling was bad for his bootlegging racket, and anybody who started anything from then on could expect to have his booze guards turned loose on them. Whisper didn't look impressed. Neither did Reno."

"They wouldn't be," the girl said. "What did you do to Noonan? I mean how did you strip him and Reno?"

"I told the others that he had known all along that MacSwain killed Tim. That was the only lie I told them. Then I told them about the bank stick-up being turned by Reno and the chief, with Jerry taken along and dropped on the premises to tie the job to Whisper. I knew that's the way it was if what you told me was right, about Jerry getting out of the car, starting toward the bank and being shot. The hole was in his back. Fitting in with that, McGraw said the last seen of the stick-up car was when it turned into King Street. The boys would be returning to the City Hall, to their jail alibi."

"But didn't the bank watchman say he shot Jerry? That's the way it was in the papers."

"He said so, but he'd say anything and believe it. He probably emptied his gun with his eyes shut, and anything that fell was his. Didn't you see Jerry drop?"

"Yes, I did, and he was facing the bank, but it was all too confused for me to see who shot him. There were a lot of men shooting, and—"

"Yeah. They'd see to that. I also advertised the fact—at least, it looks like a fact to me—that Reno plugged Lew Yard. This Reno is a tough egg, isn't he? Noonan went watery, but all they got out of Reno was a 'What of it?' It was all nice and gentlemanly. They were evenly divided—Pete and Whisper against Noonan and Reno. But none of them could count on his partner backing him up if he made a play, and by the time the meeting was over the pairs had been split. Noonan was out of the count, and Reno and Whisper, against each other, had Pete against them. So everybody sat around and behaved and watched everybody else while I juggled death and destruction.

"Whisper was the first to leave, and he seems to have had time to collect some rods in front of Noonan's house by the time the chief reached home. The chief was shot down. If Pete the Finn meant what he said—and he has the look of a man who would—he'll be out after Whisper. Reno was as much to blame for Jerry's death as Noonan, so Whisper ought to be gunning for him. Knowing it, Reno will be out to get Whisper first, and that will set Pete on his trail. Besides that, Reno will likely have his hands full standing off those of the late Lew Yard's underlings who don't fancy Reno as boss. All in all it's one swell dish."

Dinah Brand reached across the table and patted my hand. Her eyes were uneasy. She said:

"It's not your fault, darling. You said yourself that there was nothing else you could do. Finish your drink and we'll have another."

"There was plenty else I could do," I contradicted her. "Old Elihu ran out on me at first simply because these birds had too much on him for him to risk a break unless he was sure they could be wiped out. He couldn't see how I could do it, so he played with them. He's not exactly their brand of cut-throat, and, besides, he thinks the city is his personal property, and he doesn't like the way they've taken it away from him.

"I could have gone to him this afternoon and showed him that I had them ruined. He'd have listened to reason. He'd have come over to my side, have given me the support I needed to swing the play legally. I could have done that. But it's easier to have them killed off, easier and surer, and, now that I'm feeling this way, more satisfying. I don't know how I'm going to come out with the Agency. The Old Man will boil me in oil if he ever finds out what I've been doing. It's this damned town. Poisonville is right. It's poisoned me.

"Look. I sat at Willsson's table tonight and played them like you'd play trout, and got just as much fun out of it. I looked at Noonan and knew he hadn't a chance in a thousand of living another day because of what I had done to him, and I laughed, and felt warm and happy inside. That's not me. I've got hard skin all over what's left of my soul, and after twenty years of messing around with crime I can look at any sort of a murder without seeing anything in it but my bread and butter, the day's work. But this getting a rear out of planning deaths is not natural to me. It's what this place has done to me."

She smiled too softly and spoke too indulgently:

"You exaggerate so, honey. They deserve all they get. I wish you wouldn't look like that. You make me feel creepy."

I grinned, picked up the glasses, and went out to the kitchen for more gin. When I came back she frowned at me over anxious dark eyes and asked:

"Now what did you bring the ice pick in for?"

"To show you how my mind's running. A couple of days ago, if I thought about it at all, it was as a good tool to pry off chunks of ice." I ran a finger down its half-foot of round steel blade to the needle point. "Not a bad thing to pin a man to his clothes with. That's the way I'm betting, on the level. I can't even see a mechanical cigar lighter without thinking of filling one with nitroglycerine for somebody you don't like. There's a piece of copper wire lying in the gutter in front of your house —thin, soft, and just long enough to go around a neck with two ends to hold on. I had one hell of a time to keep from picking it up and stuffing it in my pocket, just in case—"

"You're crazy."

"I know it. That's what I've been telling you. I'm going blood-simple."

"Well, I don't like it. Put that thing back in the kitchen and sit down and be sensible."

I obeyed two-thirds of the order.

"The trouble with you is," she scolded me, "your nerves are shot. You've been through too much excitement in the last few days. Keep it up and you're going to have the heebie-jeebies for fair, a nervous breakdown."

I held up a hand with spread fingers. It was steady enough.

She looked at it and said:

"That doesn't mean anything. It's inside you. Why don't you sneak off for a couple of days' rest? You've got things here so they'll run themselves. Let's go down to Salt Lake. It'll do you good."

"Can't, sister. Somebody's got to stay here to count the dead. Besides, the whole program is based on the present combination of people and events. Our going out of town would change that, and the chances are the whole thing would have to be gone over again."

"Nobody would have to know you were gone, and I've got nothing to do with it."

"Since when?"

She leaned forward, made her eyes small, and asked:

"Now what are you getting at?"

"Nothing. Just wondering how you got to be a disinterested bystander all of a sudden. Forgotten that Donald Willsson was killed because of you, starting the whole thing? Forgotten that it was the dope you gave me on Whisper that kept the job from petering out in the middle?"

"You know just as well as I do that none of that was my fault," she said indignantly. "And it's all past, anyway. You're just bringing it up because you're in a rotten humor and want to argue."

"It wasn't past last night, when you were scared stiff Whisper was going to kill you."

"Will you stop talking about killing!"

"Young Albury once told me Bill Quint had threatened to kill you," I said.

"Stop it."

"You seem to have a gift for stirring up murderous notions in your boy friends. There's Albury waiting trial for killing Willsson. There's Whisper who's got you shivering in corners. Even I haven't escaped your influence. Look at the way I've turned. And I've always had a private notion that Dan Rolff's going to have a try at you some day."

"Dan! You're crazy. Why, I—"

"Yeah. He was a lunger and down and out, and you took him in. You gave him a home and all the laudanum he wants. You use him for errand boy, you slap his face in front of me, and slap him around in front of others. He's in love with you. One of these mornings you're going to wake up and find he's whittled your neck away."

She shivered, got up and laughed.

"I'm glad one of us knows what you're talking about, if you do," she said as she carried our empty glasses through the kitchen door.

I lit a cigarette and wondered why I felt the way I did, wondered if I were getting psychic, wondered whether there was anything in this presentiment business or whether my nerves were just ragged.

"The next best thing for you to do if you won't go away," the girl advised me when she returned with full glasses, "is to get plastered and forget everything for a few hours. I put a double slug of gin in yours. You need it."

"It's not me," I said, wondering why I was saying it, but somehow enjoying it. "It's you. Every time I mention killing, you jump on me. You're a woman. You think if nothing's said about it, maybe none of the God only knows how many people in town who might want to will kill you. That's silly. Nothing we say or don't say is going to make Whisper, for instance—"

"Please, please stop! I am silly. I am afraid of the words. I'm afraid of him. I— Oh, why didn't you put him out of the way when I asked you?"

"Sorry," I said, meaning it.

"Do you think he—?"

"I don't know," I told her, "and I reckon you're right. There's no use talking about it. The thing to do is drink, though there doesn't seem to be much body to this gin."

"That's you, not the gin. Do you want an honest to God rear?"

"I'd drink nitroglycerine tonight."

"That's just about what you're going to get," she promised me.

She rattled bottles in the kitchen and brought me in a glass of what looked like the stuff we had been drinking. I sniffed at it and said:

"Some of Dan's laudanum, huh? He still in the hospital?"

"Yes. I think his skull is fractured. There's your kick, mister, if that's what you want."

I put the doped gin down my throat. Presently I felt more comfortable. Time went by as we drank and talked in a world that was rosy, cheerful, and full of fellowship and peace on earth.

Dinah stuck to gin. I tried that for a while too, and then had another gin and laudanum.

For a while after that I played a game, trying to hold my eyes open as if I were awake, even though I couldn't see anything out of them. When the trick wouldn't fool her any more I gave it up.

The last thing I remembered was her helping me on to the living room Chesterfield.

XXI · *The Seventeenth Murder*

I dreamed I was sitting on a bench, in Baltimore, facing the tumbling fountain in Harlem Park, beside a woman who wore a veil. I had come there with her. She was somebody I knew well. But I had suddenly forgotten who she was. I couldn't see her face because of the long black veil.

I thought that if I said something to her I would recognize her voice when she answered. But I was very embarrassed and was a long time finding anything to say. Finally I asked her if she knew a man named Carroll T. Harris.

She answered me, but the roar and swish of the tumbling fountain smothered her voice, and I could hear nothing.

Fire engines went out Edmondson Avenue. She left me to run after them. As she ran she cried, "Fire! Fire!" I recognized her voice then and knew who she was, and knew she was someone important to me. I ran after her, but it was too late. She and the fire engines were gone.

I walked streets hunting for her, half the streets in the United States, Gay Street and Mount Royal Avenue in Baltimore, Colfax Avenue in Denver, Aetna Road and St. Clair Avenue in Cleveland, McKinney Avenue in Dallas, Lemartine and Cornell and Amory Streets in Boston, Berry Boulevard in Louisville, Lexington Avenue in New York, until I came to Victoria Street in Jacksonville, where I heard her voice again, though I still could not see her.

I walked more streets, listening to her voice. She was calling a name, not mine, one strange to me, but no matter how fast I walked or in what direction, I could get no nearer her voice. It was the same distance from me in the street that runs past the Federal Building in El Paso as in Detroit's Grand Circus Park. Then the voice stopped.

Tired and discouraged, I went into the lobby of the hotel that faces the railroad station in Rocky Mount, North Carolina, to rest. While I sat there a train came in. She got off it and came into the lobby, over to me, and began kissing me. I was very uncomfortable because everybody stood around looking at us and laughing.

That dream ended there.

I dreamed I was in a strange city hunting for a man I hated. I had an open knife in my pocket and meant to kill him with it when I found him. It was Sunday morning. Church bells were ringing, crowds of people were in the streets, going to and from church. I walked almost as far as in the first dream, but always in this same strange city.

Then the man I was after yelled at me, and I saw him. He was a small brown man who wore an immense sombrero. He was standing on the steps of a tall building on the far side of a wide plaza, laughing at me. Between us, the plaza was crowded with people, packed shoulder to shoulder.

Keeping one hand on the open knife in my pocket, I ran toward the little brown man, running on the heads and shoulders of the people in the plaza. The heads and shoulders were of unequal heights and not evenly spaced. I slipped and floundered over them.

The little brown man stood on the steps and laughed until I had almost reached him. Then he ran into the tall building. I chased him up miles of spiral stairway, always just an inch more than a hand's reach behind him. We came to the roof. He ran straight across to the edge and jumped just as one of my hands touched him.

His shoulder slid out of my fingers. My hand knocked his sombrero off, and closed on his head. It was a smooth hard round head no larger than a large egg. My fingers went all the way around it. Squeezing his head in one hand, I tried to bring the knife out of my pocket with the other—and realized that I had gone off the edge of the roof with him. We dropped giddily down toward the millions of upturned faces in the plaza, miles down.

∴

I opened my eyes in the dull light of morning sun filtered through drawn blinds.

I was lying face down on the dining room floor, my head resting on my left forearm. My right arm was stretched straight out. My right hand held the round blue and white handle of Dinah Brand's ice pick. The pick's six-inch needle-sharp blade was buried in Dinah Brand's left breast.

She was lying on her back, dead. Her long muscular legs were stretched out toward the kitchen door. There was a run down the front of her right stocking.

Slowly, gently, as if afraid of awakening her, I let go the ice pick, drew in my arm, and got up.

My eyes burned. My throat and mouth were hot, wooly. I went into the kitchen, found a bottle of gin, tilted it to my mouth, and kept it there until I had to breathe. The kitchen clock said seven-forty-one.

With the gin in me I returned to the dining room, switched on the lights, and looked at the dead girl.

Not much blood was in sight: a spot the size of a silver dollar around the hole the ice pick made in her blue silk dress. There was a bruise on her right cheek, just under the cheek bone. Another bruise, finger-made, was on her right wrist. Her hands were empty. I moved her enough to see that nothing was under her.

I examined the room. So far as I could tell, nothing had been changed in it. I went back to the kitchen and found no recognizable changes there.

The spring lock on the back door was fastened, and had no marks to show it had been monkeyed with. I went to the front door and failed to find any marks on it. I went through the house from top to bottom, and learned nothing. The windows were all right. The girl's jewelry, on her dressing table (except the two diamond rings on her hands), and four hundred odd dollars in her handbag, on a bedroom chair, were undisturbed.

In the dining room again, I knelt beside the dead girl and used my handkerchief to wipe the ice pick handle clean of any prints my fingers had left on it. I did the same to glasses, bottles, doors, light buttons, and the pieces of furniture I had touched, or was likely to have touched.

Then I washed my hands, examined my clothes for blood, made sure I was leaving none of my property behind, and went to the front door. I opened it, wiped the inner knob, closed it behind me, wiped the outer knob, and went away.

∴

From a drug store in upper Broadway I telephoned Dick Foley and asked him to come over to my hotel. He arrived a few minutes after I got there.

"Dinah Brand was killed in her house last night or early this morning," I told him. "Stabbed with an ice pick. The police don't know it yet. I've told you enough about her for you to know that there are any number of people who might have had reason for killing her. There are three I want looked up first—Whisper, Dan Rolff and Bill Quint, the radical fellow. You've got their descriptions. Rolff is in the hospital with a dented skull. I don't know which hospital. Try the City first. Get hold of Mickey Linehan—he's still camped on Pete the Finn's trail—and have him let Pete rest while he gives you a hand on this. Find out where those three birds were last night. And time means something."

The little Canadian op had been watching me curiously while I talked. Now he started to say something, changed his mind, grunted, "Righto," and departed.

∴

I went out to look for Reno Starkey. After an hour of searching I located him, by telephone, in a Ronney Street rooming house.

"By yourself?" he asked when I had said I wanted to see him.

"Yeah."

He said I could come out, and told me how to get there. I took a taxi. It was a dingy two-story house near the edge of town.

A couple of men loitered in front of a grocer's on the corner above. Another pair sat on the low wooden steps of the house down at the next corner. None of the four was conspicuously refined in appearance.

When I rang the bell two men opened the door. They weren't so mild looking either.

I was taken upstairs to a front room where Reno, collarless and in shirt-sleeves and vest, sat tilted back in a chair with his feet on the window sill.

He nodded his sallow horse face and said:

"Pull a chair over."

The men who had brought me up went away, closing the door. I sat down and said:

"I want an alibi. Dinah Brand was killed last night after I left her. There's no chance of my being copped for it, but with Noonan dead I don't know how I'm hitched up with the department. I don't want to give them any openings to even try to hang anything on me. If I've got to I can prove where I was last night, but you can save me a lot of trouble if you will."

Reno looked at me with dull eyes and asked:

"Why pick on me?"

"You phoned me there last night. You're the only person who knows I was there the first part of the night. I'd have to fix it with you even if I got the alibi somewhere else, wouldn't I?"

He asked:

"You didn't croak her, did you?"

I said, "No," casually.

He stared out the window a little while before he spoke. He asked:

"What made you think I'd give you the lift? Do I owe you anything for what you done to me at Willsson's last night?"

I said:

"I didn't hurt you any. The news was half-out anyhow. Whisper knew enough to guess the rest. I only gave you a show-down. What do you care? You can take care of yourself."

"I aim to try," he agreed. "All right. You was at the Tanner House in Tanner. That's a little burg twenty-thirty miles up the hill. You went up there after you left Willsson's and stayed till morning. A guy named Ricker that hangs around Murry's with a hire heap drove you up and back. You ought to know what you was doing up there. Give me your sig and I'll have it put on the register."

"Thanks," I said as I unscrewed my fountain pen.

"Don't say them. I'm doing this because I need all the friends I can get. When the time comes that you sit in with me and Whisper and Pete, I don't expect the sour end of it."

"You won't get it," I promised. "Who's going to be chief of police?"

"McGraw's acting chief. He'll likely cinch it."

"How'll he play?"

"With the Finn. Rough stuff will hurt his shop just like it does Pete's. It'll have to be hurt some. I'd be a swell mutt to sit still while a guy like Whisper is on the loose. It's me or him. Think he croaked the broad?"

"He had reason enough," I said as I gave him the slip of paper on which I had written my name. "She double-crossed him, sold him out, plenty."

"You and her was kind of thick, wasn't you?" he asked.

I let the question alone, lighting a cigarette. Reno waited a while and then said:

"You better hunt up Ricker and·let him get a look at you so's he'll know how to describe you if he's asked."

A long-legged youngster of twenty-two or so with a thin freckled face around reckless eyes opened the door and came into the room. Reno introduced him to me as Hank O'Marra. I stood up to shake his hand, and then asked Reno:

"Can I reach you here if I need to?"

"Know Peak Murry?"

"I've met him, and I know his joint."

"Anything you give him will get to me," he said. "We're getting out of here. It's not so good. That Tanner lay is all set."

"Right. Thanks." I went out of the house.

XXII · *The Ice Pick*

DOWNTOWN, I went first to police headquarters. McGraw was holding down the chief's desk. His blond-lashed eyes looked suspiciously at me, and the lines in his leathery face were even deeper and sourer than usual.

"When'd you see Dinah Brand last?" he asked without any preliminaries, not even a nod. His voice rasped disagreeably through his bony nose.

"Ten-forty last night, or thereabout," I said. "Why?"

"Where?"

"Her house."

"How long were you there?"

"Ten minutes, maybe fifteen."

"Why?"

"Why what?"

"Why didn't you stay any longer than that?"

"What," I asked, sitting down in the chair he hadn't offered me, "makes it any of your business?"

He glared at me while he filled his lungs so he could yell, "Murder!" in my face.

I laughed and said:

"You don't think she had anything to do with Noonan's killing?"

I wanted a cigarette, but cigarettes were too well known as first aids to the nervous for me to take a chance on one just then.

McGraw was trying to look through my eyes. I let him look, having all sorts of confidence in my belief that, like a lot of people, I looked most honest when I was lying. Presently he gave up the eye-study and asked:

"Why not?"

That was weak enough. I said, "All right, why not?" indifferently, offered him a cigarette, and took one myself. Then I added: "My guess is that Whisper did it."

"Was he there?" For once McGraw cheated his nose, snapping the words off his teeth.

"Was he where?"

"At Brand's?"

"No," I said, wrinkling my forehead. "Why should he be—if he was off killing Noonan?"

"Damn Noonan!" the acting chief exclaimed irritably. "What do you keep dragging him in for?"

I tried to look at him as if I thought him crazy.

He said:

"Dinah Brand was murdered last night."

I said: "Yeah?"

"Now will you answer my questions?"

"Of course. I was at Willsson's with Noonan and the others. After I left there, around ten-thirty, I dropped in at her house to tell her I had to go up to Tanner. I had a half-way date with her. I stayed there about ten minutes, long enough to have a drink. There was nobody else there, unless they were hiding. When was she killed? And how?"

McGraw told me he had sent a pair of his dicks—Shepp and Vanaman—to see the girl that morning, to see how much help she could and would give the department in copping Whisper for Noonan's murder. The dicks got to her house at nine-thirty. The front door was ajar. Nobody answered their ringing. They went in and found the girl lying on her back in the dining room, dead, with a stab wound in her left breast.

The doctor who examined the body said she had been killed with a slender, round, pointed blade about six inches in length, at about three o'clock in the morning. Bureaus, closets, trunks, and so on, had apparently been skilfully and thoroughly ransacked. There was no money in the girl's handbag, or elsewhere in the house. The jewel case on her dressing table was empty. Two diamond rings were on her fingers.

The police hadn't found the weapon with which she had been stabbed. The fingerprint experts hadn't turned up anything they could use. Neither doors nor windows seemed to have been forced. The kitchen showed that the girl had been drinking with a guest or guests.

"Six inches, round, slim, pointed," I repeated the weapon's description. "That sounds like her ice pick."

McGraw reached for the phone and told somebody to send Shepp and Vanaman in. Shepp was a stoop-shouldered tall man whose wide mouth had a grimly honest look that probably came from bad teeth. The other detective was short, stocky, with purplish veins in his nose and hardly any neck.

McGraw introduced us and asked them about the ice pick. They had not seen it, were positive it hadn't been there. They wouldn't have overlooked an article of its sort.

"Was it there last night?" McGraw asked me.

"I stood beside her while she chipped off pieces of ice with it."

I described it. McGraw told the dicks to search her house again, and then to try to find the pick in the vicinity of the house.

"You knew her," he said when Shepp and Vanaman had gone. "What's your slant on it?"

"Too new for me to have one," I dodged the question. "Give me an hour or two to think it over. What do you think?"

He fell back into sourness, growling, "How the hell do I know?"

But the fact that he let me go away without asking me any more questions told me he had already made up his mind that Whisper had killed the girl.

I wondered if the little gambler had done it, or if this was another of the wrong raps that Poisonville police chiefs liked to hang on him. It didn't seem to make much difference now. It was a cinch he had—personally or by deputy—put Noonan out, and they could only hang him once.

.·.

There were a lot of men in the corridor when I left McGraw. Some of these men were quite young—just kids—quite a few were foreigners, and most of them were every bit as tough looking as any men should be.

Near the street door I met Donner, one of the coppers who had been on the Cedar Hill expedition.

"Hello," I greeted him. "What's the mob? Emptying the can to make room for more?"

"Them's our new specials," he told me, speaking as if he didn't think much of them. "We're going to have a augmented force."

"Congratulations," I said and went on out.

In his pool room I found Peak Murry sitting at a desk behind the cigar counter talking to three men. I sat down on the other side of the room and watched two kids knock balls around. In a few minutes the lanky proprietor came over to me.

"If you see Reno some time," I told him, "you might let him know that Pete the Finn's having his mob sworn in as special coppers."

"I might," Murry agreed.

∴

Mickey Linehan was sitting in the lobby when I got back to my hotel. He followed me up to my room, and reported:

"Your Dan Rolff pulled a sneak from the hospital somewhere after midnight last night. The croakers are kind of steamed up about it. Seems they were figuring on pulling a lot of little pieces of bone out of his brain this morning. But him and his duds were gone. We haven't got a line on Whisper yet. Dick's out now trying to place Bill Quint. What's what on this girl's carving? Dick tells me you got it before the coppers."

"It—"

The telephone bell rang.

A man's voice, carefully oratorical, spoke my name with a question mark after it.

I said: "Yeah."

The voice said:

"This is Mr. Charles Proctor Dawn speaking. I think you will find it well worth your while to appear at my offices at your earliest convenience."

"Will I? Who are you?"

"Mr. Charles Proctor Dawn, attorney-at-law. My suite is in the Rutledge Block, 310 Green Street. I think you will find it well—"

"Mind telling me part of what it's about?" I asked.

"There are affairs best not discussed over the telephone. I think you will find—"

"All right," I interrupted him again. "I'll be around to see you this afternoon if I get a chance."

"You will find it very, very advisable," he assured me.

I hung up on that.

Mickey said:

"You were going to give me the what's what on the Brand slaughter."

I said:

"I wasn't. I started to say it oughtn't to be hard to trace Rolff— running around with a fractured skull and probably a lot of bandages. Suppose you try it. Give Hurricane Street a play first."

Mickey grinned all the way across his comedian's red face, said, "Don't tell me anything that's going on—I'm only working with you," picked up his hat, and left me.

I spread myself on the bed, smoked cigarettes end to end, and thought about last night—my frame of mind, my passing out, my dreams, and the situation into which I woke. The thinking was unpleasant enough to make me glad when it was interrupted.

Fingernails scratched the outside of my door. I opened the door.

The man who stood there was a stranger to me. He was young, thin, and gaudily dressed. He had heavy eyebrows and a small mustache that were coal-black against a very pale, nervous, but not timid, face.

"I'm Ted Wright," he said, holding out a hand as if I were glad to meet him. "I guess you've heard Whisper talk about me."

I gave him my hand, let him in, closed the door, and asked:

"You're a friend of Whisper's?"

"You bet." He held up two thin fingers pressed tightly together. "Just like that, me and him."

I didn't say anything. He looked around the room, smiled nervously, crossed to the open bathroom door, peeped in, came back to me, rubbed his lips with his tongue, and made his proposition:

"I'll knock him off for you for half a grand."

"Whisper?"

"Yep, and it's dirt cheap."

"Why do I want him killed?" I asked.

"He un-womaned you, didn't he?"

"Yeah?"

"You ain't that dumb."

A notion stirred in my noodle. To give it time to crawl around I said: "Sit down. This needs talking over."

"It don't need nothing," he said, looking at me sharply, not moving toward either chair. "You either want him knocked off or you don't."

"Then I don't."

He said something I didn't catch, down in his throat, and turned to the door. I got between him and it. He stopped, his eyes fidgeting.

I said:

"So Whisper's dead?"

He stepped back and put a hand behind him. I poked his jaw, leaning my hundred and ninety pounds on the poke.

He got his legs crossed and went down.

I pulled him up by the wrists, yanked his face close to mine, and growled:

"Come through. What's the racket?"

"I ain't done nothing to you."

"Let me catch you. Who got Whisper?"

"I don't know nothing a—"

I let go of one of his wrists, slapped his face with my open hand, caught his wrist again, and tried my luck at crunching both of them while I repeated:

"Who got Whisper?"

"Dan Rolff," he whined. "He walked up to him and stuck him with the same skewer Whisper had used on the twist. That's right."

"How do you know it was the one Whisper killed the girl with?"

"Dan said so."

"What did Whisper say?"

"Nothing. He looked funny as hell, standing there with the butt of the sticker sticking out his side. Then he flashes the rod and puts two pills in Dan just like one, and the both of them go down together, cracking heads, Dan's all bloody through the bandages."

"And then what?"

"Then nothing. I roll them over, and they're a pair of stiffs. Every word I'm telling you is gospel."

"Who else was there?"

"Nobody else. Whisper was hiding out, with only me to go between him and the mob. He killed Noonan hisself, and he didn't want to have to trust nobody for a couple of days, till he could see what was what, excepting me."

"So you, being a smart boy, thought you could run around to his enemies and pick up a little dough for killing him after he was dead?"

"I was clean, and this won't be no place for Whisper's pals when the word gets out that he's croaked," Wright whined. "I had to raise a getaway stake."

"How'd you make out so far?"

"I got a century from Pete and a century and a half from Peak Murry—for Reno—with more promised from both when I turn the trick." The whine changed into boasting as he talked. "I bet you I could get McGraw to come across too, and I thought you'd kick in with something."

"They must be high in the air to toss dough at a woozy racket like that."

"I don't know," he said superiorly. "It ain't such a lousy one at that." He became humble again. "Give me a chance, chief. Don't gum it on me. I'll give you fifty bucks now and a split of whatever I get from McGraw if you'll keep your clam shut till I can put it over and grab a rattler."

"Nobody but you knows where Whisper is?"

"Nobody else, except Dan, that's as dead as he is."

"Where are they?"

"The old Redman warehouse down on Porter Street. In the back, upstairs, Whisper had a room fixed up with a bed, stove, and some grub. Give me a chance. Fifty bucks now and a cut on the rest."

I let go of his arm and said:

"I don't want the dough, but go ahead. I'll lay off for a couple of hours. That ought to be long enough."

"Thanks, chief. Thanks, thanks," and he hurried away from me.

..

I put on my coat and hat, went out, found Green Street and the Rutledge Block. It was a wooden building a long while past any prime it might ever have had. Mr. Charles Proctor Dawn's establishment was on the second floor. There was no elevator. I climbed a worn and rickety flight of wooden steps.

The lawyer had two rooms, both dingy, smelly, and poorly lighted. I waited in the outer one while a clerk who went well with the rooms carried my name in to the lawyer. Half a minute later the clerk opened the door and beckoned me in.

Mr. Charles Proctor Dawn was a little fat man of fifty-something. He had prying triangular eyes of a very light color, a short fleshy nose, and a fleshier mouth whose greediness was only partly hidden between a ragged gray mustache and a ragged gray Vandyke beard. His clothes were dark and unclean looking without actually being dirty.

He didn't get up from his desk, and throughout my visit he kept his right hand on the edge of a desk drawer that was some six inches open.

He said:

"Ah, my dear sir, I am extremely gratified to find that you had the good judgment to recognize the value of my counsel."

His voice was even more oratorical than it had been over the wire.

I didn't say anything.

Nodding his whiskers as if my not saying anything was another exhibition of good judgment, he continued:

"I may say, in all justice, that you will find it the invariable part of sound judgment to follow the dictates of my counsel in all cases. I may say this, my dear sir, without false modesty, appreciating with both fitting humility and a deep sense of true and lasting values, my responsibilities as well as my prerogatives as a—and why should I stoop to conceal the fact that there are those who feel justified in preferring to substitute the definite article for the indefinite?—recognized and accepted leader of the bar in this thriving state."

He knew a lot of sentences like those, and he didn't mind using them on me. Finally he got along to:

"Thus, that conduct which in a minor practitioner might seem irregular, becomes, when he who exercises it occupies such indisputable prominence in his community—and, I might say, not merely the immediate community—as serves to place him above fear of reproach, simply that greater ethic which scorns the pettier conventionalities when confronted with an opportunity to serve mankind through one of its individual representatives. Therefore, my dear sir, I have not hesitated to brush aside scornfully all trivial considerations of accepted precedent, to summon you, to say to you frankly and candidly, my dear sir, that your interests will best be served by and through retaining me as your legal representative."

I asked:

"What'll it cost?"

"That," he said loftily, "is of but secondary importance. However, it is a detail which has its deserved place in our relationship, and must be not overlooked or neglected. We shall say, a thousand dollars now. Later, no doubt—"

He ruffled his whiskers and didn't finish the sentence.

I said I hadn't, of course, that much money on me.

"Naturally, my dear sir. Naturally. But that is of not the least importance in any degree. None whatever. Any time will do for that, any time up to ten o'clock tomorrow morning."

"At ten tomorrow," I agreed. "Now I'd like to know why I'm supposed to need legal representatives."

He made an indignant face.

"My dear sir, this is no matter for jesting, of that I assure you."

I explained that I hadn't been joking, that I really was puzzled.

He cleared his throat, frowned more or less importantly, said:

"It may well be, my dear sir, that you do not fully comprehend the peril that surrounds you, but it is indubitably preposterous that you should expect me to suppose that you are without any inkling of the difficulties—the legal difficulties, my dear sir—with which you are about to be confronted, growing, as they do, out of occurrences that took place at no more remote time than last night, my dear sir, last night. However, there is no time to go into that now. I have a pressing appointment with Judge Leffner. On the morrow I shall be glad to go more thoroughly into each least ramification of the situation—and I assure you they are many —with you. I shall expect you at ten tomorrow morning."

I promised to be there, and went out. I spent the evening in my room, drinking unpleasant whiskey, thinking unpleasant thoughts, and waiting for reports that didn't come from Mickey and Dick. I went to sleep at midnight.

XXIII · Mr. Charles Proctor Dawn

I was half dressed the next morning when Dick Foley came in. He reported, in his word-saving manner, that Bill Quint had checked out of the Miners' Hotel at noon the previous day, leaving no forwarding address.

A train left Personville for Ogden at twelve-thirty-five. Dick had wired the Continental's Salt Lake branch to send a man up to Ogden to try to trace Quint.

"We can't pass up any leads," I said, "but I don't think Quint's the man we want. She gave him the air long ago. If he had meant to do anything about it he would have done it before this. My guess is that when he heard she had been killed he decided to duck, being a discarded lover who had threatened her."

Dick nodded and said:

"Gun play out the road last night. Hijacking. Four trucks of hooch nailed, burned."

That sounded like Reno Starkey's answer to the news that the big bootlegger's mob had been sworn in as special coppers.

Mickey Linehan arrived by the time I had finished dressing.

"Dan Rolff was at the house, all right," he reported. "The Greek grocer on the corner saw him come out around nine yesterday morning. He went down the street wobbling and talking to himself. The Greek thought he was drunk."

"Howcome the Greek didn't tell the police? Or did he?"

"Wasn't asked. A swell department this burg's got. What do we do: find him for them and turn him in with the job all tacked up?"

"McGraw has decided Whisper killed her," I said, "and he's not bothering himself with any leads that don't lead that way. Unless he came back later for the ice pick, Rolff didn't turn the trick. She was killed at three in the morning. Rolff wasn't there at eight-thirty, and the pick was still sticking in her. It was—"

Dick Foley came over to stand in front of me and ask:

"How do you know?"

I didn't like the way he looked or the way he spoke. I said:

"You know because I'm telling you."

Dick didn't say anything. Mickey grinned his halfwit's grin and asked:

"Where do we go from here? Let's get this thing polished off."

"I've got a date for ten," I told them. "Hang around the hotel till I get back. Whisper and Rolff are probably dead—so we won't have to hunt for them." I scowled at Dick and said: "I was told that. I didn't kill either of them."

The little Canadian nodded without lowering his eyes from mine.

I ate breakfast alone, and then set out for the lawyer's office.

Turning off King Street, I saw Hank O'Marra's freckled face in an automobile that was going up Green Street. He was sitting beside a man I didn't know. The long-legged youngster waved an arm at me and stopped the car. I went over to him.

He said:

"Reno wants to see you."

"Where will I find him?"

"Jump in."

"I can't go now," I said. "Probably not till afternoon."

"See Peak when you're ready."

I said I would. O'Marra and his companion drove on up Green Street. I walked half a block south to the Rutledge Block.

With a foot on the first of the rickety steps that led up to the lawyer's floor, I stopped to look at something.

It was barely visible back in a dim corner of the first floor. It was a shoe. It was lying in a position that empty shoes don't lie in.

I took my foot off the step and went toward the shoe. Now I could see an ankle and the cuff of a black pants-leg above the shoe-top.

That prepared me for what I found.

I found Mr. Charles Proctor Dawn huddled among two brooms, a mop and a bucket, in a little alcove formed by the back of the stairs and a corner of the wall. His Vandyke beard was red with blood from a cut that ran diagonally across his forehead. His head was twisted sidewise and backward at an angle that could only be managed with a broken neck.

I quoted Noonan's, "What's got to be done has got to be done," to myself, and, gingerly pulling one side of the dead man's coat out of the way, emptied his inside coat pocket, transferring a black book and a sheaf of papers to my own pocket. In two of his other pockets I found nothing I wanted. The rest of his pockets couldn't be got at without moving him, and I didn't care to do that.

∴

Five minutes later I was back in the hotel, going in through a side door, to avoid Dick and Mickey in the lobby, and walking up to the mezzanine to take an elevator.

In my room I sat down and examined my loot.

I took the book first, a small imitation-leather memoranda book of the sort that sells for not much money in any stationery store. It held some fragmentary notes that meant nothing to me, and thirty-some names and addresses that meant as little, with one exception:

Helen Albury
1229A Hurricane St.

That was interesting because, first, a young man named Robert Albury was in prison, having confessed that he shot and killed Donald Willsson in a fit of jealousy aroused by Willsson's supposed success with Dinah Brand; and, second, Dinah Brand had lived, and had been murdered, at 1232 Hurricane Street, across the street from 1229A.

I did not find my name in the book.

I put the book aside and began unfolding and reading the papers I had taken with it. Here too I had to wade through a lot that didn't mean anything to find something that did.

This find was a group of four letters held together by a rubber band.

The letters were in slitted envelopes that had postmarks dated a week apart, on the average. The latest was a little more than six months old. The letters were addressed to Dinah Brand. The first—that is, the earliest—wasn't so bad, for a love letter. The second was a bit goofier. The third and fourth were swell examples of how silly an ardent and unsuccessful wooer can be, especially if he's getting on in years. The four letters were signed by Elihu Willsson.

I had not found anything to tell me definitely why Mr. Charles Proctor Dawn had thought he could blackmail me out of a thousand dollars, but I had found plenty to think about. I encouraged my brain with two Fatimas, and then went downstairs.

"Go out and see what you can raise on a lawyer named Charles Proctor Dawn," I told Mickey. "He's got offices in Green Street. Stay away from them. Don't put in a lot of time on him. I just want a rough line quick."

I told Dick to give me a five-minute start and then follow me out to the neighborhood of 1229A Hurricane Street.

．．

1229A was the upper flat in a two-story building almost directly opposite Dinah's house. 1229 was divided into two flats, with a private entrance for each. I rang the bell at the one I wanted.

The door was opened by a thin girl of eighteen or nineteen with dark eyes set close together in a shiny yellowish face under short-cut brown hair that looked damp.

She opened the door, made a choked, frightened sound in her throat, and backed away from me, holding both hands to her open mouth.

"Miss Helen Albury?" I asked.

She shook her head violently from side to side. There was no truthfulness in it. Her eyes were crazy.

I said:

"I'd like to come in and talk to you a few minutes," going in as I spoke, closing the door behind me.

She didn't say anything. She went up the steps in front of me, her head twisted around so she could watch me with her scary eyes.

We went into a scantily furnished living room. Dinah's house could be seen from its windows.

The girl stood in the center of the floor, her hands still to her mouth.

I wasted time and words trying to convince her that I was harmless.

It was no good. Everything I said seemed to increase her panic. It was a damned nuisance. I quit trying, and got down to business.

"You are Robert Albury's sister?" I asked.

No reply, nothing but the senseless look of utter fear.

I said:

"After he was arrested for killing Donald Willsson you took this flat so you could watch her. What for?"

Not a word from her. I had to supply my own answer:

"Revenge. You blamed Dinah Brand for your brother's trouble. You watched for your chance. It came the night before last. You sneaked into her house, found her drunk, stabbed her with the ice pick you found there."

She didn't say anything. I hadn't succeeded in jolting the blankness out of her frightened face. I said:

"Dawn helped you, engineered it for you. He wanted Elihu Willsson's letters. Who was the man he sent to get them, the man who did the actual killing? Who was he?"

That got me nothing. No change in her expression, or lack of expression. No word. I thought I would like to spank her. I said:

"I've given you your chance to talk. I'm willing to listen to your side of the story. But suit yourself."

She suited herself by keeping quiet. I gave it up. I was afraid of her, afraid she would do something even crazier than her silence if I pressed her further. I went out of the flat not sure that she had understood a single word I had said.

At the corner I told Dick Foley:

"There's a girl in there, Helen Albury, eighteen, five six, skinny, not more than a hundred, if that, eyes close together, brown, yellow skin, brown short hair, straight, got on a gray suit now. Tail her. If she cuts up on you throw her in the can. Be careful—she's crazy as a bedbug."

. .

I set out for Peak Murry's dump, to locate Reno and see what he wanted. Half a block from my destination I stepped into an office building doorway to look the situation over.

A police patrol wagon stood in front of Murry's. Men were being led, dragged, carried, from pool room to wagon. The leaders, draggers, and carriers did not look like regular coppers. They were, I supposed, Pete the Finn's crew, now special officers. Pete, with McGraw's help, apparently was making good his threat to give Whisper and Reno all the war they wanted.

While I watched, an ambulance arrived, was loaded, and drove away. I was too far away to recognize anybody or any bodies. When the height

of the excitement seemed past I circled a couple of blocks and returned
to my hotel.

Mickey Linehan was there with information about Mr. Charles
Proctor Dawn.

"He's the guy that the joke was wrote about: 'Is he a criminal lawyer?' 'Yes, very.' This fellow Albury that you nailed, some of his family
hired this bird Dawn to defend him. Albury wouldn't have anything to
do with him when Dawn came to see him. This three-named shyster nearly
went over himself last year, on a blackmail rap, something to do with a
parson named Hill, but squirmed out of it. Got some property out on
Libert Street, wherever that is. Want me to keep digging?"

"That'll do. We'll stick around till we hear from Dick."

Mickey yawned and said that was all right with him, never being
one that had to run around a lot to keep his blood circulating, and asked
if I knew we were getting nationally famous.

I asked him what he meant by that.

"I just ran into Tommy Robins," he said. "The Consolidated Press
sent him here to cover the doings. He tells me some of the other press
associations and a big-city paper or two are sending in special correspon-
dents, beginning to play our troubles up."

I was making one of my favorite complaints—that newspapers were
good for nothing except to hash things up so nobody could unhash them
—when I heard a boy chanting my name. For a dime he told me I was
wanted on the phone.

Dick Foley:

"She showed right away. To 310 Green Street. Full of coppers.
Mouthpiece named Dawn killed. Police took her to the Hall."

"She still there?"

"Yes, in the chief's office."

"Stick, and get anything you pick up to me quick."

I went back to Mickey Linehan and gave him my room key and
instructions:

"Camp in my room. Take anything that comes for me and pass it on.
I'll be at the Shannon around the corner, registered as J. W. Clark. Tell
Dick and nobody."

Mickey asked, "What the hell?" got no answer, and moved his loose-
jointed bulk toward the elevators.

XXIV · *Wanted*

I went around to the Shannon Hotel, registered my alias, paid my day's rent, and was taken to room 321.

An hour passed before the phone rang.

Dick Foley said he was coming up to see me.

He arrived within five minutes. His thin worried face was not friendly. Neither was his voice. He said:

"Warrants out for you. Murder. Two counts—Brand and Dawn. I phoned. Mickey said he'd stick. Told me you were here. Police got him. Grilling him now."

"Yeah, I expected that."

"So did I," he said sharply.

I said, making myself drawl the words:

"You think I killed them, don't you, Dick?"

"If you didn't, it's a good time to say so."

"Going to put the finger on me?" I asked.

He pulled his lips back over his teeth. His face changed from tan to buff.

I said:

"Go back to San Francisco, Dick. I've got enough to do without having to watch you."

He put his hat on very carefully and very carefully closed the door behind him when he went out.

At four o'clock I had some lunch, cigarettes, and an *Evening Herald* sent up to me.

Dinah Brand's murder, and the newer murder of Charles Proctor Dawn, divided the front page of the *Herald*, with Helen Albury connecting them.

Helen Albury was, I read, Robert Albury's sister, and she was, in spite of his confession, thoroughly convinced that her brother was not guilty of murder, but the victim of a plot. She had retained Charles Proctor Dawn to defend him. (I could guess that the late Charles Proctor had hunted her up, and not she him.) The brother refused to have Dawn or any other lawyer, but the girl (properly encouraged by Dawn, no doubt) had not given up the fight.

Finding a vacant flat across the street from Dinah Brand's house, Helen Albury had rented it, and had installed herself therein with a pair of field glasses and one idea—to prove that Dinah and her associates were guilty of Donald Willsson's murder.

I, it seems, was one of the "associates." The *Herald* called me "a man supposed to be a private detective from San Francisco, who has been in the city for several days, apparently on intimate terms with Max ('Whisper') Thaler, Daniel Rolff, Oliver ('Reno') Starkey, and Dinah Brand." We were the plotters who had framed Robert Albury.

The night that Dinah had been killed, Helen Albury, peeping through her window, had seen things that were, according to the *Herald,* extremely significant when considered in connection with the subsequent finding of Dinah's dead body. As soon as the girl heard of the murder, she took her important knowledge to Charles Proctor Dawn. He, the police learned from his clerks, immediately sent for me, and had been closeted with me that afternoon. He had later told his clerks that I was to return the next—this—morning at ten. This morning I had not appeared to keep my appointment. At twenty-five minutes past ten, the janitor of the Rutledge Block had found Charles Proctor Dawn's body in a corner behind the staircase, murdered. It was believed that valuable papers had been taken from the dead man's pockets.

At the very moment that the janitor was finding the dead lawyer, I, it seems, was in Helen Albury's flat, having forced an entrance, and was threatening her. After she succeeded in throwing me out, she hurried to Dawn's offices, arriving while the police were there, telling them her story. Police sent to my hotel had not found me there, but in my room they had found one Michael Linehan, who also represented himself to be a San Francisco private detective. Michael Linehan was still being questioned by the police. Whisper, Reno, Rolff and I were being hunted by the police, charged with murder. Important developments were expected.

Page two held an interesting half-column. Detectives Shepp and Vanaman, the discoverers of Dinah Brand's body, had mysteriously vanished. Foul play on the part of us "associates" was feared.

There was nothing in the paper about last night's hijacking, nothing about the raid on Peak Murry's joint.

．．

I went out after dark. I wanted to get in touch with Reno.

From a drug store I phoned Peak Murry's pool room.

"Is Peak there?" I asked.

"This is Peak," said a voice that didn't sound anything at all like his. "Who's talking?"

I said disgustedly, "This is Lillian Gish," hung up the receiver, and removed myself from the neighborhood.

I gave up the idea of finding Reno and decided to go calling on my client, old Elihu, and try to blackjack him into good behavior with the love letters he had written Dinah Brand, and which I had stolen from Dawn's remains.

I walked, keeping to the darker side of the darkest streets. It was a fairly long walk for a man who sneers at exercise. By the time I reached Willsson's block I was in bad enough humor to be in good shape for the sort of interviews he and I usually had. But I wasn't to see him for a little while yet.

I was two pavements from my destination when somebody *S-s-s-s'd* at me.

I probably didn't jump twenty feet.

" 'S all right," a voice whispered.

It was dark there. Peeping out under my bush—I was on my hands and knees in somebody's front yard—I could make out the form of a man crouching close to a hedge, on my side of it.

My gun was in my hand now. There was no special reason why I shouldn't take his word for it that it was all right.

I got up off my knees and went to him. When I got close enough I recognized him as one of the men who had let me into the Ronney Street house the day before.

I sat on my heels beside him and asked:

"Where'll I find Reno? Hank O'Marra said he wanted to see me."

"He does that. Know where Kid McLeod's place is at?"

"No."

"It's on Martin Street above King, corner the alley. Ask for the Kid. Go back that-away three blocks, and then down. You can't miss it."

I said I'd try not to, and left him crouching behind his hedge, watching my client's place, waiting, I guessed, for a shot at Pete the Finn, Whisper, or any of Reno's other unfriends who might happen to call on old Elihu.

Following directions, I came to a soft drink and rummy establishment with red and yellow paint all over it. Inside I asked for Kid McLeod. I was taken into a back room, where a fat man with a dirty collar, a lot of gold teeth, and only one ear, admitted he was McLeod.

"Reno sent for me," I said. "Where'll I find him?"

"And who does that make you?" he asked.

I told him who I was. He went out without saying anything. I waited ten minutes. He brought a boy back with him, a kid of fifteen or so with a vacant expression on a pimply red face.

"Go with Sonny," Kid McLeod told me.

I followed the boy out a side door, down two blocks of back street, across a sandy lot, through a ragged gate, and up to the back door of a frame house.

The boy knocked on the door and was asked who he was.

"Sonny, with a guy the Kid sent," he replied.

The door was opened by long-legged O'Marra. Sonny went away. I went into a kitchen where Reno Starkey and four other men sat around a table that had a lot of beer on it. I noticed that two automatic pistols hung on nails over the top of the door through which I had come. They would be handy if any of the house's occupants opened the door, found an enemy with a gun there, and were told to put up their hands.

Reno poured me a glass of beer and led me through the dining room into a front room. A man lay on his belly there, with one eye to the crack between the drawn blind and the bottom of the window, watching the street.

"Go back and get yourself some beer," Reno told him.

He got up and went away. We made ourselves comfortable in adjoining chairs.

"When I fixed up that Tanner alibi for you," Reno said, "I told you I was doing it because I needed all the friends I could get."

"You got one."

"Crack the alibi yet?" he asked.

"Not yet."

"It'll hold," he assured me, "unless they got too damned much on you. Think they have?"

I did think so. I said:

"No. McGraw's just feeling playful. That'll take care of itself. How's your end holding up?"

He emptied his glass, wiped his mouth on the back of a hand, and said:

"I'll make out. But that's what I wanted to see you about. Here's how she stacks up. Pete's throwed in with McGraw. That lines coppers and beer mob up against me and Whisper. But hell! Me and Whisper are busier trying to put the chive in each other than bucking the combine. That's a sour racket. While we're tangling, them bums will eat us up."

I said I had been thinking the same thing. He went on:

"Whisper'll listen to you. Find him, will you? Put it to him. Here's the proposish: he means to get me for knocking off Jerry Hooper, and I mean to get him first. Let's forget that for a couple of days. Nobody won't have to trust nobody else. Whisper don't ever show in any of his jobs anyways. He just sends the boys. I'll do the same this time. We'll just put the mobs together to swing the caper. We run them together, rub out that damned Finn, and then we'll have plenty of time to go gunning among ourselves.

"Put it to him cold. I don't want him to get any ideas that I'm dodging a rumpus with him or any other guy. Tell him I say if we put Pete out of the way we'll have more room to do our own scrapping in. Pete's holed-up down in Whiskeytown. I ain't got enough men to go down there and pull him out. Neither has Whisper. The two of us together has. Put it to him."

"Whisper," I said, "is dead."

Reno said, "Is that so?" as if he thought it wasn't.

"Dan Rolff killed him yesterday morning, down in the old Redman warehouse, stuck him with the ice pick Whisper had used on the girl."

Reno asked:

"You know this? You're not just running off at the head?"

"I know it."

"Damned funny none of his mob act like he was gone," he said, but he was beginning to believe me.

"They don't know it. He was hiding out, with Ted Wright the only one in on the where. Ted knew it. He cashed in on it. He told me he got a hundred or a hundred and fifty from you, through Peak Murry."

"I'd have given the big umpchay twice that for the straight dope," Reno grumbled. He rubbed his chin and said: "Well, that settles the Whisper end."

I said: "No."

"What do you mean, no?"

"If his mob don't know where he is," I suggested, "let's tell them. They blasted him out of the can when Noonan copped him. Think they'd try it again if the news got around that McGraw had picked him up on the quiet?"

"Keep talking," Reno said.

"If his friends try to crack the hoosegow again, thinking he's in it, that'll give the department, including Pete's specials, something to do. While they're doing it, you could try your luck in Whiskeytown."

"Maybe," he said slowly, "maybe we'll try just that thing."

"It ought to work," I encouraged him, standing up. "I'll see you—"

"Stick around. This is as good a spot as any while there's a reader out for you. And we'll need a good guy like you on the party."

I didn't like that so much. I knew enough not to say so. I sat down again.

Reno got busy arranging the rumor. The telephone was worked overtime. The kitchen door was worked as hard, letting men in and out. More came in than went out. The house filled with men, smoke, tension.

XXV · Whiskeytown

AT half-past one Reno turned from answering a phone call to say:

"Let's take a ride."

He went upstairs. When he came down he carried a black valise. Most of the men had gone out the kitchen door by then.

Reno gave me the black valise, saying:

"Don't wrastle it around too much."

It was heavy.

The seven of us left in the house went out the front door and got into a curtained touring car that O'Marra had just driven up to the curb. Reno sat beside O'Marra. I was squeezed in between men in the back seat, with the valise squeezed between my legs.

Another car came out of the first cross street to run ahead of us. A third followed us. Our speed hung around forty, fast enough to get us somewhere, not fast enough to get us a lot of attention.

We had nearly finished the trip before we were bothered.

The action started in a block of one-story houses of the shack type, down in the southern end of the city.

A man put his head out of a door, put his fingers in his mouth, and whistled shrilly.

Somebody in the car behind us shot him down.

At the next corner we ran through a volley of pistol bullets.

Reno turned around to tell me:

"If they pop the bag, we'll all of us hit the moon. Get it open. We got to work fast when we get there."

I had the fasteners unsnapped by the time we came to rest at the curb in front of a dark three-story brick building.

Men crawled all over me, opening the valise, helping themselves to the contents, bombs made of short sections of two-inch pipe, packed in sawdust in the bag. Bullets bit chunks out of the car's curtains.

Reno reached back for one of the bombs, hopped out to the sidewalk, paid no attention to a streak of blood that suddenly appeared in the middle of his left cheek, and heaved his piece of stuffed pipe at the brick building's door.

A sheet of flame was followed by deafening noise. Hunks of things pelted us while we tried to keep from being knocked over by the concussion. Then there was no door to keep anybody out of the red brick building.

A man ran forward, swung his arm, let a pipeful of hell go through the doorway. The shutters came off the downstairs windows, fire and glass flying behind them.

The car that had followed us was stationary up the street, trading shots with the neighborhood. The car that had gone ahead of us had turned into a side street. Pistol shots from behind the red brick building, between the explosions of our cargo, told us that our advance car was covering the back door.

O'Marra, out in the middle of the street, bent far over, tossed a bomb to the brick building's roof. It didn't explode. O'Marra put one foot high in the air, clawed at his throat, and fell solidly backward.

Another of our party went down under the slugs that were cutting at us from a wooden building next to the brick one.

Reno cursed stolidly and said:

"Burn them out, Fat."

Fat spit on a bomb, ran around the back of our car, and swung his arm.

We picked ourselves up off the sidewalk, dodged flying things, and saw that the frame house was all out of whack, with flames climbing its torn edges.

"Any left?" Reno asked as we looked around, enjoying the novelty of not being shot at.

"Here's the last one," Fat said, holding out a bomb.

Fire was dancing inside the upper windows of the brick house. Reno looked at it, took the bomb from Fat, and said:

"Back off. They'll be coming out."

We moved away from the front of the house.

A voice indoors yelled:

"Reno!"

Reno slipped into the shadow of our car before he called back:

"Well?"

"We're done," a heavy voice shouted. "We're coming out. Don't shoot."

Reno asked: "Who's we're?"

"This is Pete," the heavy voice said. "There's four left of us."

"You come first," Reno ordered, "with your mitts on the top of your head. The others come out one at a time, same way, after you. And half a minute apart is close enough. Come on."

We waited a moment, and then Pete the Finn appeared in the dyna-mited doorway, his hands holding the top of his bald head. In the glare from the burning next-door house we could see that his face was cut, his clothes almost all torn off.

Stepping over wreckage, the bootlegger came slowly down the steps to the sidewalk.

Reno called him a lousy fish-eater and shot him four times in face and body.

Pete went down. A man behind me laughed.

Reno hurled the remaining bomb through the doorway.

We scrambled into our car. Reno took the wheel. The engine was dead. Bullets had got to it.

Reno worked the horn while the rest of us piled out.

The machine that had stopped at the corner came for us. Waiting for it, I looked up and down the street that was bright with the glow of two burning buildings. There were a few faces at windows, but whoever besides us was in the street had taken to cover. Not far away, firebells sounded.

The other machine slowed up for us to climb aboard. It was already full. We packed it in layers, with the overflow hanging on the running boards.

We bumped over dead Hank O'Marra's legs and headed for home. We covered one block of the distance with safety if not comfort. After that we had neither.

A limousine turned into the street ahead of us, came half a block toward us, put its side to us, and stopped. Out of the side, gun-fire.

Another car came around the limousine and charged us. Out of it, gun-fire.

We did our best, but we were too damned amalgamated for good fighting. You can't shoot straight holding a man in your lap, another hanging on your shoulder, while a third does his shooting from an inch behind your ear.

Our other car—the one that had been around at the building's rear—came up and gave us a hand. But by then two more had joined the opposition. Apparently Thaler's mob's attack on the jail was over, one way or the other, and Pete's army, sent to help there, had returned in time to spoil our get-away. It was a sweet mess.

I leaned over a burning gun and yelled in Reno's ear:

"This is the bunk. Let's us extras get out and do our wrangling from the street."

He thought that a good idea, and gave orders:

"Pile out, some of you hombres, and take them from the pavements."

I was the first man out, with my eye on a dark alley entrance.

Fat followed me to it. In my shelter, I turned on him and growled:

"Don't pile up on me. Pick your own hole. There's a cellarway that looks good."

He agreeably trotted off toward it, and was shot down at his third step.

I explored my alley. It was only twenty feet long, and ended against a high board fence with a locked gate.

A garbage can helped me over the gate into a brick-paved yard. The side fence of that yard let me into another, and from that I got into another, where a fox terrier raised hell at me.

I kicked the pooch out of the way, made the opposite fence, untangled myself from a clothes line, crossed two more yards, got yelled at from a window, had a bottle thrown at me, and dropped into a cobblestoned back street.

The shooting was behind me, but not far enough. I did all I could to remedy that. I must have walked as many streets as I did in my dreams the night Dinah was killed.

My watch said it was three-thirty a. m. when I looked at it on Elihu Willsson's front steps.

XXVI · *Blackmail*

I had to push my client's doorbell a lot before I got any play on it.

Finally the door was opened by the tall sunburned chauffeur. He was dressed in undershirt and pants, and had a billiard cue in one fist.

"What do you want?" he demanded, and then, when he got another look at me: "It's you, is it? Well, what do you want?"

"I want to see Mr. Willsson."

"At four in the morning? Go on with you," and he started to close the door.

I put a foot against it. He looked from my foot to my face, hefted the billiard cue, and asked:

"You after getting your kneecap cracked?"

"I'm not playing," I insisted. "I've got to see the old man. Tell him."

"I don't have to tell him. He told me no later than this afternoon that if you come around he didn't want to see you."

"Yeah?" I took the four love letters out of my pocket, picked out the first and least idiotic of them, held it out to the chauffeur, and said: "Give him that and tell him I'm sitting on the steps with the rest of them. Tell him I'll sit here five minutes and then carry the rest of them to Tommy Robins of the Consolidated Press."

The chauffeur scowled at the letter, said, "To hell with Tommy Robins and his blind aunt!" took the letter, and closed the door.

Four minutes later he opened the door again and said:

"Inside, you."

I followed him upstairs to old Elihu's bedroom.

My client sat up in bed with his love letter crushed in one round pink fist, its envelope in the other.

His short white hair bristled. His round eyes were as much red as blue. The parallel lines of his mouth and chin almost touched. He was in a lovely humor.

As soon as he saw me he shouted:

"So after all your brave talking you had to come back to the old pirate to have your neck saved, did you?"

I said I didn't anything of the sort. I said if he was going to talk like a sap he ought to lower his voice so the people in Los Angeles wouldn't learn what a sap he was.

The old boy let his voice out another notch, bellowing:

"Because you've stolen a letter or two that don't belong to you, you needn't think you—"

I put fingers in my ears. They didn't shut out the noise, but they insulted him into cutting the bellowing short.

I took the fingers out and said:

"Send the flunkey away so we can talk. You won't need him. I'm not going to hurt you."

He said, "Get out," to the chauffeur.

The chauffeur, looking at me without fondness, left us, closing the door.

Old Elihu gave me the rush act, demanding that I surrender the rest of the letters immediately, wanting to know loudly and profanely where I had got them, what I was doing with them, threatening me with this, that, and the other, but mostly just cursing me.

I didn't surrender the letters. I said:

"I took them from the man you hired to recover them. A tough break for you that he had to kill the girl."

Enough red went out of the old man's face to leave it normally pink. He worked his lips over his teeth, screwed up his eyes at me, and said:

"Is that the way you're going to play it?"

His voice came comparatively quiet from his chest. He had settled down to fight.

I pulled a chair over beside the bed, sat down, put as much amusement as I could in a grin, and said:

"That's one way."

He watched me, working his lips, saying nothing. I said:

"You're the damndest client I ever had. What do you do? You hire me to clean town, change your mind, run out on me, work against me until I begin to look like a winner, then get on the fence, and now when you think I'm licked again, you don't even want to let me in the house. Lucky for me I happened to run across those letters."

He said: "Blackmail."

I laughed and said:

"Listen who's naming it. All right, call it that." I tapped the edge of the bed with a forefinger. "I'm not licked, old top. I've won. You came crying to me that some naughty men had taken your little city away from you. Pete the Finn, Lew Yard, Whisper Thaler, and Noonan. Where are they now?

"Yard died Tuesday morning, Noonan the same night, Whisper

Wednesday morning, and the Finn a little while ago. I'm giving your city back to you whether you want it or not. If that's blackmail, O. K. Now here's what you're going to do. You're going to get hold of your mayor, I suppose the lousy village has got one, and you and he are going to phone the governor— Keep still until I get through.

"You're going to tell the governor that your city police have got out of hand, what with bootleggers sworn in as officers, and so on. You're going to ask him for help—the national guard would be best. I don't know how various ruckuses around town have come out, but I do know the big boys —the ones you were afraid of—are dead. The ones that had too much on you for you to stand up to them. There are plenty of busy young men working like hell right now, trying to get into the dead men's shoes. The more, the better. They'll make it easier for the white-collar soldiers to take hold while everything is disorganized. And none of the substitutes are likely to have enough on you to do much damage.

"You're going to have the mayor, or the governor, whichever it comes under, suspend the whole Personville police department, and let the mail-order troops handle things till you can organize another. I'm told that the mayor and the governor are both pieces of your property. They'll do what you tell them. And that's what you're going to tell them. It can be done, and it's got to be done.

"Then you'll have your city back, all nice and clean and ready to go to the dogs again. If you don't do it, I'm going to turn these love letters of yours over to the newspaper buzzards, and I don't mean your *Herald* crew —the press associations. I got the letters from Dawn. You'll have a lot of fun proving that you didn't hire him to recover them, and that he didn't kill the girl doing it. But the fun you'll have is nothing to the fun people will have reading these letters. They're hot. I haven't laughed so much over anything since the hogs ate my kid brother."

I stopped talking.

The old man was shaking, but there was no fear in his shaking. His face was purple again. He opened his mouth and roared:

"Publish them and be damned!"

I took them out of my pocket, dropped them on his bed, got up from my chair, put on my hat, and said:

"I'd give my right leg to be able to believe that the girl was killed by somebody you sent to get the letters. By God, I'd like to top off the job by sending you to the gallows!"

He didn't touch the letters. He said:

"You told me the truth about Thaler and Pete?"

"Yeah. But what difference does it make? You'll only be pushed around by somebody else."

He threw the bedclothes aside and swung his stocky pajamaed legs and pink feet over the edge of the bed.

"Have you got the guts," he barked, "to take the job I offered you once before—chief of police?"

"No. I lost my guts out fighting your fights while you were hiding in bed and thinking up new ways of disowning me. Find another wet nurse."

He glared at me. Then shrewd wrinkles came around his eyes.

He nodded his old head and said:

"You're afraid to take the job. So you did kill the girl?"

I left him as I had left him the last time, saying, "Go to hell!" and walking out.

The chauffeur, still toting his billiard cue, still regarding me without fondness, met me on the ground floor and took me to the door, looking as if he hoped I would start something. I didn't. He slammed the door after me.

.·.

The street was gray with the beginning of daylight.

Up the street a black coupé stood under some trees. I couldn't see if anyone was in it. I played safe by walking in the opposite direction. The coupé moved after me.

There is nothing in running down streets with automobiles in pursuit. I stopped, facing this one. It came on. I took my hand away from my side when I saw Mickey Linehan's red face through the windshield.

He swung the door open for me to get in.

"I thought you might come up here," he said as I sat beside him, "but I was a second or two too late. I saw you go in, but was too far away to catch you."

"How'd you make out with the police?" I asked. "Better keep driving while we talk."

"I didn't know anything, couldn't guess anything, didn't have any idea of what you were working on, just happened to hit town and meet you. Old friends—that line. They were still trying when the riot broke. They had me in one of the little offices across from the assembly room. When the circus cut loose I back-windowed them."

"How'd the circus wind up?" I asked.

"The coppers shot hell out of them. They got the tip-off half an hour ahead of time, and had the whole neighborhood packed with specials. Seems it was a juicy row while it lasted—no duck soup for the coppers at that. Whisper's mob, I hear."

"Yeah. Reno and Pete the Finn tangled tonight. Hear anything about it?"

"Only that they'd had it."

"Reno killed Pete and ran into an ambush on the get-away. I don't know what happened after that. Seen Dick?"

"I went up to his hotel and was told he'd checked out to catch the evening train."

"I sent him back home," I explained. "He seemed to think I'd killed Dinah Brand. He was getting on my nerves with it."

"Well?"

"You mean, did I kill her? I don't know, Mickey. I'm trying to find out. Want to keep riding with me, or want to follow Dick back to the Coast?"

Mickey said:

"Don't get so cocky over one lousy murder that maybe didn't happen. But what the hell? You know you didn't lift her dough and pretties."

"Neither did the killer. They were still there after eight that morning, when I left. Dan Rolff was in and out between then and nine. He wouldn't have taken them. The— I've got it! The coppers that found the body— Shepp and Vanaman—got there at nine-thirty. Besides the jewelry and money, some letters old Willsson had written the girl were—must have been—taken. I found them later in Dawn's pocket. The two dicks disappeared just about then. See it?

"When Shepp and Vanaman found the girl dead they looted the joint before they turned in the alarm. Old Willsson being a millionaire, his letters looked good to them, so they took them along with the other valuables, and turned them—the letters—over to the shyster to peddle back to Elihu. But Dawn was killed before he could do anything on that end. I took the letters. Shepp and Vanaman, whether they did or didn't know that the letters were not found in the dead man's possession, got cold feet. They were afraid the letters would be traced to them. They had the money and jewelry. They lit out."

"Sounds fair enough," Mickey agreed, "but it don't seem to put any fingers on any murderers."

"It clears the way some. We'll try to clear it some more. See if you can find Porter Street and an old warehouse called Redman. The way I got it, Rolff killed Whisper there, walked up to him and stabbed him with the ice pick he had found in the girl. If he did it that way, then Whisper hadn't killed her. Or he would have been expecting something of the sort, and wouldn't have let the lunger get that close to him. I'd like to look at their remains and check up."

"Porter's over beyond King," Mickey said. "We'll try the south end first. It's nearer and more likely to have warehouses. Where do you set this Rolff guy?"

"Out. If he killed Whisper for killing the girl, that marks him off. Besides, she had bruises on her wrist and cheek, and he wasn't strong enough to rough her. My notion is that he left the hospital, spent the night God knows where, showed up at the girl's house after I left that morning, let himself in with his key, found her, decided Whisper had done the trick, took the sticker out of her, and went hunting Whisper."

"So?" Mickey said. "Now where do you get the idea that you might be the boy who put it over?"

"Stop it," I said grouchily as we turned into Porter Street. "Let's find our warehouse."

XXVII · *Warehouses*

WE rode down the street, jerking our eyes around, hunting for buildings that looked like deserted warehouses. It was light enough by now to see well.

Presently I spotted a big square rusty-red building set in the center of a weedy lot. Disuse stuck out all over lot and building. It had the look of a likely candidate.

"Pull up at the next corner," I said. "That looks like the dump. You stick with the heap while I scout it."

I walked two unnecessary blocks so I could come into the lot behind the building. I crossed the lot carefully, not sneaking, but not making any noises I could avoid.

I tried the back door cautiously. It was locked, of course. I moved over to a window, tried to look in, couldn't because of gloom and dirt, tried the window, and couldn't budge it.

I went to the next window with the same luck. I rounded the corner of the building and began working my way along the north side. The first window had me beaten. The second went up slowly with my push, and didn't make much noise doing it.

Across the inside of the window frame, from top to bottom, boards were nailed. They looked solid and strong from where I stood.

I cursed them, and remembered hopefully that the window hadn't made much noise when I raised it. I climbed up on the sill, put a hand against the boards, and tried them gently.

They gave.

I put more weight behind my hand. The boards went away from the left side of the frame, showing me a row of shiny nail points.

I pushed them back farther, looked past them, saw nothing but darkness, heard nothing.

With my gun in my right fist, I stepped over the sill, down into the building. Another step to the left put me out of the window's gray light.

I switched my gun to my left hand and used my right to push the boards back over the window.

A full minute of breathless listening got me nothing. Holding my gun-arm tight to my side, I began exploring the joint. Nothing but the floor came under my feet as I inch-by-inched them forward. My groping left hand felt nothing until it touched a rough wall. I seemed to have crossed a room that was empty.

I moved along the wall, hunting for a door. Half a dozen of my undersized steps brought me to one. I leaned an ear against it, and heard no sound.

I found the knob, turned it softly, eased the door back.

Something swished.

I did four things all together: let go the knob, jumped, pulled trigger, and had my left arm walloped with something hard and heavy as a tombstone.

The flare of my gun showed me nothing. It never does, though it's easy to think you've seen things. Not knowing what else to do, I fired again, and once more.

An old man's voice pleaded:

"Don't do that, partner. You don't have to do that."

I said: "Make a light."

A match spluttered on the floor, kindled, and put flickering yellow light on a battered face. It was an old face of the useless, characterless sort that goes well with park benches. He was sitting on the floor, his stringy legs sprawled far apart. He didn't seem hurt anywhere. A table-leg lay beside him.

"Get up and make a light," I ordered, "and keep matches burning until you've done it."

He struck another match, sheltered it carefully with his hands as he got up, crossed the room, and lit a candle on a three-legged table.

I followed him, keeping close. My left arm was numb or I would have taken hold of him for safety.

"What are you doing here?" I asked when the candle was burning.

I didn't need his answer. One end of the room was filled with wooden cases piled six high, branded *Perfection Maple Syrup*.

While the old man explained that as God was his keeper he didn't know nothing about it, that all he knew was that a man named Yates had two days ago hired him as night watchman, and if anything was wrong he was as innocent as innocent, I pulled part of the top off one case.

The bottles inside had Canadian Club labels that looked as if they had been printed with a rubber stamp.

I left the cases and, driving the old man in front of me with the candle, searched the building. As I expected, I found nothing to indicate that this was the warehouse Whisper had occupied.

By the time we got back to the room that held the liquor my left arm was strong enough to lift a bottle. I put it in my pocket and gave the old man some advice:

"Better clear out. You were hired to take the place of some of the men Pete the Finn turned into special coppers. But Pete's dead now and his racket has gone blooey."

When I climbed out the window the old man was standing in front of the cases, looking at them with greedy eyes while he counted on his fingers.

∴

"Well?" Mickey asked when I returned to him and his coupé.

I took out the bottle of anything but Canadian Club, pulled the cork, passed it to him, and then put a shot into my own system.

He asked, "Well?" again.

I said: "Let's try to find the old Redman warehouse."

He said: "You're going to ruin yourself some time telling people too much," and started the car moving.

Three blocks farther up the street we saw a faded sign, *Redman & Company*. The building under the sign was long, low, and narrow, with corrugated iron roof and few windows.

"We'll leave the boat around the corner," I said. "And you'll go with me this time. I didn't have a whole lot of fun by myself last trip."

When we climbed out of the coupé, an alley ahead promised a path to the warehouse's rear. We took it.

A few people were wandering through the streets, but it was still too early for the factories that filled most of this part of town to come to life.

At the rear of our building we found something interesting. The back door was closed. Its edge, and the edge of the frame, close to the lock, were scarred. Somebody had worked there with a jimmy.

Mickey tried the door. It was unlocked. Six inches at a time, with pauses between, he pushed it far enough back to let us squeeze in.

When we squeezed in we could hear a voice. We couldn't make out what the voice was saying. All we could hear was the faint rumble of a distant man's voice, with a suggestion of quarrelsomeness in it.

Mickey pointed a thumb at the door's scar and whispered.

"Not coppers."

I took two steps inside, keeping my weight on my rubber heels. Mickey followed, breathing down the back of my neck.

Ted Wright had told me Whisper's hiding place was in the back, upstairs. The distant rumbling voice could have been coming from there.

I twisted my face around to Mickey and asked:

"Flashlight?"

He put it in my left hand. I had my gun in my right. We crept forward.

The door, still a foot open, let in enough light to show us the way

across this room to a doorless doorway. The other side of the doorway was
black.

I flicked the light across the blackness, found a door, shut off the
light, and went forward. The next squirt of light showed us steps leading
up.

We went up the steps as if we were afraid they would break under
our feet.

The rumbling voice had stopped. There was something else in the
air. I didn't know what. Maybe a voice not quite loud enough to be heard,
if that means anything.

I had counted nine steps when a voice spoke clearly above us. It said:
"Sure, I killed the bitch."

A gun said something, the same thing four times, roaring like a 16-
inch rifle under the iron roof.

The first voice said: "All right."

By that time Mickey and I had put the rest of the steps behind us,
had shoved a door out of the way, and were trying to pull Reno Starkey's
hands away from Whisper's throat.

It was a tough job and a useless one. Whisper was dead.

Reno recognized me and let his hands go limp.

His eyes were as dull, his horse face as wooden, as ever.

Mickey carried the dead gambler to the cot that stood in one end of
the room, spreading him on it.

The room, apparently once an office, had two windows. In their light
I could see a body stowed under the cot—Dan Rolff. A Colt's service
automatic lay in the middle of the floor.

Reno bent his shoulders, swaying.

"Hurt?" I asked.

"He put all four in me," he said calmly, bending to press both forearms against his lower body.

"Get a doc," I told Mickey.

"No good," Reno said. "I got no more belly left than Peter Collins."

I pulled a folding chair over and sat him down on it, so he could
lean forward and hold himself together.

Mickey ran out and down the stairs.

"Did you know he wasn't croaked?" Reno asked.

"No. I gave it to you the way I got it from Ted Wright."

"Ted left too soon," he said. "I was leary of something like that, and
came to make sure. He trapped me pretty, playing dead till I was under
the gun." He stared dully at Whisper's corpse. "Game at that, damn him.
Dead, but wouldn't lay down, bandaging hisself, laying here waiting by
hisself." He smiled, the only smile I had ever seen him use. "But he's just
meat and not much of it now."

His voice was thickening. A little red puddle formed under the edge of his chair. I was afraid to touch him. Only the pressure of his arms, and his bent-forward position, were keeping him from falling apart.

He stared at the puddle and asked:

"How the hell did you figure you didn't croak her?"

"I had to take it out in hoping I hadn't, till just now," I said. "I had you pegged for it, but couldn't be sure. I was all hopped up that night, and had a lot of dreams, with bells ringing and voices calling, and a lot of stuff like that. I got an idea maybe it wasn't straight dreaming so much as hop-head nightmares stirred up by things that were happening around me.

"When I woke up, the lights were out. I didn't think I killed her, turned off the light, and went back to take hold of the ice pick. But it could have happened other ways. You knew I was there that night. You gave me my alibi without stalling. That got me thinking. Dawn tried blackmailing me after he heard Helen Albury's story. The police, after hearing her story, tied you, Whisper, Rolff and me together. I found Dawn dead after seeing O'Marra half a block away. It looked like the shyster had tried blackmailing you. That and the police tying us together started me thinking the police had as much on the rest of you as on me. What they had on me was that Helen Albury had seen me go in or out or both that night. It was a good guess they had the same on the rest of you. There were reasons for counting Whisper and Rolff out. That left you— and me. But why you killed her's got me puzzled."

"I bet you," he said, watching the red puddle grow on the floor. "It was her own damned fault. She calls me up, tells me Whisper's coming to see her, and says if I get there first I can bushwhack him. I'd like that. I go over there, stick around, but he don't show."

He stopped, pretending interest in the shape the red puddle was taking. I knew pain had stopped him, but I knew he would go on talking as soon as he got himself in hand. He meant to die as he had lived, inside the same tough shell. Talking could be torture, but he wouldn't stop on that account, not while anybody was there to see him. He was Reno Starkey who could take anything the world had without batting an eye, and he would play it out that way to the end.

"I got tired of waiting," he went on after a moment. "I hit her door and asked howcome. She takes me in, telling me there's nobody there. I'm doubtful, but she swears she's alone, and we go back in the kitchen. Knowing her, I'm beginning to think maybe it's me and not Whisper that's being trapped."

Mickey came in, telling us he had phoned for an ambulance.

Reno used the interruption to rest his voice, and then continued with his story:

"Later, I find that Whisper did phone her he was coming, and got there before me. You were coked. She was afraid to let him in, so he beat it. She don't tell me that, scared I'll go and leave her. You're hopped and she wants protection against Whisper coming back. I don't know none of that then. I'm leary that I've walked into something, knowing her. I think I'll take hold of her and slap the truth out of her. I try it, and she grabs the pick and screams. When she squawks, I hear a man's feet hitting the floor. The trap's sprung, I think."

He spoke slower, taking more time and pains to turn each word out calmly and deliberately, as talking became harder. His voice had become blurred, but if he knew it he pretended he didn't.

"I don't mean to be the only one that's hurt. I twist the pick out of her hand and stick it in her. You gallop out, coked to the edges, charging at the whole world with both eyes shut. She tumbles into you. You go down, roll around till your hand hits the butt of the pick. Holding on to that, you go to sleep, peaceful as she is. I see it then, what I've done. But hell! she's croaked. There's nothing to do about it. I turn off the lights and go home. When you—"

A tired looking ambulance crew—Poisonville gave them plenty of work—brought a litter into the room, ending Reno's tale. I was glad of it. I had all the information I wanted, and sitting there listening to and watching him talk himself to death wasn't pleasant.

I took Mickey over to a corner of the room and muttered in his ear:

"The job's yours from now on. I'm going to duck. I ought to be in the clear, but I know my Poisonville too well to take any chances. I'll drive your car to some way station where I can catch a train for Ogden. I'll be at the Roosevelt Hotel there, registered as P. F. King. Stay with the job, and let me know when it's wise to either take my own name again or a trip to Honduras."

I spent most of my week in Ogden trying to fix up my reports so they would not read as if I had broken as many Agency rules, state laws and human bones as I had.

Mickey arrived on the sixth night.

He told me that Reno was dead, that I was no longer officially a criminal, that most of the First National Bank stick-up loot had been recovered, that MacSwain had confessed killing Tim Noonan, and that Personville, under martial law, was developing into a sweet-smelling and thornless bed of roses.

Mickey and I went back to San Francisco.

I might just as well have saved the labor and sweat I had put into trying to make my reports harmless. They didn't fool the Old Man. He gave me merry hell.

THE
DAIN CURSE

TO ALBERT S. SAMUELS

THE DAIN CURSE

Part One: The Dains

I · *Eight Diamonds*

It was a diamond all right, shining in the grass half a dozen feet from the blue brick walk. It was small, not more than a quarter of a carat in weight, and unmounted. I put it in my pocket and began searching the lawn as closely as I could without going at it on all fours.

I had covered a couple of square yards of sod when the Leggetts' front door opened.

A woman came out on the broad stone top step and looked down at me with good-humored curiosity.

She was a woman of about my age, forty, with darkish blond hair, a pleasant plump face, and dimpled pink cheeks. She had on a lavender-flowered white housedress.

I stopped poking at the grass and went up to her, asking: "Is Mr. Leggett in?"

"Yes." Her voice was placid as her face. "You wish to see him?"

I said I did.

She smiled at me and at the lawn.

"You're another detective, aren't you?"

I admitted that.

She took me up to a green, orange, and chocolate room on the second floor, put me in a brocaded chair, and went to call her husband from his laboratory. While I waited, I looked around the room, deciding that the dull orange rug under my feet was probably both genuinely oriental and genuinely ancient, that the walnut furniture hadn't been ground out by machinery, and that the Japanese pictures on the wall hadn't been selected by a prude.

Edgar Leggett came in saying: "I'm sorry to have kept you waiting, but I couldn't break off till now. Have you learned something?"

His voice was unexpectedly harsh, rasping, though his manner was friendly enough. He was a dark-skinned erect man in his middle forties, muscularly slender and of medium height. He would have been handsome if his brown face hadn't been so deeply marked with sharp, hard lines across the forehead and from nostrils down across mouth-corners. Dark hair, worn rather long, curled above and around the broad, grooved forehead. Red-brown eyes were abnormally bright behind horn-rimmed spectacles. His nose was long, thin, and high-bridged. His lips were thin, sharp, nimble, over a small, bony chin. His black and white clothes were well made and cared for.

"Not yet," I said to his question. "I'm not a police detective—Continental Agency—for the insurance company—and I'm just starting."

"Insurance company?" He seemed surprised, raising dark eyebrows above the dark tops of his spectacles.

"Yeah. Didn't—?"

"Surely," he said, smiling, stopping my words with a small flourish of one hand. It was a long, narrow hand with over-developed finger-tips, ugly as most trained hands are. "Surely. They would have been insured. I hadn't thought of that. They weren't my diamonds, you know; they were Halstead's."

"Halstead and Beauchamp? I didn't get any details from the insurance company. You had the diamonds on approval?"

"No. I was using them experimentally. Halstead knew of my work with glass—coloring it, staining or dyeing it, after its manufacture—and he became interested in the possibility of the process being adapted to diamonds, particularly in improving off-color stones, removing yellowish and brownish tinges, emphasizing blues. He asked me to try it and five weeks ago gave me those diamonds to work on. There were eight of them, none especially valuable. The largest weighed only a trifle more than half a carat, some of the others only a quarter, and except for two they were all of poor color. They're the stones the burglar got."

"Then you hadn't succeeded?" I asked.

"Frankly," he said, "I hadn't made the slightest progress. This was a more delicate matter, and on more obdurate material."

"Where'd you keep them?"

"Usually they were left lying around in the open—always in the laboratory, of course—but for several days now they had been locked in the cabinet—since my last unsuccessful experiment."

"Who knew about the experiments?"

"Anyone, everyone—there was no occasion for secrecy."

"They were stolen from the cabinet?"

"Yes. This morning we found our front door open, the cabinet drawer forced, and the diamonds gone. The police found marks on the kitchen door. They say the burglar came in that way and left by the front door. We heard nothing last night. And nothing else was taken."

"The front door was ajar when I came downstairs this morning," Mrs.

Leggett said from the doorway. "I went upstairs and awakened Edgar, and we searched the house and found the diamonds gone. The police think the man I saw must have been the burglar."

I asked about the man she had seen.

"It was last night, around midnight, when I opened the bedroom windows before going to bed. I saw a man standing upon the corner. I can't say, even now, that there was anything very suspicious-looking about him. He was standing there as if waiting for somebody. He was looking down this way, but not in a way to make me think he was watching this house. He was a man past forty, I should say, rather short and broad—somewhat of your build—but he had a bristly brown mustache and was pale. He wore a soft hat and overcoat—dark—I think they were brown. The police think that's the same man Gabrielle saw."

"Who?"

"My daughter Gabrielle," she said. "Coming home late one night—Saturday night, I think it was—she saw a man and thought he had come from our steps; but she wasn't sure and didn't think anything more of it until after the burglary."

"I'd like to talk to her. Is she home?"

Mrs. Leggett went out to get her.

I asked Leggett: "Were the diamonds loose?"

"They were unset, of course, and in small manila envelopes—Halstead and Beauchamp's—each in a separate envelope, with a number and the weight of the stone written in pencil. The envelopes are missing too."

Mrs. Leggett returned with her daughter, a girl of twenty or less in a sleeveless white silk dress. Of medium height, she looked more slender than she actually was. She had hair as curly as her father's, and no longer, but of a much lighter brown. She had a pointed chin and extremely white, smooth skin, and of her features only the green-brown eyes were large: forehead, mouth, and teeth were remarkably small. I stood up to be introduced to her, and asked about the man she had seen.

"I'm not positive that he came from the house," she said, "or even from the lawn." She was sullen, as if she didn't like being questioned. "I thought he might have, but I only saw him walking up the street."

"What sort of looking man was he?"

"I don't know. It was dark. I was in the car, he was walking up the street. I didn't examine him closely. He was about your size. It might have been you, for all I know."

"It wasn't. That was Saturday night?"

"Yes—that is, Sunday morning."

"What time?"

"Oh, three o'clock or after," she said impatiently.

"Were you alone?"

"Hardly."

I asked her who was with her and finally got a name: Eric Collinson had driven her home. I asked where I could find Eric Collinson. She frowned, hesitated, and said he was employed by Spear, Camp and Duffy, stockbrokers. She also said she had a putrid headache and she hoped I would excuse her now, as she knew I couldn't have any more questions to ask her. Then, without waiting for any reply I might have made to that, she turned and went out of the room. Her ears, I noticed when she turned, had no lobes, and were queerly pointed at the top.

"How about your servants?" I asked Mrs. Leggett.

"We've only one—Minnie Hershey, a Negress. She doesn't sleep here, and I'm sure she had nothing to do with it. She's been with us for nearly two years and I can vouch for her honesty."

I said I'd like to talk to Minnie, and Mrs. Leggett called her in. The servant was a small, wiry mulatto girl with the straight black hair and brown features of an Indian. She was very polite and very insistent that she had nothing to do with the theft of the diamonds and had known nothing about the burglary until she arrived at the house that morning. She gave me her home address, in San Francisco's darktown.

Leggett and his wife took me up to the laboratory, a large room that covered all but a small fifth of the third story. Charts hung between the windows on the whitewashed wall. The wooden floor was uncovered. An X-ray machine—or something similar—four or five smaller machines, a forge, a wide sink, a large zinc table, some smaller porcelain ones, stands, racks of glassware, siphon-shaped metal tanks—that sort of stuff filled most of the room.

The cabinet the diamonds had been taken from was a green-painted steel affair with six drawers all locking together. The second drawer from the top—the one the diamonds had been in—was open. Its edge was dented where a jimmy or chisel had been forced between it and the frame. The other drawers were still locked. Leggett said the forcing of the diamond drawer had jammed the locking mechanism so that he would have to get a mechanic to open the others.

We went downstairs, through a room where the mulatto was walking around behind a vacuum cleaner, and into the kitchen. The back door and its frame were marked much as the cabinet was, apparently by the same tool.

When I had finished looking at the door, I took the diamond out of my pocket and showed it to the Leggetts, asking: "Is this one of them?"

Leggett picked it out of my palm with forefinger and thumb, held it up to the light, turned it from side to side, and said: "Yes. It has that cloudy spot down at the culet. Where did you get it?"

"Out front, in the grass."

"Ah, our burglar dropped some of his spoils in his haste."

I said I doubted it.

Leggett pulled his brows together behind his glasses, looked at me with smaller eyes, and asked sharply: "What do you think?"

"I think it was planted there. Your burglar knew too much. He knew which drawer to go to. He didn't waste time on anything else. Detectives always say: 'Inside job,' because it saves work if they can find a victim right on the scene; but I can't see anything else here."

Minnie came to the door, still holding the vacuum cleaner, and began to cry that she was an honest girl, and nobody had any right to accuse her of anything, and they could search her and her home if they wanted to, and just because she was a colored girl was no reason, and so on and so on; and not all of it could be made out, because the vacuum cleaner was still humming in her hand and she sobbed while she talked. Tears ran down her cheeks.

Mrs. Leggett went to her, patted her shoulder, and said: "There, there. Don't cry, Minnie. I know you hadn't anything to do with it, and so does everybody else. There, there." Presently she got the girl's tears turned off and sent her upstairs.

Leggett sat on a corner of the kitchen table and asked: "You suspect someone in this house?"

"Somebody who's been in it, yeah."

"Whom?"

"Nobody yet."

"That"—he smiled, showing white teeth almost as small as his daughter's—"means everybody—all of us?"

"Let's take a look at the lawn," I suggested. "If we find any more diamonds I'll say maybe I'm mistaken about the inside angle."

Half-way through the house, as we went towards the front door, we met Minnie Hershey in a tan coat and violet hat, coming to say good-bye to her mistress. She wouldn't, she said tearfully, work anywhere where anybody thought she had stolen anything. She was just as honest as anybody else, and more than some, and just as much entitled to respect, and if she couldn't get it one place she could another, because she knew places where people wouldn't accuse her of stealing things after she had worked for them for two long years without ever taking so much as a slice of bread.

Mrs. Leggett pleaded with her, reasoned with her, scolded her, and commanded her, but none of it was any good. The brown girl's mind was made up, and away she went.

Mrs. Leggett looked at me, making her pleasant face as severe as she could, and said reprovingly: "Now see what you've done."

I said I was sorry, and her husband and I went out to examine the lawn. We didn't find any more diamonds.

II · *Long-nose*

I put in a couple of hours canvassing the neighborhood, trying to place the man Mrs. and Miss Leggett had seen. I didn't have any
luck with that one, but I picked up news of another. A Mrs. Priestly—a
pale semi-invalid who lived three doors below the Leggetts—gave me the
first line on him.

Mrs. Priestly often sat at a front window at night when she couldn't
sleep. On two of these nights she had seen the man. She said he was a tall
man, and young, she thought, and he walked with his head thrust forward. The street was too poorly lighted for her to describe his coloring and
clothes.

She had first seen him a week before. He had passed up and down on
the other side of the street five or six times, at intervals of fifteen or twenty
minutes, with his face turned as if watching something—or looking for
something—on Mrs. Priestly's—and the Leggetts'—side of the street. She
thought it was between eleven and twelve o'clock that she had seen him
the first time that night, and around one o'clock the last. Several nights
later—Saturday—she had seen him again, not walking this time, but standing on the corner below, looking up the street, at about midnight. He went
away after half an hour, and she had not seen him again.

Mrs. Priestly knew the Leggetts by sight, but knew very little about
them, except that the daughter was said to be a bit wild. They seemed to
be nice people, but kept to themselves. He had moved into the house in
1921, alone except for the housekeeper—a Mrs. Begg, who, Mrs. Priestly
understood, was now with a family named Freemander in Berkeley. Mrs.
Leggett and Gabrielle had not come to live with Leggett until 1923.

Mrs. Priestly said she had not been at her window the previous night
and therefore had not seen the man Mrs. Leggett had seen on the corner.

A man named Warren Daley, who lived on the opposite side of the
street, down near the corner where Mrs. Priestly had seen her man, had,
when locking up the house Sunday night, surprised a man—apparently the
same man—in the vestibule. Daley was not at home when I called, but,
after telling me this much, Mrs. Daley got him on the phone for me.

Daley said the man had been standing in the vestibule, either hiding
from or watching someone up the street. As soon as Daley opened the
door, the man ran away, down the street, paying no attention to Daley's
"What are you doing there?" Daley said he was a man of thirty-two or

three, fairly well dressed in dark clothes, and had a long, thin, and sharp nose.

That was all I could shake the neighborhood down for. I went to the Montgomery Street offices of Spear, Camp and Duffy and asked for Eric Collinson.

He was young, blond, tall, broad, sunburned, and dressy, with the good-looking unintelligent face of one who would know everything about polo, or shooting, or flying, or something of that sort—maybe even two things of that sort—but not much about anything else. We sat on a fatted leather seat in the customers' room, now, after market hours, empty except for a weedy boy juggling numbers on the board. I told Collinson about the burglary and asked him about the man he and Miss Leggett had seen Saturday night.

"He was an ordinary-looking chap, as far as I could see. It was dark. Short and chunky. You think he took them?"

"Did he come from the Leggett house?" I asked.

"From the lawn, at least. He seemed jumpy—that's why I thought perhaps he'd been nosing around where he shouldn't. I suggested I go after him and ask him what he was up to, but Gaby wouldn't have it. Might have been a friend of her father's. Did you ask him? He goes in for odd eggs."

"Wasn't that late for a visitor to be leaving?"

He looked away from me, so I asked: "What time was it?"

"Midnight, I dare say."

"Midnight?"

"That's the word. The time when the graves give up their dead, and ghosts walk."

"Miss Leggett said it was after three o'clock."

"You see how it is!" he exclaimed, blandly triumphant, as if he had demonstrated something we had been arguing about. "She's half blind and won't wear glasses for fear of losing beauty. She's always making mistakes like that. Plays abominable bridge—takes deuces for aces. It was probably a quarter after twelve, and she looked at the clock and got the hands mixed."

I said: "That's too bad," and "Thanks," and went up to Halstead and Beauchamp's store in Geary Street.

Watt Halstead was a suave, pale, bald, fat man, with tired eyes and a too tight collar. I told him what I was doing and asked him how well he knew Leggett.

"I know him as a desirable customer and by reputation as a scientist. Why do you ask?"

"His burglary's sour—in spots anyway."

"Oh, you're mistaken. That is, you're mistaken if you think a man of his caliber would be mixed up in anything like that. A servant, of course; yes, that's possible: it often happens, doesn't it? But not Leggett. He is a scientist of some standing—he has done some remarkable work with color —and, unless our credit department has been misinformed, a man of more than moderate means. I don't mean that he is wealthy in the modern sense of the word, but too wealthy for a thing of that sort. And, confidentially, I happen to know that his present balance in the Seaman's National Bank is in excess of ten thousand dollars. Well—the eight diamonds were worth no more than a thousand or twelve or thirteen hundred dollars."

"At retail? Then they cost you five or six hundred?"

"Well," smiling, "seven fifty would be nearer."

"How'd you come to give him the diamonds?"

"He's a customer of ours, as I've told you, and when I learned what he had done with glass, I thought what a wonderful thing it would be if the same method could be applied to diamonds. Fitzstephan—it was largely through him that I learned of Leggett's work with glass—was skeptical, but I thought it worth trying—still think so—and persuaded Leggett to try."

Fitzstephan was a familiar name. I asked: "Which Fitzstephan was that?"

"Owen, the writer. You know him?"

"Yeah, but I didn't know he was on the coast. We used to drink out of the same bottle. Do you know his address?"

Halstead found it in the telephone book for me, a Nob Hill apartment.

From the jeweler's I went to the vicinity of Minnie Hershey's home. It was a Negro neighborhood, which made the getting of reasonably accurate information twice as unlikely as it always is.

What I managed to get added up to this: The girl had come to San Francisco from Winchester, Virginia, four or five years ago, and for the last half-year had been living with a Negro called Rhino Tingley. One told me Rhino's first name was Ed, another Bill, but they agreed that he was young, big, and black and could easily be recognized by the scar on his chin. I was also told that he depended for his living on Minnie and pool; that he was not bad except when he got mad—then he was supposed to be a holy terror; and that I could get a look at him the early part of almost any evening in either Bunny Mack's barber-shop or Big-foot Gerber's cigar-store.

I learned where these joints were and then went downtown again, to the police detective bureau in the Hall of Justice. Nobody was in the pawnshop detail office. I crossed the corridor and asked Lieutenant Duff whether anybody had been put on the Leggett job.

He said: "See O'Gar."

I went into the assembly room, looking for O'Gar and wondering what he—a homicide detail detective-sergeant—had to do with my job.

Neither O'Gar nor Pat Reddy, his partner, was in. I smoked a cigarette, tried to guess who had been killed, and decided to phone Leggett.

"Any police detectives been in since I left?" I asked when his harsh voice was in my ear.

"No, but the police called up a little while ago and asked my wife and daughter to come to a place in Golden Gate Avenue to see if they could identify a man there. They left a few minutes ago. I didn't accompany them, not having seen the supposed burglar."

"Whereabouts in Golden Gate Avenue?"

He didn't remember the number, but he knew the block—above Van Ness Avenue. I thanked him and went out there.

In the designated block I found a uniformed copper standing in the doorway of a small apartment house. I asked him if O'Gar was there.

"Up in three ten," he said.

I rode up in a rickety elevator. When I got out on the third floor, I came face to face with Mrs. Leggett and her daughter, leaving.

"Now I hope you're satisfied that Minnie had nothing to do with it," Mrs. Leggett said chidingly.

"The police found your man?"

"Yes."

I said to Gabrielle Leggett: "Eric Collinson says it was only midnight, or a few minutes later, that you got home Saturday night."

"Eric," she said irritably, passing me to enter the elevator, "is an ass."

Her mother, following her into the elevator, reprimanded her amiably: "Now, dear."

I walked down the hall to a doorway where Pat Reddy stood talking to a couple of reporters, said hello, squeezed past them into a short passage-way, and went through that to a shabbily furnished room where a dead man lay on a wall bed.

Phels, of the police identification bureau, looked up from his magnifying glass to nod at me and then went on with his examination of a mission table's edge.

O'Gar pulled his head and shoulders in the open window and growled: "So we got to put up with you again?"

O'Gar was a burly, stolid man of fifty, who wore wide-brimmed black hats of the movie-sheriff sort. There was a lot of sense in his hard bullet-head, and he was comfortable to work with.

I looked at the corpse—a man of forty or so, with a heavy, pale face, short hair touched with gray, a scrubby, dark mustache, and stocky arms and legs. There was a bullet hole just over his navel, and another high on the left side of his chest.

"It's a man," O'Gar said as I put the blankets over him again. "He's dead."

"What else did somebody tell you?" I asked.

"Looks like him and another guy glaumed the ice, and then the other guy decided to take a one-way split. The envelopes are here"—O'Gar took them out of his pocket and ruffled them with a thumb—"but the diamonds ain't. They went down the fire-escape with the other guy a little while back. People spotted him making the sneak, but lost him when he cut through the alley. Tall guy with a long nose. This one"—he pointed the envelopes at the bed—"has been here a week. Name of Louis Upton, with New York labels. We don't know him. Nobody in the dump'll say they ever saw him with anybody else. Nobody'll say they know Long-nose."

Pat Reddy came in. He was a big, jovial youngster, with almost brains enough to make up for his lack of experience. I told him and O'Gar what I had turned up on the job so far.

"Long-nose and this bird taking turns watching Leggett's?" Reddy suggested.

"Maybe," I said, "but there's an inside angle. How many envelopes have you got there, O'Gar?"

"Seven."

"Then the one for the planted diamond is missing."

"How about the yellow girl?" Reddy asked.

"I'm going out for a look at her man tonight," I said. "You people trying New York on this Upton?"

"Uh-huh," O'Gar said.

III · *Something Black*

AT the Nob Hill address Halstead had given me, I told my name to the boy at the switchboard and asked him to pass it on to Fitzstephan. I remembered Fitzstephan as a long, lean, sorrel-haired man of thirty-two, with sleepy gray eyes, a wide, humorous mouth, and carelessly worn clothes; a man who pretended to be lazier than he was, would rather talk than do anything else, and had a lot of what seemed to be accurate information and original ideas on any subject that happened to come up, as long as it was a little out of the ordinary.

I had met him five years before, in New York, where I was digging dirt on a chain of fake mediums who had taken a coal-and-ice dealer's widow for a hundred thousand dollars. Fitzstephan was plowing the same field for literary material. We became acquainted and pooled forces. I got more out of the combination than he did, since he knew the spook racket inside and out; and, with his help, I cleaned up my job in a couple of weeks. We were fairly chummy for a month or two after that, until I left New York.

"Mr. Fitzstephan says to come right up," the switchboard boy said.

His apartment was on the sixth floor. He was standing at its door when I got out of the elevator.

"By God," he said, holding out a lean hand, "it *is* you!"

"None other."

He hadn't changed any. We went into a room where half a dozen bookcases and four tables left little room for anything else. Magazines and books in various languages, papers, clippings, proof sheets, were scattered everywhere—all just as it used to be in his New York rooms.

We sat down, found places for our feet between table-legs, and accounted roughly for our lives since we had last seen one another. He had been in San Francisco for a little more than a year—except, he said, for week-ends, and two months hermiting in the country, finishing a novel. I had been there nearly five years. He liked San Francisco, he said, but wouldn't oppose any movement to give the West back to the Indians.

"How's the literary grift go?" I asked.

He looked at me sharply, demanding: "You haven't been reading me?"

"No. Where'd you get that funny idea?"

"There was something in your tone, something proprietary, as in the voice of one who has bought an author for a couple of dollars. I haven't met it often enough to be used to it. Good God! Remember once I offered you a set of my books as a present?" He had always liked to talk that way.

"Yeah. But I never blamed you. You were drunk."

"On sherry—Elsa Donne's sherry. Remember Elsa? She showed us a picture she had just finished, and you said it was pretty. Sweet God, wasn't she furious! You said it so vapidly and sincerely and as if you were so sure that she would like your saying it. Remember? She put us out, but we'd both already got plastered on her sherry. But you weren't tight enough to take the books."

"I was afraid I'd read them and understand them," I explained, "and then you'd have felt insulted."

A Chinese boy brought us cold white wine.

Fitzstephan said: "I suppose you're still hounding the unfortunate evil-doer?"

"Yeah. That's how I happened to locate you. Halstead tells me you know Edgar Leggett."

A gleam pushed through the sleepiness in his gray eyes, and he sat up a little in his chair, asking: "Leggett's been up to something?"

"Why do you say that?"

"I didn't say it. I asked it." He made himself limp in the chair again, but the gleam didn't go out of his eyes. "Come on, out with it. Don't try to be subtle with me, my son; that's not your style at all. Try it and you're sunk. Out with it: what's Leggett been up to?"

"We don't do it that way," I said. "You're a storywriter. I can't trust you not to build up on what I tell you. I'll save mine till after you've spoken your piece, so yours won't be twisted to fit mine. How long have you known him?"

"Since shortly after I came here. He's always interested me. There's something obscure in him, something dark and inviting. He is, for instance, physically ascetic—neither smoking or drinking, eating meagerly, sleeping, I'm told, only three or four hours a night—but mentally, or spiritually, sensual—does that mean anything to you?—to the point of decadence. You used to think I had an abnormal appetite for the fantastic. You should know him. His friends—no, he hasn't any—his choice companions are those who have the most outlandish ideas to offer: Marquard and his insane figures that aren't figures, but the boundaries of areas in space that are the figures; Denbar Curt and his algebraism; the Haldorns and their Holy Grail sect; crazy Laura Joines; Farnham—"

"And you," I put in, "with explanations and descriptions that explain and describe nothing. I hope you don't think any of what you've said means anything to me."

"I remember you now: you were always like that." He grinned at me, running thin fingers through his sorrel hair. "Tell me what's up while I try to find one-syllable words for you."

I asked him if he knew Eric Collinson. He said he did; there was nothing to know about him except that he was engaged to Gabrielle Leggett, that his father was the lumber Collinson, and that Eric was Princeton, stocks and bonds, and hand-ball, a nice boy.

"Maybe," I said, "but he lied to me."

"Isn't that like a sleuth?" Fitzstephan shook his head, grinning. "You must have had the wrong fellow—somebody impersonating him. The Chevalier Bayard doesn't lie, and, besides, lying requires imagination. You've—or wait! Was a woman involved in your question?"

I nodded.

"You're correct, then," Fitzstephan assured me. "I apologize. The Chevalier Bayard always lies when a woman is involved, even if it's unnecessary and puts her to a lot of trouble. It's one of the conventions of Bayardism, something to do with guarding her honor or the like. Who was the woman?"

"Gabrielle Leggett," I said, and told him all I knew about the Leggetts, the diamonds, and the dead man in Golden Gate Avenue. Disappointment deepened in his face while I talked.

"That's trivial, dull," he complained when I had finished. "I've been thinking of Leggett in terms of Dumas, and you bring me a piece of gimcrackery out of O. Henry. You've let me down, you and your shabby diamonds. But"—his eyes brightened again—"this may lead to something.

Leggett may or may not be criminal, but there's more to him than a two-penny insurance swindle."

"You mean," I asked, "that he's one of these master minds? So you read newspapers? What do you think he is? King of the bootleggers? Chief of an international crime syndicate? A white-slave magnate? Head of a dope ring? Or queen of the counterfeiters in disguise?"

"Don't be an idiot," he said. "But he's got brains, and there's something black in him. There's something he doesn't want to think about, but must not forget. I've told you that he's thirsty for all that's dizziest in thought, yet he's cold as a fish, but with a bitter-dry coldness. He's a neurotic who keeps his body fit and sensitive and ready—for what?—while he drugs his mind with lunacies. Yet he's cold and sane. If a man has a past that he wants to forget, he can easiest drug his mind against memory through his body, with sensuality if not with narcotics. But suppose the past is not dead, and this man must keep himself fit to cope with it should it come into the present. Well, then he would be wisest to anæsthetize his mind directly, letting his body stay strong and ready."

"And this past?"

Fitzstephan shook his head, saying: "If I don't know—and I don't —it isn't my fault. Before you're through, you'll know how difficult it is to get information out of that family."

"Did you try?"

"Certainly. I'm a novelist. My business is with souls and what goes on in them. He's got one that attracts me, and I've always considered myself unjustly treated by his not turning himself inside out for me. You know, I doubt if Leggett's his name. He's French. He told me once he came from Atlanta, but he's French in outlook, in quality of mind, in everything except admission."

"What of the rest of the family?" I asked. "Gabrielle's cuckoo, isn't she?"

"I wonder." Fitzstephan looked curiously at me. "Are you saying that carelessly, or do you really think she's off?"

"I don't know. She's odd, an uncomfortable sort of person. And, then, she's got animal ears, hardly any forehead; and her eyes shift from green to brown and back without ever settling on one color. How much of her affairs have you turned up in your snooping around?"

"Are you—who make your living snooping—sneering at my curiosity about people and my attempts to satisfy it?"

"We're different," I said. "I do mine with the object of putting people in jail, and I get paid for it, though not as much as I should."

"That's not different," he said. "I do mine with the object of putting people in books, and I get paid for it, though not as much as I should."

"Yeah, but what good does that do?"

"God knows. What good does putting them in jail do?"

"Relieves congestion," I said. "Put enough people in jail, and cities wouldn't have traffic problems. What do you know about this Gabrielle?"

"She hates her father. He worships her."

"How come the hate?"

"I don't know; perhaps because he worships her."

"There's no sense to that," I complained. "You're just being literary. What about Mrs. Leggett?"

"You've never eaten one of her meals, I suppose? You'd have no doubts if you had. None but a serene, sane soul ever achieved such cooking. I've often wondered what she thinks of the weird creatures who are her husband and daughter, though I imagine she simply accepts them as they are without even being conscious of their weirdness."

"All this is well enough in its way," I said, "but you still haven't told me anything definite."

"No, I haven't," he replied, "and that, my boy, is it. I've told you what I know and what I imagine, and none of it is definite. That's the point—in a year of trying I've learned nothing definite about Leggett. Isn't that—remembering my curiosity and my usual skill in satisfying it —enough to convince you that the man is hiding something and knows how to hide it?"

"Is it? I don't know. But I know I've wasted enough time learning nothing that anybody can be jailed for. Dinner tomorrow night? Or the next?"

"The next. About seven o'clock?"

I said I would stop for him, and went out. It was then after five o'clock. Not having had any luncheon, I went up to Blanco's for food, and then to darktown for a look at Rhino Tingley.

I found him in Big-foot Gerber's cigar-store, rolling a fat cigar around in his mouth, telling something to the other Negroes—four of them—in the place.

". . . says to him: 'Nigger, you talking yourself out of skin,' and I reaches out my hand for him, and, 'fore God, there weren't none of him there excepting his footprints in the ce-ment pavement, eight feet apart and leading home."

Buying a package of cigarettes, I weighed him in while he talked. He was a chocolate man of less than thirty years, close to six feet tall and weighing two hundred pounds plus, with big yellow-balled pop eyes, a broad nose, a big blue-lipped and blue-gummed mouth, and a ragged black scar running from his lower lip down behind his blue and white striped collar. His clothes were new enough to look new, and he wore them sportily. His voice was a heavy bass that shook the glass of the show-cases when he laughed with his audience.

I went out of the store while they were laughing, heard the laughter stop short behind me, resisted the temptation to look back, and moved down the street towards the building where he and Minnie lived. He came abreast of me when I was half a block from the flat.

I said nothing while we took seven steps side by side.

Then he said: "You the man that been inquirying around about me?"

The sour odor of Italian wine was thick enough to be seen.

I considered, and said: "Yeah."

"What you got to do with me?" he asked, not disagreeably, but as if he wanted to know.

Across the street Gabrielle Leggett, in brown coat and brown and yellow hat, came out of Minnie's building and walked south, not turning her face towards us. She walked swiftly and her lower lip was between her teeth.

I looked at the Negro. He was looking at me. There was nothing in his face to show that he had seen Gabrielle Leggett, or that the sight of her meant anything to him.

I said: "You've got nothing to hide, have you? What do you care who asks about you?"

"All the same, I'm the party to come to if you wants to know about me. You the man that got Minnie fired?"

"She wasn't fired. She quit."

"Minnie don't have to take nobody's lip. She—"

"Let's go over and talk to her," I suggested, leading the way across the street. At the front door he went ahead, up a flight of stairs, down a dark hall to a door which he opened with one of the twenty or more keys on his ring.

Minnie Hershey, in a pink kimono trimmed with yellow ostrich feathers that looked like little dead ferns, came out of the bedroom to meet us in the living-room. Her eyes got big when she saw me.

Rhino said: "You know this gentleman, Minnie."

Minnie said: "Y-yes."

I said: "You shouldn't have left the Leggetts' that way. Nobody thinks you had anything to do with the diamonds. What did Miss Leggett want here?"

"There been no Miss Leggetts here," she told me. "I don't know what you talking about."

"She came out as we were coming in."

"Oh! *Miss* Leggett. I thought you said *Mrs.* Leggett. I beg your pardon. Yes, sir. Miss Gabrielle was sure enough here. She wanted to know if I wouldn't come back there. She thinks a powerful lot of me, Miss Gabrielle does."

"That," I said, "is what you ought to do. It was foolish, leaving like that."

Rhino took the cigar out of his mouth and pointed the red end at the girl.

"You away from them," he boomed, "and you stay away from them. You don't have to take nothing from nobody." He put a hand in his pants pocket, lugged out a thick bundle of paper money, thumped it down on the table, and rumbled: "What for you have to work for folks?"

He was talking to the girl, but looking at me, grinning, gold teeth shining against purplish mouth. The girl looked at him scornfully, said: "Lead him around, *vino*," and turned to me again, her brown face tense, anxious to be believed, saying earnestly: "Rhino got that money in a crap game, mister. Hope to die if he didn't."

Rhino said: "Ain't nobody's business where I got my money. I got it. I got—" He put his cigar on the edge of the table, picked up the money, wet a thumb as big as a heel on a tongue like a bath-mat, and counted his roll bill by bill down on the table. "Twenty—thirty—eighty—hundred —hundred and ten—two hundred and ten—three hundred and ten—three hundred and thirty—three hundred and thirty-five—four hundred and thirty-five—five hundred and thirty-five—five hundred and eighty-five—six hundred and five—six hundred and ten—six hundred and twenty—seven hundred and twenty—seven hundred and seventy—eight hundred and twenty—eight hundred and thirty—eight hundred and forty—nine hundred and forty—nine hundred and sixty—nine hundred and seventy—nine hundred and seventy-five—nine hundred and ninety-five—ten hundred and fifteen—ten hundred and twenty—eleven hundred and twenty—eleven hundred and seventy. Anybody want to know what I got, that's what I got —eleven hundred and seventy dollars. Anybody want to know where I get it, maybe I tell them, maybe I don't. Just depend on how I feel about it."

Minnie said: "He won it in a crap game, mister, up the Happy Day Social Club. Hope to die if he didn't."

"Maybe I did," Rhino said, still grinning widely at me. "But supposing I didn't?"

"I'm no good at riddles," I said, and, after again advising Minnie to return to the Leggetts, left the flat. Minnie closed the door behind me. As I went down the hall I could hear her voice scolding and Rhino's chesty bass laughter.

In a downtown Owl drug-store I turned to the Berkeley section of the telephone directory, found only one Freemander listed, and called the number. Mrs. Begg was there and consented to see me if I came over on the next ferry.

The Freemander house was set off a road that wound uphill towards the University of California.

Mrs. Begg was a scrawny, big-boned woman, with not much gray hair packed close around a bony skull, hard gray eyes, and hard, capable hands. She was sour and severe, but plain-spoken enough to let us talk turkey without a lot of preliminary hemming and hawing.

I told her about the burglary and my belief that the thief had been helped, at least with information, by somebody who knew the Leggett household, winding up: "Mrs. Priestly told me you had been Leggett's housekeeper, and she thought you could help me."

Mrs. Begg said she doubted whether she could tell me anything that would pay me for my trip from the city, but she was willing to do what she could, being an honest woman and having nothing to conceal from anybody. Once started, she told me a great deal, damned near talking me earless. Throwing out the stuff that didn't interest me, I came away with this information:

Mrs. Begg had been hired by Leggett, through an employment agency, as housekeeper in the spring of 1921. At first she had a girl to help her, but there wasn't enough work for two, so, at Mrs. Begg's suggestion, they let the girl go. Leggett was a man of simple tastes and spent nearly all his time on the top floor, where he had his laboratory and a cubbyhole bedroom. He seldom used the rest of the house except when he had friends in for an evening. Mrs. Begg didn't like his friends, though she could say nothing against them except that the way they talked was a shame and a disgrace. Edgar Leggett was as nice a man as a person could want to know, she said, only so secretive that it made a person nervous. She was never allowed to go up on the third floor, and the door of the laboratory was always kept locked. Once a month a Jap would come in to clean it up under Leggett's supervision. Well, she supposed he had a lot of scientific secrets, and maybe dangerous chemicals, that he didn't want people poking into, but just the same it made a person uneasy. She didn't know anything about her employer's personal or family affairs and knew her place too well to ask him any questions.

In August 1923—it was a rainy morning, she remembered—a woman and a girl of fifteen, with a lot of suit-cases, had come to the house. She let them in and the woman asked for Mr. Leggett. Mrs. Begg went up to the laboratory door and told him, and he came down. Never in all her born days had she seen such a surprised man as he was when he saw them. He turned absolutely white, and she thought he was going to fall down, he shook that bad. She didn't know what Leggett and the woman and the girl said to one another that morning, because they jabbered away in some foreign language, though the lot of them could talk English as good as anybody else, and better than most, especially that Gabrielle when she got to cursing. Mrs. Begg had left them and gone on about her business. Pretty soon Leggett came out to the kitchen and told her his visitors were a Mrs. Dain, his sister-in-law, and her daughter, neither of whom he had seen for ten years; and that they were going to stay there with him. Mrs. Dain later told Mrs. Begg that they were English, but had been living in New York for several years. Mrs. Begg said she liked Mrs. Dain, who was a sensible woman and a first-rate housewife, but that Gabrielle was a tartar. Mrs. Begg always spoke of the girl as "that Gabrielle."

With the Dains there, and with Mrs. Dain's ability as a housekeeper, there was no longer any place for Mrs. Begg. They had been very liberal, she said, helping her find a new place and giving her a generous bonus when she left. She hadn't seen any of them since, but, thanks to the careful watch she habitually kept on the marriage, death, and birth notices in the morning papers, she had learned, a week after she left, that a marriage license had been issued to Edgar Leggett and Alice Dain.

IV · *The Vague Harpers*

WHEN I arrived at the agency at nine the next morning, Eric Collinson was sitting in the reception room. His sunburned face was dingy without pinkness, and he had forgotten to put stickum on his hair.

"Do you know anything about Miss Leggett?" he asked, jumping up and meeting me at the door. "She wasn't home last night, and she's not home yet. Her father wouldn't say he didn't know where she was, but I'm sure he didn't. He told me not to worry, but how can I help worrying? Do you know anything about it?"

I said I didn't and told him about seeing her leave Minnie Hershey's the previous evening. I gave him the mulatto's address and suggested that he ask her. He jammed his hat on his head and hurried off.

Getting O'Gar on the phone, I asked him if he had heard from New York yet.

"Uh-huh," he said. "Upton—that's his right name—was once one of you private dicks—had a agency of his own—till '23, when him and a guy named Harry Ruppert were sent over for trying to fix a jury. How'd you make out with the shine?"

"I don't know. This Rhino Tingley's carrying an eleven-hundred-case roll. Minnie says he got it with the rats and mice. Maybe he did: it's twice what he could have peddled Leggett's stuff for. Can you try to have it checked? He's supposed to have got it at the Happy Day Social Club."

O'Gar promised to do what he could and hung up.

I sent a wire to our New York branch, asking for more dope on Upton and Ruppert, and then went up to the county clerk's office in the municipal building, where I dug into the August and September 1923 marriage-license file. The application I wanted was dated August 26 and bore Edgar Leggett's statement that he was born in Atlanta, Georgia, on March 6, 1883, and that this was his second marriage; and Alice Dain's statement that she was born in London, England, on October 22, 1888, and that she had not been married before.

When I returned to the agency, Eric Collinson, his yellow hair still further disarranged, was again lying in wait for me.

"I saw Minnie," he said excitedly, "and she couldn't tell me anything. She said Gaby was there last night to ask her to come back to work, but that's all she knew about her. But she—she's wearing an emerald ring that I'm positive is Gaby's."

"Did you ask her about it?"

"Who? Minnie? No. How could I? It would have been—you know."

"That's right," I agreed, thinking of Fitzstephan's Chevalier Bayard, "we must always be polite. Why did you lie to me about the time you and Miss Leggett got home the other night?"

Embarrassment made his face more attractive-looking and less intelligent.

"That was silly of me," he stammered, "but I didn't—you know—I thought you—I was afraid—"

He wasn't getting anywhere. I suggested: "You thought that was a late hour and didn't want me to get wrong notions about her?"

"Yes, that's it."

I shooed him out and went into the operatives' room, where Mickey Linehan—big, loose-hung, red-faced—and Al Mason—slim, dark, sleek— were swapping lies about the times they had been shot at, each trying to pretend he had been more frightened than the other. I told them who was who and what was what on the Leggett job—as far as my knowledge went, and it didn't go far when I came to putting it in words—and sent Al out to keep an eye on the Leggetts' house, Mickey to see how Minnie and Rhino behaved.

Mrs. Leggett, her pleasant face shadowed, opened the door when I rang the bell an hour later. We went into the green, orange, and chocolate room, where we were joined by her husband. I passed on to them the information about Upton that O'Gar had received from New York and told them I had wired for more dope on Ruppert.

"Some of your neighbors saw a man who was not Upton loitering around," I said, "and a man who fits the same description ran down the fire-escape from the room Upton was killed in. We'll see what Ruppert looks like."

I was watching Leggett's face. Nothing changed in it. His too bright red-brown eyes held interest and nothing else.

I asked: "Is Miss Leggett in?"

He said: "No."

"When will she be in?"

"Probably not for several days. She's gone out of town."

"Where can I find her?" I asked, turning to Mrs. Leggett. "I've some questions to ask her."

Mrs. Leggett avoided my gaze, looking at her husband.

His metallic voice answered my question: "We don't know, exactly. Friends of hers, a Mr. and Mrs. Harper, drove up from Los Angeles and asked her to go along on a trip up in the mountains. I don't know which route they intended taking, and doubt if they had any definite destination."

I asked questions about the Harpers. Leggett admitted knowing very little about them. Mrs. Harper's first name was Carmel, he said, and everybody called the man Bud, but Leggett wasn't sure whether his name was Frank or Walter. Nor did he know the Harpers' Los Angeles address. He thought they had a house somewhere in Pasadena, but wasn't sure, having, in fact, heard something about their selling the house, or perhaps only intending to. While he told me this nonsense, his wife sat staring at the floor, lifting her blue eyes twice to look swiftly, pleadingly, at her husband.

I asked her: "Don't you know anything more about them than that?"

"No," she said weakly, darting another glance at her husband's face, while he, paying no attention to her, stared levelly at me.

"When did they leave?" I asked.

"Early this morning," Leggett said. "They were staying at one of the hotels—I don't know which—and Gabrielle spent the night with them so they could start early."

I had enough of the Harpers. I asked: "Did either of you—any of you—know anything about Upton—have any dealings with him of any sort —before this affair?"

Leggett said: "No."

I had other questions, but the kind of replies I was drawing didn't mean anything, so I stood up to go. I was tempted to tell him what I thought of him, but there was no profit in that.

He got up too, smiling politely, and said: "I'm sorry to have caused the insurance company all this trouble through what was, after all, probably my carelessness. I should like to ask your opinion: do you really think I should accept responsibility for the loss of the diamonds and make it good?"

"The way it stands," I said, "I think you should; but that wouldn't stop the investigation."

Mrs. Leggett put her handkerchief to her mouth quickly.

Leggett said: "Thanks." His voice was casually polite. "I'll have to think it over."

On my way back to the agency I dropped in on Fitzstephan for half an hour. He was writing, he told me, an article for the *Psychopathological Review*—that's probably wrong, but it was something on that order— condemning the hypothesis of an unconscious or subconscious mind as a snare and a delusion, a pitfall for the unwary and a set of false whiskers for the charlatan, a gap in psychology's roof that made it impossible, or nearly, for the sound scholar to smoke out such faddists as, for example, the psychoanalyst and the behaviorist, or words to that effect. He went on like that for ten minutes or more, finally coming back to the United

States with: "But how are you getting along with the problem of the elusive diamonds?"

"This way and that way," I said, and told him what I had learned and done so far.

"You've certainly," he congratulated me when I finished, "got it all as tangled and confused as possible."

"It'll be worse before it's better," I predicted. "I'd like to have ten minutes alone with Mrs. Leggett. Away from her husband, I imagine things could be done with her. Could you get anything out of her? I'd like to know why Gabrielle has gone, even if I can't learn where."

"I'll try," Fitzstephan said willingly. "Suppose I go out there tomorrow afternoon—to borrow a book. Waite's *Rosy Cross* will do it. They know I'm interested in that sort of stuff He'll be working in the laboratory, and I'll refuse to disturb him. I'll have to go at it in an offhand way, but maybe I can get something out of her."

"Thanks," I said. "See you tomorrow night."

I spent most of the afternoon putting my findings and guesses on paper and trying to fit them together in some sort of order. Eric Collinson phoned twice to ask if I had any news of his Gabrielle. Neither Mickey Linehan nor Al Mason reported anything. At six o'clock I called it a day.

V · *Gabrielle*

THE next day brought happenings.

Early in the morning there was a telegram from our New York office. Decoded, it read:

LOUIS UPTON FORMER PROPRIETOR DETECTIVE AGENCY HERE STOP ARRESTED SEPTEMBER FIRST ONE NINE TWO THREE FOR BRIBING TWO JURORS IN SEXTON MURDER TRIAL STOP TRIED TO SAVE HIMSELF BY IMPLICATING HARRY RUPPERT OPERATIVE IN HIS EMPLOY STOP BOTH MEN CONVICTED STOP BOTH RELEASED FROM SING SING FEBRUARY SIX THIS YEAR STOP RUPPERT SAID TO HAVE THREATENED TO KILL UPTON STOP RUPPERT THIRTY TWO YEARS FIVE FEET ELEVEN INCHES HUNDRED FIFTY POUNDS BROWN HAIR AND EYES SALLOW COMPLEXION THIN FACE LONG THIN NOSE WALKS WITH STOOP AND CHIN OUT STOP MAILING PHOTOGRAPHS

That placed Ruppert definitely enough as the man Mrs. Priestly and Daley had seen and the man who had probably killed Upton.

O'Gar called me on the phone to tell me: "That dinge of yours —Rhino Tingley—was picked up in a hock shop last night trying to unload some jewelry. None of it was loose diamonds. We haven't been able to crack him yet, just got him identified. I sent a man out to Leggett's with some of the stuff, thinking it might be theirs, but they said no."

That didn't fit in anywhere. I suggested: "Try Halstead and Beauchamp. Tell them you think the stuff is Leggett's. Don't tell them he said it wasn't."

Half an hour later the detective-sergeant phoned me again, from the jewelers', to tell me that Halstead had positively identified two pieces—a string of pearls and a topaz brooch—as articles Leggett had purchased there for his daughter.

"That's swell," I said. "Now will you do this? Go out to Rhino's flat and put the screws on his woman, Minnie Hershey. Frisk the joint, rough her up; the more you scare her, the better. She may be wearing an emerald ring. If she is, or if it—or any other jewelry that might be the Leggetts'—is there, you can take it away with you; but don't stay too long and don't bother her afterwards. I've got her covered. Just stir her up and beat it."

"I'll turn her white," O'Gar promised.

Dick Foley was in the operatives' room, writing his report on a warehouse robbery that had kept him up all night. I chased him out to help Mickey with the mulatto.

"Both of you tail her if she leaves her joint after the police are through," I said, "and as soon as you put her in anywhere, one of you get to a phone and let me know."

I went back to my office and burned cigarettes. I was ruining the third one when Eric Collinson phoned to ask if I had found his Gabrielle yet.

"Not quite, but I've got prospects. If you aren't busy, you might come over and go along with me—if it so happens that there turns out to be some place to go."

He said, very eagerly, that he would do that.

A few minutes later Mickey Linehan phoned: "The high yellow's gone visiting," and gave me a Pacific Avenue address.

The phone rang again before I got it out of my hand.

"This is Watt Halstead," a voice said. "Can you come down to see me for a minute or two?"

"Not now. What is it?"

"It's about Edgar Leggett, and it's quite puzzling. The police brought some jewelry in this morning, asking whether we knew whose it was. I recognized a string of pearls and a brooch that Edgar Leggett bought from us for his daughter last year—the brooch in the spring, the pearls at Christmas. After the police had gone, I, quite naturally, phoned Leggett; and he took the most peculiar attitude. He waited until I had told him about

it, then said: 'I thank you very much for your interference in my affairs,'
and hung up. What do you suppose is the matter with him?"

"God knows. Thanks. I've got to run now, but I'll stop in when I get
a chance."

I hunted up Owen Fitzstephan's number, called it, and heard his
drawled: "Hello."

"You'd better get busy on your book-borrowing if any good's to come
of it," I said.

"Why? Are things taking place?"

"Things are."

"Such as?" he asked.

"This and that, but it's no time for anybody who wants to poke his
nose into the Leggett mysteries to be dilly-dallying with pieces about unconscious minds."

"Right," he said: "I'm off to the front now."

Eric Collinson had come in while I was talking to the novelist.

"Come on," I said, leading the way out towards the elevators. "This
might not be a false alarm."

"Where are we going?" he asked impatiently. "Have you found her?
Is she all right?"

I replied to the only one of his questions that I had the answer to
by giving him the Pacific Avenue address Mickey had given me. It meant
something to Collinson. He said: "That's Joseph's place."

We were in the elevator with half a dozen other people. I held my
response down to a "Yeah?"

He had a Chrysler roadster parked around the corner. We got into
it and began bucking traffic and traffic signals towards Pacific Avenue.

I asked: "Who is Joseph?"

"Another cult. He's the head of it. He calls his place the Temple of
the Holy Grail. It's the fashionable one just now. You know how they
come and go in California. I don't like having Gabrielle there, if that's
where she is—though—I don't know—they may be all right. He's one of
Mr. Leggett's queer friends. Do you know that she's there?"

"Maybe. Is she a member of the cult?"

"She goes there, yes. I've been there with her."

"What sort of a layout is it?"

"Oh, it seems to be all right," he said somewhat reluctantly. "The
right sort of people: Mrs. Payson Laurence, and the Ralph Colemans, and
Mrs. Livingston Rodman, people like that. And the Haldorns—that's Joseph and his wife Aaronia—seem to be quite all right, but—but I don't like
the idea of Gabrielle going there like this." He missed the end of a cable
car with the Chrysler's right wheel. "I don't think it's good for her to
come too much under their influence."

"You've been there; what is their brand of hocus-pocus?" I asked.

"It isn't hocus-pocus, really," he replied, wrinkling his forehead. "I don't know very much about their creed; or anything like that, but I've been to their services with Gabrielle, and they're quite as dignified, as beautiful even, as either Episcopalian or Catholic services. You mustn't think that this is the Holy Roller or House of David sort of thing. It isn't at all. Whatever it is, it is quite first-rate. The Haldorns are people of—of —well, more culture than I."

"Then what's the matter with them?"

He shook his head gloomily. "I honestly don't know that anything is. I don't like it. I don't like having Gabrielle go off like this without letting anybody know where she's gone. Do you think her parents knew where she had gone?"

"No."

"I don't think so either," he said.

From the street the Temple of the Holy Grail looked like what it had originally been, a six-story yellow brick apartment building. There was nothing about its exterior to show that it wasn't still that. I made Collinson drive past it to the corner where Mickey Linehan was leaning his lop-sided bulk against a stone wall. He came to the car as it stopped at the curb.

"The dark meat left ten minutes ago," he reported, "with Dick behind her. Nobody else that looks like anybody you listed has been out."

"Camp here in the car and watch the door," I told him. "We're going in," I said to Collinson. "Let me do most of the talking."

When we reached the Temple door I had to caution him: "Try not breathing so hard. Everything will probably be oke."

I rang the bell. The door was opened immediately by a broad-shouldered, meaty woman of some year close to fifty. She was a good three inches taller than my five feet six. Flesh hung in little bags on her face, but there was neither softness nor looseness in her eyes and mouth. Her long upper lip had been shaved. She was dressed in black, black clothes that covered her from chin and ear-lobes to within less than an inch of the floor.

"We want to see Miss Leggett," I said.

She pretended she hadn't understood me.

"We want to see Miss Leggett," I repeated, "Miss Gabrielle Leggett."

"I don't know." Her voice was bass. "But come in."

She took us not very cheerfully into a small, dimly lighted reception room to one side of the foyer, told us to wait there, and went away.

"Who's the village blacksmith?" I asked Collinson.

He said he didn't know her. He fidgeted around the room. I sat down. Drawn blinds let in too little light for me to make out much of the room, but the rug was soft and thick, and what I could see of the furniture leaned towards luxury rather than severity.

Except for Collinson's fidgeting, no sound came from anywhere in the building. I looked at the open door and saw that we were being examined. A small boy of twelve or thirteen stood there staring at us with big dark eyes that seemed to have lights of their own in the semi-darkness.

I said: "Hello, son."

Collinson jumped around at the sound of my voice.

The boy said nothing. He stared at me for at least another minute with the blank, unblinking, embarrassing stare that only children can manage completely, then turned his back on me and walked away, making no more noise going than he had made coming.

"Who's that?" I asked Collinson.

"It must be the Haldorns' son Manuel. I've never seen him before."

Collinson walked up and down. I sat and watched the door. Presently a woman, walking silently on the thick carpet, appeared there and came into the reception room. She was tall, graceful; and her dark eyes seemed to have lights of their own, like the boy's. That was all I could see clearly then.

I stood up.

She addressed Collinson: "How do you do? This is Mr. Collinson, isn't it?" Her voice was the most musical I had ever heard.

Collinson mumbled something or other and introduced me to the woman, calling her Mrs. Haldorn. She gave me a warm, firm hand and then crossed the room to raise a blind, letting in a fat rectangle of afternoon sun. While I blinked at her in the sudden brightness, she sat down and motioned us into chairs.

I saw her eyes first. They were enormous, almost black, warm, and heavily fringed with almost black lashes. They were the only live, human, real things in her face. There was warmth and there was beauty in her oval, olive-skinned face, but, except for the eyes, it was warmth and beauty that didn't seem to have anything to do with reality. It was as if her face were not a face, but a mask that she had worn until it had almost become a face. Even her mouth, which was a mouth to talk about, looked not so much like flesh as like a too perfect imitation of flesh, softer and redder and maybe warmer than genuine flesh, but not genuine flesh. Above this face, or mask, uncut black hair was tied close to her head, parted in the middle, and drawn across temples and upper ears to end in a knot on the nape of her neck. Her neck was long, strong, slender; her body tall, fully fleshed, supple; her clothes dark and silky, part of her body.

I said: "We want to see Miss Leggett, Mrs. Haldorn."

She asked curiously: "Why do you think she is here?"

"That doesn't make any difference, does it?" I replied quickly, before Collinson could say something wrong. "She is. We'd like to see her."

"I don't think you can," she said slowly. "She isn't well, and she came here to rest, particularly to get away from people for a while."

"Sorry," I said, "but it's a case of have to. We wouldn't have come like this if it hadn't been important."

"It is important?"

"Yeah."

She hesitated, said: "Well, I'll see," excused herself, and left us.

"I wouldn't mind moving in here myself," I told Collinson.

He didn't know what I was talking about. His face was flushed and excited.

"Gabrielle may not like our coming here like this," he said.

I said that would be too bad.

Aaronia Haldorn returned to us.

"I'm really very sorry," she said, standing in the doorway, smiling politely, "but Miss Leggett doesn't wish to see you."

"I'm sorry she doesn't," I said, "but we'll have to see her."

She drew herself up straight and her smile went away.

"I beg your pardon?" she said.

"We'll have to see her," I repeated, keeping my voice amiable. "It's important, as I told you."

"I am sorry." Even the iciness she got into her voice didn't keep it from being beautiful. "You cannot see her."

I said: "Miss Leggett's an important witness, as you probably know, in a robbery and murder job. Well, we've got to see her. If it suits you better, I'm willing to wait half an hour till we can get a policeman up here with whatever authority you make necessary. We're going to see her."

Collinson said something unintelligible, though it sounded apologetic.

Aaronia Haldorn made the slightest of bows.

"You may do as you see fit," she said coldly. "I do not approve of your disturbing Miss Leggett against her wishes, and so far as my permission is concerned, I do not give it. If you insist, I cannot prevent you."

"Thanks. Where is she?"

"Her room is on the fifth floor, just beyond the stairs, to the left."

She bent her head a little once more and went away.

Collinson put a hand on my arm, mumbling: "I don't know whether I—whether we ought to do this. Gabrielle's not going to like it. She won't—"

"Suit yourself," I growled, "but I'm going up. Maybe she won't like it, but neither do I like having people running away and hiding when I want to ask them about stolen diamonds."

He frowned, chewed his lips, and made uncomfortable faces, but he went along with me. We found an automatic elevator, rode to the fifth floor, and went down a purple-carpeted corridor to the door just beyond the stairs on the left-hand side.

I tapped the door with the back of my hand. There was no answer from inside. I tapped again, louder.

A voice sounded inside the room. It might have been anybody's voice, though probably a woman's. It was too faint for us to know what it said and too smothered for us to know who was saying it.

I poked Collinson with my elbow and ordered: "Call her."

He pulled at his collar with a forefinger and called hoarsely: "Gaby, it's Eric."

That didn't bring an answer.

I thumped the wood again, calling: "Open the door."

The voice inside said something that was nothing to me. I repeated my thumping and calling. Down the corridor a door opened and a sallow thin-haired old man's head stuck out and asked: "What's the matter?" I said: "None of your damned business," and pounded the door again.

The inside voice came strong enough now to let us know that it was complaining, though no words could be made out yet. I rattled the knob and found that the door was unlocked. Rattling the knob some more, I worked the door open an inch or so. Then the voice was clearer. I heard soft feet on the floor. I heard a choking sob. I pushed the door open.

Eric Collinson made a noise in his throat that was like somebody very far away yelling horribly.

Gabrielle Leggett stood beside the bed, swaying a little, holding the white foot-rail of the bed with one hand. Her face was white as lime. Her eyes were all brown, dull, focused on nothing, and her small forehead was wrinkled. She looked as if she knew there was something in front of her and was wondering what it was. She had on one yellow stocking, a brown velvet skirt that had been slept in, and a yellow chemise. Scattered around the room were a pair of brown slippers, the other stocking, a brown and gold blouse, a brown coat, and a brown and yellow hat.

Everything else in the room was white: white-papered walls and white-painted ceiling; white-enameled chairs, bed, table, fixtures—even to the telephone—and woodwork; white felt on the floor. None of the furniture was hospital furniture, but solid whiteness gave it that appearance. There were two windows, and two doors besides the one I had opened. The door on the left opened into a bathroom, the one on the right into a small dressing-room.

I pushed Collinson into the room, followed him, and closed the door. There was no key in it, and no place for a key, no lock of any fixable sort. Collinson stood gaping at the girl, his jaw sagging, his eyes as vacant as hers; but there was more horror in his face. She leaned against the foot of the bed and stared at nothing with dark, blank eyes in a ghastly, puzzled face.

I put an arm around her and sat her on the side of the bed, telling Collinson: "Gather up her clothes." I had to tell him twice before he came out of his trance.

He brought me her things and I began dressing her. He dug his fingers into my shoulder and protested in a voice that would have been appropriate if I had been robbing a poor-box:

"No! You can't—"

"What the hell?" I asked, pushing his hand away. "You can have the job if you want it."

He was sweating. He gulped and stuttered: "No, no! I couldn't—it—" He broke off and walked to the window.

"She told me you were an ass," I said to his back, and discovered I was putting the brown and gold blouse on her backwards. She might as well have been a wax figure, for all the help she gave me, but at least she didn't struggle when I wrestled her around, and she stayed where I shoved her.

By the time I had got her into coat and hat, Collinson had come away from the window and was spluttering questions at me. What was the matter with her? Oughtn't we to get a doctor? Was it safe to take her out? And when I stood up, he took her away from me, supporting her with his long, thick arms, babbling: "It's Eric, Gaby. Don't you know me? Speak to me. What is the matter, dear?"

"There's nothing the matter except that she's got a skinful of dope," I said. "Don't try to bring her out of it. Wait till we get her home. You take this arm and I'll take that. She can walk all right. If we run into anybody, just keep going and let me handle them. Let's go."

We didn't meet anybody. We went out to the elevator, down in it to the ground floor, across the foyer, and into the street without seeing a single person.

We went down to the corner where we had left Mickey in the Chrysler.

"That's all for you," I told him.

He said: "Right, so long," and went away.

Collinson and I wedged the girl between us in the roadster, and he put it in motion.

We rode three blocks. Then he asked: "Are you sure home's the best place for her?"

I said I was. He didn't say anything for five more blocks and then repeated his question, adding something about a hospital.

"Why not a newspaper office?" I sneered.

Three blocks of silence, and he started again: "I know a doctor who—"

"I've got work to do," I said; "and Miss Leggett home now, in the shape she's in now, will help me get it done. So she goes home."

He scowled, accusing me angrily: "You'd humiliate her, disgrace her, endanger her life, for the sake of—"

"Her life's in no more danger than yours or mine. She's simply got a little more of the junk in her than she can stand up under. And she took it. I didn't give it to her."

The girl we were talking about was alive and breathing between us —even sitting up with her eyes open—but knowing no more of what was going on than if she had been in Finland.

We should have turned to the right at the next corner. Collinson held the car straight and stepped it up to forty-five miles an hour, staring ahead, his face hard and lumpy.

"Take the next turn," I commanded.

"No," he said, and didn't. The speedometer showed a 50, and people on the sidewalks began looking after us as we whizzed by.

"Well?" I asked, wriggling an arm loose from the girl's side.

"We're going down the peninsula," he said firmly. "She's not going home in her condition."

I grunted: "Yeah?" and flashed my free hand at the controls. He knocked it aside, holding the wheel with one hand, stretching the other out to block me if I tried again.

"Don't do that," he cautioned me, increasing our speed another half-dozen miles. "You know what will happen to all of us if you—"

I cursed him, bitterly, fairly thoroughly, and from the heart. His face jerked around to me, full of righteous indignation because, I suppose, my language wasn't the kind one should use in a lady's company.

And that brought it about.

A blue sedan came out of a cross-street a split second before we got there. Collinson's eyes and attention got back to his driving in time to twist the roadster away from the sedan, but not in time to make a neat job of it. We missed the sedan by a couple of inches, but as we passed behind it our rear wheels started sliding out of line. Collinson did what he could, giving the roadster its head, going with the skid, but the corner curb wouldn't co-operate. It stood stiff and hard where it was. We hit it side-wise and rolled over on the lamp-post behind it. The lamp-post snapped, crashed down on the sidewalk. The roadster, over on its side, spilled us out around the lamp-post. Gas from the broken post roared up at our feet.

Collinson, most of the skin scraped from one side of his face, crawled back on hands and knees to turn off the roadster's engine. I sat up, raising the girl, who was on my chest, with me. My right shoulder and arm were out of whack, dead. The girl was making whimpering noises in her chest, but I couldn't see any marks on her except a shallow scratch on one cheek. I had been her cushion, had taken the jolt for her. The soreness of my chest, belly, and back, the lameness of my shoulder and arm, told me how much I had saved her.

People helped us up. Collinson stood with his arms around the girl, begging her to say she wasn't dead, and so on. The smash had jarred her into semi-consciousness, but she still didn't know whether there had been an accident or what. I went over and helped Collinson hold her up— though neither needed help—saying earnestly to the gathering crowd: "We've got to get her home. Who can—?"

A pudgy man in plus fours offered his services. Collinson and I got in the back of his car with the girl, and I gave the pudgy man her address. He said something about a hospital, but I insisted that home was the place for her. Collinson was too upset to say anything. Twenty minutes later we took the girl out of the car in front of her house. I thanked the pudgy man profusely, giving him no opportunity to follow us indoors.

VI · *The Man from Devil's Island*

AFTER some delay—I had to ring twice—the Leggetts' door was opened by Owen Fitzstephan. There was no sleepiness in his eyes: they were hot and bright, as they were when he found life interesting. Knowing the sort of things that interested him, I wondered what had happened.

"What have you been doing?" he asked, looking at our clothes, at Collinson's bloody face, at the girl's scratched cheek.

"Automobile accident," I said. "Nothing serious. Where's everybody?"

"Everybody," he said, with peculiar emphasis on the word, "is up in the laboratory;" and then to me: "Come here."

I followed him across the reception hall to the foot of the stairs, leaving Collinson and the girl standing just inside the street door. Fitzstephan put his mouth close to my ear and whispered:

"Leggett's committed suicide."

I was more annoyed than surprised. I asked: "Where is he?"

"In the laboratory. Mrs. Leggett and the police are up there. It happened only half an hour ago."

"We'll all go up," I said.

"Isn't it rather unnecessary," he asked, "taking Gabrielle up there?"

"Might be tough on her," I said irritably, "but it's necessary enough. Anyway, she's coked-up and better able to stand the shock than she will be later, when the stuff's dying out in her." I turned to Collinson. "Come on, we'll go up to the laboratory."

I went ahead, letting Fitzstephan help Collinson with the girl. There were six people in the laboratory: a uniformed copper—a big man with a red mustache—standing beside the door; Mrs. Leggett, sitting on a wooden chair in the far end of the room, her body bent forward, her hands holding a handkerchief to her face, sobbing quietly; O'Gar and Reddy, standing by one of the windows, close together, their heads rubbing over a sheaf of papers that the detective-sergeant held in his thick fists; a gray-faced, dandified man in dark clothes, standing beside the zinc table, twiddling eye-glasses on a black ribbon in his hand; and Edgar Leggett, seated on a chair at the table, his head and upper body resting on the table, his arms sprawled out.

O'Gar and Reddy looked up from their reading as I came in. Passing the table on my way to join them at the window, I saw blood, a small black automatic pistol lying close to one of Leggett's hands, and seven unset diamonds grouped by his head.

O'Gar said, "Take a look," and handed me part of his sheaf of paper —four stiff white sheets covered with very small, precise, and regular handwriting in black ink. I was getting interested in what was written there when Fitzstephan and Collinson came in with Gabrielle Leggett.

Collinson looked at the dead man at the table. Collinson's face went white. He put his big body between the girl and her father.

"Come in," I said.

"This is no place for Miss Leggett now," he said hotly, turning to take her away.

"We ought to have everybody in here," I told O'Gar. He nodded his bullet head at the policeman. The policeman put a hand on Collinson's shoulder and said: "You'll have to come in, the both of you."

Fitzstephan placed a chair by one of the end windows for the girl. She sat down and looked around the room—at the dead man, at Mrs. Leggett, at all of us—with eyes that were dull but no longer completely blank. Collinson stood beside her, glaring at me. Mrs. Leggett hadn't looked up from her handkerchief.

I spoke to O'Gar, clearly enough for the others to hear: "Let's read the letter out loud."

He screwed up his eyes, hesitated, then thrust the rest of his sheaf at me, saying: "Fair enough. You read it."

I read:

"To the police:—

"My name is Maurice Pierre de Mayenne. I was born in Fécamp, department of Seine-Inférieure, France, on March 6, 1883, but was chiefly educated in England. In 1903 I went to Paris to study painting, and there, four years later, I made the acquaintance of Alice and Lily Dain, orphan daughters of a British naval officer. I married Lily the following year, and in 1909 our daughter Gabrielle was born.

"Shortly after my marriage I had discovered that I had made a most horrible mistake, that it was Alice, and not my wife Lily, whom I really loved. I kept this discovery to myself until the child was past the most difficult baby years; that is, until she was nearly five, and then told my wife, asking that she divorce me so I could marry Alice. She refused.

"On June 6, 1913, I murdered Lily and fled with Alice and Gabrielle to London, where I was soon arrested and returned to Paris, to be tried, found guilty, and sentenced to life imprisonment on the Iles du Salut. Alice, who had had no part in the murder, no knowledge of it until after it was done, and who had accompanied us to London only because of her love for Gabrielle, was also tried, but justly acquitted. All this is a matter of record in Paris.

"In 1918 I escaped from the islands with a fellow convict named Jacques Labaud, on a flimsy raft. I do not know—we never knew—how long we were adrift on the ocean, nor, toward the last, how long we went without food and water. Then Labaud could stand no more, and died. He died of starvation and exposure. I did not kill him. No living creature could have been feeble enough for me to have killed it, no matter what my desire. But when Labaud was dead there was enough food for one, and I lived to be washed ashore in the Golfo Triste.

"Calling myself Walter Martin, I secured employment with a British copper mining company at Aroa, and within a few months had become private secretary to Philip Howart, the resident manager. Shortly after this promotion I was approached by a cockney named John Edge, who outlined to me a plan by which we could defraud the company of a hundred-odd pounds monthly. When I refused to take part in the fraud, Edge revealed his knowledge of my identity, and threatened exposure unless I assisted him. That Venezuela had no extradition treaty with France might save me from being returned to the islands, Edge said; but that was not my chief danger: Labaud's body had been cast ashore, undecomposed enough to show what had happened to him, and I, an escaped murderer, would be under the necessity of proving to a Venezuelan court that I had not killed Labaud in Venezuelan waters to keep from starving.

"I still refused to join Edge in his fraud, and prepared to go away. But while I was making my preparations he killed Howart and looted the company safe. He urged me to flee with him, arguing that I could not face the police investigation even if he did not expose me. That was true enough: I went with him. Two months later, in Mexico City, I learned why Edge had been so desirous of my company. He had a firm hold on me, through his knowledge of my identity, and a great—an unjustified—opinion of my ability; and he intended using me to commit crimes that were beyond his grasp. I was determined, no matter what happened, no matter what became necessary, never to return to the Iles du Salut; but neither did I intend becoming a professional criminal. I attempted to desert Edge in Mexico City; he found me; we fought; and I killed him. I killed him in self-defense: he struck me first.

"In 1920 I came to the United States, to San Francisco, changed my name once more—to Edgar Leggett—and began making a new place for myself in the world, developing experiments with color that I had attempted as a young artist in Paris. In 1923, believing that Edgar Leggett could never now be connected with Maurice de Mayenne, I sent for Alice and Gabrielle, who were then living in New York, and Alice and I were married. But the past was not dead, and there was no unbridgeable chasm between Leggett and Mayenne. Alice, not hearing from me after my escape, not knowing what had happened to me, employed a private detective to find me, a Louis Upton. Upton sent a man named Ruppert to South America, and Ruppert succeeded in tracing me step by step from my landing in the Golfo Triste up to, but no farther than, my departure from Mexico City after Edge's death. In doing this, Ruppert of course learned of the deaths of Labaud, Howart and Edge; three deaths of which I was guiltless, but of which—or at least of one or more of which—I most certainly, my record being what it is, would be convicted if tried.

"I do not know how Upton found me in San Francisco. Possibly he traced Alice and Gabrielle to me. Late last Saturday night he called upon me and demanded money as the price of silence. Having no money available at the time, I put him off until Tuesday, when I gave him the diamonds as part payment. But I was desperate. I knew what being at Upton's mercy would mean, having experienced the same thing with Edge. I determined to kill him. I decided to pretend the diamonds had been stolen, and to so inform you, the police. Upton, I was confident, would thereupon immediately communicate with me. I would make an appointment with him and shoot him down in cold blood, confident that I would have no difficulty in arranging a story that would make me seem justified in having killed this known burglar, in whose possession, doubtless, the stolen diamonds would be found.

"I think the plan would have been successful. However, Ruppert—pursuing Upton with a grudge of his own to settle—saved me from killing Upton by himself killing him. Ruppert, the man who had traced my course from Devil's Island to Mexico City, had also, either from Upton or by spying on Upton, learned that Mayenne was Leggett, and, with the police after him for Upton's murder, he came here, demanding that I shelter him, returning the diamonds, claiming money in their stead.

"I killed him. His body is in the cellar. Out front, a detective is watching my house. Other detectives are busy elsewhere inquiring into my affairs. I have not been able satisfactorily to explain certain of my actions, nor to avoid contradictions, and, now that I am actually suspect, there is little chance of the past's being kept secret. I have always known—have known it most surely when I would not admit it to myself—that this would one day happen. I am not going back to Devil's Island. My wife and daughter had neither knowledge of nor part in Ruppert's death.

"Maurice de Mayenne."

VII · *The Curse*

NOBODY said anything for some minutes after I had finished reading. Mrs. Leggett had taken her handkerchief from her face to listen, sobbing softly now and then. Gabrielle Leggett was looking jerkily around the room, light fighting cloudiness in her eyes, her lips twitching as if she was trying to get words out but couldn't.

I went to the table, bent over the dead man, and ran my hand over his pockets. The inside coat pocket bulged. I reached under his arm, unbuttoned and pulled open his coat, taking a brown wallet from the pocket. The wallet was thick with paper money—fifteen thousand dollars when we counted it later.

Showing the others the wallet's contents, I asked:

"Did he leave any message besides the one I read?"

"None that's been found," O'Gar said. "Why?"

"Any that you know of, Mrs. Leggett?" I asked.

She shook her head.

"Why?" O'Gar asked again.

"He didn't commit suicide," I said. "He was murdered."

Gabrielle Leggett screamed shrilly and sprang out of her chair, pointing a sharp-nailed white finger at Mrs. Leggett.

"She killed him," the girl shrieked. "She said, 'Come back here,' and held the kitchen door open with one hand, and picked up the knife from the drain-board with the other, and when he went past her she pushed it in his back. I saw her do it. She killed him. I wasn't dressed, and when I heard them coming I hid in the pantry, and I saw her do it."

Mrs. Leggett got to her feet. She staggered, and would have fallen if Fitzstephan hadn't gone over to steady her. Amazement washed her swollen face empty of grief.

The gray-faced dandified man by the table—Doctor Riese, I learned later—said, in a cold, crisp voice:

"There is no stab wound. He was shot through the temple by a bullet from this pistol, held close, slanting up. Clearly suicide, I should say."

Collinson forced Gabrielle down to her chair again, trying to calm her. She was working her hands together and moaning.

I disagreed with the doctor's last statement, and said so while turning something else over in my mind:

"Murder. He had this money in his pocket. He was going away. He wrote that letter to the police to clear his wife and daughter, so they wouldn't be punished for complicity in his crimes. Did it," I asked O'Gar, "sound to you like the dying statement of a man who was leaving a wife and daughter he loved? No message, no word, to them—all to the police."

"Maybe you're right," the bullet-headed man said; "but supposing he was going away, he still didn't leave them any—"

"He would have told them—either on paper or talking—something before he went, if he had lived long enough. He was winding up his affairs, preparing to go away, and— Maybe he *was* going to commit suicide, though the money and the tone of the letter make me doubt it; but even in that case my guess is that he didn't, that he was killed before he had finished his preparations—maybe because he was taking too long a time. How was he found?"

"I heard," Mrs. Leggett sobbed; "I heard the shot, and ran up here, and he—he was like that. And I went down to the telephone, and the bell—the doorbell—rang, and it was Mr. Fitzstephan, and I told him. It couldn't—there was nobody else in the house to—to kill him."

"You killed him," I said to her. "He was going away. He wrote this statement, shouldering your crimes. You killed Ruppert down in the kitchen. That's what the girl was talking about. Your husband's letter sounded enough like a suicide letter to pass for one, you thought; so you murdered him—murdered him because you thought his confession and death would hush up the whole business, keep us from poking into it any further."

Her face didn't tell me anything. It was distorted, but in a way that might have meant almost anything. I filled my lungs and went on, not exactly bellowing, but getting plenty of noise out:

"There are half a dozen lies in your husband's statement—half a dozen that I can peg now. He didn't send for you and his daughter. You traced him here. Mrs. Begg said he was the most surprised man she had ever seen when you arrived from New York. He didn't give Upton the diamonds. His account of why he gave them to Upton and of what he intended doing afterwards is ridiculous: it's simply the best story he could think of on short notice to cover you up. Leggett would have given him money or he would have given him nothing; he wouldn't have been foolish enough to give him somebody else's diamonds and have all this stink raised.

"Upton traced you here and he came to you with his demand—not to your husband. You had hired Upton to find Leggett; you were the one he knew; he and Ruppert had traced Leggett for you, not only to Mexico

City, but all the way here. They'd have squeezed you before this if they hadn't been sent to Sing Sing for another trick. When they got out, Upton came here and made his play. You framed the burglary; you gave Upton the diamonds; and you didn't tell your husband anything about it. Your husband thought the burglary was on the level. Otherwise, would he—a man with his record—have risked reporting it to the police?

"Why didn't you tell him about Upton? Didn't you want him to know that you had had him traced step by step from Devil's Island to San Francisco? Why? His southern record was a good additional hold on him, if you needed one? You didn't want him to know you knew about Labaud and Howart and Edge?"

I didn't give her a chance to answer any of these questions, but sailed ahead, turning my voice loose:

"Maybe Ruppert, following Upton here, got in touch with you, and you had him kill Upton, a job he was willing to do on his own hook. Probably, because he did kill him and he did come to you afterwards, and you thought it necessary to put the knife into him down in the kitchen. You didn't know the girl, hiding in the pantry, saw you; but you did know that you were getting out of your depth. You knew that your chances of getting away with Ruppert's murder were slim. Your house was too much in the spotlight. So you played your only out. You went to your husband with the whole story—or as much of it as could be arranged to persuade him—and got him to shoulder it for you. And then you handed him this— here at the table.

"He shielded you. He had always shielded you. *You*," I thundered, my voice in fine form by now, "killed your sister Lily, his first wife, and let him take the fall for you. *You* went to London with him after that. Would you have gone with your sister's murderer if you had been innocent? *You* had him traced here, and *you* came here after him, and *you* married him. *You* were the one who decided he had married the wrong sister, and *you* killed her."

"She did! She did!" cried Gabrielle Leggett, trying to get up from the chair in which Collinson was holding her. "She—"

Mrs. Leggett drew herself up straight, and smiled, showing strong yellowish teeth set edge to edge. She took two steps toward the center of the room. One hand was on her hip, the other hanging loosely at her side. The housewife—Fitzstephan's serene sane soul—was suddenly gone. This was a blonde woman whose body was rounded, not with the plumpness of contented, well-cared-for early middle age, but with the cushioned, soft-sheathed muscles of the hunting cats, whether in jungle or alley.

I picked up the pistol from the table and put it in my pocket.

"You wish to know who killed my sister?" Mrs. Leggett asked softly, speaking to me, her teeth clicking together between words, her mouth smiling, her eyes burning. "She, the dope fiend, Gabrielle—she killed her mother. She is the one he shielded."

The girl cried out something unintelligible.

"Nonsense," I said. "She was a baby."

"Oh, but it is not nonsense," the woman said. "She was nearly five, a child of five playing with a pistol that she had taken from a drawer while her mother slept. The pistol went off and Lily died. An accident, of course, but Maurice was too sensitive a soul to bear the thought of her growing up knowing that she had killed her mother. Besides, it was likely that Maurice would have been convicted in any event. It was known that he and I were intimate, that he wanted his freedom from Lily; and he was at the door of Lily's bedroom when the shot was fired. But that was a slight matter to him: his one desire was to save the child from memory of what she had done, so her life might not be blackened by the knowledge that she had, however accidentally, killed her mother."

What made this especially nasty was the niceness with which the woman smiled as she talked, and the care—almost fastidious—with which she selected her words, mouthing them daintily. She went on:

"Gabrielle was always, even before she became addicted to drugs, a child of, one might say, limited mentality; and so, by the time the London police had found us, we had succeeded in quite emptying her mind of the last trace of memory, that is, of this particular memory. This is, I assure you, the entire truth. She killed her mother; and her father, to use your expression, took the fall for her."

"Fairly plausible," I conceded, "but it doesn't hang together right. There's a chance that you made Leggett believe that, but I doubt it. I think you're trying to hurt your step-daughter because she's told us of seeing you knife Ruppert downstairs."

She pulled her lips back from her teeth and took a quick step toward me, her eyes wide and white-ringed; then she checked herself, laughed sharply, and the glare went from her eyes—or maybe went back through them, to smolder behind them. She put her hands on her hips and smiled playfully, airily, at me and spoke playfully to me, while mad hatred glowed behind eyes, smile, and voice.

"Am I? Then I must tell you this, which I should not tell you unless it was true. I taught her to kill her mother. Do you understand? I taught her, trained her, drilled her, rehearsed her. Do you understand that? Lily and I were true sisters, inseparable, hating one another poisonously. Maurice, he wished to marry neither of us—why should he?—though he was intimate enough with both. You are to try to understand that literally. But we were poverty-ridden and he was not, and, because we were and he wasn't, Lily wished to marry him. And I, I wished to marry him because she did. We were true sisters, like that in all things. But Lily got him, first—trapped him—that is crude but exact—into matrimony.

"Gabrielle was born six or seven months later. What a happy little family we were. I lived with them—weren't Lily and I inseparable?—and from the first Gabrielle had more love for me than for her mother. I saw to that: there was nothing her Aunt Alice wouldn't do for her dear niece; because her preferring me infuriated Lily, not that Lily herself loved the child so much, but that we were sisters; and whatever one wanted the other wanted, not to share, but exclusively.

"Gabrielle had hardly been born before I began planning what I should some day do; and when she was nearly five I did it. Maurice's pistol, a small one, was kept in a locked drawer high in a chiffonier. I unlocked the drawer, unloaded the pistol, and taught Gabrielle an amusing little game. I would lie on Lily's bed, pretending to sleep. The child would push a chair to the chiffonier, climb up on it, take the pistol from the drawer, creep over to the bed, put the muzzle of the pistol to my head, and press the trigger. When she did it well, making little or no noise, holding the pistol correctly in her tiny hands, I would reward her with candy, cautioning her against saying anything about the game to her mother or to anyone else, as we were going to surprise her mother with it.

"We did. We surprised her completely one afternoon when, having taken aspirin for a headache, Lily was sleeping in her bed. That time I unlocked the drawer but did not unload the pistol. Then I told the child she might play the game with her mother; and I went to visit friends on the floor below, so no one would think I had had any part in my dear sister's demise. I thought Maurice would be away all afternoon. I intended, when I heard the shot, to rush upstairs with my friends and find with them that the child playing with the pistol had killed her mother.

"I had little fear of the child's talking afterwards. Of, as I have said, limited mentality, loving and trusting me as she did, and in my hands both before and during any official inquiry that might be made, I knew I could very easily control her, make sure that she said nothing to reveal my part in the—ah—enterprise. But Maurice very nearly spoiled the whole thing. Coming home unexpectedly, he reached the bedroom door just as Gabrielle pressed the trigger. The tiniest fraction of a second earlier, and he would have been in time to save his wife's life.

"Well, that was unfortunate in that it led to his being convicted; but it certainly prevented his ever suspecting me; and his subsequent desire to wipe from the child's mind all remembrance of the deed relieved me of any further anxiety or effort. I did follow him to this country after his escape from Devil's Island, and I did follow him to San Francisco when Upton had found him for me; and I used Gabrielle's love for me and her hatred of him—I had carefully cultivated that with skilfully clumsy attempts to persuade her to forgive him for murdering her mother—and the necessity of keeping her in ignorance of the truth, and my record of faithfulness to him and her, to make him marry me, to make him think that marrying me would in some sense salvage our ruined lives. The day he married Lily I swore I would take him away from her. And I did. And I hope my dear sister in hell knows it."

The smile was gone. Mad hatred was no longer *behind* eyes and voice: it was *in* them, and in the set of her features, the pose of her body. This mad hatred—and she as part of it—seemed the only live thing in the room. The eight of us who looked at and listened to her didn't, for the moment, count: we were alive to her, but not to each other, nor to anything but her.

She turned from me to fling an arm out at the girl on the other side of the room; and now her voice was throaty, vibrant, with savage triumph in it; and her words were separated into groups by brief pauses, so that she seemed to be chanting them.

"You're her daughter," she cried; "and you're cursed with the same black soul and rotten blood that she and I and all the Dains have had; and you're cursed with your mother's blood on your hands in babyhood; and with the twisted mind and the need for drugs that are my gifts to you; and your life will be black as your mother's and mine were black; and the lives of those you touch will be black as Maurice's was black; and your—"

"Stop!" Eric Collinson gasped. "Make her stop."

Gabrielle Leggett, both hands to her ears, her face twisted with terror, screamed once—horribly—and fell forward out of her chair.

Pat Reddy was young at manhunting, but O'Gar and I should have known better than to stop watching Mrs. Leggett even for a half-second, no matter how urgently the girl's scream and fall pulled at our attention. But we did look at the girl—if for less than half a second—and that was long enough. When we looked at Mrs. Leggett again, she had a gun in her hand, and she had taken her first step towards the door.

Nobody was between her and the door: the uniformed copper had gone to help Collinson with Gabrielle Leggett. Nobody was behind her: her back was to the door and by turning she had brought Fitzstephan into her field of vision. She glared over the black gun, burning eyes darting from one to another of us, taking another step backward, snarling: "Don't you move."

Pat Reddy shifted his weight to the balls of his feet. I frowned at him, shaking my head. The hall and stairs were better places in which to catch her: in here somebody would die.

She backed over the sill, blew breath between her teeth with a hissing, spitting sound, and was gone down the hall.

Owen Fitzstephan was first through the door after her. The policeman got in my way, but I was second out. The woman had reached the head of the stairs, at the other end of the dim hall, with Fitzstephan, not far behind, rapidly overtaking her.

He caught her on the between-floors landing, just as I reached the top of the stairs. He pinned one of her arms to her body, but the other, with the gun, was free. He grabbed at it and missed. She twisted the muzzle in to his body as I—with my head bent to miss the edge of the floor—leaped down at them.

I landed on them just in time, crashing into them, smashing them into the corner of the wall, sending her bullet, meant for the sorrel-haired man, into a step.

We weren't standing up. I caught with both hands at the flash of her gun, missed, and had her by the waist. Close to my chin Fitzstephan's lean fingers closed on her gun-hand wrist.

She twisted her body against my right arm. My right arm was still lame from our spill out of the Chrysler. It wouldn't hold. Her thick body went up, turning over on me.

Gunfire roared in my ear, burnt my cheek.

The woman's body went limp.

When O'Gar and Reddy pulled us apart she lay still. The second bullet had gone through her throat.

I went up to the laboratory. Gabrielle Leggett, with the doctor and Collinson kneeling beside her, was lying on the floor.

I told the doctor: "Better take a look at Mrs. Leggett. She's on the stairs. Dead, I think, but you'd better take a look."

The doctor went out. Collinson, chafing the unconscious girl's hands, looked at me as if I were something there ought to be a law against, and said:

"I hope you're satisfied with the way your work got done."

"It got done," I said.

VIII · But and If

FITZSTEPHAN and I ate one of Mrs. Schindler's good dinners that evening in her low-ceilinged basement, and drank her husband's good beer. The novelist in Fitzstephan was busy trying to find what he called Mrs. Leggett's psychological basis.

"The killing of her sister is plain enough, knowing her character as we now do," he said, "and so are the killing of her husband, her attempt to ruin her niece's life when she was exposed, and even her determination to kill herself on the stairs rather than be caught. But the quiet years in between—where do they fit in?"

"It's Leggett's murder that doesn't fit in," I argued. "The rest is all one piece. She wanted him. She killed her sister—or had her killed—in a way to tie him to her; but the law pulled them apart. There was nothing she could do about that, except wait and hope for the chance that always existed, that he would be freed some day. We don't know of anything else she wanted then. Why shouldn't she be quiet, holding Gabrielle as her hostage against the chance she hoped for, living comfortably enough, no doubt, on his money? When she heard of his escape, she came to America and set about finding him. When her detectives located him here she came to him. He was willing to marry her. She had what she wanted. Why should she be anything but quiet? She wasn't a trouble-maker for the fun of it—one of these people who act out of pure mischief. She was simply a woman who wanted what she wanted and was willing to go to any length to get it. Look how patiently, and for how many years, she hid her hatred from the girl. And her wants weren't even very extravagant. You won't find the key to her in any complicated derangements. She was simple as an animal, with an animal's simple ignorance of right and wrong, dislike for being thwarted, and spitefulness when trapped."

Fitzstephan drank beer and asked:

"You'd reduce the Dain curse, then, to a primitive strain in the blood?"

"To less than that, to words in an angry woman's mouth."

"It's fellows like you that take all the color out of life." He sighed behind cigarette smoke. "Doesn't Gabrielle's being made the tool of her mother's murder convince you of the necessity—at least the poetic necessity—of the curse?"

"Not even if she *was* the tool, and that's something I wouldn't bet on. Apparently Leggett didn't doubt it. He stuffed his letter with those ancient details to keep her covered up. But we've only got Mrs. Leggett's word that he actually saw the child kill her mother. On the other hand, Mrs. Leggett said, in front of Gabrielle, that Gabrielle had been brought up to believe her father the murderer—so we can believe that. And it isn't likely—though it's possible—that he would have gone that far except to save her from knowledge of her own guilt. But, from that point on, one guess at the truth is about as good as another. Mrs. Leggett wanted him and she got him. Then why in hell did she kill him?"

"You jump around so," Fitzstephan complained. "You answered that back in the laboratory. Why don't you stick to your answer? You said she killed him because the letter sounded enough like a pre-suicide statement to pass, and she thought it and his death would ensure her safety."

"That was good enough to say then," I admitted; "but not now, in cold blood, with more facts to fit in. She had worked and waited for years to get him. He must have had some value to her."

"But she didn't love him, or there is no reason to suppose she did. He hadn't that value to her. He was to her no more than a trophy of the hunt; and that's a value not affected by death—one has the head embalmed and nailed on the wall."

"Then why did she keep Upton away from him? Why did she kill Ruppert? Why should she have carried the load for him there? It was his danger. Why did she make it hers if he had no value to her? Why did she risk all that to keep him from learning that the past had come to life again?"

"I think I see what you're getting at," Fitzstephan said slowly. "You think—"

"Wait—here's another thing. I talked to Leggett and his wife together a couple of times. Neither of them addressed a word to the other either time, though the woman did a lot of acting to make me think she would have told me something about her daughter's disappearance if it had not been for him."

"Where did you find Gabrielle?"

"After seeing Ruppert murdered, she beat it to the Haldorns' with what money she had and her jewelry, turning the jewelry over to Minnie Hershey to raise money on. Minnie bought a couple of pieces for herself —her man had picked himself up a lot of dough in a crap game a night or two before: the police checked that—and sent the man out to peddle the rest. He was picked up in a hock-shop, just on general suspicion."

"Gabrielle was leaving home for good?" he asked.

"You can't blame her—thinking her father a murderer, and now catching her step-mother in the act. Who'd want to live in a home like that?"

"And you think Leggett and his wife were on bad terms? That may be: I hadn't seen much of them lately, and wasn't intimate enough with them to have been let in on a condition of that sort if it had existed. Do you think he had perhaps learned something—some of the truth about her?"

"Maybe, but not enough to keep him from taking the fall for her on Ruppert's murder; and what he had learned wasn't connected with this recent affair, because the first time I saw him he really believed in the burglary. But then—"

"Aw, shut up! You're never satisfied until you've got two buts and an if attached to everything. I don't see any reason for doubting Mrs. Leggett's story. She told us the whole thing quite gratuitously. Why should we suppose that she'd lie to implicate herself?"

"You mean in her sister's murder? She'd been acquitted of that, and I suppose the French system's like ours in that she couldn't be tried again for it, no matter what she confessed. She didn't give anything away, brother."

"Always belittling," he said. "You need more beer to expand your soul."

At the Leggett-Ruppert inquests I saw Gabrielle Leggett again, but was not sure that she even recognized me. She was with Madison Andrews, who had been Leggett's attorney and was now his estate's executor. Eric Collinson was there, but, peculiarly, apparently not with Gabrielle. He gave me nods and nothing else.

The newspapers got hold of what Mrs. Leggett had said happened in

Paris in 1913, and made a couple-day fuss over it. The recovery of Halstead and Beauchamp's diamonds let the Continental Detective Agency out: we wrote *Discontinued* at the bottom of the Leggett record. I went up in the mountains to snoop around for a gold-mine-owner who thought his employes were gypping him.

I expected to be in the mountains for at least a month: inside jobs of that sort take time. On the evening of my tenth day there I had a long-distance call from the Old Man, my boss.

"I'm sending Foley up to relieve you," he said. "Don't wait for him. Catch tonight's train back. The Leggett matter is active again."

Part Two: The Temple

IX · *Tad's Blind Man*

MADISON ANDREWS was a tall gaunt man of sixty with ragged white hair, eyebrows, and mustache that exaggerated the ruddiness of his bony hard-muscled face. He wore his clothes loose, chewed tobacco, and had twice in the past ten years been publicly named co-respondent in divorce suits.

"I dare say young Collinson has babbled all sorts of nonsense to you," he said. "He seems to think I'm in my second childhood, as good as told me so."

"I haven't seen him," I said. "I've only been back in town a couple of hours, long enough to go to the office and then come here."

"Well," he said, "he is her fiancé, but I am responsible for her, and I preferred following Doctor Riese's counsel. He is her physician. He said that letting her go to the Temple for a short stay would do more to restore her to mental health than anything else we could do. I couldn't disregard his advice. The Haldorns may be, probably are, charlatans, but Joseph Haldorn is certainly the only person to whom Gabrielle has willingly talked, and in whose company she has seemed at peace, since her parents' deaths. Doctor Riese said that to cross her in her desire to go to the Temple would be to send her mind deeper into its illness. Could I snap my fingers at his opinion because young Collinson didn't like it?"

I said: "No."

"I have no illusions concerning the cult," he went on defending himself. "It is probably as full of quackery as any other. But we are not concerned with its religious aspect. We're interested in it as therapeutics, as a cure for Gabrielle's mind. Even if the character of its membership were not such that I could count with certainty on Gabrielle's safety, I should still have been tempted to let her go. Her recovery is, as I see it, the thing with which we should be most concerned, and nothing else should be allowed to interfere with that."

He was worried. I nodded and kept quiet, waiting to learn what was worrying him. I got it little by little as he went on talking around in circles.

On Doctor Riese's advice and over Collinson's protests he had let Gabrielle Leggett go to the Temple of the Holy Grail to stay awhile. She had wanted to go, no less prominently respectable a person than Mrs. Livingston Rodman was staying there at the time, the Haldorns had been Edgar Leggett's friends: Andrews let her go. That had been six days ago. She had taken the mulatto, Minnie Hershey, with her as maid. Doctor Riese had gone to see her each day. On four days he had found her improved. On the fifth day her condition had alarmed him. Her mind was more completely dazed than it had ever been, and she had the symptoms of one who had been subjected to some sort of shock. He couldn't get anything out of her. He couldn't get anything out of Minnie. He couldn't get anything out of the Haldorns. He had no way of learning what had happened, or if anything had happened.

Eric Collinson had held Riese up for daily reports on Gabrielle. Riese told him the truth about his last visit. Collinson hit the ceiling. He wanted the girl taken away from the Temple immediately: the Haldorns were preparing to murder her, according to his notion. He and Andrews had a swell row. Andrews thought that the girl had simply suffered a relapse from which she would most speedily recover if left where she wished to stay. Riese was inclined to agree with Andrews. Collinson didn't. He threatened to create a stink if they didn't yank her away *pronto*.

That worried Andrews. It wouldn't look so good for him, the hardheaded lawyer, letting his ward go to such a place, if anything happened to her. On the other hand, he said he really believed it was for her benefit to stay there. And he didn't want anything to happen to her. He finally reached a compromise with Collinson. Gabrielle should be allowed to remain in the Temple for a few more days at least, but somebody should be put in there to keep an eye on her, and to see that the Haldorns weren't playing any tricks on her.

Riese had suggested me: my luck in hitting on the manner of Leggett's death had impressed him. Collinson had objected that my brutality was largely responsible for Gabrielle's present condition, but he had finally given in. I already knew Gabrielle and her history, and I hadn't made such a total mess of that first job: my efficiency offset my brutality, or words to that effect. So Andrews had phoned the Old Man, offered him a high enough rate to justify pulling me off another job, and there I was.

"The Haldorns know you are coming," Andrews wound up. "It doesn't matter what they think about it. I simply told them that Doctor Riese and I had decided that, until Gabrielle's mind became more settled, it would be best to have a competent man on hand in case of emergency, as much perhaps to safeguard others as her. There is no need of my giving you instructions. It is simply a matter of taking every precaution."

"Does Miss Leggett know I'm coming?"

"No, and I don't think we need say anything to her about it. You'll make your watch over her as unobtrusive as possible, of course, and I doubt that she will, in her present state of mind, pay enough attention to your presence to resent it. If she does—well, we'll see."

Andrews gave me a note to Aaronia Haldorn.

An hour and a half later I was sitting opposite her in the Temple reception room while she read it. She put it aside and offered me long Russian cigarettes in a white jade box. I apologized for sticking to my Fatimas, and worked the lighter on the smoking stand she pushed out between us. When our cigarettes were burning, she said:

"We shall try to make you as comfortable as possible. We are neither barbarians nor fanatics. I explain this because so many people are surprised to find us neither. This is a temple, but none of us supposes that happiness, comfort, or any of the ordinary matters of civilized living, will desecrate it. You are not one of us. Perhaps—I hope—you will become one of us. However—do not squirm—you won't, I assure you, be annoyed. You may attend our services or not, as you choose, and you may come and go as you wish. You will show us, I am sure, the same consideration we show you, and I am equally sure that you will not interfere in any way with anything you may see—no matter how peculiar you may think it—so long as it does not promise to affect your—patient."

"Of course not," I promised.

She smiled, as if to thank me, rubbed her cigarette's end in the ash tray, and stood up, saying: "I'll show you your room."

Not a word had been said by either of us about my previous visit.

Carrying my hat and gladstone bag, I followed her to the elevator. We got out at the fifth floor.

"That is Miss Leggett's room," Aaronia Haldorn said, indicating the door that Collinson and I had taken turns knocking a couple of weeks before. "And this is yours." She opened the door that faced Gabrielle's across the corridor.

My room was a duplicate of hers, except that it was without a dressing-room. My door, like hers, had no lock.

"Where does her maid sleep?" I asked.

"In one of the servant's rooms on the top floor. Doctor Riese is with Miss Leggett now, I think. I'll tell him you have arrived."

I thanked her. She went out of my room, closing the door.

Fifteen minutes later Doctor Riese knocked and came in.

"I am glad you are here," he said, shaking hands. He had a crisp, precise way of turning out his words, sometimes emphasizing them by gesturing with the black-ribboned glasses in his hand. I never saw the glasses on his nose. "We shan't need your professional skill, I trust, but I am glad you are here."

"What's wrong?" I asked in what was meant for a tone that invited confidences.

He looked sharply at me, tapped his glasses on his left thumb-nail, and said:

"What is wrong is, so far as I know, altogether in my sphere. I know of nothing else wrong." He shook my hand again. "You'll find your part quite boring, I hope."

"But yours isn't?" I suggested.

He stopped turning away towards the door, frowned, tapped his glasses with his thumb-nail again, and said:

"No, it is not." He hesitated, as if deciding whether to say something more, decided not to, and moved to the door.

"I've a right to know what you honestly think about it," I said.

He looked sharply at me again. "I don't know what I honestly think about it." A pause. "I am not satisfied." He didn't look satisfied. "I'll be in again this evening."

He went out and shut the door. Half a minute later he opened the door, said, "Miss Leggett is extremely ill," shut the door again and went away.

I grumbled, "This is going to be a lot of fun," to myself, sat down at a window and smoked a cigarette.

A maid in black and white knocked on the door and asked me what I wanted for luncheon. She was a hearty pink and plump blonde somewhere in the middle twenties, with blue eyes that looked curiously at me and had jokes in them. I took a shot of Scotch from the bottle in my bag, ate the luncheon the maid presently returned with, and spent the afternoon in my room.

By keeping my ears open I managed to catch Minnie as she came out of her mistress's room at a little after four. The mulatto's eyes jerked wide when she saw me standing in my doorway.

"Come in," I said. "Didn't Doctor Riese tell you I was here?"

"No, sir. Are—are you—? You're not wanting anything with Miss Gabrielle?"

"Just looking out for her, seeing that nothing happens to her. And if you'll keep me wised up, let me know what she says and does, and what others say and do, you'll be helping me, and helping her; because then I won't have to bother her."

The mulatto said, "Yes, yes," readily enough, but, as far as I could learn from her brown face, my coöperative idea wasn't getting across any too well.

"How is she this afternoon?" I asked.

"She's right cheerful this afternoon, sir. She like this place."

"How'd she spend the afternoon?"

"She—I don't know, sir. She just kind of spent it—quiet like."

Not much news there. I said:

"Doctor Riese thinks she'll be better off not knowing I'm here, so you needn't say anything to her about me."

"No, sir, I sure won't," she promised, but it sounded more polite than sincere.

In the early evening Aaronia Haldorn came in and invited me down to dinner. The dining-room was paneled and furnished in dark walnut. There were ten of us at the table.

Joseph Haldorn was tall, built like a statue, and wore a black silk robe. His hair was thick, long, white, and glossy. His thick beard, trimmed round, was white and glossy. Aaronia Haldorn introduced me to him, calling him, "Joseph," as if he had no last name. All the others addressed him in the same way. He gave me a white even-toothed smile and a warm strong hand. His face, healthily pink, was without line or wrinkle. It was a tranquil face, especially the clear brown eyes, somehow making you feel at peace with the world. The same soothing quality was in his baritone voice.

He said: "We are happy to have you here."

The words were merely polite, meaningless, yet, as he said them, I actually believed that for some reason he was happy. Now I understood Gabrielle Leggett's desire to come to this place. I said that I, too, was happy to be there, and while I was saying it I actually thought I was.

Besides Joseph and his wife and their son at the table there was Mrs. Rodman, a tall frail woman with transparent skin, faded eyes, and a voice that never rose above a murmur; a man named Fleming, who was young,, dark, very thin, and wore a dark mustache and the detached air of one busy with his own thoughts; Major Jeffries, a well-tailored, carefully mannered man, stout and bald and sallow; his wife, a pleasant sort of person in spite of a kittenishness thirty years too young for her; a Miss Hillen, sharp of chin and voice, with an intensely eager manner; and Mrs. Pavlov, who was quite young, had a high-cheek-boned dark face, and avoided everybody's eyes.

The food, served by two Filipino boys, was good. There was not much conversation and none of it was religious. It wasn't so bad.

After dinner I returned to my room. I listened at Gabrielle Leggett's door for a few minutes, but heard nothing. In my room I fidgeted and smoked and waited for Doctor Riese to show up as he had promised. He didn't show up. I supposed that one of the emergencies that are regular parts of doctors' lives had kept him elsewhere, but his not coming made me irritable. Nobody went in or out of Gabrielle's room. I tiptoed over to listen at her door a couple of times. Once I heard nothing. Once I heard faint meaningless rustling sounds.

At a little after ten o'clock I heard some of the inmates going past my door, probably on their way to their rooms for the night.

At five minutes past eleven I heard Gabrielle's door open. I opened mine. Minnie Hershey was going down the corridor toward the rear of the building. I was tempted to call her, but didn't. My last attempt to get anything out of her had been a flop, and I wasn't feeling tactful enough now to stand much chance of having better luck.

By this time I had given up hopes of seeing Riese before the following day.

I switched off my lights, left my door open, and sat there in the dark, looking at the girl's door and cursing the world. I thought of Tad's blind man in a dark room hunting for a black hat that wasn't there, and knew how he felt.

At a little before midnight Minnie Hershey, in hat and coat as if she had just come in from the street, returned to Gabrielle's room. She didn't seem to see me. I stood up silently and tried to peep past her when she opened the door, but didn't have any luck.

Minnie remained there until nearly one o'clock, and when she came out she closed the door very softly, walking tiptoe. That was an unnecessary precaution on the thick carpet. Because it was unnecessary it made me nervous. I went to my door and called in a low voice:

"Minnie."

Maybe she didn't hear me. She went on tiptoeing down the corridor. That increased my jumpiness. I went after her quickly and stopped her by catching one of her wiry wrists.

Her Indian face was expressionless.

"How is she?" I asked.

"Miss Gabrielle's all right, sir. You just leave her alone," she mumbled.

"She's not all right. What's she doing now?"

"She's sleeping."

"Coked?"

She raised angry maroon eyes and let them drop again, saying nothing.

"She sent you out to get dope?" I demanded, tightening my grip on her wrist.

"She sent me out to get some—some medicine—yes, sir."

"And took some and went to sleep?"

"Y-yes, sir."

"We'll go back and take a look at her," I said.

The mulatto tried to jerk her wrist free. I held it. She said:

"You leave me alone, Mister, or else I'll yell."

"I'll leave you alone after we've had our look, maybe," I said, turning her around with my other hand on her shoulder. "So if you're going to yell you can get started right now."

She wasn't willing to go back to her mistress's room, but she didn't make me drag her. Gabrielle Leggett was lying on her side in bed, sleeping quietly, the bedclothes stirring gently with her breathing. Her small white face, at rest, with brown curls falling over it, looked like a sick child's.

I turned Minnie loose and went back to my room. Sitting there in the dark I understood why people bit their fingernails. I sat there for an hour or more, and then, God-damning myself for an old woman, I took off my shoes, picked the most comfortable chair, put my feet on another, hung a blanket over me, and went to sleep facing Gabrielle Leggett's door through my open doorway.

X · Dead Flowers

I opened my eyes drowsily, decided that I had dozed off for only a moment, closed my eyes, drifted back into slumber, and then roused myself sluggishly again. Something wasn't right.

I forced my eyes open, then closed them, and opened them again. Whatever wasn't right had to do with that. Blackness was there when they were open and when they were closed. That should have been reasonable enough: the night was dark, and my windows were out of the street lights' range. That should have been reasonable enough, but it wasn't: I remembered that I had left my door open, and the corridor lights had been on. Facing me was no pale rectangle of light framed by my doorway, with Gabrielle's door showing through.

I was too awake by now to jump up suddenly. I held my breath and listened, hearing nothing but the tick of my wrist-watch. Cautiously moving my hand, I looked at the luminous dial—3:17. I had been asleep longer than I had supposed, and the corridor light had been put out.

My head was numb, my body stiff and heavy, and there was a bad taste in my mouth. I got out from under the blanket, and out of my chairs, moving awkwardly, my muscles stubborn. I crept on stockinged feet to the door, and bumped into the door. It had been closed. When I opened it the corridor light was burning as before. The air that came in from the corridor seemed surprisingly fresh, sharp, pure.

I turned my face back into the room, sniffing. There was an odor of flowers, faint, stuffy, more the odor of a closed place in which flowers had died than of flowers themselves. Lilies of the valley, moonflowers, perhaps another one or two. I spent time trying to divide the odor into its parts, seriously trying to determine whether a trace of honeysuckle was actually present. Then I vaguely remembered having dreamed of a funeral. Trying to recall exactly what I had dreamed, I leaned against the door-frame and let sleep come into me again.

The jerking up of my neck muscles when my head had sunk too low aroused me. I wrestled my eyes open, standing there on legs that weren't part of me, stupidly wondering why I didn't go to bed. While I drowsed over the idea that there might be some reason why I shouldn't sleep, if I could only think of it, I put a hand against the wall to steady myself. The hand touched the light button. I had sense enough to push it.

Light scorched my eyes. Squinting, I could see a world that was real to me, and could remember that I had work to do. I made for the bathroom, where cold water on head and face left me still stupid and muddled, but at least partly conscious.

I turned off my lights, crossed to Gabrielle's door, listened, and heard nothing. I opened the door, stepped inside, and closed the door. My flashlight showed me an empty bed with covers thrown down across the foot. I put a hand in the hollow her body had made in the bed—cold. There was nobody in bathroom or dressing-alcove. Under the edge of the bed lay a pair of green mules, and a green dressing-gown, or something of the sort, was hanging over the back of a chair.

I went to my room for my shoes, and then walked down the front stairs, intending to go through the house from bottom to top. I would go silently first, and then, if, as was likely enough, I ran across nothing, I could start kicking in doors, turning people out of bed, and raising hell till I turned up the girl. I wanted to find her as soon as possible, but she had too long a start for a few minutes to make much difference now; so if I didn't waste any time, neither did I run.

I was half-way between the second and first floors when I saw something move below—or, rather, saw the movement of something without actually seeing it. It moved from the direction of the street-door towards the interior of the house. I was looking towards the elevator at the time as I walked down the stairs. The banister shut off my view of the street-door. What I saw was a flash of movement across half a dozen of the spaces between the banister's uprights. By the time I had brought my eyes into focus there, there was nothing to see. I thought I had seen a face, but that's what anybody would have thought in my position, and all I had actually seen was the movement of something pale.

The lobby, and what I could see of the corridors, were vacant when I reached the ground-floor. I started towards the rear of the building, and stopped. I heard, for the first time since I had awakened, a noise that I hadn't made. A shoe-sole had scuffed on the stone steps the other side of the street-door.

I walked to the front door, got one hand on the bolt, the other hand on the latch, snapped them back together, and yanked the door open with my left hand, letting my right hang within a twist of my gun.

Eric Collinson stood on the top step.

"What the hell are you doing here?" I asked sourly.

It was a long story, and he was too excited to make it a clear one. As nearly as I could untangle it from his words, he had been in the habit of phoning Doctor Riese daily for reports on Gabrielle's progress. Today —or rather yesterday—and last night, he had failed to get the doctor on the wire. He had called up as late as two o'clock this morning. Doctor Riese was not at home, he had been told, and none of the household knew where he was or why he was not at home. Collinson had then, after the two-o'clock call, come to the neighborhood of the Temple, on the chance that he might see me and get some word of the girl. He hadn't intended, he said, coming to the door until he saw me looking out.

"Until you did what?" I asked.

"Saw you."

"When?"

"A minute ago, when you looked out."

"You didn't see me," I said. "What did you see?"

"Somebody looking out, peeping out. I thought it was you, and came up from the corner where I was sitting in the car. Is Gabrielle all right?"

"Sure," I said. There was no use telling him I was hunting for her, and have him blow up on me. "Don't talk so loud. Riese's people don't know where he is?"

"No—they seem worried. But that's all right if Gabrielle's all right." He put a hand on my upper arm. "Could—could I see her? Just for a second? I won't say anything. She needn't even know I've seen her. I don't mean now—but can't you arrange it?"

This bird was young, tall, strong, and perfectly willing to have himself broken into pieces for Gabrielle Leggett. I knew something was wrong. I didn't know what. I didn't know what I would have to do to make it right, and how much help I would need. I couldn't afford to turn him away. On the other hand, I couldn't give him the low-down on the racket —that would have turned him into a wild man. I said:

"Come in. I'm on an inspection trip. You can go along if you keep quiet, and afterwards we'll see what we can do."

He came in, looking and acting as if I were St. Peter letting him into Heaven. I closed the door and led him through the lobby, down the main corridor. So far as we could see we had the joint to ourselves. And then we didn't.

Gabrielle Leggett came around a corner just ahead of us. She was barefooted. Her only clothing was a yellow silk nightgown that was splashed with dark stains. In both hands, held out in front of her as she walked, she carried a large dagger, almost a sword. It was red and wet. Her hands and bare arms were red and wet. There was a dab of blood on one of her cheeks. Her eyes were clear, bright, and calm. Her small forehead was smooth, her mouth and chin firmly set.

She walked up to me, her untroubled gaze holding my probably troubled one, and said evenly, just as if she had expected to find me there, had come there to find me:

"Take it. It is evidence. I killed him."

I said: "Huh?"

Still looking straight into my eyes, she said:

"You are a detective. Take me to where they will hang me."

It was easier to move my hand than my tongue. I took the bloody dagger from her. It was a broad, thick-bladed weapon, double-edged, with a bronze hilt like a cross.

Eric Collinson pushed past me, babbling words that nobody could have made out, going for the girl with shaking outstretched hands. She shrank over against the wall, away from him, fear in her face.

"Don't let him touch me," she begged.

"Gabrielle," he cried, reaching for her.

"No, no," she panted.

I walked into his arms, my body between him and her, facing him, pressing him back with a hand against his chest, growling at him: "Be still, you."

He took my shoulders in his big brown hands and began pushing me out of the way. I got ready to rap him on the chin with the heavy bronze dagger hilt. But we didn't have to go that far: looking over me at the girl he forgot his intentions of forcing me out of his path, and his hands went loose on my shoulders. I leaned on the hand that I had on his chest, moving him back until he was against the wall; and then stepped away from him, a little to one side, so I could see both him and her facing each other from opposite walls.

"Be still till we see what's happened," I told him, and turned to the girl, pointing the dagger at her. "What's happened?"

She was calm again.

"Come," she said. "I'll show you. Don't let Eric come, please."

"He won't bother you," I promised.

She nodded at that, gravely, and led us back down the corridor, around the corner, and up to a small iron door that stood ajar. She went through first. I followed her. Collinson was at my heels. Fresh air hit us when we went through the door. I looked up and saw dim stars in a dark sky. I looked down again. In the light that came through the open door behind us I saw that we were walking on a floor of white marble, or pentagonal tiles that imitated white marble. The place was dark except for the light from behind us. I took my flashlight out.

Walking unhurriedly on bare feet that must have found the tiled floor chilly, she led us straight to a square grayish shape that loomed up ahead. When she halted close to it and said, "There," I clicked on my light.

The light glittered and glistened on a wide altar of brilliant white, crystal, and silver.

On the lowest of the three altar steps Doctor Riese lay dead on his back.

His face was composed, as if he were sleeping. His arms were straight down at his sides. His clothes were not rumpled, though his coat and vest were unbuttoned. His shirt was all blood. There were four holes in his shirt-front, all alike, all the size and shape that the weapon the girl had given me would have made. No blood was coming from his wounds now, but when I put a hand on his forehead I found it not quite cold. There was blood on the altar steps, and on the floor below, where his noseglasses, unbroken, on the end of their black ribbon, lay.

I straightened up and swung the beam of my light into the girl's face. She blinked and squinted, but her face showed nothing except that physical discomfort.

"You killed him?" I asked.

Young Collinson came out of his trance to bawl: "No."

"Shut up." I told him, stepping closer to the girl, so he couldn't wedge himself between us. "Did you?" I asked her again.

"Are you surprised?" she inquired quietly. "You were there when my step-mother told of the cursed Dain blood in me, and of what it had done and would do to me and those who touched me. Is this," she asked, pointing at the dead man, "anything you should not have expected?"

"Don't be silly," I said while I tried to figure out her calmness. I had seen her coked to the ears before, but this wasn't that. I didn't know what this was. "Why did you kill him?"

Collinson grabbed my arm and yanked me around to face him. He was all on fire.

"We can't stand here talking," he cried. "We've got to get her out of here, away from this. We've got to hide the body, or put it some place where they'll think somebody else did it. You know how those things are done. I'll take her home. You fix it."

"Yeah?" I asked. "What'll I do? Frame it on one of the Filipino boys, so they'll hang him instead of her?"

"Yes, that's it. You know how to—"

"Like hell that's it," I said. "You've got nice ideas."

His face got redder. He stammered: "I didn't—didn't mean so they'll hang anybody, really. I wouldn't want you to do that. But couldn't it be fixed for him to get away? I—I'd make it worth his while. He could—"

"Turn it off," I growled. "You're wasting our time."

"But you've got to," he insisted. "You came here to see that nothing happened to Gabrielle and you've got to go through with it."

"Yeah? You're a smart boy."

"I know it's a lot to ask, but I'll pay—"

"Stop it." I took my arm out of his hands and turned to the girl again, asking: "Who else was here when it happened?"

"No one."

I played my light around, on the corpse and altar, all over the floor, on the walls, and saw nothing I hadn't seen before. The walls were white, smooth, and unbroken except for the door we had come through and another, exactly like it, on the other side. These four straight whitewashed walls, undecorated, rose six stories to the sky.

I put the dagger beside Riese's body, snapped off the light, and told Collinson: "We'll take Miss Leggett up to her room."

"For God's sake let's get her out of here—out of this house—now, while there's time!"

I said she'd look swell running through the streets barefooted and with nothing on but a bloodstained nightie.

I turned on the light again when I heard him making noises. He was jerking his arms out of his overcoat. He said: "I've got the car at the corner, and I can carry her to it," and started towards her with the coat held out.

She ran around to the other side of me, moaning: "Oh, don't let him touch me."

I put out an arm to stop him. It wasn't strong enough. The girl got behind me. Collinson pursued her and she came around in front. I felt like the center of a merry-go-round, and didn't like the feel of it. When Collinson came in front of me, I drove my shoulder into his side, sending him staggering over against the side of the altar. Following him, I planted myself in front of the big sap and blew off steam: "Stop it. If you want to play with us you've got to stop cutting up, and do what you're told, and let her alone. Yes or no?"

He straightened his legs under him and began: "But, man, you can't—"

"Let her alone," I said. "Let me alone. The next break you make I'm going to sock your jaw with the flat of a gun. If you want it now, say so. Will you behave?"

He muttered: "All right."

I turned around to see the girl, a gray shadow, running towards the open door, her bare feet making little noise on the tiles. My shoes made an ungodly racket as I went after her. Just inside the door I caught her with an arm around her waist. The next moment my arm was jerked away, and I was flung aside, smacking into the wall, slipping down on one knee. Collinson, looking eight feet tall in the darkness, stood close to me, storming down at me, but all I could pick out of his many words was a "damn you."

I was in a swell mood when I got up from my knee. Playing nurse-maid to a crazy girl wasn't enough: I had to be chucked around by her boy friend. I put all the hypocrisy I had into my voice when I said casually, "You oughtn't to do that," to him and went over to where the girl was standing by the door.

"We'll go up to your room now," I told her.

"Not Eric," she protested.

"He won't bother you," I promised again, hoping there'd be more truth to it this time. "Go ahead."

She hesitated, then went through the doorway. Collinson, looking partly sheepish, partly savage, and altogether discontented, followed me through. I closed the door, asking the girl if she had the key. "No," she said, as if she hadn't known there was a key.

We rode up in the elevator, the girl keeping me always between her and her fiancé, if that's what he still was. He stared fixedly at nothing. I studied her face, still trying to dope her out, to decide whether she had been shocked back into sanity or farther away from it. Looking at her, the first guess seemed likely, but I had a hunch it wasn't. We saw nobody between the altar and her room. I switched on her lights and we went in. I closed the door and put my back against it. Collinson put his overcoat and hat on a chair and stood beside them, folding his arms, looking at Gabrielle. She sat on the edge of the bed and looked at my feet.

"Tell us the whole thing, quick," I commanded.

She looked up at my face and said: "I should like to go to sleep now."

That settled the question of her sanity, so far as I was concerned: she hadn't any. But now I had another thing to worry me. This room was not exactly as it had been before. Something had been changed in it since I had been there not many minutes ago. I shut my eyes, trying to shake up my memory for a picture of it then; I opened my eyes, looking at it now.

"Can't I?" she asked.

I let her question wait while I put my gaze around the room, checking it up item by item, as well as I could. The only change I could put my finger on was Collinson's coat and hat on the chair. There was no mystery to their presence; and the chair, I decided, was what had bothered me. It still did. I went to it and picked up his coat. There was nothing under it. That's what was wrong: a green dressing-gown, or something of the sort, had been there before, and was not there now. I didn't see it elsewhere in the room, and didn't have enough confidence in its being there to search for it. The green mules were under the bed.

I said to the girl:

"Not now. Go in the bathroom and wash the blood off, and then get dressed. Take your clothes in there with you. When you're dressed, give your nightgown to Collinson." I turned to him. "Put it in your pocket and keep it there. Don't go out of the room until I come back, and don't let anybody in. I won't be gone long. Got a gun?"

"No," he said, "but I—"

The girl got up from the bed, came over to stand close in front of me, and interrupted him.

"You can't leave me here with him," she said earnestly. "I won't have it. Isn't it enough that I've killed one man tonight? Don't make me kill another." She was earnest, but not excited, speaking as if her words were quite reasonable.

"I've got to go out for a while," I said. "And you can't stay alone. Do what I tell you."

"Do you know what you're doing?" she asked in a thin, tired voice. "You can't know, or you wouldn't do it." Her back was to Collinson. She lifted her face so that I saw rather than heard the nearly soundless words her lips formed: "Not Eric. Let him go."

She had me woozy: a little more of it and I would have been ready for the cell next to hers: I was actually tempted to let her have her way. I jerked a thumb at the bathroom and said: "You can stay in there till I come back, if you want, but he'll have to stay here."

She nodded hopelessly and went into the dressing-alcove. When she crossed from there to the bathroom, carrying clothes in her arms, a tear was shiny beneath each eye.

I gave my gun to Collinson. The hand in which he took it was tight and shaky. He was making a lot of noise with his breath. I said: "Now don't be a sap. Give me some help instead of trouble for once. Nobody in or out: if you have to shoot, shoot."

He tried to say something, couldn't, grabbed my nearest hand, and did his best to disable it. I took it away from him and went down to the scene of Doctor Riese's murder. I had some difficulty in getting there. The iron door through which we had passed a few minutes ago was now locked. The lock seemed simple enough. I went at it with the fancy attachments on my pocketknife, and presently had the door open.

I didn't find the green gown inside. I didn't find Riese's body on the altar steps. It was nowhere in sight. The dagger was gone. Every trace of blood, except where the pool on the white floor had left a faintly yellow stain, was gone. Somebody had been tidying up.

XI · God

I went back to the lobby, to a recess where I had seen a telephone. The phone was there, but dead. I put it down and set out for Minnie Hershey's room on the sixth floor. I hadn't been able to do much with the mulatto so far, but she was apparently devoted to her mistress, and, with the telephone useless, I needed a messenger.

I opened the mulatto's door—lockless as the others—and went in, closing it behind me. Holding a hand over the lens of my flashlight, I snapped it on. Enough light leaked through my fingers to show me the brown girl in her bed, sleeping. The windows were closed, the atmosphere heavy, with a faint stuffiness that was familiar, the odor of a place where flowers had died.

I looked at the girl in bed. She was on her back, breathing through open mouth, her face more like an Indian's than ever with the heaviness of sleep on it. Looking at her, I felt drowsy myself. It seemed a shame to turn her out. Perhaps she was dreaming of—I shook my head, trying to clear it of the muddle settling there. Lilies of the valley, moonflowers—flowers that had died—was honeysuckle one of the flowers? The question seemed to be important. The flashlight was heavy in my hand, too heavy. Hell with it: I let it drop. It hit my foot, puzzling me: who had touched my foot? Gabrielle Leggett, asking to be saved from Eric Collinson? That didn't make sense, or did it? I tried to shake my head again, tried desperately. It weighed a ton, and would barely move from side to side. I felt myself swaying; put out a foot to steady myself. The foot and leg were weak, limber, doughy. I had to take another step or fall, took it, forced my head up and my eyes open, hunting for a place to fall, and saw the window six inches from my face.

I swayed forward till the sill caught my thighs, holding me up. My hands were on the sill. I tried to find the handles on the bottom of the window, wasn't sure that I had found them, but put everything I had into an upward heave. The window didn't budge. My hands seemed nailed down. I think I sobbed then; and, holding the sill with my right hand, I beat the glass from the center of the pane with my open left.

Air that stung like ammonia came through the opening. I put my face to it, hanging to the sill with both hands, sucking air in through mouth, nose, eyes, ears, and pores, laughing, with water from my stinging eyes trickling down into my mouth. I hung there drinking air until I was reasonably sure of my legs under me again, and of my eyesight, until I knew myself able to think and move again, though neither speedily nor surely. I couldn't afford to wait longer. I put a handkerchief over my mouth and nose and turned away from the window.

Not more than three feet away, there in the black room, a pale bright thing like a body, but not like flesh, stood writhing before me.

It was tall, yet not so tall as it seemed, because it didn't stand on the floor, but hovered with its feet a foot or more above the floor. Its feet—it had feet, but I don't know what their shape was. They had no shape, just as the thing's legs and torso, arms and hands, head and face, had no shape, no fixed form. They writhed, swelling and contracting, stretching and shrinking, not greatly, but without pause. An arm drifted into the body, was swallowed by the body, came out again as if poured out. The nose stretched down over the gaping shapeless mouth, shrank back up into the face till it was flush with the pulpy cheeks, grew out again. Eyes spread until they were one gigantic eye that blotted out the whole upper face, diminished until there was no eye, and opened in their places again. The legs were now one leg like a twisting, living pedestal, and then three, and then two. No feature or member ever stopped twisting, quivering, writhing long enough for its average outline, its proper shape, to be seen. The thing was a thing like a man who floated above the floor, with a horrible grimacing greenish face and pale flesh that was not flesh, that was visible in the dark, and that was as fluid and as unresting and as transparent as tidal water.

I knew—then—that I was off-balance from breathing the dead-flower stuff, but I couldn't—though I tried to—tell myself that I did not see this thing. It was there. It was there within reach of my hand if I leaned forward, shivering, writhing, between me and the door. I didn't believe in the supernatural—but what of that? The thing was there. It was there and it was not, I knew, a trick of luminous paint, a man with a sheet over him. I gave it up. I stood there with my handkerchief jammed to my nose and mouth, not stirring, not breathing, possibly not even letting my blood run through me. I was there, and the thing was there, and I stayed where I was.

The thing spoke, though I could not say that I actually heard the words: it was as if I simply became, through my entire body, conscious of the words:

"Down, enemy of the Lord God; down on your knees."

I stirred then, to lick my lips with a tongue drier than they were.

"Down, accursed of the Lord God, before the blow falls."

An argument was something I understood. I moved my handkerchief sufficiently to say: "Go to hell." It had a silly sound, especially in the creaking voice I had used.

The thing's body twisted convulsively, swayed, and bent towards me.

I dropped my handkerchief and reached for the thing with both hands. I got hold of the thing, and I didn't. My hands were on it, *in* it to the wrists, into the center of it, and shut on it. And there was nothing in my hands but dampness without temperature, neither warm nor cold.

That same dampness came into my face when the thing's face floated into mine. I bit at its face—yes—and my teeth closed on nothing, though I could see and feel that my face was *in* its face. And in my hands, on my arms, against my body, the thing squirmed and writhed, shuddered and shivered, swirling wildly now, breaking apart, reuniting madly in the black air.

Through the thing's transparent flesh I could see my hands clenched in the center of its damp body. I opened them, struck up and down inside it with stiff crooked fingers, trying to gouge it open; and I could see it being torn apart, could see it flowing together after my clawing fingers had passed; but all I could feel was its dampness.

Now another feeling came to me, growing quickly once it had started —of an immense suffocating weight bearing me down. This thing that had no solidity had weight, weight that was pressing me down, smothering me. My knees were going soft. I spit its face out of my mouth, tore my right hand free from its body and struck up at its face, and felt nothing but its dampness brushing my fist.

I clawed at its insides again with my left hand, tearing at this substance that was so plainly seen, so faintly felt. And then on my left hand I saw something else—blood. Blood that was dark and thick and real covered my hand, dripped from it, running out between my fingers.

I laughed and got strength to straighten my back against the monstrous weight on me, wrenching at the thing's insides again, croaking: "I'll gut you plenty." More blood came through my fingers. I tried to laugh again, triumphantly, and couldn't, choking instead. The thing's weight on me was twice what it had been. I staggered back, sagging against the wall, flattening myself against it to keep from sliding down it.

Air from the broken window, cold, pure, bitter, came over my shoulder to sting my nostrils, to tell me—by its difference from the air I had been breathing—that not the thing's weight, but the poisonous flower-smelling stuff, had been bearing me down.

The thing's greenish pale dampness squirmed over my face and body. Coughing, I stumbled through the thing, to the door, got the door open, and sprawled out in the corridor that was now as dark as the room I had just left.

As I fell, somebody fell over me. But this was no indescribable thing. It was human. The knees that hit my back were human, sharp. The grunt that blew hot breath in my ear was human, surprised. The arm my fingers caught was human, thin. I thanked God for its thinness. The corridor air was doing me a lot of good, but I was in no shape to do battle with an athlete.

I put what strength I had into my grip on the thin arm, dragging it under me as I rolled over on as much of the rest of its owner as I could cover. My other hand, flung out across the man's thin body as I rolled, struck something that was hard and metallic on the floor. Bending my wrist, I got my fingers on it, and recognized its feel: it was the over-size dagger with which Riese had been killed. The man I was lolling on had, I guessed, stood beside the door of Minnie's room, waiting to carve me when I came out; and my fall had saved me, making him miss me with the blade, tripping him. Now he was kicking, jabbing, and butting up at me from his face-down position on the floor, with my hundred and ninety pounds anchoring him there.

Holding on to the dagger, I took my right hand from his arm and spread it over the back of his head, grinding his face into the carpet, taking it easy, waiting for more of the strength that was coming back into me with each breath. A minute or two more and I would be ready to pick him up and get words out of him.

But I wasn't allowed to wait that long. Something hard pounded my right shoulder, then my back, and then struck the carpet close to our heads. Somebody was swinging a club at me.

I rolled off the skinny man. The club-swinger's feet stopped my rolling. I looped my right arm above the feet, took another rap on the back, missed the legs with my circling arm, and felt skirts against my hand. Surprised, I pulled my hand back. Another chop of the club—on my side this time—reminded me that this was no place for gallantry. I made a fist of my hand and struck back at the skirt. It folded around my fist: a meaty shin stopped my fist. The shin's owner snarled above me and backed off before I could hit out again.

Scrambling up on hands and knees, I bumped my head into wood— a door. A hand on the knob helped me up. Somewhere inches away in the dark the club swished again. The knob turned in my hand. I went in with the door, into the room, and made as little noise as I could, practically none, shutting the door.

Behind me in the room a voice said, very softly, but also very earnestly:

"Go right out of here or I'll shoot you."

It was the plump blonde maid's voice, frightened. I turned, bending low in case she did shoot. Enough of the dull gray of approaching daylight came into this room to outline a shadow sitting up in bed, holding something small and dark in one outstretched hand.

"It's me," I whispered.

"Oh, you!" She didn't lower the thing in her hand.

"You in on the racket?" I asked, risking a slow step towards the bed.

"I do what I'm told and I keep my mouth shut, but I'm not going in for strong-arm work, not for the money they're paying me."

"Swell," I said, taking more and quicker steps towards the bed. "Could I get down through this window to the floor below if I tied a couple of sheets together?"

"I don't know— Ouch! Stop!"

I had her gun—a .32 automatic—in my right hand, her wrist in my left, and was twisting them. "Let go," I ordered, and she did. Releasing her hand, I stepped back, picking up the dagger I had dropped on the foot of the bed.

I tiptoed to the door and listened. I couldn't hear anything. I opened the door slowly, and couldn't hear anything, couldn't see anything in the dim grayness that went through the door. Minnie Hershey's door was open, as I had left it when I tumbled out. The thing I had fought wasn't there. I went into Minnie's room, switching on the lights. She was lying as she had lain before, sleeping heavily. I pocketed my gun, pulled down the covers, picked Minnie up, and carried her over to the maid's room.

"See if you can bring her to life," I told the maid, dumping the mulatto on the bed beside her.

"She'll come around all right in a little while: they always do."

I said, "Yeah?" and went out, down to the fifth floor, to Gabrielle Leggett's room.

Gabrielle's room was empty. Collinson's hat and overcoat were gone; so were the clothes she had taken into the bathroom; and so was the bloody nightgown.

I cursed the pair of them, trying to show no favoritism, but probably concentrating most on Collinson; snapped off the lights; and ran down the front stairs, feeling as violent as I must have looked, battered and torn and bruised, with a red dagger in one hand, a gun in the other. For four flights of down-going I heard nothing, but when I reached the second floor a noise like small thunder was audible below me. Dashing down the remaining flight, I identified it as somebody's knocking on the front door. I hoped the somebody wore a uniform. I went to the door, unlocked it, and pulled it open.

Eric Collinson was there, wild-eyed, white-faced, and frantic.

"Where's Gaby?" he gasped.

"God damn you," I said and hit him in the face with the gun.

He drooped, bending forward, stopped himself with hands on the vestibule's opposite walls, hung there a moment, and slowly pulled himself upright again. Blood leaked from a corner of his mouth.

"Where's Gaby?" he repeated doggedly.

"Where'd you leave her?"

"Here. I was taking her away. She asked me to. She sent me out first to see if anybody was in the street. Then the door closed."

"You're a smart boy," I grumbled. "She tricked you, still trying to save you from that lousy curse. Why in hell couldn't you do what I told you? But come on; we'll have to find her."

She wasn't in any of the reception rooms off the lobby. We left the lights on in them and hurried down the main corridor.

A small figure in white pajamas sprang out of a doorway and fastened itself on me, tangling itself in my legs, all but upsetting me. Unintelligible words came out of it. I pulled it loose from me and saw that it was the boy Manuel. Tears wet his panic-stricken face and crying ruined all the words he was trying to speak.

"Take it easy, son," I said. "I can't understand a word you're saying."

I understood, "Don't let him kill her."

"Who kill who?" I asked. "And take your time."

He didn't take his time, but I managed to hear "father" and "mama."

"Your father's trying to kill your mother?" I asked, since that seemed the most likely combination.

His head went up and down.

"Where?" I asked.

He fluttered a hand at the iron door ahead. I started towards it, and stopped.

"Listen, son," I bargained. "I'd like to help your mother, but I've got to know where Miss Leggett is first. Do you know where she is?"

"In there with them," he cried. "Oh, hurry, do hurry!"

"Right. Come on, Collinson," and we raced for the iron door.

The door was closed, but not locked. I yanked it open. The altar was glaring white, crystal, and silver in an immense beam of blue-white light that slanted down from an edge of the roof.

At one end of the altar Gabrielle crouched, her face turned up into the beam of light. Her face was ghastly white and expressionless in the harsh light. Aaronia Haldorn lay on the altar step where Riese had lain. There was a dark bruise on her forehead. Her hands and feet were tied with broad white bands of cloth, her arms tied to her body. Most of her clothes had been torn off.

Joseph, white-robed, stood in front of the altar, and of his wife. He stood with both arms held high and wide-spread, his back and neck bent so that his bearded face was lifted to the sky. In his right hand he held an ordinary horn-handled carving knife, with a long curved blade. He was talking to the sky, but his back was to us, and we couldn't hear his words. As we came through the door, he lowered his arms and bent over his wife. We were still a good thirty feet from him. I bellowed:

"Joseph!"

He straightened again, turning, and when the knife came into view I saw that it was still clean, shiny.

"Who calls Joseph, a name that is no more?" he asked, and I'd be a liar if I didn't admit that, standing there—for I had halted ten feet from him, with Collinson beside me—looking at him, listening to his voice, I didn't begin to feel that perhaps, after all, nothing very terrible had been about to happen. "There is no Joseph," he went on, not waiting for an answer to his question. "You may now know, as the world shall soon know, that he who went among you as Joseph was not Joseph, but God Himself. Now that you know, go."

I should have said, "Bunk," and jumped him. To any other man, I would have. To this one I didn't. I said: "I'll have to take Miss Leggett and Mrs. Haldorn with me," and said it indecisively, almost apologetically.

He drew himself up taller, and his white-bearded face was stern.

"Go," he commanded; "go from me before your defiance leads to destruction."

Aaronia Haldorn spoke from where she lay tied on the step, spoke to me:

"Shoot. Shoot now—quick. Shoot."

I said to the man:

"I don't care what your right name is. You're going to the can. Now put your knife down."

"Blasphemer," he thundered, and took a step towards me. "Now you will die."

That should have been funny. It wasn't.

I yelled, "Stop," at him. He wouldn't stop. I was afraid. I fired. The bullet hit his cheek. I saw the hole it made. No muscle twitched in his face; not even his eyes blinked. He walked deliberately, not hurrying, towards me.

I worked the automatic's trigger, pumping six more bullets into his face and body. I saw them go in. And he came on steadily, showing in no way that he was conscious of them. His eyes and face were stern, but not angry. When he was close to me the knife in his hand went up high above his head. That's no way to fight with a knife; but he wasn't fighting: he was bringing retribution to me, and he paid as little attention to my attempts to stop him as a parent does to those of a small child he's punishing.

I was fighting. When the knife, shining over our heads, started down I went in under it, bending my right forearm against his knife-arm, driving the dagger in my left hand at his throat. I drove the heavy blade into his throat, in till the hilt's cross stopped it. Then I was through.

I didn't know I had closed my eyes until I found myself opening them. The first thing I saw was Eric Collinson kneeling beside Gabrielle Leggett, turning her face from the glaring light-beam, trying to rouse her. Next I saw Aaronia Haldorn, apparently unconscious on the altar step, with the boy Manuel crying on her and pulling with too nervous hands at her bonds. Then I saw that I was standing with my legs apart, and that Joseph was lying between my feet, dead, with the dagger through his neck.

"Thank God he wasn't really God," I mumbled to myself.

A brown body in white brushed past me, and Minnie Hershey was throwing herself down in front of Gabrielle Leggett, crying:

"Oh, Miss Gabrielle, I thought that devil had come alive and was after you again."

I went over to the mulatto and took her by the shoulder, lifting her up, asking her: "How could he? Didn't you kill him dead?"

"Yes, sir, but—"

"But you thought he might have come back in another shape?"

"Y-yes, sir. I thought he was—" She stopped and worked her lips together.

"Me?" I asked.

She nodded, not looking at me.

XII · *The Unholy Grail*

OWEN FITZSTEPHAN and I ate another of Mrs. Schindler's good dinners that evening, though my eating was a matter of catching bites between words. His curiosity poked at me with questions, requests to have this or that point made clear, and orders to keep talking whenever I stopped for breath or food.

"You could have got me in on it," he had complained before our soup was in front of us. "I knew the Haldorns, you know, or, at least, had met them once or twice at Leggett's. You could have used that as an excuse for somehow letting me in on the affair, so that I'd now have first-hand knowledge of what happened, and why; instead of having to depend on what I can get out of you and what the newspapers imagine their readers would like to think had happened."

"I had," I said, "enough grief with the one guy I did let in on it—Eric Collinson."

"Whatever trouble you had with him was your own fault, for selecting the wrong assistant, when such a better one was available. But come, my boy, I'm listening. Let's have the story, and then I can tell you where you erred."

"Sure," I agreed, "you'll be able to do that. Well, the Haldorns were originally actors. Most of what I can tell you comes from her, so a lot of maybes will have to be hung on it in spots. Fink won't talk at all; and the other help—maids, Filipino boys, Chinese cook, and the like—don't seem to know anything that helps much. None of them seems to have been let in on the trick stuff.

"As actors, Aaronia Haldorn says, she and Joseph were just pretty good, not getting on as well as they wanted to. About a year ago she ran into an old acquaintance—a one-time trouper—who had chucked the stage for the pulpit, and had made a go of it, now riding in Packards instead of day-coaches. That gave her something to think about. Thinking in that direction meant, pretty soon, thinking about Aimee, Buchman, Jeddu what's-his-name, and the other headliners. And in the end her thinking came to, why not us? They—or she: Joseph was a lightweight—rigged up a cult that pretended to be the revival of an old Gaelic church, dating from King Arthur's time, or words to that effect."

"Yes," said Fitzstephan; "Arthur Machen's. But go on."

"They brought their cult to California because everybody does, and picked San Francisco because it held less competition than Los Angeles. With them they brought a little fellow named Tom Fink who had at one time or another been in charge of the mechanical end of most of the well-known stage magicians' and illusionists' acts; and Fink's wife, a big village-smith of a woman.

"They didn't want a mob of converts: they wanted them few but wealthy. The racket got away to a slow start—until they landed Mrs. Rod-man. She fell plenty. They took her for one of her apartment buildings, and she also footed the remodeling bill. The stage mechanic Fink was in charge of the remodeling, and did a neat job. They didn't need the kitch-ens that were dotted, one to an apartment, through the building, and Fink knew how to use part of that scattered kitchen-space for concealed rooms and cabinets; and he knew how to adapt the gas and water pipes, and the electric wiring, to his hocus-pocus.

"I can't give you the mechanical details now; not till we've had time to take the joint apart. It's going to be interesting. I saw some of their work—mingled right in with it—a ghost made by an arrangement of lights thrown up on steam rising from a padded pipe that had been pushed into a dark room through a concealed opening in the wainscoating under a bed. The part of the steam that wasn't lighted was invisible in the darkness, showing only a man-shape that quivered and writhed, and that was damp and real to the touch, without any solidity. You can take my word for its being a weird stunt, especially when you've been filled up with the stuff they pumped into the room before they turned their spook loose on you. I don't know whether they used ether or chloroform or what: its odor was nicely disguised with some sort of flower perfume. This spook—I fought with it, on the level, and even thought I had it bleeding, not knowing I had cut my hand breaking a window to let air in. It was a beaut: it made a few minutes seem like a lot of hours to me.

"Till the very last, when Haldorn went wild, there wasn't anything crude about their work. They kept the services—the whole public end of the cult—as dignified and orderly and restrained as possible. The hocus-pocusing was all done in the privacy of the victim's bedroom. First the perfumed gas was pumped in. Then the illuminated steam spook was sicked on him, with a voice coming out of the same pipe—or maybe there was another arrangement for that—to give him his orders, or whatever was to be given. The gas kept him from being too sharp-eyed and suspicious, and also weakened his will, so he'd be more likely to do what he was told. It was slick enough; and I imagine they squeezed themselves out a lot of pennies that way.

"Happening in the victim's room, when he was alone, these visions had a lot of authority, and the Haldorns gave them more by the attitude they took towards them. Discussion of these visions was not absolutely prohibited, but was discouraged. They were supposed—these spook sessions —to be confidential between the victim and his God, to be too sacred to be bragged about. Mentioning them, even to Joseph, unless there was some special reason for having to mention them, was considered in bad taste, indelicate. See how nicely that would work out? The Haldorns seemed to be *not* trying to capitalize on these spook sessions, seemed not to know what took place in them, and therefore to have no interest in whether the victim carried out his spook-given instructions or not. Their stand was that that was simply and strictly a concern of the victim's and his God's."

"That's very good," Fitzstephan said, smiling delightedly, "a neat reversal of the usual cult's—the usual sect's, for that matter—insistence on confession, public testimony, or some other form of advertising the mysteries. Go on."

I tried to eat. He said:

"What of the members, the customers? How do they like their cult now? You've talked to some of them, haven't you?"

"Yeah," I said; "but what can you do with people like them? Half of them are still willing to string along with Aaronia Haldorn. I showed Mrs. Rodman one of the pipes that the spooks came out of. When she had gasped once and gulped twice she offered to take us to the cathedral and show us that the images there, including the one on the cross, were made out of even more solid and earthly materials than steam; and asked us if we would arrest the bishop on proof that no actual flesh and blood—whether divine or not—was in the monstrance. I thought O'Gar, who's a good Catholic, would blackjack her."

"The Colemans weren't there, were they? The Ralph Colemans?"

"No."

"Too bad," he said, grinning. "I must look Ralph up and question him. He'll be in hiding by now, of course, but he's worth hunting out. He always has the most consistently logical and creditable reasons for having done the most idiotic things. He is"—as if that explained it—"an advertising man." Fitzstephan frowned at the discovery that I was eating again, and said impatiently: "Talk, my boy, talk."

"You've met Haldorn," I said. "What did you think of him?"

"I saw him twice, I think. He was, undoubtedly, impressive."

"He was," I agreed. "He had what he needed. Ever talk to him?"

"No; that is, not except to exchange the polite equivalents of 'pleased to meet you.'"

"Well, he looked at you and spoke to you, and things happened inside you. I'm not the easiest guy in the world to dazzle, I hope; but he had me going. I came damned near to believing he was God toward the last. He was quite young—in his thirties: they'd had the coloring—the pigment—in his hair and beard killed to give him that Father Joseph front. His wife says she used to hypnotize him before he went into action, and that without being hypnotized he wasn't so effective on people. Later he got so that he could hypnotize himself without her help, and toward the last it became a permanent condition with him.

"She didn't know her husband had fallen for Gabrielle till after the girl had come to stay in the Temple. Until then she thought that Gabrielle was to him, as to her, just another customer—one whose recent troubles made her a very likely prospect. But Joseph had fallen for her, and wanted her. I don't know how far he had worked on her, nor even how he had worked on her, but I suppose he was sewing her up by using his hocus-pocus against her fear of the Dain curse. Anyway, Doctor Riese finally discovered that everything wasn't going well with her. Yesterday morning he told me he was coming back to see her that evening, and he did come back, but he didn't see her; and I didn't see him—not then.

"He went back to see Joseph before he came up to the girl's room, and managed to overhear Joseph giving instructions to the Finks. That should have been fine, but wasn't. Riese was foolish enough to let Joseph know he had overheard him. Joseph locked Riese up—a prisoner.

"They had cut loose on Minnie from the very beginning. She was a mulatto, and therefore susceptible to that sort of game, and she was de-voted to Gabrielle Leggett. They had chucked visions and voices at the poor girl until she was dizzy. Now they decided to make her kill Riese. They drugged him and put him on the altar. They ghosted her into think-ing that he was Satan—this is serious: they did this—come up from hell to carry Gabrielle down and keep her from becoming a saint. Minnie was ripe for it—poor boogie—and when the spirit told her that she had been selected to save her mistress, that she'd find the anointed weapon on her table, she followed the instructions the spirit gave her. She got out of bed, picked up the dagger that had been put on her table, went down to the altar, and killed Riese.

"To play safe, they pumped some of the gas into my room, to keep me slumbering while Minnie was at work. But I had been nervous, jumpy, and was sleeping in a chair in the center of the room, instead of on the bed, close to the gas-pipe; so I came out of the dope before the night was far gone.

"By this time, Aaronia Haldorn had made a couple of discoveries: first, that her husband's interest in the girl wasn't altogether financial; and second, that he had gone off center, was a dangerous maniac. Going around hypnotized all the time, what brains he had—not a whole lot to start with, she says—had become completely scrambled. His success in flimflamming his followers had gone to his head. He thought he could do anything, get away with anything. He had dreams, she says, of the entire world deluded into belief in his divinity: he didn't see why that would be any—or much —more difficult than fooling the handful that he had fooled. She thinks he actually had insane notions of his own divinity. I don't go that far. I think he knew well enough that he wasn't divine, but thought he could kid the rest of the world. These details don't make much difference: the thing is that he was a nut who saw no limit to his power.

"Aaronia Haldorn had, she says, no knowledge of Riese's murder until after it was done. Joseph, using the vision-and-voice trick, sent Gabrielle down to see the corpse on the altar step. That would fit in, you see, with his original scheme to tie her to him by playing his divinity against her curse. Apparently, he intended joining her there, and putting on an act of some sort for her. But Collinson and I interrupted that. Joseph and Gabrielle heard us talking at the door, so Joseph held back, not joining her at the altar, and she came to meet us. Joseph's plan was successful this far: the girl actually believed the curse had been responsible for Riese's death. She told us she had killed him and ought to be hanged for it.

"As soon as I saw Riese's body I knew she hadn't killed him. He was lying in an orderly position. It was plain he had been doped before being killed. Then the door leading to the altar, which I imagined was kept locked, was open, and she didn't know anything about the key. There was a chance that she had been in on the killing, but none that she had done it alone as she confessed.

"The place was scientifically equipped for eavesdropping: both of the Haldorns heard her confession. Aaronia got busy manufacturing evidence to fit the confession. She went up to Gabrielle's room and got her dressing-gown; got the bloody dagger from where I had dropped it beside the body after taking it from the girl; wrapped the dagger in the dressing-gown, and stuck them in a corner where the police could find them easy enough. Meanwhile, Joseph is working in another direction. He doesn't—as his wife does—want Gabrielle carried off to jail or the booby-hatch. He wants her. He wants her belief in her guilt and responsibility to tie her to him, not take her away. He removes Riese's remains—tucking them in one of the concealed cabinets—and has the Finks clean up the mess. He's overheard Collinson trying to persuade me to hush up the doings, and so he knows he can count on the boy—the only other exactly sane witness—to keep quiet if I'm taken care of.

"Kill yourself into a hole, and the chances are a time comes when you have to kill yourself out. To this nut Joseph now, 'taking care of' me is simply a matter of another murder. He and the Finks—though I don't think we're going to prove their part—went to work on Minnie with the spooks again. She had killed Riese docilely enough: why not me? You see, they were handicapped by not being equipped for this wholesale murdering into which they had all of a sudden plunged. For instance, except for my gun and one of the maids'—which they didn't know anything about—there wasn't a firearm in the place; and the dagger was the only other weapon—until they got to dragging in carving sets and plumber's helpers. Then, too, I suppose, there were the sleeping customers to consider—Mrs. Rodman's probable dislike for being roused by the noise of her spiritual guides ganging up on a roughneck sleuth. Anyway, the idea was that Minnie could be induced to walk up to me and stick the dagger into me in a quiet way.

"They had found the dagger again, in the dressing-gown, where Aaronia had stuck it; and Joseph began suspecting that his wife was double-crossing him. When he caught her in the acting of turning on the dead-flower stuff so strong in Minnie's room that it knocked her completely out—put her so soundly asleep that a dozen ghosts couldn't have stirred her into action—he was sure of her treachery; and, up to his neck now, decided to kill *her*."

"His wife?" Fitzstephan asked.

"Yeah, but what difference does that make? It might as well have been anybody else for all the sense it makes. I hope you're not trying to keep this nonsense straight in your mind. You know damned well all this didn't happen "

"Then what," he asked, looking puzzled, "did happen?"

"I don't know. I don't think anybody knows. I'm telling you what I saw plus the part of what Aaronia Haldorn told me which fits in with what I saw. To fit in with what I saw, most of it must have happened very nearly as I've told you. If you want to believe that it did, all right. I don't. I'd rather believe I saw things that weren't there."

"Not now," he pleaded. "Later, after you've finished the story, you can attach your ifs and buts to it, distorting and twisting it, making it as cloudy and confusing and generally hopeless as you like. But first please finish it, so I'll see it at least once in its original state before you start improving it."

"You actually believe what I've told you so far?" I asked.

He nodded, grinning, and said that he not only believed it but liked it.

"What a childish mind you've got," I said. "Let me tell you the story about the wolf that went to the little girl's grandmother's house and—"

"I always liked that one, too; but finish this one now. Joseph had decided to kill his wife."

"All right. There's not much more. While Minnie was being worked on, I popped into her room, intending to rouse her and send her for help. Before I did any rousing, I was needing some myself: I had a couple of lungfuls of the gas. The Finks must have turned the ghost loose on me, because Joseph was probably on his way downstairs with his wife at that time. He had faith enough in his divinity-shield, or he was nutty enough, to take her down and tie her on the altar before he carved her. Or maybe he had a way of fitting that stunt into his scheme, or maybe he simply had a liking for bloody theatricals. Anyway, he probably took her down there while I was up in Minnie's room going around and around with the ghost.

"The ghost had me sweating ink, and when I finally left him and tottered out into the corridor, the Finks jumped me. I say they did, and know it; but it was too dark for me to see them. I beat them off, got a gun, and went downstairs. Collinson and Gabrielle were gone from where I had left them. I found Collinson: Gabrielle had put him outside and shut the door on him. The Haldorns' son—a kid of thirteen or so—came to us with the news that Papa was about to kill Mama, and that Gabrielle was with them. I killed Haldorn, but I almost didn't. I put seven bullets in him. Hard-coated .32's go in clean, without much of a thump, true enough; but I put seven of them in him—in his face and body—standing close and firing pointblank—and he didn't even know it. That's how completely he had himself hypnotized. I finally got him down by driving the dagger through his neck."

I stopped. Fitzstephan asked: "Well?"

"Well what?"

"What happened after that?"

"Nothing," I said. "That's the kind of a story it is. I warned you there was no sense to it."

"But what was Gabrielle doing there?"

"Crouching beside the altar, looking up at the pretty spotlight."

"But why was she there? What was her reason for being there? Had she been called there again? Or was she there of her own free will? How did she come to be there? What was she there for?"

"I don't know. She didn't know. I asked her. She didn't know she was there."

"But surely you could learn something from the others?"

"Yeah," I said; "what I've told you, chiefly from Aaronia Haldorn. She and her husband ran a cult, and he went crazy and began murdering people, and how could she help it? Fink won't talk. He's a mechanic, yes; and he put in his trick-machinery for the Haldorns and operated it; but he doesn't know what happened last night. He heard a lot of noises, but it was none of his business to go poking his nose out to see what it was: the first he knew anything was wrong was when some police came and started giving him hell. Mrs. Fink's gone. The other employes probably don't really know anything, though it's a gut they could make some good guesses. Manuel, the little boy, is too frightened to talk—and will be sure to know nothing when he gets over his fright. What we're up against is this: if Joseph went crazy and committed some murders on his own hook, the others, even though they unknowingly helped him, are in the clear. The worst any of them can draw is a light sentence for taking part in the cult swindle. But if any of them admits knowing anything, then he lets himself in for trouble as an accomplice in the murder. Nobody's likely to do that."

"I see," Fitzstephan said slowly. "Joseph is dead, so Joseph did everything. How will you get around that?"

"I won't," I said; "though the police will at least try to. My end's done, so Madison Andrews told me a couple of hours ago."

"But if, as you say, you aren't satisfied that you've learned the whole truth of the affair, I should think you—"

"It's not me," I said. "There's a lot I'd like to do yet, but I was hired, this time, by Andrews, to guard her while she was in the Temple. She isn't there now, and Andrews doesn't think there's anything further to be learned about what happened there. And, as far as guarding her is necessary, her husband ought to be able to do that."

"Her what?"

"Husband."

Fitzstephan thumped his stein down on the table so that beer sloshed over the sides.

"Now there you are," he said accusingly. "You didn't tell me anything about that. God only knows how much else there is that you've not told me."

"Collinson took advantage of the confusion to carry her off to Reno, where they won't have to wait the Californian three days for their license. I didn't know they'd gone till Andrews jumped on my neck three or four hours later. He was kind of unpleasant about it, which is one of the ways we came to stop being client and operative."

"I didn't know he was opposed to Collinson as a husband for her."

"I don't know that he is, but he didn't think this the time, nor that the way, for their wedding."

"I can understand that," he said as we got up from the table. "Andrews likes to have his way in most things."

Part Three: Quesada

XIII · *The Cliff Road*

ERIC COLLINSON wired me from Quesada:

COME IMMEDIATELY STOP NEED YOU STOP TROUBLE DANGER STOP
MEET ME AT SUNSET HOTEL STOP DO NOT COMMUNICATE STOP
GABRIELLE MUST NOT KNOW STOP HURRY

                                        ERIC CARTER

The telegram came to the agency on Friday morning.

I wasn't in San Francisco that morning. I was up in Martinez dickering with a divorced wife of Phil Leach, alias a lot of names. We wanted him for spreading reams of orphan paper through the Northwest, and we wanted him badly. This ex-wife—a sweet-looking little blonde telephone operator—had a fairly recent photograph of Phil, and was willing to sell it.

"He never thought enough of me to risk passing any bum checks so I could have things," she complained. "I had to bring in my own share of the nut. So why shouldn't I make something out of him now, when I guess some tramp's getting plenty? Now how much will you give for it?"

She had an exaggerated idea of how much the photograph was worth to us, of course, but I finally made the deal with her. But it was after six when I returned to the city, too late for a train that would put me in Quesada that night. I packed a bag, got my car from the garage, and drove down.

Quesada was a one-hotel town pasted on the rocky side of a young mountain that sloped into the Pacific Ocean some eighty miles from San Francisco. Quesada's beach was too abrupt and hard and jagged for bathing, so Quesada had never got much summer-resort money. For a while it had been a hustling rum-running port, but that racket was dead now: bootleggers had learned there was more profit and less worry in handling domestic hooch than imported. Quesada had gone back to sleep.

I got there at eleven-something that night, garaged my car, and crossed the street to the Sunset Hotel. It was a low, sprawled-out, yellow building. The night clerk was alone in the lobby, a small effeminate man well past sixty who went to a lot of trouble to show me that his fingernails were rosy and shiny.

When he had read my name on the register he gave me a sealed envelope—hotel stationery—addressed to me in Eric Collinson's handwriting. I tore it open and read:

> Do not leave the hotel
> until I have seen you.
> E. C.

"How long has this been here?" I asked.

"Since about eight o'clock. Mr. Carter waited for you for more than an hour, until after the last stage came in from the railroad."

"He isn't staying here?"

"Oh, dear, no. He and his bride have got the Tooker place, down in the cove."

Collinson wasn't the sort of person to whose instructions I'd pay a whole lot of attention. I asked:

"How do you get there?"

"You'd never be able to find it at night," the clerk assured me, "unless you went all the way around by the East road, and not then, I'm sure, unless you knew the country."

"Yeah? How do you get there in the daytime?"

"You go down this street to the end, take the fork of the road on the ocean side, and follow that up along the cliff. It isn't really a road, more of a path. It's about three miles to the house, a brown house, shingled all over, on a little hill. It's easily enough found in the daytime if you remember to keep to the right, to the ocean side, all the way down. But you'd never, never in the world, be able to find—"

"Thanks," I said, not wanting to hear the story all over again.

He led me up to a room, promised to call me at five, and I was asleep by midnight.

The morning was dull, ugly, foggy, and cold when I climbed out of bed to say, "All right, thanks," into the phone. It hadn't improved much by the time I had got dressed and gone downstairs. The clerk said there was not a chance in the world of getting anything to eat in Quesada before seven o'clock.

I went out of the hotel, down the street until it became a dirt road, kept to the dirt road until it forked, and turned into the branch that bent toward the ocean. This branch was never really a road from its beginning, and soon was nothing but a rocky path climbing along the side of a rocky ledge that kept pushing closer to the water's edge. The side of the ledge became steeper and steeper, until the path was simply an irregular shelf on the face of a cliff—a shelf eight or ten feet wide in places, no more than four or five in others. Above and behind the path, the cliff rose sixty or seventy feet; below and in front, it slanted down a hundred or more to ravel out in the ocean. A breeze from the general direction of China was pushing fog over the top of the cliff, making noisy lather of sea water at its bottom.

Rounding a corner where the cliff was steepest—was, in fact, for a hundred yards or so, straight up and down—I stopped to look at a small ragged hole in the path's outer rim. The hole was perhaps six inches across, with fresh loose earth piled in a little semicircular mound on one side, scattered on the other. It wasn't exciting to look at, but it said plainly to even such a city man as I was: here a bush was uprooted not so long ago.

There was no uprooted bush in sight. I chucked my cigarette away and got down on hands and knees, putting my head out over the path's rim, looking down. I saw the bush twenty feet below. It was perched on the top of a stunted tree that grew almost parallel to the cliff, fresh brown earth sticking to the bush's roots. The next thing that caught my eye was also brown—a soft hat lying upside down between two pointed gray rocks, half-way down to the water. I looked at the bottom of the cliff and saw the feet and legs.

They were a man's feet and legs, in black shoes and dark trousers. The feet lay on the top of a water-smoothed boulder, lay on their sides, six inches apart, both pointing to the left. From the feet, dark-trousered legs slanted down into the water, disappearing beneath the surface a few inches above the knees. That was all I could see from the cliff road.

I went down the cliff, though not at that point. It was a lot too steep there to be tackled by a middle-aged fat man. A couple of hundred yards back, the path had crossed a crooked ravine that creased the cliff diagonally from top to bottom. I returned to the ravine and went down it, stumbling, sliding, sweating and swearing, but reaching the bottom all in one piece, with nothing more serious the matter with me than torn fingers, dirty clothes, and ruined shoes.

The fringe of rock that lay between cliff and ocean wasn't meant to be walked on, but I managed to travel over it most of the way, having to wade only once or twice, and then not up to my knees. But when I came to the spot where the feet and legs were I had to go waist-deep into the Pacific to lift the body, which rested on its back on the worn slanting side of a mostly submerged boulder, covered from thighs up by frothing water. I got my hands under the armpits, found solid ground for my feet, and lifted.

It was Eric Collinson's body. Bones showed through flesh and clothing on his shattered back. The back of his head—that half of it—was crushed. I dragged him out of the water and put him down on dry rocks. His dripping pockets contained a hundred and fifty-four dollars and eighty-two cents, a watch, a knife, a gold pen and pencil, papers, a couple of letters, and a memoranda book. I spread out the papers, letters, and book; and read them; and learned nothing except that what was written in them hadn't anything to do with his death. I couldn't find anything else —on him or near him—to tell me more about his death than the uprooted bush, the hat caught between rocks, and the position of his body had told me.

I left him there and went back to the ravine, panting and heaving myself up it to the cliff path, returning to where the bush had grown. I didn't find anything there in the way of significant marks, footprints, or the like. The path was chiefly hard rock. I went on along it. Presently the cliff began to bend away from the ocean, lowering the path along its side. After another half-mile there was no cliff at all, merely a bush-grown ridge at whose foot the path ran. There was no sun yet. My pants stuck disagreeably to my chilly legs. Water squunched in my torn shoes. I hadn't had any breakfast. My cigarettes had got wet. My left knee ached from a twist it had got sliding down the ravine. I cursed the detective business and slopped on along the path.

The path took me away from the sea for a while, across the neck of a wooded point that pushed the ocean back, down into a small valley, up the side of a low hill; and then I saw the house the night clerk had described.

It was a rather large two-story building, roof and walls brown-shingled, set on a hump in the ground close to where the ocean came in to take a quarter-mile u-shaped bite out of the coast. The house faced the water. I was behind it. There was nobody in sight. The ground-floor windows were closed, with drawn blinds. The second-story windows were open. Off to one side were some smaller farm buildings.

I went around to the front of the house. Wicker chairs and a table were on the screened front porch. The screened porch-door was hooked on the inside. I rattled it noisily. I rattled it off and on for at least five minutes, and got no response. I went around to the rear again, and knocked on the back door. My knocking knuckles pushed the door open half a foot. Inside was a dark kitchen and silence. I opened the door wider, knocking on it again, loudly. More silence.

I called: "Mrs. Collinson."

When no answer came I went through the kitchen and a darker dining room, found a flight of stairs, climbed them, and began poking my head into rooms.

There was nobody in the house.

In one bedroom, a .38 automatic pistol lay in the center of the floor. There was an empty shell close to it, another under a chair across the room, and a faint odor of burnt gunpowder in the air. In one corner of the ceiling was a hole that a .38 bullet could have made, and, under it on the floor, a few crumbs of plaster. The bed-clothes were smooth and undisturbed. Clothes in the closet, things on and in table and bureau, told me this was Eric Collinson's bedroom.

Next to it, according to the same sort of evidence, was Gabrielle's bedroom. Her bed had not been slept in, or had been made since being slept in. On the floor of her closet I found a black satin dress, a once-white handkerchief, and a pair of black suede slippers, all wet and muddy—the handkerchief also wet with blood. In her bathroom—in the tub—were a bath-towel and a face-towel, both stained with mud and blood, and still damp. On her dressing-table was a small piece of thick white paper that had been folded. White powder clung to one crease. I touched it with the end of my tongue—morphine.

I went back to Quesada, changed my shoes and socks, got breakfast and a supply of dry cigarettes, and asked the clerk—a dapper boy, this one —who was responsible for law and order there.

"The marshal's Dick Cotton," he told me; "but he went up to the city last night. Ben Rolly's deputy sheriff. You can likely find him over at his old man's office."

"Where's that?"

"Next door to the garage."

I found it, a one-story red brick building with wide glass windows labeled *J. King Rolly, Real Estate, Mortgages, Loans, Stocks and Bonds, Insurance, Notes, Employment Agency, Notary Public, Moving and Storage*, and a lot more that I've forgotten.

Two men were inside, sitting with their feet on a battered desk behind a battered counter. One was a man of fifty-and, with hair, eyes, and skin of indefinite, washed-out tan shades—an amiable, aimless-looking man in shabby clothes. The other was twenty years younger and in twenty years would look just like him.

"I'm hunting," I said, "for the deputy sheriff."

"Me," the younger man said, easing his feet from desk to floor. He didn't get up. Instead, he put a foot out, hooked a chair by its rounds, pulled it from the wall, and returned his feet to the desk-top. "Set down. This is Pa," wiggling a thumb at the other man. "You don't have to mind him."

"Know Eric Carter?" I asked.

"The fellow honeymooning down to the Tooker place? I didn't know his front name was Eric."

"Eric Carter," the elder Rolly said; "that's the way I made out the rent receipt for him."

"He's dead," I told them. "He fell off the cliff road last night or this morning. It could have been an accident."

The father looked at the son with round tan eyes. The son looked at me with questioning tan eyes and said: "Tch, tch, tch."

I gave him a card. He read it carefully, turning it over to see that there was nothing on its back, and passed it to his father.

"Go down and take a look at him?" I suggested.

"I guess I ought to," the deputy sheriff agreed, getting up from his chair. He was a larger man than I had supposed—as big as the dead Collinson boy—and, in spite of his slouchiness, he had a nicely muscled body.

I followed him out to a dusty car in front of the office. Rolly senior didn't go with us.

"Somebody told you about it?" the deputy sheriff asked when we were riding.

"I stumbled on him. Know who the Carters are?"

"Somebody special?"

"You heard about the Riese murder in the San Francisco temple?"

"Uh-huh, I read the papers."

"Mrs. Carter was the Gabrielle Leggett mixed up in that, and Carter was the Eric Collinson."

"Tch, tch, tch," he said.

"And her father and step-mother were killed a couple of weeks before that."

"Tch, tch, tch," he said. "What's the matter with them?"

"A family curse."

"Sure enough?"

I didn't know how seriously he meant that question, though he seemed serious enough. I hadn't got him sized up yet. However, clown or not, he was the deputy sheriff stationed at Quesada, and this was his party. He was entitled to the facts. I gave them to him as we bounced over the lumpy road, gave him all I had, from Paris in 1913 to the cliff road a couple of hours ago.

"When they came back from being married in Reno, Collinson dropped in to see me. They had to stick around for the Haldorn bunch's trial, and he wanted a quiet place to take the girl: she was still in a daze. You know Owen Fitzstephan?"

"The writer fellow that was down here a while last year? Uh-huh."

"Well, he suggested this place."

"I know. The old man mentioned it. But what'd they take them aliases for?"

"To dodge publicity, and, partly, to try to dodge something like this."

He frowned vaguely and asked:

"You mean they expected something like this?"

"Well, it's easy to say, 'I told you so,' after things happen, but I've never thought we had the answer to either of the two mix-ups she's been in. And not having the answer—how could you tell what to expect? I didn't think so much of their going off into seclusion like this while whatever was hanging over her—if anything was—was still hanging over her, but Collinson was all for it. I made him promise to wire me if he saw anything funny. Well, he did."

Rolly nodded three or four times, then asked:

"What makes you think he didn't fall off the cliff?"

"He sent for me. Something was wrong. Outside of that, too many things have happened around his wife for me to believe in accidents."

"There's the curse, though," he said.

"Yeah," I agreed, studying his indefinite face, still trying to figure him out. "But the trouble with it is it's worked out too well, too regularly. It's the first one I ever ran across that did."

He frowned over my opinion for a couple of minutes, and then stopped the car. "We'll have to get out here: the road ain't so good the rest of the way." None of it had been. "Still and all, you do hear of them working out. There's things that happen that makes a fellow think there's things in the world—in life—that he don't know much about." He frowned again as we set off afoot, and found a word he liked. "It's inscrutable," he wound up.

I let that go at that.

He went ahead up the cliff path, stopping of his own accord where the bush had been torn up, a detail I hadn't mentioned. I didn't say anything while he stared down at Collinson's body, looked searchingly up and down the face of the cliff, and then went up and down the path, bent far over, his tan eyes intent on the ground.

He wandered around for ten minutes or more, then straightened up and said: "There's nothing here that I can find. Let's go down."

I started back toward the ravine, but he said there was a better way ahead. There was. We went down it to the dead man.

Rolly looked from the corpse to the edge of the path high above us, and complained: "I don't hardly see how he could have landed just that-away."

"He didn't. I pulled him out of the water," I said, showing the deputy exactly where I had found the body.

"That would be more like it," he decided.

I sat on a rock and smoked a cigarette while he went around examining, touching, moving rocks, pebbles, and sand. He didn't seem to have any luck.

XIV · *The Crumpled Chrysler*

WE climbed to the path again and went on to the Collinsons' house. I showed Rolly the stained towels, handkerchief, dress, and slippers; the paper that had held morphine; the gun on Collinson's floor, the hole in the ceiling, and the empty shells on the floor.

"That shell under the chair is where it was," I said; "but the other —the one in the corner—was here, close to the gun, when I saw it before."

"You mean it's been moved since you were here?"

"Yeah."

"But what good would that do anybody?" he objected.

"None that I know of, but it's been moved."

He had lost interest. He was looking at the ceiling. He said:

"Two shots and one hole. I wonder. Maybe the other went out the window."

He went back to Gabrielle Collinson's bedroom and examined the black velvet gown. There were some torn places in it—down near the bottom—but no bullet-holes. He put the dress down and picked up the morphine paper from the dressing-table.

"What do you suppose this is doing here?" he asked.

"She uses it. It's one of the things her step-mother taught her."

"Tch, tch, tch. Kind of looks like she might have done it."

"Yeah?"

"You know it does. She's a dope fiend, ain't she? They had had trouble, and he sent for you, and—" He broke off, pursed his lips, then asked: "What time do you reckon he was killed?"

"I don't know. Maybe last night, on his way home from waiting for me."

"You were in the hotel all night?"

"From eleven-something till five this morning. Of course I could have sneaked out for long enough to pull a murder between those hours."

"I didn't mean nothing like that," he said. "I was just wondering. What kind of looking woman is this Mrs. Collinson-Carter? I never saw her."

"She's about twenty; five feet four or five; looks thinner than she really is; light brown hair, short and curly; big eyes that are sometimes brown and sometimes green; white skin; hardly any forehead; small mouth and teeth; pointed chin; no lobes on her ears, and they're pointed on top; been sick for a couple of months and looks it."

"Oughtn't be hard to pick her up," he said, and began poking into drawers, closets, trunks, and so on. I had poked into them on my first visit, and hadn't found anything interesting either.

"Don't look like she did any packing or took much of anything with her," he decided when he came back to where I was sitting by the dressing-table. He pointed a thick finger at the monogrammed silver toilet-set on the table. "What's the G. D. L. for?"

"Her name was Gabrielle Something Leggett before she was married."

"Oh, yes. She went away in the car, I reckon. Huh?"

"Did they have one down here?" I asked.

"He used to come to town in a Chrysler roadster when he didn't walk. She could only have took it out by the East road. We'll go out that-away and see."

Outside, I waited while he made circles around the house, finding nothing. In front of a shed where a car obviously had been kept he pointed at some tracks, and said, "Drove out this morning." I took his word for it.

We walked along a dirt road to a gravel one, and along that perhaps a mile to a gray house that stood in a group of red farm buildings. A small-boned, high-shouldered man who limped slightly was oiling a pump behind the house. Rolly called him Debro.

"Sure, Ben," he replied to Rolly's question. "She went by here about seven this morning, going like a bat out of hell. There wasn't anybody else in the car."

"How was she dressed?" I asked.

"She didn't have on any hat and a tan coat."

I asked him what he knew about the Carters: he was their nearest neighbor. He didn't know anything about them. He had talked to Carter two or three times, and thought him an agreeable enough young fellow. Once he had taken the missus over to call on Mrs. Carter, but Carter told them she was lying down, not feeling well. None of the Debros had ever seen her except at a distance, walking or riding with her husband.

"I don't guess there's anybody around here that's talked to her," he wound up, "except of course Mary Nunez."

"Mary working for them?" the deputy asked.

"Yes. What's the matter, Ben? Something the matter over there?"

"He fell off the cliff last night, and she's gone away without saying anything to anybody."

Debro whistled.

Rolly went into the house to use Debro's phone, reporting to the sheriff. I stayed outside with Debro, trying to get more—if only his opinions—out of him. All I got were expressions of amazement.

"We'll go over and see Mary," the deputy said when he came from the phone; and then, when we had left Debro, had crossed the road, and were walking through a field towards a cluster of trees: "Funny she wasn't there."

"Who is she?"

"A Mex. Lives down in the hollow with the rest of them. Her man, Pedro Nunez, is doing a life-stretch in Folsom for killing a bootlegger named Dunne in a hijacking two-three years back."

"Local killing?"

"Uh-huh. It happened down in the cove in front of the Tooker place."

We went through the trees and down a slope to where half a dozen shacks—shaped, sized, and red-leaded to resemble box-cars—lined the side of a stream, with vegetable gardens spread out behind them. In front of one of the shacks a shapeless Mexican woman in a pink-checkered dress sat on an empty canned-soup box smoking a corncob pipe and nursing a brown baby. Ragged and dirty children played between the buildings, with ragged and dirty mongrels helping them make noise. In one of the gardens a brown man in overalls that had once been blue was barely moving a hoe.

The children stopped playing to watch Rolly and me cross the stream on conveniently placed stones. The dogs came yapping to meet us, snarling and snapping around us until one of the boys chased them. We stopped in front of the woman with the baby. The deputy grinned down at the baby and said:

"Well, well, ain't he getting to be a husky son-of-a-gun!"

The woman took the pipe from her mouth long enough to complain stolidly:

"Colic all the time."

"Tch, tch, tch. Where's Mary Nunez?"

The pipe-stem pointed at the next shack.

"I thought she was working for them people at the Tooker place," he said.

"Sometimes," the woman replied indifferently.

We went to the next shack. An old woman in a gray wrapper had come to the door, watching us while stirring something in a yellow bowl.

"Where's Mary?" the deputy asked.

She spoke over her shoulder into the shack's interior, and moved aside to let another woman take her place in the doorway. This other woman was short and solidly built, somewhere in her early thirties, with intelligent dark eyes in a wide, flat face. She held a dark blanket together at her throat. The blanket hung to the floor all around her.

"Howdy, Mary," Rolly greeted her. "Why ain't you over to the Carters'?"

"I'm sick, Mr. Rolly." She spoke without accent. "Chills—so I just stayed home today."

"Tch, tch, tch. That's too bad. Have you had the doc?"

She said she hadn't. Rolly said she ought to. She said she didn't need him: she had chills often. Rolly said that might be so, but that was all the more reason for having him: it was best to play safe and have things like that looked after. She said yes but doctors took so much money, and it was bad enough being sick without having to pay for it. He said in the long run it was likely to cost folks more not having a doctor than having him. I had begun to think they were going to keep it up all day when Rolly finally brought the talk around to the Carters again, asking the woman about her work there.

She told us she had been hired two weeks ago, when they took the house. She went there each morning at nine—they never got up before ten—cooked their meals, did the housework, and left after washing the dinner dishes in the evening—usually somewhere around seven-thirty. She seemed surprised at the news that Collinson—Carter to her—had been killed and his wife had gone away. She told us that Collinson had gone out by himself, for a walk, he said, right after dinner the previous night. That was at about half-past six, dinner having been, for no especial reason, a little early. When she left for home, at a few minutes past seven, Mrs. Carter had been reading a book in the front second-story room.

Mary Nunez couldn't, or wouldn't, tell us anything on which I could base a reasonable guess at Collinson's reason for sending for me. She knew, she insisted, nothing about them except that Mrs. Carter didn't seem happy—wasn't happy. She—Mary Nunez—had figured it all out to her own satisfaction: Mrs. Carter loved someone else, but her parents had made her marry Carter; and so, of course, Carter had been killed by the other man, with whom Mrs. Carter had now run away. I couldn't get her to say that she had any grounds for this belief other than her woman's intuition, so I asked her about the Carters' visitors.

She said she had never seen any.

Rolly asked her if the Carters ever quarreled. She started to say, "No," and then, rapidly, said they did, often, and were never on good terms. Mrs. Carter didn't like to have her husband near her, and several times had told him, in Mary's hearing, that if he didn't go away from her and stay away she would kill him. I tried to pin Mary down to details, asking what had led up to these threats, how they had been worded, but she wouldn't be pinned down. All she remembered positively, she told us, was that Mrs. Carter had threatened to kill Mr. Carter if he didn't go away from her.

"That pretty well settles that," Rolly said contentedly when we had crossed the stream again and were climbing the slope toward Debro's.

"What settles what?"

"That his wife killed him."

"Think she did?"

"So do you."

I said: "No."

Rolly stopped walking and looked at me with vague worried eyes.

"Now how can you say that?" he remonstrated. "Ain't she a dope fiend? And cracked in the bargain, according to your own way of telling it? Didn't she run away? Wasn't them things she left behind torn and dirty and bloody? Didn't she threaten to kill him so much that he got scared and sent for you?"

"Mary didn't hear threats," I said. "They were warnings—about the curse. Gabrielle Collinson really believed in it, and thought enough of him to try to save him from it. I've been through that before with her. That's why she wouldn't have married him if he hadn't carried her off while she was too rattled to know what she was doing. And she was afraid on that account afterwards."

"But who's going to believe—?"

"I'm not asking anybody to believe anything," I growled, walking on again. "I'm telling you what I believe. And while I'm at it I'll tell you I believe Mary Nunez is lying when she says she didn't go to the house this morning. Maybe she didn't have anything to do with Collinson's death. Maybe she simply went there, found the Collinsons gone, saw the bloody things and the gun—kicking that shell across the floor without knowing it —and then beat it back to her shack, fixing up that chills story to keep herself out of it; having had enough of that sort of trouble when her husband was sent over. Maybe not. Anyway, that would be how nine out of ten women of her sort in her place would have played it; and I want more proof before I believe her chills just happened to hit her this morning."

"Well," the deputy sheriff asked; "if she didn't have nothing to do with it, what difference does all that make anyway?"

The answers I thought up to that were profane and insulting. I kept them to myself.

At Debro's again, we borrowed a loose-jointed touring car of at least three different makes, and drove down the East road, trying to trace the girl in the Chrysler. Our first stop was at the house of a man named Claude Baker. He was a lanky sallow person with an angular face three or four days behind the razor. His wife was probably younger than he, but looked older—a tired and faded thin woman who might have been pretty at one time. The oldest of their six children was a bowlegged, freckled girl of ten; the youngest was a fat and noisy infant in its first year. Some of the in-betweens were boys and some girls, but they all had colds in their heads. The whole Baker family came out on the porch to receive us. They hadn't seen her, they said: they were never up as early as seven o'clock. They knew the Carters by sight, but knew nothing about them. They asked more questions than Rolly and I did.

Shortly beyond the Baker house the road changed from gravel to asphalt. What we could see of the Chrysler's tracks seemed to show that it had been the last car over the road. Two miles from Baker's we stopped in front of a small bright green house surrounded by rose bushes. Rolly bawled:

"Harve! Hey, Harve!"

A big-boned man of thirty-five or so came to the door, said, "Hullo, Ben," and walked between the rose bushes to our car. His features, like his voice, were heavy, and he moved and spoke deliberately. His last name was Whidden. Rolly asked him if he had seen the Chrysler.

"Yes, Ben, I saw them," he said. "They went past around a quarter after seven this morning, hitting it up."

"They?" I asked, while Rolly asked: "Them?"

"There was a man and a woman—or a girl—in it. I didn't get a good look at them—just saw them whizz past. She was driving, a kind of small woman she looked like from here, with brown hair."

"What did the man look like?"

"Oh, he was maybe forty, and didn't look like he was very big either. A pinkish face, he had, and gray coat and hat."

"Ever see Mrs. Carter?" I asked.

"The bride living down the cove? No. I seen him, but not her. Was that her?"

I said we thought it was.

"The man wasn't him," he said. "He was somebody I never seen before."

"Know him again if you saw him?"

"I reckon I would—if I saw him going past like that."

Four miles beyond Whidden's we found the Chrysler. It was a foot or two off the road, on the left-hand side, standing on all fours with its radiator jammed into a eucalyptus tree. All its glass was shattered, and the front third of its metal was pretty well crumpled. It was empty. There was no blood in it. The deputy sheriff and I seemed to be the only people in the vicinity.

We ran around in circles, straining our eyes at the ground, and when we got through we knew what we had known at the beginning—the Chrysler had run into a eucalyptus tree. There were tire-marks on the road, and marks that could have been footprints on the ground by the car; but it was possible to find the same sort of marks in a hundred places along that, or any other, road. We got into our borrowed car again and drove on, asking questions wherever we found someone to question; and all the answers were: No, we didn't see her or them.

"What about this fellow Baker?" I asked Rolly as we turned around to go back. "Debro saw her alone. There was a man with her when she passed Whidden's. The Bakers saw nothing, and it was in their territory that the man must have joined her."

"Well," he said, argumentatively; "it could of happened that way, couldn't it?"

"Yeah, but it might be a good idea to do some more talking to them."

"If you want to," he consented without enthusiasm. "But don't go dragging me into any arguments with them. He's my wife's brother."

That made a difference. I asked:

"What sort of man is he?"

"Claude's kind of shiftless, all right. Like the old man says, he don't manage to raise nothing much but kids on that farm of his, but I never heard tell that he did anybody any harm."

"If you say he's all right, that's enough for me," I lied. "We won't bother him."

XV · *I've Killed Him*

SHERIFF FEENEY, fat, florid, and with a lot of brown mustache, and district attorney Vernon, sharp-featured, aggressive, and hungry for fame, came over from the county seat. They listened to our stories, looked the ground over, and agreed with Rolly that Gabrielle Collinson had killed her husband. When Marshal Dick Cotton—a pompous, unintelligent man in his forties—returned from San Francisco, he added his vote to the others. The coroner and his jury came to the same opinion, though officially they limited themselves to the usual "person or persons unknown," with recommendations involving the girl.

The time of Collinson's death was placed between eight and nine o'clock Friday night. No marks not apparently caused by his fall had been found on him. The pistol found in his room had been identified as his. No fingerprints were on it. I had an idea that some of the county officials half suspected me of having seen to that, though nobody said anything of that sort. Mary Nunez stuck to her story of being kept home by chills. She had a flock of Mexican witnesses to back it up. I couldn't find any to knock holes in it. We found no further trace of the man Whidden had seen. I tried the Bakers again, by myself, with no luck. The marshal's wife, a frail youngish woman with a weak pretty face and nice shy manners, who worked in the telegraph office, said Collinson had sent off his wire to me early Friday morning. He was pale and shaky, she said, with dark-rimmed, bloodshot eyes. She had supposed he was drunk, though she hadn't smelled alcohol on his breath.

Collinson's father and brother came down from San Francisco. Hubert Collinson, the father, was a big calm man who looked capable of taking as many more millions out of Pacific Coast lumber as he wanted. Laurence Collinson was a year or two older than his dead brother, and much like him in appearance. Both Collinsons were careful to say nothing that could be interpreted as suggesting they thought Gabrielle had been responsible for Eric's death, but there was little doubt that they did think so.

Hubert Collinson said quietly to me, "Go ahead; get to the bottom of it;" and thus became the fourth client for whom the agency had been concerned with Gabrielle's affairs.

Madison Andrews came down from San Francisco. He and I talked in my hotel room. He sat on a chair by the window, cut a cube of tobacco from a yellowish plug, put it in his mouth, and decided that Collinson had committed suicide.

I sat on the side of the bed, set fire to a Fatima, and contradicted him:

"He wouldn't have torn up the bush if he'd gone over willingly."

"Then it was an accident. That was a dangerous road to be walked in the dark."

"I've stopped believing in accidents," I said. "And he had sent me an SOS. And there was the gun that had been fired in his room."

He leaned forward in his chair. His eyes were hard and watchful. He was a lawyer cross-examining a witness.

"You think Gabrielle was responsible?"

I wouldn't go that far. I said:

"He was murdered. He was murdered by— I told you two weeks ago that we weren't through with that damned curse, and that the only way to get through with it was to have the Temple business sifted to the bottom."

"Yes, I remember," he said without quite sneering. "You advanced the theory that there was some connecting link between her parents' deaths and the trouble she had at the Haldorns'; but, as I recall it, you had no idea what the link might be. Don't you think that deficiency has a tendency to make your theory a little—say—vaporous?"

"Does it? Her father, step-mother, physician, and husband have been killed, one after the other, in less than two months; and her maid jailed for murder. All the people closest to her. Doesn't that look like a program? And"—I grinned at him—"are you sure it's not going further? And if it does, aren't you the next closest person to her?"

"Preposterous!" He was very much annoyed now. "We know about her parents' deaths, and about Riese's, and that there was no link between them. We know that those responsible for Riese's murder are now either dead or in prison. There's no getting around that. It's simply preposterous to say there are links between one and another of these crimes when we know there's none."

"We don't know anything of the kind," I insisted. "All we know is that we haven't found the links. Who profits—or could hope to profit—by what has happened?"

"Not a single person so far as I know."

"Suppose she died? Who'd get the estate?"

"I don't know. There are distant relations in England or France, I dare say."

"That doesn't get us very far," I growled. "Anyway, nobody's tried to kill her. It's her friends who get the knock-off."

The lawyer reminded me sourly that we couldn't say that nobody had tried to kill her—or had succeeded—until we found her. I couldn't argue with him about that. Her trail still ended where the eucalyptus tree had stopped the Chrysler.

I gave him a piece of advice before he left:

"Whatever you believe, there's no sense in your taking unnecessary chances: remember that there might be a program, and you might be next on it. It won't hurt to be careful."

He didn't thank me. He suggested, unpleasantly, that doubtless I thought he should hire private detectives to guard him.

Madison Andrews had offered a thousand-dollar reward for information leading to discovery of the girl's whereabouts. Hubert Collinson had offered another thousand, with an additional twenty-five hundred for the arrest and conviction of his son's murderer. Half the population of the county had turned bloodhound. Anywhere you went you found men walking, or even crawling, around, searching fields, paths, hills, and valleys for clues, and in the woods you were likely to find more amateur gumshoes than trees.

Her photographs had been distributed and published widely. The newspapers, from San Diego to Vancouver, gave us a tremendous play, whooping it up in all the colored ink they had. All the San Francisco and Los Angeles Continental operatives who could be pulled off other jobs were checking Quesada's exits, hunting, questioning, finding nothing. Radio broadcasters helped. The police everywhere, all the agency's branches, were stirred up.

And by Monday all this hubbub had brought us exactly nothing.

Monday afternoon I went back to San Francisco and told all my troubles to the Old Man. He listened politely, as if to some moderately interesting story that didn't concern him personally, smiled his meaningless smile, and, instead of any assistance, gave me his pleasantly expressed opinion that I'd eventually succeed in working it all out to a satisfactory conclusion.

Then he told me that Fitzstephan had phoned, trying to get in touch with me. "It may be important. He would have gone down to Quesada to find you if I hadn't told him I expected you."

I called Fitzstephan's number.

"Come up," he said. "I've got something. I don't know whether it's a fresh puzzle, or the key to a puzzle; but it's something."

I rode up Nob Hill on a cable car and was in his apartment within fifteen minutes.

"All right, spring it," I said as we sat down in his paper-, magazine-, and book-littered living room.

"Any trace of Gabrielle yet?" he asked.

"No. But spring the puzzle. Don't be literary with me, building up to climaxes and the like. I'm too crude for that—it'd only give me a bellyache. Just spread it out for me."

"You'll always be what you are," he said, trying to seem disappointed and disgusted, but not succeeding because he was—inwardly—too excited over something. "Somebody—a man—called me up early Saturday morning —half-past one—on the phone. He asked: 'Is this Fitzstephan?' I said: 'Yes;' and then the voice said: 'Well, I've killed him.' He said it just like that. I'm sure of those exact words, though they weren't very clear. There was a lot of noise on the line, and the voice seemed distant.

"I didn't know who it was—what he was talking about. I asked: 'Killed who? Who is this?' I couldn't understand any of his answer except the word 'money.' He said something about money, repeating it several times, but I could understand only that one word. There were some people here—the Marquards, Laura Joines with some man she'd brought, Ted and Sue Van Slack—and we had been in the middle of a literary free-for-all. I had a wisecrack on my tongue—something about Cabell being a romanticist in the same sense that the wooden horse was Trojan—and didn't want to be robbed of my opportunity to deliver it by this drunken joker, or whoever he was, on the phone. I couldn't make heads or tails of what he was saying, so I hung up and went back to my guests.

"It never occurred to me that the phone conversation could have had any meaning until yesterday morning, when I read about Collinson's death. I was at the Colemans', up in Ross. I went up there Saturday morning, for the week-end, having finally run Ralph to earth." He grinned. "And I made him glad enough to see me leave this morning." He became serious again. "Even after hearing of Collinson's death, I wasn't convinced that my phone call was of any importance, had any meaning. It was such a silly sort of thing. But of course I meant to tell you about it. But look—this was in my mail when I got home this morning."

He took an envelope from his pocket and tossed it over to me. It was a cheap and shiny white envelope of the kind you can buy anywhere. Its corners were dark and curled, as if it had been carried in a pocket for some time. Fitzstephan's name and address had been printed on it, with a hard pencil, by someone who was a rotten printer, or who wanted to be thought so. It was postmarked San Francisco, nine o'clock Saturday morning. Inside was a soiled and crookedly torn piece of brown wrapping paper, with one sentence—as poorly printed with pencil as the address— on it:

ANY BODY THAT WANTS MRS. CARTER
CAN HAVE SAME BY PAYING $10000——

There was no date, no salutation, no signature.

"She was seen driving away alone as late as seven Saturday morning," I said. "This was mailed here, eighty miles away, in time to be post-marked at nine—taken from the box in the first morning collection, say. That's one to get wrinkles over. But even that's not as funny as its coming to you instead of to Andrews, who's in charge of her affairs, or her father-in-law, who's got the most money."

"It is funny and it isn't," Fitzstephan replied. His lean face was eager. "There may be a point of light there. You know I recommended Quesada to Collinson, having spent a couple of months there last spring finishing *The Wall of Ashdod*, and gave him a card to a real estate dealer named Rolly—the deputy sheriff's father—there, introducing him as Eric Carter. A native of Quesada might not know she was Gabrielle Collinson, née Leggett. In that case he wouldn't know how to reach her people except through me, who had sent her and her husband there. So the letter is sent to me, but starts off *Anybody that*, to be passed on to the interested persons."

"A native might have done that," I said slowly; "or a kidnapper who wanted us to think he was a native, didn't want us to think he knew the Collinsons."

"Exactly. And as far as I know none of the natives knew my address here."

"How about Rolly?"

"Not unless Collinson gave it to him. I simply scribbled the introduction on the back of a card."

"Said anything to anybody else about the phone call and this letter?" I asked.

"I mentioned the call to the people who were here Friday night—when I thought it was a joke or a mistake. I haven't shown this to anybody else. In fact," he said, "I was a little doubtful about showing it at all—and still am. Is it going to make trouble for me?"

"Yeah, it will. But you oughtn't mind that. I thought you liked first-hand views of trouble. Better give me the names and addresses of your guests. If they and Coleman account for your whereabouts Friday night and over the week-end, nothing serious will happen to you; though you'll have to go down to Quesada and let the county officials third-degree you."

"Shall we go now?"

"I'm going back tonight. Meet me at the Sunset Hotel there in the morning. That'll give me time to work on the officials—so they won't throw you in the dungeon on sight."

I went back to the agency and put in a Quesada call. I couldn't get hold of Vernon or the sheriff, but Cotton was reachable. I gave him the information I had got from Fitzstephan, promising to produce the novelist for questioning the next morning.

The marshal said the search for the girl was still going on without results. Reports had come in that she had been seen—practically simultaneously—in Los Angeles, Eureka, Carson City, Denver, Portland, Tijuana, Ogden, San Jose, Vancouver, Porterville, and Hawaii. All except the most ridiculous reports were being run out.

The telephone company could tell me that Owen Fitzstephan's Saturday morning phone-call had not been a long distance call, and that nobody in Quesada had called a San Francisco number either Friday night or Saturday morning.

Before I left the agency I visited the Old Man again, asking him if he would try to persuade the district attorney to turn Aaronia Haldorn and Tom Fink loose on bail.

"They're not doing us any good in jail," I explained, "and, loose, they might lead us somewhere if we shadowed them. He oughtn't to mind: he knows he hasn't a chance in the world of hanging murder-raps on them as things now stack up."

The Old Man promised to do his best, and to put an operative behind each of our suspects if they were sprung.

I went over to Madison Andrews' office. When I had told him about Fitzstephan's messages, and had given him our explanation of them, the lawyer nodded his bony white-thatched head and said:

"And whether that's the true explanation or not, the county authorities will now have to give up their absurd theory that Gabrielle killed her husband."

I shook my head sidewise.

"What?" he asked explosively.

"They're going to think the messages were cooked up to clear her," I predicted.

"Is that what you think?" His jaws got lumpy in front of his ears, and his tangled eyebrows came down over his eyes.

"I hope they weren't," I said; "because if it's a trick it's a damned childish one."

"How could it be?" he demanded loudly. "Don't talk nonsense. None of us knew anything then. The body hadn't been found when—"

"Yeah," I agreed; "and that's why, if it turns out to have been a stunt, it'll hang Gabrielle."

"I don't understand you," he said disagreeably. "One minute you're talking about somebody persecuting the girl, and the next minute you're talking as if you thought she was the murderer. Just what do you think?"

"Both can be true," I replied, no less disagreeably. "And what difference does it make what I think? It'll be up to the jury when she's found. The question now is: what are you going to do about the ten-thousand-dollar demand—if it's on the level?"

"What I'm going to do is increase the reward for her recovery, with an additional reward for the arrest of her abductor."

"That's the wrong play," I said. "Enough reward money has been posted. The only way to handle a kidnapping is to come across. I don't like it any more than you do, but it's the only way. Uncertainty, nervousness, fear, disappointment, can turn even a mild kidnapper into a maniac. Buy the girl free, and then do your fighting. Pay what's asked when it's asked."

He tugged at his ragged mustache, his jaw set obstinately, his eyes worried. But the jaw won out.

"I'm damned if I'll knuckle down," he said.

"That's your business." I got up and reached for my hat. "Mine's finding Collinson's murderer, and having her killed is more likely to help me than not."

He didn't say anything.

I went down to Hubert Collinson's office. He wasn't in, but I told Laurence Collinson my story, winding up:

"Will you urge your father to put up the money? And to have it ready to pass over as soon as the kidnapper's instructions come?"

"It won't be necessary to urge him," he said immediately. "Of course we shall pay whatever is required to ensure her safety."

XVI · *The Night Hunt*

I caught the 5:25 train south. It put me in Poston, a dusty town twice Quesada's size, at 7:30; and a rattle-trap stage, in which I was the only passenger, got me to my destination half an hour later. Rain was beginning to fall as I was leaving the stage across the street from the hotel.

Jack Santos, a San Francisco reporter, came out of the telegraph office and said: "Hello. Anything new?"

"Maybe, but I'll have to give it to Vernon first."

"He's in his room in the hotel, or was ten minutes ago. You mean the ransom letter that somebody got?"

"Yeah. He's already given it out?"

"Cotton started to, but Vernon headed him off, told us to let it alone."

"Why?"

"No reason at all except that it was Cotton giving it to us." Santos pulled the corners of his thin lips down. "It's been turned into a contest between Vernon, Feeney, and Cotton to see which can get his name and picture printed most."

"They been doing anything except that?"

"How can they?" he asked disgustedly. "They spend ten hours a day trying to make the front page, ten more trying to keep the others from making it, and they've got to sleep some time."

In the hotel I gave "nothing new" to some more reporters, registered again, left my bag in my room, and went down the hall to 204. Vernon opened the door when I had knocked. He was alone, and apparently had been reading the newspapers that made a pink, green, and white pile on the bed. The room was blue-gray with cigar smoke.

This district attorney was a thirty-year-old dark-eyed man who carried his chin up and out so that it was more prominent than nature had intended, bared all his teeth when he talked, and was very conscious of being a go-getter. He shook my hand briskly and said:

"I'm glad you're back. Come in. Sit down. Are there any new developments?"

"Cotton pass you the dope I gave him?"

"Yes." Vernon posed in front of me, hands in pockets, feet far apart. "What importance do you attach to it?"

"I advised Andrews to get the money ready. He won't. The Collinsons will."

"They will," he said, as if confirming a guess I had made. "And?" He held his lips back so that his teeth remained exposed.

"Here's the letter." I gave it to him. "Fitzstephan will be down in the morning."

He nodded emphatically, carried the letter closer to the light, and examined it and its envelope minutely. When he had finished he tossed it contemptuously to the table.

"Obviously a fraud," he said. "Now what, exactly, is this Fitzstephan's—is that the name?—story?"

I told him, word for word. When that was done, he clicked his teeth together, turned to the telephone, and told someone to tell Feeney that he—Mr. Vernon, district attorney—wished to see him immediately. Ten minutes later the sheriff came in wiping rain off his big brown mustache.

Vernon jerked a thumb at me and ordered: "Tell him."

I repeated what Fitzstephan had told me. The sheriff listened with an attentiveness that turned his florid face purple and had him panting. As the last word left my mouth, the district attorney snapped his fingers and said:

"Very well. He claims there were people in his apartment when the phone call came. Make a note of their names. He claims to have been in Ross over the week-end, with the—who were they? Ralph Coleman? Very well. Sheriff, see that those things are checked up. We'll learn how much truth there is to it."

I gave the sheriff the names and addresses Fitzstephan had given me. Feeney wrote them on the back of a laundry list and puffed out to get the county's crime-detecting machinery going on them.

Vernon hadn't anything to tell me. I left him to his newspapers and went downstairs. The effeminate night clerk beckoned me over to the desk and said:

"Mr. Santos asked me to tell you that services are being held in his room tonight."

I thanked the clerk and went up to Santos' room. He, three other newshounds, and a photographer were there. The game was stud. I was sixteen dollars ahead at twelve-thirty, when I was called to the phone to listen to the district attorney's aggressive voice:

"Will you come to my room immediately?"

"Yeah." I gathered up my hat and coat, telling Santos: "Cash me in. Important call. I always have one when I get a little ahead of the game."

"Vernon?" he asked as he counted my chips.

"Yeah."

"It can't be much," he sneered, "or he'd 've sent for Red too," nodding at the photographer, "so tomorrow's readers could see him holding it in his hand."

Cotton, Feeney, and Rolly were with the district attorney. Cotton —a medium-sized man with a round dull face dimpled in the chin—was dressed in black rubber boots, slicker, and hat that were wet and muddy. He stood in the middle of the room, his round eyes looking quite proud of their owner. Feeney, straddling a chair, was playing with his mustache; and his florid face was sulky. Rolly, standing beside him, rolling a cigarette, looked vaguely amiable as usual.

Vernon closed the door behind me and said irritably:

"Cotton thinks he's discovered something. He thinks—"

Cotton came forward, chest first, interrupting:

"I don't think nothing. I know durned well—"

Vernon snapped his fingers between the marshal and me, saying, just as snappishly:

"Never mind that. We'll go out there and see."

I stopped at my room for raincoat, gun, and flashlight. We went downstairs and climbed into a muddy car. Cotton drove. Vernon sat beside him. The rest of us sat in back. Rain beat on top and curtains, trickling in through cracks.

"A hell of a night to be chasing pipe dreams," the sheriff grumbled, trying to dodge a leak.

"Dick'd do a sight better minding his own business," Rolly agreed. "What's he got to do with what don't happen in Quesada?"

"If he'd take more care of what does happen there, he wouldn't have to worry about what's down the shore," Feeney said, and he and his deputy sniggered together.

Whatever point there was to this conversation was over my head. I asked:

"What's he up to?"

"Nothing," the sheriff told me. "You'll see that it's nothing, and, by God! I'm going to give him a piece of my mind. I don't know what's the matter with Vernon, paying any attention to him at all."

That didn't mean anything to me. I peeped out between curtains. Rain and darkness shut out the scenery, but I had an idea that we were headed for some point on the East road. It was a rotten ride—wet, noisy, and bumpy. It ended in as dark, wet, and muddy a spot as any we had gone through.

Cotton switched off the lights and got out, the rest of us following, slipping and slopping in wet clay up to our ankles.

"This is too damned much," the sheriff complained.

Vernon started to say something, but the marshal was walking away, down the road. We plodded after him, keeping together more by the sound of our feet squashing in the mud than by sight. It was black.

Presently we left the road, struggled over a high wire fence, and went on with less mud under our feet, but slippery grass. We climbed a hill. Wind blew rain down it into our faces. The sheriff was panting. I was sweating. We reached the top of the hill and went down its other side, with the rustle of sea-water on rocks ahead of us. Boulders began crowding grass out of our path as the descent got steeper. Once Cotton slipped to his knees, tripping Vernon, who saved himself by grabbing me. The sheriff's panting sounded like groaning now. We turned to the left, going along in single file, the surf close beside us. We turned to the left again, climbed a slope, and halted under a low shed without walls—a wooden roof propped on a dozen posts. Ahead of us a larger building made a black blot against the almost black sky.

Cotton whispered: "Wait till I see if his car's here."

He went away. The sheriff blew out his breath and grunted: "Damn such a expedition!" Rolly sighed.

The marshal returned jubilant.

"It ain't there, so he ain't here," he said. "Come on, it'll get us out of the wet anyways."

We followed him up a muddy path between bushes to the black house, up on its back porch. We stood there while he got a window open, climbed through, and unlocked the door. Our flashlights, used for the first time now, showed us a small neat kitchen. We went in, muddying the floor.

Cotton was the only member of the party who showed any enthusiasm. His face, from hat-brim to dimpled chin, was the face of a master of ceremonies who is about to spring what he is sure will be a delightful surprise. Vernon regarded him skeptically, Feeney disgustedly, Rolly indifferently, and I—who didn't know what we were there for—no doubt curiously.

It developed that we were there to search the house. We did it, or at least Cotton did it while the rest of us pretended to help him. It was a small house. There was only one room on the ground-floor besides the kitchen, and only one—an unfinished bedroom—above. A grocer's bill and a tax-receipt in a table-drawer told me whose house it was—Harvey Whidden's. He was the big-boned deliberate man who had seen the stranger in the Chrysler with Gabrielle Collinson.

We finished the ground-floor with a blank score, and went upstairs. There, after ten minutes of poking around, we found something. Rolly pulled it out from between bed-slats and mattress. It was a small flat bundle wrapped in a white linen towel.

Cotton dropped the mattress, which he had been holding up for the deputy to look under, and joined us as we crowded around Rolly's package. Vernon took it from the deputy sheriff and unrolled it on the bed. Inside the towel were a package of hair-pins, a lace-edged white handkerchief, a silver hair-brush and comb engraved G. D. L., and a pair of black kid gloves, small and feminine.

I was more surprised than anyone else could have been.

"G. D. L.," I said, to be saying something, "could be Gabrielle Something Leggett—Mrs. Collinson's name before she was married."

Cotton said triumphantly: "You're durned right it could."

A heavy voice said from the doorway:

"Have you got a search-warrant? What the hell are you doing here if you haven't? It's burglary, and you know it."

Harvey Whidden was there. His big body, in a yellow slicker, filled the doorway. His heavy-featured face was dark and angry.

Vernon began: "Whidden, I—"

The marshal screamed, "It's him!" and pulled a gun from under his coat.

I pushed his arm as he fired at the man in the doorway. The bullet hit the wall.

Whidden's face was now more astonished than angry. He jumped back through the doorway and ran downstairs. Cotton, upset by my push, straightened himself up, cursed me, and ran out after Whidden. Vernon, Feeney, and Rolly stood staring after them.

I said: "This is good clean sport, but it makes no sense to me. What's it all about?"

Nobody told me. I said: "This comb and brush were on Mrs. Collinson's table when we searched the house, Rolly."

The deputy sheriff nodded uncertainly, still staring at the door. No noise came through it now. I asked:

"Would there be any special reason for Cotton framing Whidden?"

The sheriff said: "They ain't good friends." (I had noticed that.) "What do you think, Vern?"

The district attorney took his gaze from the door, rolled the things in their towel again, and stuffed the bundle in his pocket. "Come on," he snapped, and strode downstairs.

The front door was open. We saw nothing, heard nothing, of Cotton and Whidden. A Ford—Whidden's—stood at the front gate soaking up rain. We got into it. Vernon took the wheel, and drove to the house in the cove. We hammered at its door until it was opened by an old man in gray underwear, put there as caretaker by the sheriff.

The old man told us that Cotton had been there at eight o'clock that night, just, he said, to look around again. He, the caretaker, didn't know no reason why the marshal had to be watched, so he hadn't bothered him, letting him do what he wanted, and, so far as he knew, the marshal hadn't taken any of the Collinsons' property, though of course he might of.

Vernon and Feeney gave the old man hell, and we went back to Quesada.

Rolly was with me on the back seat. I asked him:

"Who is this Whidden? Why should Cotton pick on him?"

"Well, for one thing, Harve's got kind of a bad name, from being mixed up in the rum-running that used to go on here, and from being in trouble now and then."

"Yeah? And for another thing?"

The deputy sheriff frowned, hesitating, hunting for words; and before he had found them we were stopping in front of a vine-covered cottage on a dark street corner. The district attorney led the way to its front porch and rang the bell.

After a little while a woman's voice sounded overhead:

"Who's there?"

We had to retreat to the steps to see her—Mrs. Cotton at a second-story window.

"Dick got home yet?" Vernon asked.

"No, Mr. Vernon, he hasn't. I was getting worried. Wait a minute; I'll come down."

"Don't bother," he said. "We won't wait. I'll see him in the morning."

"No. Wait," she said urgently and vanished from the window.

A moment later she opened the front door. Her blue eyes were dark and excited. She had on a rose bathrobe.

"You needn't have bothered," the district attorney said. "There was nothing special. We got separated from him a little while ago, and just wanted to know if he'd got back yet. He's all right."

"Was—?" Her hands worked folds of her bathrobe over her thin breasts. "Was he after—after Harvey—Harvey Whidden?"

Vernon didn't look at her when he said, "Yes;" and he said it without showing his teeth. Feeney and Rolly looked as uncomfortable as Vernon.

Mrs. Cotton's face turned pink. Her lower lip trembled, blurring her words.

"Don't believe him, Mr. Vernon. Don't believe a word he tells you. Harve didn't have anything to do with those Collinsons, with neither one of them. Don't let Dick tell you he did. He didn't."

Vernon looked at his feet and didn't say anything. Rolly and Feeney were looking intently out through the open door—we were standing just inside it—at the rain. Nobody seemed to have any intention of speaking.

I asked, "No?" putting more doubt in my voice than I actually felt.

"No, he didn't," she cried, turning her face to me. "He couldn't. He couldn't have had anything to do with it." The pink went out of her face, leaving it white and desperate. "He—he was here that night—all night—from before seven until daylight."

"Where was your husband?"

"Up in the city, at his mother's."

"What's her address?"

She gave it to me, a Noe Street number.

"Did anybody—?"

"Aw, come on," the sheriff protested, still staring at the rain. "Ain't that enough?"

Mrs. Cotton turned from me to the district attorney again, taking hold of one of his arms.

"Don't tell it on me, please, Mr. Vernon," she begged. "I don't know what I'd do if it came out. But I had to tell you. I couldn't let him put it on Harve. Please, you won't tell anybody else?"

The district attorney swore that under no circumstances would he, or any of us, repeat what she had told us to anybody; and the sheriff and his deputy agreed with vigorous red-faced nods.

But when we were in the Ford again, away from her, they forgot their embarrassment and became manhunters again. Within ten minutes they had decided that Cotton, instead of going to San Francisco to his mother's Friday night, had remained in Quesada, had killed Collinson, had gone to the city to phone Fitzstephan and mail the letter, and then had returned to Quesada in time to kidnap Mrs. Collinson; planning from the first to plant the evidence against Whidden, with whom he had long been on bad terms, having always suspected what everybody else knew—that Whidden was Mrs. Cotton's lover.

The sheriff—he whose chivalry had kept me from more thoroughly questioning the woman a few minutes ago—now laughed his belly up and down.

"That's rich," he gurgled. "Him out framing Harve, and Harve getting himself a alibi in *his* bed. Dick's face ought to be a picture for Puck when we spring that on him. Let's find him tonight."

"Better wait," I advised. "It won't hurt to check up his San Francisco trip before we put it to him. All we've got on him so far is that he tried to frame Whidden. If he's the murderer and kidnapper he seems to have gone to a lot of unnecessary foolishness."

Feeney scowled at me and defended their theory:

"Maybe he was more interested in framing Harve than anything else."

"Maybe," I said; "but it won't hurt to give him a little more rope and see what he does with it."

Feeney was against that. He wanted to grab the marshal *pronto;* but Vernon reluctantly backed me up. We dropped Rolly at his house and returned to the hotel.

In my room, I put in a phone-call for the agency in San Francisco. While I was waiting for the connection knuckles tapped my door. I opened it and let in Jack Santos, pajamaed, bathrobed, and slippered.

"Have a nice ride?" he asked, yawning.

"Swell."

"Anything break?"

"Not for publication, but—under the hat—the new angle is that our marshal is trying to hang the job on his wife's boy friend—with home-made evidence. The other big officials think Cotton turned the trick himself."

"That ought to get them all on the front page." Santos sat on the foot of my bed and lit a cigarette. "Ever happen to hear that Feeney was Cotton's rival for the telegraphing hand of the present Mrs. Cotton, until she picked the marshal—the triumph of dimples over mustachios?"

"No," I admitted. "What of it?"

"How do I know? I just happened to pick it up. A fellow in the garage told me."

"How long ago?"

"That they were rival suitors? Less than a couple of years."

I got my San Francisco call, and told Field—the agency night-man—to have somebody check up the marshal's Noe Street visit. Santos yawned and went out while I was talking. I went to bed when I had finished.

XVII · *Below Dull Point*

THE telephone bell brought me out of sleep a little before ten the following morning. Mickey Linehan, talking from San Francisco, told me Cotton had arrived at his mother's house at between seven and seven-thirty Saturday morning. The marshal had slept for five or six hours —telling his mother he had been up all night laying for a burglar—and had left for home at six that evening.

Cotton was coming in from the street when I reached the lobby. He was red-eyed and weary, but still determined.

"Catch Whidden?" I asked.

"No, durn him, but I will. Say, I'm glad you jiggled my arm, even if it did let him get away. I—well, sometimes a fellow's enthusiasm gets the best of his judgment."

"Yeah. We stopped at your house on our way back, to see how you'd made out."

"I ain't been home yet," he said. "I put in the whole durned night hunting for that fellow. Where's Vern and Feeney?"

"Pounding their ears. Better get some sleep yourself," I suggested. "I'll ring you up if anything happens."

He set off for home. I went into the café for breakfast. I was half through when Vernon joined me there. He had telegrams from the San Francisco police department and the Marin County sheriff's office, confirming Fitzstephan's alibis.

"I got my report on Cotton," I said. "He reached his mother's at seven or a little after Saturday morning, and left at six that evening."

"Seven or a little after?" Vernon didn't like that. If the marshal had been in San Francisco at that time he could hardly have been abducting the girl. "Are you sure?"

"No, but that's the best we've been able to do so far. There's Fitzstephan now." Looking through the café door, I had seen the novelist's lanky back at the hotel desk. "Excuse me a moment."

I went over and got Fitzstephan, bringing him back to the table with me, and introducing him to Vernon. The district attorney stood up to shake hands with him, but was too busy with thoughts of Cotton to bother now with anything else. Fitzstephan said he had had breakfast before leaving the city, and ordered a cup of coffee. Just then I was called to the phone.

Cotton's voice, but excited almost beyond recognition:

"For God's sake get Vernon and Feeney and come up here."

"What's the matter?" I asked.

"Hurry! Something awful's happened. Hurry!" he cried, and hung up.

I went back to the table and told Vernon about it. He jumped up, upsetting Fitzstephan's coffee. Fitzstephan got up too, but hesitated, looking at me.

"Come on," I invited him. "Maybe this'll be one of the things you like."

Fitzstephan's car was in front of the hotel. The marshal's house was only seven blocks away. Its front door was open. Vernon knocked on the frame as we went in, but we didn't wait for an answer.

Cotton met us in the hall. His eyes were round and bloodshot in a face as hard-white as marble. He tried to say something, but couldn't get the words past his tight-set teeth. He gestured towards the door behind him with a fist that was clenched on a piece of brown paper.

Through the doorway we saw Mrs. Cotton. She was lying on the blue-carpeted floor. She had on a pale blue dress. Her throat was covered with dark bruises. Her lips and tongue—the tongue, swollen, hung out—were darker than the bruises. Her eyes were wide open, bulging, up-turned, and dead. Her hand, when I touched it, was still warm.

Cotton, following us into the room, held out the brown paper in his hand. It was an irregularly torn piece of wrapping paper, covered on both sides with writing—nervously, unevenly, hastily scribbled in pencil. A softer pencil had been used than on Fitzstephan's message, and the paper was a darker brown.

I was closest to Cotton. I took the paper, and read it aloud hurriedly, skipping unnecessary words:

"Whidden came last night . . . said husband after him . . . frame him for Collinson trouble . . . I hid him in garret . . . he said only way to save him was to say he was here Friday night . . . said if I didn't they'd hang him . . . when Mr. Vernon came Harve said he'd kill me if I didn't . . . so I said it . . . but he wasn't here that night . . . I didn't know he was guilty then . . . told me afterwards . . . tried to kidnap her Thursday night . . . husband nearly caught him . . . came in office after Collinson sent telegram and saw it . . . followed him and killed him . . . went to San Francisco, drinking whiskey . . . decided to go through with kid-napping anyway . . . phoned man who knew her to try to learn who he could get money from . . . too drunk to talk good . . . wrote letter and came back . . . met her on road . . . took her to old bootleggers' hiding place somewhere below Dull Point . . . goes in boat . . . afraid he'll kill me . . . locked in garret . . . writing while he's down getting food . . . murderer . . . I won't help him . . . Daisy Cotton."

The sheriff and Rolly had arrived while I was reading it. Feeney's face was as white and set as Cotton's.

Vernon bared his teeth at the marshal, snarling:

"You wrote that."

Feeney grabbed it from my hands, looked at it, shook his head, and said hoarsely:

"No, that's her writing, all right."

Cotton was babbling:

"No, before God, I didn't. I planted that stuff on him, I'll admit that, but that was all. I come home and find her like this. I swear to God!"

"Where were you Friday night?" Vernon asked.

"Here, watching the house. I thought—I thought he might— But he wasn't here that night. I watched till daybreak and then went to the city. I didn't—"

The sheriff's bellow drowned the rest of Cotton's words. The sheriff was waving the dead woman's letter. He bellowed:

"Below Dull Point! What are we waiting for?"

He plunged out of the house, the rest of us following. Cotton and Rolly rode to the waterfront in the deputy's car. Vernon, the sheriff, and

I rode with Fitzstephan. The sheriff cried throughout the short trip, tears splashing on the automatic pistol he held in his lap.

At the waterfront we changed from the cars to a green and white motor boat run by a pink-cheeked, tow-headed youngster called Tim. Tim said he didn't know anything about any bootleggers' hiding places below Dull Point, but if there was one there he could find it. In his hands the boat produced a lot of speed, but not enough for Feeney and Cotton. They stood together in the bow, guns in their fists, dividing their time between straining forward and yelling back for more speed.

Half an hour from the dock, we rounded a blunt promontory that the others called Dull Point, and Tim cut down our speed, putting the boat in closer to the rocks that jumped up high and sharp at the water's edge. We were now all eyes—eyes that soon ached from staring under the noon sun but kept on staring. Twice we saw clefts in the rock-walled shore, pushed hopefully in to them, saw that they were blind, leading nowhere, opening into no hiding-places.

The third cleft was even more hopeless-looking at first sight, but, now that Dull Point was some distance behind us, we couldn't pass up anything. We slid in to the cleft, got close enough to decide that it was another blind one, gave it up, and told Tim to go on. We were washed another couple of feet nearer before the tow-headed boy could bring the boat around.

Cotton, in the bow, bent forward from the waist and yelled:

"Here it is."

He pointed his gun at one side of the cleft. Tim let the boat drift in another foot or so. Craning our necks, we could see that what we had taken for the shore-line on that side was actually a high, thin, saw-toothed ledge of rock, separated from the cliff at this end by twenty feet of water.

"Put her in," Feeney ordered.

Tim frowned at the water, hesitated, said: "She can't make it."

The boat backed him up by shuddering suddenly under our feet, with an unpleasant rasping noise.

"That be damned!" the sheriff bawled. "Put her in."

Tim took a look at the sheriff's wild face, and put her in.

The boat shuddered under our feet again, more violently, and now there was a tearing sound in with the rasping, but we went through the opening and turned down behind the saw-tooth ledge.

We were in a v-shaped pocket, twenty feet wide where we had come in, say eighty feet long, high-walled, inaccessible by land, accessible by sea only as we had come. The water that floated us—and was coming in rapidly to sink us—ran a third of the way down the pocket. White sand paved the other two thirds. A small boat was resting its nose on the edge of the sand. It was empty. Nobody was in sight. There didn't seem to be anywhere for anybody to hide. There were footprints, large and small, in the sand, empty tin cans, and the remains of a fire.

"Harve's," Rolly said, nodding at the boat.

Our boat grounded beside it. We jumped, splashed, ashore—Cotton ahead, the others spread out behind him.

As suddenly as if he had sprung out of the air, Harvey Whidden appeared in the far end of the v, standing in the sand, a rifle in his hands. Anger and utter astonishment were mixed in his heavy face, and in his voice when he yelled:

"You God-damned double-crossing—" The noise his rifle made blotted out the rest of his words.

Cotton had thrown himself down sideways. The rifle bullet missed him by inches, sang between Fitzstephan and me, nicking his hat-brim, and splattered on the rocks behind. Four of our guns went off together, some more than once.

Whidden went over backwards, his feet flying in the air. He was dead when we got to him—three bullets in his chest, one in his head.

We found Gabrielle Collinson cowering back in the corner of a narrow-mouthed hole in the rock wall—a long triangular cave whose mouth had been hidden from our view by the slant at which it was set. There were blankets in there, spread over a pile of dried seaweed, some canned goods, a lantern, and another rifle.

The girl's small face was flushed and feverish, and her voice was hoarse: she had a cold in her chest. She was too frightened at first to tell us anything coherent, and apparently recognized neither Fitzstephan nor me.

The boat we had come in was out of commission. Whidden's boat couldn't be trusted to carry more than three with safety through the surf. Tim and Rolly set off for Quesada in it, to get us a larger vessel. It was an hour-and-a-half's round trip. While they were gone we worked on the girl, soothing her, assuring her that she was among friends, that there was nothing to be afraid of now. Her eyes gradually became less scary, her breathing easier, and her nails less tightly pressed into her palms. At the end of an hour she was answering our questions.

She said she knew nothing of Whidden's attempt to kidnap her Thursday night, nothing of the telegram Eric had sent me. She sat up all Friday night waiting for him to return from his walk, and at daylight, frantic at his failure to return, had gone to look for him. She found him—as I had. Then she went back to the house and tried to commit suicide—to put an end to the curse by shooting herself.

"I tried twice," she whispered; "but I couldn't. I couldn't. I was too much a coward. I couldn't keep the pistol pointing at myself while I did it. I tried the first time to shoot myself in the temple, and then in the breast; but I hadn't the courage. Each time I jerked it away just before I fired. And after the second time I couldn't even get courage to try again."

She changed her clothes then—evening clothes, now muddy and torn from her search—and drove away from the house. She didn't say where she had intended going. She didn't seem to know. Probably she hadn't had any destination—was simply going away from the place where the curse had settled on her husband.

She hadn't driven far when she had seen a machine coming towards her, driven by the man who had brought her here. He had turned his car across the road in front of her, blocking the road. Trying to avoid hitting his car, she had run into a tree—and hadn't known anything else until she had awakened in the cave. She had been here since then. The man had left her here alone most of the time. She had neither strength nor courage to escape by swimming, and there was no other way out.

The man had told her nothing, had asked her nothing, had addressed no words to her except to say, "Here's some food," or, "Till I bring you some water, you'll have to get along on canned tomatoes when you're thirsty," or other things of that sort. She never remembered having seen him before. She didn't know his name. He was the only man she had seen since her husband's death.

"What did he call you?" I asked. "Mrs. Carter? Or Mrs. Collinson?"

She frowned thoughtfully, then shook her head, saying:

"I don't think he ever called me by name. He never spoke unless he had to, and he wasn't here very much. I was usually alone."

"How long had he been here this time?"

"Since before daylight. The noise of his boat woke me up."

"Sure? This is important. Are you sure he's been here since daylight?"

"Yes."

I was sitting on my heels in front of her. Cotton was standing on my left, beside the sheriff. I looked up at the marshal and said:

"That puts it up to you, Cotton. Your wife was still warm when we saw her—after eleven."

He goggled at me, stammering: "Wh-what's that you say?"

On the other side of me I heard Vernon's teeth click together sharply.

I said:

"Your wife was afraid Whidden would kill her, and wrote that statement. But he didn't kill her. He's been here since daylight. You found the statement, learned from it that they *had* been too friendly. Well, what did you do then?"

"That's a lie," he cried. "There ain't a word of truth in it. She was dead there when I found her. I never—"

"You killed her," Vernon barked at him over my head. "You choked her, counting on that statement to throw suspicion on Whidden."

"That's a lie," the marshal cried again, and made the mistake of trying to get his gun out.

Feeney slugged him, dropping him, and had handcuffs on his wrists before he could get up again.

XVIII · *The Pineapple*

"It doesn't make sense," I said. "It's dizzy. When we grab our man—or woman—we're going to find it's a goof, and Napa will get it instead of the gallows."

"That," Owen Fitzstephan said, "is characteristic of you. You're stumped, bewildered, flabbergasted. Do you admit you've met your master, have run into a criminal too wily for you? Not you. He's outwitted you: therefore he's an idiot or a lunatic. Now really. Of course there's a certain unexpected modesty to that attitude."

"But he's got to be goofy," I insisted. "Look: Mayenne marries—"

"Are you," he asked disgustedly, "going to recite that catalogue again?"

"You've got a flighty mind. That's no good in this business. You don't catch murderers by amusing yourself with interesting thoughts. You've got to sit down to all the facts you can get and turn them over and over till they click."

"If that's your technic, you'll have to put up with it," he said; "but I'm damned if I see why I should suffer. You recited the Mayenne-Leggett-Collinson history step by step last night at least half a dozen times. You've done nothing else since breakfast this morning. I'm getting enough of it. Nobody's mysteries ought to be as tiresome as you're making this one."

"Hell," I said; "I sat up half the night after you went to bed and recited it to myself. You got to turn them over and over, my boy, till they click."

"I like the Nick Carter school better. Aren't you even threatened with any of the conclusions that this turning-them-over-and-over is supposed to lead to?"

"Yeah, I've got one. It's that Vernon and Feeney are wrong in thinking that Cotton was working with Whidden on the kidnapping, and double-crossed him. According to them, Cotton thought up the plan and persuaded Whidden to do the rough stuff while the marshal used his official position to cover him up. Collinson stumbled on the plan and was killed. Then Cotton made his wife write that statement—it's phony, right enough, was dictated to her—killed her, and led us to Whidden. Cotton was the first man ashore when we got to the hiding place—to make sure Whidden was killed resisting arrest before he could talk."

Fitzstephan ran long fingers through his sorrel hair and asked:

"Don't you think jealousy would have given Cotton motive enough?"

"Yeah. But where's Whidden's motive for putting himself in Cotton's hands? Besides, where does that layout fit in with the Temple racket?"

"Are you sure," Fitzstephan asked, "that you're right in thinking there must be a connection?"

"Yeah. Gabrielle's father, step-mother, physician, and husband have been slaughtered in less than a handful of weeks—all the people closest to her. That's enough to tie it all together for me. If you want more links, I can point them out to you. Upton and Ruppert were the apparent instigators of the first trouble, and got killed. Haldorn of the second, and got killed. Whidden of the third, and got killed. Mrs. Leggett killed her husband; Cotton apparently killed his wife; and Haldorn would have killed his if I hadn't blocked him. Gabrielle, as a child, was made to kill her mother; Gabrielle's maid was made to kill Riese, and nearly me. Leggett left behind him a statement explaining—not altogether satisfactorily —everything, and was killed. So did and was Mrs. Cotton. Call any of these pairs coincidences. Call any couple of pairs coincidences. You'll still have enough left to point at somebody who's got a system he likes, and sticks to it."

Fitzstephan squinted thoughtfully at me, agreeing:

"There may be something in that. It does, as you put it, look like the work of one mind."

"And a goofy one."

"Be obstinate about it," he said. "But even your goof must have a motive."

"Why?"

"Damn your sort of mind," he said with good-natured impatience. "If he had no motive connected with Gabrielle, why should his crimes be connected with her?"

"We don't know that all of them are," I pointed out. "We only know of the ones that are."

He grinned and said:

"You'll go any distance to disagree, won't you?"

I said:

"Then again, maybe the goof's crimes are connected with Gabrielle because he is."

Fitzstephan let his gray eyes go sleepy over that, pursing his mouth, looking at the door closed between my room and Gabrielle's.

"All right," he said, looking at me again. "Who's your maniac close to Gabrielle?"

"The closest and goofiest person to Gabrielle is Gabrielle herself."

Fitzstephan got up and crossed the hotel room—I was sitting on the edge of the bed—to shake my hand with solemn enthusiasm.

"You're wonderful," he said. "You amaze me. Ever have night sweats? Put out your tongue and say, 'Ah.'"

"Suppose," I began, but was interrupted by a feeble tapping on the corridor door.

I went to the door and opened it. A thin man of my own age and height in wrinkled black clothes stood in the corridor. He was breathing heavily through a red-veined nose, and his small brown eyes were timid.

"You know me," he said apologetically.

"Yeah. Come in." I introduced him to Fitzstephan: "This is the Tom Fink who was one of Haldorn's helpers in the Temple of the Holy Grail."

Fink looked reproachfully at me, then dragged his crumpled hat from his head and crossed the room to shake Fitzstephan's hand. That done, he returned to me and said, almost whispering:

"I come down to tell you something."

"Yeah?"

He fidgeted, turning his hat around and around in his hands. I winked at Fitzstephan and went out with Fink. In the corridor, I closed the door and stopped, saying: "Let's have it."

Fink rubbed his lips with his tongue and then with the back of one scrawny hand. He said, in his half-whisper:

"I come down to tell you something I thought you ought to know."

"Yeah?"

"It's about this fellow Whidden that was killed."

"Yeah?"

"He was—"

The door to my room split open. Floors, walls, and ceiling wriggled under, around, and over us. There was too much noise to be heard—a roar that was felt bodily. Tom Fink was carried away from me, backward. I had sense enough to throw myself down as I was blown in the opposite direction, and got nothing worse out of it than a bruised shoulder when I hit the wall. A door-frame stopped Fink, wickedly, its edge catching the back of his head. He came forward again, folding over to lie face-down on the floor, still except for blood running from his head.

I got up and made for my room. Fitzstephan was a mangled pile of flesh and clothing in the center of the floor. My bed was burning. There was neither glass nor wire netting left in the window. I saw these things mechanically as I staggered toward Gabrielle's room. The connecting door was open—perhaps blown open.

She was crouching on all fours in bed, facing the foot, her feet on the pillows. Her nightdress was torn at one shoulder. Her green-brown eyes—glittering under brown curls that had tumbled down to hide her forehead—were the eyes of an animal gone trap-crazy. Saliva glistened on her pointed chin. There was nobody else in the room.

"Where's the nurse?" My voice was choked.

The girl said nothing. Her eyes kept their crazy terror focused on me.

"Get under the covers," I ordered. "Want to get pneumonia?"

She didn't move. I walked around to the side of the bed, lifting an end of the covers with one hand, reaching out the other to help her, saying:

"Come on, get inside."

She made a queer noise deep in her chest, dropped her head, and put her sharp teeth into the back of my hand. It hurt. I put her under the covers, returned to my room, and was pushing my burning mattress through the window when people began to arrive.

"Get a doctor," I called to the first of them; "and stay out of here."

I had got rid of the mattress by the time Mickey Linehan pushed through the crowd that was now filling the corridor. Mickey blinked at what was left of Fitzstephan, at me, and asked:

"What the hell?"

His big loose mouth sagged at the ends, looking like a grin turned upside down.

I licked burnt fingers and asked unpleasantly:

"What the hell does it look like?"

"More trouble, sure." The grin turned right side up on his red face. "Sure—you're here."

Ben Rolly came in. "Tch, tch, tch," he said, looking around. "What do you suppose happened?"

"Pineapple," I said.

"Tch, tch, tch."

Doctor George came in and knelt beside the wreck of Fitzstephan. George had been Gabrielle's physician since her return from the cave the previous day. He was a short, chunky, middle-aged man with a lot of black hair everywhere except on his lips, cheeks, chin, and nose-bridge. His hairy hands moved over Fitzstephan.

"What's Fink been doing?" I asked Mickey.

"Hardly any. I got on his tail when they sprung him yesterday noon. He went from the hoosegow to a hotel on Kearny Street and got himself a room. He spent most of the afternoon in the Public Library, reading the newspaper files on the girl's troubles, from beginning to date. He ate after that, and went back to the hotel. He could have back-doored me. If he didn't, he camped in his room all night. It was dark at midnight when I knocked off so I could be on the job again at six a. m. He showed at seven-something, got breakfast, and grabbed a rattler for Poston, changed to the stage for here, and came straight to the hotel, asking for you. That's the crop."

"Damn my soul!" the kneeling doctor exclaimed. "The man's not dead."

I didn't believe him. Fitzstephan's right arm was gone, and most of his right leg. His body was too twisted to see what was left of it, but there was only one side to his face. I said:

"There's another one out in the hall, with his head knocked in."

"Oh, he's all right," the doctor muttered without looking up. "But this one—well, damn my soul!"

He scrambled to his feet and began ordering this and that. He was excited. A couple of men came in from the corridor. The woman who had been nursing Gabrielle Collinson—a Mrs. Herman—joined them, and another man with a blanket. They took Fitzstephan away.

"That fellow out in the hall Fink?" Rolly asked.

"Yeah." I told him what Fink had told me, adding: "He hadn't finished when the blow-up came."

"Suppose the bomb was meant for him, meant to keep him from finishing?"

Mickey said: "Nobody followed him down from the city, except me."

"Maybe," I said. "Better see what they're doing with him, Mick."

Mickey went out.

"This window was closed," I told Rolly. "There was no noise as of something being thrown through the glass just before the explosion; and there's no broken window-glass inside the room. The screen was over it, too, so we can say the pineapple wasn't chucked in through the window."

Rolly nodded vaguely, looking at the door to Gabrielle's room.

"Fink and I were in the corridor talking," I went on. "I ran straight back through here to her room. Nobody could have got out of her room after the explosion without my seeing them—or hearing them. There wasn't finger-snapping time between my losing sight of her corridor-door from the outside, and seeing it again from the inside. The screen over her window is still O K."

"Mrs. Herman wasn't in there with her?" Rolly asked.

"She was supposed to be, but wasn't. We'll find out about that. There's no use thinking Mrs. Collinson chucked the bomb. She's been in bed since we brought her back from Dull Point yesterday. She couldn't have had the bomb planted there because she had no way of knowing that she was going to occupy the room. Nobody's been in there since except you, Feeney, Vernon, the doctor, the nurse, and me."

"I wasn't going to say she had anything to do with it," the deputy sheriff mumbled. "What does she say?"

"Nothing yet. We'll try her now, though I doubt if it'll get us much."

It didn't. Gabrielle lay in the middle of the bed, the covers gathered close to her chin as if she was prepared to duck down under them at the first alarm, and shook her head No to everything we asked, whether the answer fit or didn't.

The nurse came in, a big-breasted, red-haired woman of forty-something with a face that seemed honest because it was homely, freckled, and blue-eyed. She swore on the Gideon Bible that she had been out of the room for less than five minutes, just going downstairs for some stationery, intending to write a letter to her nephew in Vallejo while her patient was sleeping; and that was the only time she had been out of the room all day. She had met nobody in the corridor, she said.

"You left the door unlocked?" I asked.

"Yes, so I wouldn't be as likely to wake her when I came back."

"Where's the stationery you got?"

"I didn't get it. I heard the explosion and ran back upstairs." Fear came into her face, turning the freckles to ghastly spots. "You don't think—!"

"Better look after Mrs. Collinson," I said gruffly.

XIX · *The Degenerate*

ROLLY and I went back to my room, closing the connecting door. He said:

"Tch, tch, tch. I'd of thought Mrs. Herman was the last person in the world to—"

"You ought to've," I grumbled. "You recommended her. Who is she?"

"She's Tod Herman's wife. He's got the garage. She used to be a trained nurse before she married Tod. I thought she was all right."

"She got a nephew in Vallejo?"

"Uh-huh; that would be the Schultz kid that works at Mare Island. How do you suppose she come to get mixed up in—?"

"Probably didn't, or she would have had the writing paper she went after. Put somebody here to keep people out till we can borrow a San Francisco bomb-expert to look it over."

The deputy called one of the men in from the corridor, and we left him looking important in the room. Mickey Linehan was in the lobby when we got there.

"Fink's got a cracked skull. He's on his way to the county hospital with the other wreck."

"Fitzstephan dead yet?" I asked.

"Nope, and the doc thinks if they get him over where they got the right kind of implements they can keep him from dying. God knows what for—the shape he's in! But that's just the kind of stuff a croaker thinks is a lot of fun."

"Was Aaronia Haldorn sprung with Fink?" I asked.

"Yes. Al Mason's tailing her."

"Call up the Old Man and see if Al's reported anything on her. Tell the Old Man what's happened here, and see if they've found Andrews."

"Andrews?" Rolly asked as Mickey headed for the phone. "What's the matter with him?"

"Nothing that I know of; only we haven't been able to find him to tell him Mrs. Collinson has been rescued. His office hasn't seen him since yesterday morning, and nobody will say they know where he is."

"Tch, tch, tch. Is there any special reason for wanting him?"

"I don't want her on my hands the rest of my life," I said. "He's in charge of her affairs, he's responsible for her, and I want to turn her over to him."

Rolly nodded vaguely.

We went outside and asked all the people we could find all the questions we could think of. None of the answers led anywhere, except to repeated assurance that the bomb hadn't been chucked through the window. We found six people who had been in sight of that side of the hotel immediately before, and at the time of, the explosion; and none of them had seen anything that could be twisted into bearing on the bomb-throwing.

Mickey came away from the phone with the information that Aaronia Haldorn, when released from the city prison, had gone to the home of a family named Jeffries in San Mateo, and had been there ever since; and that Dick Foley, hunting for Andrews, had hopes of locating him in Sausalito.

District attorney Vernon and sheriff Feeney, with a horde of reporters and photographers close behind them, arrived from the county seat. They went through a lot of detecting motions that got them nowhere except on the front pages of all the San Francisco and Los Angeles papers —the place they liked best.

I had Gabrielle Collinson moved into another room in the hotel, and posted Mickey Linehan next door, with the connecting door unlocked. Gabrielle talked now, to Vernon, Feeney, Rolly, and me. What she said didn't help us much. She had been asleep, she said; had been awakened by a terrible noise and a terrible jarring of her bed; and then I had come in. That was all she knew.

Late in the afternoon McCracken, a San Francisco police department bomb-expert, arrived. After examining all the fragments of this and that which he could sweep up, he gave us a preliminary verdict that the bomb had been a small one, of aluminum, charged with a low-grade nitroglycerine, and exploded by a crude friction device.

"Amateur or professional job?" I asked.

McCracken spit out loose shreds of tobacco—he was one of the men who chew their cigarettes—and said:

"I'd say it was made by a guy that knew his stuff, but had to work with what he could get his hands on. I'll tell you more when I've worked this junk over in the lab."

"No timer on it?" I asked.

"No signs of one."

Doctor George returned from the county seat with the news that what was left of Fitzstephan still breathed. The doctor was tickled pink. I had to yell at him to make him hear my questions about Fink and Gabrielle. Then he told me Fink's life wasn't in danger, and the girl's cold was enough better that she might get out of bed if she wished. I asked about her nerves, but he was in too much of a hurry to get back to Fitzstephan to pay much attention to anything else.

"Hm-m-m, yes, certainly," he muttered, edging past me towards his car. "Quiet, rest, freedom from anxiety," and he was gone.

I ate dinner with Vernon and Feeney in the hotel café that evening. They didn't think I had told them all I knew about the bombing, and kept me on the witness stand throughout the meal, though neither of them accused me pointblank of holding out.

After dinner I went up to my new room. Mickey was sprawled on the bed reading a newspaper.

"Go feed yourself," I said. "How's our baby?"

"She's up. How do you figure her—only fifty cards to her deck?"

"Why?" I asked. "What's she been doing?"

"Nothing. I was just thinking."

"That's from having an empty stomach. Better go eat."

"Aye, aye, Mr. Continental," he said and went out.

The next room was quiet. I listened at the door and then tapped it. Mrs. Herman's voice said: "Come in."

She was sitting beside the bed making gaudy butterflies on a piece of yellowish cloth stretched on hoops. Gabrielle Collinson sat in a rocking chair on the other side of the room, frowning at hands clasped in her lap —clasped hard enough to whiten the knuckles and spread the finger-ends. She had on the tweed clothes in which she had been kidnapped. They were still rumpled, but had been brushed clean of mud. She didn't look up when I came in. The nurse did, pushing her freckles together in an uneasy smile.

"Good evening," I said, trying to make a cheerful entrance. "Looks like we're running out of invalids."

That brought no response from the girl, too much from the nurse.

"Yes, indeed," Mrs. Herman exclaimed with exaggerated enthusiasm. "We can't call Mrs. Collinson an invalid now—now that she's up and about—and I'm almost sorry that she is—he-he-he—because I certainly never did have such a nice patient in every way; but that's what we girls used to say at the hospital when we were in training: the nicer the patient was, the shorter the time we'd have him, while you take a disagreeable one and she'd live—I mean, be there—forever and a day, it seems like. I remember once when—"

I made a face at her and wagged my head at the door. She let the rest of her words die inside her open mouth. Her face turned red, then white. She dropped her embroidery and got up, saying idiotically: "Yes, yes, that's the way it always is. Well, I've got to go see about those—you know—what do you call them. Pardon me for a few minutes, please." She went out quickly, sidewise, as if afraid I'd sneak up behind her and kick her.

When the door had closed, Gabrielle looked up from her hands and said:

"Owen is dead."

She didn't ask, she said it; but there was no way of treating it except as a question.

"No." I sat down in the nurse's chair and fished out cigarettes. "He's alive."

"Will he live?" Her voice was still husky from her cold.

"The doctors think so," I exaggerated.

"If he lives, will he—?" She left the question unfinished, but her husky voice seemed impersonal enough.

"He'll be pretty badly maimed."

She spoke more to herself than to me:

"That should be even more satisfactory."

I grinned. If I was as good an actor as I thought, there was nothing in the grin but good-humored amusement.

"Laugh," she said gravely. "I wish you could laugh it away. But you can't. It's there. It will always be there." She looked down at her hands and whispered: "Cursed."

Spoken in any other tone, that last word would have been melodramatic, ridiculously stagey. But she said it automatically, without any feeling, as if saying it had become a habit. I could see her lying in bed in the dark, whispering it to herself hour after hour, whispering it to her body when she put on her clothes, to her face reflected in mirrors, day after day.

I squirmed in my chair and growled:

"Stop it. Just because a bad-tempered woman works off her hatred and rage in a ten-twenty-thirty speech about—"

"No, no; my step-mother merely put in words what I have always known. I hadn't known it was in the Dain blood, but I knew it was in mine. How could I help knowing? Hadn't I the physical marks of degeneracy?" She crossed the room to stand in front of me, turning her head sidewise, holding back her curls with both hands. "Look at my ears—without lobes, pointed tops. People don't have ears like that. Animals do." She turned her face to me again, still holding back her hair. "Look at my forehead—its smallness, its shape—animal. My teeth." She bared them—white, small, pointed. "The shape of my face." Her hands left her hair and slid down her cheeks, coming together under her oddly pointed small chin.

"Is that all?" I asked. "Haven't you got cloven hoofs? All right. Say these things are as peculiar as you seem to think they are. What of it? Your step-mother was a Dain, and she was poison, but where were her physical marks of degeneracy? Wasn't she as normal, as wholesome-looking as any woman you're likely to find?"

"But that's no answer." She shook her head impatiently. "She didn't have the physical marks perhaps. I have, and the mental ones too. I—" She sat down on the side of the bed close to me, elbows on knees, tortured white face between hands. "I've not ever been able to think clearly, as other people do, even the simplest thoughts. Everything is always so confused in my mind. No matter what I try to think about, there's a fog that gets between me and it, and other thoughts get between us, so I barely catch a glimpse of the thought I want before I lose it again, and have to hunt through the fog, and at last find it, only to have the same thing happen again and again and again. Can you understand how horrible that can become: going through life like that—year after year—knowing you will always be like that—or worse?"

"I can't," I said. "It sounds normal as hell to me. Nobody thinks clearly, no matter what they pretend. Thinking's a dizzy business, a matter of catching as many of those foggy glimpses as you can and fitting them together the best you can. That's why people hang on so tight to their beliefs and opinions; because, compared to the haphazard way in which they're arrived at, even the goofiest opinion seems wonderfully clear, sane, and self-evident. And if you let it get away from you, then you've got to dive back into that foggy muddle to wangle yourself out another to take its place."

She took her face out of her hands and smiled shyly at me, saying:

"It's funny I didn't like you before." Her face became serious again. "But—"

"But nothing," I said. "You're old enough to know that everybody except very crazy people and very stupid people suspect themselves now and then—or whenever they happen to think about it—of not being exactly sane. Evidence of goofiness is easily found: the more you dig into yourself, the more you turn up. Nobody's mind could stand the sort of examination you've been giving yours. Going around trying to prove yourself cuckoo! It's a wonder you haven't driven yourself nuts."

"Perhaps I have."

"No. Take my word for it, you're sane. Or don't take my word for it. Look. You got a hell of a start in life. You got into bad hands at the very beginning. Your step-mother was plain poison, and did her best to ruin you, and in the end succeeded in convincing you that you were smeared with a very special family curse. In the past couple of months—the time I've known you—all the calamities known to man have been piled up on you, and your belief in your curse has made you hold yourself responsible for every item in the pile. All right. How's it affected you? You've been dazed a lot of the time, hysterical part of the time, and when your husband was killed you tried to kill yourself, but weren't unbalanced enough to face the shock of the bullet tearing through your flesh.

"Well, good God, sister! I'm only a hired man with only a hired man's interest in your troubles, and some of them have had me groggy. Didn't I try to bite a ghost back in that Temple? And I'm supposed to be old and toughened to crime. This morning—after all you'd been through —somebody touches off a package of nitroglycerine almost beside your bed. Here you are this evening, up and dressed, arguing with me about your sanity.

"If you aren't normal, it's because you're tougher, saner, cooler than normal. Stop thinking about your Dain blood and think about the Mayenne blood in you. Where do you suppose you got your toughness, except from him? It's the same toughness that carried him through Devil's Island, Central America, and Mexico, and kept him standing up till the end. You're more like him than like the one Dain I saw. Physically, you take after your father, and if you've got any physical marks of degeneracy —whatever that means—you got them from him."

She seemed to like that. Her eyes were almost happy. But I had talked myself out of words for the moment, and while I was hunting for more behind a cigarette the shine went out of her eyes.

"I'm glad—I'm grateful to you for what you've said, if you've meant it." Hopelessness was in her tone again, and her face was back between her hands. "But, whatever I am, she was right. You can't say she wasn't. You can't deny that my life has been cursed, blackened, and the lives of everyone who's touched me."

"I'm one answer to that," I said. "I've been around you a lot recently, and I've mixed into your affairs enough, and nothing's happened to me that a night's sleep wouldn't fix up."

"But in a different way," she protested slowly, wrinkling her forehead. "There's no personal relationship with you. It's professional with you— your work. That makes a difference."

I laughed and said:

"That won't do. There's Fitzstephan. He knew your family, of course, but he was here through me, on my account, and was actually, then, a step further removed from you than I. Why shouldn't I have gone down first? Maybe the bomb was meant for me? Maybe. But that brings us to a human mind behind it—one that can bungle—and not your infallible curse."

"You are mistaken," she said, staring at her knees. "Owen loved me."

I decided not to appear surprised. I asked:

"Had you—?"

"No, please! Please don't ask me to talk about it. Not now—after what happened this morning." She jerked her shoulders up high and straight, said crisply: "You said something about an infallible curse. I don't know whether you misunderstand me, or are pretending to, to make me seem foolish. But I don't believe in an infallible curse, one coming from the devil or God, like Job's, say." She was earnest now, no longer talking to change the conversation. "But can't there be—aren't there people who are so thoroughly—fundamentally—evil that they poison—bring out the worst in—everybody they touch? And can't that—?"

"There are people who can," I half-agreed, "when they want to."

"No, no! Whether they want to or not. When they desperately don't want to. It is so. It is. I loved Eric because he was clean and fine. You know he was. You knew him well enough, and you know men well enough, to know he was. I loved him that way, wanted him that way. And then, when we were married—"

She shuddered and gave me both of her hands. The palms were dry and hot, the ends of her fingers cold. I had to hold them tight to keep the nails out of my flesh. I asked:

"You were a virgin when you married him?"

"Yes, I was. I am. I—"

"It's nothing to get excited about," I said. "You are, and have the usual silly notions. And you use dope, don't you?"

She nodded. I went on:

"That would cut your own interest in sex to below normal, so that a perfectly natural interest in it on somebody else's part would seem abnormal. Eric was too young, too much in love with you, maybe too inexperienced, to keep from being clumsy. You can't make anything horrible out of that."

"But it wasn't only Eric," she explained. "Every man I've known. Don't think me conceited. I know I'm not beautiful. But I don't want to be evil. I don't. Why do men—? Why have all the men I've—?"

"Are you," I asked, "talking about me?"

"No—you know I'm not. Don't make fun of me, please."

"Then there are exceptions? Any others? Madison Andrews, for instance?"

"If you know him at all well, or have heard much about him, you don't have to ask that."

"No," I agreed. "But you can't blame the curse with him—it's habit. Was he very bad?"

"He was very funny," she said bitterly.

"How long ago was it?"

"Oh, possibly a year and a half. I didn't say anything to my father and step-mother. I was—I was ashamed that men were like that to me, and that—"

"How do you know," I grumbled, "that most men aren't like that to most women? What makes you think your case is so damned unique? If your ears were sharp enough, you could listen now and hear a thousand

women in San Francisco making the same complaint, and—God knows—
maybe half of them would be thinking themselves sincere."

She took her hands away from me and sat up straight on the bed.
Some pink came into her face.

"Now you *have* made me feel silly," she said.

"Not much sillier than I do. I'm supposed to be a detective. Since
this job began, I've been riding around on a merry-go-round, staying the
same distance behind your curse, suspecting what it'd look like if I could
get face to face with it, but never getting there. I will now. Can you stand
another week or two?"

"You mean—?"

"I'm going to show you that your curse is a lot of hooey, but it'll
take a few days, maybe a couple of weeks."

She was round-eyed and trembling, wanting to believe me, afraid to.
I said:

"That's settled. What are you going to do now?"

"I—I don't know. Do you mean what you've said? That this can be
ended? That I'll have no more—? That you can—?"

"Yeah. Could you go back to the house in the cove for a while? It
might help things along, and you'll be safe enough there. We could take
Mrs. Herman with us, and maybe an op or two."

"I'll go," she said.

I looked at my watch and stood up saying:

"Better go back to bed. We'll move down tomorrow. Good night."

She chewed her lower lip, wanting to say something, not wanting to
say it, finally blurting it out:

"I'll have to have morphine down there."

"Sure. What's your day's ration?"

"Five—ten grains."

"That's mild enough," I said, and then, casually: "Do you like using
the stuff?"

"I'm afraid it's too late for my liking or not liking it to matter."

"You've been reading the Hearst papers," I said. "If you want to
break off, and we've a few days to spare down there, we'll use them wean-
ing you. It's not so tough."

She laughed shakily, with a queer twitching of her mouth.

"Go away," she cried. "Don't give me any more assurances, any more
of your promises, please. I can't stand any more tonight. I'm drunk on
them now. Please go away."

"All right. Night."

"Good night—and thanks."

I went into my room, closing the door. Mickey was unscrewing the
top of a flask. His knees were dusty. He turned his half-wit's grin on me
and said:

"What a swell dish you are. What are you trying to do? Win yourself a home?"

"Sh-h-h. Anything new?"

"The master minds have gone back to the county seat. The red-head nurse was getting a load at the keyhole when I came back from feeding. I chased her."

"And took her place?" I asked, nodding at his dusty knees.

You couldn't embarrass Mickey. He said:

"Hell, no. She was at the other door, in the hall."

XX · *The House in the Cove*

I got Fitzstephan's car from the garage and drove Gabrielle and Mrs. Herman down to the house in the cove late the following morning. The girl was in low spirits. She made a poor job of smiling when spoken to, and had nothing to say on her own account. I thought she might be depressed by the thought of returning to the house she had shared with Collinson, but when we got there she went in with no appearance of reluctance, and being there didn't seem to increase her depression.

After luncheon—Mrs. Herman turned out to be a good cook—Gabrielle decided she wanted to go outdoors, so she and I walked over to the Mexican settlement to see Mary Nunez. The Mexican woman promised to come back to work the next day. She seemed fond of Gabrielle, but not of me.

We returned home by way of the shore, picking a path between scattered rocks. We walked slowly. The girl's forehead was puckered between her eyebrows. Neither of us said anything until we were within a quarter of a mile of the house. Then Gabrielle sat down on the rounded top of a boulder that was warm in the sun.

"Can you remember what you told me last night?" she asked, running her words together in her hurry to get them out. She looked frightened.

"Yeah."

"Tell me again," she begged, moving over to one end of her boulder. "Sit down and tell me again—all of it."

I did. According to me, it was as foolish to try to read character from the shape of ears as from the position of stars, tea-leaves, or spit in the sand; anybody who started hunting for evidence of insanity in himself would certainly find plenty, because all but stupid minds were jumbled affairs; she was, as far as I could see, too much like her father to have much Dain blood in her, or to have been softened much by what she had, even if you wanted to believe that things like that could be handed down; there was nothing to show that her influence on people was any worse than anybody else's, it being doubtful that many people had a very good influence on those of the opposite sex, and, anyway, she was too young, inexperienced, and self-centered to judge how she varied from the normal in this respect; I would show her in a few days that there was for her difficulties a much more tangible, logical, and jailable answer than any curse; and she wouldn't have much trouble breaking away from morphine, since she was a fairly light user of the stuff and had a temperament favorable to a cure.

I spent three-quarters of an hour working these ideas over for her, and didn't make such a lousy job of it. The fear went out of her eyes as I talked. Toward the last she smiled to herself. When I had finished she jumped up, laughing, working her fingers together.

"Thank you. Thank you," she babbled. "Please don't let me ever stop believing you. Make me believe you even if— No. It *is* true. Make me believe it always. Come on. Let's walk some more."

She almost ran me the rest of the way to the house, chattering all the way. Mickey Linehan was on the porch. I stopped there with him while the girl went in.

"Tch, tch, tch, as Mr. Rolly says." He shook his grinning face at me. "I ought to tell her what happened to that poor girl up in Poisonville that got so she thought she could trust you."

"Bring any news down from the village with you?" I asked.

"Andrews has turned up. He was at the Jeffries' place in San Mateo, where Aaronia Haldorn's staying. She's still there. Andrews was there from Tuesday afternoon till last night. Al was watching the place and saw him go in, but didn't peg him till he came out. The Jeffries are away— San Diego. Dick's tailing Andrews now. Al says the Haldorn broad hasn't been off the place. Rolly tells me Fink's awake, but don't know anything about the bomb. Fitzstephan's still hanging on to life."

"I think I'll run over and talk to Fink this afternoon," I said. "Stick around here. And—oh, yeah—you'll have to act respectful to me when Mrs. Collinson's around. It's important that she keep on thinking I'm hot stuff."

"Bring back some booze," Mickey said. "I can't do it sober."

Fink was propped up in bed when I got to him, looking out under bandages. He insisted that he knew nothing about the bomb, that all he had come down for was to tell me that Harvey Whidden was his step-son, the missing village-blacksmith's son by a former marriage.

"Well, what of it?" I asked.

"I don't know what of it, except that he was, and I thought you'd want to know about it."

"Why should I?"

"The papers said you said there was some kind of connection between what happened here and what happened up there, and that heavy-set detective said you said I knew more about it than I let on. And I don't want any more trouble, so I thought I'd just come down and tell you, so you couldn't say I hadn't told all I knew."

"Yeah? Then tell me what you know about Madison Andrews."

"I don't know anything about him. I don't know him. He's her guardian or something, ain't he? I read that in the newspapers. But I don't know him."

"Aaronia Haldorn does."

"Maybe she does, mister, but I don't. I just worked for the Haldorns. It wasn't anything to me but a job."

"What was it to your wife?"

"The same thing, a job."

"Where is she?"

"I don't know."

"Why'd she run away from the Temple?"

"I told you before, I don't know. Didn't want to get in trouble, I— Who wouldn't of run away if they got a chance?"

The nurse who had been fluttering around became a nuisance by this time, so I left the hospital for the district attorney's office in the court house. Vernon pushed aside a stack of papers with a the-world-can-wait gesture, and said, "Glad to see you; sit down," nodding vigorously, showing me all his teeth.

I sat down and said:

"Been talking to Fink. I couldn't get anything out of him, but he's our meat. The bomb couldn't have got in there except by him."

Vernon frowned for a moment, then shook his chin at me, and snapped:

"What was his motive? And you were there. You say you were looking at him all the time he was in the room. You say you saw nothing."

"What of that?" I asked. "He could outsmart me there. He was a magician's mechanic. He'd know how to make a bomb, and how to put it down without my seeing it. That's his game. We don't know what Fitz-stephan saw. They tell me he'll pull through. Let's hang on to Fink till he does."

Vernon clicked his teeth together and said: "Very well, we'll hold him."

I went down the corridor to the sheriff's office. Feeney wasn't in, but his chief deputy—a lanky, pockmarked man named Sweet—said he knew from the way Feeney had spoken of me that he—Feeney—would want me to be given all the help I asked for.

"That's fine," I said. "What I'm interested in now is picking up a couple of bottles of—well, gin, Scotch—whatever happens to be best in this part of the country."

Sweet scratched his Adam's apple and said:

"I wouldn't know about that. Maybe the elevator boy. I guess his gin would be safest. Say, Dick Cotton's crying his head off wanting to see you. Want to talk to him?"

"Yeah, though I don't know what for."

"Well, come back in a couple of minutes."

I went out and rang for the elevator. The boy—he had an age-bent back and a long yellow-gray mustache—was alone in it.

"Sweet said maybe you'd know where I could get a gallon of the white," I said.

"He's crazy," the boy grumbled, and then, when I kept quiet: "You'll be going out this way?"

"Yeah, in a little while."

He closed the door. I went back to Sweet. He took me down an inclosed walk that connected the court house with the prison behind, and left me alone with Cotton in a small boiler-plate cell. Two days in jail hadn't done the marshal of Quesada any good. He was gray-faced and jumpy, and the dimple in his chin kept squirming as he talked. He hadn't anything to tell me except that he was innocent.

All I could think of to say to him was: "Maybe, but you brought it on yourself. What evidence there is is against you. I don't know whether it's enough to convict you or not—depends on your lawyer."

"What did he want?" Sweet asked when I had gone back to him.

"To tell me that he's innocent."

The deputy scratched his Adam's apple again and asked:

"It's supposed to make any difference to you?"

"Yeah, it's been keeping me awake at night. See you later."

I went out to the elevator. The boy pushed a newspaper-wrapped gallon jug at me and said: "Ten bucks." I paid him, stowed the jug in Fitzstephan's car, found the local telephone office, and put in a call for Vic Dallas's drug-store in San Francisco's Mission district.

"I want," I told Vic, "fifty grains of M. and eight of those calomel-ipecac-atropine-strychnine-cascara shots. I'll have somebody from the agency pick up the package tonight or in the morning. Right?"

"If you say so, but if you kill anybody with it don't tell them where you got the stuff."

"Yeah," I said; "they'll die just because I haven't got a lousy pill-roller's diploma."

I put in another San Francisco call, for the agency, talking to the Old Man.

"Can you spare me another op?" I asked.

"MacMan is available, or he can relieve Drake. Whichever you prefer."

"MacMan'll do. Have him stop at Dallas's drug-store for a package on the way down. He knows where it is."

The Old Man said he had no new reports on Aaronia Haldorn and Andrews.

I drove back to the house in the cove. We had company. Three strange cars were standing empty in the driveway, and half a dozen newshounds were sitting and standing around Mickey on the porch. They turned their questions on me.

"Mrs. Collinson's here for a rest," I said. "No interviews, no posing for pictures. Let her alone. If anything breaks here I'll see that you get it, those of you who lay off her. The only thing I can tell you now is that Fink's being held for the bombing."

"What did Andrews come down for?" Jack Santos asked.

That wasn't a surprise to me: I had expected him to turn up now that he had come out of seclusion.

"Ask him," I suggested. "He's administering Mrs. Collinson's estate. You can't make a mystery out of his coming down to see her."

"Is it true that they're on bad terms?"

"No."

"Then why didn't he show up before this—yesterday, or the day before?"

"Ask him."

"Is it true that he's up to his tonsils in debt, or was before the Leggett estate got into his hands?"

"Ask him."

Santos smiled with thinned lips and said:

"We don't have to: we asked some of his creditors. Is there anything to the report that Mrs. Collinson and her husband had quarreled over her being too friendly with Whidden, a couple of days before her husband was killed?"

"Anything but the truth," I said. "Tough. You could do a lot with a story like that."

"Maybe we will," Santos said. "Is it true that she and her husband's family are on the outs, that old Hubert has said he's willing to spend all he's got to see that she pays for any part she had in his son's death?"

I didn't know. I said:

"Don't be a chump. We're working for Hubert now, taking care of her."

"Is it true that Mrs. Haldorn and Tom Fink were released because they had threatened to tell all they knew if they were held for trial?"

"Now you're kidding me, Jack," I said. "Is Andrews still here?"

"Yes."

I went indoors and called Mickey in, asking him: "Seen Dick?"

"He drove past a couple of minutes after Andrews came."

"Sneak away and find him. Tell him not to let the newspaper gang make him, even if he has to risk losing Andrews for a while. They'd go crazy all over their front pages if they learned we were shadowing him, and I don't want them to go that crazy."

Mrs. Herman was coming down the stairs. I asked her where Andrews was.

"Up in the front room."

I went up there. Gabrielle, in a low-cut dark silk gown, was sitting stiff and straight on the edge of a leather rocker. Her face was white and sullen. She was looking at a handkerchief stretched between her hands. She looked up at me as if glad I had come in. Andrews stood with his back to the fireplace. His white hair, eyebrows, and mustache stood out every which way from his bony pink face. He shifted his scowl from the girl to me, and didn't seem glad I had come in.

I said, "Hullo," and found a table-corner to prop myself on.

He said: "I've come to take Mrs. Collinson back to San Francisco."

She didn't say anything. I said:

"Not to San Mateo?"

"What do you mean by that?" The white tangles of his brows came down to hide all but the bottom halves of his blue eyes.

"God knows. Maybe my mind's been corrupted by the questions the newspapers have been asking me."

He didn't quite wince. He said, slowly, deliberately:

"Mrs. Haldorn sent for me professionally. I went to see her to explain how impossible it would be, in the circumstances, for me to advise or represent her."

"That's all right with me," I said. "And if it took you thirty hours to explain that to her, it's nobody's business."

"Precisely."

"But—I'd be careful how I told the reporters waiting downstairs that. You know how suspicious they are—for no reason at all."

He turned to Gabrielle again, speaking quietly, but with some impatience:

"Well, Gabrielle, are you going with me?"

"Should I?" she asked me.

"Not unless you especially want to."

"I—I don't."

"Then that's settled," I said.

Andrews nodded and went forward to take her hand, saying:

"I'm sorry, but I must get back to the city now, my dear. You should have a phone put in, so you can reach me in case you need to."

He declined her invitation to stay to dinner, said, "Good evening," not unpleasantly, to me, and went out. Through a window I could see him presently getting into his car, giving as little attention as possible to the newspaper men gathered around him.

Gabrielle was frowning at me when I turned away from the window. "What did you mean by what you said about San Mateo?" she asked.

"How friendly are he and Aaronia Haldorn?" I asked.

"I haven't any idea. Why? Why did you talk to him as you did?"

"Detective business. For one thing, there's a rumor that getting control of the estate may have helped him keep his own head above water. Maybe there's nothing in it. But it won't hurt to give him a little scare, so he'll get busy straightening things out—if he has done any juggling—between now and clean-up day. No use of you losing money along with the rest of your troubles."

"Then he—?" she began.

"He's got a week—several days at least—to unjuggle in. That ought to be enough."

"But—"

Mrs. Herman, calling us to dinner, ended the conversation.

Gabrielle ate very little. She and I had to do most of the talking until I got Mickey started telling about a job he had been on up in Eureka, where he posed as a foreigner who knew no English. Since English was the only language he did know, and Eureka normally held at least one specimen of every nationality there is, he'd had a hell of a time keeping people from finding out just what he was supposed to be. He made a long and laughable story of it. Maybe some of it was the truth: he always got a lot of fun out of acting like the other half of a half-wit.

After the meal he and I strolled around outside while the spring night darkened the grounds.

"MacMan will be down in the morning," I told him. "You and he will have to do the watchdog. Divide it between you anyway you want, but one will have to be on the job all the time."

"Don't give yourself any of the worst of it," he complained. "What's this supposed to be down here—a trap?"

"Maybe."

"Maybe. Uh-huh. You don't know what the hell you're doing. You're stalling around waiting for the horseshoe in your pocket to work."

"The outcome of successful planning always looks like luck to saps. Did Dick have any news?"

"No. He tailed Andrews straight here from his house."

The front door opened, throwing yellow light across the porch. Gabrielle, a dark cape on her shoulders, came into the yellow light, shut the door, and came down the gravel walk.

"Take a nap now if you want," I told Mickey. "I'll call you when I turn in. You'll have to stand guard till morning."

"You're a darb." He laughed in the dark. "By God, you're a darb."

"There's a gallon of gin in the car."

"Huh? Why didn't you say so instead of wasting my time just talking?" The lawn grass swished against his shoes as he walked away.

I moved towards the gravel walk, meeting the girl.

"Isn't it a lovely night?" she said.

"Yeah. But you're not supposed to go roaming around alone in the dark, even if your troubles are practically over."

"I didn't intend to," she said, taking my arm. "And what does practically over mean?"

"That there are a few details to be taken care of—the morphine, for instance."

She shivered and said:

"I've only enough left for tonight. You promised to—"

"Fifty grains coming in the morning."

She kept quiet, as if waiting for me to say something else. I didn't say anything else. Her fingers wriggled on my sleeve.

"You said it wouldn't be hard to cure me." She spoke half-questioningly, as if expecting me to deny having said anything of the sort.

"It wouldn't."

"You said, perhaps . . ." letting the words fade off.

"We'd do it while we were here?"

"Yes."

"Want to?" I asked. "It's no go if you don't."

"Do I want to?" She stood still in the road, facing me. "I'd give—" A sob ended that sentence. Her voice came again, high-pitched, thin: "Are you being honest with me? Are you? Is what you've told me—all you told me last night and this afternoon—as true as you made it sound? Do I believe in you because you're sincere? Or because you've learned how—as a trick of your business—to make people believe in you?"

She might have been crazy, but she wasn't so stupid. I gave her the answer that seemed best at the time:

"Your belief in me is built on mine in you. If mine's unjustified, so is yours. So let me ask you a question first: were you lying when you said, 'I don't want to be evil'?"

"Oh, I don't. I don't."

"Well, then," I said with an air of finality, as if that settled it. "Now if you want to get off the junk, off we'll get you."

"How—how long will it take?"

"Say a week, to be safe. Maybe less."

"Do you mean that? No longer than that?"

"That's all for the part that counts. You'll have to take care of yourself for some time after, till your system's hitting on all eight again, but you'll be off the junk."

"Will I suffer—much?"

"A couple of bad days; but they won't be as bad as you'll think they are, and your father's toughness will carry you through them."

"If," she said slowly, "I should find out in the middle of it that I can't go through with it, can I—?"

"There'll be nothing you can do about it," I promised cheerfully. "You'll stay in till you come out the other end."

She shivered again and asked:

"When shall we start?"

"Day after tomorrow. Take your usual snort tomorrow, but don't try to stock up. And don't worry about it. It'll be tougher on me than on you: I'll have to put up with you."

"And you'll make allowances—you'll understand—if I'm not always nice while I'm going through it? Even if I'm nasty?"

"I don't know." I didn't want to encourage her to cut up on me. "I don't think so much of niceness that can be turned into nastiness by a little grief."

"Oh, but—" She stopped, wrinkled her forehead, said: "Can't we send Mrs. Herman away? I don't want to—I don't want her looking at me."

"I'll get rid of her in the morning."

"And if I'm—you won't let anybody else see me—if I'm not—if I'm too terrible?"

"No," I promised. "But look here: you're preparing to put on a show for me. Stop thinking about that end of it. You're going to behave. I don't want a lot of monkey-business out of you."

She laughed suddenly, asking:

"Will you beat me if I'm bad?"

I said she might still be young enough for a spanking to do her good.

XXI · Aaronia Haldorn

MARY NUNEZ arrived at half-past seven the next morning. Mickey Linehan drove Mrs. Herman to Quesada, leaving her there, returning with MacMan and a load of groceries.

MacMan was a square-built, stiff-backed ex-soldier. Ten years of the island had baked his tight-mouthed, solid-jawed, grim face a dark oak. He was the perfect soldier: he went where you sent him, stayed where you put him, and had no ideas of his own to keep him from doing exactly what you told him.

He gave me the druggist's package. I took ten grains of morphine up to Gabrielle. She was eating breakfast in bed. Her eyes were watery, her face damp and grayish. When she saw the bindles in my hand she pushed her tray aside and held her hands out eagerly, wriggling her shoulders.

"Come back in five minutes?" she asked.

"You can take your jolt in front of me. I won't blush."

"But I would," she said, and did.

I went out, shut the door, and leaned against it, hearing the crackle of paper and the clink of a spoon on the water-glass. Presently she called: "All right."

I went in again. A crumpled ball of white paper in the tray was all that remained of one bindle. The others weren't in sight. She was leaning back against her pillows, eyes half closed, as comfortable as a cat full of goldfish. She smiled lazily at me and said:

"You're a dear. Know what I'd like to do today? Take some lunch and go out on the water—spend the whole day floating in the sun."

"That ought to be good for you. Take either Linehan or MacMan with you. You're not to go out alone."

"What are you going to do?"

"Ride up to Quesada, over to the county seat, maybe as far as the city."

"Mayn't I go with you?"

I shook my head, saying: "I've got work to do, and you're supposed to be resting."

She said, "Oh," and reached for her coffee. I turned to the door. "The rest of the morphine." She spoke over the edge of her cup. "You've put it in a safe place, where nobody will find it?"

"Yeah," I said, grinning at her, patting my coat-pocket.

In Quesada I spent half an hour talking to Rolly and reading the San Francisco papers. They were beginning to poke at Andrews with hints and questions that stopped just short of libel. That was so much to the good. The deputy sheriff hadn't anything to tell me.

I went over to the county seat. Vernon was in court. Twenty minutes of the sheriff's conversation didn't add anything to my education. I called up the agency and talked to the Old Man. He said Hubert Collinson, our client, had expressed some surprise at our continuing the operation, having supposed that Whidden's death had cleared up the mystery of his son's murder.

"Tell him it didn't," I said. "Eric's murder was tied up with Gabrielle's troubles, and we can't get to the bottom of one except through the other. It'll probably take another week. Collinson's all right," I assured the Old Man. "He'll stand for it when it's explained to him."

The Old Man said, "I certainly hope so," rather coldly, not enthusiastic over having five operatives at work on a job that the supposed client might not want to pay for.

I drove up to San Francisco, had dinner at the St. Germain, stopped at my rooms to collect another suit and a bagful of clean shirts and the like, and got back to the house in the cove a little after midnight. Mac-Man came out of the darkness while I was tucking the car—we were still using Fitzstephan's—under the shed. He said nothing had happened in my absence. We went into the house together. Mickey was in the kitchen, yawning and mixing himself a drink before relieving MacMan on sentry duty.

"Mrs. Collinson gone to bed?" I asked.

"Her light's still on. She's been in her room all day."

MacMan and I had a drink with Mickey and then went upstairs. I knocked at the girl's door.

"Who is it?" she asked. I told her. She said: "Yes?"

"No breakfast in the morning."

"Really?" Then, as if it were something she had almost forgotten: "Oh, I've decided not to put you to all the trouble of curing me." She opened the door and stood in the opening, smiling too pleasantly at me, a finger holding her place in a book. "Did you have a nice ride?"

"All right," I said, taking the rest of the morphine from my pocket and holding it out to her. "There's no use of my carrying this around."

She didn't take it. She laughed in my face and said:

"You *are* a brute, aren't you?"

"Well, it's your cure, not mine." I put the stuff back in my pocket. "If you—" I broke off to listen. A board had creaked down the hall. Now there was a soft sound, as of a bare foot dragging across the floor.

"That's Mary watching over me," Gabrielle whispered gaily. "She made a bed in the attic and refused to go home. She doesn't think I'm safe with you and your friends. She warned me against you, said you were —what was it?—oh, yes—wolves. Are you?"

"Practically. Don't forget—no breakfast in the morning."

The following afternoon I gave her the first dose of Vic Dallas's mixture, and three more at two-hour intervals. She spent that day in her room. That was Saturday.

On Sunday she had ten grains of morphine and was in high spirits all day, considering herself as good as cured already.

On Monday she had the remainder of Vic's concoction, and the day was pretty much like Saturday. Mickey Linehan returned from the county seat with the news that Fitzstephan was conscious, but too weak and too bandaged to have talked if the doctors had let him; that Andrews had been to San Mateo to see Aaronia Haldorn again; and that she had been to the hospital to see Fink, but had been refused permission by the sheriff's office.

Tuesday was a more exciting day.

Gabrielle was up and dressed when I carried her orange-juice breakfast in. She was bright-eyed, restless, talkative, and laughed easily and often until I mentioned—off-hand—that she was to have no more morphine.

"Ever, you mean?" Her face and voice were panicky. "No, you don't mean that?"

"Yeah."

"But I'll die." Tears filled her eyes, ran down her small white face, and she wrung her hands. It was childishly pathetic. I had to remind myself that tears were one of the symptoms of morphine withdrawal. "You know that's not the way. I don't expect as much as usual. I know I'll get less and less each day. But you can't stop it like this. You're joking. That would kill me." She cried some more at the thought of being killed.

I made myself laugh as if I were sympathetic but amused.

"Nonsense," I said cheerfully. "The chief trouble you're going to have is in being too alive. A couple of days of that, and you'll be all set."

She bit her lips, finally managed a smile, holding out both hands to me.

"I'm going to believe you," she said. "I do believe you. I'm going to believe you no matter what you say."

Her hands were clammy. I squeezed them and said:

"That'll be swell. Now back to bed. I'll look in every now and then, and if you want anything in between, sing out."

"You're not going off today?"

"No," I promised.

She stood the gaff pretty well all afternoon. Of course, there wasn't much heartiness in the way she laughed at herself between attacks when the sneezing and yawning hit her, but the thing was that she tried to laugh.

Madison Andrews came between five and half-past. Having seen him drive in, I met him on the porch. The ruddiness of his face had been washed out to a weak orange.

"Good evening," he said politely. "I wish to see Mrs. Collinson."

"I'll deliver any message to her," I offered.

He pulled his white eyebrows down and some of his normal ruddiness came back.

"I wish to see her." It was a command.

"She doesn't wish to see you. Is there any message?"

All of his ruddiness was back now. His eyes were hot. I was standing between him and the door. He couldn't go in while I stood there. For a moment he seemed about to push me out of the way. That didn't worry me: he was carrying a handicap of twenty pounds and twenty years.

He pulled his jaw into his neck and spoke in the voice of authority:

"Mrs. Collinson must return to San Francisco with me. She cannot stay here. This is a preposterous arrangement."

"She's not going to San Francisco," I said. "If necessary, the district attorney can hold her here as a material witness. Try upsetting that with any of your court orders, and we'll give you something else to worry about. I'm telling you this so you'll know how we stand. We'll prove that she might be in danger from you. How do we know you haven't played marbles with the estate? How do we know you don't mean to take advantage of her present upset condition to shield yourself from trouble over the estate? Why, man, you might even be planning to send her to an insane-asylum so the estate will stay under your control."

He was sick behind his eyes, though the rest of him stood up well enough under this broadside. When he had got his breath and had swallowed, he demanded:

"Does Gabrielle believe this?" His face was magenta.

"Who said anybody believed it?" I was trying to be bland. "I'm just telling you what we'll go into court with. You're a lawyer. You know there's not necessarily any connection between what's true and what you go into court with—or into the newspapers."

The sickness spread from behind his eyes, pushing the color from his face, the stiffness from his bones; but he held himself tall and he found a level voice.

"You may tell Mrs. Collinson," he said, "that I shall return my letters testamentary to the court this week, with an accounting of the estate, and a request that I be relieved."

"That'll be swell," I said, but I felt sorry for the old boy shuffling down to his car, climbing slowly into it.

I didn't tell Gabrielle he had been there.

She was whining a little now between her yawning and sneezing, and her eyes were running water. Face, body, and hands were damp with sweat. She couldn't eat. I kept her full of orange juice. Noises and odors—no matter how faint, how pleasant—were becoming painful to her, and she twitched and jerked continually in her bed.

"Will it get much worse than this?" she asked.

"Not much. There'll be nothing you can't stand."

Mickey Linehan was waiting for me when I got downstairs.

"The spick's got herself a chive," he said pleasantly.

"Yeah?"

"Yeah. It's the one I've been using to shuck lemons to take the stink out of that bargain-counter gin you bought—or did you just borrow it, the owner knowing you'd return it because nobody could drink it? It's a paring knife—four or five inches of stainless steel blade—so you won't get rust-marks on your undershirt when she sticks it in your back. I couldn't find it, and asked her about it, and she didn't look at me like I was a well-poisoner when she said she didn't know anything about it, and that's the first time she never looked at me that way, so I knew she had it."

"Smart of you," I said. "Well, keep an eye on her. She don't like us much."

"I'm to do that?" Mickey grinned. "My idea would be for everybody to look out for himself, seeing that you're the lad she dog-eyes most, and it's most likely you that'll get whittled on. What'd you ever do to her?

THE DAIN CURSE [275

You haven't been dumb enough to fool with a Mex lady's affections, have you?"

I didn't think he was funny, though he may have been.

Aaronia Haldorn arrived just before dark, in a Lincoln limousine driven by a Negro who turned the siren loose when he brought the car into the drive. I was in Gabrielle's room when the thing howled. She all but jumped out of bed, utterly terrorized by what must have been an ungodly racket to her too sensitive ears.

"What was it? What was it?" she kept crying between rattling teeth, her body shaking the bed.

"Sh-h-h," I soothed her. I was acquiring a pretty fair bedside manner. "Just an automobile horn. Visitors. I'll go down and head them off."

"You won't let anybody see me?" she begged.

"No. Be a good girl till I get back."

Aaronia Haldorn was standing beside the limousine talking to Mac-Man when I came out. In the dim light, her face was a dusky oval mask between black hat and black fur coat—but her luminous eyes were real enough.

"How do you do?" she said, holding out a hand. Her voice was a thing to make warm waves run up your back. "I'm glad for Mrs. Collinson's sake that you're here. She and I have had excellent proof of your protective ability, both owing our lives to it."

That was all right, but it had been said before. I made a gesture that was supposed to indicate modest distaste for the subject, and beat her to the first tap with:

"I'm sorry she can't see you. She isn't well."

"Oh, but I should so like to see her, if only for a moment. Don't you think it might be good for her?"

I said I was sorry. She seemed to accept that as final, though she said: "I came all the way from the city to see her."

I tried that opening with:

"Didn't Mr. Andrews tell you . . . ?" letting it ravel out.

She didn't say whether he had. She turned and began walking slowly across the grass. There was nothing for me to do but walk along beside her. Full darkness was only a few minutes away. Presently, when we had gone thirty or forty feet from the car, she said:

"Mr. Andrews thinks you suspect him."

"He's right."

"Of what do you suspect him?"

"Juggling the estate. Mind, I don't know, but I do suspect him."

"Really?"

"Really," I said; "and not of anything else."

"Oh, I should suppose that was quite enough."

"It's enough for me. I didn't think it was enough for you."

"I beg your pardon?"

I didn't like the ground I was on with this woman. I was afraid of her. I piled up what facts I had, put some guesses on them, and took a jump from the top of the heap into space:

"When you got out of prison, you sent for Andrews, pumped him for all he knew, and then, when you learned he was playing with the girl's pennies, you saw what looked to you like a chance to confuse things by throwing suspicion on him. The old boy's woman-crazy: he'd be duck-soup for a woman like you. I don't know what you're planning to do with him, but you've got him started, and have got the papers started after him. I take it you gave them the tip-off on his high financing? It's no good, Mrs. Haldorn. Chuck it. It won't work. You can stir him up, all right, and make him do something criminal, get him into a swell jam: he's desperate enough now that he's being poked at. But whatever he does now won't hide what somebody else did in the past. He's promised to get the estate in order and hand it over. Let him alone. It won't work."

She didn't say anything while we took another dozen steps. A path came under our feet. I said:

"This is the path that runs up the cliff, the one Eric Collinson was pushed from. Did you know him?"

She drew in her breath sharply, with almost a sob in her throat, but her voice was steady, quiet and musical, when she replied:

"You know I did. Why should you ask?"

"Detectives like questions they already know the answers to. Why did you come down here, Mrs. Haldorn?"

"Is that another whose answer you know?"

"I know you came for one or both of two reasons."

"Yes?"

"First, to learn how close we were to our riddle's answer. Right?"

"I've my share of curiosity, naturally," she confessed.

"I don't mind making that much of your trip a success. I know the answer."

She stopped in the path, facing me, her eyes phosphorescent in the deep twilight. She put a hand on my shoulder: she was taller than I. The other hand was in her coat-pocket. She put her face nearer mine. She spoke very slowly, as if taking great pains to be understood:

"Tell me truthfully. Don't pretend. I don't want to do an unnecessary wrong. Wait, wait—think before you speak—and believe me when I say this isn't the time for pretending, for lying, for bluffing. Now tell me the truth: do you know the answer?"

"Yeah."

She smiled faintly, taking her hand from my shoulder, saying:

"Then there's no use of our fencing."

I jumped at her. If she had fired from her pocket she might have plugged me. But she tried to get the gun out. By then I had a hand on her wrist. The bullet went into the ground between our feet. The nails of her free hand put three red ribbons down the side of my face. I tucked my head under her chin, turned my hip to her before her knee came up, brought her body hard against mine with one arm around her, and bent her gun-hand behind her. She dropped the gun as we fell. I was on top. I stayed there until I had found the gun. I was getting up when MacMan arrived.

"Everything's eggs in the coffee," I told him, having trouble with my voice.

"Have to plug her?" he asked, looking at the woman lying still on the ground.

"No, she's all right. See that the chauffeur's behaving."

MacMan went away. The woman sat up, tucked her legs under her, and rubbed her wrist. I said:

"That's the second reason for your coming, though I thought you meant it for Mrs. Collinson."

She got up, not saying anything. I didn't help her up, not wanting her to know how shaky I was. I said:

"Since we've gone this far, it won't do any harm and it might do some good to talk."

"I don't think anything will do any good now." She set her hat straight. "You say you know. Then lies are worthless, and only lies would help." She shrugged. "Well, what now?"

"Nothing now, if you'll promise to remember that the time for being desperate is past. This kind of thing splits up in three parts—being caught, being convicted, and being punished. Admit it's too late to do anything about the first, and—well, you know what California courts and prison boards are."

She looked curiously at me and asked: "Why do you tell me this?"

"Because being shot at's no treat to me, and because when a job's done I like to get it cleaned up and over with. I'm not interested in trying to convict you for your part in the racket, and it's a nuisance having you horning in now, trying to muddy things up. Go home and behave."

Neither of us said anything more until we had walked back to the limousine. Then she turned, put out her hand to me, and said:

"I think—I don't know yet—I think I owe you even more now than before."

I didn't say anything and I didn't take her hand. Perhaps it was because she was holding her hand out that she asked:

"May I have my pistol now?"

"No."

"Will you give my best wishes to Mrs. Collinson, and tell her I'm so sorry I couldn't see her?"

"Yeah."

She said, "Goodbye," and got into the car; I took off my hat and she rode away.

XXII · *Confessional*

MICKEY LINEHAN opened the front door for me. He looked
at my scratched face and laughed:

"You do have one hell of a time with your women. Why don't you
ask them instead of trying to take it away from them? It'd save you a lot
of skin." He poked a thumb at the ceiling. "Better go up and negotiate
with that one. She's been raising hell."

I went up to Gabrielle's room. She was sitting in the middle of the
wallowed-up bed. Her hands were in her hair, tugging at it. Her soggy
face was thirty-five years old. She was making hurt-animal noises in her
throat.

"It's a fight, huh?" I said from the door.

She took her hands out of her hair.

"I won't die?" The question was a whimper between edge-to-edge
teeth.

"Not a chance."

She sobbed and lay down. I straightened the covers over her. She
complained that there was a lump in her throat, that her jaws and the
hollows behind her knees ached.

"Regular symptoms," I assured her. "They won't bother you much,
and you'll miss the cramps."

Fingernails scratched the door. Gabrielle jumped up in bed, crying:
"Don't go away again."

"No farther than the door," I promised, and went to it.

MacMan was there.

"That Mexican Mary," he whispered, "was hiding in the bushes
watching you and the woman. I spotted her when she came out, and tailed
her across to the road below. She stopped the limousine and talked with
the woman—five-ten minutes. I couldn't get near enough to hear any of it."

"Where is she now?"

"In the kitchen. She came back. The woman in the heap went on.
Mickey says the Mex is packing a knife and is going to make grief for us.
Reckon he's right?"

"He generally is," I said. "She's strong for Mrs. Collinson, and
doesn't think we mean her any good. Why in hell can't she mind her own
business? It adds up that she peeped and saw Mrs. Haldorn wasn't for us,
figured she was for Mrs. Collinson, and braced her. I hope Mrs. Haldorn

had sense enough to tell her to behave. Anyway, there's nothing we can do but watch her. No use giving her the gate: we've got to have a cook."

When MacMan had gone Gabrielle remembered we had had a visitor, and asked me about it, and about the shot she had heard and my scratched face.

"It was Aaronia Haldorn," I told her; "and she lost her head. No harm done. She's gone now."

"She came here to kill me," the girl said, not excitedly, but as if she knew certainly.

"Maybe. She wouldn't admit anything. Why should she kill you?"

I didn't get an answer to that.

It was a long bad night. I spent most of it in the girl's room, in a leather rocker dragged in from the front room. She got perhaps an hour and a half of sleep, in three instalments. Nightmares brought her screaming out of all three. I dozed when she let me. Off and on through the night I heard stealthy sounds in the hall—Mary Nunez watching over her mistress, I supposed.

Wednesday was a longer and worse day. By noon my jaws were as sore as Gabrielle's, from going around holding my back teeth together. She was getting the works now. Light was positive, active pain to her eyes, sound to her ears, odors of any sort to her nostrils. The weight of her silk nightgown, the touch of sheets over and under her, tortured her skin. Every nerve she had yanked every muscle she had, continually. Promises that she wasn't going to die were no good now: life wasn't nice enough.

"Stop fighting it, if you want," I said. "Let yourself go. I'll take care of you."

She took me at my word, and I had a maniac on my hands. Once her shrieks brought Mary Nunez to the door, snarling and spitting at me in Mex-Spanish. I was holding Gabrielle down in bed by the shoulders, sweating as much as she was.

"Get out of here," I snarled back at the Mexican woman.

She put a brown hand into the bosom of her dress and came a step into the room. Mickey Linehan came up behind her, pulled her back into the hall, and shut the door.

Between the high spots, Gabrielle lay on her back, panting, twitching, staring at the ceiling with hopeless suffering eyes. Sometimes her eyes closed, but the jerking of her body didn't stop.

Rolly came down from Quesada that afternoon with word that Fitzstephan had come sufficiently alive to be questioned by Vernon. Fitzstephan had told the district attorney that he had not seen the bomb, had seen nothing to show when, where, and how it came into the room; but that he had an indistinct memory of hearing a tinkling, as of broken glass falling, and a thud on the floor close to him just after Fink and I had left the room.

I told Rolly to tell Vernon I'd try to get over to see him the next day, and to hang on to Fink. The deputy sheriff promised to deliver the message, and left. Mickey and I were standing on the porch. We didn't have anything to say to each other, hadn't all day. I was lighting a cigarette when the girl's voice came from indoors. Mickey turned away, saying something with the name of God in it.

I scowled at him and asked angrily:

"Well, am I right or wrong?"

He glared back at me, said, "I'd a damned sight rather be wrong," and walked away.

I cursed him and went inside. Mary Nunez, starting up the front stairs, retreated towards the kitchen when she saw me, walking backwards, her eyes watching me crazily. I cursed her and went upstairs to where I had left MacMan at the girl's door. He wouldn't look at me, so I made it unanimous by cursing him.

Gabrielle spent the balance of the afternoon shrieking, begging, and crying for morphine. That evening she made a complete confession:

"I told you I didn't want to be evil," she said, wadding the bedclothes in feverish hands. "That was a lie. I did. I've always wanted to, always have been. I wanted to do to you what I did to the others; but now I don't want you: I want morphine. They won't hang me: I know that. And I don't care what else they do to me, if I get morphine."

She laughed viciously and went on:

"You were right when you said I brought out the worst in men because I wanted to. I did want to; and I did—except, I failed with Doctor Riese, and with Eric. I don't know what was the matter with them. But I failed with both of them, and in failing let them learn too much about me. And that's why they were killed. Joseph drugged Doctor Riese, and I killed him myself, and then we made Minnie think she had. And I persuaded Joseph to kill Aaronia, and he would have done it—he would have done anything I asked—if you hadn't interfered. I got Harvey to kill Eric for me. I was tied to Eric—legally—a good man who wanted to make a good woman of me."

She laughed again, licking her lips.

"Harvey and I had to have money, and I couldn't—I was too afraid of being suspected—get enough from Andrews; so we pretended I had been kidnapped, to get it that way. It was a shame you killed Harvey: he was a glorious beast. I had that bomb, had had it for months. I took it from father's laboratory, when he was making some experiments for a moving picture company. It wasn't very large, and I always carried it with me—just in case. I meant it for you in the hotel room. There was nothing between Owen and me—that was another lie—he didn't love me. I meant it for you, because you were—because I was afraid you were getting at the truth. I was feverish, and when I heard two men go out, leaving one in your room, I was sure the one was you. I didn't see that it was Owen till too late—till I had opened the door a little and thrown the bomb in. Now you've got what you want. Give me morphine. There's no reason for your playing with me any longer. Give me morphine. You've succeeded. Have what I've told you written out: I'll sign it. You can't pretend now I'm worth curing, worth saving. Give me morphine."

Now it was my turn to laugh, asking:

"And aren't you going to confess to kidnapping Charlie Ross and blowing up the *Maine?*"

We had some more hell—a solid hour of it—before she exhausted herself again. The night dragged through. She got a little more than two hours' sleep, a half-hour gain over the previous night. I dozed in the chair when I could.

Sometime before daylight I woke to the feel of a hand on my coat. Keeping my breathing regular, I pushed my eyelids far enough apart to squint through the lashes. We had a very dim light in the room, but I thought Gabrielle was in bed, though I couldn't see whether she was asleep or awake. My head was tilted back to rest on the back of the chair. I couldn't see the hand that was exploring my inside coat-pocket, nor the arm that came down over my shoulder; but they smelled of the kitchen, so I knew they were brown.

The Mexican woman was standing behind me. Mickey had told me she had a knife. Imagination told me she was holding it in her other hand. Good judgment told me to let her alone. I did that, closing my eyes again. Paper rustled between her fingers, and her hand left my pocket.

I moved my head sleepily then, and changed a foot's position. When I heard the door close quietly behind me, I sat up and looked around. Gabrielle was sleeping. I counted the bindles in my pocket and found that eight of them had been taken.

Presently Gabrielle opened her eyes. This was the first time since the cure started that she had awakened quietly. Her face was haggard, but not wild-eyed. She looked at the window and asked:

"Isn't day coming yet?"

"It's getting light." I gave her some orange juice. "We'll get some solid food in you today."

"I don't want food. I want morphine."

"Don't be silly. You'll get food. You won't get morphine. Today won't be like yesterday. You're over the hump, and the rest of it's downhill going, though you may hit a couple of rough spots. It's silly to ask for morphine now. What do you want to do? Have nothing to show for the hell you've been through? You've got it licked now: stay with it."

"Have I—have I really got it licked?"

"Yeah. All you've got to buck now is nervousness, and the memory of how nice it felt to have a skinful of hop."

"I can do it," she said. "I can do it because you say I can."

She got along fine till late in the morning, when she blew up for an hour or two. But it wasn't so bad, and I got her straightened out again. When Mary brought up her luncheon I left them together and went downstairs for my own.

Mickey and MacMan were already at the dining room table. Neither of them spoke a word—to one another or to me—during the meal. Since they kept quiet, I did.

When I went back upstairs, Gabrielle, in a green bathrobe, was sitting in the leather rocker that had been my bed for two nights. She had brushed her hair and powdered her face. Her eyes were mostly green, with a lift to the lower lids as if she was hiding a joke. She said with mock solemnity:

"Sit down. I want to talk seriously to you."

I sat down.

"Why did you go through all this with—for me?" She was really serious now. "You didn't have to, and it couldn't have been pleasant. I was —I don't know how bad I was." She turned red from forehead to chest. "I know I was revolting, disgusting. I know how I must seem to you now. Why—why did you?"

I said:

"I'm twice your age, sister; an old man. I'm damned if I'll make a chump of myself by telling you why I did it, why it was neither revolting nor disgusting, why I'd do it again and be glad of the chance."

She jumped out of her chair, her eyes round and dark, her mouth trembling.

"You mean—?"

"I don't mean anything that I'll admit," I said; "and if you're going to parade around with that robe hanging open you're going to get yourself some bronchitis. You ex-hopheads have to be careful about catching cold."

She sat down again, put her hands over her face, and began crying. I let her cry. Presently she giggled through her fingers and asked:

"Will you go out and let me be alone all afternoon?"

"Yeah, if you'll keep warm."

I drove over to the county seat, went to the county hospital, and argued with people until they let me into Fitzstephan's room.

He was ninety per cent bandages, with only an eye, an ear, and one side of his mouth peeping out. The eye and the half-mouth smiled through linen at me, and a voice came through:

"No more of your hotel rooms for me." It wasn't a clear voice because it had to come out sidewise, and he couldn't move his jaw; but there was plenty of vitality in it. It was the voice of a man who meant to keep on living.

I smiled at him and said:

"No hotel rooms this time, unless you think San Quentin's a hotel. Strong enough to stand up under a third-degree, or shall we wait a day or two?"

"I ought to be at my best now," he said. "Facial expressions won't betray me."

"Good. Now here's the first point: Fink handed you that bomb when he shook hands with you. That's the only way it could have got in without my seeing it. His back was to me then. You didn't know what he was handing you, but you had to take it, just as you have to deny it now, or tip us off that you were tied up with the Holy Grail mob, and that Fink had reasons for killing you."

Fitzstephan said: "You say the most remarkable things. I'm glad he had reasons, though."

"You engineered Riese's murder. The others were your accomplices. When Joseph died the blame was put all on him, the supposed madman. That's enough to let the others out, or ought to be. But here you are killing Collinson and planning God knows what else. Fink knows that if you keep it up you're going to let the truth out about the Temple murder, and he'll swing with you. So, scared panicky, he tries to stop you."

Fitzstephan said: "Better and better. So I killed Collinson?"

"You had him killed—hired Whidden and then didn't pay him. He kidnapped the girl then, holding her for his money, knowing she was what you wanted. It was you his bullet came closest to when we cornered him."

Fitzstephan said: "I'm running out of exclamatory phrases. So I was after her? I wondered about my motive."

"You must have been pretty rotten with her. She'd had a bad time with Andrews, and even with Eric, but she didn't mind talking about them. But when I tried to learn the details of your wooing she shuddered and shut up. I suppose she slammed you down so hard you bounced, and you're the sort of egoist to be driven to anything by that."

Fitzstephan said: "I suppose. You know, I've had more than half an idea at times that you were secretly nursing some exceptionally idiotic theory."

"Well, why shouldn't I? You were standing beside Mrs. Leggett when she suddenly got that gun. Where'd she get it? Chasing her out of the laboratory and down the stairs wasn't in character—not for you. Your hand was on her gun when that bullet hit her neck. Was I supposed to be deaf, dumb, and blind? There was, as you agreed, one mind behind all Gabrielle's troubles. You're the one person who has that sort of a mind, whose connection with each episode can be traced, and who has the necessary motive. The motive held me up: I couldn't be sure of it till I'd had my first fair chance to pump Gabrielle—after the explosion. And another thing that held me up was my not being able to tie you to the Temple crowd till Fink and Aaronia Haldorn did it for me."

Fitzstephan said: "Ah, Aaronia helped tie me? What has she been up to?" He said it absent-mindedly, and his one visible gray eye was small, as if he was busy with other thoughts behind it.

"She's done her best to cover you up by gumming the works, creating confusion, setting us after Andrews, even trying to shoot me. I mentioned Collinson just after she'd learned that the Andrews false-trail was no good. She gave me a half-concealed gasp and sob, just on the off-chance that it'd lead me astray, overlooking no bets. I like her: she's shifty."

"She's so headstrong," Fitzstephan said lightly, not having listened to half I had said, busy with his own thoughts. He turned his head on the pillow so that his eye looked at the ceiling, narrow and brooding.

I said: "And so ends the Great Dain Curse."

He laughed then, as well as he could with one eye and a fraction of a mouth, and said:

"Suppose, my boy, I were to tell you I'm a Dain?"

I said: "Huh?"

He said: "My mother and Gabrielle's maternal grandfather were brother and sister."

I said: "I'll be damned."

"You'll have to go away and let me think," he said. "I don't know yet what I shall do. Understand, at present I admit nothing. But the chances are I shall insist on the curse, shall use it to save my dear neck. In that event, my son, you're going to see a most remarkable defense, a circus that will send the nation's newspapers into happy convulsions. I shall be a Dain, with the cursed Dain blood in me, and the crimes of Cousin Alice and Cousin Lily and Second-cousin Gabrielle and the Lord knows how many other criminal Dains shall be evidence in my behalf. The number of my own crimes will be to my advantage, on the theory that nobody but a lunatic could have committed so many. And won't they be many? I'll produce crimes and crimes, dating from the cradle.

"Even literature shall help me. Didn't most reviewers agree that *The Pale Egyptian* was the work of a sub-Mongolian? And, as I remember, the consensus was that my *Eighteen Inches* bore all the better known indications of authorial degeneracy. Evidence, son, to save my sweet neck. And I shall wave my mangled body at them—an arm gone, a leg gone, parts of my torso and face—a ruin whose crimes and high Heaven have surely brought sufficient punishment upon him. And perhaps the bomb shocked me into sanity again, or, at least, out of criminal insanity. Perhaps I'll even have become religious. It'll be a splendid circus. It tempts me. But I must think before I commit myself."

He panted through the uncovered half of his mouth, exhausted by his speech, looking at me with a gray eye that held triumphant mirth.

"You'll probably make a go of it," I said as I prepared to leave. "And I'm satisfied if you do. You've taken enough of a licking. And, legally, you're entitled to beat the jump if ever anybody was."

"Legally entitled?" he repeated, the mirth going out of his eye. He looked away, and then at me again, uneasily. "Tell me the truth. Am I?"

I nodded.

"But, damn it, that spoils it," he complained, fighting to keep the uneasiness out of his eye, fighting to retain his usual lazily amused manner, and not making such a poor job of it. "It's no fun if I'm really cracked."

When I got back to the house in the cove, Mickey and MacMan were sitting on the front steps. MacMan said, "Hello," and Mickey said: "Get any fresh woman-scars while you were away? Your little playmate's been asking for you." I supposed from this—from my being readmitted to the white race—that Gabrielle had had a good afternoon.

She was sitting up in bed with pillows behind her back, her face still—or again—powdered, her eyes shining happily.

"I didn't mean for you to go away forever," she scolded. "It was nasty of you. I've got a surprise for you and I've nearly burst waiting."

"Well, here I am. What is it?"

"Shut your eyes."

I shut them.

"Open your eyes."

I opened them. She was holding out to me the eight bindles that Mary Nunez had picked my pocket for.

"I've had them since noon," she said proudly; "and they've got finger-marks and tear-marks on them, but not one of them has been opened. It—honestly—it wasn't so hard not to."

"I knew it wouldn't be, for you," I said. "That's why I didn't take them away from Mary."

"You knew? You trusted me that much—to go away and leave me with them?"

Nobody but an idiot would have confessed that for two days the folded papers had held powdered sugar instead of the original morphine.

"You're the nicest man in the world." She caught one of my hands and rubbed her cheek into it, then dropped it quickly, frowned her face out of shape, and said: "Except! You sat there this noon and deliberately tried to make me think you were in love with me."

"Well?" I asked, trying to keep my face straight.

"You hypocrite. You deceiver of young girls. It would serve you right if I made you marry me—or sued you for breach of promise. I honestly believed you all afternoon—and it *did* help me. I believed you until you came in just now, and then I saw—" She stopped.

"Saw what?"

"A monster. A nice one, an especially nice one to have around when you're in trouble, but a monster just the same, without any human foolishness like love in him, and— What's the matter? Have I said something I shouldn't?"

"I don't think you should have," I said. "I'm not sure I wouldn't trade places with Fitzstephan now—if that big-eyed woman with the voice was part of the bargain."

"Oh, dear!" she said.

XXIII · *The Circus*

OWEN FITZSTEPHAN never spoke to me again. He refused to see me, and when, as a prisoner, he couldn't help himself there, he shut his mouth and kept it shut. This sudden hatred of me—for it amounted to that—had grown, I supposed, out of his knowing I thought him insane. He wanted the rest of the world, or at least the dozen who would represent the world on his jury, to think he had been crazy—and did make them think so—but he didn't want me to agree with them. As a sane man who, by pretending to be a lunatic, had done as he pleased and escaped punishment, he had a joke—if you wanted to call it that—on the world. But if he was a lunatic who, ignorant of his craziness, thought he was pretending to be a lunatic, then the joke—if you wanted to call it that—was on him. And my having such a joke on him was more than his egotism could stomach, even though it's not likely he ever admitted to himself that he was, or might be, actually crazy. Whatever he thought, he never spoke to me after the hospital interview in which I had said he was legally entitled to escape hanging.

His trial, when he was well enough to appear in court some months later, was every bit of the circus he had promised, and the newspapers had their happy convulsions. He was tried in the county court house for Mrs. Cotton's murder. Two new witnesses had been found, who had seen him walking away from the rear of the Cotton house that morning, and a third who identified his car as the one that had been parked four blocks away all—or all the latter part of—the previous night. The city and county district attorneys agreed that this evidence made the Cotton case the strongest against him.

Fitzstephan's plea was *Not guilty by reason of insanity,* or whatever the legal wording was. Since Mrs. Cotton's murder had been the last of his crimes, his lawyers could, and did, introduce, as proof of his insanity, all that he had done in the others. They made a high, wide, and handsome job of it, carrying out his original idea that the best way to prove him crazy was to show he had committed more crimes than any sane man could have. Well, it was plain enough that he had.

He had known Alice Dain, his cousin, in New York when she and Gabrielle, then a child, were living there. Gabrielle couldn't corroborate this: we had only Fitzstephan's word for it; but it may have been so. He said they concealed his relationship from the others because they did not want the girl's father—for whom Alice was then searching—to know that she was bringing with her any links with the dangerous past. Fitzstephan said Alice had been his mistress in New York: that could have been true, but didn't matter.

After Alice and Gabrielle left New York for San Francisco, Fitzstephan and the woman exchanged letters occasionally, but with no definite purpose. Fitzstephan then met the Haldorns. The cult was his idea: he organized it, financed it, and brought it to San Francisco, though he kept his connection with it a secret, since everyone who knew him knew his skepticism; and his interest in it would have advertised it as the fake it was. To him, he said, the cult was a combination of toy and meal-ticket: he liked influencing people, especially in obscure ways, and people didn't seem to like buying his books.

Aaronia Haldorn was his mistress. Joseph was a puppet, in the family as in the Temple.

In San Francisco Fitzstephan and Alice arranged so that he became acquainted with her husband and Gabrielle through other friends of the family. Gabrielle was now a young woman. Her physical peculiarities, which he interpreted pretty much as she had, fascinated him; and he tried his luck with her. He didn't have any. That made him doubly determined to land her: he was that way. Alice was his ally. She knew him and she hated the girl—so she wanted him to have her. Alice had told Fitzstephan the family history. The girl's father did not know at this time that she had been taught to think him her mother's murderer. He knew she had a deep aversion to him, but did not know on what it was based. He thought that what he had gone through in prison and since had marked him with a hardness naturally enough repellant to a young girl who was, in spite of their relationship, actually only a recent acquaintance.

He learned the truth about it when, surprising Fitzstephan in further attempts to make Gabrielle—as Fitzstephan put it—listen to reason, he had got into a three-cornered row with the pair of them. Leggett now began to understand what sort of a woman he was married to. Fitzstephan was no longer invited to the Leggett house, but kept in touch with Alice and waited his time.

His time came when Upton arrived with his demand for blackmail. Alice went to Fitzstephan for advice. He gave it to her—poisonously. He urged her to handle Upton herself, concealing his demand—his knowledge of the Leggett past—from Leggett. He told her she should above all else continue to keep her knowledge of Leggett's Central American and Mexican history concealed from him—a valuable hold on him now that he hated her because of what she'd taught the girl. Giving Upton the diamonds, and faking the burglary evidence, were Fitzstephan's ideas. Poor Alice didn't mean anything to him: he didn't care what happened to her so long as he could ruin Leggett and get Gabrielle.

He succeeded in the first of those aims: guided by him, Alice completely demolished the Leggett household, thinking, until the very last, when he pursued her after giving her the pistol in the laboratory, that he had a clever plan by which they would be saved; that is, she and he would: her husband didn't count with her any more than she with Fitzstephan. Fitzstephan had had to kill her, of course, to keep her from exposing him when she found that his clever plan was a trap for her.

Fitzstephan said he killed Leggett himself. When Gabrielle left the house after seeing Ruppert's murder, she left a note saying she had gone for good. That broke up the arrangement as far as Leggett was concerned. He told Alice he was through, was going away, and offered of his own accord to write a statement assuming responsibility for what she had done. Fitzstephan tried to persuade Alice to kill him, but she wouldn't. He did. He wanted Gabrielle, and he didn't think a live Leggett, even though a fugitive from justice, would let him have her.

Fitzstephan's success in getting rid of Leggett, and in escaping detection by killing Alice, encouraged him. He went blithely on with his plan to get the girl. The Haldorns had been introduced to the Leggetts some months before, and already had her nibbling at their hook. She had gone to them when she ran away from home. Now they persuaded her to come to the Temple again. The Haldorns didn't know what Fitzstephan was up to, what he had done to the Leggetts: they thought that the girl was only another of the likely prospects he fed them. But Doctor Riese, hunting for Joseph in Joseph's part of the Temple the day I got there, opened a door that should have been locked, and saw Fitzstephan and the Haldorns in conference.

That was dangerous: Riese couldn't be kept quiet, and, once Fitzstephan's connection with the Temple was known, as likely as not the truth about his part in the Leggett riot would come out. He had two easily handled tools—Joseph and Minnie. He had Riese killed. But that woke Aaronia up to his true interest in Gabrielle. Aaronia, jealous, could and would either make him give up the girl or ruin him. He persuaded Joseph that none of them was safe from the gallows while Aaronia lived. When I saved Aaronia by killing her husband, I also saved Fitzstephan for the time: Aaronia and Fink had to keep quiet about Riese's death if they wanted to save themselves from being charged with complicity in it.

By this time Fitzstephan had hit his stride. He looked on Gabrielle now as his property, bought with the deaths he had caused. Each death had increased her price, her value to him. When Eric carried her off and married her, Fitzstephan hadn't hesitated. Eric was to be killed.

Nearly a year before, Fitzstephan had wanted a quiet place where he could go to finish a novel. Mrs. Fink, my village-blacksmith, had recommended Quesada. She was a native of the village, and her son by a former marriage, Harvey Whidden, was living there. Fitzstephan went to Quesada for a couple of months, and became fairly well acquainted with Whidden. Now that there was another murder to be done, Fitzstephan remembered Whidden as a man who might do it, for a price.

When Fitzstephan heard that Collinson wanted a quiet place where his wife could rest and recuperate while they were waiting for the Haldorns' trial, he suggested Quesada. Well, it was a quiet place, probably the quietest in California. Then Fitzstephan went to Whidden with an offer of a thousand dollars for Eric's murder. Whidden refused at first, but he wasn't nimble-witted, and Fitzstephan could be persuasive enough, so the bargain had been made.

Whidden bungled a try at it Thursday night, frightening Collinson into wiring me, saw the wire in the telegraph office, and thought he had to go through with it then to save himself. So he fortified himself with whiskey, followed Collinson Friday night, and shoved him off the cliff. Then he took some more whiskey and came to San Francisco, considering himself by this time a hell of a desperate guy. He phoned his employer, saying: "Well, I killed him easy enough and dead enough. Now I want my money."

Fitzstephan's phone came through the house switchboard: he didn't know who might have heard Whidden talking. He decided to play safe. He pretended he didn't know who was talking nor what he was talking about. Thinking Fitzstephan was double-crossing him, knowing what the novelist wanted, Whidden decided to take the girl and hold her for, not his original thousand dollars, but ten thousand. He had enough drunken cunning to disguise his handwriting when he wrote his note to Fitzstephan, not to sign it, and to so word it that Fitzstephan couldn't tell the police who had sent it without explaining how he knew who had sent it.

Fitzstephan wasn't sitting any too pretty. When he got Whidden's note, he decided to play his hand boldly, pushing his thus-far-solid luck. He told me about the phone-call and gave me the letter. That entitled him to show himself in Quesada with an excellent reason for being there. But he came down ahead of time, the night before he joined me, and went to the marshal's house to ask Mrs. Cotton—whose relation to Whidden he knew—where he could find the man. Whidden was there, hiding from the marshal. Whidden wasn't nimble-witted, and Fitzstephan was persuasive enough when he wanted to be: Fitzstephan explained how Whidden's recklessness had forced him to pretend to not understand the phone-call. Fitzstephan had a scheme by which Whidden could now collect his ten thousand dollars in safety, or so he made Whidden think.

Whidden went back to his hiding-place. Fitzstephan remained with Mrs. Cotton. She, poor woman, now knew too much, and didn't like what she knew. She was doomed: killing people was the one sure and safe way of keeping them quiet: his whole recent experience proved it. His experience with Leggett told him that if he could get her to leave behind a statement in which various mysterious points were satisfactorily—and not too truthfully—explained, his situation would be still further improved. She suspected his intentions, and didn't want to help him carry them out. She finally wrote the statement he dictated, but not until late in the morning. His description of how he finally got it from her wasn't pleasant; but he got it, and then strangled her, barely finishing when her husband arrived home from his all-night hunt.

Fitzstephan escaped by the back door—the witnesses who had seen him go away from the house didn't come forward until his photograph in the papers jogged their memories—and joined Vernon and me at the hotel. He went with us to Whidden's hiding-place below Dull Point. He knew Whidden, knew the dull man's probable reaction to this second betrayal. He knew that neither Cotton nor Feeney would be sorry to have to shoot Whidden. Fitzstephan believed he could trust to his luck and what gamblers call the percentage of the situation. That failing, he meant to stumble when he stepped from the boat, accidentally shooting Whidden with the gun in his hand. (He remembered how neatly he had disposed of Mrs. Leggett.) He might have been blamed for that, might even have been suspected, but he could hardly have been convicted of anything.

Once again his luck held. Whidden, seeing Fitzstephan with us, had flared up and tried to shoot him, and we had killed Whidden.

That was the story with which this crazy man, thinking himself sane, tried to establish his insanity, and succeeded. The other charges against him were dropped. He was sent to the state asylum at Napa. A year later he was discharged. I don't suppose the asylum officials thought him cured: they thought he was too badly crippled ever to be dangerous again.

Aaronia Haldorn carried him off to an island in Puget Sound, I've heard.

She testified at his trial, as one of his witnesses, but was not herself tried for anything. The attempt of her husband and Fitzstephan to kill her had, for all practical purposes, removed her from among the guilty.

We never found Mrs. Fink.

Tom Fink drew a five-to-fifteen-years jolt in San Quentin for what he had done to Fitzstephan. Neither of them seemed to blame the other now, and each tried to cover the other up on the witness stand. Fink's professed motive for the bombing was to avenge his step-son's death, but nobody swallowed that. He had tried to check Fitzstephan's activities before Fitzstephan brought the whole works down on their ears.

Released from prison, finding himself shadowed, Fink had seen both reason for fear and a means to safety in that shadow. He *had* back-doored Mickey that night, slipping out to get the material for his bomb, and then in again, working all night on the bomb. The news he had brought me was supposed to account for his presence in Quesada. The bomb wasn't large—its outer cover was an aluminum soap container wrapped in white paper—and neither he nor Fitzstephan had had any difficulty in concealing it from me when it passed between them during their hand-shaking. Fitzstephan had thought it something Aaronia was sending him, something important enough to justify the risk in sending it. He couldn't have refused to take it without attracting my attention, without giving away the connection between him and Fink. He had concealed it until we had left the room, and then had opened it—to wake up in the hospital. Tom Fink had thought himself safe, with Mickey to testify that he had shadowed him from the time he had left the prison, and me to account for his behavior on the scene of the bombing.

Fitzstephan said that he did not think Alice Leggett's account of the killing of her sister Lily was the truth, that he thought she—Alice—had done the killing herself and had lied to hurt Gabrielle. Everybody took it for granted that he was right—everybody, including Gabrielle—though he didn't have any evidence to support what was after all only his guess. I was tempted to have the agency's Paris correspondent see what he could dig up on that early affair, but decided not to. It was nobody's business except Gabrielle's, and she seemed happy enough with what had already been dug up.

She was in the Collinsons' hands now. They had come to Quesada for her as soon as the newspapers put out their first extra accusing Fitzstephan of Eric's murder. The Collinsons hadn't had to be crude about it—to admit that they'd ever suspected her of anything: when Andrews had surrendered his letters testamentary, and another administrator—Walter Fielding—had been appointed, the Collinsons had simply seemed to pick her up, as was their right as her closest relations, where Andrews had put her down.

Two months in the mountains topped off her cure, and she came back to the city looking like nothing that she had been. The difference was not only in appearance.

"I can't really make myself believe that all that actually happened to me," she told me one noon when she, Laurence Collinson, and I were lunching together between morning and afternoon court-sessions. "Is it, do you think, because there was so much of it that I became callous?"

"No. Remember you were going around coked up most of the time. That saved you from the sharp edge. Lucky for you you were. Stay away from the morphine now and it'll always be a hazy sort of dream. Any time you want to bring it back clear and vivid, take a jolt."

"I won't, I won't, ever," she said; "not even to give you the—the fun of bullying me through a cure again. He enjoyed himself awfully," she told Laurence Collinson. "He used to curse me, ridicule me, threaten me with the most terrible things, and then, at the last, I think he tried to seduce me. And if I'm uncouth at times, Laurence, you'll have to blame him: he positively hadn't a refining influence."

She seemed to have come back far enough.

Laurence Collinson laughed with us, but not from any farther down than his chin. I had an idea he thought I hadn't a refining influence.

THE
MALTESE FALCON

TO *JOSE*

THE MALTESE FALCON

I · Spade & Archer

SAMUEL SPADE's jaw was long and bony, his chin a jutting v under the more flexible v of his mouth. His nostrils curved back to make another, smaller, v. His yellow-grey eyes were horizontal. The v *motif* was picked up again by thickish brows rising outward from twin creases above a hooked nose, and his pale brown hair grew down—from high flat temples —in a point on his forehead. He looked rather pleasantly like a blond satan.

He said to Effie Perine: "Yes, sweetheart?"

She was a lanky sunburned girl whose tan dress of thin woolen stuff clung to her with an effect of dampness. Her eyes were brown and playful in a shiny boyish face. She finished shutting the door behind her, leaned against it, and said: "There's a girl wants to see you. Her name's Wonderly."

"A customer?"

"I guess so. You'll want to see her anyway: she's a knockout."

"Shoo her in, darling," said Spade. "Shoo her in."

Effie Perine opened the door again, following it back into the outer office, standing with a hand on the knob while saying: "Will you come in, Miss Wonderly?"

A voice said, "Thank you," so softly that only the purest articulation made the words intelligible, and a young woman came through the doorway. She advanced slowly, with tentative steps, looking at Spade with cobalt-blue eyes that were both shy and probing.

She was tall and pliantly slender, without angularity anywhere. Her body was erect and high-breasted, her legs long, her hands and feet narrow. She wore two shades of blue that had been selected because of her eyes. The hair curling from under her blue hat was darkly red, her full lips more brightly red. White teeth glistened in the crescent her timid smile made.

Spade rose bowing and indicating with a thick-fingered hand the oaken armchair beside his desk. He was quite six feet tall. The steep rounded slope of his shoulders made his body seem almost conical—no broader than it was thick—and kept his freshly pressed grey coat from fitting very well.

Miss Wonderly murmured, "Thank you," softly as before and sat down on the edge of the chair's wooden seat.

Spade sank into his swivel-chair, made a quarter-turn to face her, smiled politely. He smiled without separating his lips. All the v's in his face grew longer.

The tappity-tap-tap and the thin bell and muffled whir of Effie Perine's typewriting came through the closed door. Somewhere in a neighboring office a power-driven machine vibrated dully. On Spade's desk a limp cigarette smoldered in a brass tray filled with the remains of limp cigarettes. Ragged grey flakes of cigarette-ash dotted the yellow top of the desk and the green blotter and the papers that were there. A buff-curtained window, eight or ten inches open, let in from the court a current of air faintly scented with ammonia. The ashes on the desk twitched and crawled in the current.

Miss Wonderly watched the grey flakes twitch and crawl. Her eyes were uneasy. She sat on the very edge of the chair. Her feet were flat on the floor, as if she were about to rise. Her hands in dark gloves clasped a flat dark handbag in her lap.

Spade rocked back in his chair and asked: "Now what can I do for you, Miss Wonderly?"

She caught her breath and looked at him. She swallowed and said hurriedly: "Could you—? I thought—I—that is—" Then she tortured her lower lip with glistening teeth and said nothing. Only her dark eyes spoke now, pleading.

Spade smiled and nodded as if he understood her, but pleasantly, as if nothing serious were involved. He said: "Suppose you tell me about it, from the beginning, and then we'll know what needs doing. Better begin as far back as you can."

"That was in New York."

"Yes."

"I don't know where she met him. I mean I don't know where in New York. She's five years younger than I—only seventeen—and we didn't have the same friends. I don't suppose we've ever been as close as sisters should be. Mama and Papa are in Europe. It would kill them. I've got to get her back before they come home."

"Yes," he said.

"They're coming home the first of the month."

Spade's eyes brightened. "Then we've two weeks," he said.

"I didn't know what she had done until her letter came. I was frantic." Her lips trembled. Her hands mashed the dark handbag in her lap.

"I was too afraid she had done something like this to go to the police, and the fear that something had happened to her kept urging me to go. There wasn't anyone I could go to for advice. I didn't know what to do. What could I do?"

"Nothing, of course," Spade said, "but then her letter came?"

"Yes, and I sent her a telegram asking her to come home. I sent it to General Delivery here. That was the only address she gave me. I waited a whole week, but no answer came, not another word from her. And Mama and Papa's return was drawing nearer and nearer. So I came to San Francisco to get her. I wrote her I was coming. I shouldn't have done that, should I?"

"Maybe not. It's not always easy to know what to do. You haven't found her?"

"No, I haven't. I wrote her that I would go to the St. Mark, and I begged her to come and let me talk to her even if she didn't intend to go home with me. But she didn't come. I waited three days, and she didn't come, didn't even send me a message of any sort."

Spade nodded his blond satan's head, frowned sympathetically, and tightened his lips together.

"It was horrible," Miss Wonderly said, trying to smile. "I couldn't sit there like that—waiting—not knowing what had happened to her, what might be happening to her." She stopped trying to smile. She shuddered. "The only address I had was General Delivery. I wrote her another letter, and yesterday afternoon I went to the Post Office. I stayed there until after dark, but I didn't see her. I went there again this morning, and still didn't see Corinne, but I saw Floyd Thursby."

Spade nodded again. His frown went away. In its place came a look of sharp attentiveness.

"He wouldn't tell me where Corinne was," she went on, hopelessly. "He wouldn't tell me anything, except that she was well and happy. But how can I believe that? That is what he would tell me anyhow, isn't it?"

"Sure," Spade agreed. "But it might be true."

"I hope it is. I do hope it is," she exclaimed. "But I can't go back home like this, without having seen her, without even having talked to her on the phone. He wouldn't take me to her. He said she didn't want to see me. I can't believe that. He promised to tell her he had seen me, and to bring her to see me—if she would come—this evening at the hotel. He said he knew she wouldn't. He promised to come himself if she wouldn't. He—"

She broke off with a startled hand to her mouth as the door opened.

The man who had opened the door came in a step, said, "Oh, excuse me!" hastily took his brown hat from his head, and backed out.

"It's all right, Miles," Spade told him. "Come in. Miss Wonderly, this is Mr. Archer, my partner."

Miles Archer came into the office again, shutting the door behind him, ducking his head and smiling at Miss Wonderly, making a vaguely polite gesture with the hat in his hand. Hè was of medium height, solidly built, wide in the shoulders, thick in the neck, with a jovial heavy-jawed red face and some grey in his close-trimmed hair. He was apparently as many years past forty as Spade was past thirty.

Spade said: "Miss Wonderly's sister ran away from New York with a fellow named Floyd Thursby. They're here. Miss Wonderly has seen Thursby and has a date with him tonight. Maybe he'll bring the sister with him. The chances are he won't. Miss Wonderly wants us to find the sister and get her away from him and back home." He looked at Miss Wonderly. "Right?"

"Yes," she said indistinctly. The embarrassment that had gradually been driven away by Spade's ingratiating smiles and nods and assurances was pinkening her face again. She looked at the bag in her lap and picked nervously at it with a gloved finger.

Spade winked at his partner.

Miles Archer came forward to stand at a corner of the desk. While the girl looked at her bag he looked at her. His little brown eyes ran their bold appraising gaze from her lowered face to her feet and up to her face again. Then he looked at Spade and made a silent whistling mouth of appreciation.

Spade lifted two fingers from the arm of his chair in a brief warning gesture and said:

"We shouldn't have any trouble with it. It's simply a matter of having a man at the hotel this evening to shadow him away when he leaves, and shadow him until he leads us to your sister. If she comes with him, and you persuade her to return with you, so much the better. Otherwise —if she doesn't want to leave him after we've found her—well, we'll find a way of managing that."

Archer said: "Yeh." His voice was heavy, coarse.

Miss Wonderly looked up at Spade, quickly, puckering her forehead between her eyebrows.

"Oh, but you must be careful!" Her voice shook a little, and her lips shaped the words with nervous jerkiness. "I'm deathly afraid of him, of what he might do. She's so young and his bringing her here from New York is such a serious— Mightn't he—mightn't he do—something to her?"

Spade smiled and patted the arms of his chair.

"Just leave that to us," he said. "We'll know how to handle him."

"But mightn't he?" she insisted.

"There's always a chance." Spade nodded judicially. "But you can trust us to take care of that."

"I do trust you," she said earnestly, "but I want you to know that he's a dangerous man. I honestly don't think he'd stop at anything. I don't

believe he'd hesitate to—to kill Corinne if he thought it would save him.
Mightn't he do that?"

"You didn't threaten him, did you?"

"I told him that all I wanted was to get her home before Mama and
Papa came so they'd never know what she had done. I promised him I'd
never say a word to them about it if he helped me, but if he didn't Papa
would certainly see that he was punished. I—I don't suppose he believed
me, altogether."

"Can he cover up by marrying her?" Archer asked.

The girl blushed and replied in a confused voice: "He has a wife
and three children in England. Corinne wrote me that, to explain why
she had gone off with him."

"They usually do," Spade said, "though not always in England." He
leaned forward to reach for pencil and pad of paper. "What does he look
like?"

"Oh, he's thirty-five years old, perhaps, and as tall as you, and either
naturally dark or quite sunburned. His hair is dark too, and he has thick
eyebrows. He talks in a rather loud, blustery way and has a nervous, irritable manner. He gives the impression of being—of violence."

Spade, scribbling on the pad, asked without looking up: "What color
eyes?"

"They're blue-grey and watery, though not in a weak way. And—oh,
yes—he has a marked cleft in his chin."

"Thin, medium, or heavy build?"

"Quite athletic. He's broad-shouldered and carries himself erect, has
what could be called a decidedly military carriage. He was wearing a
light grey suit and a grey hat when I saw him this morning."

"What does he do for a living?" Spade asked as he laid down his
pencil.

"I don't know," she said. "I haven't the slightest idea."

"What time is he coming to see you?"

"After eight o'clock."

"All right, Miss Wonderly, we'll have a man there. It'll help if—"

"Mr. Spade, could either you or Mr. Archer?" She made an appealing
gesture with both hands. "Could either of you look after it personally?
I don't mean that the man you'd send wouldn't be capable, but—oh!—I'm
so afraid of what might happen to Corinne. I'm afraid of him. Could you?
I'd be—I'd expect to be charged more, of course." She opened her handbag with nervous fingers and put two hundred-dollar bills on Spade's
desk. "Would that be enough?"

"Yeh," Archer said, "and I'll look after it myself."

Miss Wonderly stood up, impulsively holding a hand out to him.

"Thank you! Thank you!" she exclaimed, and then gave Spade her
hand, repeating: "Thank you!"

"Not at all," Spade said over it. "Glad to. It'll help some if you either meet Thursby downstairs or let yourself be seen in the lobby with him at some time."

"I will," she promised, and thanked the partners again.

"And don't look for me," Archer cautioned her. "I'll see you all right."

Spade went to the corridor-door with Miss Wonderly. When he returned to his desk Archer nodded at the hundred-dollar bills there, growled complacently, "They're right enough," picked one up, folded it, and tucked it into a vest-pocket. "And they had brothers in her bag."

Spade pocketed the other bill before he sat down. Then he said: "Well, don't dynamite her too much. What do you think of her?"

"Sweet! And you telling me not to dynamite her." Archer guffawed suddenly without merriment. "Maybe you saw her first, Sam, but I spoke first." He put his hands in his trousers-pockets and teetered on his heels.

"You'll play hell with her, you will." Spade grinned wolfishly, showing the edges of teeth far back in his jaw. "You've got brains, yes you have." He began to make a cigarette.

II · Death in the Fog

A telephone-bell rang in darkness. When it had rung three times bed-springs creaked, fingers fumbled on wood, something small and hard thudded on a carpeted floor, the springs creaked again, and a man's voice said:

"Hello. . . . Yes, speaking. . . . Dead? . . . Yes. . . . Fifteen minutes. Thanks."

A switch clicked and a white bowl hung on three gilded chains from the ceiling's center filled the room with light. Spade, barefooted in green and white checked pajamas, sat on the side of his bed. He scowled at the telephone on the table while his hands took from beside it a packet of brown papers and a sack of Bull Durham tobacco.

Cold steamy air blew in through two open windows, bringing with it half a dozen times a minute the Alcatraz foghorn's dull moaning. A tinny alarm-clock, insecurely mounted on a corner of Duke's *Celebrated Criminal Cases of America*—face down on the table—held its hands at five minutes past two.

Spade's thick fingers made a cigarette with deliberate care, sifting a measured quantity of tan flakes down into curved paper, spreading the flakes so that they lay equal at the ends with a slight depression in the middle, thumbs rolling the paper's inner edge down and up under the outer edge as forefingers pressed it over, thumbs and fingers sliding to the paper cylinder's ends to hold it even while tongue licked the flap, left forefinger and thumb pinching their end while right forefinger and thumb smoothed the damp seam, right forefinger and thumb twisting their end and lifting the other to Spade's mouth.

He picked up the pigskin and nickel lighter that had fallen to the floor, manipulated it, and with the cigarette burning in a corner of his mouth stood up. He took off his pajamas. The smooth thickness of his arms, legs, and body, the sag of his big rounded shoulders, made his body like a bear's. It was like a shaved bear's: his chest was hairless. His skin was childishly soft and pink.

He scratched the back of his neck and began to dress. He put on a thin white union-suit, grey socks, black garters, and dark brown shoes. When he had fastened his shoes he picked up the telephone, called Graystone 4500, and ordered a taxicab. He put on a green-striped white shirt, a soft white collar, a green necktie, the grey suit he had worn that day, a loose tweed overcoat, and a dark grey hat. The street-door-bell rang as he stuffed tobacco, keys, and money into his pockets.

Where Bush Street roofed Stockton before slipping downhill to Chinatown, Spade paid his fare and left the taxicab. San Francisco's night-fog, thin, clammy, and penetrant, blurred the street. A few yards from where Spade had dismissed the taxicab a small group of men stood looking up an alley. Two women stood with a man on the other side of Bush Street, looking at the alley. There were faces at windows.

Spade crossed the sidewalk between iron-railed hatchways that opened above bare ugly stairs, went to the parapet, and, resting his hands on the damp coping, looked down into Stockton Street.

An automobile popped out of the tunnel beneath him with a roaring swish, as if it had been blown out, and ran away. Not far from the tunnel's mouth a man was hunkered on his heels before a billboard that held advertisements of a moving picture and a gasoline across the front of a gap between two store-buildings. The hunkered man's head was bent almost to the sidewalk so he could look under the billboard. A hand flat on the paving, a hand clenched on the billboard's green frame, held him in this grotesque position. Two other men stood awkwardly together at one end of the billboard, peeping through the few inches of space between it and the building at that end. The building at the other end had a blank grey sidewall that looked down on the lot behind the billboard. Lights flickered on the sidewall, and the shadows of men moving among lights.

Spade turned from the parapet and walked up Bush Street to the alley where men were grouped. A uniformed policeman chewing gum under an enameled sign that said *Burritt St.* in white against dark blue put out an arm and asked:

"What do you want here?"

"I'm Sam Spade. Tom Polhaus phoned me."

"Sure you are." The policeman's arm went down. "I didn't know you at first. Well, they're back there." He jerked a thumb over his shoulder. "Bad business."

"Bad enough," Spade agreed, and went up the alley.

Half-way up it, not far from the entrance, a dark ambulance stood. Behind the ambulance, to the left, the alley was bounded by a waist-high fence, horizontal strips of rough boarding. From the fence dark ground fell away steeply to the billboard on Stockton Street below.

A ten-foot length of the fence's top rail had been torn from a post at one end and hung dangling from the other. Fifteen feet down the slope a flat boulder stuck out. In the notch between boulder and slope Miles Archer lay on his back. Two men stood over him. One of them held the beam of an electric torch on the dead man. Other men with lights moved up and down the slope.

One of them hailed Spade, "Hello, Sam," and clambered up to the alley, his shadow running up the slope before him. He was a barrel-bellied tall man with shrewd small eyes, a thick mouth, and carelessly shaven dark jowls. His shoes, knees, hands, and chin were daubed with brown loam.

"I figured you'd want to see it before we took him away," he said as he stepped over the broken fence.

"Thanks, Tom," Spade said. "What happened?" He put an elbow on a fence-post and looked down at the men below, nodding to those who nodded to him.

Tom Polhaus poked his own left breast with a dirty finger. "Got him right through the pump—with this." He took a fat revolver from his coat-pocket and held it out to Spade. Mud inlaid the depressions in the revolver's surface. "A Webley. English, ain't it?"

Spade took his elbow from the fence-post and leaned down to look at the weapon, but he did not touch it.

"Yes," he said, "Webley-Fosbery automatic revolver. That's it. Thirty-eight, eight shot. They don't make them any more. How many gone out of it?"

"One pill." Tom poked his breast again. "He must've been dead when he cracked the fence." He raised the muddy revolver. "Ever seen this before?"

Spade nodded. "I've seen Webley-Fosberys," he said without interest, and then spoke rapidly: "He was shot up here, huh? Standing where you are, with his back to the fence. The man that shot him stands here." He went around in front of Tom and raised a hand breast-high with leveled forefinger. "Lets him have it and Miles goes back, taking the top off the fence and going on through and down till the rock catches him. That it?"

"That's it," Tom replied slowly, working his brows together. "The blast burnt his coat."

"Who found him?"

"The man on the beat, Shilling. He was coming down Bush, and just as he got here a machine turning threw headlights up here, and he saw the top off the fence. So he came up to look at it, and found him."

"What about the machine that was turning around?"

"Not a damned thing about it, Sam. Shilling didn't pay any attention to it, not knowing anything was wrong then. He says nobody didn't come out of here while he was coming down from Powell or he'd've seen them. The only other way out would be under the billboard on Stockton. Nobody went that way. The fog's got the ground soggy, and the only marks are where Miles slid down and where this here gun rolled."

"Didn't anybody hear the shot?"

"For the love of God, Sam, we only just got here. Somebody must've heard it, when we find them." He turned and put a leg over the fence. "Coming down for a look at him before he's moved?"

Spade said: "No."

Tom halted astride the fence and looked back at Spade with surprised small eyes.

Spade said: "You've seen him. You'd see everything I could."

Tom, still looking at Spade, nodded doubtfully and withdrew his leg over the fence.

"His gun was tucked away on his hip," he said. "It hadn't been fired. His overcoat was buttoned. There's a hundred and sixty-some bucks in his clothes. Was he working, Sam?"

Spade, after a moment's hesitation, nodded.

Tom asked: "Well?"

"He was supposed to be tailing a fellow named Floyd Thursby," Spade said, and described Thursby as Miss Wonderly had described him.

"What for?"

Spade put his hands into his overcoat-pockets and blinked sleepy eyes at Tom.

Tom repeated impatiently: "What for?"

"He was an Englishman, maybe. I don't know what his game was, exactly. We were trying to find out where he lived." Spade grinned faintly and took a hand from his pocket to pat Tom's shoulder. "Don't crowd me " He put the hand in his pocket again. "I'm going out to break the news to Miles's wife." He turned away.

Tom, scowling, opened his mouth, closed it without having said anything, cleared his throat, put the scowl off his face, and spoke with a husky sort of gentleness:

"It's tough, him getting it like that. Miles had his faults same as the rest of us, but I guess he must've had some good points too."

"I guess so," Spade agreed in a tone that was utterly meaningless, and went out of the alley.

In an all-night drug-store on the corner of Bush and Taylor Streets, Spade used a telephone.

"Precious," he said into it a little while after he had given a number, "Miles has been shot. . . . Yes, he's dead. . . . Now don't get excited. . . . Yes. . . . You'll have to break it to Iva. . . . No, I'm damned if I will. You've got to do it. . . . That's a good girl. . . . And keep her away from the office. . . . Tell her I'll see her—uh—some time. . . . Yes, but don't tie me up to anything. . . . That's the stuff. You're an angel. 'Bye."

Spade's tinny alarm-clock said three-forty when he turned on the light in the suspended bowl again. He dropped his hat and overcoat on the bed and went into his kitchen, returning to the bedroom with a wine-glass and a tall bottle of Bacardi. He poured a drink and drank it standing. He put bottle and glass on the table, sat on the side of the bed facing them, and rolled a cigarette. He had drunk his third glass of Bacardi and was lighting his fifth cigarette when the street-door-bell rang. The hands of the alarm-clock registered four-thirty.

Spade sighed, rose from the bed, and went to the telephone-box beside his bathroom door. He pressed the button that released the street-door-lock. He muttered, "Damn her," and stood scowling at the black telephone-box, breathing irregularly while a dull flush grew in his cheeks.

The grating and rattling of the elevator-door opening and closing came from the corridor. Spade sighed again and moved towards the corridor-door. Soft heavy footsteps sounded on the carpeted floor outside, the footsteps of two men. Spade's face brightened. His eyes were no longer harassed. He opened the door quickly.

"Hello, Tom," he said to the barrel-bellied tall detective with whom he had talked in Burritt Street, and, "Hello, Lieutenant," to the man beside Tom. "Come in."

They nodded together, neither saying anything, and came in. Spade shut the door and ushered them into his bedroom. Tom sat on an end of the sofa by the windows. The Lieutenant sat on a chair beside the table.

The Lieutenant was a compactly built man with a round head under short-cut grizzled hair and a square face behind a short-cut grizzled mustache. A five-dollar gold-piece was pinned to his necktie and there was a small elaborate diamond-set secret-society-emblem on his lapel.

Spade brought two wine-glasses in from the kitchen, filled them and his own with Bacardi, gave one to each of his visitors, and sat down with his on the side of the bed. His face was placid and uncurious. He raised his glass, and said, "Success to crime," and drank it down.

Tom emptied his glass, set it on the floor beside his feet, and wiped his mouth with a muddy forefinger. He stared at the foot of the bed as if trying to remember something of which it vaguely reminded him.

The Lieutenant looked at his glass for a dozen seconds, took a very small sip of its contents, and put the glass on the table at his elbow. He examined the room with hard deliberate eyes, and then looked at Tom.

Tom moved uncomfortably on the sofa and, not looking up, asked: "Did you break the news to Miles's wife, Sam?"

Spade said: "Uh-huh."

"How'd she take it?"

Spade shook his head. "I don't know anything about women."

Tom said softly: "The hell you don't."

The Lieutenant put his hands on his knees and leaned forward. His greenish eyes were fixed on Spade in a peculiarly rigid stare, as if their focus were a matter of mechanics, to be changed only by pulling a lever or pressing a button.

"What kind of gun do you carry?" he asked.

"None. I don't like them much. Of course there are some in the office."

"I'd like to see one of them," the Lieutenant said. "You don't happen to have one here?"

"No."

"You sure of that?"

"Look around." Spade smiled and waved his empty glass a little. "Turn the dump upside-down if you want. I won't squawk—if you've got a search-warrant."

Tom protested: "Oh, hell, Sam!"

Spade set his glass on the table and stood up facing the Lieutenant. "What do you want, Dundy?" he asked in a voice hard and cold as his eyes.

Lieutenant Dundy's eyes had moved to maintain their focus on Spade's. Only his eyes had moved.

Tom shifted his weight on the sofa again, blew a deep breath out through his nose, and growled plaintively: "We're not wanting to make any trouble, Sam."

Spade, ignoring Tom, said to Dundy: "Well, what do you want? Talk turkey. Who in hell do you think you are, coming in here trying to rope me?"

"All right," Dundy said in his chest, "sit down and listen."

"I'll sit or stand as I damned please," said Spade, not moving.

"For Christ's sake be reasonable," Tom begged. "What's the use of us having a row? If you want to know why we didn't talk turkey it's because when I asked you who this Thursby was you as good as told me it was none of my business. You can't treat us that way, Sam. It ain't right and it won't get you anywheres. We got our work to do."

Lieutenant Dundy jumped up, stood close to Spade, and thrust his square face up at the taller man's.

"I've warned you your foot was going to slip one of these days," he said.

Spade made a depreciative mouth, raising his eyebrows. "Everybody's foot slips sometime," he replied with derisive mildness.

"And this is yours."

Spade smiled and shook his head. "No, I'll do nicely, thank you." He stopped smiling. His upper lip, on the left side, twitched over his eyetooth. His eyes became narrow and sultry. His voice came out deep as the Lieutenant's. "I don't like this. What are you sucking around for? Tell me, or get out and let me go to bed."

"Who's Thursby?" Dundy demanded.

"I told Tom what I knew about him."

"You told Tom damned little."

"I knew damned little."

"Why were you tailing him?"

"I wasn't. Miles was—for the swell reason that we had a client who was paying good United States money to have him tailed."

"Who's the client?"

Placidity came back to Spade's face and voice. He said reprovingly: "You know I can't tell you that until I've talked it over with the client."

"You'll tell it to me or you'll tell it in court," Dundy said hotly. "This is murder and don't you forget it."

"Maybe. And here's something for you to not forget, sweetheart. I'll tell it or not as I damned please. It's a long while since I burst out crying because policemen didn't like me."

Tom left the sofa and sat on the foot of the bed. His carelessly shaven mud-smeared face was tired and lined.

"Be reasonable, Sam," he pleaded. "Give us a chance. How can we turn up anything on Miles's killing if you won't give us what you've got?"

"You needn't get a headache over that," Spade told him. "I'll bury my dead."

Lieutenant Dundy sat down and put his hands on his knees again. His eyes were warm green discs.

"I thought you would," he said. He smiled with grim content. "That's just exactly why we came to see you. Isn't it, Tom?"

Tom groaned, but said nothing articulate.

Spade watched Dundy warily.

"That's just exactly what I said to Tom," the Lieutenant went on. "I said: 'Tom, I've got a hunch that Sam Spade's a man to keep the family-troubles in the family.' That's just what I said to him."

The wariness went out of Spade's eyes. He made his eyes dull with boredom. He turned his face around to Tom and asked with great care-lessness: "What's itching your boy-friend now?"

Dundy jumped up and tapped Spade's chest with the ends of two bent fingers.

"Just this," he said, taking pains to make each word distinct, em-phasizing them with his tapping finger-ends: "Thursby was shot down in front of his hotel just thirty-five minutes after you left Burritt Street."

Spade spoke, taking equal pains with his words: "Keep your God-damned paws off me."

Dundy withdrew the tapping fingers, but there was no change in his voice: "Tom says you were in too much of a hurry to even stop for a look at your partner."

Tom growled apologetically: "Well, damn it, Sam, you did run off like that."

"And you didn't go to Archer's house to tell his wife," the Lieutenant said. "We called up and that girl in your office was there, and she said you sent her."

Spade nodded. His face was stupid in its calmness.

Lieutenant Dundy raised his two bent fingers towards Spade's chest, quickly lowered them, and said: "I give you ten minutes to get to a phone and do your talking to the girl. I give you ten minutes to get to Thursby's joint—Geary near Leavenworth—you could do it easy in that time, or fifteen at the most. And that gives you ten or fifteen minutes of waiting before he showed up."

"I knew where he lived?" Spade asked. "And I knew he hadn't gone straight home from killing Miles?"

"You knew what you knew," Dundy replied stubbornly. "What time did you get home?"

"Twenty minutes to four. I walked around thinking things over."

The Lieutenant wagged his round head up and down. "We knew you weren't home at three-thirty. We tried to get you on the phone. Where'd you do your walking?"

"Out Bush Street a way and back."

"Did you see anybody that—?"

"No, no witnesses," Spade said and laughed pleasantly. "Sit down, Dundy. You haven't finished your drink. Get your glass, Tom."

Tom said: "No, thanks, Sam."

Dundy sat down, but paid no attention to his glass of rum.

Spade filled his own glass, drank, set the empty glass on the table, and returned to his bedside-seat.

"I know where I stand now," he said, looking with friendly eyes from one of the police-detectives to the other. "I'm sorry I got up on my hind legs, but you birds coming in and trying to put the work on me made me nervous. Having Miles knocked off bothered me, and then you birds cracking foxy. That's all right now, though, now that I know what you're up to."

Tom said: "Forget it."

The Lieutenant said nothing.

Spade asked: "Thursby die?"

While the Lieutenant hesitated Tom said: "Yes."

Then the Lieutenant said angrily: "And you might just as well know it—if you don't—that he died before he could tell anybody anything."

Spade was rolling a cigarette. He asked, not looking up: "What do you mean by that? You think I did know it?"

"I meant what I said," Dundy replied bluntly.

Spade looked up at him and smiled, holding the finished cigarette in one hand, his lighter in the other.

"You're not ready to pinch me yet, are you, Dundy?" he asked.

Dundy looked with hard green eyes at Spade and did not answer him.

"Then," said Spade, "there's no particular reason why I should give a damn what you think, is there, Dundy?"

Tom said: "Aw, be reasonable, Sam."

Spade put the cigarette in his mouth, set fire to it, and laughed smoke out.

"I'll be reasonable, Tom," he promised. "How did I kill this Thursby? I've forgotten."

Tom grunted disgust. Lieutenant Dundy said: "He was shot four times in the back, with a forty-four or forty-five, from across the street, when he started to go in the hotel. Nobody saw it, but that's the way it figures."

"And he was wearing a Luger in a shoulder-holster," Tom added. "It hadn't been fired."

"What do the hotel-people know about him?" Spade asked.

"Nothing except that he'd been there a week."

"Alone?"

"Alone."

"What did you find on him? or in his room?"

Dundy drew his lips in and asked: "What'd you think we'd find?"

Spade made a careless circle with his limp cigarette. "Something to tell you who he was, what his story was. Did you?"

"We thought you could tell us that."

Spade looked at the Lieutenant with yellow-grey eyes that held an almost exaggerated amount of candor. "I've never seen Thursby, dead or alive."

Lieutenant Dundy stood up looking dissatisfied. Tom rose yawning and stretching.

"We've asked what we came to ask," Dundy said, frowning over eyes hard as green pebbles. He held his mustached upper lip tight to his teeth, letting his lower lip push the words out. "We've told you more than you've told us. That's fair enough. You know me, Spade. If you did or you didn't you'll get a square deal out of me, and most of the breaks. I don't know that I'd blame you a hell of a lot—but that wouldn't keep me from nailing you."

"Fair enough," Spade replied evenly. "But I'd feel better about it if you'd drink your drink."

Lieutenant Dundy turned to the table, picked up his glass, and slowly emptied it. Then he said, "Good night," and held out his hand. They shook hands ceremoniously. Tom and Spade shook hands ceremoniously. Spade let them out. Then he undressed, turned off the lights, and went to bed.

III · *Three Women*

WHEN Spade reached his office at ten o'clock the following morning Effie Perine was at her desk opening the morning's mail. Her boyish face was pale under its sunburn. She put down the handful of envelopes and the brass paper-knife she held and said: "She's in there." Her voice was low and warning.

"I asked you to keep her away," Spade complained. He too kept his voice low.

Effie Perine's brown eyes opened wide and her voice was irritable as his: "Yes, but you didn't tell me how." Her eyelids went together a little and her shoulders drooped. "Don't be cranky, Sam," she said wearily. "I had her all night."

Spade stood beside the girl, put a hand on her head, and smoothed her hair away from its parting. "Sorry, angel, I haven't—" He broke off as the inner door opened. "Hello, Iva," he said to the woman who had opened it.

"Oh, Sam!" she said.

She was a blonde woman of a few more years than thirty. Her facial prettiness was perhaps five years past its best moment. Her body for all its sturdiness was finely modeled and exquisite. She wore black clothes from hat to shoes. They had as mourning an impromptu air. Having spoken, she stepped back from the door and stood waiting for Spade.

He took his hand from Effie Perine's head and entered the inner office, shutting the door. Iva came quickly to him, raising her sad face for his kiss. Her arms were around him before his held her. When they had kissed he made a little movement as if to release her, but she pressed her face to his chest and began sobbing.

He stroked her round back, saying: "Poor darling." His voice was tender. His eyes, squinting at the desk that had been his partner's, across the room from his own, were angry. He drew his lips back over his teeth in an impatient grimace and turned his chin aside to avoid contact with the crown of her hat. "Did you send for Miles's brother?" he asked.

"Yes, he came over this morning." The words were blurred by her sobbing and his coat against her mouth.

He grimaced again and bent his head for a surreptitious look at the watch on his wrist. His left arm was around her, the hand on her left shoulder. His cuff was pulled back far enough to leave the watch uncovered. It showed ten-ten.

The woman stirred in his arms and raised her face again. Her blue eyes were wet, round, and white-ringed. Her mouth was moist.

"Oh, Sam," she moaned, "did you kill him?"

Spade stared at her with bulging eyes. His bony jaw fell down. He took his arms from her and stepped back out of her arms. He scowled at her and cleared his throat.

She held her arms up as he had left them. Anguish clouded her eyes, partly closed them under eyebrows pulled up at the inner ends. Her soft damp red lips trembled.

Spade laughed a harsh syllable, "Ha!" and went to the buff-curtained window. He stood there with his back to her looking through the curtain into the court until she started towards him. Then he turned quickly and went to his desk. He sat down, put his elbows on the desk, his chin between his fists, and looked at her. His yellowish eyes glittered between narrowed lids.

"Who," he asked coldly, "put that bright idea in your head?"

"I thought—" She lifted a hand to her mouth and fresh tears came to her eyes. She came to stand beside the desk, moving with easy sure-footed grace in black slippers whose smallness and heel-height were extreme. "Be kind to me, Sam," she said humbly.

He laughed at her, his eyes still glittering. "You killed my husband, Sam, be kind to me." He clapped his palms together and said: "Jesus Christ."

She began to cry audibly, holding a white handkerchief to her face.

He got up and stood close behind her. He put his arms around her. He kissed her neck between ear and coat-collar. He said: "Now, Iva, don't." His face was expressionless. When she had stopped crying he put his mouth to her ear and murmured: "You shouldn't have come here today, precious. It wasn't wise. You can't stay. You ought to be home."

She turned around in his arms to face him and asked: "You'll come tonight?"

He shook his head gently. "Not tonight."

"Soon?"

"Yes."

"How soon?"

"As soon as I can."

He kissed her mouth, led her to the door, opened it, said, "Good-bye, Iva," bowed her out, shut the door, and returned to his desk.

He took tobacco and cigarette-papers from his vest-pockets, but did not roll a cigarette. He sat holding the papers in one hand, the tobacco in the other, and looked with brooding eyes at his dead partner's desk.

Effie Perine opened the door and came in. Her brown eyes were uneasy. Her voice was careless. She asked: "Well?"

Spade said nothing. His brooding gaze did not move from his partner's desk.

The girl frowned and came around to his side. "Well," she asked in a louder voice, "how did you and the widow make out?"

"She thinks I shot Miles," he said. Only his lips moved.

"So you could marry her?"

Spade made no reply to that.

The girl took his hat from his head and put it on the desk. Then she leaned over and took the tobacco-sack and the papers from his inert fingers.

"The police think I shot Thursby," he said.

"Who is he?" she asked, separating a cigarette-paper from the packet, sifting tobacco into it.

"Who do you think I shot?" he asked.

When she ignored that question he said: "Thursby's the guy Miles was supposed to be tailing for the Wonderly girl."

Her thin fingers finished shaping the cigarette. She licked it, smoothed it, twisted its ends, and placed it between Spade's lips. He said, "Thanks, honey," put an arm around her slim waist, and rested his cheek wearily against her hip, shutting his eyes.

"Are you going to marry Iva?" she asked, looking down at his pale brown hair.

"Don't be silly," he muttered. The unlighted cigarette bobbed up and down with the movement of his lips.

"She doesn't think it's silly. Why should she—the way you've played around with her?"

He sighed and said: "I wish to Christ I'd never seen her."

"Maybe you do now." A trace of spitefulness came into the girl's voice. "But there was a time."

"I never know what to do or say to women except that way," he grumbled, "and then I didn't like Miles."

"That's a lie, Sam," the girl said. "You know I think she's a louse, but I'd be a louse too if it would give me a body like hers."

Spade rubbed his face impatiently against her hip, but said nothing.

Effie Perine bit her lip, wrinkled her forehead, and, bending over for a better view of his face, asked: "Do you suppose she could have killed him?"

Spade sat up straight and took his arm from her waist. He smiled at her. His smile held nothing but amusement. He took out his lighter, snapped on the flame, and applied it to the end of his cigarette. "You're an angel," he said tenderly through smoke, "a nice rattle-brained angel."

She smiled a bit wryly. "Oh, am I? Suppose I told you that your Iva hadn't been home many minutes when I arrived to break the news at three o'clock this morning?"

"Are you telling me?" he asked. His eyes had become alert though his mouth continued to smile.

"She kept me waiting at the door while she undressed or finished undressing. I saw her clothes where she had dumped them on a chair. Her hat and coat were underneath. Her singlette, on top, was still warm. She said she had been asleep, but she hadn't. She had wrinkled up the bed, but the wrinkles weren't mashed down."

Spade took the girl's hand and patted it. "You're a detective, darling, but"—he shook his head—"she didn't kill him."

Effie Perine snatched her hand away. "That louse wants to marry you, Sam," she said bitterly.

He made an impatient gesture with his head and one hand.

She frowned at him and demanded: "Did you see her last night?"

"No."

"Honestly?"

"Honestly. Don't act like Dundy, sweetheart. It ill becomes you."

"Has Dundy been after you?"

"Uh-huh. He and Tom Polhaus dropped in for a drink at four o'clock."

"Do they really think you shot this what's-his-name?"

"Thursby." He dropped what was left of his cigarette into the brass tray and began to roll another.

"Do they?" she insisted.

"God knows." His eyes were on the cigarette he was making. "They did have some such notion. I don't know how far I talked them out of it."

"Look at me, Sam."

He looked at her and laughed so that for the moment merriment mingled with the anxiety in her face.

"You worry me," she said, seriousness returning to her face as she talked. "You always think you know what you're doing, but you're too slick for your own good, and some day you're going to find it out."

He sighed mockingly and rubbed his cheek against her arm. "That's what Dundy says, but you keep Iva away from me, sweet, and I'll manage to survive the rest of my troubles." He stood up and put on his hat. "Have the *Spade & Archer* taken off the door and *Samuel Spade* put on. I'll be back in an hour, or phone you."

Spade went through the St. Mark's long purplish lobby to the desk and asked a red-haired dandy whether Miss Wonderly was in. The red-haired dandy turned away, and then back shaking his head. "She checked out this morning, Mr. Spade."

"Thanks."

Spade walked past the desk to an alcove off the lobby where a plump young-middle-aged man in dark clothes sat at a flat-topped mahogany desk. On the edge of the desk facing the lobby was a triangular prism of mahogany and brass inscribed *Mr. Freed.*

The plump man got up and came around the desk holding out his hand.

"I was awfully sorry to hear about Archer, Spade," he said in the tone of one trained to sympathize readily without intrusiveness. "I've just seen it in the *Call*. He was in here last night, you know."

"Thanks, Freed. Were you talking to him?"

"No. He was sitting in the lobby when I came in early in the evening. I didn't stop. I thought he was probably working and I know you fellows like to be left alone when you're busy. Did that have anything to do with his—?"

"I don't think so, but we don't know yet. Anyway, we won't mix the house up in it if it can be helped."

"Thanks."

"That's all right. Can you give me some dope on an ex-guest, and then forget that I asked for it?"

"Surely."

"A Miss Wonderly checked out this morning. I'd like to know the details."

"Come along," Freed said, "and we'll see what we can learn."

Spade stood still, shaking his head. "I don't want to show in it."

Freed nodded and went out of the alcove. In the lobby he halted suddenly and came back to Spade.

"Harriman was the house-detective on duty last night," he said. "He's sure to have seen Archer. Shall I caution him not to mention it?"

Spade looked at Freed from the corners of his eyes. "Better not. That won't make any difference as long as there's no connection shown with this Wonderly. Harriman's all right, but he likes to talk, and I'd as lief not have him think there's anything to be kept quiet."

Freed nodded again and went away. Fifteen minutes later he returned.

"She arrived last Tuesday, registering from New York. She hadn't a trunk, only some bags. There were no phone-calls charged to her room, and she doesn't seem to have received much, if any, mail. The only one anybody remembers having seen her with was a tall dark man of thirty-six or so. She went out at half-past nine this morning, came back an hour later, paid her bill, and had her bags carried out to a car. The boy who carried them says it was a Nash touring car, probably a hired one. She left a forwarding address—the Ambassador, Los Angeles."

Spade said, "Thanks a lot, Freed," and left the St. Mark.

When Spade returned to his office Effie Perine stopped typing a letter to tell him: "Your friend Dundy was in. He wanted to look at your guns."

"And?"

"I told him to come back when you were here."

"Good girl. If he comes back again let him look at them."

"And Miss Wonderly called up."

"It's about time. What did she say?"

"She wants to see you." The girl picked up a slip of paper from her desk and read the memorandum penciled on it: "She's at the Coronet, on California Street, apartment one thousand and one. You're to ask for Miss Leblanc."

Spade said, "Give me," and held out his hand. When she had given him the memorandum he took out his lighter, snapped on the flame, set it to the slip of paper, held the paper until all but one corner was curling black ash, dropped it on the linoleum floor, and mashed it under his shoe-sole.

The girl watched him with disapproving eyes.

He grinned at her, said, "That's just the way it is, dear," and went out again.

IV · *The Black Bird*

MISS WONDERLY, in a belted green crêpe silk dress, opened the door of apartment 1001 at the Coronet. Her face was flushed. Her dark red hair, parted on the left side, swept back in loose waves over her right temple, was somewhat tousled.

Spade took off his hat and said: "Good morning."

His smile brought a fainter smile to her face. Her eyes, of blue that was almost violet, did not lose their troubled look. She lowered her head and said in a hushed, timid voice: "Come in, Mr. Spade."

She led him past open kitchen-, bathroom-, and bedroom-doors into a cream and red living-room, apologizing for its confusion: "Everything is upside-down. I haven't even finished unpacking."

She laid his hat on a table and sat down on a walnut settee. He sat on a brocaded oval-backed chair facing her.

She looked at her fingers, working them together, and said: "Mr. Spade, I've a terrible, terrible confession to make."

Spade smiled a polite smile, which she did not lift her eyes to see, and said nothing.

"That—that story I told you yesterday was all—a story," she stammered, and looked up at him now with miserable frightened eyes.

"Oh, that," Spade said lightly. "We didn't exactly believe your story."

"Then—?" Perplexity was added to the misery and fright in her eyes.

"We believed your two hundred dollars."

"You mean—?" She seemed to not know what he meant.

"I mean that you paid us more than if you'd been telling the truth," he explained blandly, "and enough more to make it all right."

Her eyes suddenly lighted up. She lifted herself a few inches from the settee, settled down again, smoothed her skirt, leaned forward, and spoke eagerly: "And even now you'd be willing to—?"

Spade stopped her with a palm-up motion of one hand. The upper part of his face frowned. The lower part smiled. "That depends," he said. "The hell of it is, Miss—— Is your name Wonderly or Leblanc?"

She blushed and murmured: "It's really O'Shaughnessy—Brigid O'Shaughnessy."

"The hell of it is, Miss O'Shaughnessy, that a couple of murders"—she winced—"coming together like this get everybody stirred up, make the police think they can go the limit, make everybody hard to handle and expensive. It's not—"

He stopped talking because she had stopped listening and was waiting for him to finish.

"Mr. Spade, tell me the truth." Her voice quivered on the verge of hysteria. Her face had become haggard around desperate eyes. "Am I to blame for—for last night?"

Spade shook his head. "Not unless there are things I don't know about," he said. "You warned us that Thursby was dangerous. Of course you lied to us about your sister and all, but that doesn't count: we didn't believe you." He shrugged his sloping shoulders. "I wouldn't say it was your fault."

She said, "Thank you," very softly, and then moved her head from side to side. "But I'll always blame myself." She put a hand to her throat. "Mr. Archer was so—so alive yesterday afternoon, so solid and hearty and—"

"Stop it," Spade commanded. "He knew what he was doing. They're the chances we take."

"Was—was he married?"

"Yes, with ten thousand insurance, no children, and a wife who didn't like him."

"Oh, please don't!" she whispered.

Spade shrugged again. "That's the way it was." He glanced at his watch and moved from his chair to the settee beside her. "There's no time for worrying about that now." His voice was pleasant but firm. "Out there a flock of policemen and assistant district attorneys and reporters are running around with their noses to the ground. What do you want to do?"

"I want you to save me from—from it all," she replied in a thin tremulous voice. She put a timid hand on his sleeve. "Mr. Spade, do they know about me?"

"Not yet. I wanted to see you first."

"What—what would they think if they knew about the way I came to you—with those lies?"

"It would make them suspicious. That's why I've been stalling them till I could see you. I thought maybe we wouldn't have to let them know all of it. We ought to be able to fake a story that will rock them to sleep, if necessary."

"You don't think I had anything to do with the—the murders—do you?"

Spade grinned at her and said: "I forgot to ask you that. Did you?"

"No."

"That's good. Now what are we going to tell the police?"

She squirmed on her end of the settee and her eyes wavered between heavy lashes, as if trying and failing to free their gaze from his. She seemed smaller, and very young and oppressed.

"Must they know about me at all?" she asked. "I think I'd rather die than that, Mr. Spade. I can't explain now, but can't you somehow manage so that you can shield me from them, so I won't have to answer their questions? I don't think I could stand being questioned now. I think I would rather die. Can't you, Mr. Spade?"

"Maybe," he said, "but I'll have to know what it's all about."

She went down on her knees at his knees. She held her face up to him. Her face was wan, taut, and fearful over tight-clasped hands.

"I haven't lived a good life," she cried. "I've been bad—worse than you could know—but I'm not all bad. Look at me, Mr. Spade. You know I'm not all bad, don't you? You can see that, can't you? Then can't you trust me a little? Oh, I'm so alone and afraid, and I've got nobody to help me if you won't help me. I know I've no right to ask you to trust me if I won't trust you. I do trust you, but I can't tell you. I can't tell you now. Later I will, when I can. I'm afraid, Mr. Spade. I'm afraid of trusting you. I don't mean that. I do trust you, but—I trusted Floyd and— I've nobody else, nobody else, Mr. Spade. You can help me. You've said you can help me. If I hadn't believed you could save me I would have run away today instead of sending for you. If I thought anybody else could save me would

I be down on my knees like this? I know this isn't fair of me. But be generous, Mr. Spade, don't ask me to be fair. You're strong, you're resourceful, you're brave. You can spare me some of that strength and resourcefulness and courage, surely. Help me, Mr. Spade. Help me because I need help so badly, and because if you don't where will I find anyone who can, no matter how willing? Help me. I've no right to ask you to help me blindly, but I do ask you. Be generous, Mr. Spade. You can help me. Help me."

Spade, who had held his breath through much of this speech, now emptied his lungs with a long sighing exhalation between pursed lips and said: "You won't need much of anybody's help. You're good. You're very good. It's chiefly your eyes, I think, and that throb you get into your voice when you say things like 'Be generous, Mr. Spade.'"

She jumped up on her feet. Her face crimsoned painfully, but she held her head erect and she looked Spade straight in the eyes.

"I deserve that," she said. "I deserve it, but—oh!—I did want your help so much. I do want it, and need it, so much. And the lie was in the way I said it, and not at all in what I said." She turned away, no longer holding herself erect. "It is my own fault that you can't believe me now."

Spade's face reddened and he looked down at the floor, muttering: "Now you are dangerous."

Brigid O'Shaughnessy went to the table and picked up his hat. She came back and stood in front of him holding the hat, not offering it to him, but holding it for him to take if he wished. Her face was white and thin.

Spade looked at his hat and asked: "What happened last night?"

"Floyd came to the hotel at nine o'clock, and we went out for a walk. I suggested that so Mr. Archer could see him. We stopped at a restaurant in Geary Street, I think it was, for supper and to dance, and came back to the hotel at about half-past twelve. Floyd left me at the door and I stood inside and watched Mr. Archer follow him down the street, on the other side."

"Down? You mean towards Market Street?"

"Yes."

"Do you know what they'd be doing in the neighborhood of Bush and Stockton, where Archer was shot?"

"Isn't that near where Floyd lived?"

"No. It would be nearly a dozen blocks out of his way if he was going from your hotel to his. Well, what did you do after they had gone?"

"I went to bed. And this morning when I went out for breakfast I saw the headlines in the papers and read about—you know. Then I went up to Union Square, where I had seen automobiles for hire, and got one and went to the hotel for my luggage. After I found my room had been searched yesterday I knew I would have to move, and I had found this place yesterday afternoon. So I came up here and then telephoned your office."

"Your room at the St. Mark was searched?" he asked.

"Yes, while I was at your office." She bit her lip. "I didn't mean to tell you that."

"That means I'm not supposed to question you about it?"

She nodded shyly.

He frowned.

She moved his hat a little in her hands.

He laughed impatiently and said: "Stop waving the hat in my face. Haven't I offered to do what I can?"

She smiled contritely, returned the hat to the table, and sat beside him on the settee again.

He said: "I've got nothing against trusting you blindly except that I won't be able to do you much good if I haven't some idea of what it's all about. For instance, I've got to have some sort of a line on your Floyd Thursby."

"I met him in the Orient." She spoke slowly, looking down at a pointed finger tracing eights on the settee between them. "We came here from Hongkong last week. He was—he had promised to help me. He took advantage of my helplessness and dependence on him to betray me."

"Betray you how?"

She shook her head and said nothing.

Spade, frowning with impatience, asked: "Why did you want him shadowed?"

"I wanted to learn how far he had gone. He wouldn't even let me know where he was staying. I wanted to find out what he was doing, whom he was meeting, things like that."

"Did he kill Archer?"

She looked up at him, surprised. "Yes, certainly," she said.

"He had a Luger in a shoulder-holster. Archer wasn't shot with a Luger."

"He had a revolver in his overcoat-pocket," she said.

"You saw it?"

"Oh, I've seen it often. I know he always carries one there. I didn't see it last night, but I know he never wears an overcoat without it."

"Why all the guns?"

"He lived by them. There was a story in Hongkong that he had come out there, to the Orient, as bodyguard to a gambler who had had to leave the States, and that the gambler had since disappeared. They said Floyd knew about his disappearing. I don't know. I do know that he always went heavily armed and that he never went to sleep without covering the floor around his bed with crumpled newspaper so nobody could come silently into his room."

"You picked a nice sort of playmate."

"Only that sort could have helped me," she said simply, "if he had been loyal."

"Yes, if." Spade pinched his lower lip between finger and thumb and looked gloomily at her. The vertical creases over his nose deepened, drawing his brows together. "How bad a hole are you actually in?"

"As bad," she said, "as could be."

"Physical danger?"

"I'm not heroic. I don't think there's anything worse than death."

"Then it's that?"

"It's that as surely as we're sitting here"—she shivered—"unless you help me."

He took his fingers away from his mouth and ran them through his hair. "I'm not Christ," he said irritably. "I can't work miracles out of thin air." He looked at his watch. "The day's going and you're giving me nothing to work with. Who killed Thursby?"

She put a crumpled handkerchief to her mouth and said, "I don't know," through it.

"Your enemies or his?"

"I don't know. His, I hope, but I'm afraid—I don't know."

"How was he supposed to be helping you? Why did you bring him here from Hongkong?"

She looked at him with frightened eyes and shook her head in silence. Her face was haggard and pitifully stubborn.

Spade stood up, thrust his hands into the pockets of his jacket, and scowled down at her. "This is hopeless," he said savagely. "I can't do anything for you. I don't know what you want done. I don't even know if you know what you want."

She hung her head and wept.

He made a growling animal noise in his throat and went to the table for his hat.

"You won't," she begged in a small choked voice, not looking up, "go to the police?"

"Go to them!" he exclaimed, his voice loud with rage. "They've been running me ragged since four o'clock this morning. I've made myself God knows how much trouble standing them off. For what? For some crazy notion that I could help you. I can't. I won't try." He put his hat on his head and pulled it down tight. "Go to them? All I've got to do is stand still and they'll be swarming all over me. Well, I'll tell them what I know and you'll have to take your chances."

She rose from the settee and held herself straight in front of him though her knees were trembling, and she held her white panic-stricken face up high though she couldn't hold the twitching muscles of mouth and chin still. She said: "You've been patient. You've tried to help me. It is hopeless, and useless, I suppose." She stretched out her right hand. "I thank you for what you have done. I—I'll have to take my chances."

Spade made the growling animal noise in his throat again and sat down on the settee. "How much money have you got?" he asked.

The question startled her. Then she pinched her lower lip between her teeth and answered reluctantly: "I've about five hundred dollars left."

"Give it to me."

She hesitated, looking timidly at him. He made angry gestures with mouth, eyebrows, hands, and shoulders. She went into her bedroom, returning almost immediately with a sheaf of paper money in one hand.

He took the money from her, counted it, and said: "There's only four hundred here."

"I had to keep some to live on," she explained meekly, putting a hand to her breast.

"Can't you get any more?"

"No."

"You must have something you can raise money on," he insisted.

"I've some rings, a little jewelry."

"You'll have to hock them," he said, and held out his hand. "The Remedial's the best place—Mission and Fifth."

She looked pleadingly at him. His yellow-grey eyes were hard and implacable. Slowly she put her hand inside the neck of her dress, brought out a slender roll of bills, and put them in his waiting hand.

He smoothed the bills out and counted them—four twenties, four tens, and a five. He returned two of the tens and the five to her. The others he put in his pocket. Then he stood up and said: "I'm going out and see what I can do for you. I'll be back as soon as I can with the best news I can manage. I'll ring four times—long, short, long, short—so you'll know it's me. You needn't go to the door with me. I can let myself out."

He left her standing in the center of the floor looking after him with dazed blue eyes.

Spade went into a reception-room whose door bore the legend *Wise, Merican & Wise.* The red-haired girl at the switchboard said: "Oh, hello, Mr. Spade."

"Hello, darling," he replied. "Is Sid in?"

He stood beside her with a hand on her plump shoulder while she manipulated a plug and spoke into the mouthpiece: "Mr. Spade to see you, Mr. Wise." She looked up at Spade. "Go right in."

He squeezed her shoulder by way of acknowledgment, crossed the reception-room to a dully lighted inner corridor, and passed down the corridor to a frosted glass door at its far end. He opened the frosted glass door and went into an office where a small olive-skinned man with a tired oval face under thin dark hair dotted with dandruff sat behind an immense desk on which bales of paper were heaped.

The small man flourished a cold cigar-stub at Spade and said: "Pull a chair around. So Miles got the big one last night?" Neither his tired face nor his rather shrill voice held any emotion.

"Uh-huh, that's what I came in about." Spade frowned and cleared his throat. "I think I'm going to have to tell a coroner to go to hell, Sid. Can I hide behind the sanctity of my clients' secrets and identities and what-not, all the same priest or lawyer?"

Sid Wise lifted his shoulders and lowered the ends of his mouth. "Why not? An inquest is not a court-trial. You can try, anyway. You've gotten away with more than that before this."

"I know, but Dundy's getting snotty, and maybe it is a little bit thick this time. Get your hat, Sid, and we'll go see the right people. I want to be safe."

Sid Wise looked at the papers massed on his desk and groaned, but he got up from his chair and went to the closet by the window. "You're a son of a gun, Sammy," he said as he took his hat from its hook.

Spade returned to his office at ten minutes past five that evening. Effie Perine was sitting at his desk reading *Time*. Spade sat on the desk and asked: "Anything stirring?"

"Not here. You look like you'd swallowed the canary."

He grinned contentedly. "I think we've got a future. I always had an idea that if Miles would go off and die somewhere we'd stand a better chance of thriving. Will you take care of sending flowers for me?"

"I did."

"You're an invaluable angel. How's your woman's intuition today?"

"Why?"

"What do you think of Wonderly?"

"I'm for her," the girl replied without hesitation.

"She's got too many names," Spade mused, "Wonderly, Leblanc, and she says the right one's O'Shaughnessy."

"I don't care if she's got all the names in the phone-book. That girl is all right, and you know it."

"I wonder." Spade blinked sleepily at Effie Perine. He chuckled. "Anyway she's given up seven hundred smacks in two days, and that's all right."

Effie Perine sat up straight and said: "Sam, if that girl's in trouble and you let her down, or take advantage of it to bleed her, I'll never forgive you, never have any respect for you, as long as I live."

Spade smiled unnaturally. Then he frowned. The frown was unnatural. He opened his mouth to speak, but the sound of someone's entrance through the corridor-door stopped him.

Effie Perine rose and went into the outer office. Spade took off his hat and sat in his chair. The girl returned with an engraved card—*Mr. Joel Cairo.*

"This guy is queer," she said.

"In with him, then, darling," said Spade.

Mr. Joel Cairo was a small-boned dark man of medium height. His hair was black and smooth and very glossy. His features were Levantine. A square-cut ruby, its sides paralleled by four baguette diamonds, gleamed against the deep green of his cravat. His black coat, cut tight to narrow shoulders, flared a little over slightly plump hips. His trousers fitted his round legs more snugly than was the current fashion. The uppers of his patent-leather shoes were hidden by fawn spats. He held a black derby hat in a chamois-gloved hand and came towards Spade with short, mincing, bobbing steps. The fragrance of *chypre* came with him.

Spade inclined his head at his visitor and then at a chair, saying: "Sit down, Mr. Cairo."

Cairo bowed elaborately over his hat, said, "I thank you," in a high-pitched thin voice and sat down. He sat down primly, crossing his ankles, placing his hat on his knees, and began to draw off his yellow gloves.

Spade rocked back in his chair and asked: "Now what can I do for you, Mr. Cairo?" The amiable negligence of his tone, his motion in the chair, were precisely as they had been when he had addressed the same question to Brigid O'Shaughnessy on the previous day.

Cairo turned his hat over, dropping his gloves into it, and placed it bottom-up on the corner of the desk nearest him. Diamonds twinkled on the second and fourth fingers of his left hand, a ruby that matched the one in his tie even to the surrounding diamonds on the third finger of his right hand. His hands were soft and well cared for. Though they were not large their flaccid bluntness made them seem clumsy. He rubbed his palms together and said over the whispering sound they made: "May a stranger offer condolences for your partner's unfortunate death?"

"Thanks."

"May I ask, Mr. Spade, if there was, as the newspapers inferred, a certain—ah—relationship between that unfortunate happening and the death a little later of the man Thursby?"

Spade said nothing in a blank-faced definite way.

Cairo rose and bowed. "I beg your pardon." He sat down and placed his hands side by side, palms down, on the corner of the desk. "More than idle curiosity made me ask that, Mr. Spade. I am trying to recover an —ah—ornament that has been—shall we say?—mislaid. I thought, and hoped, you could assist me."

Spade nodded with eyebrows lifted to indicate attentiveness.

"The ornament is a statuette," Cairo went on, selecting and mouthing his words carefully, "the black figure of a bird."

Spade nodded again, with courteous interest.

"I am prepared to pay, on behalf of the figure's rightful owner, the sum of five thousand dollars for its recovery." Cairo raised one hand from the desk-corner and touched a spot in the air with the broad-nailed tip of an ugly forefinger. "I am prepared to promise that—what is the phrase?—

no questions will be asked." He put his hand on the desk again beside the other and smiled blandly over them at the private detective.

"Five thousand is a lot of money," Spade commented, looking thoughtfully at Cairo. "It—"

Fingers drummed lightly on the door.

When Spade had called, "Come in," the door opened far enough to admit Effie Perine's head and shoulders. She had put on a small dark felt hat and a dark coat with a grey fur collar.

"Is there anything else?" she asked.

"No. Good night. Lock the door when you go, will you?"

"Good night," she said and disappeared behind the closing door.

Spade turned in his chair to face Cairo again, saying: "It's an interesting figure."

The sound of the corridor-door's closing behind Effie Perine came to them.

Cairo smiled and took a short compact flat black pistol out of an inner pocket. "You will please," he said, "clasp your hands together at the back of your neck."

V · *The Levantine*

SPADE did not look at the pistol. He raised his arms and, leaning back in his chair, intertwined the fingers of his two hands behind his head. His eyes, holding no particular expression, remained focused on Cairo's dark face.

Cairo coughed a little apologetic cough and smiled nervously with lips that had lost some of their redness. His dark eyes were humid and bashful and very earnest. "I intend to search your offices, Mr. Spade. I warn you that if you attempt to prevent me I shall certainly shoot you."

"Go ahead." Spade's voice was as empty of expression as his face.

"You will please stand," the man with the pistol instructed him at whose thick chest the pistol was aimed. "I shall have to make sure that you are not armed."

Spade stood up pushing his chair back with his calves as he straightened his legs.

Cairo went around behind him. He transferred the pistol from his right hand to his left. He lifted Spade's coat-tail and looked under it. Holding the pistol close to Spade's back, he put his right hand around

Spade's side and patted his chest. The Levantine face was then no more than six inches below and behind Spade's right elbow.

Spade's elbow dropped as Spade spun to the right. Cairo's face jerked back not far enough: Spade's right heel on the patent-leathered toes anchored the smaller man in the elbow's path. The elbow struck him beneath the cheek-bone, staggering him so that he must have fallen had he not been held by Spade's foot on his foot. Spade's elbow went on past the astonished dark face and straightened when Spade's hand struck down at the pistol. Cairo let the pistol go the instant that Spade's fingers touched it. The pistol was small in Spade's hand.

Spade took his foot off Cairo's to complete his about-face. With his left hand Spade gathered together the smaller man's coat-lapels—the ruby-set green tie bunching out over his knuckles—while his right hand stowed the captured weapon away in a coat-pocket. Spade's yellow-grey eyes were somber. His face was wooden, with a trace of sullenness around the mouth.

Cairo's face was twisted by pain and chagrin. There were tears in his dark eyes. His skin was the complexion of polished lead except where the elbow had reddened his cheek.

Spade by means of his grip on the Levantine's lapels turned him slowly and pushed him back until he was standing close in front of the chair he had lately occupied. A puzzled look replaced the look of pain in the lead-colored face. Then Spade smiled. His smile was gentle, even dreamy. His right shoulder raised a few inches. His bent right arm was driven up by the shoulder's lift. Fist, wrist, forearm, crooked elbow, and upper arm seemed all one rigid piece, with only the limber shoulder giving them motion. The fist struck Cairo's face, covering for a moment one side of his chin, a corner of his mouth, and most of his cheek between cheek-bone and jaw-bone.

Cairo shut his eyes and was unconscious.

Spade lowered the limp body into the chair, where it lay with sprawled arms and legs, the head lolling back against the chair's back, the mouth open.

Spade emptied the unconscious man's pockets one by one, working methodically, moving the lax body when necessary, making a pile of the pockets' contents on the desk. When the last pocket had been turned out he returned to his own chair, rolled and lighted a cigarette, and began to examine his spoils. He examined them with grave unhurried thoroughness.

There was a large wallet of dark soft leather. The wallet contained three hundred and sixty-five dollars in United States bills of several sizes; three five-pound notes; a much-visaed Greek passport bearing Cairo's name and portrait; five folded sheets of pinkish onion-skin paper covered with what seemed to be Arabic writing; a raggedly clipped newspaper-account of the finding of Archer's and Thursby's bodies; a post-card-photograph of a dusky woman with bold cruel eyes and a tender drooping mouth; a large silk handkerchief, yellow with age and somewhat cracked along its folds; a thin sheaf of Mr. Joel Cairo's engraved cards; and a ticket for an orchestra seat at the Geary Theatre that evening.

Besides the wallet and its contents there were three gaily colored silk handkerchiefs fragrant of *chypre*; a platinum Longines watch on a platinum and red gold chain, attached at the other end to a small pear-shaped pendant of some white metal; a handful of United States, British, French, and Chinese coins; a ring holding half a dozen keys; a silver and onyx fountain-pen; a metal comb in a leatherette case; a nail-file in a leatherette case; a small street-guide to San Francisco; a Southern Pacific baggage-check; a half-filled package of violet pastilles; a Shanghai insurance-broker's business-card; and four sheets of Hotel Belvedere writing paper, on one of which was written in small precise letters Samuel Spade's name and the addresses of his office and his apartment.

Having examined these articles carefully—he even opened the back of the watch-case to see that nothing was hidden inside—Spade leaned over and took the unconscious man's wrist between finger and thumb, feeling his pulse. Then he dropped the wrist, settled back in his chair, and rolled and lighted another cigarette. His face while he smoked was, except for occasional slight and aimless movements of his lower lip, so still and reflective that it seemed stupid; but when Cairo presently moaned and fluttered his eyelids Spade's face became bland, and he put the beginning of a friendly smile into his eyes and mouth.

Joel Cairo awakened slowly. His eyes opened first, but a full minute passed before they fixed their gaze on any definite part of the ceiling. Then he shut his mouth and swallowed, exhaling heavily through his nose afterward. He drew in one foot and turned a hand over on his thigh. Then he raised his head from the chair-back, looked around the office in confusion, saw Spade, and sat up. He opened his mouth to speak, started, clapped a hand to his face where Spade's fist had struck and where there was now a florid bruise.

Cairo said through his teeth, painfully: "I could have shot you, Mr. Spade."

"You could have tried," Spade conceded.

"I did not try."

"I know."

"Then why did you strike me after I was disarmed?"

"Sorry," Spade said, and grinned wolfishly, showing his jaw-teeth, "but imagine my embarrassment when I found that five-thousand-dollar offer was just hooey."

"You are mistaken, Mr. Spade. That was, and is, a genuine offer."

"What the hell?" Spade's surprise was genuine.

"I am prepared to pay five thousand dollars for the figure's return." Cairo took his hand away from his bruised face and sat up prim and business-like again. "You have it?"

"No."

"If it is not here"—Cairo was very politely skeptical—"why should you have risked serious injury to prevent my searching for it?"

"I should sit around and let people come in and stick me up?" Spade flicked a finger at Cairo's possessions on the desk. "You've got my apartment-address. Been up there yet?"

"Yes, Mr. Spade. I am ready to pay five thousand dollars for the figure's return, but surely it is natural enough that I should try first to spare the owner that expense if possible."

"Who is he?"

Cairo shook his head and smiled. "You will have to forgive my not answering that question."

"Will I?" Spade leaned forward smiling with tight lips. "I've got you by the neck, Cairo. You've walked in and tied yourself up, plenty strong enough to suit the police, with last night's killings. Well, now you'll have to play with me or else."

Cairo's smile was demure and not in any way alarmed. "I made somewhat extensive inquiries about you before taking any action," he said, "and was assured that you were far too reasonable to allow other considerations to interfere with profitable business relations."

Spade shrugged. "Where are they?" he asked.

"I have offered you five thousand dollars for—"

Spade thumped Cairo's wallet with the backs of his fingers and said: "There's nothing like five thousand dollars here. You're betting your eyes. You could come in and say you'd pay me a million for a purple elephant, but what in hell would that mean?"

"I see, I see," Cairo said thoughtfully, screwing up his eyes. "You wish some assurance of my sincerity." He brushed his red lower lip with a fingertip. "A retainer, would that serve?"

"It might."

Cairo put his hand out towards his wallet, hesitated, withdrew the hand, and said: "You will take, say, a hundred dollars?"

Spade picked up the wallet and took out a hundred dollars. Then he frowned, said, "Better make it two hundred," and did.

Cairo said nothing.

"Your first guess was that I had the bird," Spade said in a crisp voice when he had put the two hundred dollars into his pocket and had dropped the wallet on the desk again. "There's nothing in that. What's your second?"

"That you know where it is, or, if not exactly that, that you know it is where you can get it."

Spade neither denied nor affirmed that: he seemed hardly to have heard it. He asked: "What sort of proof can you give me that your man is the owner?"

"Very little, unfortunately. There is this, though: nobody else can give you any authentic evidence of ownership at all. And if you know as much about the affair as I suppose—or I should not be here—you know that the means by which it was taken from him shows that his right to it was more valid than anyone else's—certainly more valid than Thursby's."

"What about his daughter?" Spade asked.

Excitement opened Cairo's eyes and mouth, turned his face red, made his voice shrill. "*He* is not the owner!"

Spade said, "Oh," mildly and ambiguously.

"Is he here, in San Francisco, now?" Cairo asked in a less shrill, but still excited, voice.

Spade blinked his eyes sleepily and suggested: "It might be better all around if we put our cards on the table."

Cairo recovered composure with a little jerk. "I do not think it would be better." His voice was suave now. "If you know more than I, I shall profit by your knowledge, and so will you to the extent of five thousand dollars. If you do not then I have made a mistake in coming to you, and to do as you suggest would be simply to make that mistake worse."

Spade nodded indifferently and waved his hand at the articles on the desk, saying: "There's your stuff"; and then, when Cairo was returning them to his pockets: "It's understood that you're to pay my expenses while I'm getting this black bird for you, and five thousand dollars when it's done?"

"Yes, Mr. Spade; that is, five thousand dollars less whatever moneys have been advanced to you—five thousand in all."

"Right. And it's a legitimate proposition." Spade's face was solemn except for wrinkles at the corners of his eyes. "You're not hiring me to do any murders or burglaries for you, but simply to get it back if possible in an honest and lawful way."

"If possible," Cairo agreed. His face also was solemn except for the eyes. "And in any event with discretion." He rose and picked up his hat. "I am at the Hotel Belvedere when you wish to communicate with me—room six-thirty-five. I confidently expect the greatest mutual benefit from our association, Mr. Spade." He hesitated. "May I have my pistol?"

"Sure. I'd forgotten it."

Spade took the pistol out of his coat-pocket and handed it to Cairo.

Cairo pointed the pistol at Spade's chest.

"You will please keep your hands on the top of the desk," Cairo said earnestly. "I intend to search your offices."

Spade said: "I'll be damned." Then he laughed in his throat and said: "All right. Go ahead. I won't stop you."

VI · *The Undersized Shadow*

FOR half an hour after Joel Cairo had gone Spade sat alone, still and frowning, at his desk. Then he said aloud in the tone of one dismissing a problem, "Well, they're paying for it," and took a bottle of Manhattan cocktail and a paper drinking-cup from a desk-drawer. He filled the cup two-thirds full, drank, returned the bottle to the drawer, tossed the cup into the wastebasket, put on his hat and overcoat, turned off the lights, and went down to the night-lit street.

An undersized youth of twenty or twenty-one in neat grey cap and overcoat was standing idly on the corner below Spade's building.

Spade walked up Sutter Street to Kearny, where he entered a cigar-store to buy two sacks of Bull Durham. When he came out the youth was one of four people waiting for a street-car on the opposite corner.

Spade ate dinner at Herbert's Grill in Powell Street. When he left the Grill, at a quarter to eight, the youth was looking into a nearby haber-dasher's window.

Spade went to the Hotel Belvedere, asking at the desk for Mr. Cairo. He was told that Cairo was not in. The youth sat in a chair in a far corner of the lobby.

Spade went to the Geary Theatre, failed to see Cairo in the lobby, and posted himself on the curb in front, facing the theatre. The youth loitered with other loiterers before Marquard's restaurant below.

At ten minutes past eight Joel Cairo appeared, walking up Geary Street with his little mincing bobbing steps. Apparently he did not see Spade until the private detective touched his shoulder. He seemed moder-ately surprised for a moment, and then said: "Oh, yes, of course you saw the ticket."

"Uh-huh. I've got something I want to show you." Spade drew Cairo back towards the curb a little away from the other waiting theatre-goers. "The kid in the cap down by Marquard's."

Cairo murmured, "I'll see," and looked at his watch. He looked up Geary Street. He looked at a theatre-sign in front of him on which George Arliss was shown costumed as Shylock, and then his dark eyes crawled sidewise in their sockets until they were looking at the kid in the cap, at his cool pale face with curling lashes hiding lowered eyes.

"Who is he?" Spade asked.

Cairo smiled up at Spade. "I do not know him."

"He's been tailing me around town."

Cairo wet his lower lip with his tongue and asked: "Do you think it was wise, then, to let him see us together?"

"How do I know?" Spade replied. "Anyway, it's done."

Cairo removed his hat and smoothed his hair with a gloved hand. He replaced his hat carefully on his head and said with every appearance of candor: "I give you my word I do not know him, Mr. Spade. I give you my word I have nothing to do with him. I have asked nobody's assistance except yours, on my word of honor."

"Then he's one of the others?"

"That may be."

"I just wanted to know, because if he gets to be a nuisance I may have to hurt him."

"Do as you think best. He is not a friend of mine."

"That's good. There goes the curtain. Good night," Spade said, and crossed the street to board a westbound street-car.

The youth in the cap boarded the same car.

Spade left the car at Hyde Street and went up to his apartment. His rooms were not greatly upset, but showed unmistakable signs of having been searched. When Spade had washed and had put on a fresh shirt and collar he went out again, walked up to Sutter Street, and boarded a westbound car. The youth boarded it also.

Within half a dozen blocks of the Coronet Spade left the car and went into the vestibule of a tall brown apartment-building. He pressed three bell-buttons together. The street-door-lock buzzed. He entered, passed the elevator and stairs, went down a long yellow-walled corridor to the rear of the building, found a back door fastened by a Yale lock, and let himself out into a narrow court. The court led to a dark back street, up which Spade walked for two blocks. Then he crossed over to California Street and went to the Coronet. It was not quite half-past nine o'clock.

The eagerness with which Brigid O'Shaughnessy welcomed Spade suggested that she had been not entirely certain of his coming. She had put on a satin gown of the blue shade called Artoise that season, with chalcedony shoulder-straps, and her stockings and slippers were Artoise.

The red and cream sitting-room had been brought to order and livened with flowers in squat pottery vases of black and silver. Three small rough-barked logs burned in the fireplace. Spade watched them burn while she put away his hat and coat.

"Do you bring me good news?" she asked when she came into the room again. Anxiety looked through her smile, and she held her breath.

"We won't have to make anything public that hasn't already been made public."

"The police won't have to know about me?"

"No."

She sighed happily and sat on the walnut settee. Her face relaxed and her body relaxed. She smiled up at him with admiring eyes. "However did you manage it?" she asked more in wonder than in curiosity.

"Most things in San Francisco can be bought, or taken."

"And you won't get into trouble? Do sit down." She made room for him on the settee.

"I don't mind a reasonable amount of trouble," he said with not too much complacence.

He stood beside the fireplace and looked at her with eyes that studied, weighed, judged her without pretense that they were not studying, weighing, judging her. She flushed slightly under the frankness of his scrutiny, but she seemed more sure of herself than before, though a becoming shyness had not left her eyes. He stood there until it seemed plain that he meant to ignore her invitation to sit beside her, and then crossed to the settee.

"You aren't," he asked as he sat down, "exactly the sort of person you pretend to be, are you?"

"I'm not sure I know what you mean," she said in her hushed voice, looking at him with puzzled eyes.

"Schoolgirl manner," he explained, "stammering and blushing and all that."

She blushed and replied hurriedly, not looking at him: "I told you this afternoon that I've been bad—worse than you could know."

"That's what I mean," he said. "You told me that this afternoon in the same words, same tone. It's a speech you've practiced."

After a moment in which she seemed confused almost to the point of tears she laughed and said: "Very well, then, Mr. Spade, I'm not at all the sort of person I pretend to be. I'm eighty years old, incredibly wicked, and an iron-molder by trade. But if it's a pose it's one I've grown into, so you won't expect me to drop it entirely, will you?"

"Oh, it's all right," he assured her. "Only it wouldn't be all right if you were actually that innocent. We'd never get anywhere."

"I won't be innocent," she promised with a hand on her heart.

"I saw Joel Cairo tonight," he said in the manner of one making polite conversation.

Gaiety went out of her face. Her eyes, focused on his profile, became frightened, then cautious. He had stretched his legs out and was looking at his crossed feet. His face did not indicate that he was thinking about anything.

There was a long pause before she asked uneasily:

"You—you know him?"

"I saw him tonight." Spade did not look up and he maintained his light conversational tone. "He was going to see George Arliss."

"You mean you talked to him?"

"Only for a minute or two, till the curtain-bell rang."

She got up from the settee and went to the fireplace to poke the fire. She changed slightly the position of an ornament on the mantelpiece, crossed the room to get a box of cigarettes from a table in a corner, straightened a curtain, and returned to her seat. Her face now was smooth and unworried.

Spade grinned sidewise at her and said: "You're good. You're very good."

Her face did not change. She asked quietly: "What did he say?"

"About what?"

She hesitated. "About me."

"Nothing." Spade turned to hold his lighter under the end of her cigarette. His eyes were shiny in a wooden satan's face.

"Well, what did he say?" she asked with half-playful petulance.

"He offered me five thousand dollars for the black bird."

She started, her teeth tore the end of her cigarette, and her eyes, after a swift alarmed glance at Spade, turned away from him.

"You're not going to go around poking at the fire and straightening up the room again, are you?" he asked lazily.

She laughed a clear merry laugh, dropped the mangled cigarette into a tray, and looked at him with clear merry eyes. "I won't," she promised. "And what did you say?"

"Five thousand dollars is a lot of money."

She smiled, but when, instead of smiling, he looked gravely at her, her smile became faint, confused, and presently vanished. In its place came a hurt, bewildered look. "Surely you're not really considering it," she said.

"Why not? Five thousand dollars is a lot of money."

"But, Mr. Spade, you promised to help me." Her hands were on his arm. "I trusted you. You can't—" She broke off, took her hands from his sleeve and worked them together.

Spade smiled gently into her troubled eyes. "Don't let's try to figure out how much you've trusted me," he said. "I promised to help you—sure —but you didn't say anything about any black birds."

"But you must've known or—or you wouldn't have mentioned it to me. You do know now. You won't—you can't—treat me like that." Her eyes were cobalt-blue prayers.

"Five thousand dollars is," he said for the third time, "a lot of money."

She lifted her shoulders and hands and let them fall in a gesture that accepted defeat. "It is," she agreed in a small dull voice. "It is far more than I could ever offer you, if I must bid for your loyalty."

Spade laughed. His laughter was brief and somewhat bitter. "That is good," he said, "coming from you. What have you given me besides money? Have you given me any of your confidence? any of the truth? any help in helping you? Haven't you tried to buy my loyalty with money and nothing else? Well, if I'm peddling it, why shouldn't I let it go to the highest bidder?"

"I've given you all the money I have." Tears glistened in her white-ringed eyes. Her voice was hoarse, vibrant. "I've thrown myself on your mercy, told you that without your help I'm utterly lost. What else is there?" She suddenly moved close to him on the settee and cried angrily: "Can I buy you with my body?"

Their faces were few inches apart. Spade took her face between his hands and he kissed her mouth roughly and contemptuously. Then he sat back and said: "I'll think it over." His face was hard and furious.

She sat still holding her numb face where his hands had left it.

He stood up and said: "Christ! there's no sense to this." He took two steps towards the fireplace and stopped, glowering at the burning logs, grinding his teeth together.

She did not move.

He turned to face her. The two vertical lines above his nose were deep clefts between red wales. "I don't give a damn about your honesty," he told her, trying to make himself speak calmly. "I don't care what kind of tricks you're up to, what your secrets are, but I've got to have something to show that you know what you're doing."

"I do know. Please believe that I do, and that it's all for the best, and—"

"Show me," he ordered. "I'm willing to help you. I've done what I could so far. If necessary I'll go ahead blindfolded, but I can't do it without more confidence in you than I've got now. You've got to convince me that you know what it's all about, that you're not simply fiddling around by guess and by God, hoping it'll come out all right somehow in the end."

"Can't you trust me just a little longer?"

"How much is a little? And what are you waiting for?"

She bit her lip and looked down. "I must talk to Joel Cairo," she said almost inaudibly.

"You can see him tonight," Spade said, looking at his watch. "His show will be out soon. We can get him on the phone at his hotel."

She raised her eyes, alarmed. "But he can't come here. I can't let him know where I am. I'm afraid."

"My place," Spade suggested.

She hesitated, working her lips together, then asked: "Do you think he'd go there?"

Spade nodded.

"All right," she exclaimed, jumping up, her eyes large and bright. "Shall we go now?"

She went into the next room. Spade went to the table in the corner and silently pulled the drawer out. The drawer held two packs of playing-cards, a pad of score-cards for bridge, a brass screw, a piece of red string, and a gold pencil. He had shut the drawer and was lighting a cigarette when she returned wearing a small dark hat and a grey kidskin coat, carrying his hat and coat.

Their taxicab drew up behind a dark sedan that stood directly in front of Spade's street-door. Iva Archer was alone in the sedan, sitting at the wheel. Spade lifted his hat to her and went indoors with Brigid O'Shaughnessy. In the lobby he halted beside one of the benches and asked: "Do you mind waiting here a moment? I won't be long."

"That's perfectly all right," Brigid O'Shaughnessy said, sitting down. "You needn't hurry."

Spade went out to the sedan. When he had opened the sedan's door Iva spoke quickly: "I've got to talk to you, Sam. Can't I come in?" Her face was pale and nervous.

"Not now."

Iva clicked her teeth together and asked sharply: "Who is she?"

"I've only a minute, Iva," Spade said patiently. "What is it?"

"Who is she?" she repeated, nodding at the street-door.

He looked away from her, down the street. In front of a garage on the next corner an undersized youth of twenty or twenty-one in neat grey cap and overcoat loafed with his back against a wall. Spade frowned and returned his gaze to Iva's insistent face. "What is the matter?" he asked. "Has anything happened? You oughtn't to be here at this time of night."

"I'm beginning to believe that," she complained. "You told me I oughtn't to come to the office, and now I oughtn't to come here. Do you mean I oughtn't to chase after you? If that's what you mean why don't you say it right out?"

"Now, Iva, you've got no right to take that attitude."

"I know I haven't. I haven't any rights at all, it seems, where you're concerned. I thought I did. I thought your pretending to love me gave me—"

Spade said wearily: "This is no time to be arguing about that, precious. What was it you wanted to see me about?"

"I can't talk to you here, Sam. Can't I come in?"

"Not now."

"Why can't I?"

Spade said nothing.

She made a thin line of her mouth, squirmed around straight behind the wheel, and started the sedan's engine, staring angrily ahead.

When the sedan began to move Spade said, "Good night, Iva," shut the door, and stood at the curb with his hat in his hand until it had been driven away. Then he went indoors again.

Brigid O'Shaughnessy rose smiling cheerfully from the bench and they went up to his apartment.

VII · G in the Air

IN his bedroom that was a living-room now the wall-bed was up, Spade took Brigid O'Shaughnessy's hat and coat, made her comfortable in a padded rocking chair, and telephoned the Hotel Belvedere. Cairo had not returned from the theatre. Spade left his telephone-number with the request that Cairo call him as soon as he came in.

Spade sat down in the armchair beside the table and without any preliminary, without an introductory remark of any sort, began to tell the girl about a thing that had happened some years before in the Northwest. He talked in a steady matter-of-fact voice that was devoid of emphasis or pauses, though now and then he repeated a sentence slightly rearranged, as if it were important that each detail be related exactly as it had happened.

At the beginning Brigid O'Shaughnessy listened with only partial attentiveness, obviously more surprised by his telling the story than interested in it, her curiosity more engaged with his purpose in telling the story than with the story he told; but presently, as the story went on, it caught her more and more fully and she became still and receptive.

A man named Flitcraft had left his real-estate-office, in Tacoma, to go to luncheon one day and had never returned. He did not keep an engagement to play golf after four that afternoon, though he had taken the initiative in making the engagement less than half an hour before he went out to luncheon. His wife and children never saw him again. His wife and he were supposed to be on the best of terms. He had two children, boys, one five and the other three. He owned his house in a Tacoma suburb, a new Packard, and the rest of the appurtenances of successful American living.

Flitcraft had inherited seventy thousand dollars from his father, and, with his success in real estate, was worth something in the neighborhood of two hundred thousand dollars at the time he vanished. His affairs were in order, though there were enough loose ends to indicate that he had not been setting them in order preparatory to vanishing. A deal that would have brought him an attractive profit, for instance, was to have been concluded the day after the one on which he disappeared. There was nothing to suggest that he had more than fifty or sixty dollars in his immediate possession at the time of his going. His habits for months past could be accounted for too thoroughly to justify any suspicion of secret vices, or even of another woman in his life, though either was barely possible.

"He went like that," Spade said, "like a fist when you open your hand."

When he had reached this point in his story the telephone-bell rang.

"Hello," Spade said into the instrument. "Mr. Cairo? . . . This is Spade. Can you come up to my place—Post Street—now? . . . Yes, I think it is." He looked at the girl, pursed his lips, and then said rapidly: "Miss O'Shaughnessy is here and wants to see you."

Brigid O'Shaughnessy frowned and stirred in her chair, but did not say anything.

Spade put the telephone down and told her: "He'll be up in a few minutes. Well, that was in 1922. In 1927 I was with one of the big detective agencies in Seattle. Mrs. Flitcraft came in and told us somebody had seen a man in Spokane who looked a lot like her husband. I went over there. It was Flitcraft, all right. He had been living in Spokane for a couple of years as Charles—that was his first name—Pierce. He had an automobile-business that was netting him twenty or twenty-five thousand a year, a wife, a baby son, owned his home in a Spokane suburb, and usually got away to play golf after four in the afternoon during the season."

Spade had not been told very definitely what to do when he found Flitcraft. They talked in Spade's room at the Davenport. Flitcraft had no feeling of guilt. He had left his first family well provided for, and what he had done seemed to him perfectly reasonable. The only thing that bothered him was a doubt that he could make that reasonableness clear to Spade. He had never told anybody his story before, and thus had not had to attempt to make its reasonableness explicit. He tried now.

"I got it all right," Spade told Brigid O'Shaughnessy, "but Mrs. Flitcraft never did. She thought it was silly. Maybe it was. Anyway, it came out all right. She didn't want any scandal, and, after the trick he had played on her—the way she looked at it—she didn't want him. So they were divorced on the quiet and everything was swell all around.

"Here's what had happened to him. Going to lunch he passed an office-building that was being put up—just the skeleton. A beam or something fell eight or ten stories down and smacked the sidewalk alongside him. It brushed pretty close to him, but didn't touch him, though a piece of the sidewalk was chipped off and flew up and hit his cheek. It only took a piece of skin off, but he still had the scar when I saw him. He rubbed it with his finger—well, affectionately—when he told me about it. He was scared stiff of course, he said, but he was more shocked than really frightened He felt like somebody had taken the lid off life and let him look at the works."

Flitcraft had been a good citizen and a good husband and father, not by any outer compulsion, but simply because he was a man who was most comfortable in step with his surroundings. He had been raised that way. The people he knew were like that. The life he knew was a clean orderly sane responsible affair. Now a falling beam had shown him that life was fundamentally none of these things. He, the good citizen-husband-father, could be wiped out between office and restaurant by the accident of a falling beam. He knew then that men died at haphazard like that, and lived only while blind chance spared them.

It was not, primarily, the injustice of it that disturbed him: he accepted that after the first shock. What disturbed him was the discovery that in sensibly ordering his affairs he had got out of step, and not into step, with life. He said he knew before he had gone twenty feet from the fallen beam that he would never know peace again until he had adjusted himself to this new glimpse of life. By the time he had eaten his luncheon he had found his means of adjustment. Life could be ended for him at random by a falling beam: he would change his life at random by simply going away. He loved his family, he said, as much as he supposed was usual, but he knew he was leaving them adequately provided for, and his love for them was not of the sort that would make absence painful.

"He went to Seattle that afternoon," Spade said, "and from there by boat to San Francisco. For a couple of years he wandered around and then drifted back to the Northwest, and settled in Spokane and got married. His second wife didn't look like the first, but they were more alike than they were different. You know, the kind of women that play fair games of golf and bridge and like new salad-recipes. He wasn't sorry for what he had done. It seemed reasonable enough to him. I don't think he even knew he had settled back naturally into the same groove he had jumped out of in Tacoma. But that's the part of it I always liked. He adjusted himself to beams falling, and then no more of them fell, and he adjusted himself to them not falling."

"How perfectly fascinating," Brigid O'Shaughnessy said. She left her chair and stood in front of him, close. Her eyes were wide and deep. "I don't have to tell you how utterly at a disadvantage you'll have me, with him here, if you choose."

Spade smiled slightly without separating his lips. "No, you don't have to tell me," he agreed.

"And you know I'd never have placed myself in this position if I hadn't trusted you completely." Her thumb and forefinger twisted a black button on his blue coat.

Spade said, "That again!" with mock resignation.

"But you know it's so," she insisted.

"No, I don't know it." He patted the hand that was twisting the button. "My asking for reasons why I should trust you brought us here. Don't let's confuse things. You don't have to trust me, anyhow, as long as you can persuade me to trust you."

She studied his face. Her nostrils quivered.

Spade laughed. He patted her hand again and said: "Don't worry about that now. He'll be here in a moment. Get your business with him over, and then we'll see how we'll stand."

"And you'll let me go about it—with him—in my own way?"

"Sure."

She turned her hand under his so that her fingers pressed his. She said softly: "You're a God-send."

Spade said: "Don't overdo it."

She looked reproachfully at him, though smiling, and returned to the padded rocker.

Joel Cairo was excited. His dark eyes seemed all irises and his high-pitched thin-voiced words were tumbling out before Spade had the door half-open.

"That boy is out there watching the house, Mr. Spade, that boy you showed me, or to whom you showed me, in front of the theatre. What am I to understand from that, Mr. Spade? I came here in good faith, with no thought of tricks or traps."

"You were asked in good faith." Spade frowned thoughtfully. "But I ought to've guessed he might show up. He saw you come in?"

"Naturally. I could have gone on, but that seemed useless, since you had already let him see us together."

Brigid O'Shaughnessy came into the passageway behind Spade and asked anxiously: "What boy? What is it?"

Cairo removed his black hat from his head, bowed stiffly, and said in a prim voice: "If you do not know, ask Mr. Spade. I know nothing about it except through him."

"A kid who's been trying to tail me around town all evening," Spade said carelessly over his shoulder, not turning to face the girl. "Come on in, Cairo. There's no use standing here talking for all the neighbors."

Brigid O'Shaughnessy grasped Spade's arm above the elbow and demanded: "Did he follow you to my apartment?"

"No. I shook him before that. Then I suppose he came back here to try to pick me up again."

Cairo, holding his black hat to his belly with both hands, had come into the passageway. Spade shut the corridor-door behind him and they went into the living-room. There Cairo bowed stiffly over his hat once more and said: "I am delighted to see you again, Miss O'Shaughnessy."

"I was sure you would be, Joe," she replied, giving him her hand.

He made a formal bow over her hand and released it quickly.

She sat in the padded rocker she had occupied before. Cairo sat in the armchair by the table. Spade, when he had hung Cairo's hat and coat in the closet, sat on an end of the sofa in front of the windows and began to roll a cigarette.

Brigid O'Shaughnessy said to Cairo: "Sam told me about your offer for the falcon. How soon can you have the money ready?"

Cairo's eyebrows twitched. He smiled. "It is ready." He continued to smile at the girl for a little while after he had spoken, and then looked at Spade.

Spade was lighting his cigarette. His face was tranquil.

"In cash?" the girl asked.

"Oh, yes," Cairo replied.

She frowned, put her tongue between her lips, withdrew it, and asked: "You are ready to give us five thousand dollars, now, if we give you the falcon?"

Cairo held up a wriggling hand. "Excuse me," he said. "I expressed myself badly. I did not mean to say that I have the money in my pockets, but that I am prepared to get it on a very few minutes' notice at any time during banking hours."

"Oh!" She looked at Spade.

Spade blew cigarette-smoke down the front of his vest and said: "That's probably right. He had only a few hundred in his pockets when I frisked him this afternoon."

When her eyes opened round and wide he grinned.

The Levantine bent forward in his chair. He failed to keep eagerness from showing in his eyes and voice. "I can be quite prepared to give you the money at, say, half-past ten in the morning. Eh?"

Brigid O'Shaughnessy smiled at him and said: "But I haven't got the falcon."

Cairo's face was darkened by a flush of annoyance. He put an ugly hand on either arm of his chair, holding his small-boned body erect and stiff between them. His dark eyes were angry. He did not say anything.

The girl made a mock-placatory face at him. "I'll have it in a week at the most, though," she said.

"Where is it?" Cairo used politeness of mien to express skepticism.

"Where Floyd hid it."

"Floyd? Thursby?"

She nodded.

"And you know where that is?" he asked.

"I think I do."

"Then why must we wait a week?"

"Perhaps not a whole week. Whom are you buying it for, Joe?"

Cairo raised his eyebrows. "I told Mr. Spade. For its owner."

Surprise illuminated the girl's face. "So you went back to him?"

"Naturally I did."

She laughed softly in her throat and said: "I should have liked to have seen that."

Cairo shrugged. "That was the logical development." He rubbed the back of one hand with the palm of the other. His upper lids came down to shade his eyes. "Why, if I in turn may ask a question, are you willing to sell to me?"

"I'm afraid," she said simply, "after what happened to Floyd. That's why I haven't it now. I'm afraid to touch it except to turn it over to somebody else right away."

Spade, propped on an elbow on the sofa, looked at and listened to them impartially. In the comfortable slackness of his body, in the easy stillness of his features, there was no indication of either curiosity or impatience.

"Exactly what," Cairo asked in a low voice, "happened to Floyd?"

The tip of Brigid O'Shaughnessy's right forefinger traced a swift G in the air.

Cairo said, "I see," but there was something doubting in his smile. "Is he here?"

"I don't know." She spoke impatiently. "What difference does it make?"

The doubt in Cairo's smile deepened. "It might make a world of difference," he said, and rearranged his hands in his lap so that, intentionally or not, a blunt forefinger pointed at Spade.

The girl glanced at the pointing finger and made an impatient motion with her head. "Or me," she said, "or you."

"Exactly, and shall we add more certainly the boy outside?"

"Yes," she agreed and laughed. "Yes, unless he's the one you had in Constantinople."

Sudden blood mottled Cairo's face. In a shrill enraged voice he cried: "The one you couldn't make?"

Brigid O'Shaughnessy jumped up from her chair. Her lower lip was between her teeth. Her eyes were dark and wide in a tense white face. She took two quick steps towards Cairo. He started to rise. Her right hand went out and cracked sharply against his cheek, leaving the imprint of fingers there.

Cairo grunted and slapped her cheek, staggering her sidewise, bringing from her mouth a brief muffled scream.

Spade, wooden of face, was up from the sofa and close to them by then. He caught Cairo by the throat and shook him. Cairo gurgled and put a hand inside his coat. Spade grasped the Levantine's wrist, wrenched it away from the coat, forced it straight out to the side, and twisted it until the clumsy flaccid fingers opened to let the black pistol fall down on the rug.

Brigid O'Shaughnessy quickly picked up the pistol.

Cairo, speaking with difficulty because of the fingers on his throat, said: "This is the second time you've put your hands on me." His eyes, though the throttling pressure on his throat made them bulge, were cold and menacing.

"Yes," Spade growled. "And when you're slapped you'll take it and like it." He released Cairo's wrist and with a thick open hand struck the side of his face three times, savagely.

Cairo tried to spit in Spade's face, but the dryness of the Levantine's mouth made it only an angry gesture. Spade slapped the mouth, cutting the lower lip.

The door-bell rang.

Cairo's eyes jerked into focus on the passageway that led to the corridor-door. His eyes had become unangry and wary. The girl had gasped and turned to face the passageway. Her face was frightened. Spade stared gloomily for a moment at the blood trickling from Cairo's lip, and then stepped back, taking his hand from the Levantine's throat.

"Who is it?" the girl whispered, coming close to Spade; and Cairo's eyes jerked back to ask the same question.

Spade gave his answer irritably: "I don't know."

The bell rang again, more insistently.

"Well, keep quiet," Spade said, and went out of the room, shutting the door behind him.

Spade turned on the light in the passageway and opened the door to the corridor. Lieutenant Dundy and Tom Polhaus were there.

"Hello, Sam," Tom said. "We thought maybe you wouldn't've gone to bed yet."

Dundy nodded, but said nothing.

Spade said good-naturedly: "Hello. You guys pick swell hours to do your visiting in. What is it this time?"

Dundy spoke then, quietly: "We want to talk to you, Spade."

"Well?" Spade stood in the doorway, blocking it. "Go ahead and talk."

Tom Polhaus advanced saying: "We don't have to do it standing here, do we?"

Spade stood in the doorway and said: "You can't come in." His tone was very slightly apologetic.

Tom's thick-featured face, even in height with Spade's, took on an expression of friendly scorn, though there was a bright gleam in his small shrewd eyes. "What the hell, Sam?" he protested and put a big hand playfully on Spade's chest.

Spade leaned against the pushing hand, grinned wolfishly, and asked: "Going to strong-arm me, Tom?"

Tom grumbled, "Aw, for God's sake," and took his hand away.

Dundy clicked his teeth together and said through them: "Let us in."

Spade's lip twitched over his eyetooth. He said: "You're not coming in. What do you want to do about it? Try to get in? Or do your talking here? Or go to hell?"

Tom groaned.

Dundy, still speaking through his teeth, said: "It'd pay you to play

along with us a little, Spade. You've got away with this and you've got
away with that, but you can't keep it up forever."

"Stop me when you can," Spade replied arrogantly.

"That's what I'll do." Dundy put his hands behind him and thrust
his hard face up towards the private detective's. "There's talk going
around that you and Archer's wife were cheating on him."

Spade laughed. "That sounds like something you thought up yourself."

"Then there's not anything to it?"

"Not anything."

"The talk is," Dundy said, "that she tried to get a divorce out of him
so's she could put in with you, but he wouldn't give it to her. Anything
to that?"

"No."

"There's even talk," Dundy went on stolidly, "that that's why he was
put on the spot."

Spade seemed mildly amused. "Don't be a hog," he said. "You
oughtn't try to pin more than one murder at a time on me. Your first
idea that I knocked Thursby off because he'd killed Miles falls apart if
you blame me for killing Miles too."

"You haven't heard me say you killed anybody," Dundy replied.
"You're the one that keeps bringing that up. But suppose I did. You could
have blipped them both. There's a way of figuring it."

"Uh-huh. I could've butchered Miles to get his wife, and then
Thursby so I could hang Miles's killing on him. That's a hell of a swell
system, or will be when I can give somebody else the bump and hang
Thursby's on them. How long am I supposed to keep that up? Are you
going to put your hand on my shoulder for all the killings in San Francisco
from now on?"

Tom said: "Aw, cut the comedy, Sam. You know damned well we
don't like this any more than you do, but we got our work to do."

"I hope you've got something to do besides pop in here early every
morning with a lot of damned fool questions."

"And get damned lying answers," Dundy added deliberately.

"Take it easy," Spade cautioned him.

Dundy looked him up and down and then looked him straight in
the eyes. "If you say there was nothing between you and Archer's wife,"
he said, "you're a liar, and I'm telling you so."

A startled look came into Tom's small eyes.

Spade moistened his lips with the tip of his tongue and asked: "Is
that the hot tip that brought you here at this ungodly time of night?"

"That's one of them."

"And the others?"

Dundy pulled down the corners of his mouth. "Let us in." He
nodded significantly at the doorway in which Spade stood.

Spade frowned and shook his head.

Dundy's mouth-corners lifted in a smile of grim satisfaction. "There must've been something to it," he told Tom.

Tom shifted his feet and, not looking at either man, mumbled: "God knows."

"What's this?" Spade asked. "Charades?"

"All right, Spade, we're going." Dundy buttoned his overcoat. "We'll be in to see you now and then. Maybe you're right in bucking us. Think it over."

"Uh-huh," Spade said, grinning. "Glad to see you any time, Lieutenant, and whenever I'm not busy I'll let you in."

A voice in Spade's living-room screamed: "Help! Help! Police! Help!" The voice, high and thin and shrill, was Joel Cairo's.

Lieutenant Dundy stopped turning away from the door, confronted Spade again, and said decisively: "I guess we're going in."

The sounds of a brief struggle, of a blow, of a subdued cry, came to them.

Spade's face twisted into a smile that held little joy. He said, "I guess you are," and stood out of the way.

When the police-detectives had entered he shut the corridor-door and followed them back to the living-room.

VIII · Horse Feathers

BRIGID O'SHAUGHNESSY was huddled in the armchair by the table. Her forearms were up over her cheeks, her knees drawn up until they hid the lower part of her face. Her eyes were white-circled and terrified.

Joel Cairo stood in front of her, bending over her, holding in one hand the pistol Spade had twisted out of his hand. His other hand was clapped to his forehead. Blood ran through the fingers of that hand and down under them to his eyes. A smaller trickle from his cut lip made three wavy lines across his chin.

Cairo did not heed the detectives. He was glaring at the girl huddled in front of him. His lips were working spasmodically, but no coherent sound came from between them.

Dundy, the first of the three into the living-room, moved swiftly to Cairo's side, put a hand on his own hip under his overcoat, a hand on the Levantine's wrist, and growled: "What are you up to here?"

Cairo took the red-smeared hand from his head and flourished it close to the Lieutenant's face. Uncovered by the hand, his forehead showed a three-inch ragged tear. "This is what she has done," he cried. "Look at it."

The girl put her feet down on the floor and looked warily from Dundy, holding Cairo's wrist, to Tom Polhaus, standing a little behind them, to Spade, leaning against the door-frame. Spade's face was placid. When his gaze met hers his yellow-grey eyes glinted for an instant with malicious humor and then became expressionless again.

"Did you do that?" Dundy asked the girl, nodding at Cairo's cut head.

She looked at Spade again. He did not in any way respond to the appeal in her eyes. He leaned against the door-frame and observed the occupants of the room with the polite detached air of a disinterested spectator.

The girl turned her eyes up to Dundy's. Her eyes were wide and dark and earnest. "I had to," she said in a low throbbing voice. "I was all alone in here with him when he attacked me. I couldn't—I tried to keep him off. I—I couldn't make myself shoot him."

"Oh, you liar!" Cairo cried, trying unsuccessfully to pull the arm that held his pistol out of Dundy's grip. "Oh, you dirty filthy liar!" He twisted himself around to face Dundy. "She's lying awfully. I came here in good faith and was attacked by both of them, and when you came he went out to talk to you, leaving her here with this pistol, and then she said they were going to kill me after you left, and I called for help, so you wouldn't leave me here to be murdered, and then she struck me with the pistol."

"Here, give me this thing," Dundy said, and took the pistol from Cairo's hand. "Now let's get this straight. What'd you come here for?"

"He sent for me." Cairo twisted his head around to stare defiantly at Spade. "He called me up on the phone and asked me to come here."

Spade blinked sleepily at the Levantine and said nothing.

Dundy asked: "What'd he want you for?"

Cairo withheld his reply until he had mopped his bloody forehead and chin with a lavender-barred silk handkerchief. By then some of the indignation in his manner had been replaced by caution. "He said he wanted—they wanted—to see me. I didn't know what about."

Tom Polhaus lowered his head, sniffed the odor of *chypre* that the mopping handkerchief had released in the air, and turned his head to scowl interrogatively at Spade. Spade winked at him and went on rolling a cigarette.

Dundy asked: "Well, what happened then?"

"Then they attacked me. She struck me first, and then he choked me and took the pistol out of my pocket. I don't know what they would have done next if you hadn't arrived at that moment. I dare say they would have murdered me then and there. When he went out to answer the bell he left her here with the pistol to watch over me."

Brigid O'Shaughnessy jumped out of the armchair crying, "Why don't you make him tell the truth?" and slapped Cairo on the cheek.

Cairo yelled inarticulately.

Dundy pushed the girl back into the chair with the hand that was not holding the Levantine's arm and growled: "None of that now."

Spade, lighting his cigarette, grinned softly through smoke and told Tom: "She's impulsive."

"Yeah," Tom agreed.

Dundy scowled down at the girl and asked: "What do you want us to think the truth is?"

"Not what he said," she replied. "Not anything he said." She turned to Spade. "Is it?"

"How do I know?" Spade responded. "I was out in the kitchen mixing an omelette when it all happened, wasn't I?"

She wrinkled her forehead, studying him with eyes that perplexity clouded.

Tom grunted in disgust.

Dundy, still scowling at the girl, ignored Spade's speech and asked her: "If he's not telling the truth, how come he did the squawking for help, and not you?"

"Oh, he was frightened to death when I struck him," she replied, looking contemptuously at the Levantine.

Cairo's face flushed where it was not blood-smeared. He exclaimed: "Pfoo! Another lie!"

She kicked his leg, the high heel of her blue slipper striking him just below the knee. Dundy pulled him away from her while big Tom came to stand close to her, rumbling: "Behave, sister. That's no way to act."

"Then make him tell the truth," she said defiantly.

"We'll do that all right," he promised. "Just don't get rough."

Dundy, looking at Spade with green eyes hard and bright and satisfied, addressed his subordinate: "Well, Tom, I don't guess we'll go wrong pulling the lot of them in."

Tom nodded gloomily.

Spade left the door and advanced to the center of the room, dropping his cigarette into a tray on the table as he passed it. His smile and manner were amiably composed. "Don't be in a hurry," he said. "Everything can be explained."

"I bet you," Dundy agreed, sneering.

Spade bowed to the girl. "Miss O'Shaughnessy," he said, "may I present Lieutenant Dundy and Detective-sergeant Polhaus." He bowed to Dundy. "Miss O'Shaughnessy is an operative in my employ."

Joel Cairo said indignantly: "That isn't so. She—"

Spade interrupted him in a quite loud, but still genial, voice: "I hired her just recently, yesterday. This is Mr. Joel Cairo, a friend—an acquaintance, at any rate—of Thursby's. He came to me this afternoon and tried to hire me to find something Thursby was supposed to have on him when he was bumped off. It looked funny, the way he put it to me, so I wouldn't touch it. Then he pulled a gun—well, never mind that unless it comes to a point of laying charges against each other. Anyway, after talking it over with Miss O'Shaughnessy, I thought maybe I could get something out of him about Miles's and Thursby's killings, so I asked him to come up here. Maybe we put the questions to him a little rough, but he wasn't hurt any, not enough to have to cry for help. I'd already had to take his gun away from him again."

As Spade talked anxiety came into Cairo's reddened face. His eyes moved jerkily up and down, shifting their focus uneasily between the floor and Spade's bland face.

Dundy confronted Cairo and bruskly demanded: "Well, what've you got to say to that?"

Cairo had nothing to say for nearly a minute while he stared at the Lieutenant's chest. When he lifted his eyes they were shy and wary. "I don't know what I should say," he murmured. His embarrassment seemed genuine.

"Try telling the facts," Dundy suggested.

"The facts?" Cairo's eyes fidgeted, though their gaze did not actually leave the Lieutenant's. "What assurance have I that the facts will be believed?"

"Quit stalling. All you've got to do is swear to a complaint that they took a poke at you and the warrant-clerk will believe you enough to issue a warrant that'll let us throw them in the can."

Spade spoke in an amused tone: "Go ahead, Cairo. Make him happy. Tell him you'll do it, and then we'll swear to one against you, and he'll have the lot of us."

Cairo cleared his throat and looked nervously around the room, not into the eyes of anyone there.

Dundy blew breath through his nose in a puff that was not quite a snort and said: "Get your hats."

Cairo's eyes, holding worry and a question, met Spade's mocking gaze. Spade winked at him and sat on the arm of the padded rocker. "Well, boys and girls," he said, grinning at the Levantine and at the girl with nothing but delight in his voice and grin, "we put it over nicely."

Dundy's hard square face darkened the least of shades. He repeated peremptorily: "Get your hats."

Spade turned his grin on the Lieutenant, squirmed into a more comfortable position on the chair-arm, and asked lazily: "Don't you know when you're being kidded?"

Tom Polhaus's face became red and shiny.

Dundy's face, still darkening, was immobile except for lips moving stiffly to say: "No, but we'll let that wait till we get down to the Hall."

Spade rose and put his hands in his trousers-pockets. He stood erect so he might look that much farther down at the Lieutenant. His grin was a taunt and self-certainty spoke in every line of his posture.

"I dare you to take us in, Dundy," he said. "We'll laugh at you in every newspaper in San Francisco. You don't think any of us is going to swear to any complaints against the others, do you? Wake up. You've been kidded. When the bell rang I said to Miss O'Shaughnessy and Cairo: 'It's those damned bulls again. They're getting to be nuisances. Let's play a joke on them. When you hear them going one of you scream, and then we'll see how far we can string them along before they tumble.' And—"

Brigid O'Shaughnessy bent forward in her chair and began to laugh hysterically.

Cairo started and smiled. There was no vitality in his smile, but he held it fixed on his face.

Tom, glowering, grumbled: "Cut it out, Sam."

Spade chuckled and said: "But that's the way it was. We—"

"And the cut on his head and mouth?" Dundy asked scornfully. "Where'd they come from?"

"Ask him," Spade suggested. "Maybe he cut himself shaving."

Cairo spoke quickly, before he could be questioned, and the muscles of his face quivered under the strain of holding his smile in place while he spoke. "I fell. We intended to be struggling for the pistol when you came in, but I fell. I tripped on the end of the rug and fell while we were pretending to struggle."

Dundy said: "Horse feathers."

Spade said: "That's all right, Dundy, believe it or not. The point is that that's our story and we'll stick to it. The newspapers will print it whether they believe it or not, and it'll be just as funny one way as the other, or more so. What are you going to do about it? It's no crime to kid a copper, is it? You haven't got anything on anybody here. Everything we told you was part of the joke. What are you going to do about it?"

Dundy put his back to Spade and gripped Cairo by the shoulders. "You can't get away with that," he snarled, shaking the Levantine. "You belched for help and you've got to take it."

"No, sir," Cairo sputtered. "It was a joke. He said you were friends of his and would understand."

Spade laughed.

Dundy pulled Cairo roughly around, holding him now by one wrist and the nape of his neck. "I'll take you along for packing the gun, anyway," he said. "And I'll take the rest of you along to see who laughs at the joke."

Cairo's alarmed eyes jerked sidewise to focus on Spade's face.

Spade said: "Don't be a sap, Dundy. The gun was part of the plant. It's one of mine." He laughed. "Too bad it's only a thirty-two, or maybe you could find it was the one Thursby and Miles were shot with."

Dundy released Cairo, spun on his heel, and his right fist clicked on Spade's chin.

Brigid O'Shaughnessy uttered a short cry.

Spade's smile flickered out at the instant of the impact, but returned immediately with a dreamy quality added. He steadied himself with a short backward step and his thick sloping shoulders writhed under his coat. Before his fist could come up Tom Polhaus had pushed himself between the two men, facing Spade, encumbering Spade's arms with the closeness of his barrel-like belly and his own arms.

"No, no, for Christ's sake!" Tom begged.

After a long moment of motionlessness Spade's muscles relaxed. "Then get him out of here quick," he said. His smile had gone away again, leaving his face sullen and somewhat pale.

Tom, staying close to Spade, keeping his arms on Spade's arms, turned his head to look over his shoulder at Lieutenant Dundy. Tom's small eyes were reproachful.

Dundy's fists were clenched in front of his body and his feet were planted firm and a little apart on the floor, but the truculence in his face was modified by thin rims of white showing between green irises and upper eyelids.

"Get their names and addresses," he ordered.

Tom looked at Cairo, who said quickly: "Joel Cairo, Hotel Belvedere."

Spade spoke before Tom could question the girl. "You can always get in touch with Miss O'Shaughnessy through me."

Tom looked at Dundy. Dundy growled: "Get her address."

Spade said: "Her address is in care of my office."

Dundy took a step forward, halting in front of the girl. "Where do you live?" he asked.

Spade addressed Tom: "Get him out of here. I've had enough of this."

Tom looked at Spade's eyes—hard and glittering—and mumbled: "Take it easy, Sam." He buttoned his coat and turned to Dundy, asking, in a voice that aped casualness, "Well, is that all?" and taking a step towards the door.

Dundy's scowl failed to conceal indecision.

Cairo moved suddenly towards the door, saying: "I'm going too, if Mr. Spade will be kind enough to give me my hat and coat."

Spade asked: "What's the hurry?"

Dundy said angrily: "It was all in fun, but just the same you're afraid to be left here with them."

"Not at all," the Levantine replied, fidgeting, looking at neither of them, "but it's quite late and—and I'm going. I'll go out with you if you don't mind."

Dundy put his lips together firmly and said nothing. A light was glinting in his green eyes.

Spade went to the closet in the passageway and fetched Cairo's hat and coat. Spade's face was blank. His voice held the same blankness when he stepped back from helping the Levantine into his coat and said to Tom: "Tell him to leave the gun."

Dundy took Cairo's pistol from his overcoat-pocket and put it on the table. He went out first, with Cairo at his heels. Tom halted in front of Spade, muttering, "I hope to God you know what you're doing," got no response, sighed, and followed the others out. Spade went after them as far as the bend in the passageway, where he stood until Tom had closed the corridor-door.

IX · Brigid

SPADE returned to the living-room and sat on an end of the sofa, elbows on knees, cheeks in hands, looking at the floor and not at Brigid O'Shaughnessy smiling weakly at him from the armchair. His eyes were sultry. The creases between brows over his nose were deep. His nostrils moved in and out with his breathing.

Brigid O'Shaughnessy, when it became apparent that he was not going to look up at her, stopped smiling and regarded him with growing uneasiness.

Red rage came suddenly into his face and he began to talk in a harsh guttural voice. Holding his maddened face in his hands, glaring at the floor, he cursed Dundy for five minutes without break, cursed him obscenely, blasphemously, repetitiously, in a harsh guttural voice.

Then he took his face out of his hands, looked at the girl, grinned sheepishly, and said: "Childish, huh? I know, but, by God, I do hate being hit without hitting back." He touched his chin with careful fingers. "Not that it was so much of a sock at that." He laughed and lounged back on the sofa, crossing his legs. "A cheap enough price to pay for winning." His brows came together in a fleeting scowl. "Though I'll remember it."

The girl, smiling again, left her chair and sat on the sofa beside him. "You're absolutely the wildest person I've ever known," she said. "Do you always carry on so high-handed?"

"I let him hit me, didn't I?"

"Oh, yes, but a police official."

"It wasn't that," Spade explained. "It was that in losing his head and slugging me he overplayed his hand. If I'd mixed it with him then he couldn't've backed down. He'd've had to go through with it, and we'd've had to tell that goofy story at headquarters." He stared thoughtfully at the girl, and asked: "What did you do to Cairo?"

"Nothing." Her face became flushed. "I tried to frighten him into keeping still until they had gone and he either got too frightened or stubborn and yelled."

"And then you smacked him with the gun?"

"I had to. He attacked me."

"You don't know what you're doing." Spade's smile did not hide his annoyance. "It's just what I told you: you're fumbling along by guess and by God."

"I'm sorry," she said, face and voice soft with contrition, "Sam."

"Sure you are." He took tobacco and papers from his pockets and began to make a cigarette. "Now you've had your talk with Cairo. Now you can talk to me."

She put a fingertip to her mouth, staring across the room at nothing with widened eyes, and then, with narrower eyes, glanced quickly at Spade. He was engrossed in the making of his cigarette. "Oh, yes," she began, "of course—" She took the finger away from her mouth and smoothed her blue dress over her knees. She frowned at her knees.

Spade licked his cigarette, sealed it, and asked, "Well?" while he felt for his lighter.

"But I didn't," she said, pausing between words as if she were selecting them with great care, "have time to finish talking to him." She stopped frowning at her knees and looked at Spade with clear candid eyes. "We were interrupted almost before we had begun."

Spade lighted his cigarette and laughed his mouth empty of smoke. "Want me to phone him and ask him to come back?"

She shook her head, not smiling. Her eyes moved back and forth between her lids as she shook her head, maintaining their focus on Spade's eyes. Her eyes were inquisitive.

Spade put an arm across her back, cupping his hand over the smooth bare white shoulder farthest from him. She leaned back into the bend of his arm. He said: "Well, I'm listening."

She twisted her head around to smile up at him with playful insolence, asking: "Do you need your arm there for that?"

"No." He removed his hand from her shoulder and let his arm drop down behind her.

"You're altogether unpredictable," she murmured.

He nodded and said amiably: "I'm still listening."

"Look at the time!" she exclaimed, wriggling a finger at the alarm-clock perched atop the book saying two-fifty with its clumsily shaped hands.

"Uh-huh, it's been a busy evening."

"I must go." She rose from the sofa. "This is terrible."

Spade did not rise. He shook his head and said: "Not until you've told me about it."

"But look at the time," she protested, "and it would take hours to tell you."

"It'll have to take them then."

"Am I a prisoner?" she asked gaily.

"Besides, there's the kid outside. Maybe he hasn't gone home to sleep yet."

Her gaiety vanished. "Do you think he's still there?"

"It's likely."

She shivered. "Could you find out?"

"I could go down and see."

"Oh, that's—will you?"

Spade studied her anxious face for a moment and then got up from the sofa saying: "Sure." He got a hat and overcoat from the closet. "I'll be gone about ten minutes."

"Do be careful," she begged as she followed him to the corridor-door. He said, "I will," and went out.

Post Street was empty when Spade issued into it. He walked east a block, crossed the street, walked west two blocks on the other side, re-crossed it, and returned to his building without having seen anyone except two mechanics working on a car in a garage.

When he opened his apartment-door Brigid O'Shaughnessy was standing at the bend in the passageway, holding Cairo's pistol straight down at her side.

"He's still there," Spade said.

She bit the inside of her lip and turned slowly, going back into the living-room. Spade followed her in, put his hat and overcoat on a chair, said, "So we'll have time to talk," and went into the kitchen.

He had put the coffee-pot on the stove when she came to the door, and was slicing a slender loaf of French bread. She stood in the doorway and watched him with preoccupied eyes. The fingers of her left hand idly caressed the body and barrel of the pistol her right hand still held.

"The table-cloth's in there," he said, pointing the bread-knife at a cupboard that was one breakfast-nook partition.

She set the table while he spread liverwurst on, or put cold corned beef between, the small ovals of bread he had sliced. Then he poured the coffee, added brandy to it from a squat bottle, and they sat at the table. They sat side by side on one of the benches. She put the pistol down on the end of the bench nearer her.

"You can start now, between bites," he said.

She made a face at him, complained, "You're the most insistent person," and bit a sandwich.

"Yes, and wild and unpredictable. What's this bird, this falcon, that everybody's all steamed up about?"

She chewed the beef and bread in her mouth, swallowed it, looked attentively at the small crescent its removal had made in the sandwich's rim, and asked: "Suppose I wouldn't tell you? Suppose I wouldn't tell you anything at all about it? What would you do?"

"You mean about the bird?"

"I mean about the whole thing."

"I wouldn't be too surprised," he told her, grinning so that the edges of his jaw-teeth were visible, "to know what to do next."

"And that would be?" She transferred her attention from the sandwich to his face. "That's what I wanted to know: what would you do next?"

He shook his head.

Mockery rippled in a smile on her face. "Something wild and unpredictable?"

"Maybe. But I don't see what you've got to gain by covering up now. It's coming out bit by bit anyhow. There's a lot of it I don't know, but there's some of it I do, and some more that I can guess at, and, give me another day like this, I'll soon be knowing things about it that you don't know."

"I suppose you do now," she said, looking at her sandwich again, her face serious. "But—oh!—I'm so tired of it, and I do so hate having to talk about it. Wouldn't it—wouldn't it be just as well to wait and let you learn about it as you say you will?"

Spade laughed. "I don't know. You'll have to figure that out for yourself. My way of learning is to heave a wild and unpredictable monkey-wrench into the machinery. It's all right with me, if you're sure none of the flying pieces will hurt you."

She moved her bare shoulders uneasily, but said nothing. For several minutes they ate in silence, he phlegmatically, she thoughtfully. Then she said in a hushed voice: "I'm afraid of you, and that's the truth."

He said: "That's not the truth."

"It is," she insisted in the same low voice. "I know two men I'm afraid of and I've seen both of them tonight."

"I can understand your being afraid of Cairo," Spade said. "He's out of your reach."

"And you aren't?"

"Not that way," he said and grinned.

She blushed. She picked up a slice of bread encrusted with grey liverwurst. She put it down on her plate. She wrinkled her white forehead and she said: "It's a black figure, as you know, smooth and shiny, of a bird, a hawk or falcon, about that high." She held her hands a foot apart.

"What makes it important?"

She sipped coffee and brandy before she shook her head. "I don't know," she said. "They'd never tell me. They promised me five hundred pounds if I helped them get it. Then Floyd said afterward, after we'd left Joe, that he'd give me seven hundred and fifty."

"So it must be worth more than seventy-five hundred dollars?"

"Oh, much more than that," she said. "They didn't pretend that they were sharing equally with me. They were simply hiring me to help them."

"To help them how?"

She lifted her cup to her lips again. Spade, not moving the domineering stare of his yellow-grey eyes from her face, began to make a cigarette. Behind them the percolator bubbled on the stove.

"To help them get it from the man who had it," she said slowly when she had lowered her cup, "a Russian named Kemidov."

"How?"

"Oh, but that's not important," she objected, "and wouldn't help you"—she smiled impudently—"and is certainly none of your business."

"This was in Constantinople?"

She hesitated, nodded, and said: "Marmora."

He waved his cigarette at her, saying: "Go ahead, what happened then?"

"But that's all. I've told you. They promised me five hundred pounds to help them and I did and then we found that Joe Cairo meant to desert us, taking the falcon with him and leaving us nothing. So we did exactly that to him, first. But then I wasn't any better off than I had been before, because Floyd hadn't any intention at all of paying me the seven hundred and fifty pounds he had promised me. I had learned that by the time we got here. He said we would go to New York, where he would sell it and give me my share, but I could see he wasn't telling me the truth." Indignation had darkened her eyes to violet. "And that's why I came to you to get you to help me learn where the falcon was."

"And suppose you'd got it? What then?"

"Then I'd have been in a position to talk terms with Mr. Floyd Thursby."

Spade squinted at her and suggested: "But you wouldn't have known where to take it to get more money than he'd give you, the larger sum that you knew he expected to sell it for?"

"I did not know," she said.

Spade scowled at the ashes he had dumped on his plate. "What makes it worth all that money?" he demanded. "You must have some idea, at least be able to guess."

"I haven't the slightest idea."

He directed the scowl at her. "What's it made of?"

"Porcelain or black stone. I don't know. I've never touched it. I've only seen it once, for a few minutes. Floyd showed it to me when we'd first got hold of it."

Spade mashed the end of his cigarette in his plate and made one draught of the coffee and brandy in his cup. His scowl had gone away. He wiped his lips with his napkin, dropped it crumpled on the table, and spoke casually: "You *are* a liar."

She got up and stood at the end of the table, looking down at him with dark abashed eyes in a pinkening face. "I am a liar," she said. "I have always been a liar."

"Don't brag about it. It's childish." His voice was good-humored. He came out from between table and bench. "Was there any truth at all in that yarn?"

She hung her head. Dampness glistened on her dark lashes. "Some," she whispered.

"How much?"

"Not—not very much."

Spade put a hand under her chin and lifted her head. He laughed into her wet eyes and said: "We've got all night before us. I'll put some more brandy in some more coffee and we'll try again."

Her eyelids drooped. "Oh, I'm so tired," she said tremulously, "so tired of it all, of myself, of lying and thinking up lies, and of not knowing what is a lie and what is the truth. I wish I—"

She put her hands up to Spade's cheeks, put her open mouth hard against his mouth, her body flat against his body.

Spade's arms went around her, holding her to him, muscles bulging his blue sleeves, a hand cradling her head, its fingers half lost among red hair, a hand moving groping fingers over her slim back. His eyes burned yellowly.

X · *The Belvedere Divan*

BEGINNING day had reduced night to a thin smokiness when Spade sat up. At his side Brigid O'Shaughnessy's soft breathing had the regularity of utter sleep. Spade was quiet leaving bed and bedroom and shutting the bedroom-door. He dressed in the bathroom. Then he examined the sleeping girl's clothes, took a flat brass key from the pocket of her coat, and went out.

He went to the Coronet, letting himself into the building and into her apartment with the key. To the eye there was nothing furtive about his going in: he entered boldly and directly. To the ear his going in was almost unnoticeable: he made as little sound as might be.

In the girl's apartment he switched on all the lights. He searched the place from wall to wall. His eyes and thick fingers moved without apparent haste, and without ever lingering or fumbling or going back, from one inch of their fields to the next, probing, scrutinizing, testing with expert certainty. Every drawer, cupboard, cubbyhole, box, bag, trunk—locked or unlocked—was opened and its contents subjected to examination by eyes and fingers. Every piece of clothing was tested by hands that felt for telltale bulges and ears that listened for the crinkle of paper between pressing fingers. He stripped the bed of bedclothes. He looked under rugs and at the under side of each piece of furniture. He pulled down blinds to see that nothing had been rolled up in them for concealment. He leaned through windows to see that nothing hung below them on the outside. He poked with a fork into powder and cream-jars on the dressing-table. He held atomizers and bottles up against the light. He examined dishes and pans and food and food-containers. He emptied the garbage-can on spread sheets of newspaper. He opened the top of the flush-box in the bathroom, drained the box, and peered down into it. He examined and tested the metal screens over the drains of bathtub, wash-bowl, sink, and laundry tub.

He did not find the black bird. He found nothing that seemed to have any connection with a black bird. The only piece of writing he found was a week-old receipt for the month's apartment-rent Brigid O'Shaughnessy had paid. The only thing he found that interested him enough to delay his search while he looked at it was a double-handful of rather fine jewelry in a polychrome box in a locked dressing-table-drawer.

When he had finished he made and drank a cup of coffee. Then he unlocked the kitchen-window, scarred the edge of its lock a little with his pocket-knife, opened the window—over a fire-escape—got his hat and overcoat from the settee in the living-room, and left the apartment as he had come.

On his way home he stopped at a store that was being opened by a puffy-eyed shivering plump grocer and bought oranges, eggs, rolls, butter, and cream.

Spade went quietly into his apartment, but before he had shut the corridor-door behind him Brigid O'Shaughnessy cried: "Who is that?"

"Young Spade bearing breakfast."

"Oh, you frightened me!"

The bedroom-door he had shut was open. The girl sat on the side of the bed, trembling, with her right hand out of sight under a pillow.

Spade put his packages on the kitchen-table and went into the bedroom. He sat on the bed beside the girl, kissed her smooth shoulder, and said: "I wanted to see if that kid was still on the job, and to get stuff for breakfast."

"Is he?"

"No."

She sighed and leaned against him. "I awakened and you weren't here and then I heard someone coming in. I was terrified."

Spade combed her red hair back from her face with his fingers and said: "I'm sorry, angel. I thought you'd sleep through it. Did you have that gun under your pillow all night?"

"No. You know I didn't. I jumped up and got it when I was frightened."

He cooked breakfast—and slipped the flat brass key into her coat-pocket again—while she bathed and dressed.

She came out of the bathroom whistling *En Cuba.* "Shall I make the bed?" she asked.

"That'd be swell. The eggs need a couple of minutes more."

Their breakfast was on the table when she returned to the kitchen. They sat where they had sat the night before and ate heartily.

"Now about the bird?" Spade suggested presently as they ate.

She put her fork down and looked at him. She drew her eyebrows together and made her mouth small and tight. "You can't ask me to talk about that this morning of all mornings," she protested. "I don't want to and I won't."

"It's a stubborn damned hussy," he said sadly and put a piece of roll into his mouth.

The youth who had shadowed Spade was not in sight when Spade and Brigid O'Shaughnessy crossed the sidewalk to the waiting taxicab. The taxicab was not followed. Neither the youth nor another loiterer was visible in the vicinity of the Coronet when the taxicab arrived there.

Brigid O'Shaughnessy would not let Spade go in with her. "It's bad enough to be coming home in evening dress at this hour without bringing company. I hope I don't meet anybody."

"Dinner tonight?"

"Yes."

They kissed. She went into the Coronet. He told the chauffeur: "Hotel Belvedere."

When he reached the Belvedere he saw the youth who had shadowed him sitting in the lobby on a divan from which the elevators could be seen. Apparently the youth was reading a newspaper.

At the desk Spade learned that Cairo was not in. He frowned and pinched his lower lip. Points of yellow light began to dance in his eyes. "Thanks," he said softly to the clerk and turned away.

Sauntering, he crossed the lobby to the divan from which the elevators could be seen and sat down beside—not more than a foot from—the young man who was apparently reading a newspaper.

The young man did not look up from his newspaper. Seen at this scant distance, he seemed certainly less than twenty years old. His features were small, in keeping with his stature, and regular. His skin was very fair. The whiteness of his cheeks was as little blurred by any considerable growth of beard as by the glow of blood. His clothing was neither new nor of more than ordinary quality, but it, and his manner of wearing it, was marked by a hard masculine neatness.

Spade asked casually, "Where is he?" while shaking tobacco down into a brown paper curved to catch it.

The boy lowered his paper and looked around, moving with a purposeful sort of slowness, as of a more natural swiftness restrained. He looked with small hazel eyes under somewhat long curling lashes at Spade's chest. He said, in a voice as colorless and composed and cold as his young face: "What?"

"Where is he?" Spade was busy with his cigarette.

"Who?"

"The fairy."

The hazel eyes' gaze went up Spade's chest to the knot of his maroon tie and rested there. "What do you think you're doing, Jack?" the boy demanded. "Kidding me?"

"I'll tell you when I am." Spade licked his cigarette and smiled amiably at the boy. "New York, aren't you?"

The boy stared at Spade's tie and did not speak. Spade nodded as if the boy had said yes and asked: "Baumes rush?"

The boy stared at Spade's tie for a moment longer, then raised his newspaper and returned his attention to it. "Shove off," he said from the side of his mouth.

Spade lighted his cigarette, leaned back comfortably on the divan, and spoke with good-natured carelessness: "You'll have to talk to me before you're through, sonny—some of you will—and you can tell G. I said so."

The boy put his paper down quickly and faced Spade, staring at his necktie with bleak hazel eyes. The boy's small hands were spread flat over his belly. "Keep asking for it and you're going to get it," he said, "plenty." His voice was low and flat and menacing. "I told you to shove off. Shove off."

Spade waited until a bespectacled pudgy man and a thin-legged blonde girl had passed out of hearing. Then he chuckled and said: "That would go over big back on Seventh Avenue. But you're not in Romeville now. You're in my burg." He inhaled cigarette-smoke and blew it out in a long pale cloud. "Well, where is he?"

The boy spoke two words, the first a short guttural verb, the second "you."

"People lose teeth talking like that." Spade's voice was still amiable though his face had become wooden. "If you want to hang around you'll be polite."

The boy repeated his two words.

Spade dropped his cigarette into a tall stone jar beside the divan and with a lifted hand caught the attention of a man who had been standing at an end of the cigar-stand for several minutes. The man nodded and came towards them. He was a middle-aged man of medium height, round and sallow of face, compactly built, tidily dressed in dark clothes.

"Hello, Sam," he said as he came up.

"Hello, Luke."

They shook hands and Luke said: "Say, that's too bad about Miles."

"Uh-huh, a bad break." Spade jerked his head to indicate the boy on the divan beside him. "What do you let these cheap gunmen hang out in your lobby for, with their tools bulging their clothes?"

"Yes?" Luke examined the boy with crafty brown eyes set in a suddenly hard face. "What do you want here?" he asked.

The boy stood up. Spade stood up. The boy looked at the two men, at their neckties, from one to the other. Luke's necktie was black. The boy looked like a schoolboy standing in front of them.

Luke said: "Well, if you don't want anything, beat it, and don't come back."

The boy said, "I won't forget you guys," and went out.

They watched him go out. Spade took off his hat and wiped his damp forehead with a handkerchief.

The hotel-detective asked: "What is it?"

"Damned if I know," Spade replied. "I just happened to spot him. Know anything about Joel Cairo—six-thirty-five?"

"Oh, that one!" The hotel-detective leered.

"How long's he been here?"

"Four days. This is the fifth."

"What about him?"

"Search me, Sam. I got nothing against him but his looks."

"Find out if he came in last night?"

"Try to," the hotel-detective promised and went away. Spade sat on the divan until he returned. "No," Luke reported, "he didn't sleep in his room. What is it?"

"Nothing."

"Come clean. You know I'll keep my clam shut, but if there's anything wrong we ought to know about it so's we can collect our bill."

"Nothing like that," Spade assured him. "As a matter of fact, I'm doing a little work for him. I'd tell you if he was wrong."

"You'd better. Want me to kind of keep an eye on him?"

"Thanks, Luke. It wouldn't hurt. You can't know too much about the men you're working for these days."

It was twenty-one minutes past eleven by the clock over the elevator-doors when Joel Cairo came in from the street. His forehead was bandaged. His clothes had the limp unfreshness of too many hours' consecutive wear. His face was pasty, with sagging mouth and eyelids.

Spade met him in front of the desk. "Good morning," Spade said easily.

Cairo drew his tired body up straight and the drooping lines of his face tightened. "Good morning," he responded without enthusiasm.

There was a pause.

Spade said: "Let's go some place where we can talk."

Cairo raised his chin. "Please excuse me," he said. "Our conversations in private have not been such that I am anxious to continue them. Pardon my speaking bluntly, but it is the truth."

"You mean last night?" Spade made an impatient gesture with head and hands. "What in hell else could I do? I thought you'd see that. If you pick a fight with her, or let her pick one with you, I've got to throw in with her. I don't know where that damned bird is. You don't. She does. How in hell are we going to get it if I don't play along with her?"

Cairo hesitated, said dubiously: "You have always, I must say, a smooth explanation ready."

Spade scowled. "What do you want me to do? Learn to stutter? Well, we can talk over here." He led the way to the divan. When they were seated he asked: "Dundy take you down to the Hall?"

"Yes."

"How long did they work on you?"

"Until a very little while ago, and very much against my will." Pain and indignation were mixed in Cairo's face and voice. "I shall certainly take the matter up with the Consulate General of Greece and with an attorney."

"Go ahead, and see what it gets you. What did you let the police shake out of you?"

There was prim satisfaction in Cairo's smile. "Not a single thing. I adhered to the course you indicated earlier in your rooms." His smile went away. "Though I certainly wished you had devised a more reasonable story. I felt decidedly ridiculous repeating it."

Spade grinned mockingly. "Sure," he said, "but its goofiness is what makes it good. You sure you didn't give them anything?"

"You may rely upon it, Mr. Spade, I did not."

Spade drummed with his fingers on the leather seat between them. "You'll be hearing from Dundy again. Stay dummied-up on him and you'll be all right. Don't worry about the story's goofiness. A sensible one would've had us all in the cooler." He rose to his feet. "You'll want sleep if you've been standing up under a police-storm all night. See you later."

Effie Perine was saying, "No, not yet," into the telephone when Spade entered his outer office. She looked around at him and her lips shaped a silent word: "Iva." He shook his head. "Yes, I'll have him call you as soon as he comes in," she said aloud and replaced the receiver on its prong. "That's the third time she's called up this morning," she told Spade.

He made an impatient growling noise.

The girl moved her brown eyes to indicate the inner office. "Your Miss O'Shaughnessy's in there. She's been waiting since a few minutes after nine."

Spade nodded as if he had expected that and asked: "What else?"

"Sergeant Polhaus called up. He didn't leave any message."

"Get him for me."

"And G. called up."

Spade's eyes brightened. He asked: "Who?"

"G. That's what he said." Her air of personal indifference to the subject was flawless. "When I told him you weren't in he said: 'When he comes in, will you please tell him that G., who got his message, phoned and will phone again?'."

Spade worked his lips together as if tasting something he liked. "Thanks, darling," he said. "See if you can get Tom Polhaus." He opened the inner door and went into his private office, pulling the door to behind him.

Brigid O'Shaughnessy, dressed as on her first visit to the office, rose from a chair beside his desk and came quickly towards him. "Somebody has been in my apartment," she exclaimed. "It is all upside-down, every which way."

He seemed moderately surprised. "Anything taken?"

"I don't think so. I don't know. I was afraid to stay. I changed as fast as I could and came down here. Oh, you must've let that boy follow you there!"

Spade shook his head. "No, angel." He took an early copy of an afternoon paper from his pocket, opened it, and showed her a quarter-column headed SCREAM ROUTS BURGLAR.

A young woman named Carolin Beale, who lived alone in a Sutter Street apartment, had been awakened at four that morning by the sound of somebody moving in her bedroom. She had screamed. The mover had run away. Two other women who lived alone in the same building had discovered, later in the morning, signs of the burglar's having visited their apartments. Nothing had been taken from any of the three.

"That's where I shook him," Spade explained. "I went into that building and ducked out the back door. That's why all three were women who lived alone. He tried the apartments that had women's names in the vesti-bule-register, hunting for you under an alias."

"But he was watching your place when we were there," she objected.

Spade shrugged. "There's no reason to think he's working alone. Or maybe he went to Sutter Street after he had begun to think you were go-ing to stay all night in my place. There are a lot of maybes, but I didn't lead him to the Coronet."

She was not satisfied. "But he found it, or somebody did."

"Sure." He frowned at her feet. "I wonder if it could have been Cairo. He wasn't at his hotel all night, didn't get in till a few minutes ago. He told me he had been standing up under a police-grilling all night. I won-der." He turned, opened the door, and asked Effie Perine: "Got Tom yet?"

"He's not in. I'll try again in a few minutes."

"Thanks." Spade shut the door and faced Brigid O'Shaughnessy.

She looked at him with cloudy eyes. "You went to see Joe this morn-ing?" she asked.

"Yes."

She hesitated. "Why?"

"Why?" He smiled down at her. "Because, my own true love, I've got to keep in some sort of touch with all the loose ends of this dizzy affair if I'm ever going to make heads or tails of it." He put an arm around her shoulders and led her over to his swivel-chair. He kissed the tip of her nose lightly and set her down in the chair. He sat on the desk in front of her. He said: "Now we've got to find a new home for you, haven't we?"

She nodded with emphasis. "I won't go back there."

He patted the desk beside his thighs and made a thoughtful face. "I think I've got it," he said presently. "Wait a minute." He went into the outer office, shutting the door.

Effie Perine reached for the telephone, saying: "I'll try again."

"Afterwards. Does your woman's intuition still tell you that she's a madonna or something?"

She looked sharply up at him. "I still believe that no matter what kind of trouble she's gotten into she's all right, if that's what you mean."

"That's what I mean," he said. "Are you strong enough for her to give her a lift?"

"How?"

"Could you put her up for a few days?"

"You mean at home?"

"Yes. Her joint's been broken into. That's the second burglary she's had this week. It'd be better for her if she wasn't alone. It would help a lot if you could take her in."

Effie Perine leaned forward, asking earnestly: "Is she really in danger, Sam?"

"I think she is."

She scratched her lip with a fingernail. "That would scare Ma into a green hemorrhage. I'll have to tell her she's a surprise-witness or something that you're keeping under cover till the last minute."

"You're a darling," Spade said. "Better take her out there now. I'll get her key from her and bring whatever she needs over from her apartment. Let's see. You oughtn't to be seen leaving here together. You go home now. Take a taxi, but make sure you aren't followed. You probably won't be, but make sure. I'll send her out in another in a little while, making sure she isn't followed."

XI · *The Fat Man*

THE telephone-bell was ringing when Spade returned to his office after sending Brigid O'Shaughnessy off to Effie Perine's house. He went to the telephone.

"Hello. . . . Yes, this is Spade. . . . Yes, I got it. I've been waiting to hear from you. . . . Who? . . . Mr. Gutman? Oh, yes, sure! . . . Now —the sooner the better. . . . Twelve C. . . . Right. Say fifteen minutes. . . . Right."

Spade sat on the corner of his desk beside the telephone and rolled a cigarette. His mouth was a hard complacent v. His eyes, watching his fingers make the cigarette, smoldered over lower lids drawn up straight.

The door opened and Iva Archer came in.

Spade said, "Hello, honey," in a voice as lightly amiable as his face had suddenly become.

"Oh, Sam, forgive me! forgive me!" she cried in a choked voice. She stood just inside the door, wadding a black-bordered handkerchief in her small gloved hands, peering into his face with frightened red and swollen eyes.

He did not get up from his seat on the desk-corner. He said: "Sure. That's all right. Forget it."

"But, Sam," she wailed, "I sent those policemen there. I was mad, crazy with jealousy, and I phoned them that if they'd go there they'd learn something about Miles's murder."

"What made you think that?"

"Oh, I didn't! But I was mad, Sam, and I wanted to hurt you."

"It made things damned awkward." He put his arm around her and drew her nearer. "But it's all right now, only don't get any more crazy notions like that."

"I won't," she promised, "ever. But you weren't nice to me last night.

You were cold and distant and wanted to get rid of me, when I had come down there and waited so long to warn you, and you—"

"Warn me about what?"

"About Phil. He's found out about—about you being in love with me, and Miles had told him about my wanting a divorce, though of course *he* never knew what for, and now Phil thinks we—you killed his brother because he wouldn't give me the divorce so we could get married. He told me he believed that, and yesterday he went and told the police."

"That's nice," Spade said softly. "And you came to warn me, and because I was busy you got up on your ear and helped this damned Phil Archer stir things up."

"I'm sorry," she whimpered, "I know you won't forgive me. I—I'm sorry, sorry, sorry."

"You ought to be," he agreed, "on your own account as well as mine. Has Dundy been to see you since Phil did his talking? Or anybody from the bureau?"

"No." Alarm opened her eyes and mouth.

"They will," he said, "and it'd be just as well to not let them find you here. Did you tell them who you were when you phoned?"

"Oh, no! I simply told them that if they'd go to your apartment right away they'd learn something about the murder and hung up."

"Where'd you phone from?"

"The drug-store up above your place. Oh, Sam, dearest, I—"

He patted her shoulder and said pleasantly: "It was a dumb trick, all right, but it's done now. You'd better run along home and think up things to tell the police. You'll be hearing from them. Maybe it'd be best to say 'no' right across the board." He frowned at something distant. "Or maybe you'd better see Sid Wise first." He removed his arm from around her, took a card out of his pocket, scribbled three lines on its back, and gave it to her. "You can tell Sid everything." He frowned. "Or almost everything. Where were you the night Miles was shot?"

"Home," she replied without hesitating.

He shook his head, grinning at her.

"I was," she insisted.

"No," he said, "but if that's your story it's all right with me. Go see Sid. It's up on the next corner, the pinkish building, room eight-twenty-seven."

Her blue eyes tried to probe his yellow-grey ones. "What makes you think I wasn't home?" she asked slowly.

"Nothing except that I know you weren't."

"But I was, I was." Her lips twisted and anger darkened her eyes. "Effie Perine told you that," she said indignantly. "I saw her looking at my clothes and snooping around. You know she doesn't like me, Sam. Why do you believe things she tells you when you know she'd do anything to make trouble for me?"

"Jesus, you women," Spade said mildly. He looked at the watch on his wrist. "You'll have to trot along, precious. I'm late for an appointment now. You do what you want, but if I were you I'd tell Sid the truth or nothing. I mean leave out the parts you don't want to tell him, but don't make up anything to take its place."

"I'm not lying to you, Sam," she protested.

"Like hell you're not," he said and stood up.

She strained on tiptoe to hold her face nearer his. "You don't believe me?" she whispered.

"I don't believe you."

"And you won't forgive me for—for what I did?"

"Sure I do." He bent his head and kissed her mouth. "That's all right. Now run along."

She put her arms around him. "Won't you go with me to see Mr. Wise?"

"I can't, and I'd only be in the way." He patted her arms, took them from around his body, and kissed her left wrist between glove and sleeve. He put his hands on her shoulders, turned her to face the door, and released her with a little push. "Beat it," he ordered.

The mahogany door of suite 12-C at the Alexandria Hotel was opened by the boy Spade had talked to in the Belvedere lobby. Spade said, "Hello," good-naturedly. The boy did not say anything. He stood aside holding the door open.

Spade went in. A fat man came to meet him.

The fat man was flabbily fat with bulbous pink cheeks and lips and chins and neck, with a great soft egg of a belly that was all his torso, and pendant cones for arms and legs. As he advanced to meet Spade all his bulbs rose and shook and fell separately with each step, in the manner of clustered soap-bubbles not yet released from the pipe through which they had been blown. His eyes, made small by fat puffs around them, were dark and sleek. Dark ringlets thinly covered his broad scalp. He wore a black cutaway coat, black vest, black satin Ascot tie holding a pinkish pearl, striped grey worsted trousers, and patent-leather shoes.

His voice was a throaty purr. "Ah, Mr. Spade," he said with enthusiasm and held out a hand like a fat pink star.

Spade took the hand and smiled and said: "How do you do, Mr. Gutman?"

Holding Spade's hand, the fat man turned beside him, put his other hand to Spade's elbow, and guided him across a green rug to a green plush chair beside a table that held a siphon, some glasses, and a bottle of Johnnie Walker whiskey on a tray, a box of cigars—Coronas del Ritz—two newspapers, and a small and plain yellow soapstone box.

Spade sat in the green chair. The fat man began to fill two glasses from bottle and siphon. The boy had disappeared. Doors set in three of the room's walls were shut. The fourth wall, behind Spade, was pierced by two windows looking out over Geary Street.

"We begin well, sir," the fat man purred, turning with a proffered glass in his hand. "I distrust a man that says when. If he's got to be careful not to drink too much it's because he's not to be trusted when he does."

Spade took the glass and, smiling, made the beginning of a bow over it.

The fat man raised his glass and held it against a window's light. He nodded approvingly at the bubbles running up in it. He said: "Well, sir, here's to plain speaking and clear understanding."

They drank and lowered their glasses.

The fat man looked shrewdly at Spade and asked: "You're a close-mouthed man?"

Spade shook his head. "I like to talk."

"Better and better!" the fat man exclaimed. "I distrust a close-mouthed man. He generally picks the wrong time to talk and says the wrong things. Talking's something you can't do judiciously unless you keep in practice." He beamed over his glass. "We'll get along, sir, that we will." He set his glass on the table and held the box of Coronas del Ritz out to Spade. "A cigar, sir."

Spade took a cigar, trimmed the end of it, and lighted it. Meanwhile the fat man pulled another green plush chair around to face Spade's within convenient distance and placed a smoking-stand within reach of both chairs. Then he took his glass from the table, took a cigar from the box, and lowered himself into his chair. His bulbs stopped jouncing and settled into flabby rest. He sighed comfortably and said: "Now, sir, we'll talk if you like. And I'll tell you right out that I'm a man who likes talking to a man that likes to talk."

"Swell. Will we talk about the black bird?"

The fat man laughed and his bulbs rode up and down on his laughter. "Will we?" he asked and, "We will," he replied. His pink face was shiny with delight. "You're the man for me, sir, a man cut along my own lines. No beating about the bush, but right to the point. 'Will we talk about the black bird?' We will. I like that, sir. I like that way of doing business. Let us talk about the black bird by all means, but first, sir, answer me a question, please, though maybe it's an unnecessary one, so we'll understand each other from the beginning. You're here as Miss O'Shaughnessy's representative?"

Spade blew smoke above the fat man's head in a long slanting plume. He frowned thoughtfully at the ash-tipped end of his cigar. He replied deliberately: "I can't say yes or no. There's nothing certain about it either way, yet." He looked up at the fat man and stopped frowning. "It depends."

"It depends on—?"

Spade shook his head. "If I knew what it depends on I could say yes or no."

The fat man took a mouthful from his glass, swallowed it, and suggested: "Maybe it depends on Joel Cairo?"

Spade's prompt "Maybe" was noncommittal. He drank.

The fat man leaned forward until his belly stopped him. His smile was ingratiating and so was his purring voice. "You could say, then, that the question is which one of them you'll represent?"

"You could put it that way."

"It will be one or the other?"

"I didn't say that."

The fat man's eyes glistened. His voice sank to a throaty whisper asking: "Who else is there?"

Spade pointed his cigar at his own chest. "There's me," he said.

The fat man sank back in his chair and let his body go flaccid. He blew his breath out in a long contented gust. "That's wonderful, sir," he purred. "That's wonderful. I do like a man that tells you right out he's looking out for himself. Don't we all? I don't trust a man that says he's not. And the man that's telling the truth when he says he's not I distrust most of all, because he's an ass and an ass that's going contrary to the laws of nature."

Spade exhaled smoke. His face was politely attentive. He said: "Uh-huh. Now let's talk about the black bird."

The fat man smiled benevolently. "Let's," he said. He squinted so that fat puffs crowding together left nothing of his eyes but a dark gleam visible. "Mr. Spade, have you any conception of how much money can be made out of that black bird?"

"No."

The fat man leaned forward again and put a bloated pink hand on the arm of Spade's chair. "Well, sir, if I told you—by Gad, if I told you half!—you'd call me a liar."

Spade smiled. "No," he said, "not even if I thought it. But if you won't take the risk just tell me what it is and I'll figure out the profits."

The fat man laughed. "You couldn't do it, sir. Nobody could do it that hadn't had a world of experience with things of that sort, and"—he paused impressively—"there aren't any other things of that sort." His bulbs jostled one another as he laughed again. He stopped laughing, abruptly. His fleshy lips hung open as laughter had left them. He stared at Spade with an intentness that suggested myopia. He asked: "You mean you don't know what it is?" Amazement took the throatiness out of his voice.

Spade made a careless gesture with his cigar. "Oh, hell," he said lightly, "I know what it's supposed to look like. I know the value in life you people put on it. I don't know what it is."

"She didn't tell you?"

"Miss O'Shaughnessy?"

"Yes. A lovely girl, sir."

"Uh-huh. No."

The fat man's eyes were dark gleams in ambush behind pink puffs of flesh. He said indistinctly, "She must know," and then, "And Cairo didn't either?"

"Cairo is cagey. He's willing to buy it, but he won't risk telling me anything I don't know already."

The fat man moistened his lips with his tongue. "How much is he willing to buy it for?" he asked.

"Ten thousand dollars."

The fat man laughed scornfully. "Ten thousand, and dollars, mind you, not even pounds. That's the Greek for you. Humph! And what did you say to that?"

"I said if I turned it over to him I'd expect the ten thousand."

"Ah, yes, *if!* Nicely put, sir." The fat man's forehead squirmed in a flesh-blurred frown. "They must know," he said only partly aloud, then: "Do they? Do they know what the bird is, sir? What was your impression?"

"I can't help you there," Spade confessed. "There's not much to go by. Cairo didn't say he did and he didn't say he didn't. She said she didn't, but I took it for granted that she was lying."

"That was not an injudicious thing to do," the fat man said, but his mind was obviously not on his words. He scratched his head. He frowned until his forehead was marked by raw red creases. He fidgeted in his chair as much as his size and the size of the chair permitted fidgeting. He shut his eyes, opened them suddenly—wide—and said to Spade: "Maybe they don't." His bulbous pink face slowly lost its worried frown and then, more quickly, took on an expression of ineffable happiness. "If they don't," he cried, and again: "If they don't I'm the only one in the whole wide sweet world who does!"

Spade drew his lips back in a tight smile. "I'm glad I came to the right place," he said.

The fat man smiled too, but somewhat vaguely. Happiness had gone out of his face, though he continued to smile, and caution had come into his eyes. His face was a watchful-eyed smiling mask held up between his thoughts and Spade. His eyes, avoiding Spade's, shifted to the glass at Spade's elbow. His face brightened. "By Gad, sir," he said, "your glass is empty." He got up and went to the table and clattered glasses and siphon and bottle mixing two drinks.

Spade was immobile in his chair until the fat man, with a flourish and a bow and a jocular "Ah, sir, this kind of medicine will never hurt you!" had handed him his refilled glass. Then Spade rose and stood close to the fat man, looking down at him, and Spade's eyes were hard and bright. He raised his glass. His voice was deliberate, challenging: "Here's to plain speaking and clear understanding."

The fat man chuckled and they drank. The fat man sat down. He held his glass against his belly with both hands and smiled up at Spade. He said: "Well, sir, it's surprising, but it well may be a fact that neither of them does know exactly what that bird is, and that nobody in all this whole wide sweet world knows what it is, saving and excepting only your humble servant, Casper Gutman, Esquire."

"Swell." Spade stood with legs apart, one hand in his trousers-pocket, the other holding his glass. "When you've told me there'll only be two of us who know."

"Mathematically correct, sir"—the fat man's eyes twinkled—"but"—his smile spread—"I don't know for certain that I'm going to tell you."

"Don't be a damned fool," Spade said patiently. "You know what it is. I know where it is. That's why we're here."

"Well, sir, where is it?"

Spade ignored the question.

The fat man bunched his lips, raised his eyebrows, and cocked his head a little to the left. "You see," he said blandly, "I must tell you what I know, but you will not tell me what you know. That is hardly equitable, sir. No, no, I do not think we can do business along those lines."

Spade's face became pale and hard. He spoke rapidly in a low furious voice: "Think again and think fast. I told that punk of yours that you'd have to talk to me before you got through. I'll tell you now that you'll do your talking today or you are through. What are you wasting my time for? You and your lousy secret! Christ! I know exactly what that stuff is that they keep in the subtreasury vaults, but what good does that do me? I can get along without you. God damn you! Maybe you could have got along without me if you'd kept clear of me. You can't now. Not in San Francisco. You'll come in or you'll get out—and you'll do it today."

He turned and with angry heedlessness tossed his glass at the table. The glass struck the wood, burst apart, and splashed its contents and glittering fragments over table and floor. Spade, deaf and blind to the crash, wheeled to confront the fat man again.

The fat man paid no more attention to the glass's fate than Spade did: lips pursed, eyebrows raised, head cocked a little to the left, he had maintained his pink-faced blandness throughout Spade's angry speech, and he maintained it now.

Spade, still furious, said: "And another thing, I don't want—"

The door to Spade's left opened. The boy who had admitted Spade came in. He shut the door, stood in front of it with his hands flat against his flanks, and looked at Spade. The boy's eyes were wide open and dark with wide pupils. Their gaze ran over Spade's body from shoulders to knees, and up again to settle on the handkerchief whose maroon border peeped from the breast-pocket of Spade's brown coat.

"Another thing," Spade repeated, glaring at the boy: "Keep that gunsel away from me while you're making up your mind. I'll kill him. I don't like him. He makes me nervous. I'll kill him the first time he gets in my way. I won't give him an even break. I won't give him a chance. I'll kill him."

The boy's lips twitched in a shadowy smile. He neither raised his eyes nor spoke.

The fat man said tolerantly: "Well, sir, I must say you have a most violent temper."

"Temper?" Spade laughed crazily. He crossed to the chair on which he had dropped his hat, picked up the hat, and set it on his head. He held out a long arm that ended in a thick forefinger pointing at the fat man's belly. His angry voice filled the room. "Think it over and think like hell. You've got till five-thirty to do it in. Then you're either in or out, for keeps." He let his arm drop, scowled at the bland fat man for a moment, scowled at the boy, and went to the door through which he had entered. When he opened the door he turned and said harshly: "Five-thirty—then the curtain."

The boy, staring at Spade's chest, repeated the two words he had twice spoken in the Belvedere lobby. His voice was not loud. It was bitter.

Spade went out and slammed the door.

XII · *Merry-Go-Round*

SPADE rode down from Gutman's floor in an elevator. His lips were dry and rough in a face otherwise pale and damp. When he took out his handkerchief to wipe his face he saw his hand trembling. He grinned at it and said, "Whew!" so loudly that the elevator-operator turned his head over his shoulder and asked: "Sir?"

Spade walked down Geary Street to the Palace Hotel, where he ate luncheon. His face had lost its pallor, his lips their dryness, and his hand its trembling by the time he had sat down. He ate hungrily without haste, and then went to Sid Wise's office.

When Spade entered, Wise was biting a fingernail and staring at the window. He took his hand from his mouth, screwed his chair around to face Spade, and said: " 'Lo. Push a chair up."

Spade moved a chair to the side of the big paper-laden desk and sat down. "Mrs. Archer come in?" he asked.

"Yes." The faintest of lights flickered in Wise's eyes. "Going to marry the lady, Sammy?"

Spade sighed irritably through his nose. "Christ, now you start that!" he grumbled.

A brief tired smile lifted the corners of the lawyer's mouth. "If you don't," he said, "you're going to have a job on your hands."

Spade looked up from the cigarette he was making and spoke sourly: "You mean you are? Well, that's what you're for. What did she tell you?"

"About you?"

"About anything I ought to know."

Wise ran fingers through his hair, sprinkling dandruff down on his shoulders. "She told me she had tried to get a divorce from Miles so she could—"

"I know all that," Spade interrupted him. "You can skip it. Get to the part I don't know."

"How do I know how much she—?"

"Quit stalling, Sid." Spade held the flame of his lighter to the end of his cigarette. "What did she tell you that she wanted kept from me?"

Wise looked reprovingly at Spade. "Now, Sammy," he began, "that's not—"

Spade looked heavenward at the ceiling and groaned: "Dear God, he's my own lawyer that's got rich off me and I have to get down on my knees and beg him to tell me things!" He lowered at Wise. "What in hell do you think I sent her to you for?"

Wise made a weary grimace. "Just one more client like you," he complained, "and I'd be in a sanitarium—or San Quentin."

"You'd be with most of your clients. Did she tell you where she was the night he was killed?"

"Yes."

"Where?"

"Following him."

Spade sat up straight and blinked. He exclaimed incredulously: "Jesus, these women!" Then he laughed, relaxed, and asked: "Well, what did she see?"

Wise shook his head. "Nothing much. When he came home for dinner that evening he told her he had a date with a girl at the St. Mark, ragging her, telling her that was her chance to get the divorce she wanted. She thought at first he was just trying to get under her skin. He knew—"

"I know the family history," Spade said. "Skip it. Tell me what she did."

"I will if you'll give me a chance. After he had gone out she began to think that maybe he might have had that date. You know Miles. It would have been like him to—"

"You can skip Miles's character too."

"I oughtn't to tell you a damned thing," the lawyer said. "So she got their car from the garage and drove down to the St. Mark, sitting in the car across the street. She saw him come out of the hotel and she saw that he was shadowing a man and a girl—she says she saw the same girl with you last night—who had come out just ahead of him. She knew then that he was working, had been kidding her. I suppose she was disappointed, and mad—she sounded that way when she told me about it. She followed Miles long enough to make sure he was shadowing the pair, and then she went up to your apartment. You weren't home."

"What time was that?" Spade asked.

"When she got to your place? Between half-past nine and ten the first time."

"The first time?"

"Yes. She drove around for half an hour or so and then tried again. That would make it, say, ten-thirty. You were still out, so she drove back downtown and went to a movie to kill time until after midnight, when she thought she'd be more likely to find you in."

Spade frowned. "She went to a movie at ten-thirty?"

"So she says—the one on Powell Street that stays open till one in the morning. She didn't want to go home, she said, because she didn't want to be there when Miles came. That always made him mad, it seems, especially if it was around midnight. She stayed in the movie till it closed." Wise's words came out slower now and there was a sardonic glint in his eye. "She says she had decided by then not to go back to your place again. She says she didn't know whether you'd like having her drop in that late. So she went to Tait's—the one on Ellis Street—had something to eat and then went home—alone." Wise rocked back in his chair and waited for Spade to speak.

Spade's face was expressionless. He asked: "You believe her?"

"Don't you?" Wise replied.

"How do I know? How do I know it isn't something you fixed up between you to tell me?"

Wise smiled. "You don't cash many checks for strangers, do you, Sammy?"

"Not basketfuls. Well, what then? Miles wasn't home. It was at least two o'clock by then—must've been—and he was dead."

"Miles wasn't home," Wise said. "That seems to have made her mad again—his not being home first to be made mad by her not being home. So she took the car out of the garage again and went back to your place."

"And I wasn't home. I was down looking at Miles's corpse. Jesus, what a swell lot of merry-go-round riding. Then what?"

"She went home, and her husband still wasn't there, and while she was undressing your messenger came with the news of his death."

Spade didn't speak until he had with great care rolled and lighted another cigarette. Then he said: "I think that's an all right spread. It seems to click with most of the known facts. It ought to hold."

Wise's fingers, running through his hair again, combed more dandruff down on his shoulders. He studied Spade's face with curious eyes and asked: "But you don't believe it?"

Spade plucked his cigarette from between his lips. "I don't believe it or disbelieve it, Sid. I don't know a damned thing about it."

A wry smile twisted the lawyer's mouth. He moved his shoulders wearily and said: "That's right—I'm selling you out. Why don't you get an honest lawyer—one you can trust?"

"That fellow's dead." Spade stood up. He sneered at Wise. "Getting touchy, huh? I haven't got enough to think about: now I've got to remember to be polite to you. What did I do? Forget to genuflect when I came in?"

Sid Wise smiled sheepishly. "You're a son of a gun, Sammy," he said.

Effie Perine was standing in the center of Spade's outer office when he entered. She looked at him with worried brown eyes and asked: "What happened?"

Spade's face grew stiff. "What happened where?" he demanded.

"Why didn't she come?"

Spade took two long steps and caught Effie Perine by the shoulders. "She didn't get there?" he bawled into her frightened face.

She shook her head violently from side to side. "I waited and waited and she didn't come, and I couldn't get you on the phone, so I came down."

Spade jerked his hands away from her shoulders, thrust them far down in his trousers-pockets, said, "Another merry-go-round," in a loud enraged voice, and strode into his private office. He came out again. "Phone your mother," he commanded. "See if she's come yet."

He walked up and down the office while the girl used the telephone. "No," she said when she had finished. "Did—did you send her out in a taxi?"

His grunt probably meant yes.

"Are you sure she— Somebody must have followed her!"

Spade stopped pacing the floor. He put his hands on his hips and glared at the girl. He addressed her in a loud savage voice: "Nobody followed her. Do you think I'm a God-damned schoolboy? I made sure of it before I put her in the cab, I rode a dozen blocks with her to be more sure, and I checked her another half-dozen blocks after I got out."

"Well, but—"

"But she didn't get there. You've told me that. I believe it. Do you think I think she did get there?"

Effie Perine sniffed. "You certainly act like a God-damned schoolboy," she said.

Spade made a harsh noise in his throat and went to the corridor-door. "I'm going out and find her if I have to dig up sewers," he said. "Stay here till I'm back or you hear from me. For Christ's sake let's do something right."

He went out, walked half the distance to the elevators, and retraced his steps. Effie Perine was sitting at her desk when he opened the door. He said: "You ought to know better than to pay any attention to me when I talk like that."

"If you think I pay any attention to you you're crazy," she replied, "only"—she crossed her arms and felt her shoulders, and her mouth twitched uncertainly—"I won't be able to wear an evening gown for two weeks, you big brute."

He grinned humbly, said, "I'm no damned good, darling," made an exaggerated bow, and went out again.

Two yellow taxicabs were at the corner-stand to which Spade went. Their chauffeurs were standing together talking. Spade asked: "Where's the red-faced blond driver that was here at noon?"

"Got a load," one of the chauffeurs said.

"Will he be back here?"

"I guess so."

The other chauffeur ducked his head to the east. "Here he comes now."

Spade walked down to the corner and stood by the curb until the red-faced blond chauffeur had parked his cab and got out. Then Spade went up to him and said: "I got into your cab with a lady at noontime. We went out Stockton Street and up Sacramento to Jones, where I got out."

"Sure," the red-faced man said, "I remember that."

"I told you to take her to a Ninth-Avenue-number. You didn't take her there. Where did you take her?"

The chauffeur rubbed his cheek with a grimy hand and looked doubtfully at Spade. "I don't know about this."

"It's all right," Spade assured him, giving him one of his cards. "If you want to play safe, though, we can ride up to your office and get your superintendent's OK."

"I guess it's all right. I took her to the Ferry Building."

"By herself?"

"Yeah. Sure."

"Didn't take her anywhere else first?"

"No. It was like this: after we dropped you I went on out Sacramento, and when we got to Polk she rapped on the glass and said she wanted to get a newspaper, so I stopped at the corner and whistled for a kid, and she got her paper."

"Which paper?"

"The *Call*. Then I went on out Sacramento some more, and just after we'd crossed Van Ness she knocked on the glass again and said take her to the Ferry Building."

"Was she excited or anything?"

"Not so's I noticed."

"And when you got to the Ferry Building?"

"She paid me off, and that was all."

"Anybody waiting for her there?"

"I didn't see them if they was."

"Which way did she go?"

"At the Ferry? I don't know. Maybe upstairs, or towards the stairs."

"Take the newspaper with her?"

"Yeah, she had it tucked under her arm when she paid me."

"With the pink sheet outside, or one of the white?"

"Hell, Cap, I don't remember that."

Spade thanked the chauffeur, said, "Get yourself a smoke," and gave him a silver dollar.

Spade bought a copy of the *Call* and carried it into an office-building-vestibule to examine it out of the wind.

His eyes ran swiftly over the front-page-headlines and over those on the second and third pages. They paused for a moment under SUSPECT ARRESTED AS COUNTERFEITER on the fourth page, and again on page five under BAY YOUTH SEEKS DEATH WITH BULLET. Pages six and seven held nothing to interest him. On eight 3 BOYS ARRESTED AS S. F. BURGLARS AFTER SHOOTING held his attention for a moment, and after that nothing until he reached the thirty-fifth page, which held news of the weather, shipping, produce, finance, divorce, births, marriages, and deaths. He read the list of dead, passed over pages thirty-six and thirty-seven—financial news—found nothing to stop his eyes on the thirty-eighth and last page, sighed, folded the newspaper, put it in his coat-pocket, and rolled a cigarette.

For five minutes he stood there in the office-building-vestibule smoking and staring sulkily at nothing. Then he walked up to Stockton Street, hailed a taxicab, and had himself driven to the Coronet.

He let himself into the building and into Brigid O'Shaughnessy's apartment with the key she had given him. The blue gown she had worn the previous night was hanging across the foot of her bed. Her blue stockings and slippers were on the bedroom floor. The polychrome box that had held jewelry in her dressing-table-drawer now stood empty on the dressing-table-top. Spade frowned at it, ran his tongue across his lips, strolled through the rooms, looking around but not touching anything, then left the Coronet and went downtown again.

In the doorway of Spade's office-building he came face to face with the boy he had left at Gutman's. The boy put himself in Spade's path, blocking the entrance, and said: "Come on. He wants to see you."

The boy's hands were in his overcoat-pockets. His pockets bulged more than his hands need have made them bulge.

Spade grinned and said mockingly: "I didn't expect you till five-twenty-five. I hope I haven't kept you waiting."

The boy raised his eyes to Spade's mouth and spoke in the strained voice of one in physical pain: "Keep on riding me and you're going to be picking iron out of your navel."

Spade chuckled. "The cheaper the crook, the gaudier the patter," he said cheerfully. "Well, let's go."

They walked up Sutter Street side by side. The boy kept his hands in his overcoat-pockets. They walked a little more than a block in silence. Then Spade asked pleasantly: "How long have you been off the goose-berry lay, son?"

The boy did not show that he had heard the question.

"Did you ever—?" Spade began, and stopped. A soft light began to glow in his yellowish eyes. He did not address the boy again.

They went into the Alexandria, rode up to the twelfth floor, and walked down the corridor towards Gutman's suite. Nobody else was in the corridor.

Spade lagged a little, so that, when they were within fifteen feet of Gutman's door, he was perhaps a foot and a half behind the boy. He leaned sidewise suddenly and grasped the boy from behind by both arms, just beneath the boy's elbows. He forced the boy's arms forward so that the boy's hands, in his overcoat-pockets, lifted the overcoat up before him. The boy struggled and squirmed, but he was impotent in the big man's grip. The boy kicked back, but his feet went between Spade's spread legs.

Spade lifted the boy straight up from the floor and brought him down hard on his feet again. The impact made little noise on the thick carpet. At the moment of impact Spade's hands slid down and got a fresh grip on the boy's wrists. The boy, teeth set hard together, did not stop straining against the man's big hands, but he could not tear himself loose, could not keep the man's hands from crawling down over his own hands. The boy's teeth ground together audibly, making a noise that mingled with the noise of Spade's breathing as Spade crushed the boy's hands.

They were tense and motionless for a long moment. Then the boy's arms became limp. Spade released the boy and stepped back. In each of Spade's hands, when they came out of the boy's overcoat-pockets, there was a heavy automatic pistol.

The boy turned and faced Spade. The boy's face was a ghastly white blank. He kept his hands in his overcoat-pockets. He looked at Spade's chest and did not say anything.

Spade put the pistols in his own pockets and grinned derisively. "Come on," he said. "This will put you in solid with your boss."

They went to Gutman's door and Spade knocked.

XIII · *The Emperor's Gift*

GUTMAN opened the door. A glad smile lighted his fat face. He held out a hand and said: "Ah, come in, sir! Thank you for coming. Come in."

Spade shook the hand and entered. The boy went in behind him. The fat man shut the door. Spade took the boy's pistols from his pockets and held them out to Gutman. "Here. You shouldn't let him run around with these. He'll get himself hurt."

The fat man laughed merrily and took the pistols. "Well, well," he said, "what's this?" He looked from Spade to the boy.

Spade said: "A crippled newsie took them away from him, but I made him give them back."

The white-faced boy took the pistols out of Gutman's hands and pocketed them. The boy did not speak.

Gutman laughed again. "By Gad, sir," he told Spade, "you're a chap worth knowing, an amazing character. Come in. Sit down. Give me your hat."

The boy left the room by the door to the right of the entrance.

The fat man installed Spade in a green plush chair by the table, pressed a cigar upon him, held a light to it, mixed whiskey and carbonated water, put one glass in Spade's hand, and, holding the other, sat down facing Spade.

"Now, sir," he said, "I hope you'll let me apologize for—"

"Never mind that," Spade said. "Let's talk about the black bird."

The fat man cocked his head to the left and regarded Spade with fond eyes. "All right, sir," he agreed. "Let's." He took a sip from the glass in his hand. "This is going to be the most astounding thing you've ever heard of, sir, and I say that knowing that a man of your caliber in your profession must have known some astounding things in his time."

Spade nodded politely.

The fat man screwed up his eyes and asked: "What do you know, sir, about the Order of the Hospital of St. John of Jerusalem, later called the Knights of Rhodes and other things?"

Spade waved his cigar. "Not much—only what I remember from history in school—Crusaders or something."

"Very good. Now you don't remember that Suleiman the Magnificent chased them out of Rhodes in 1523?"

"No."

"Well, sir, he did, and they settled in Crete. And they stayed there for seven years, until 1530 when they persuaded the Emperor Charles V to give them"—Gutman held up three puffy fingers and counted them—"Malta, Gozo, and Tripoli."

"Yes?"

"Yes, sir, but with these conditions: they were to pay the Emperor each year the tribute of one"—he held up a finger—"falcon in acknowledgment that Malta was still under Spain, and if they ever left the island it was to revert to Spain. Understand? He was giving it to them, but not unless they used it, and they couldn't give or sell it to anybody else."

"Yes."

The fat man looked over his shoulders at the three closed doors, hunched his chair a few inches nearer Spade's, and reduced his voice to a husky whisper: "Have you any conception of the extreme, the immeasurable, wealth of the Order at that time?"

"If I remember," Spade said, "they were pretty well fixed."

Gutman smiled indulgently. "Pretty well, sir, is putting it mildly." His whisper became lower and more purring. "They were rolling in wealth, sir. You've no idea. None of us has any idea. For years they had preyed on the Saracens, had taken nobody knows what spoils of gems, precious metals, silks, ivories—the cream of the cream of the East. That is history, sir. We all know that the Holy Wars to them, as to the Templars, were largely a matter of loot.

"Well, now, the Emperor Charles has given them Malta, and all the rent he asks is one insignificant bird per annum, just as a matter of form. What could be more natural than for these immeasurably wealthy Knights to look around for some way of expressing their gratitude? Well, sir, that's exactly what they did, and they hit on the happy thought of sending Charles for the first year's tribute, not an insignificant live bird, but a glorious golden falcon encrusted from head to foot with the finest jewels in their coffers. And—remember, sir—they had fine ones, the finest out of Asia." Gutman stopped whispering. His sleek dark eyes examined Spade's face, which was placid. The fat man asked: "Well, sir, what do you think of that?"

"I don't know."

The fat man smiled complacently. "These are facts, historical facts, not schoolbook history, not Mr. Wells's history, but history nevertheless." He leaned forward. "The archives of the Order from the twelfth century on are still at Malta. They are not intact, but what is there holds no less than three"—he held up three fingers—"references that can't be to anything else but this jeweled falcon. In J. Delaville Le Roulx's *Les Archives de l'Ordre de Saint-Jean* there is a reference to it—oblique to be sure, but a reference still. And the unpublished—because unfinished at the time of his death—supplement to Paoli's *Dell' origine ed instituto del sacro militar ordine* has a clear and unmistakable statement of the facts I am telling you."

"All right," Spade said.

"All right, sir. Grand Master Villiers de l'Isle d'Adam had this foot-high jeweled bird made by Turkish slaves in the castle of St. Angelo and sent it to Charles, who was in Spain. He sent it in a galley commanded by a French knight named Cormier or Corvere, a member of the Order." His voice dropped to a whisper again. "It never reached Spain." He smiled with compressed lips and asked: "You know of Barbarossa, Redbeard, Khair-ed-Din? No? A famous admiral of buccaneers sailing out of Algiers then. Well, sir, he took the Knights' galley and he took the bird. The bird went to Algiers. That's a fact. That's a fact that the French historian Pierre Dan put in one of his letters from Algiers. He wrote that the bird had been there for more than a hundred years, until it was carried away by Sir Francis Verney, the English adventurer who was with the Algerian buccaneers for a while. Maybe it wasn't, but Pierre Dan believed it was, and that's good enough for me.

"There's nothing said about the bird in Lady Francis Verney's *Memoirs of the Verney Family during the Seventeenth Century*, to be sure. I looked. And it's pretty certain that Sir Francis didn't have the bird when he died in a Messina hospital in 1615. He was stony broke. But, sir, there's no denying that the bird *did* go to Sicily. It was there and it came into the possession there of Victor Amadeus II some time after he became king in 1713, and it was one of his gifts to his wife when he married in Chambéry after abdicating. That is a fact, sir. Carutti, the author of *Storia del Regno di Vittorio Amadeo II*, himself vouched for it.

"Maybe they—Amadeo and his wife—took it along with them to Turin when he tried to revoke his abdication. Be that as it may, it turned up next in the possession of a Spaniard who had been with the army that took Naples in 1734—the father of Don José Monino y Redondo, Count of Floridablanca, who was Charles III's chief minister. There's nothing to show that it didn't stay in that family until at least the end of the Carlist War in '40. Then it appeared in Paris at just about the time that Paris was full of Carlists who had had to get out of Spain. One of them must have brought it with him, but, whoever he was, it's likely he knew nothing about its real value. It had been—no doubt as a precaution during the Carlist trouble in Spain—painted or enameled over to look like nothing more than a fairly interesting black statuette. And in that disguise, sir, it was, you might say, kicked around Paris for seventy years by private owners and dealers too stupid to see what it was under the skin."

The fat man paused to smile and shake his head regretfully. Then he went on: "For seventy years, sir, this marvelous item was, as you might say, a football in the gutters of Paris—until 1911 when a Greek dealer named Charilaos Konstantinides found it in an obscure shop. It didn't take Charilaos long to learn what it was and to acquire it. No thickness of enamel could conceal value from his eyes and nose. Well, sir, Charilaos was the man who traced most of its history and who identified it as what it actually was. I got wind of it and finally forced most of the history out of him, though I've been able to add a few details since.

"Charilaos was in no hurry to convert his find into money at once. He knew that—enormous as its intrinsic value was—a far higher, a terrific, price could be obtained for it once its authenticity was established beyond doubt. Possibly he planned to do business with one of the modern descendents of the old Order—the English Order of St. John of Jerusalem, the Prussian Johanniterorden, or the Italian or German *langues* of the Sovereign Order of Malta—all wealthy orders."

The fat man raised his glass, smiled at its emptiness, and rose to fill it and Spade's. "You begin to believe me a little?" he asked as he worked the siphon.

"I haven't said I didn't."

"No," Gutman chuckled. "But how you looked." He sat down, drank generously, and patted his mouth with a white handkerchief. "Well, sir, to hold it safe while pursuing his researches into its history, Charilaos had re-enamelled the bird, apparently just as it is now. One year to the very day after he had acquired it—that was possibly three months after I'd made him confess to me—I picked up the *Times* in London and read that his establishment had been burglarized and him murdered. I was in Paris the next day." He shook his head sadly. "The bird was gone. By Gad, sir, I was wild. I didn't believe anybody else knew what it was. I didn't believe he had told anybody but me. A great quantity of stuff had been stolen. That made me think that the thief had simply taken the bird along with the rest of his plunder, not knowing what it was. Because I assure you that a thief who knew its value would not burden himself with anything else—no, sir—at least not anything less than crown jewels."

He shut his eyes and smiled complacently at an inner thought. He opened his eyes and said: "That was seventeen years ago. Well, sir, it took me seventeen years to locate that bird, but I did it. I wanted it, and I'm not a man that's easily discouraged when he wants something." His smile grew broad. "I wanted it and I found it. I want it and I'm going to have it." He drained his glass, dried his lips again, and returned his handkerchief to his pocket. "I traced it to the home of a Russian general—one Kemidov—in a Constantinople suburb. He didn't know a thing about it. It was nothing but a black enameled figure to him, but his natural contrariness—the natural contrariness of a Russian general—kept him from selling it to me when I made him an offer. Perhaps in my eagerness I was a little unskillful, though not very. I don't know about that. But I did know I wanted it and I was afraid this stupid soldier might begin to investigate his property, might chip off some of the enamel. So I sent some —ah—agents to get it. Well, sir, they got it and I haven't got it." He stood up and carried his empty glass to the table. "But I'm going to get it. Your glass, sir."

"Then the bird doesn't belong to any of you?" Spade asked, "but to a General Kemidov?"

"Belong?" the fat man said jovially. "Well, sir, you might say it belonged to the King of Spain, but I don't see how you can honestly grant anybody else clear title to it—except by right of possession." He clucked. "An article of that value that has passed from hand to hand by such means is clearly the property of whoever can get hold of it."

"Then it's Miss O'Shaughnessy's now?"

"No, sir, except as my agent."

Spade said, "Oh," ironically.

Gutman, looking thoughtfully at the stopper of the whiskey-bottle in his hand, asked: "There's no doubt that she's got it now?"

"Not much."

"Where?"

"I don't know exactly."

The fat man set the bottle on the table with a bang. "But you said you did," he protested.

Spade made a careless gesture with one hand. "I meant to say I know where to get it when the time comes."

The pink bulbs of Gutman's face arranged themselves more happily. "And you do?" he asked.

"Yes."

"Where?"

Spade grinned and said: "Leave that to me. That's my end."

"When?"

"When I'm ready."

The fat man pursed his lips and, smiling with only slight uneasiness, asked: "Mr. Spade, where is Miss O'Shaughnessy now?"

"In my hands, safely tucked away."

Gutman smiled with approval. "Trust you for that, sir," he said. "Well now, sir, before we sit down to talk prices, answer me this: how soon can you—or how soon are you willing to—produce the falcon?"

"A couple of days."

The fat man nodded. "That is satisfactory. We— But I forgot our nourishment." He turned to the table, poured whiskey, squirted charged water into it, set a glass at Spade's elbow and held his own aloft. "Well, sir, here's to a fair bargain and profits large enough for both of us."

They drank. The fat man sat down. Spade asked: "What's your idea of a fair bargain?"

Gutman held his glass up to the light, looked affectionately at it, took another long drink, and said: "I have two proposals to make, sir, and either is fair. Take your choice. I will give you twenty-five thousand dollars when you deliver the falcon to me, and another twenty-five thousand as soon as I get to New York; or I will give you one quarter—twenty-five per cent—of what I realize on the falcon. There you are, sir: an almost immediate fifty thousand dollars or a vastly greater sum within, say, a couple of months."

Spade drank and asked: "How much greater?"

"Vastly," the fat man repeated. "Who knows how much greater? Shall I say a hundred thousand, or a quarter of a million? Will you believe me if I name the sum that seems the probable minimum?"

"Why not?"

The fat man smacked his lips and lowered his voice to a purring murmur. "What would you say, sir, to half a million?"

Spade narrowed his eyes. "Then you think the dingus is worth two million?"

Gutman smiled serenely. "In your own words, why not?" he asked.

Spade emptied his glass and set it on the table. He put his cigar in his mouth, took it out, looked at it, and put it back in. His yellow-grey eyes were faintly muddy. He said: "That's a hell of a lot of dough."

The fat man agreed: "That's a hell of a lot of dough." He leaned forward and patted Spade's knee. "That is the absolute rock-bottom minimum—or Charilaos Konstantinides was a blithering idiot—and he wasn't."

Spade removed the cigar from his mouth again, frowned at it with distaste, and put it on the smoking-stand. He shut his eyes hard, opened them again. Their muddiness had thickened. He said: "The—the minimum, huh? And the maximum?" An unmistakable *sh* followed the x in maximum as he said it.

"The maximum?" Gutman held his empty hand out, palm up. "I refuse to guess. You'd think me crazy. I don't know. There's no telling how high it could go, sir, and that's the one and only truth about it."

Spade pulled his sagging lower lip tight against the upper. He shook his head impatiently. A sharp frightened gleam awoke in his eyes—and was smothered by the deepening muddiness. He stood up, helping himself up with his hands on the arms of his chair. He shook his head again and took an uncertain step forward. He laughed thickly and muttered: "God damn you."

Gutman jumped up and pushed his chair back. His fat globes jiggled. His eyes were dark holes in an oily pink face.

Spade swung his head from side to side until his dull eyes were pointed at—if not focused on—the door. He took another uncertain step.

The fat man called sharply: "Wilmer!"

A door opened and the boy came in.

Spade took a third step. His face was grey now, with jaw-muscles standing out like tumors under his ears. His legs did not straighten again after his fourth step and his muddy eyes were almost covered by their lids. He took his fifth step.

The boy walked over and stood close to Spade, a little in front of him, but not directly between Spade and the door. The boy's right hand was inside his coat over his heart. The corners of his mouth twitched.

Spade essayed his sixth step.

The boy's leg darted out across Spade's leg, in front. Spade tripped over the interfering leg and crashed face-down on the floor. The boy, keeping his right hand under his coat, looked down at Spade. Spade tried to get up. The boy drew his right foot far back and kicked Spade's temple. The kick rolled Spade over on his side. Once more he tried to get up, could not, and went to sleep.

XIV · *La Paloma*

SPADE, coming around the corner from the elevator at a few minutes past six in the morning, saw yellow light glowing through the frosted glass of his office-door. He halted abruptly, set his lips together, looked up and down the corridor, and advanced to the door with swift quiet strides.

He put his hand on the knob and turned it with care that permitted neither rattle nor click. He turned the knob until it would turn no farther: the door was locked. Holding the knob still, he changed hands, taking it now in his left hand. With his right hand he brought his keys out of his pocket, carefully, so they could not jingle against one another. He separated the office-key from the others and, smothering the others together in his palm, inserted the office-key in the lock. The insertion was soundless. He balanced himself on the balls of his feet, filled his lungs, clicked the door open, and went in.

Effie Perine sat sleeping with her head on her forearms, her forearms on her desk. She wore her coat and had one of Spade's overcoats wrapped cape-fashion around her.

Spade blew his breath out in a muffled laugh, shut the door behind him, and crossed to the inner door. The inner office was empty. He went over to the girl and put a hand on her shoulder.

She stirred, raised her head drowsily, and her eyelids fluttered. Suddenly she sat up straight, opening her eyes wide. She saw Spade, smiled, leaned back in her chair, and rubbed her eyes with her fingers. "So you finally got back?" she said. "What time is it?"

"Six o'clock. What are you doing here?"

She shivered, drew Spade's overcoat closer around her, and yawned. "You told me to stay till you got back or phoned."

"Oh, you're the sister of the boy who stood on the burning deck?"

"I wasn't going to—" She broke off and stood up, letting his coat slide down on the chair behind her. She looked with dark excited eyes at his temple under the brim of his hat and exclaimed: "Oh, your head! What happened?"

His right temple was dark and swollen.

"I don't know whether I fell or was slugged. I don't think it amounts to much, but it hurts like hell." He barely touched it with his fingers, flinched, turned his grimace into a grim smile, and explained: "I went visiting, was fed knockout-drops, and came to twelve hours later all spread out on a man's floor."

She reached up and removed his hat from his head. "It's terrible," she said. "You'll have to get a doctor. You can't walk around with a head like that."

"It's not as bad as it looks, except for the headache, and that might be mostly from the drops." He went to the cabinet in the corner of the office and ran cold water on a handkerchief. "Anything turn up after I left?"

"Did you find Miss O'Shaughnessy, Sam?"

"Not yet. Anything turn up after I left?"

"The District Attorney's office phoned. He wants to see you."

"Himself?"

"Yes, that's the way I understood it. And a boy came in with a message—that Mr. Gutman would be delighted to talk to you before five-thirty."

Spade turned off the water, squeezed the handkerchief, and came away from the cabinet holding the handkerchief to his temple. "I got that," he said. "I met the boy downstairs, and talking to Mr. Gutman got me this."

"Is that the G. who phoned, Sam?"

"Yes."

"And what—?"

Spade stared through the girl and spoke as if using speech to arrange his thoughts: "He wants something he thinks I can get. I persuaded him I could keep him from getting it if he didn't make the deal with me before five-thirty. Then—uh-huh—sure—it was after I'd told him he'd have to wait a couple of days that he fed me the junk. It's not likely he thought I'd die. He'd know I'd be up and around in ten or twelve hours. So maybe the answer's that he figured he could get it without my help in that time if I was fixed so I couldn't butt in." He scowled. "I hope to Christ he was wrong." His stare became less distant. "You didn't get any word from the O'Shaughnessy?"

The girl shook her head no and asked: "Has this got anything to do with her?"

"Something."

"This thing he wants belongs to her?"

"Or to the King of Spain. Sweetheart, you've got an uncle who teaches history or something over at the University?"

"A cousin. Why?"

"If we brightened his life with an alleged historical secret four centuries old could we trust him to keep it dark awhile?"

"Oh, yes, he's good people."

"Fine. Get your pencil and book."

She got them and sat in her chair. Spade ran more cold water on his handkerchief and, holding it to his temple, stood in front of her and dictated the story of the falcon as he had heard it from Gutman, from Charles V's grant to the Hospitallers up to—but no further than—the enameled bird's arrival in Paris at the time of the Carlist influx. He stumbled over the names of authors and their works that Gutman had mentioned, but managed to achieve some sort of phonetic likeness. The rest of the history he repeated with the accuracy of a trained interviewer.

When he had finished the girl shut her notebook and raised a flushed smiling face to him. "Oh, isn't this thrilling?" she said. "It's—"

"Yes, or ridiculous. Now will you take it over and read it to your cousin and ask him what he thinks of it? Has he ever run across anything that might have some connection with it? Is it probable? Is it possible— even barely possible? Or is it the bunk? If he wants more time to look it up, O K, but get some sort of opinion out of him now. And for God's sake make him keep it under his hat."

"I'll go right now," she said, "and you go see a doctor about that head."

"We'll have breakfast first."

"No, I'll eat over in Berkeley. I can't wait to hear what Ted thinks of this."

"Well," Spade said, "don't start boo-hooing if he laughs at you."

After a leisurely breakfast at the Palace, during which he read both morning papers, Spade went home, shaved, bathed, rubbed ice on his bruised temple, and put on fresh clothes.

He went to Brigid O'Shaughnessy's apartment at the Coronet. Nobody was in the apartment. Nothing had been changed in it since his last visit.

He went to the Alexandria Hotel. Gutman was not in. None of the other occupants of Gutman's suite was in. Spade learned that these other occupants were the fat man's secretary, Wilmer Cook, and his daughter

Rhea, a brown-eyed fair-haired smallish girl of seventeen whom the hotel-staff said was beautiful. Spade was told that the Gutman party had arrived at the hotel, from New York, ten days before, and had not checked out.

Spade went to the Belvedere and found the hotel-detective eating in the hotel-café.

"Morning, Sam. Set down and bite an egg." The hotel-detective stared at Spade's temple. "By God, somebody maced you plenty!"

"Thanks, I've had mine," Spade said as he sat down, and then, referring to his temple: "It looks worse than it is. How's my Cairo's conduct?"

"He went out not more than half an hour behind you yesterday and I ain't seen him since. He didn't sleep here again last night."

"He's getting bad habits."

"Well, a fellow like that alone in a big city. Who put the slug to you, Sam?"

"It wasn't Cairo." Spade looked attentively at the small silver dome covering Luke's toast. "How's chances of giving his room a casing while he's out?"

"Can do. You know I'm willing to go all the way with you all the time." Luke pushed his coffee back, put his elbows on the table, and screwed up his eyes at Spade. "But I got a hunch you ain't going all the way with me. What's the honest-to-God on this guy, Sam? You don't have to kick back on me. You know I'm regular."

Spade lifted his eyes from the silver dome. They were clear and candid. "Sure, you are," he said. "I'm not holding out. I gave you it straight. I'm doing a job for him, but he's got some friends that look wrong to me and I'm a little leery of him."

"The kid we chased out yesterday was one of his friends."

"Yes, Luke, he was."

"And it was one of them that shoved Miles across."

Spade shook his head. "Thursby killed Miles."

"And who killed him?"

Spade smiled. "That's supposed to be a secret, but, confidentially, I did," he said, "according to the police."

Luke grunted and stood up saying: "You're a tough one to figure out, Sam. Come on, we'll have that look-see."

They stopped at the desk long enough for Luke to "fix it so we'll get a ring if he comes in," and went up to Cairo's room. Cairo's bed was smooth and trim, but paper in wastebasket, unevenly drawn blinds, and a couple of rumpled towels in the bathroom showed that the chambermaid had not yet been in that morning.

Cairo's luggage consisted of a square trunk, a valise, and a gladstone bag. His bathroom-cabinet was stocked with cosmetics—boxes, cans, jars, and bottles of powders, creams, ungents, perfumes, lotions, and tonics.

Two suits and an overcoat hung in the closet over three pairs of carefully treed shoes.

The valise and smaller bag were unlocked. Luke had the trunk unlocked by the time Spade had finished searching elsewhere.

"Blank so far," Spade said as they dug down into the trunk.

They found nothing there to interest them.

"Any particular thing we're supposed to be looking for?" Luke asked as he locked the trunk again.

"No. He's supposed to have come here from Constantinople. I'd like to know if he did. I haven't seen anything that says he didn't."

"What's his racket?"

Spade shook his head. "That's something else I'd like to know." He crossed the room and bent down over the wastebasket. "Well, this is our last shot."

He took a newspaper from the basket. His eyes brightened when he saw it was the previous day's *Call.* It was folded with the classified-advertising-page outside. He opened it, examined that page, and nothing there stopped his eyes.

He turned the paper over and looked at the page that had been folded inside, the page that held financial and shipping news, the weather, births, marriages, divorces, and deaths. From the lower left-hand corner, a little more than two inches of the bottom of the second column had been torn out.

Immediately above the tear was a small caption *Arrived Today* followed by:

12:20 A. M.—Capac from Astoria.
5:05 A. M.—Helen P. Drew from Greenwood.
5:06 A. M.—Albarado from Bandon.

The tear passed through the next line, leaving only enough of its letters to make *from Sydney* inferable.

Spade put the *Call* down on the desk and looked into the wastebasket again. He found a small piece of wrapping-paper, a piece of string, two hosiery tags, a haberdasher's sale-ticket for half a dozen pairs of socks, and, in the bottom of the basket, a piece of newspaper rolled into a tiny ball.

He opened the ball carefully, smoothed it out on the desk, and fitted it into the torn part of the *Call.* The fit at the sides was exact, but between the top of the crumpled fragment and the inferable *from Sydney* half an inch was missing, sufficient space to have held announcement of six or seven boats' arrival. He turned the sheet over and saw that the other side of the missing portion could have held only a meaningless corner of a stockbroker's advertisement.

Luke, leaning over his shoulder, asked: "What's this all about?"

"Looks like the gent's interested in a boat."

"Well, there's no law against that, or is there?" Luke said while Spade was folding the torn page and the crumpled fragment together and putting them into his coat-pocket. "You all through here now?"

"Yes. Thanks a lot, Luke. Will you give me a ring as soon as he comes in?"

"Sure."

Spade went to the Business Office of the *Call*, bought a copy of the previous day's issue, opened it to the shipping-news-page, and compared it with the page taken from Cairo's wastebasket. The missing portion had read:

5:17 A. M.–Tahiti from Sydney and Papeete.
6:05 A. M.–Admiral Peoples from Astoria.
8:07 A. M.–Caddopeak from San Pedro.
8:17 A. M.–Silverado from San Pedro.
8:05 A. M.–La Paloma from Hongkong.
9:03 A. M.–Daisy Gray from Seattle.

He read the list slowly and when he had finished he underscored *Hongkong* with a fingernail, cut the list of arrivals from the paper with his pocket-knife, put the rest of the paper and Cairo's sheet into the wastebasket, and returned to his office.

He sat down at his desk, looked up a number in the telephone-book, and used the telephone.

"Kearny one four o one, please. . . . Where is the *Paloma*, in from Hongkong yesterday morning, docked?" He repeated the question. "Thanks."

He held the receiver-hook down with his thumb for a moment, released it, and said: "Davenport two o two o, please. . . . Detective bureau, please. . . . Is Sergeant Polhaus there? . . . Thanks. . . . Hello, Tom, this is Sam Spade. . . . Yes, I tried to get you yesterday afternoon. . . . Sure, suppose you go to lunch with me. . . . Right."

He kept the receiver to his ear while his thumb worked the hook again.

"Davenport o one seven o, please. . . . Hello, this is Samuel Spade. My secretary got a phone-message yesterday that Mr. Bryan wanted to see me. Will you ask him what time's the most convenient for him? . . . Yes, Spade, S-p-a-d-e." A long pause. "Yes. . . . Two-thirty? All right. Thanks."

He called a fifth number and said: "Hello, darling, let me talk to Sid? . . . Hello, Sid—Sam. I've got a date with the District Attorney at half-past two this afternoon. Will you give me a ring—here or there—around four, just to see that I'm not in trouble? . . . Hell with your Saturday afternoon golf: your job's to keep me out of jail. . . . Right, Sid. 'Bye."

He pushed the telephone away, yawned, stretched, felt his bruised temple, looked at his watch, and rolled and lighted a cigarette. He smoked sleepily until Effie Perine came in.

Effie Perine came in smiling, bright-eyed and rosy-faced. "Ted says it could be," she reported, "and he hopes it is. He says he's not a specialist in that field, but the names and dates are all right, and at least none of your authorities or their works are out-and-out fakes. He's all excited over it."

"That's swell, as long as he doesn't get too enthusiastic to see through it if it's phoney."

"Oh, he wouldn't—not Ted! He's too good at his stuff for that."

"Uh-huh, the whole damned Perine family's wonderful," Spade said, "including you and the smudge of soot on your nose."

"He's not a Perine, he's a Christy." She bent her head to look at her nose in her vanity-case-mirror. "I must've got that from the fire." She scrubbed the smudge with the corner of a handkerchief.

"The Perine-Christy enthusiasm ignite Berkeley?" he asked.

She made a face at him while patting her nose with a powdered pink disc. "There was a boat on fire when I came back. They were towing it out from the pier and the smoke blew all over our ferry-boat."

Spade put his hands on the arms of his chair. "Were you near enough to see the name of the boat?" he asked.

"Yes. *La Paloma.* Why?"

Spade smiled ruefully. "I'm damned if I know why, sister," he said.

XV · *Every Crackpot*

SPADE and Detective-sergeant Polhaus ate pickled pigs' feet at one of big John's tables at the States Hof Brau.

Polhaus, balancing pale bright jelly on a fork half-way between plate and mouth, said: "Hey, listen, Sam! Forget about the other night. He was dead wrong, but you know anybody's liable to lose their head if you ride them thataway."

Spade looked thoughtfully at the police-detective. "Was that what you wanted to see me about?" he asked.

Polhaus nodded, put the forkful of jelly into his mouth, swallowed it, and qualified his nod: "Mostly."

"Dundy send you?"

Polhaus made a disgusted mouth. "You know he didn't. He's as bullheaded as you are."

Spade smiled and shook his head. "No, he's not, Tom," he said. "He just thinks he is."

Tom scowled and chopped at his pig's foot with a knife. "Ain't you ever going to grow up?" he grumbled. "What've you got to beef about? He didn't hurt you. You came out on top. What's the sense of making a grudge of it? You're just making a lot of grief for yourself."

Spade placed his knife and fork carefully together on his plate, and put his hands on the table beside his plate. His smile was faint and devoid of warmth. "With every bull in town working overtime trying to pile up grief for me a little more won't hurt. I won't even know it's there."

Polhaus's ruddiness deepened. He said: "That's a swell thing to say to me."

Spade picked up his knife and fork and began to eat. Polhaus ate.

Presently Spade asked: "See the boat on fire in the bay?"

"I saw the smoke. Be reasonable, Sam. Dundy was wrong and he knows it. Why don't you let it go at that?"

"Think I ought to go around and tell him I hope my chin didn't hurt his fist?"

Polhaus cut savagely into his pig's foot.

Spade said: "Phil Archer been in with any more hot tips?"

"Aw, hell! Dundy didn't think you shot Miles, but what else could he do except run the lead down? You'd've done the same thing in his place, and you know it."

"Yes?" Malice glittered in Spade's eyes. "What made him think I didn't do it? What makes you think I didn't? Or don't you?"

Polhaus's ruddy face flushed again. He said: "Thursby shot Miles."

"You think he did."

"He did. That Webley was his, and the slug in Miles came out of it."

"Sure?" Spade demanded.

"Dead sure," the police-detective replied. "We got hold of a kid—a bellhop at Thursby's hotel—that had seen it in his room just that morning. He noticed it particular because he'd never saw one just like it before. I never saw one. You say they don't make them any more. It ain't likely there'd be another around and—anyway—if that wasn't Thursby's what happened to his? And that's the gun the slug in Miles come out of." He started to put a piece of bread into his mouth, withdrew it, and asked: "You say you've seen them before: where was that at?" He put the bread into his mouth.

"In England before the war."

"Sure, there you are."

Spade nodded and said: "Then that leaves Thursby the only one I killed."

Polhaus squirmed in his chair and his face was red and shiny.

"Christ's sake, ain't you never going to forget that?" he complained earnestly. "That's out. You know it as well as I do. You'd think you wasn't a dick yourself the way you bellyache over things. I suppose you don't never pull the same stuff on anybody that we pulled on you?"

"You mean that you tried to pull on me, Tom—just tried."

Polhaus swore under his breath and attacked the remainder of his pig's foot.

Spade said: "All right. You know it's out and I know it's out. What does Dundy know?"

"He knows it's out."

"What woke him up?"

"Aw, Sam, he never really thought you'd—" Spade's smile checked Polhaus. He left the sentence incomplete and said: "We dug up a record on Thursby."

"Yes? Who was he?"

Polhaus's shrewd small brown eyes studied Spade's face. Spade exclaimed irritably: "I wish to God I knew half as much about this business as you smart guys think I do!"

"I wish we all did," Polhaus grumbled. "Well, he was a St. Louis gunman the first we hear of him. He was picked up a lot of times back there for this and that, but he belonged to the Egan mob, so nothing much was ever done about any of it. I don't know howcome he left that shelter, but they got him once in New York for knocking over a row of stuss-games—his twist turned him up—and he was in a year before Fallon got him sprung. A couple of years later he did a short hitch in Joliet for pistol-whipping another twist that had given him the needle, but after that he took up with Dixie Monahan and didn't have any trouble getting out whenever he happened to get in. That was when Dixie was almost as big a shot as Nick the Greek in Chicago gambling. This Thursby was Dixie's bodyguard and he took the run-out with him when Dixie got in wrong with the rest of the boys over some debts he couldn't or wouldn't pay off. That was a couple of years back—about the time the Newport Beach Boating Club was shut up. I don't know if Dixie had any part in that. Anyways, this is the first time him or Thursby's been seen since."

"Dixie's been seen?" Spade asked.

Polhaus shook his head. "No." His small eyes became sharp, prying. "Not unless you've seen him or know somebody's seen him."

Spade lounged back in his chair and began to make a cigarette. "I haven't," he said mildly. "This is all new stuff to me."

"I guess it is," Polhaus snorted.

Spade grinned at him and asked: "Where'd you pick up all this news about Thursby?"

"Some of it's on the records. The rest—well—we got it here and there."

"From Cairo, for instance?" Now Spade's eyes held the prying gleam.

Polhaus put down his coffee-cup and shook his head. "Not a word of it. You poisoned that guy for us."

Spade laughed. "You mean a couple of high-class sleuths like you and Dundy worked on that lily-of-the-valley all night and couldn't crack him?"

"What do you mean—all night?" Polhaus protested. "We worked on him for less than a couple of hours. We saw we wasn't getting nowhere, and let him go."

Spade laughed again and looked at his watch. He caught John's eye and asked for the check. "I've got a date with the D. A. this afternoon," he told Polhaus while they waited for his change.

"He send for you?"

"Yes."

Polhaus pushed his chair back and stood up, a barrel-bellied tall man, solid and phlegmatic. "You won't be doing me any favor," he said, "by telling him I've talked to you like this."

A lathy youth with salient ears ushered Spade into the District Attorney's office. Spade went in smiling easily, saying easily: "Hello, Bryan!"

District Attorney Bryan stood up and held his hand out across his desk. He was a blond man of medium stature, perhaps forty-five years old, with aggressive blue eyes behind black-ribboned nose-glasses, the over-large mouth of an orator, and a wide dimpled chin. When he said, "How do you do, Spade?" his voice was resonant with latent power.

They shook hands and sat down.

The District Attorney put his finger on one of the pearl buttons in a battery of four on his desk, said to the lathy youth who opened the door again, "Ask Mr. Thomas and Healy to come in," and then, rocking back in his chair, addressed Spade pleasantly: "You and the police haven't been hitting it off so well, have you?"

Spade made a negligent gesture with the fingers of his right hand. "Nothing serious," he said lightly. "Dundy gets too enthusiastic."

The door opened to admit two men. The one to whom Spade said, "Hello, Thomas!" was a sunburned stocky man of thirty in clothing and hair of a kindred unruliness. He clapped Spade on the shoulder with a freckled hand, asked, "How's tricks?" and sat down beside him. The second man was younger and colorless. He took a seat a little apart from the others and balanced a stenographer's notebook on his knee, holding a green pencil over it.

Spade glanced his way, chuckled, and asked Bryan: "Anything I say will be used against me?"

The District Attorney smiled. "That always holds good." He took his glasses off, looked at them, and set them on his nose again. He looked through them at Spade and asked: "Who killed Thursby?"

Spade said: "I don't know."

Bryan rubbed his black eyeglass-ribbon between thumb and fingers and said knowingly: "Perhaps you don't, but you certainly could make an excellent guess."

"Maybe, but I wouldn't."

The District Attorney raised his eyebrows.

"I wouldn't," Spade repeated. He was serene. "My guess might be excellent, or it might be crummy, but Mrs. Spade didn't raise any children dippy enough to make guesses in front of a district attorney, an assistant district attorney, and a stenographer."

"Why shouldn't you, if you've nothing to conceal?"

"Everybody," Spade responded mildly, "has something to conceal."

"And you have—?"

"My guesses, for one thing."

The District Attorney looked down at his desk and then up at Spade. He settled his glasses more firmly on his nose. He said: "If you'd prefer not having the stenographer here we can dismiss him. It was simply as a matter of convenience that I brought him in."

"I don't mind him a damned bit," Spade replied. "I'm willing to have anything I say put down and I'm willing to sign it."

"We don't intend asking you to sign anything," Bryan assured him. "I wish you wouldn't regard this as a formal inquiry at all. And please don't think I've any belief—much less confidence—in those theories the police seem to have formed."

"No?"

"Not a particle."

Spade sighed and crossed his legs. "I'm glad of that." He felt in his pockets for tobacco and papers. "What's your theory?"

Bryan leaned forward in his chair and his eyes were hard and shiny as the lenses over them. "Tell me who Archer was shadowing Thursby for and I'll tell you who killed Thursby."

Spade's laugh was brief and scornful. "You're as wrong as Dundy," he said.

"Don't misunderstand me, Spade," Bryan said, knocking on the desk with his knuckles. "I don't say your client killed Thursby or had him killed, but I do say that, knowing who your client is, or was, I'll mighty soon know who killed Thursby."

Spade lighted his cigarette, removed it from his lips, emptied his lungs of smoke, and spoke as if puzzled: "I don't exactly get that."

"You don't? Then suppose I put it this way: where is Dixie Monahan?"

Spade's face retained its puzzled look. "Putting it that way doesn't help much," he said. "I still don't get it."

The District Attorney took his glasses off and shook them for emphasis. He said: "We know Thursby was Monahan's bodyguard and went with him when Monahan found it wise to vanish from Chicago. We know Monahan welshed on something like two-hundred-thousand-dollars' worth of bets when he vanished. We don't know—not yet—who his creditors were." He put the glasses on again and smiled grimly. "But we all know what's likely to happen to a gambler who welshes, and to his bodyguard, when his creditors find him. It's happened before."

Spade ran his tongue over his lips and pulled his lips back over his teeth in an ugly grin. His eyes glittered under pulled-down brows. His reddening neck bulged over the rim of his collar. His voice was low and hoarse and passionate. "Well, what do you think? Did I kill him for his creditors? Or just find him and let them do their own killing?"

"No, no!" the District Attorney protested. "You misunderstand me."

"I hope to Christ I do," Spade said.

"He didn't mean that," Thomas said.

"Then what did he mean?"

Bryan waved a hand. "I only mean that you might have been involved in it without knowing what it was. That could—"

"I see," Spade sneered. "You don't think I'm naughty. You just think I'm dumb."

"Nonsense," Bryan insisted: "Suppose someone came to you and engaged you to find Monahan, telling you they had reasons for thinking he was in the city. The someone might give you a completely false story—any one of a dozen or more would do—or might say he was a debtor who had run away, without giving you any of the details. How could you tell what was behind it? How would you know it wasn't an ordinary piece of detective work? And under those circumstances you certainly couldn't be held responsible for your part in it unless"—his voice sank to a more impressive key and his words came out spaced and distinct—"you made yourself an accomplice by concealing your knowledge of the murderer's identity or information that would lead to his apprehension."

Anger was leaving Spade's face. No anger remained in his voice when he asked: "That's what you meant?"

"Precisely."

"All right. Then there's no hard feelings. But you're wrong."

"Prove it."

Spade shook his head. "I can't prove it to you now. I can tell you."

"Then tell me."

"Nobody ever hired me to do anything about Dixie Monahan."

Bryan and Thomas exchanged glances. Bryan's eyes came back to Spade and he said: "But, by your own admission, somebody did hire you to do something about his bodyguard Thursby."

"Yes, about his ex-bodyguard Thursby."

"Ex?"

"Yes, ex."

"You know that Thursby was no longer associated with Monahan? You know that positively?"

Spade stretched out his hand and dropped the stub of his cigarette into an ashtray on the desk. He spoke carelessly: "I don't know anything positively except that my client wasn't interested in Monahan, had never been interested in Monahan. I heard that Thursby took Monahan out to the Orient and lost him."

Again the District Attorney and his assistant exchanged glances.

Thomas, in a tone whose matter-of-factness did not quite hide excitement, said: "That opens another angle. Monahan's friends could have knocked Thursby off for ditching Monahan."

"Dead gamblers don't have any friends," Spade said.

"It opens up two new lines," Bryan said. He leaned back and stared at the ceiling for several seconds, then sat upright quickly. His orator's face was alight. "It narrows down to three things. Number one: Thursby was killed by the gamblers Monahan had welshed on in Chicago. Not knowing Thursby had sloughed Monahan—or not believing it—they killed him because he had been Monahan's associate, or to get him out of the way so they could get to Monahan, or because he had refused to lead them to Monahan. Number two: he was killed by friends of Monahan. Or number three: he sold Monahan out to his enemies and then fell out with them and they killed him."

"Or number four," Spade suggested with a cheerful smile: "he died of old age. You folks aren't serious, are you?"

The two men stared at Spade, but neither of them spoke. Spade turned his smile from one to the other of them and shook his head in mock pity. "You've got Arnold Rothstein on the brain," he said.

Bryan smacked the back of his left hand down into the palm of his right. "In one of those three categories lies the solution." The power in his voice was no longer latent. His right hand, a fist except for protruding forefinger, went up and then down to stop with a jerk when the finger was leveled at Spade's chest. "And you can give us the information that will enable us to determine the category."

Spade said, "Yes?" very lazily. His face was somber. He touched his lower lip with a finger, looked at the finger, and then scratched the back of his neck with it. Little irritable lines had appeared in his forehead. He blew his breath out heavily through his nose and his voice was an ill-humored growl. "You wouldn't want the kind of information I could give you, Bryan. You couldn't use it. It'd poop this gambler's-revenge-scenario for you."

Bryan sat up straight and squared his shoulders. His voice was stern without blustering. "You are not the judge of that. Right or wrong, I am nonetheless the District Attorney."

Spade's lifted lip showed his eyetooth. "I thought this was an informal talk."

"I am a sworn officer of the law twenty-four hours a day," Bryan said, "and neither formality nor informality justifies your withholding

from me evidence of crime, except of course"—he nodded meaningly—
"on certain constitutional grounds."

"You mean if it might incriminate me?" Spade asked. His voice was
placid, almost amused, but his face was not. "Well, I've got better grounds
than that, or grounds that suit me better. My clients are entitled to a
decent amount of secrecy. Maybe I can be made to talk to a Grand Jury
or even a Coroner's Jury, but I haven't been called before either yet, and
it's a cinch I'm not going to advertise my clients' business until I have to.
Then again, you and the police have both accused me of being mixed up
in the other night's murders. I've had trouble with both of you before. As
far as I can see, my best chance of clearing myself of the trouble you're
trying to make for me is by bringing in the murderers—all tied up. And
my only chance of ever catching them and tying them up and bringing
them in is by keeping away from you and the police, because neither of
you show any signs of knowing what in hell it's all about." He rose and
turned his head over his shoulder to address the stenographer: "Getting
this all right, son? Or am I going too fast for you?"

The stenographer looked at him with startled eyes and replied: "No,
sir, I'm getting it all right."

"Good work," Spade said and turned to Bryan again. "Now if you
want to go to the Board and tell them I'm obstructing justice and ask
them to revoke my license, hop to it. You've tried it before and it didn't
get you anything but a good laugh all around." He picked up his hat.

Bryan began: "But look here—"

Spade said: "And I don't want any more of these informal talks. I've
got nothing to tell you or the police and I'm God-damned tired of being
called things by every crackpot on the city payroll. If you want to see me,
pinch me or subpœna me or something and I'll come down with my lawyer." He put his hat on his head, said, "See you at the inquest, maybe,"
and stalked out.

XVI · *The Third Murder*

SPADE went into the Hotel Sutter and telephoned the Alexandria. Gutman was not in. No member of Gutman's party was in. Spade
telephoned the Belvedere. Cairo was not in, had not been in that day.

Spade went to his office.

A swart greasy man in notable clothes was waiting in the outer room.
Effie Perine, indicating the swart man, said: "This gentleman wishes to
see you, Mr. Spade."

Spade smiled and bowed and opened the inner door. "Come in."
Before following the man in Spade asked Effie Perine: "Any news on that
other matter?"

"No, sir."

The swart man was the proprietor of a moving-picture-theater in
Market Street. He suspected one of his cashiers and a doorman of collud-
ing to defraud him. Spade hurried him through the story, promised to
"take care of it," asked for and received fifty dollars, and got rid of him in
less than half an hour.

When the corridor-door had closed behind the showman Effie Perine
came into the inner office. Her sunburned face was worried and questioning. "You haven't found her yet?" she asked.

He shook his head and went on stroking his bruised temple lightly
in circles with his fingertips.

"How is it?" she asked.

"All right, but I've got plenty of headache."

She went around behind him, put his hand down, and stroked his
temple with her slender fingers. He leaned back until the back of his head
over the chair-top rested against her breast. He said: "You're an angel."

She bent her head forward over his and looked down into his face.
"You've got to find her, Sam. It's more than a day and she—"

He stirred and impatiently interrupted her: "I haven't got to do anything, but if you'll let me rest this damned head a minute or two I'll go
out and find her."

She murmured, "Poor head," and stroked it in silence awhile. Then
she asked: "You know where she is? Have you any idea?"

The telephone-bell rang. Spade picked up the telephone and said:
"Hello. . . . Yes, Sid, it came out all right, thanks. . . . No. . . . Sure.
He got snotty, but so did I. . . . He's nursing a gambler's-war pipe-dream.
. . . Well, we didn't kiss when we parted. I declared my weight and
walked out on him. . . . That's something for you to worry about. . . .
Right. 'Bye." He put the telephone down and leaned back in his chair
again.

Effie Perine came from behind him and stood at his side. She demanded: "Do you think you know where she is, Sam?"

"I know where she went," he replied in a grudging tone.

"Where?" She was excited.

"Down to the boat you saw burning."

Her eyes opened until their brown was surrounded by white. "You
went down there." It was not a question.

"I did not," Spade said.

"Sam," she cried angrily, "she may be—"

"She went down there," he said in a surly voice. "She wasn't taken.
She went down there instead of to your house when she learned the boat

was in. Well, what the hell? Am I supposed to run around after my clients begging them to let me help them?"

"But, Sam, when I told you the boat was on fire!"

"That was at noon and I had a date with Polhaus and another with Bryan."

She glared at him between tightened lids. "Sam Spade," she said, "you're the most contemptible man God ever made when you want to be. Because she did something without confiding in you you'd sit here and do nothing when you know she's in danger, when you know she might be—"

Spade's face flushed. He said stubbornly: "She's pretty capable of taking care of herself and she knows where to come for help when she thinks she needs it, and when it suits her."

"That's spite," the girl cried, "and that's all it is! You're sore because she did something on her own hook, without telling you. Why shouldn't she? You're not so damned honest, and you haven't been so much on the level with her, that she should trust you completely."

Spade said: "That's enough of that."

His tone brought a brief uneasy glint into her hot eyes, but she tossed her head and the glint vanished. Her mouth was drawn taut and small. She said: "If you don't go down there this very minute, Sam, I will and I'll take the police down there." Her voice trembled, broke, and was thin and wailing. "Oh, Sam, go!"

He stood up cursing her. Then he said: "Christ! It'll be easier on my head than sitting here listening to you squawk." He looked at his watch. "You might as well lock up and go home."

She said: "I won't. I'm going to wait right here till you come back."

He said, "Do as you damned please," put his hat on, flinched, took it off, and went out carrying it in his hand.

An hour and a half later, at twenty minutes past five, Spade returned. He was cheerful. He came in asking: "What makes you so hard to get along with, sweetheart?"

"Me?"

"Yes, you." He put a finger on the tip of Effie Perine's nose and flattened it. He put his hands under her elbows, lifted her straight up, and kissed her chin. He set her down on the floor again and asked: "Anything doing while I was gone?"

"Luke—what's his name?—at the Belvedere called up to tell you Cairo has returned. That was about half an hour ago."

Spade snapped his mouth shut, turned with a long step, and started for the door.

"Did you find her?" the girl called.

"Tell you about it when I'm back," he replied without pausing and hurried out.

A taxicab brought Spade to the Belvedere within ten minutes of his departure from his office. He found Luke in the lobby. The hotel-detective came grinning and shaking his head to meet Spade. "Fifteen minutes latc," he said. "Your bird has fluttered."

Spade cursed his luck.

"Checked out—gone bag and baggage," Luke said. He took a battered memorandum-book from a vest-pocket, licked his thumb, thumbed pages, and held the book out open to Spade. "There's the number of the taxi that hauled him. I got that much for you."

"Thanks." Spade copied the number on the back of an envelope. "Any forwarding address?"

"No. He just come in carrying a big suitcase and went upstairs and packed and come down with his stuff and paid his bill and got a taxi and went without anybody being able to hear what he told the driver."

"How about his trunk?"

Luke's lower lip sagged. "By God," he said, "I forgot that! Come on."

They went up to Cairo's room. The trunk was there. It was closed, but not locked. They raised the lid. The trunk was empty.

Luke said: "What do you know about that!"

Spade did not say anything.

Spade went back to his office. Effie Perine looked up at him, inquisitively.

"Missed him," Spade grumbled and passed into his private room.

She followed him in. He sat in his chair and began to roll a cigarette. She sat on the desk in front of him and put her toes on a corner of his chair-seat.

"What about Miss O'Shaughnessy?" she demanded.

"I missed her too," he replied, "but she had been there."

"On the *La Paloma?*"

"*The La* is a lousy combination," he said.

"Stop it. Be nice, Sam. Tell me."

He set fire to his cigarette, pocketed his lighter, patted her shins, and said: "Yes, *La Paloma*. She got down there at a little after noon yesterday." He pulled his brows down. "That means she went straight there after leaving the cab at the Ferry Building. It's only a few piers away. The Captain wasn't aboard. His name's Jacobi and she asked for him by name. He was uptown on business. That would mean he didn't expect her, or not at that time anyway. She waited there till he came back at four o'clock. They spent the time from then till meal-time in his cabin and she ate with him."

He inhaled and exhaled smoke, turned his head aside to spit a yellow tobacco-flake off his lip, and went on: "After the meal Captain Jacobi had three more visitors. One of them was Gutman and one was Cairo and one was the kid who delivered Gutman's message to you yesterday. Those three came together while Brigid was there and the five of them did a lot of talking in the Captain's cabin. It's hard to get anything out of the crew, but they had a row and somewhere around eleven o'clock that night a gun went off there, in the Captain's cabin. The watchman beat it down there, but the Captain met him outside and told him everything was all right. There's a fresh bullet-hole in one corner of the cabin, up high enough to make it likely that the bullet didn't go through anybody to get there. As far as I could learn there was only the one shot. But as far as I could learn wasn't very far."

He scowled and inhaled smoke again. "Well, they left around midnight—the Captain and his four visitors all together—and all of them seem to have been walking all right. I got that from the watchman. I haven't been able to get hold of the Custom-House-men who were on duty there then. That's all of it. The Captain hasn't been back since. He didn't keep a date he had this noon with some shipping-agents, and they haven't found him to tell him about the fire."

"And the fire?" she asked.

Spade shrugged. "I don't know. It was discovered in the hold, aft—in the rear basement—late this morning. The chances are it got started some time yesterday. They got it out all right, though it did damage enough. Nobody liked to talk about it much while the Captain's away. It's the—"

The corridor-door opened. Spade shut his mouth. Effie Perine jumped down from the desk, but a man opened the connecting door before she could reach it.

"Where's Spade?" the man asked.

His voice brought Spade up erect and alert in his chair. It was a voice harsh and rasping with agony and with the strain of keeping two words from being smothered by the liquid bubbling that ran under and behind them.

Effie Perine, frightened, stepped out of the man's way.

He stood in the doorway with his soft hat crushed between his head and the top of the door-frame: he was nearly seven feet tall. A black overcoat cut long and straight and like a sheath, buttoned from throat to knees, exaggerated his leanness. His shoulders stuck out, high, thin, angular. His bony face—weather-coarsened, age-lined—was the color of wet sand and was wet with sweat on cheeks and chin. His eyes were dark and bloodshot and mad above lower lids that hung down to show pink inner membrane. Held tight against the left side of his chest by a black-sleeved arm that ended in a yellowish claw was a brown-paper-wrapped parcel bound with thin rope—an ellipsoid somewhat larger than an American football.

The tall man stood in the doorway and there was nothing to show that he saw Spade. He said, "You know—" and then the liquid bubbling came up in his throat and submerged whatever else he said. He put his other hand over the hand that held the ellipsoid. Holding himself stiffly straight, not putting his hands out to break his fall, he fell forward as a tree falls.

Spade, wooden-faced and nimble, sprang from his chair and caught the falling man. When Spade caught him the man's mouth opened and a little blood spurted out, and the brown-wrapped parcel dropped from the man's hands and rolled across the floor until a foot of the desk stopped it. Then the man's knees bent and he bent at the waist and his thin body became limber inside the sheathlike overcoat, sagging in Spade's arms so that Spade could not hold it up from the floor.

Spade lowered the man carefully until he lay on the floor on his left side. The man's eyes—dark and bloodshot, but not now mad—were wide open and still. His mouth was open as when blood had spurted from it, but no more blood came from it, and all his long body was as still as the floor it lay on.

Spade said: "Lock the door."

While Effie Perine, her teeth chattering, fumbled with the corridor-door's lock Spade knelt beside the thin man, turned him over on his back, and ran a hand down inside his overcoat. When he withdrew the hand presently it came out smeared with blood. The sight of his bloody hand brought not the least nor briefest of changes to Spade's face. Holding that hand up where it would touch nothing, he took his lighter out of his pocket with his other hand. He snapped on the flame and held the flame close to first one and then the other of the thin man's eyes. The eyes—lids, balls, irises, and pupils—remained frozen, immobile.

Spade extinguished the flame and returned the lighter to his pocket. He moved on his knees around to the dead man's side and, using his one clean hand, unbuttoned and opened the tubular overcoat. The inside of the overcoat was wet with blood and the double-breasted blue jacket beneath it was sodden. The jacket's lapels, where they crossed over the man's chest, and both sides of his coat immediately below that point, were pierced by soggy ragged holes.

Spade rose and went to the washbowl in the outer office.

Effie Perine, wan and trembling and holding herself upright by means of a hand on the corridor-door's knob and her back against its glass, whispered: "Is—is he—?"

"Yes. Shot through the chest, maybe half a dozen times." Spade began to wash his hands.

"Oughtn't we—?" she began, but he cut her short: "It's too late for a doctor now and I've got to think before we do anything." He finished washing his hands and began to rinse the bowl. "He couldn't have come far with those in him. If he— Why in hell couldn't he have stood up long enough to say something?" He frowned at the girl, rinsed his hands again, and picked up a towel. "Pull yourself together. For Christ's sake don't get sick on me now!" He threw the towel down and ran fingers through his hair. "We'll have a look at that bundle."

He went into the inner office again, stepped over the dead man's legs, and picked up the brown-paper-wrapped parcel. When he felt its weight his eyes glowed. He put it on his desk, turning it over so that the knotted part of the rope was uppermost. The knot was hard and tight. He took out his pocket-knife and cut the rope.

The girl had left the door and, edging around the dead man with her face turned away, had come to Spade's side. As she stood there—hands on a corner of the desk—watching him pull the rope loose and push aside brown paper, excitement began to supplant nausea in her face. "Do you think it is?" she whispered.

"We'll soon know," Spade said, his big fingers busy with the inner husk of coarse grey paper, three sheets thick, that the brown paper's removal had revealed. His face was hard and dull. His eyes were shining. When he had put the grey paper out of the way he had an egg-shaped mass of pale excelsior, wadded tight. His fingers tore the wad apart and then he had the foot-high figure of a bird, black as coal and shiny where its polish was not dulled by wood-dust and fragments of excelsior.

Spade laughed. He put a hand down on the bird. His wide-spread fingers had ownership in their curving. He put his other arm around Effie Perine and crushed her body against his. "We've got the damned thing, angel," he said.

"Ouch!" she said, "you're hurting me."

He took his arm away from her, picked the black bird up in both hands, and shook it to dislodge clinging excelsior. Then he stepped back holding it up in front of him and blew dust off it, regarding it triumphantly.

Effie Perine made a horrified face and screamed, pointing at his feet.

He looked down at his feet. His last backward step had brought his left heel into contact with the dead man's hand, pinching a quarter-inch of flesh at a side of the palm between heel and floor. Spade jerked his foot away from the hand.

The telephone-bell rang.

He nodded at the girl. She turned to the desk and put the receiver to her ear. She said: "Hello. . . . Yes. . . . Who? . . . Oh, yes!" Her eyes became large. "Yes. . . . Yes. . . . Hold the line. . . ." Her mouth suddenly stretched wide and fearful. She cried: "Hello! Hello! Hello!" She rattled the prong up and down and cried, "Hello!" twice. Then she sobbed and spun around to face Spade, who was close beside her by now. "It was Miss O'Shaughnessy," she said wildly. "She wants you. She's at the Alexandria—in danger. Her voice was—oh, it was awful, Sam!—and something happened to her before she could finish. Go help her, Sam!"

Spade put the falcon down on the desk and scowled gloomily. "I've got to take care of this fellow first," he said, pointing his thumb at the thin corpse on the floor.

She beat his chest with her fists, crying: "No, no—you've got to go to her. Don't you see, Sam? He had the thing that was hers and he came to you with it. Don't you see? He was helping her and they killed him and now she's— Oh, you've got to go!"

"All right." Spade pushed her away and bent over his desk, putting the black bird back into its nest of excelsior, bending the paper around it, working rapidly, making a larger and clumsy package. "As soon as I've gone phone the police. Tell them how it happened, but don't drag any names in. You don't know. I got the phone-call and I told you I had to go out, but I didn't say where." He cursed the rope for being tangled, yanked it into straightness, and began to bind the package. "Forget this thing. Tell it as it happened, but forget he had a bundle." He chewed his lower lip. "Unless they pin you down. If they seem to know about it you'll have to admit it. But that's not likely. If they do then I took the bundle away with me, unopened." He finished tying the knot and straightened up with the parcel under his left arm. "Get it straight, now. Everything happened the way it did happen, but without this dingus unless they already know about it. Don't deny it—just don't mention it. And I got the phone-call— not you. And you don't know anything about anybody else having any connection with this fellow. You don't know anything about him and you can't talk about my business until you see me. Got it?"

"Yes, Sam. Who—do you know who he is?"

He grinned wolfishly. "Uh-uh," he said, "but I'd guess he was Captain Jacobi, master of *La Paloma*." He picked up his hat and put it on. He looked thoughtfully at the dead man and then around the room.

"Hurry, Sam," the girl begged.

"Sure," he said absent-mindedly, "I'll hurry. Might not hurt to get those few scraps of excelsior off the floor before the police come. And maybe you ought to try to get hold of Sid. No." He rubbed his chin. "We'll leave him out of it awhile. It'll look better. I'd keep the door locked till they come." He took his hand from his chin and rubbed her cheek. "You're a damned good man, sister," he said and went out.

XVII · *Saturday Night*

CARRYING the parcel lightly under his arm, walking briskly, with only the ceaseless shifting of his eyes to denote wariness, Spade went, partly by way of an alley and a narrow court, from his office-building to Kearny and Post Streets, where he hailed a passing taxicab.

The taxicab carried him to the Pickwick Stage terminal in Fifth Street. He checked the bird at the Parcel Room there, put the check into a stamped envelope, wrote M. F. Holland and a San Francisco Post Office box-number on the envelope, sealed it, and dropped it into a mail-box. From the stage-terminal another taxicab carried him to the Alexandria Hotel.

Spade went up to suite 12-C and knocked on the door. The door was opened, when he had knocked a second time, by a small fair-haired girl in a shimmering yellow dressing-gown—a small girl whose face was white and dim and who clung desperately to the inner doorknob with both hands and gasped: "Mr. Spade?"

Spade said, "Yes," and caught her as she swayed.

Her body arched back over his arm and her head dropped straight back so that her short fair hair hung down her scalp and her slender throat was a firm curve from chin to chest.

Spade slid his supporting arm higher up her back and bent to get his other arm under her knees, but she stirred then, resisting, and between parted lips that barely moved blurred words came: "No! Ma' me wa'!"

Spade made her walk. He kicked the door shut and he walked her up and down the green-carpeted room from wall to wall. One of his arms around her small body, that hand under her armpit, his other hand gripping her other arm, held her erect when she stumbled, checked her swaying, kept urging her forward, but made her tottering legs bear all her weight they could bear. They walked across and across the floor, the girl falteringly, with incoördinate steps, Spade surely on the balls of his feet with balance unaffected by her staggering. Her face was chalk-white and eyeless, his sullen, with eyes hardened to watch everywhere at once.

He talked to her monotonously: "That's the stuff. Left, right, left, right. That's the stuff. One, two, three, four, one, two, three, now we turn." He shook her as they turned from the wall. "Now back again. One, two, three, four. Hold your head up. That's the stuff. Good girl. Left, right, left, right. Now we turn again." He shook her again. "That's the girl. Walk, walk, walk, walk. One, two, three, four. Now we go around." He shook her, more roughly, and increased their pace. "That's the trick. Left, right, left, right. We're in a hurry. One, two, three. . . ."

She shuddered and swallowed audibly. Spade began to chafe her arm and side and he put his mouth nearer her ear. "That's fine. You're doing fine. One, two, three, four. Faster, faster, faster, faster. That's it. Step, step, step, step. Pick them up and lay them down. That's the stuff. Now we turn. Left, right, left, right. What'd they do—dope you? The same stuff they gave me?"

Her eyelids twitched up then for an instant over dulled golden-brown eyes and she managed to say all of "Yes" except the final consonant.

They walked the floor, the girl almost trotting now to keep up with Spade, Spade slapping and kneading her flesh through yellow silk with both hands, talking and talking while his eyes remained hard and aloof

and watchful. "Left, right, left, right, left, right, turn. That's the girl.
One, two, three, four, one, two, three, four. Keep the chin up. That's the
stuff. One, two . . ."

Her lids lifted again a bare fraction of an inch and under them her
eyes moved weakly from side to side.

"That's fine," he said in a crisp voice, dropping his monotone. "Keep
them open. Open them wide—wide!" He shook her.

She moaned in protest, but her lids went farther up, though her eyes
were without inner light. He raised his hand and slapped her cheek half
a dozen times in quick succession. She moaned again and tried to break
away from him. His arm held her and swept her along beside him from
wall to wall.

"Keep walking," he ordered in a harsh voice, and then: "Who are
you?"

Her "Rhea Gutman" was thick but intelligible.

"The daughter?"

"Yes." Now she was no farther from the final consonant than *sh*.

"Where's Brigid?"

She twisted convulsively around in his arms and caught at one of his
hands with both of hers. He pulled his hand away quickly and looked at
it. Across its back was a thin red scratch an inch and a half or more in
length.

"What the hell?" he growled and examined her hands. Her left hand
was empty. In her right hand, when he forced it open, lay a three-inch
jade-headed steel bouquet-pin. "What the hell?" he growled again and
held the pin up in front of her eyes.

When she saw the pin she whimpered and opened her dressing-gown.
She pushed aside the cream-colored pajama-coat under it and showed him
her body below her left breast—white flesh crisscrossed with thin red lines,
dotted with tiny red dots, where the pin had scratched and punctured it.
"To stay awake . . . walk . . . till you came. . . . She said you'd come
. . . were so long." She swayed.

Spade tightened his arm around her and said: "Walk."

She fought against his arm, squirming around to face him again. "No
. . . tell you . . . sleep . . . save her . . ."

"Brigid?" he demanded.

"Yes . . . took her . . . Bur-Burlingame . . . twenty-six Ancho . . .
hurry . . . too late . . ." Her head fell over on her shoulder.

Spade pushed her head up roughly. "Who took her there? Your father?"

"Yes . . . Wilmer . . . Cairo." She writhed and her eyelids twitched
but did not open. ". . . kill her." Her head fell over again, and again he
pushed it up.

"Who shot Jacobi?"

She did not seem to hear the question. She tried pitifully to hold her
head up, to open her eyes. She mumbled: "Go . . . she . . ."

He shook her brutally. "Stay awake till the doctor comes."

Fear opened her eyes and pushed for a moment the cloudiness from her face. "No, no," she cried thickly, "father . . . kill me . . . swear you won't . . . he'd know . . . I did . . . for her . . . promise . . . won't . . . sleep . . . all right . . . morning . . ."

He shook her again. "You're sure you can sleep the stuff off all right?"

"Ye'." Her head fell down again.

"Where's your bed?"

She tried to raise a hand, but the effort had become too much for her before the hand pointed at anything except the carpet. With the sigh of a tired child she let her whole body relax and crumple.

Spade caught her up in his arms—scooped her up as she sank—and, holding her easily against his chest, went to the nearest of the three doors. He turned the knob far enough to release the catch, pushed the door open with his foot, and went into a passageway that ran past an open bathroom-door to a bedroom. He looked into the bathroom, saw it was empty, and carried the girl into the bedroom. Nobody was there. The clothing that was in sight and things on the chiffonier said it was a man's room.

Spade carried the girl back to the green-carpeted room and tried the opposite door. Through it he passed into another passageway, past another empty bathroom, and into a bedroom that was feminine in its accessories. He turned back the bedclothes and laid the girl on the bed, removed her slippers, raised her a little to slide the yellow dressing-gown off, fixed a pillow under her head, and put the covers up over her.

Then he opened the room's two windows and stood with his back to them staring at the sleeping girl. Her breathing was heavy but not troubled. He frowned and looked around, working his lips together. Twilight was dimming the room. He stood there in the weakening light for perhaps five minutes. Finally he shook his thick sloping shoulders impatiently and went out, leaving the suite's outer door unlocked.

Spade went to the Pacific Telephone and Telegraph Company's station in Powell Street and called Davenport 2020. "Emergency Hospital, please. . . . Hello, there's a girl in suite twelve C at the Alexandria Hotel who has been drugged. . . . Yes, you'd better send somebody to take a look at her. . . . This is Mr. Hooper of the Alexandria."

He put the receiver on its prong and laughed. He called another number and said: "Hello, Frank. This is Sam Spade. . . . Can you let me have a car with a driver who'll keep his mouth shut? . . . To go down the peninsula right away. . . . Just a couple of hours. . . . Right. Have him pick me up at John's, Ellis Street, as soon as he can make it."

He called another number—his office's—held the receiver to his ear for a little while without saying anything, and replaced it on its hook.

He went to John's Grill, asked the waiter to hurry his order of chops, baked potato, and sliced tomatoes, ate hurriedly, and was smoking a cigarette with his coffee when a thick-set youngish man with a plaid cap set askew above pale eyes and a tough cheery face came into the Grill and to his table.

"All set, Mr. Spade. She's full of gas and rearing to go."

"Swell." Spade emptied his cup and went out with the thick-set man. "Know where Ancho Avenue, or Road, or Boulevard, is in Burlingame?"

"Nope, but if she's there we can find her."

"Let's do that," Spade said as he sat beside the chauffeur in the dark Cadillac sedan. "Twenty-six is the number we want, and the sooner the better, but we don't want to pull up at the front door."

"Correct."

They rode half a dozen blocks in silence. The chauffeur said: "Your partner got knocked off, didn't he, Mr. Spade?"

"Uh-huh."

The chauffeur clucked. "She's a tough racket. You can have it for mine."

"Well, hack-drivers don't live forever."

"Maybe that's right," the thick-set man conceded, "but, just the same, it'll always be a surprise to me if I don't."

Spade stared ahead at nothing and thereafter, until the chauffeur tired of making conversation, replied with uninterested yeses and noes.

At a drug-store in Burlingame the chauffeur learned how to reach Ancho Avenue. Ten minutes later he stopped the sedan near a dark corner, turned off the lights, and waved his hand at the block ahead. "There she is," he said. "She ought to be on the other side, maybe the third or fourth house."

Spade said, "Right," and got out of the car. "Keep the engine going. We may have to leave in a hurry."

He crossed the street and went up the other side. Far ahead a lone street-light burned. Warmer lights dotted the night on either side where houses were spaced half a dozen to a block. A high thin moon was cold and feeble as the distant street-light. A radio droned through the open windows of a house on the other side of the street.

In front of the second house from the corner Spade halted. On one of the gateposts that were massive out of all proportion to the fence flanking them a 2 and a 6 of pale metal caught what light there was. A square white card was nailed over them. Putting his face close to the card, Spade could see that it was a For Sale or Rent sign. There was no gate between the posts. Spade went up the cement walk to the house. He stood still on the walk at the foot of the porch-steps for a long moment. No sound came from the house. The house was dark except for another pale square card nailed on its door.

Spade went up to the door and listened. He could hear nothing. He tried to look through the glass of the door. There was no curtain to keep his gaze out, but inner darkness. He tiptoed to a window and then to another. They, like the door, were uncurtained except by inner darkness. He tried both windows. They were locked. He tried the door. It was locked.

He left the porch and, stepping carefully over dark unfamiliar ground, walked through weeds around the house. The side-windows were too high to be reached from the ground. The back door and the one back window he could reach were locked.

Spade went back to the gatepost and, cupping the flame between his hands, held his lighter up to the *For Sale or Rent* sign. It bore the printed name and address of a San Mateo real-estate-dealer and a line penciled in blue: *Key at 31.*

Spade returned to the sedan and asked the chauffeur: "Got a flashlight?"

"Sure." He gave it to Spade. "Can I give you a hand at anything?"

"Maybe." Spade got into the sedan. "We'll ride up to number thirty-one. You can use your lights."

Number 31 was a square grey house across the street from, but a little farther up than, 26. Lights glowed in its downstairs-windows. Spade went up on the porch and rang the bell. A dark-haired girl of fourteen or fifteen opened the door. Spade, bowing and smiling, said: "I'd like to get the key to number twenty-six."

"I'll call Papa," she said and went back into the house calling: "Papa!"

A plump red-faced man, bald-headed and heavily mustached, appeared, carrying a newspaper.

Spade said: "I'd like to get the key to twenty-six."

The plump man looked doubtful. He said: "The juice is not on. You couldn't see anything."

Spade patted his pocket. "I've a flashlight."

The plump man looked more doubtful. He cleared his throat uneasily and crumpled the newspaper in his hand.

Spade showed him one of his business-cards, put it back in his pocket, and said in a low voice: "We got a tip that there might be something hidden there."

The plump man's face and voice were eager. "Wait a minute," he said. "I'll go over with you."

A moment later he came back carrying a brass key attached to a black and red tag. Spade beckoned to the chauffeur as they passed the car and the chauffeur joined them.

"Anybody been looking at the house lately?" Spade asked.

"Not that I know of," the plump man replied. "Nobody's been to me for the key in a couple of months."

The plump man marched ahead with the key until they had gone up on the porch. Then he thrust the key into Spade's hand, mumbled, "Here you are," and stepped aside.

Spade unlocked the door and pushed it open. There was silence and darkness. Holding the flashlight—dark—in his left hand, Spade entered. The chauffeur came close behind him and then, at a little distance, the plump man followed them. They searched the house from bottom to top, cautiously at first, then, finding nothing, boldly. The house was empty— unmistakably—and there was nothing to indicate that it had been visited in weeks.

Saying, "Thanks, that's all," Spade left the sedan in front of the Alexandria. He went into the hotel, to the desk, where a tall young man with a dark grave face said: "Good evening, Mr. Spade."

"Good evening." Spade drew the young man to one end of the desk. "These Gutmans—up in twelve C—are they in?"

The young man replied, "No," darting a quick glance at Spade. Then he looked away, hesitated, looked at Spade again, and murmured: "A funny thing happened in connection with them this evening, Mr. Spade. Somebody called the Emergency Hospital and told them there was a sick girl up there."

"And there wasn't?"

"Oh, no, there was nobody up there. They went out earlier in the evening."

Spade said: "Well, these practical-jokers have to have their fun. Thanks."

He went to a telephone-booth, called a number, and said: "Hello. . . . Mrs. Perine? . . . Is Effie there? . . . Yes, please. . . . Thanks.

"Hello, angel! What's the good word? . . . Fine, fine! Hold it. I'll be out in twenty minutes. . . . Right."

Half an hour later Spade rang the doorbell of a two-story brick building in Ninth Avenue. Effie Perine opened the door. Her boyish face was tired and smiling. "Hello, boss," she said. "Enter." She said in a low voice: "If Ma says anything to you, Sam, be nice to her. She's all up in the air."

Spade grinned reassuringly and patted her shoulder.

She put her hands on his arm. "Miss O'Shaughnessy?"

"No," he growled. "I ran into a plant. Are you sure it was her voice?"

"Yes."

He made an unpleasant face. "Well, it was hooey."

She took him into a bright living-room, sighed, and slumped down on one end of a Chesterfield, smiling cheerfully up at him through her weariness.

He sat beside her and asked: "Everything went O K? Nothing said about the bundle?"

"Nothing. I told them what you told me to tell them, and they seemed to take it for granted that the phone-call had something to do with it, and that you were out running it down."

"Dundy there?"

"No. Hoff and O'Gar and some others I didn't know. I talked to the Captain too."

"They took you down to the Hall?"

"Oh, yes, and they asked me loads of questions, but it was all—you know—routine."

Spade rubbed his palms together. "Swell," he said and then frowned, "though I guess they'll think up plenty to put to me when we meet. That damned Dundy will, anyway, and Bryan." He moved his shoulders. "Anybody you know, outside of the police, come around?"

"Yes." She sat up straight. "That boy—the one who brought the message from Gutman—was there. He didn't come in, but the police left the corridor-door open while they were there and I saw him standing there."

"You didn't say anything?"

"Oh, no. You had said not to. So I didn't pay any attention to him and the next time I looked he was gone."

Spade grinned at her. "Damned lucky for you, sister, that the coppers got there first."

"Why?"

"He's a bad egg, that lad—poison. Was the dead man Jacobi?"

"Yes."

He pressed her hands and stood up. "I'm going to run along. You'd better hit the hay. You're all in."

She rose. "Sam, what is—?"

He stopped her words with his hand on her mouth. "Save it till Monday," he said. "I want to sneak out before your mother catches me and gives me hell for dragging her lamb through gutters."

Midnight was a few minutes away when Spade reached his home. He put his key into the street-door's lock. Heels clicked rapidly on the sidewalk behind him. He let go the key and wheeled. Brigid O'Shaughnessy ran up the steps to him. She put her arms around him and hung on him, panting: "Oh, I thought you'd never come!" Her face was haggard, distraught, shaken by the tremors that shook her from head to foot.

With the hand not supporting her he felt for the key again, opened the door, and half lifted her inside. "You've been waiting?" he asked.

"Yes." Panting spaced her words. "In a—doorway—up the—street."

"Can you make it all right?" he asked. "Or shall I carry you?"

She shook her head against his shoulder. "I'll be—all right—when I—get where—I can—sit down."

They rode up to Spade's floor in the elevator and went around to his apartment. She left his arm and stood beside him—panting, both hands to her breast—while he unlocked his door. He switched on the passageway light. They went in. He shut the door and, with his arm around her again, took her back towards the living-room. When they were within a step of the living-room-door the light in the living-room went on.

The girl cried out and clung to Spade.

Just inside the living-room-door fat Gutman stood smiling benevolently at them. The boy Wilmer came out of the kitchen behind them. Black pistols were gigantic in his small hands. Cairo came from the bathroom. He too had a pistol.

Gutman said: "Well, sir, we're all here, as you can see for yourself. Now let's come in and sit down and be comfortable and talk."

XVIII · The Fall-Guy

SPADE, with his arms around Brigid O'Shaughnessy, smiled meagerly over her head and said: "Sure, we'll talk."

Gutman's bulbs jounced as he took three waddling backward steps away from the door.

Spade and the girl went in together. The boy and Cairo followed them in. Cairo stopped in the doorway. The boy put away one of his pistols and came up close behind Spade.

Spade turned his head far around to look down over his shoulder at the boy and said: "Get away. You're not going to frisk me."

The boy said: "Stand still. Shut up."

Spade's nostrils went in and out with his breathing. His voice was level. "Get away. Put your paw on me and I'm going to make you use the gun. Ask your boss if he wants me shot up before we talk."

"Never mind, Wilmer," the fat man said. He frowned indulgently at Spade. "You are certainly a most headstrong individual. Well, let's be seated."

Spade said, "I told you I didn't like that punk," and took Brigid O'Shaughnessy to the sofa by the windows. They sat close together, her head against his left shoulder, his left arm around her shoulders. She had stopped trembling, had stopped panting. The appearance of Gutman and his companions seemed to have robbed her of that freedom of personal movement and emotion that is animal, leaving her alive, conscious, but quiescent as a plant.

Gutman lowered himself into the padded rocking chair. Cairo chose the armchair by the table. The boy Wilmer did not sit down. He stood in the doorway where Cairo had stood, letting his one visible pistol hang down at his side, looking under curling lashes at Spade's body. Cairo put his pistol on the table beside him.

Spade took off his hat and tossed it to the other end of the sofa. He grinned at Gutman. The looseness of his lower lip and the droop of his upper eyelids combined with the v's in his face to make his grin lewd as a satyr's. "That daughter of yours has a nice belly," he said, "too nice to be scratched up with pins."

Gutman's smile was affable if a bit oily.

The boy in the doorway took a short step forward, raising his pistol as far as his hip. Everybody in the room looked at him. In the dissimilar eyes with which Brigid O'Shaughnessy and Joel Cairo looked at him there was, oddly, something identically reproving. The boy blushed, drew back his advanced foot, straightened his legs, lowered the pistol and stood as he had stood before, looking under lashes that hid his eyes at Spade's chest. The blush was pale enough and lasted for only an instant, but it was startling on his face that habitually was so cold and composed.

Gutman turned his sleek-eyed fat smile on Spade again. His voice was a suave purring. "Yes, sir, that was a shame, but you must admit that it served its purpose."

Spade's brows twitched together. "Anything would've," he said. "Naturally I wanted to see you as soon as I had the falcon. Cash customers —why not? I went to Burlingame expecting to run into this sort of a meeting. I didn't know you were blundering around, half an hour late, trying to get me out of the way so you could find Jacobi again before he found me."

Gutman chuckled. His chuckle seemed to hold nothing but satisfaction. "Well, sir," he said, "in any case, here we are having our little meeting, if that's what you wanted."

"That's what I wanted. How soon are you ready to make the first payment and take the falcon off my hands?"

Brigid O'Shaughnessy sat up straight and looked at Spade with surprised blue eyes. He patted her shoulder inattentively. His eyes were steady on Gutman's. Gutman's twinkled merrily between sheltering fat-puffs. He said: "Well, sir, as to that," and put a hand inside the breast of his coat.

Cairo, hands on thighs, leaned forward in his chair, breathing between parted soft lips. His dark eyes had the surface-shine of lacquer. They shifted their focus warily from Spade's face to Gutman's, from Gutman's to Spade's.

Gutman repeated, "Well, sir, as to that," and took a white envelope from his pocket. Ten eyes—the boy's now only half obscured by his lashes —looked at the envelope. Turning the envelope over in his swollen hands, Gutman studied for a moment its blank white front and then its back, unsealed, with the flap tucked in. He raised his head, smiled amiably, and scaled the envelope at Spade's lap.

The envelope, though not bulky, was heavy enough to fly true. It struck the lower part of Spade's chest and dropped down on his thighs. He picked it up deliberately and opened it deliberately, using both hands, having taken his left arm from around the girl. The contents of the envelope were thousand-dollar bills, smooth and stiff and new. Spade took them out and counted them. There were ten of them. Spade looked up smiling. He said mildly: "We were talking about more money than this."

"Yes, sir, we were," Gutman agreed, "but we were talking then. This is actual money, genuine coin of the realm, sir. With a dollar of this you can buy more than with ten dollars of talk." Silent laughter shook his bulbs. When their commotion stopped he said more seriously, yet not altogether seriously: "There are more of us to be taken care of now." He moved his twinkling eyes and his fat head to indicate Cairo. "And—well, sir, in short—the situation has changed."

While Gutman talked Spade had tapped the edges of the ten bills into alignment and had returned them to their envelope, tucking the flap in over them. Now, with forearms on knees, he sat hunched forward, dangling the envelope from a corner held lightly by finger and thumb down between his legs. His reply to the fat man was careless: "Sure. You're together now, but I've got the falcon."

Joel Cairo spoke. Ugly hands grasping the arms of his chair, he leaned forward and said primly in his high-pitched thin voice: "I shouldn't think it would be necessary to remind you, Mr. Spade, that though you may have the falcon yet we certainly have you."

Spade grinned. "I'm trying to not let that worry me," he said. He sat up straight, put the envelope aside—on the sofa—and addressed Gutman: "We'll come back to the money later. There's another thing that's got to be taken care of first. We've got to have a fall-guy."

The fat man frowned without comprehension, but before he could speak Spade was explaining: "The police have got to have a victim—somebody they can stick for those three murders. We—"

Cairo, speaking in a brittle excited voice, interrupted Spade. "Two—only two—murders, Mr. Spade. Thursby undoubtedly killed your partner."

"All right, two," Spade growled. "What difference does that make? The point is we've got to feed the police some—"

Now Gutman broke in, smiling confidently, talking with good-natured assurance: "Well, sir, from what we've seen and heard of you I don't think we'll have to bother ourselves about that. We can leave the handling of the police to you, all right. You won't need any of our inexpert help."

"If that's what you think," Spade said, "you haven't seen or heard enough."

"Now come, Mr. Spade. You can't expect us to believe at this late date that you are the least bit afraid of the police, or that you are not quite able to handle—"

Spade snorted with throat and nose. He bent forward, resting forearms on knees again, and interrupted Gutman irritably: "I'm not a damned bit afraid of them and I know how to handle them. That's what I'm trying to tell you. The way to handle them is to toss them a victim, somebody they can hang the works on."

"Well, sir, I grant you that's one way of doing it, but—"

"'But' hell!" Spade said. "It's the only way." His eyes were hot and earnest under a reddening forehead. The bruise on his temple was liver-colored. "I know what I'm talking about. I've been through it all before and expect to go through it again. At one time or another I've had to tell everybody from the Supreme Court down to go to hell, and I've got away with it. I got away with it because I never let myself forget that a day of reckoning was coming. I never forget that when the day of reckoning comes I want to be all set to march into headquarters pushing a victim in front of me, saying: 'Here, you chumps, is your criminal.' As long as I can do that I can put my thumb to my nose and wriggle my fingers at all the laws in the book. The first time I can't do it my name's Mud. There hasn't been a first time yet. This isn't going to be it. That's flat."

Gutman's eyes flickered and their sleekness became dubious, but he held his other features in their bulbous pink smiling complacent cast and there was nothing of uneasiness in his voice. He said: "That's a system that's got a lot to recommend it, sir—by Gad, it has! And if it was anyway practical this time I'd be the first to say: 'Stick to it by all means, sir.' But this just happens to be a case where it's not possible. That's the way it is with the best of systems. There comes a time when you've got to make exceptions, and a wise man just goes ahead and makes them. Well, sir, that's just the way it is in this case and I don't mind telling you that I think you're being very well paid for making an exception. Now maybe it will be a little more trouble to you than if you had your victim to hand over to the police, but"—he laughed and spread his hands—"you're not a man that's afraid of a little bit of trouble. You know how to do things and you know you'll land on your feet in the end, no matter what happens." He pursed his lips and partly closed one eye. "You'll manage that, sir."

Spade's eyes had lost their warmth. His face was dull and lumpy. "I know what I'm talking about," he said in a low, consciously patient, tone. "This is my city and my game. I could manage to land on my feet—sure—this time, but the next time I tried to put over a fast one they'd stop me so fast I'd swallow my teeth. Hell with that. You birds'll be in New York or Constantinople or some place else. I'm in business here."

"But surely," Gutman began, "you can—"

"I can't," Spade said earnestly. "I won't. I mean it." He sat up straight. A pleasant smile illuminated his face, erasing its dull lumpish-ness. He spoke rapidly in an agreeable, persuasive tone: "Listen to me, Gutman. I'm telling you what's best for all of us. If we don't give the police a fall-guy it's ten to one they'll sooner or later stumble on information about the falcon. Then you'll have to duck for cover with it—no matter where you are—and that's not going to help you make a fortune off it. Give them a fall-guy and they'll stop right there."

"Well, sir, that's just the point," Gutman replied, and still only in his eyes was uneasiness faintly apparent. "Will they stop right there? Or won't the fall-guy be a fresh clue that as likely as not will lead them to information about the falcon? And, on the other hand, wouldn't you say they were stopped right now, and that the best thing for us to do is leave well enough alone?"

A forked vein began to swell in Spade's forehead. "Jesus! you don't know what it's all about either," he said in a restrained tone. "They're not asleep, Gutman. They're lying low, waiting. Try to get that. I'm in it up to my neck and they know it. That's all right as long as I do something when the time comes. But it won't be all right if I don't." His voice became persuasive again. "Listen, Gutman, we've absolutely got to give them a victim. There's no way out of it. Let's give them the punk." He nodded pleasantly at the boy in the doorway. "He actually did shoot both of them—Thursby and Jacobi—didn't he? Anyway, he's made to order for the part. Let's pin the necessary evidence on him and turn him over to them."

The boy in the doorway tightened the corners of his mouth in what may have been a minute smile. Spade's proposal seemed to have no other effect on him. Joel Cairo's dark face was open-mouthed, open-eyed, yellowish, and amazed. He breathed through his mouth, his round effeminate chest rising and falling, while he gaped at Spade. Brigid O'Shaughnessy had moved away from Spade and had twisted herself around on the sofa to stare at him. There was a suggestion of hysterical laughter behind the startled confusion in her face.

Gutman remained still and expressionless for a long moment. Then he decided to laugh. He laughed heartily and lengthily, not stopping until his sleek eyes had borrowed merriment from his laughter. When he stopped laughing he said: "By Gad, sir, you're a character, that you are!" He took a white handkerchief from his pocket and wiped his eyes. "Yes, sir, there's never any telling what you'll do or say next, except that it's bound to be something astonishing."

"There's nothing funny about it." Spade did not seem offended by the fat man's laughter, nor in any way impressed. He spoke in the manner of one reasoning with a recalcitrant, but not altogether unreasonable, friend. "It's our best bet. With him in their hands, the police will—"

"But, my dear man," Gutman objected, "can't you see? If I even for a moment thought of doing it— But that's ridiculous too. I feel towards Wilmer just exactly as if he were my own son. I really do. But if I even for a moment thought of doing what you propose, what in the world do you think would keep Wilmer from telling the police every last detail about the falcon and all of us?"

Spade grinned with stiff lips. "If we had to," he said softly, "we could have him killed resisting arrest. But we won't have to go that far. Let him talk his head off. I promise you nobody'll do anything about it. That's easy enough to fix."

The pink flesh on Gutman's forehead crawled in a frown. He lowered his head, mashing his chins together over his collar, and asked: "How?" Then, with an abruptness that set all his fat bulbs to quivering and tumbling against one another, he raised his head, squirmed around to look at the boy, and laughed uproariously. "What do you think of this, Wilmer? It's funny, eh?"

The boy's eyes were cold hazel gleams under his lashes. He said in a low distinct voice: "Yes, it's funny—the son of a bitch."

Spade was talking to Brigid O'Shaughnessy: "How do you feel now, angel? Any better?"

"Yes, much better, only"—she reduced her voice until the last words would have been unintelligible two feet away—"I'm frightened."

"Don't be," he said carelessly and put a hand on her grey-stockinged knee. "Nothing very bad's going to happen. Want a drink?"

"Not now, thanks." Her voice sank again. "Be careful, Sam."

Spade grinned and looked at Gutman, who was looking at him. The fat man smiled genially, saying nothing for a moment, and then asked: "How?"

Spade was stupid. "How what?"

The fat man considered more laughter necessary then, and an explanation: "Well, sir, if you're really serious about this—this suggestion of yours, the least we can do in common politeness is to hear you out. Now how are you going about fixing it so that Wilmer"—he paused here to laugh again—"won't be able to do us any harm?"

Spade shook his head. "No," he said, "I wouldn't want to take advantage of anybody's politeness, no matter how common, like that. Forget it."

The fat man puckered up his facial bulbs. "Now come, come," he protested, "you make me decidedly uncomfortable. I shouldn't have laughed, and I apologize most humbly and sincerely. I wouldn't want to seem to ridicule anything you'd suggest, Mr. Spade, regardless of how much I disagreed with you, for you must know that I have the greatest respect and admiration for your astuteness. Now mind you, I don't see how this suggestion of yours can be in any way practical—even leaving out the fact that I couldn't feel any different towards Wilmer if he was my own flesh and blood—but I'll consider it a personal favor as well as a sign that you've accepted my apologies, sir, if you'll go ahead and outline the rest of it."

"Fair enough," Spade said. "Bryan is like most district attorneys. He's more interested in how his record will look on paper than in anything else. He'd rather drop a doubtful case than try it and have it go against him. I don't know that he ever deliberately framed anybody he believed innocent, but I can't imagine him letting himself believe them innocent if he could scrape up, or twist into shape, proof of their guilt. To be sure of convicting one man he'll let half a dozen equally guilty accomplices go free—if trying to convict them all might confuse his case.

"That's the choice we'll give him and he'll gobble it up. He wouldn't want to know about the falcon. He'll be tickled pink to persuade himself that anything the punk tells him about it is a lot of chewing-gum, an attempt to muddle things up. Leave that end to me. I can show him that if he starts fooling around trying to gather up everybody he's going to have a tangled case that no jury will be able to make heads or tails of, while if he sticks to the punk he can get a conviction standing on his head."

Gutman wagged his head sidewise in a slow smiling gesture of benign disapproval. "No, sir," he said, "I'm afraid that won't do, won't do at all. I don't see how even this District Attorney of yours can link Thursby and Jacobi and Wilmer together without having to—"

"You don't know district attorneys," Spade told him. "The Thursby angle is easy. He was a gunman and so's your punk. Bryan's already got a theory about that. There'll be no catch there. Well, Christ! they can only hang the punk once. Why try him for Jacobi's murder after he's been convicted of Thursby's? They simply close the record by writing it up against him and let it go at that. If, as is likely enough, he used the same gun on both, the bullets will match up. Everybody will be satisfied."

"Yes, but—" Gutman began, and stopped to look at the boy.

The boy advanced from the doorway, walking stiff-legged, with his legs apart, until he was between Gutman and Cairo, almost in the center of the floor. He halted there, leaning forward slightly from the waist, his shoulders raised towards the front. The pistol in his hand still hung at his side, but his knuckles were white over its grip. His other hand was a small hard fist down at his other side. The indelible youngness of his face gave an indescribably vicious—and inhuman—turn to the white-hot hatred and the cold white malevolence in his face. He said to Spade in a voice cramped by passion: "You bastard, get up on your feet and go for your heater!"

Spade smiled at the boy. His smile was not broad, but the amusement in it seemed genuine and unalloyed.

The boy said: "You bastard, get up and shoot it out if you've got the guts. I've taken all the riding from you I'm going to take."

The amusement in Spade's smile deepened. He looked at Gutman and said: "Young Wild West." His voice matched his smile. "Maybe you ought to tell him that shooting me before you get your hands on the falcon would be bad for business."

Gutman's attempt at a smile was not successful, but he kept the resultant grimace on his mottled face. He licked dry lips with a dry tongue. His voice was too hoarse and gritty for the paternally admonishing tone it tried to achieve. "Now, now, Wilmer," he said, "we can't have any of that. You shouldn't let yourself attach so much importance to these things. You—"

The boy, not taking his eyes from Spade, spoke in a choked voice out the side of his mouth: "Make him lay off me then. I'm going to fog him if he keeps it up and there won't be anything that'll stop me from doing it."

"Now, Wilmer," Gutman said and turned to Spade. His face and voice were under control now. "Your plan is, sir, as I said in the first place, not at all practical. Let's not say anything more about it."

Spade looked from one of them to the other. He had stopped smiling. His face held no expression at all. "I say what I please," he told them.

"You certainly do," Gutman said quickly, "and that's one of the things I've always admired in you. But this matter is, as I say, not at all practical, so there's not the least bit of use of discussing it any further, as you can see for yourself."

"I can't see it for myself," Spade said, "and you haven't made me see it, and I don't think you can." He frowned at Gutman. "Let's get this straight. Am I wasting time talking to you? I thought this was your show. Should I do my talking to the punk? I know how to do that."

"No, sir," Gutman replied, "you're quite right in dealing with me."

Spade said: "All right. Now I've got another suggestion. It's not as good as the first, but it's better than nothing. Want to hear it?"

"Most assuredly."

"Give them Cairo."

Cairo hastily picked up his pistol from the table beside him. He held it tight in his lap with both hands. Its muzzle pointed at the floor a little to one side of the sofa. His face had become yellowish again. His black eyes darted their gaze from face to face. The opaqueness of his eyes made them seem flat, two-dimensional.

Gutman, looking as if he could not believe he had heard what he had heard, asked: "Do what?"

"Give the police Cairo."

Gutman seemed about to laugh, but he did not laugh. Finally he exclaimed: "Well, by Gad, sir!" in an uncertain tone.

"It's not as good as giving them the punk," Spade said. "Cairo's not a gunman and he carries a smaller gun than Thursby and Jacobi were shot with. We'll have to go to more trouble framing him, but that's better than not giving the police anybody."

Cairo cried in a voice shrill with indignation: "Suppose we give them you, Mr. Spade, or Miss O'Shaughnessy? How about that if you're so set on giving them somebody?"

Spade smiled at the Levantine and answered him evenly: "You people want the falcon. I've got it. A fall-guy is part of the price I'm asking. As for Miss O'Shaughnessy"—his dispassionate glance moved to her white perplexed face and then back to Cairo and his shoulders rose and fell a fraction of an inch—"if you think she can be rigged for the part I'm perfectly willing to discuss it with you."

The girl put her hands to her throat, uttered a short strangled cry, and moved farther away from him.

Cairo, his face and body twitching with excitement, exclaimed: "You seem to forget that you are not in a position to insist on anything."

Spade laughed, a harsh derisive snort.

Gutman said, in a voice that tried to make firmness ingratiating: "Come now, gentlemen, let's keep our discussion on a friendly basis; but there certainly is"—he was addressing Spade—"something in what Mr. Cairo says. You must take into consideration the—"

"Like hell I must." Spade flung his words out with a brutal sort of carelessness that gave them more weight than they could have got from dramatic emphasis or from loudness. "If you kill me, how are you going to get the bird? If I know you can't afford to kill me till you have it, how are you going to scare me into giving it to you?"

Gutman cocked his head to the left and considered these questions. His eyes twinkled between puckered lids. Presently he gave his genial answer: "Well, sir, there are other means of persuasion besides killing and threatening to kill."

"Sure," Spade agreed, "but they're not much good unless the threat of death is behind them to hold the victim down. See what I mean? If you try anything I don't like I won't stand for it. I'll make it a matter of your having to call it off or kill me, knowing you can't afford to kill me."

"I see what you mean." Gutman chuckled. "That is an attitude, sir, that calls for the most delicate judgment on both sides, because, as you know, sir, men are likely to forget in the heat of action where their best interest lies and let their emotions carry them away."

Spade too was all smiling blandness. "That's the trick, from my side," he said, "to make my play strong enough that it ties you up, but yet not make you mad enough to bump me off against your better judgment."

Gutman said fondly: "By Gad, sir, you are a character!"

Joel Cairo jumped up from his chair and went around behind the boy and behind Gutman's chair. He bent over the back of Gutman's chair and, screening his mouth and the fat man's ear with his empty hand, whispered. Gutman listened attentively, shutting his eyes.

Spade grinned at Brigid O'Shaughnessy. Her lips smiled feebly in response, but there was no change in her eyes; they did not lose their numb stare. Spade turned to the boy: "Two to one they're selling you out, son."

The boy did not say anything. A trembling in his knees began to shake the knees of his trousers.

Spade addressed Gutman: "I hope you're not letting yourself be influenced by the guns these pocket-edition desperadoes are waving."

Gutman opened his eyes. Cairo stopped whispering and stood erect behind the fat man's chair.

Spade said: "I've practiced taking them away from both of them, so there'll be no trouble there. The punk is—"

In a voice choked horribly by emotion the boy cried, "All right!" and jerked his pistol up in front of his chest.

Gutman flung a fat hand out at the boy's wrist, caught the wrist, and bore it and the gun down while Gutman's fat body was rising in haste from the rocking chair. Joel Cairo scurried around to the boy's other side and grasped his other arm. They wrestled with the boy, forcing his arms down, holding them down, while he struggled futilely against them.

Words came out of the struggling group: fragments of the boy's incoherent speech—"right . . . go . . . bastard . . . smoke"—Gutman's "Now, now, Wilmer!" repeated many times; Cairo's "No, please, don't" and "Don't do that, Wilmer."

Wooden-faced, dreamy-eyed, Spade got up from the sofa and went over to the group. The boy, unable to cope with the weight against him, had stopped struggling. Cairo, still holding the boy's arm, stood partly in front of him, talking to him soothingly. Spade pushed Cairo aside gently and drove his left fist against the boy's chin. The boy's head snapped back as far as it could while his arms were held, and then came forward. Gutman began a desperate "Here, what—?" Spade drove his right fist against the boy's chin.

Cairo dropped the boy's arm, letting him collapse against Gutman's great round belly. Cairo sprang at Spade, clawing at his face with the curved stiff fingers of both hands. Spade blew his breath out and pushed the Levantine away. Cairo sprang at him again. Tears were in Cairo's eyes and his red lips worked angrily, forming words, but no sound came from between them.

Spade laughed, grunted, "Jesus, you're a pip!" and cuffed the side of Cairo's face with an open hand, knocking him over against the table. Cairo regained his balance and sprang at Spade the third time. Spade stopped him with both palms held out on long rigid arms against his face. Cairo, failing to reach Spade's face with his shorter arms, thumped Spade's arms.

"Stop it," Spade growled. "I'll hurt you."

Cairo cried, "Oh, you big coward!" and backed away from him.

Spade stooped to pick up Cairo's pistol from the floor, and then the boy's. He straightened up holding them in his left hand, dangling them upside-down by their trigger-guards from his forefinger.

Gutman had put the boy in the rocking chair and stood looking at him with troubled eyes in an uncertainly puckered face. Cairo went down on his knees beside the chair and began to chafe one of the boy's limp hands.

Spade felt the boy's chin with his fingers. "Nothing cracked," he said. "We'll spread him on the sofa." He put his right arm under the boy's arm and around his back, put his left forearm under the boy's knees, lifted him without apparent effort, and carried him to the sofa.

Brigid O'Shaughnessy got up quickly and Spade laid the boy there. With his right hand Spade patted the boy's clothes, found his second pistol, added it to the others in his left hand, and turned his back on the sofa. Cairo was already sitting beside the boy's head.

Spade clinked the pistols together in his hand and smiled cheerfully at Gutman. "Well," he said, "there's our fall-guy."

Gutman's face was grey and his eyes were clouded. He did not look at Spade. He looked at the floor and did not say anything.

Spade said: "Don't be a damned fool again. You let Cairo whisper to you and you held the kid while I pasted him. You can't laugh that off and you're likely to get yourself shot trying to."

Gutman moved his feet on the rug and said nothing.

Spade said: "And the other side of it is that you'll either say yes right now or I'll turn the falcon and the whole God-damned lot of you in."

Gutman raised his head and muttered through his teeth: "I don't like that, sir."

"You won't like it," Spade said. "Well?"

The fat man sighed and made a wry face and replied sadly: "You can have him."

Spade said: "That's swell."

XIX · *The Russian's Hand*

THE boy lay on his back on the sofa, a small figure that was —except for its breathing—altogether corpselike to the eye. Joel Cairo sat beside the boy, bending over him, rubbing his cheeks and wrists, smoothing his hair back from his forehead, whispering to him, and peering anxiously down at his white still face.

Brigid O'Shaughnessy stood in an angle made by table and wall. One of her hands was flat on the table, the other to her breast. She pinched her lower lip between her teeth and glanced furtively at Spade whenever he was not looking at her. When he looked at her she looked at Cairo and the boy.

Gutman's face had lost its troubled cast and was becoming rosy again. He had put his hands in his trousers-pockets. He stood facing Spade, watching him without curiosity.

Spade, idly jingling his handful of pistols, nodded at Cairo's rounded back and asked Gutman: "It'll be all right with him?"

"I don't know," the fat man replied placidly. "That part will have to be strictly up to you, sir."

Spade's smile made his v-shaped chin more salient. He said: "Cairo."

The Levantine screwed his dark anxious face around over his shoulder.

Spade said: "Let him rest awhile. We're going to give him to the police. We ought to get the details fixed before he comes to."

Cairo asked bitterly: "Don't you think you've done enough to him without that?"

Spade said: "No."

Cairo left the sofa and went close to the fat man. "Please don't do this thing, Mr. Gutman," he begged. "You must realize that—"

Spade interrupted him: "That's settled. The question is, what are you going to do about it? Coming in? Or getting out?"

Though Gutman's smile was a bit sad, even wistful in its way, he nodded his head. "I don't like it either," he told the Levantine, "but we can't help ourselves now. We really can't."

Spade asked: "What are you doing, Cairo? In or out?"

Cairo wet his lips and turned slowly to face Spade. "Suppose," he said, and swallowed. "Have I—? Can I choose?"

"You can," Spade assured him seriously, "but you ought to know that if the answer is *out* we'll give you to the police with your boy-friend."

"Oh, come, Mr. Spade," Gutman protested, "that is not—"

"Like hell we'll let him walk out on us," Spade said. "He'll either come in or he'll go in. We can't have a lot of loose ends hanging around." He scowled at Gutman and burst out irritably: "Jesus God! is this the first thing you guys ever stole? You're a fine lot of lollipops! What are you going to do next—get down and pray?" He directed his scowl at Cairo. "Well? Which?"

"You give me no choice." Cairo's narrow shoulders moved in a hopeless shrug. "I come in."

"Good," Spade said and looked at Gutman and at Brigid O'Shaughnessy. "Sit down."

The girl sat down gingerly on the end of the sofa by the unconscious boy's feet. Gutman returned to the padded rocking chair, and Cairo to the armchair. Spade put his handful of pistols on the table and sat on the table-corner beside them. He looked at the watch on his wrist and said: "Two o'clock. I can't get the falcon till daylight, or maybe eight o'clock. We've got plenty of time to arrange everything."

Gutman cleared his throat. "Where is it?" he asked and then added in haste: "I don't really care, sir. What I had in mind was that it would be best for all concerned if we did not get out of each other's sight until our business has been transacted." He looked at the sofa and at Spade again, sharply. "You have the envelope?"

Spade shook his head, looking at the sofa and then at the girl. He smiled with his eyes and said: "Miss O'Shaughnessy has it."

"Yes, I have it," she murmured, putting a hand inside her coat. "I picked it up. . . ."

"That's all right," Spade told her. "Hang on to it." He addressed Gutman: "We won't have to lose sight of each other. I can have the falcon brought here."

"That will be excellent," Gutman purred. "Then, sir, in exchange for the ten thousand dollars and Wilmer you will give us the falcon and an hour or two of grace—so we won't be in the city when you surrender him to the authorities."

"You don't have to duck," Spade said. "It'll be air-tight."

"That may be, sir, but nevertheless we'll feel safer well out of the city when Wilmer is being questioned by your District Attorney."

"Suit yourself," Spade replied. "I can hold him here all day if you want." He began to roll a cigarette. "Let's get the details fixed. Why did he shoot Thursby? And why and where and how did he shoot Jacobi?"

Gutman smiled indulgently, shaking his head and purring: "Now come, sir, you can't expect that. We've given you the money and Wilmer. That is our part of the agreement."

"I do expect it," Spade said. He held his lighter to his cigarette. "A fall-guy is what I asked for, and he's not a fall-guy unless he's a cinch to take the fall. Well, to cinch that I've got to know what's what." He pulled his brows together. "What are you bellyaching about? You're not going to be sitting so damned pretty if you leave him with an out."

Gutman leaned forward and wagged a fat finger at the pistols on the table beside Spade's legs. "There's ample evidence of his guilt, sir. Both men were shot with those weapons. It's a very simple matter for the police-department-experts to determine that the bullets that killed the men were fired from those weapons. You know that; you've mentioned it yourself. And that, it seems to me, is ample proof of his guilt."

"Maybe," Spade agreed, "but the thing's more complicated than that and I've got to know what happened so I can be sure the parts that won't fit in are covered up."

Cairo's eyes were round and hot. "Apparently you've forgotten that you assured us it would be a very simple affair," Cairo said. He turned his excited dark face to Gutman. "You see! I advised you not to do this. I don't think—"

"It doesn't make a damned bit of difference what either of you think," Spade said bluntly. "It's too late for that now and you're in too deep. Why did he kill Thursby?"

Gutman interlaced his fingers over his belly and rocked his chair. His voice, like his smile, was frankly rueful. "You are an uncommonly difficult person to get the best of," he said. "I begin to think that we made a mistake in not letting you alone from the very first. By Gad, I do, sir!"

Spade moved his hand carelessly. "You haven't done so bad. You're staying out of jail and you're getting the falcon. What do you want?" He put his cigarette in a corner of his mouth and said around it: "Anyhow you know where you stand now. Why did he kill Thursby?"

Gutman stopped rocking. "Thursby was a notorious killer and Miss O'Shaughnessy's ally. We knew that removing him in just that manner would make her stop and think that perhaps it would be best to patch up her differences with us after all, besides leaving her without so violent a protector. You see, sir, I am being candid with you?"

"Yes. Keep it up. You didn't think he might have the falcon?"

Gutman shook his head so that his round cheeks wobbled. "We didn't think that for a minute," he replied. He smiled benevolently. "We had the advantage of knowing Miss O'Shaughnessy far too well for that and, while we didn't know then that she had given the falcon to Captain Jacobi in Hongkong to be brought over on the *Paloma* while they took a faster boat, still we didn't for a minute think that, if only one of them knew where it was, Thursby was the one."

Spade nodded thoughtfully and asked: "You didn't try to make a deal with him before you gave him the works?"

"Yes, sir, we certainly did. I talked to him myself that night. Wilmer had located him two days before and had been trying to follow him to wherever he was meeting Miss O'Shaughnessy, but Thursby was too crafty for that even if he didn't know he was being watched. So that night Wilmer went to his hotel, learned he wasn't in, and waited outside for him. I suppose Thursby returned immediately after killing your partner. Be that as it may, Wilmer brought him to see me. We could do nothing with him. He was quite determinedly loyal to Miss O'Shaughnessy. Well, sir, Wilmer followed him back to his hotel and did what he did."

Spade thought for a moment. "That sounds all right. Now Jacobi."

Gutman looked at Spade with grave eyes and said: "Captain Jacobi's death was entirely Miss O'Shaughnessy's fault."

The girl gasped, "Oh!" and put a hand to her mouth.

Spade's voice was heavy and even. "Never mind that now. Tell me what happened."

After a shrewd look at Spade, Gutman smiled. "Just as you say, sir," he said. "Well, Cairo, as you know, got in touch with me—I sent for him— after he left police headquarters the night—or morning—he was up here. We recognized the mutual advantage of pooling forces." He directed his smile at the Levantine. "Mr. Cairo is a man of nice judgment. The *Paloma* was his thought. He saw the notice of its arrival in the papers that morning and remembered that he had heard in Hongkong that Jacobi and Miss O'Shaughnessy had been seen together. That was when he had been trying to find her there, and he thought at first that she had left on the *Paloma*, though later he learned that she hadn't. Well, sir, when he saw the notice of arrival in the paper he guessed just what had happened: she had given the bird to Jacobi to bring here for her. Jacobi did not know what it was, of course. Miss O'Shaughnessy is too discreet for that."

He beamed at the girl, rocked his chair twice, and went on: "Mr. Cairo and Wilmer and I went to call on Captain Jacobi and were fortunate enough to arrive while Miss O'Shaughnessy was there. In many ways it was a difficult conference, but finally, by midnight we had persuaded Miss O'Shaughnessy to come to terms, or so we thought. We then left the boat and set out for my hotel, where I was to pay Miss O'Shaughnessy and receive the bird. Well, sir, we mere men should have known better than to suppose ourselves capable of coping with her. *En route*, she and Captain Jacobi and the falcon slipped completely through our fingers." He laughed merrily. "By Gad, sir, it was neatly done."

Spade looked at the girl. Her eyes, large and dark with pleading, met his. He asked Gutman: "You touched off the boat before you left?"

"Not intentionally, no, sir," the fat man replied, "though I dare say we—or Wilmer at least—were responsible for the fire. He had been out trying to find the falcon while the rest of us were talking in the cabin and no doubt was careless with matches."

"That's fine," Spade said. "If any slip-up makes it necessary for us to try him for Jacobi's murder we can also hang an arson-rap on him. All right. Now about the shooting."

"Well, sir, we dashed around town all day trying to find them and we found them late this afternoon. We weren't sure at first that we'd found them. All we were sure of was that we'd found Miss O'Shaughnessy's apartment. But when we listened at the door we heard them moving around inside, so we were pretty confident we had them and rang the bell. When she asked us who we were and we told her—through the door—we heard a window going up.

"We knew what that meant, of course; so Wilmer hurried downstairs as fast as he could and around to the rear of the building to cover the fire-escape. And when he turned into the alley he ran right plumb smack into Captain Jacobi running away with the falcon under his arm. That was a difficult situation to handle, but Wilmer did every bit as well as he could. He shot Jacobi—more than once—but Jacobi was too tough to either fall or drop the falcon, and he was too close for Wilmer to keep out of his way. He knocked Wilmer down and ran on. And this was in broad daylight, you understand, in the afternoon. When Wilmer got up he could see a policeman coming up from the block below. So he had to give it up. He dodged into the open back door of the building next the Coronet, through into the street, and then up to join us—and very fortunate he was, sir, to make it without being seen.

"Well, sir, there we were—stumped again. Miss O'Shaughnessy had opened the door for Mr. Cairo and me after she had shut the window behind Jacobi, and she—" He broke off to smile at a memory. "We persuaded—that is the word, sir—her to tell us that she had told Jacobi to take the falcon to you. It seemed very unlikely that he'd live to go that far, even if the police didn't pick him up, but that was the only chance we had, sir. And so, once more, we persuaded Miss O'Shaughnessy to give us a little assistance. We—well—persuaded her to phone your office in an attempt to draw you away before Jacobi got there, and we sent Wilmer after him. Unfortunately it had taken us too long to decide and to persuade Miss O'Shaughnessy to—"

The boy on the sofa groaned and rolled over on his side. His eyes opened and closed several times. The girl stood up and moved into the angle of table and wall again.

"—coöperate with us," Gutman concluded hurriedly, "and so you had the falcon before we could reach you."

The boy put one foot on the floor, raised himself on an elbow, opened his eyes wide, put the other foot down, sat up, and looked around. When his eyes focused on Spade bewilderment went out of them.

Cairo left his armchair and went over to the boy. He put his arm on the boy's shoulders and started to say something. The boy rose quickly to his feet, shaking Cairo's arm off. He glanced around the room once and then fixed his eyes on Spade again. His face was set hard and he held his body so tense that it seemed drawn in and shrunken.

Spade, sitting on the corner of the table, swinging his legs carelessly, said: "Now listen, kid. If you come over here and start cutting up I'm going to kick you in the face. Sit down and shut up and behave and you'll last longer."

The boy looked at Gutman.

Gutman smiled benignly at him and said: "Well, Wilmer, I'm sorry indeed to lose you, and I want you to know that I couldn't be any fonder of you if you were my own son; but—well, by Gad!—if you lose a son it's possible to get another—and there's only one Maltese falcon."

Spade laughed.

Cairo moved over and whispered in the boy's ear. The boy, keeping his cold hazel eyes on Gutman's face, sat down on the sofa again. The Levantine sat beside him.

Gutman's sigh did not affect the benignity of his smile. He said to Spade: "When you're young you simply don't understand things."

Cairo had an arm around the boy's shoulders again and was whispering to him. Spade grinned at Gutman and addressed Brigid O'Shaughnessy: "I think it'd be swell if you'd see what you can find us to eat in the kitchen, with plenty of coffee. Will you? I don't like to leave my guests."

"Surely," she said and started towards the door.

Gutman stopped rocking. "Just a moment, my dear." He held up a thick hand. "Hadn't you better leave the envelope in here? You don't want to get grease-spots on it."

The girl's eyes questioned Spade. He said in an indifferent tone: "It's still his."

She put her hand inside her coat, took out the envelope, and gave it to Spade. Spade tossed it into Gutman's lap, saying: "Sit on it if you're afraid of losing it."

"You misunderstand me," Gutman replied suavely. "It's not that at all, but business should be transacted in a business-like manner." He opened the flap of the envelope, took out the thousand-dollar bills, counted them, and chuckled so that his belly bounced. "For instance there are only nine bills here now." He spread them out on his fat knees and thighs. "There were ten when I handed it to you, as you very well know." His smile was broad and jovial and triumphant.

Spade looked at Brigid O'Shaughnessy and asked: "Well?"

She shook her head sidewise with emphasis. She did not say anything, though her lips moved slightly, as if she had tried to. Her face was frightened.

Spade held his hand out to Gutman and the fat man put the money into it. Spade counted the money—nine thousand-dollar bills—and returned it to Gutman. Then Spade stood up and his face was dull and placid. He picked up the three pistols on the table. He spoke in a matter-of-fact voice. "I want to know about this. We"—he nodded at the girl, but without looking at her—"are going in the bathroom. The door will be open and I'll be facing it. Unless you want a three-story drop there's no way out of here except past the bathroom door. Don't try to make it."

"Really, sir," Gutman protested, "it's not necessary, and certainly not very courteous of you, to threaten us in this manner. You must know that we've not the least desire to leave."

"I'll know a lot when I'm through." Spade was patient but resolute. "This trick upsets things. I've got to find the answer. It won't take long." He touched the girl's elbow. "Come on."

In the bathroom Brigid O'Shaughnessy found words. She put her hands up flat on Spade's chest and her face up close to his and whispered: "I did not take that bill, Sam."

"I don't think you did," he said, "but I've got to know. Take your clothes off."

"You won't take my word for it?"

"No. Take your clothes off."

"I won't."

"All right. We'll go back to the other room and I'll have them taken off."

She stepped back with a hand to her mouth. Her eyes were round and horrified. "You would?" she asked through her fingers.

"I will," he said. "I've got to know what happened to that bill and I'm not going to be held up by anybody's maidenly modesty."

"Oh, it isn't that." She came close to him and put her hands on his chest again. "I'm not ashamed to be naked before you, but—can't you see?—not like this. Can't you see that if you make me you'll—you'll be killing something?"

He did not raise his voice. "I don't know anything about that. I've got to know what happened to the bill. Take them off."

She looked at his unblinking yellow-grey eyes and her face became pink and then white again. She drew herself up tall and began to undress. He sat on the side of the bathtub watching her and the open door. No sound came from the living-room. She removed her clothes swiftly, without fumbling, letting them fall down on the floor around her feet. When she was naked she stepped back from her clothing and stood looking at him. In her mien was pride without defiance or embarrassment.

He put his pistols on the toilet-seat and, facing the door, went down on one knee in front of her garments. He picked up each piece and examined it with fingers as well as eyes. He did not find the thousand-dollar bill. When he had finished he stood up holding her clothes out in his hands to her. "Thanks," he said. "Now I know."

She took the clothing from him. She did not say anything. He picked up his pistols. He shut the bathroom door behind him and went into the living-room.

Gutman smiled amiably at him from the rocking chair. "Find it?" he asked.

Cairo, sitting beside the boy on the sofa, looked at Spade with questioning opaque eyes. The boy did not look up. He was leaning forward, head between hands, elbows on knees, staring at the floor between his feet.

Spade told Gutman: "No, I didn't find it. You palmed it."

The fat man chuckled. "I palmed it?"

"Yes," Spade said, jingling the pistols in his hand. "Do you want to say so or do you want to stand for a frisk?"

"Stand for—?"

"You're going to admit it," Spade said, "or I'm going to search you. There's no third way."

Gutman looked up at Spade's hard face and laughed outright. "By Gad, sir, I believe you would. I really do. You're a character, sir, if you don't mind my saying so."

"You palmed it," Spade said.

"Yes, sir, that I did." The fat man took a crumpled bill from his vest-pocket, smoothed it on a wide thigh, took the envelope holding the nine bills from his coat-pocket, and put the smoothed bill in with the others. "I must have my little joke every now and then and I was curious to know what you'd do in a situation of that sort. I must say that you passed the test with flying colors, sir. It never occurred to me that you'd hit on such a simple and direct way of getting at the truth."

Spade sneered at him without bitterness. "That's the kind of thing I'd expect from somebody the punk's age."

Gutman chuckled.

Brigid O'Shaughnessy, dressed again except for coat and hat, came out of the bathroom, took a step towards the living-room, turned around, went to the kitchen, and turned on the light.

Cairo edged closer to the boy on the sofa and began whispering in his ear again. The boy shrugged irritably.

Spade, looking at the pistols in his hand and then at Gutman, went out into the passageway, to the closet there. He opened the door, put the pistols inside on the top of a trunk, shut the door, locked it, put the key in his trousers-pocket, and went to the kitchen door.

Brigid O'Shaughnessy was filling an aluminum percolator.

"Find everything?" Spade asked.

"Yes," she replied in a cool voice, not raising her head. Then she set the percolator aside and came to the door. She blushed and her eyes were large and moist and chiding. "You shouldn't have done that to me, Sam," she said softly.

"I had to find out, angel." He bent down, kissed her mouth lightly, and returned to the living-room.

Gutman smiled at Spade and offered him the white envelope, saying: "This will soon be yours; you might as well take it now."

Spade did not take it. He sat in the armchair and said: "There's plenty of time for that. We haven't done enough talking about the money-end. I ought to have more than ten thousand."

Gutman said: "Ten thousand dollars is a lot of money."

Spade said: "You're quoting me, but it's not all the money in the world."

"No, sir, it's not. I grant you that. But it's a lot of money to be picked up in as few days and as easily as you're getting it."

"You think it's been so damned easy?" Spade asked, and shrugged. "Well, maybe, but that's my business."

"It certainly is," the fat man agreed. He screwed up his eyes, moved his head to indicate the kitchen, and lowered his voice. "Are you sharing with her?"

Spade said: "That's my business too."

"It certainly is," the fat man agreed once more, "but"—he hesitated—"I'd like to give you a word of advice."

"Go ahead."

"If you don't—I dare say you'll give her some money in any event, but —if you don't give her as much as she thinks she ought to have, my word of advice is—be careful."

Spade's eyes held a mocking light. He asked: "Bad?"

"Bad," the fat man replied.

Spade grinned and began to roll a cigarette.

Cairo, still muttering in the boy's ear, had put his arm around the boy's shoulders again. Suddenly the boy pushed his arm away and turned on the sofa to face the Levantine. The boy's face held disgust and anger. He made a fist of one small hand and struck Cairo's mouth with it. Cairo cried out as a woman might have cried and drew back to the very end of the sofa. He took a silk handkerchief from his pocket and put it to his mouth. It came away daubed with blood. He put it to his mouth once more and looked reproachfully at the boy. The boy snarled, "Keep away from me," and put his face between his hands again. Cairo's handkerchief released the fragrance of *chypre* in the room.

Cairo's cry had brought Brigid O'Shaughnessy to the door. Spade, grinning, jerked a thumb at the sofa and told her: "The course of true love. How's the food coming along?"

"It's coming," she said and went back to the kitchen.

Spade lighted his cigarette and addressed Gutman: "Let's talk about money."

"Willingly, sir, with all my heart," the fat man replied, "but I might as well tell you frankly right now that ten thousand is every cent I can raise."

Spade exhaled smoke. "I ought to have twenty."

"I wish you could. I'd give it to you gladly if I had it, but ten thousand dollars is every cent I can manage, on my word of honor. Of course, sir, you understand that is simply the first payment. Later—"

Spade laughed. "I know you'll give me millions later," he said, "but let's stick to this first payment now. Fifteen thousand?"

Gutman smiled and frowned and shook his head. "Mr. Spade, I've told you frankly and candidly and on my word of honor as a gentleman that ten thousand dollars is all the money I've got—every penny—and all I can raise."

"But you didn't say positively."

Gutman laughed and said: "Positively."

Spade said gloomily: "That's not any too good, but if it's the best you can do—give it to me."

Gutman handed him the envelope. Spade counted the bills and was putting them in his pocket when Brigid O'Shaughnessy came in carrying a tray.

The boy would not eat. Cairo took a cup of coffee. The girl, Gutman, and Spade ate the scrambled eggs, bacon, toast, and marmalade she had prepared, and drank two cups of coffee apiece. Then they settled down to wait the rest of the night through.

Gutman smoked a cigar and read *Celebrated Criminal Cases of America*, now and then chuckling over or commenting on the parts of its contents that amused him. Cairo nursed his mouth and sulked on his end of the sofa. The boy sat with his head in his hands until a little after four o'clock. Then he lay down with his feet towards Cairo, turned his face to the window, and went to sleep. Brigid O'Shaughnessy, in the armchair, dozed, listened to the fat man's comments, and carried on wide-spaced desultory conversations with Spade.

Spade rolled and smoked cigarettes and moved, without fidgeting or nervousness, around the room. He sat sometimes on an arm of the girl's chair, on the table-corner, on the floor at her feet, on a straight-backed chair. He was wide-awake, cheerful, and full of vigor.

At half-past five he went into the kitchen and made more coffee. Half an hour later the boy stirred, awakened, and sat up yawning. Gutman looked at his watch and questioned Spade: "Can you get it now?"

"Give me another hour."

Gutman nodded and went back to his book.

At seven o'clock Spade went to the telephone and called Effie Perine's number. "Hello, Mrs. Perine? . . . This is Mr. Spade. Will you let me talk to Effie, please? . . . Yes, it is. . . . Thanks." He whistled two lines of *En Cuba*, softly. "Hello, angel. Sorry to get you up. . . . Yes, very. Here's the plot: in our Holland box at the Post Office you'll find an envelope addressed in my scribble. There's a Pickwick Stage parcel-room-check in it—for the bundle we got yesterday. Will you get the bundle and bring it to me—p. d. q.? . . . Yes, I'm home. . . . That's the girl—hustle. . . . 'Bye."

The street-door-bell rang at ten minutes of eight. Spade went to the telephone-box and pressed the button that released the lock. Gutman put down his book and rose smiling. "You don't mind if I go to the door with you?" he asked.

"O K," Spade told him.

Gutman followed him to the corridor-door. Spade opened it. Presently Effie Perine, carrying the brown-wrapped parcel, came from the elevator. Her boyish face was gay and bright and she came forward quickly, almost trotting. After one glance she did not look at Gutman. She smiled at Spade and gave him the parcel.

He took it saying: "Thanks a lot, lady. I'm sorry to spoil your day of rest, but this—"

"It's not the first one you've spoiled," she replied, laughing, and then, when it was apparent that he was not going to invite her in, asked: "Anything else?"

He shook his head. "No, thanks."

She said, "Bye-bye," and went back to the elevator.

Spade shut the door and carried the parcel into the living-room. Gutman's face was red and his cheeks quivered. Cairo and Brigid O'Shaughnessy came to the table as Spade put the parcel there. They were excited. The boy rose, pale and tense, but he remained by the sofa, staring under curling lashes at the others.

Spade stepped back from the table saying: "There you are."

Gutman's fat fingers made short work of cord and paper and excelsior, and he had the black bird in his hands. "Ah," he said huskily, "now, after seventeen years!" His eyes were moist.

Cairo licked his red lips and worked his hands together. The girl's lower lip was between her teeth. She and Cairo, like Gutman, and like Spade and the boy, were breathing heavily. The air in the room was chilly and stale, and thick with tobacco smoke.

Gutman set the bird down on the table again and fumbled at a pocket. "It's it," he said, "but we'll make sure." Sweat glistened on his round cheeks. His fingers twitched as he took out a gold pocket-knife and opened it.

Cairo and the girl stood close to him, one on either side. Spade stood back a little where he could watch the boy as well as the group at the table.

Gutman turned the bird upside-down and scraped an edge of its base with his knife. Black enamel came off in tiny curls, exposing blackened metal beneath. Gutman's knife-blade bit into the metal, turning back a thin curved shaving. The inside of the shaving, and the narrow plane its removal had left, had the soft grey sheen of lead.

Gutman's breath hissed between his teeth. His face became turgid with hot blood. He twisted the bird around and hacked at its head. There too the edge of his knife bared lead. He let knife and bird bang down on the table while he wheeled to confront Spade. "It's a fake," he said hoarsely.

Spade's face had become somber. His nod was slow, but there was no slowness in his hand's going out to catch Brigid O'Shaughnessy's wrist. He pulled her to him and grasped her chin with his other hand, raising her face roughly. "All right," he growled into her face. "You've had *your* little joke. Now tell us about it."

She cried: "No, Sam, no! That is the one I got from Kemidov. I swear—"

Joel Cairo thrust himself between Spade and Gutman and began to emit words in a shrill spluttering stream: "That's it! That's it! It was the Russian! I should have known! What a fool we thought him, and what fools he made of us!" Tears ran down the Levantine's cheeks and he danced up and down. "You bungled it!" he screamed at Gutman. "You and your stupid attempt to buy it from him! You fat fool! You let him know it was valuable and he found out how valuable and made a duplicate for us! No wonder we had so little trouble stealing it! No wonder he was so willing to send me off around the world looking for it! You imbecile! You bloated idiot!" He put his hands to his face and blubbered.

Gutman's jaw sagged. He blinked vacant eyes. Then he shook himself and was—by the time his bulbs had stopped jouncing—again a jovial fat man. "Come, sir," he said good-naturedly, "there's no need of going on like that. Everybody errs at times and you may be sure this is every bit as severe a blow to me as to anyone else. Yes, that is the Russian's hand, there's no doubt of it. Well, sir, what do you suggest? Shall we stand here and shed tears and call each other names? Or shall we"—he paused and his smile was a cherub's—"go to Constantinople?"

Cairo took his hands from his face and his eyes bulged. He stammered: "You are—?" Amazement coming with full comprehension made him speechless.

Gutman patted his fat hands together. His eyes twinkled. His voice was a complacent throaty purring: "For seventeen years I have wanted that little item and have been trying to get it. If I must spend another year on the quest—well, sir—that will be an additional expenditure in time of only"—his lips moved silently as he calculated—"five and fifteen-seventeenths per cent."

The Levantine giggled and cried: "I go with you!"

Spade suddenly released the girl's wrist and looked around the room. The boy was not there. Spade went into the passageway. The corridor-door stood open. Spade made a dissatisfied mouth, shut the door, and returned to the living-room. He leaned against the door-frame and looked at Gutman and Cairo. He looked at Gutman for a long time, sourly. Then he spoke, mimicking the fat man's throaty purr: "Well, sir, I must say you're a swell lot of thieves!"

Gutman chuckled. "We've little enough to boast about, and that's a fact, sir," he said. "But, well, we're none of us dead yet and there's not a bit of use thinking the world's come to an end just because we've run into a little setback." He brought his left hand from behind him and held it out towards Spade, pink smooth hilly palm up. "I'll have to ask you for that envelope, sir."

Spade did not move. His face was wooden. He said: "I held up my end. You got your dingus. It's your hard luck, not mine, that it wasn't what you wanted."

"Now come, sir," Gutman said persuasively, "we've all failed and there's no reason for expecting any one of us to bear the brunt of it, and—" He brought his right hand from behind him. In the hand was a small pistol, an ornately engraved and inlaid affair of silver and gold and mother-of-pearl. "In short, sir, I must ask you to return my ten thousand dollars."

Spade's face did not change. He shrugged and took the envelope from his pocket. He started to hold it out to Gutman, hesitated, opened the envelope, and took out one thousand-dollar bill. He put that bill into his trousers-pocket. He tucked the envelope's flap in over the other bills and held them out to Gutman. "That'll take care of my time and expenses," he said.

Gutman, after a little pause, imitated Spade's shrug and accepted the envelope. He said: "Now, sir, we will say good-bye to you, unless"—the fat puffs around his eyes crinkled—"you care to undertake the Constantinople expedition with us. You don't? Well, sir, frankly I'd like to have you along. You're a man to my liking, a man of many resources and nice judgment. Because we know you're a man of nice judgment we know we can say good-bye with every assurance that you'll hold the details of our little enterprise in confidence. We know we can count on you to appreciate the fact that, as the situation now stands, any legal difficulties that come to us in connection with these last few days would likewise and equally come to you and the charming Miss O'Shaughnessy. You're too shrewd not to recognize that, sir, I'm sure."

"I understand that," Spade replied.

"I was sure you would. I'm also sure that, now there's no alternative, you'll somehow manage the police without a fall-guy."

"I'll make out all right," Spade replied.

"I was sure you would. Well, sir, the shortest farewells are the best. Adieu." He made a portly bow. "And to you, Miss O'Shaughnessy, adieu. I leave you the *rara avis* on the table as a little memento."

XX · *If They Hang You*

FOR all of five minutes after the outer door had closed behind Casper Gutman and Joel Cairo, Spade, motionless, stood staring at the knob of the open living-room-door. His eyes were gloomy under a forehead drawn down. The clefts at the root of his nose were deep and red. His lips protruded loosely, pouting. He drew them in to make a hard v and went to the telephone. He had not looked at Brigid O'Shaughnessy, who stood by the table looking with uneasy eyes at him.

He picked up the telephone, set it on its shelf again, and bent to look into the telephone-directory hanging from a corner of the shelf. He turned the pages rapidly until he found the one he wanted, ran his finger down a column, straightened up, and lifted the telephone from the shelf again. He called a number and said:

"Hello, is Sergeant Polhaus there? . . . Will you call him, please? This is Samuel Spade. . . ." He stared into space, waiting. "Hello, Tom, I've got something for you. . . . Yes, plenty. Here it is: Thursby and Jacobi were shot by a kid named Wilmer Cook." He described the boy minutely. "He's working for a man named Casper Gutman." He described Gutman. "That fellow Cairo you met here is in with them too. . . . Yes, that's it. . . . Gutman's staying at the Alexandria, suite twelve C, or was. They've just left here and they're blowing town, so you'll have to move fast, but I don't think they're expecting a pinch. . . . There's a girl in it too—Gutman's daughter." He described Rhea Gutman. "Watch yourself when you go up against the kid. He's supposed to be pretty good with the gun. . . . That's right, Tom, and I've got some stuff here for you. I think I've got the guns he used. . . . That's right. Step on it—and luck to you!"

Spade slowly replaced receiver on prong, telephone on shelf. He wet his lips and looked down at his hands. Their palms were wet. He filled his deep chest with air. His eyes were glittering between straightened lids. He turned and took three long swift steps into the living-room.

Brigid O'Shaughnessy, startled by the suddenness of his approach, let her breath out in a little laughing gasp.

Spade, face to face with her, very close to her, tall, big-boned and thick-muscled, coldly smiling, hard of jaw and eye, said: "They'll talk when they're nailed—about us. We're sitting on dynamite, and we've only got minutes to get set for the police. Give me all of it—fast. Gutman sent you and Cairo to Constantinople?"

She started to speak, hesitated, and bit her lip.

He put a hand on her shoulder. "God damn you, talk!" he said. "I'm in this with you and you're not going to gum it. Talk. He sent you to Constantinople?"

"Y-yes, he sent me. I met Joe there and—and asked him to help me. Then we—"

"Wait. You asked Cairo to help you get it from Kemidov?"

"Yes."

"For Gutman?"

She hesitated again, squirmed under the hard angry glare of his eyes, swallowed, and said: "No, not then. We thought we would get it for ourselves."

"All right. Then?"

"Oh, then I began to be afraid that Joe wouldn't play fair with me, so—so I asked Floyd Thursby to help me."

"And he did. Well?"

"Well, we got it and went to Hongkong."

"With Cairo? Or had you ditched him before that?"

"Yes. We left him in Constantinople, in jail—something about a check."

"Something you fixed up to hold him there?"

She looked shamefacedly at Spade and whispered: "Yes."

"Right. Now you and Thursby are in Hongkong with the bird."

"Yes, and then—I didn't know him very well—I didn't know whether I could trust him. I thought it would be safer—anyway, I met Captain Jacobi and I knew his boat was coming here, so I asked him to bring a package for me—and that was the bird. I wasn't sure I could trust Thursby, or that Joe or—or somebody working for Gutman might not be on the boat we came on—and that seemed the safest plan."

"All right. Then you and Thursby caught one of the fast boats over. Then what?"

"Then—then I was afraid of Gutman. I knew he had people—connections—everywhere, and he'd soon know what we had done. And I was afraid he'd have learned that we had left Hongkong for San Francisco. He was in New York and I knew if he heard that by cable he would have plenty of time to get here by the time we did, or before. He did. I didn't know that then, but I was afraid of it, and I had to wait here until Captain Jacobi's boat arrived. And I was afraid Gutman would find me—or find Floyd and buy him over. That's why I came to you and asked you to watch him for—"

"That's a lie," Spade said. "You had Thursby hooked and you knew it. He was a sucker for women. His record shows that—the only falls he took were over women. And once a chump, always a chump. Maybe you didn't know his record, but you'd know you had him safe."

She blushed and looked timidly at him.

He said: "You wanted to get him out of the way before Jacobi came with the loot. What was your scheme?"

"I—I knew he'd left the States with a gambler after some trouble. I didn't know what it was, but I thought that if it was anything serious and he saw a detective watching him he'd think it was on account of the old trouble, and would be frightened into going away. I didn't think—"

"You told him he was being shadowed," Spade said confidently. "Miles hadn't many brains, but he wasn't clumsy enough to be spotted the first night."

"I told him, yes. When we went out for a walk that night I pretended to discover Mr. Archer following us and pointed him out to Floyd." She sobbed. "But please believe, Sam, that I wouldn't have done it if I had thought Floyd would kill him. I thought he'd be frightened into leaving the city. I didn't for a minute think he'd shoot him like that."

Spade smiled wolfishly with his lips, but not at all with his eyes. He said: "If you thought he wouldn't you were right, angel."

The girl's upraised face held utter astonishment.

Spade said: "Thursby didn't shoot him."

Incredulity joined astonishment in the girl's face.

Spade said: "Miles hadn't many brains, but, Christ! he had too many years' experience as a detective to be caught like that by the man he was shadowing. Up a blind alley with his gun tucked away on his hip and his overcoat buttoned? Not a chance. He was as dumb as any man ought to be, but he wasn't quite that dumb. The only two ways out of the alley could be watched from the edge of Bush Street over the tunnel. You'd told us Thursby was a bad actor. He couldn't have tricked Miles into the alley like that, and he couldn't have driven him in. He was dumb, but not dumb enough for that."

He ran his tongue over the inside of his lips and smiled affectionately at the girl. He said: "But he'd've gone up there with you, angel, if he was sure nobody else was up there. You were his client, so he would have had no reason for not dropping the shadow on your say-so, and if you caught up with him and asked him to go up there he'd've gone. He was just dumb enough for that. He'd've looked you up and down and licked his lips and gone grinning from ear to ear—and then you could've stood as close to him as you liked in the dark and put a hole through him with the gun you had got from Thursby that evening."

Brigid O'Shaughnessy shrank back from him until the edge of the

table stopped her. She looked at him with terrified eyes and cried: "Don't
—don't talk to me like that, Sam! You know I didn't! You know—"

"Stop it." He looked at the watch on his wrist. "The police will be
blowing in any minute now and we're sitting on dynamite. Talk!"

She put the back of a hand on her forehead. "Oh, why do you accuse
me of such a terrible—?"

"Will you stop it?" he demanded in a low impatient voice. "This isn't
the spot for the schoolgirl-act. Listen to me. The pair of us are sitting
under the gallows." He took hold of her wrists and made her stand up
straight in front of him. "Talk!"

"I—I— How did you know he—he licked his lips and looked—?"

Spade laughed harshly. "I knew Miles. But never mind that. Why
did you shoot him?"

She twisted her wrists out of Spade's fingers and put her hands up
around the back of his neck, pulling his head down until his mouth all
but touched hers. Her body was flat against his from knees to chest. He
put his arms around her, holding her tight to him. Her dark-lashed lids
were half down over velvet eyes. Her voice was hushed, throbbing: "I
didn't mean to, at first. I didn't, really. I meant what I told you, but when
I saw Floyd couldn't be frightened I—"

Spade slapped her shoulder. He said: "That's a lie. You asked Miles
and me to handle it ourselves. You wanted to be sure the shadower was
somebody you knew and who knew you, so they'd go with you. You got
the gun from Thursby that day—that night. You had already rented the
apartment at the Coronet. You had trunks there and none at the hotel
and when I looked the apartment over I found a rent-receipt dated five
or six days before the time you told me you rented it."

She swallowed with difficulty and her voice was humble. "Yes, that's
a lie, Sam. I did intend to if Floyd— I—I can't look at you and tell you
this, Sam." She pulled his head farther down until her cheek was against
his cheek, her mouth by his ear, and whispered: "I knew Floyd wouldn't
be easily frightened, but I thought that if he knew somebody was shadowing him either he'd— Oh, I can't say it, Sam!" She clung to him, sobbing.

Spade said: "You thought Floyd would tackle him and one or the
other of them would go down. If Thursby was the one then you were rid
of him. If Miles was, then you could see that Floyd was caught and you'd
be rid of him. That it?"

"S-something like that."

"And when you found that Thursby didn't mean to tackle him you
borrowed the gun and did it yourself. Right?"

"Yes--though not exactly."

"But exact enough. And you had that plan up your sleeve from the
first. You thought Floyd would be nailed for the killing."

"I—I thought they'd hold him at least until after Captain Jacobi had arrived with the falcon and—"

"And you didn't know then that Gutman was here hunting for you. You didn't suspect that or you wouldn't have shaken your gunman. You knew Gutman was here as soon as you heard Thursby had been shot. Then you knew you needed another protector, so you came back to me. Right?"

"Yes, but—oh, sweetheart!—it wasn't only that. I would have come back to you sooner or later. From the first instant I saw you I knew—"

Spade said tenderly: "You angel! Well, if you get a good break you'll be out of San Quentin in twenty years and you can come back to me then."

She took her cheek away from his, drawing her head far back to stare up without comprehension at him.

He was pale. He said tenderly: "I hope to Christ they don't hang you, precious, by that sweet neck." He slid his hands up to caress her throat.

In an instant she was out of his arms, back against the table, crouching, both hands spread over her throat. Her face was wild-eyed, haggard. Her dry mouth opened and closed. She said in a small parched voice: "You're not—" She could get no other words out.

Spade's face was yellow-white now. His mouth smiled and there were smile-wrinkles around his glittering eyes. His voice was soft, gentle. He said: "I'm going to send you over. The chances are you'll get off with life. That means you'll be out again in twenty years. You're an angel. I'll wait for you." He cleared his throat. "If they hang you I'll always remember you."

She dropped her hands and stood erect. Her face became smooth and untroubled except for the faintest of dubious glints in her eyes. She smiled back at him, gently. "Don't, Sam, don't say that even in fun. Oh, you frightened me for a moment! I really thought you— You know you do such wild and unpredictable things that—" She broke off. She thrust her face forward and stared deep into his eyes. Her cheeks and the flesh around her mouth shivered and fear came back into her eyes. "What—? Sam!" She put her hands to her throat again and lost her erectness.

Spade laughed. His yellow-white face was damp with sweat and though he held his smile he could not hold softness in his voice. He croaked: "Don't be silly. You're taking the fall. One of us has got to take it, after the talking those birds will do. They'd hang me sure. You're likely to get a better break. Well?"

"But—but, Sam, you can't! Not after what we've been to each other. You can't—"

"Like hell I can't."

She took a long trembling breath. "You've been playing with me? Only pretending you cared—to trap me like this? You didn't—care at all? You didn't—don't—l-love me?"

"I think I do," Spade said. "What of it?" The muscles holding his smile in place stood out like wales. "I'm not Thursby. I'm not Jacobi. I won't play the sap for you."

"That is not just," she cried. Tears came to her eyes. "It's unfair. It's contemptible of you. You know it was not that. You can't say that."

"Like hell I can't," Spade said. "You came into my bed to stop me asking questions. You led me out yesterday for Gutman with that phoney call for help. Last night you came here with them and waited outside for me and came in with me. You were in my arms when the trap was sprung —I couldn't have gone for a gun if I'd had one on me and couldn't have made a fight of it if I had wanted to. And if they didn't take you away with them it was only because Gutman's got too much sense to trust you except for short stretches when he has to and because he thought I'd play the sap for you and—not wanting to hurt you—wouldn't be able to hurt him."

Brigid O'Shaughnessy blinked her tears away. She took a step towards him and stood looking him in the eyes, straight and proud. "You called me a liar," she said. "Now you are lying. You're lying if you say you don't know down in your heart that, in spite of anything I've done, I love you."

Spade made a short abrupt bow. His eyes were becoming bloodshot, but there was no other change in his damp and yellowish fixedly smiling face. "Maybe I do," he said. "What of it? I should trust you? You who arranged that nice little trick for—for my predecessor, Thursby? You who knocked off Miles, a man you had nothing against, in cold blood, just like swatting a fly, for the sake of double-crossing Thursby? You who double-crossed Gutman, Cairo, Thursby—one, two, three? You who've never played square with me for half an hour at a stretch since I've known you? I should trust you? No, no, darling. I wouldn't do it even if I could. Why should I?"

Her eyes were steady under his and her hushed voice was steady when she replied: "Why should you? If you've been playing with me, if you do not love me, there is no answer to that. If you did, no answer would be needed."

Blood streaked Spade's eyeballs now and his long-held smile had become a frightful grimace. He cleared his throat huskily and said: "Making speeches is no damned good now." He put a hand on her shoulder. The hand shook and jerked. "I don't care who loves who I'm not going to play the sap for you. I won't walk in Thursby's and Christ knows who else's footsteps. You killed Miles and you're going over for it. I could have helped you by letting the others go and standing off the police the best way I could. It's too late for that now. I can't help you now. And I wouldn't if I could."

She put a hand on his hand on her shoulder. "Don't help me then," she whispered, "but don't hurt me. Let me go away now."

"No," he said. "I'm sunk if I haven't got you to hand over to the police when they come. That's the only thing that can keep me from going down with the others."

"You won't do that for me?"

"I won't play the sap for you."

"Don't say that, please." She took his hand from her shoulder and held it to her face. "Why must you do this to me, Sam? Surely Mr. Archer wasn't as much to you as—"

"Miles," Spade said hoarsely, "was a son of a bitch. I found that out the first week we were in business together and I meant to kick him out as soon as the year was up. You didn't do me a damned bit of harm by killing him."

"Then what?"

Spade pulled his hand out of hers. He no longer either smiled or grimaced. His wet yellow face was set hard and deeply lined. His eyes burned madly. He said: "Listen. This isn't a damned bit of good. You'll never understand me, but I'll try once more and then we'll give it up. Listen. When a man's partner is killed he's supposed to do something about it. It doesn't make any difference what you thought of him. He was your partner and you're supposed to do something about it. Then it happens we were in the detective business. Well, when one of your organization gets killed it's bad business to let the killer get away with it. It's bad all around—bad for that one organization, bad for every detective everywhere. Third, I'm a detective and expecting me to run criminals down and then let them go free is like asking a dog to catch a rabbit and let it go. It can be done, all right, and sometimes it is done, but it's not the natural thing. The only way I could have let you go was by letting Gutman and Cairo and the kid go. That's—"

"You're not serious," she said. "You don't expect me to think that these things you're saying are sufficient reason for sending me to the—"

"Wait till I'm through and then you can talk. Fourth, no matter what I wanted to do now it would be absolutely impossible for me to let you go without having myself dragged to the gallows with the others. Next, I've no reason in God's world to think I can trust you and if I did this and got away with it you'd have something on me that you could use whenever you happened to want to. That's five of them. The sixth would be that, since I've also got something on you, I couldn't be sure you wouldn't decide to shoot a hole in *me* some day. Seventh, I don't even like the idea of thinking that there might be one chance in a hundred that you'd played me for a sucker. And eighth—but that's enough. All those on one side. Maybe some of them are unimportant. I won't argue about that. But look at the number of them. Now on the other side we've got what? All we've got is the fact that maybe you love me and maybe I love you."

"You know," she whispered, "whether you do or not."

"I don't. It's easy enough to be nuts about you." He looked hungrily from her hair to her feet and up to her eyes again. "But I don't know what that amounts to. Does anybody ever? But suppose I do? What of it? Maybe next month I won't. I've been through it before—when it lasted that long. Then what? Then I'll think I played the sap. And if I did it and got sent over then I'd be sure I was the sap. Well, if I send you over I'll be sorry as hell—I'll have some rotten nights—but that'll pass. Listen." He took her by the shoulders and bent her back, leaning over her. "If that doesn't mean anything to you forget it and we'll make it this: I won't because all of me wants to—wants to say to hell with the consequences and do it—and because—God damn you—you've counted on that with me the same as you counted on that with the others." He took his hands from her shoulders and let them fall to his sides.

She put her hands up to his cheeks and drew his face down again. "Look at me," she said, "and tell me the truth. Would you have done this to me if the falcon had been real and you had been paid your money?"

"What difference does that make now? Don't be too sure I'm as crooked as I'm supposed to be. That kind of reputation might be good business—bringing in high-priced jobs and making it easier to deal with the enemy."

She looked at him, saying nothing.

He moved his shoulders a little and said: "Well, a lot of money would have been at least one more item on the other side of the scales."

She put her face up to his face. Her mouth was slightly open with lips a little thrust out. She whispered: "If you loved me you'd need nothing more on that side."

Spade set the edges of his teeth together and said through them: "I won't play the sap for you."

She put her mouth to his, slowly, her arms around him, and came into his arms. She was in his arms when the door-bell rang.

Spade, left arm around Brigid O'Shaughnessy, opened the corridor-door. Lieutenant Dundy, Detective-sergeant Tom Polhaus, and two other detectives were there.

Spade said: "Hello, Tom. Get them?"

Polhaus said: "Got them."

"Swell. Come in. Here's another one for you." Spade pressed the girl forward. "She killed Miles. And I've got some exhibits—the boy's guns, one of Cairo's, a black statuette that all the hell was about, and a thousand-dollar bill that I was supposed to be bribed with." He looked at Dundy, drew his brows together, leaned forward to peer into the Lieutenant's face, and burst out laughing. "What in hell's the matter with your little playmate, Tom? He looks heartbroken." He laughed again. "I bet, by God! when he heard Gutman's story he thought he had me at last."

"Cut it out, Sam," Tom grumbled. "We didn't think—"

"Like hell he didn't," Spade said merrily. "He came up here with his mouth watering, though you'd have sense enough to know I'd been stringing Gutman."

"Cut it out," Tom grumbled again, looking uneasily sidewise at his superior. "Anyways we got it from Cairo. Gutman's dead. The kid had just finished shooting him up when we got there."

Spade nodded. "He ought to have expected that," he said.

Effie Perine put down her newspaper and jumped out of Spade's chair when he came into the office at a little after nine o'clock Monday morning.

He said: "Morning, angel."

"Is that—what the papers have—right?" she asked.

"Yes, ma'am." He dropped his hat on the desk and sat down. His face was pasty in color, but its lines were strong and cheerful and his eyes, though still somewhat red-veined, were clear.

The girl's brown eyes were peculiarly enlarged and there was a queer twist to her mouth. She stood beside him, staring down at him.

He raised his head, grinned, and said mockingly: "So much for your woman's intuition."

Her voice was queer as the expression on her face. "You did that, Sam, to her?"

He nodded. "Your Sam's a detective." He looked sharply at her. He put his arm around her waist, his hand on her hip. "She did kill Miles, angel," he said gently, "offhand, like that." He snapped the fingers of his other hand.

She escaped from his arm as if it had hurt her. "Don't, please, don't touch me," she said brokenly. "I know—I know you're right. You're right. But don't touch me now—not now."

Spade's face became pale as his collar.

The corridor-door's knob rattled. Effie Perine turned quickly and went into the outer office, shutting the door behind her. When she came in again she shut it behind her.

She said in a small flat voice: "Iva is here."

Spade, looking down at his desk, nodded almost imperceptibly. "Yes," he said, and shivered. "Well, send her in."

THE
GLASS KEY

TO NELL MARTIN

THE GLASS KEY

I · The Body in China Street

1

GREEN dice rolled across the green table, struck the rim together, and bounced back. One stopped short holding six white spots in two equal rows uppermost. The other tumbled out to the center of the table and came to rest with a single spot on top.

Ned Beaumont grunted softly—"Uhn!"—and the winners cleared the table of money.

Harry Sloss picked up the dice and rattled them in a pale broad hairy hand. "Shoot two bits." He dropped a twenty-dollar bill and a five-dollar bill on the table.

Ned Beaumont stepped back saying: "Get on him, gamblers, I've got to refuel." He crossed the billiard-room to the door. There he met Walter Ivans coming in. He said, "'Lo, Walt," and would have gone on, but Ivans caught his elbow as he passed and turned to face him.

"D-d-did you t-talk to P-p-paul?" When Ivans said "P-p-paul" a fine spray flew out between his lips.

"I'm going up to see him now." Ivans's china-blue eyes brightened in his round fair face until Ned Beaumont, narrow of eye, added: "Don't expect much. If you could wait awhile."

Ivans's chin twitched. "B-b-but she's going to have the b-b-baby next month."

A startled look came into Ned Beaumont's dark eyes. He took his arm out of the shorter man's hand and stepped back. Then a corner of his mouth twitched under his dark mustache and he said: "It's a bad time, Walt, and—well—you'll save yourself disappointment by not looking for much before November." His eyes were narrow again and watchful.

"B-b-but if you t-tell him—"

"I'll put it to him as hot as I can and you ought to know he'll go the limit, but he's in a tough spot right now." He moved his shoulders and his face became gloomy except for the watchful brightness of his eyes.

Ivans wet his lips and blinked his eyes many times. He drew in a long breath and patted Ned Beaumont's chest with both hands. "G-g-go up now," he said in an urgent pleading voice. "I-I'll wait here f-for you."

2

Ned Beaumont went upstairs lighting a thin green-dappled cigar. At the second-floor landing, where the Governor's portrait hung, he turned towards the front of the building and knocked on the broad oaken door that shut off the corridor at that end.

When he heard Paul Madvig's "All right" he opened the door and went in.

Paul Madvig was alone in the room, standing at the window, with his hands in his trousers-pockets, his back to the door, looking through the screen down into dark China Street.

He turned around slowly and said: "Oh, here you are." He was a man of forty-five, tall as Ned Beaumont, but forty pounds heavier without softness. His hair was light, parted in the middle, and brushed flat to his head. His face was handsome in a ruddy stout-featured way. His clothes were saved from flashiness by their quality and by his manner of wearing them.

Ned Beaumont shut the door and said: "Lend me some money."

From his inner coat-pocket Madvig took a large brown wallet. "What do you want?"

"Couple of hundred."

Madvig gave him a hundred-dollar bill and five twenties, asking: "Craps?"

"Thanks." Ned Beaumont pocketed the money. "Yes."

"It's a long time since you've done any winning, isn't it?" Madvig asked as he returned his hands to his trousers-pockets.

"Not so long—a month or six weeks."

Madvig smiled. "That's a long time to be losing."

"Not for me." There was a faint note of irritation in Ned Beaumont's voice.

Madvig rattled coins in his pocket. "Much of a game tonight?" He sat on a corner of the table and looked down at his glistening brown shoes.

Ned Beaumont looked curiously at the blond man, then shook his head and said: "Peewee." He walked to the window. Above the buildings on the opposite side of the street the sky was black and heavy. He went behind Madvig to the telephone and called a number. "Hello, Bernie. This is Ned. What's the price on Peggy O'Toole? . . . Is that all? . . . Well, give me five hundred of each. . . . Sure. . . . I'm betting it's going to rain and if it does she'll beat Incinerator. . . . All right, give me a better price then. . . . Right." He put the receiver on its prong and came around in front of Madvig again.

Madvig asked: "Why don't you try laying off awhile when you hit one of these sour streaks?"

Ned Beaumont scowled. "That's no good, only spreads it out. I ought to've put that fifteen hundred on the nose instead of spreading it across the board. Might as well take your punishment and get it over with."

Madvig chuckled and raised his head to say: "If you can stand the gaff."

Ned Beaumont drew down the ends of his mouth, the ends of his mustache following them down. "I can stand anything I've got to stand," he said as he moved towards the door.

He had his hand on the door-knob when Madvig said, earnestly: "I guess you can, at that, Ned."

Ned Beaumont turned around and asked, "Can what?" fretfully.

Madvig transferred his gaze to the window. "Can stand anything," he said.

Ned Beaumont studied Madvig's averted face. The blond man stirred uncomfortably and moved coins in his pockets again. Ned Beaumont made his eyes blank and asked in an utterly puzzled tone: "Who?"

Madvig's face flushed. He rose from the table and took a step towards Ned Beaumont. "You go to hell," he said.

Ned Beaumont laughed.

Madvig grinned sheepishly and wiped his face with a green-bordered handkerchief. "Why haven't you been out to the house?" he asked. "Mom was saying last night she hadn't seen you for a month."

"Maybe I'll drop in some night this week."

"You ought to. You know how Mom likes you. Come for supper." Madvig put his handkerchief away.

Ned Beaumont moved towards the door again, slowly, watching the blond man from the ends of his eyes. With his hand on the knob he asked: "Was that what you wanted to see me about?"

Madvig frowned. "Yes, that is—" He cleared his throat. "Uh—oh—there's something else." Suddenly his diffidence was gone, leaving him apparently tranquil and self-possessed. "You know more about this stuff than I do. Miss Henry's birthday's Thursday. What do you think I ought to give her?"

Ned Beaumont took his hand from the door-knob. His eyes, by the time he was facing Madvig squarely again, had lost their shocked look. He blew cigar-smoke out and asked: "They're having some kind of birthday doings, aren't they?"

"Yes."

"You invited?"

Madvig shook his head. "But I'm going there to dinner tomorrow night."

Ned Beaumont looked down at his cigar, then up at Madvig's face again, and asked: "Are you going to back the Senator, Paul?"

"I think we will."

Ned Beaumont's smile was mild as his voice when he put his next question: "Why?"

Madvig smiled. "Because with us behind him he'll snow Roan under and with his help we can put over the whole ticket just like nobody was running against us."

Ned Beaumont put his cigar in his mouth. He asked, still mildly: "Without you"—he stressed the pronoun—"behind him could the Senator make the grade this time?"

Madvig was calmly positive. "Not a chance."

Ned Beaumont, after a little pause, asked: "Does he know that?"

"He ought to know it better than anybody else. And if he didn't know it— What the hell's the matter with you?"

Ned Beaumont's laugh was a sneer. "If he didn't know it," he suggested, "you wouldn't be going there to dinner tomorrow night?"

Madvig, frowning, asked again: "What the hell's the matter with you?"

Ned Beaumont took the cigar from his mouth. His teeth had bitten the end of it into shredded ruin. He said: "There's nothing the matter with me." He put thoughtfulness on his face: "You don't think the rest of the ticket needs his support?"

"Support's something no ticket can get too much of," Madvig replied carelessly, "but without his help we could manage to hold up our end all right."

"Have you promised him anything yet?"

Madvig pursed his lips. "It's pretty well settled."

Ned Beaumont lowered his head until he was looking up under his brows at the blond man. His face had become pale. "Throw him down, Paul," he said in a low husky voice. "Sink him."

Madvig put his fists on his hips and exclaimed softly and incredulously: "Well, I'll be damned!"

Ned Beaumont walked past Madvig and with unsteady thin fingers mashed the burning end of his cigar in the hammered copper basin on the table.

Madvig stared at the younger man's back until he straightened and turned. Then the blond man grinned at him with affection and exasperation. "What gets into you, Ned?" he complained. "You go along fine for just so long and then for no reason at all you throw an ing-bing. I'll be a dirty so-and-so if I can make you out!"

Ned Beaumont made a grimace of distaste. He said, "All right, forget it," and immediately returned to the attack with a skeptical question: "Do you think he'll play ball with you after he's re-elected?"

Madvig was not worried. "I can handle him."

"Maybe, but don't forget he's never been licked at anything in his life."

Madvig nodded in complete agreement. "Sure, and that's one of the best reasons I know for throwing in with him."

"No, it isn't, Paul," Ned Beaumont said earnestly. "It's the very worst. Think that over even if it hurts your head. How far has this dizzy blonde daughter of his got her hooks into you?"

Madvig said: "I'm going to marry Miss Henry."

Ned Beaumont made a whistling mouth, though he did not whistle. He made his eyes smaller and asked: "Is that part of the bargain?"

Madvig grinned boyishly. "Nobody knows it yet," he replied, "except you and me."

Spots of color appeared in Ned Beaumont's lean cheeks. He smiled his nicest smile and said: "You can trust me not to go around bragging about it and here's a piece of advice. If that's what you want, make them put it in writing and swear to it before a notary and post a cash bond, or, better still, insist on the wedding before election-day. Then you'll at least be sure of your pound of flesh, or she'll weigh around a hundred and ten, won't she?"

Madvig shifted his feet. He avoided Ned Beaumont's gaze while saying: "I don't know why you keep talking about the Senator like he was a yegg. He's a gentleman and—"

"Absolutely. Read about it in the *Post*—one of the few aristocrats left in American politics. And his daughter's an aristocrat. That's why I'm warning you to sew your shirt on when you go to see them, or you'll come away without it, because to them you're a lower form of animal life and none of the rules apply."

Madvig sighed and began: "Aw, Ned, don't be so damned—"

But Ned Beaumont had remembered something. His eyes were shiny with malice. He said: "And we oughtn't to forget that young Taylor Henry's an aristocrat too, which is probably why you made Opal stop playing around with him. How's that going to work out when you marry his sister and he's your daughter's uncle-in-law or something? Will that entitle him to begin playing around with her again?"

Madvig yawned. "You didn't understand me right, Ned," he said. "I didn't ask for all this. I just asked you what kind of present I ought to give Miss Henry."

Ned Beaumont's face lost its animation, became a slightly sullen mask. "How far have you got with her?" he asked in a voice that expressed nothing of what he might have been thinking.

"Nowhere. I've been there maybe half a dozen times to talk to the Senator. Sometimes I see her and sometimes I don't, but only to say 'How do you do' or something with other people around. You know, I haven't had a chance to say anything to her yet."

Amusement glinted for a moment in Ned Beaumont's eyes and vanished. He brushed back one side of his mustache with a thumb-nail and asked: "Tomorrow's your first dinner there?"

"Yes, though I don't expect it to be the last."

"And you didn't get a bid to the birthday party?"

"No." Madvig hesitated. "Not yet."

"Then the answer's one you won't like."

Madvig's face was impassive. "Such as?" he asked.

"Don't give her anything."

"Oh, hell, Ned!"

Ned Beaumont shrugged. "Do whatever you like. You asked me."

"But why?"

"You're not supposed to give people things unless you're sure they'd like to get them from you."

"But everybody likes to—"

"Maybe, but it goes deeper than that. When you give somebody something, you're saying out loud that you know they'd like to have you give—"

"I got you," Madvig said. He rubbed his chin with fingers of his right hand. He frowned and said: "I guess you're right." His face cleared. He said: "But I'll be damned if I'll pass up the chance."

Ned Beaumont said quickly: "Well, flowers then, or something like that, might be all right."

"Flowers? Jesus! I wanted—"

"Sure, you wanted to give her a roadster or a couple of yards of pearls. You'll get your chance at that later. Start little and grow."

Madvig made a wry face. "I guess you're right, Ned. You know more about this kind of stuff than I do. Flowers it is."

"And not too many of them." Then, in the same breath: "Walt Ivans's telling the world you ought to spring his brother."

Madvig pulled the bottom of his vest down. "The world can tell him Tim's going to stay indoors till after election."

"You're going to let him stand trial?"

"I am," Madvig replied, and added with more heat: "You know damned well I can't help it, Ned. With everybody up for re-election and the women's clubs on the war-path it would be jumping in the lake to have Tim's case squared now."

Ned Beaumont grinned crookedly at the blond man and made his voice drawl. "We didn't have to do much worrying about women's clubs before we joined the aristocracy."

"We do now." Madvig's eyes were opaque.

"Tim's wife's going to have a baby next month," Ned Beaumont said.

Madvig blew breath out in an impatient gust. "Anything to make it tougher," he complained. "Why don't they think of those things before they get in trouble? They've got no brains, none of them."

"They've got votes."

"That's the hell of it," Madvig growled. He glowered at the floor for a moment, then raised his head. "We'll take care of him as soon as the votes are counted, but nothing doing till then."

"That's not going over big with the boys," Ned Beaumont said, looking obliquely at the blond man. "Brains or no brains, they're used to being taken care of."

Madvig thrust his chin out a little. His eyes, round and opaquely blue, were fixed on Ned Beaumont's. In a soft voice he asked: "Well?"

Ned Beaumont smiled and kept his voice matter-of-fact. "You know it won't take a lot of this to start them saying it was different in the old days before you put in with the Senator."

"Yes?"

Ned Beaumont stood his ground with no change in voice or smile. "You know how little of this can start them saying Shad O'Rory still takes care of his boys."

Madvig, who had listened with an air of complete attentiveness, now said in a very deliberately quiet voice: "I know you won't start them talking like that, Ned, and I know I can count on you to do your best to stop any of that kind of talk you happen to hear."

For a moment after that they stood silent, looking eye into eye, and there was no change in the face of either. Ned Beaumont ended the silence. He said: "It might help some if we took care of Tim's wife and the kid."

"That's the idea." Madvig drew his chin back and his eyes lost their opaqueness. "Look after it, will you? Give them everything."

3

Walter Ivans was waiting for Ned Beaumont at the foot of the stairs, bright-eyed and hopeful. "Wh-what did he s-say?"

"It's what I told you: no can do. After election Tim's to have anything he needs to get out, but nothing stirring till then."

Walter Ivans hung his head and made a low growling noise in his chest.

Ned Beaumont put a hand on the shorter man's shoulder and said: "It's a tough break and nobody knows it better than Paul, but he can't help himself. He wants you to tell her not to pay any bills. Send them to him—rent, grocer, doctor, and hospital."

Walter Ivans jerked his head up and caught Ned Beaumont's hand in both of his. "B-by G-god that's white of him!" The china-blue eyes were wet. "B-b-but I wish he could g-get Tim out."

Ned Beaumont said, "Well, there's always a chance that something will come up to let him," freed his hand, said, "I'll be seeing you," and went around Ivans to the billiard-room door.

The billiard-room was deserted.

He got his hat and coat and went to the front door. Long oyster-colored lines of rain slanted down into China Street. He smiled and addressed the rain under his breath: "Come down, you little darlings, thirty-two hundred and fifty dollars' worth of you."

He went back and called a taxicab.

4

Ned Beaumont took his hands away from the dead man and stood up. The dead man's head rolled a little to the left, away from the curb, so that his face lay fully in the light from the corner street-lamp. It was a young face and its expression of anger was increased by the dark ridge that ran diagonally across the forehead from the edge of the curly fair hair to an eyebrow.

Ned Beaumont looked up and down China Street. As far up the street as the eye could see no person was there. Two blocks down the street, in front of the Log Cabin Club, two men were getting out of an automobile. They left the automobile standing in front of the Club, facing Ned Beaumont, and went into the Club.

Ned Beaumont, after staring down at the automobile for several seconds, suddenly twisted his head around to look up the street again and then, with a swiftness that made both movements one continuous movement, whirled and sprang upon the sidewalk in the shadow of the nearest tree. He was breathing through his mouth and though tiny points of sweat had glistened on his hands in the light he shivered now and turned up the collar of his overcoat.

He remained in the tree's shadow with one hand on the tree for perhaps half a minute. Then he straightened abruptly and began to walk towards the Log Cabin Club. He walked with increasing swiftness, leaning forward, and was moving at something more than a half-trot when he spied a man coming up the other side of the street. He immediately slackened his pace and made himself walk erect. The man entered a house before he came opposite Ned Beaumont.

By the time Ned Beaumont reached the Club he had stopped breathing through his mouth. His lips were still somewhat faded. He looked at the empty automobile without pausing, climbed the Club's steps between the two lanterns, and went indoors.

Harry Sloss and another man were crossing the foyer from the cloakroom. They halted and said together: "Hello, Ned." Sloss added: "I hear you had Peggy O'Toole today."

"Yes."

"For much?"

"Thirty-two hundred."

Sloss ran his tongue over his lower lip. "That's nice. You ought to be set for a game tonight."

"Later, maybe. Paul in?"

"I don't know. We just got in. Don't make it too late: I promised the girl I'd be home early."

Ned Beaumont said, "Right," and went over to the cloak-room. "Paul in?" he asked the attendant.

"Yes, about ten minutes ago."

Ned Beaumont looked at his wrist-watch. It was half past ten. He went up to the front second-story room. Madvig in dinner clothes was sitting at the table with a hand stretched out towards the telephone when Ned Beaumont came in.

Madvig withdrew his hand and said: "How are you, Ned?" His large handsome face was ruddy and placid.

Ned Beaumont said, "I've been worse," while shutting the door behind him. He sat on a chair not far from Madvig's. "How'd the Henry dinner go?"

The skin at the corners of Madvig's eyes crinkled. "I've been at worse," he said.

Ned Beaumont was clipping the end of a pale spotted cigar. The shakiness of his hands was incongruous with the steadiness of his voice asking: "Was Taylor there?" He looked up at Madvig without raising his head.

"Not for dinner. Why?"

Ned Beaumont stretched out crossed legs, leaned back in his chair, moved the hand holding his cigar in a careless arc, and said: "He's dead in a gutter up the street."

Madvig, unruffled, asked: "Is that so?"

Ned Beaumont leaned forward. Muscles tightened in his lean face. The wrapper of his cigar broke between his fingers with a thin crackling sound. He asked irritably: "Did you understand what I said?"

Madvig nodded slowly.

"Well?"

"Well what?"

"He was killed."

"All right," Madvig said. "Do you want me to get hysterical about it?"

Ned Beaumont sat up straight in his chair and asked: "Shall I call the police?"

Madvig raised his eyebrows a little. "Don't they know it?"

Ned Beaumont was looking steadily at the blond man. He replied: "There was nobody around when I saw him. I wanted to see you before I did anything. Is it all right for me to say I found him?"

Madvig's eyebrows came down. "Why not?" he asked blankly.

Ned Beaumont rose, took two steps towards the telephone, halted, and faced the blond man again. He spoke with slow emphasis: "His hat wasn't there."

"He won't need it now." Then Madvig scowled and said: "You're a God-damned fool, Ned."

Ned Beaumont said, "One of us is," and went to the telephone.

5

TAYLOR HENRY MURDERED
BODY OF SENATOR'S SON FOUND
IN CHINA STREET

Believed to have been the victim of a hold-up, Taylor Henry, 26, son of Senator Ralph Bancroft Henry, was found dead in China Street near the corner of Pamela Avenue at a few minutes after 10 o'clock last night.

Coroner William J. Hoops stated that young Henry's death was due to a fracture of the skull and concussion of the brain caused by hitting the back of his head against the edge of the curb after having been knocked down by a blow from a blackjack or other blunt instrument on his forehead.

The body is believed to have been first discovered by Ned Beaumont, 914 Randall Avenue, who went to the Log Cabin Club, two blocks away, to telephone the police; but before he had succeeded in getting Police Headquarters on the wire, the body had been found and reported by Patrolman Michael Smitt.

Chief of Police Frederick M. Rainey immediately ordered a wholesale round-up of all suspicious characters in the city and issued a statement to the effect that no stone will be left unturned in his effort to apprehend the murderer or murderers at once.

Members of Taylor Henry's family stated that he left his home on Charles Street at about half past nine o'clock to . . .

Ned Beaumont put the newspaper aside, swallowed the coffee that remained in his cup, put cup and saucer on the table beside his bed, and leaned back against the pillows. His face was tired and sallow. He pulled the covers up to his neck, clasped his hands together behind his head, and stared with dissatisfied eyes at the etching that hung between his bedroom-windows.

For half an hour he lay there with only his eyelids moving. Then he picked up the newspaper and reread the story. As he read, dissatisfaction spread from his eyes to all his face. He put the paper aside again, got out of bed, slowly, wearily, wrapped his lean white-pajamaed body in a small-figured brown and black kimono, thrust his feet into brown slippers, and, coughing a little, went into his living-room.

It was a large room in the old manner, high of ceiling and wide of window, with a tremendous mirror over the fireplace and much red plush on the furnishings. He took a cigar from a box on the table and sat in a wide red chair. His feet rested in a parallelogram of late morning sun and the smoke he blew out became suddenly full-bodied as it drifted into the sunlight. He frowned now and chewed a finger-nail when the cigar was not in his mouth.

Knocking sounded on his door. He sat up straight, keen of eye and alert. "Come in."

A white-jacketed waiter came in.

Ned Beaumont said, "Oh, all right," in a disappointed tone and re-laxed again against the red plush of his chair.

The waiter passed through to the bedroom, came out with a tray of dishes, and went away. Ned Beaumont threw what was left of his cigar into the fireplace and went into his bathroom. By the time he had shaved, bathed, and dressed, his face had lost its sallowness, his carriage most of its weariness.

6

It was not quite noon when Ned Beaumont left his rooms and walked eight blocks to a pale grey apartment-building in Link Street. He pressed a button in the vestibule, entered the building when the door-lock clicked, and rode to the sixth floor in a small automatic elevator.

He pressed the bell-button set in the frame of a door marked 611. The door was opened immediately by a diminutive girl who could have been only a few months out of her teens. Her eyes were dark and angry, her face white, except around her eyes, and angry. She said, "Oh, hello," and with a smile and a vaguely placatory motion of one hand apologized for her anger. Her voice had a metallic thinness. She wore a brown fur coat, but not a hat. Her short-cut hair—it was nearly black—lay smooth and shiny as enamel on her round head. The gold-set stones pendant from her ear-lobes were carnelian. She stepped back pulling the door back with her.

Ned Beaumont advanced through the doorway asking: "Bernie up yet?"

Anger burned in her face again. She said in a shrill voice: "The crummy bastard!"

Ned Beaumont shut the door behind him without turning around.

The girl came close to him, grasped his arms above the elbows, and tried to shake him. "You know what I did for that bum?" she demanded. "I left the best home any girl ever had and a mother and father that thought I was the original Miss Jesus. They told me he was no good. Everybody told me that and they were right and I was too dumb to know it. Well, I hope to tell you I know it now, the . . ." The rest was shrill obscenity.

Ned Beaumont, motionless, listened gravely. His eyes were not a well man's now. He asked, when breathlessness had stopped her words for the moment: "What's he done?"

"Done? He's taken a run-out on me, the . . ." The rest of that sentence was obscenity.

Ned Beaumont flinched. The smile into which he pushed his lips was watery. He asked: "I don't suppose he left anything for me?"

The girl clicked her teeth together and pushed her face nearer his. Her eyes widened. "Does he owe you anything?"

"I won—" He coughed. "I'm supposed to have won thirty-two hundred and fifty bucks on the fourth race yesterday."

She took her hands from his arms and laughed scornfully. "Try and get it. Look." She held out her hands. A carnelian ring was on the little finger of her left hand. She raised her hands and touched her carnelian ear-rings. "That's every stinking piece of my jewelry he left me and he wouldn't't've left me that if I hadn't had them on."

Ned Beaumont asked, in a queer detached voice: "When does this happen?"

"Last night, though I didn't find it out till this morning, but don't think I'm not going to make Mr. Son-of-a-bitch wish to God he'd never seen me." She put a hand inside her dress and brought it out a fist. She held the fist up close to Ned Beaumont's face and opened it. Three small crumpled pieces of paper lay in her hand. When he reached for them she closed her fingers over them again, stepping back and snatching her hand away.

He moved the corners of his mouth impatiently and let his hand fall down at his side.

She said excitedly: "Did you see the paper this morning about Taylor Henry?"

Ned Beaumont's reply, "Yes," was calm enough, but his chest moved out and in with a quick breath.

"Do you know what these are?" She held the three crumpled bits of paper out in her open hand once more.

Ned Beaumont shook his head. His eyes were narrow, shiny.

"They're Taylor Henry's I O Us," she said triumphantly, "twelve hundred dollars' worth of them."

Ned Beaumont started to say something, checked himself, and when he spoke his voice was lifeless. "They're not worth a nickel now he's dead."

She thrust them inside her dress again and came close to Ned Beaumont. "Listen," she said: "they never were worth a nickel and that's why he's dead."

"Is that a guess?"

"It's any damned thing you want to call it," she told him. "But let me tell you something: Bernie called Taylor up last Friday and told him he'd give him just three days to come across."

Ned Beaumont brushed a side of his mustache with a thumb-nail. "You're not just being mad, are you?" he asked cautiously.

She made an angry face. "Of course I'm mad," she said. "I'm just mad enough to take them to the police and that's what I'm going to do. But if you think it didn't happen you're just a plain damned fool."

He seemed still unconvinced. "Where'd you get them?"

"Out of the safe." She gestured with her sleek head towards the interior of the apartment.

He asked: "What time last night did he blow?"

"I don't know. I got home at half past nine and sat around most of the night expecting him. It wasn't till morning that I began to suspect something and looked around and saw he'd cleaned house of every nickel in money and every piece of my jewelry that I wasn't wearing."

He brushed his mustache with his thumb-nail again and asked: "Where do you think he'd go?"

She stamped her foot and, shaking both fists up and down, began to curse the missing Bernie again in a shrill enraged voice.

Ned Beaumont said: "Stop it." He caught her wrists and held them still. He said: "If you're not going to do anything about it but yell, give me those markers and I'll do something about it."

She tore her wrists out of his hands, crying: "I'll give you nothing. I'll give them to the police and not to another damned soul."

"All right, then do it. Where do you think he'd go, Lee?"

Lee said bitterly that she didn't know where he would go, but she knew where she would like to have him go.

Ned Beaumont said wearily: "That's the stuff. Wisecracking is going to do us a lot of good. Think he'd go back to New York?"

"How do I know?" Her eyes had suddenly become wary.

Annoyance brought spots of color into Ned Beaumont's cheeks. "What are you up to now?" he asked suspiciously.

Her face was an innocent mask. "Nothing. What do you mean?"

He leaned down towards her. He spoke with considerable earnestness, shaking his head slowly from side to side with his words. "Don't think you're not going to the police with them, Lee, because you are."

She said: "Of course I am."

7

In the drug-store that occupied part of the ground-floor of the apartment-building Ned Beaumont used a telephone. He called the Police Department's number, asked for Lieutenant Doolan, and said: "Hello. Lieutenant Doolan? . . . I'm speaking for Miss Lee Wilshire. She's in Bernie Despain's apartment at 1666 Link Street. He seems to have suddenly disappeared last night, leaving some of Taylor Henry's I O Us behind him. . . . That's right, and she says she heard him threaten him a couple of days ago. . . . Yes, and she wants to see you as soon as possible. . . . No, you'd better come up or send and as soon as you can. . . . Yes. . . . That doesn't make any difference. You don't know me. I'm just speaking for her because she didn't want to phone from his apartment. . . ." He listened a moment longer, then, without having said anything else, put the receiver on its prong and went out of the drug-store.

8

Ned Beaumont went to a neat red brick house in a row of neat red brick houses in upper Thames Street. The door was opened to his ring by a young Negress who smiled with her whole brown face, said, "How do you do, Mr. Beaumont?" and made the opening of the door a hearty invitation.

Ned Beaumont said: " 'Lo, June. Anybody home?"

"Yes, sir, they still at the dinner-table."

He walked back to the dining-room where Paul Madvig and his mother sat facing one another across a red-and-white-clothed table. There was a third chair at the table, but it was not occupied and the plate and silver in front of it had not been used.

Paul Madvig's mother was a tall gaunt woman whose blondness had been faded not quite white by her seventy-some years. Her eyes were as blue and clear and young as her son's—younger than her son's when she looked up at Ned Beaumont entering the room. She deepened the lines in her forehead, however, and said: "So here you are at last. You're a worthless boy to neglect an old woman like this."

Ned Beaumont grinned impudently at her and said: "Aw, Mom, I'm a big boy now and I've got my work to look after." He flirted a hand at Madvig. " 'Lo, Paul."

Madvig said: "Sit down and June'll scrape you up something to eat."

Ned Beaumont was bending to kiss the scrawny hand Mrs. Madvig had held out to him. She jerked it away and scolded him: "Wherever do you learn such tricks?"

"I told you I was getting to be a big boy now." He addressed Madvig: "Thanks, I'm only a few minutes past breakfast." He looked at the vacant chair. "Where's Opal?"

Mrs. Madvig replied: "She's laying down. She's not feeling good."

Ned Beaumont nodded, waited a moment, and asked politely: "Nothing serious?" He was looking at Madvig.

Madvig shook his head. "Headache or something. I think the kid dances too much."

Mrs. Madvig said: "You certainly are a fine father not to know when your daughter has headaches."

Skin crinkled around Madvig's eyes. "Now, Mom, don't be indecent," he said and turned to Ned Beaumont. "What's the good word?"

Ned Beaumont went around Mrs. Madvig to the vacant chair. He sat down and said: "Bernie Despain blew town last night with my winnings on Peggy O'Toole."

The blond man opened his eyes.

Ned Beaumont said: "He left behind him twelve hundred dollars' worth of Taylor Henry's I O Us."

The blond man's eyes jerked narrow.

Ned Beaumont said: "Lee says he called Taylor Friday and gave him three days to make good."

Madvig touched his chin with the back of a hand. "Who's Lee?"

"Bernie's girl."

"Oh." Then, when Ned Beaumont said nothing, Madvig asked: "What'd he say he was going to do about it if Taylor didn't come across?"

"I didn't hear." Ned Beaumont put a forearm on the table and leaned over it towards the blond man. "Have me made a deputy sheriff or something, Paul."

"For Christ's sake!" Madvig exclaimed, blinking. "What do you want anything like that for?"

"It'll make it easier for me. I'm going after this guy and having a buzzer may keep me from getting in a jam."

Madvig looked through worried eyes at the younger man. "What's got you all steamed up?" he asked slowly.

"Thirty-two hundred and fifty dollars."

"That's all right," Madvig said, still speaking slowly, "but something was itching you last night before you knew you'd been welshed on."

Ned Beaumont moved an impatient arm. "Do you expect me to stumble over corpses without batting an eye?" he asked. "But forget that. That doesn't count now. This does. I've got to get this guy. I've got to." His face was pale, set hard, and his voice was desperately earnest. "Listen, Paul: it's not only the money, though thirty-two hundred is a lot, but it would be the same if it was five bucks. I go two months without winning a bet and that gets me down. What good am I if my luck's gone? Then I cop, or think I do, and I'm all right again. I can take my tail out from between my legs and feel that I'm a person again and not just something that's being kicked around. The money's important enough, but it's not the real thing. It's what losing and losing and losing does to me. Can you get that? It's getting me licked. And then, when I think I've worn out the jinx, this guy takes a Mickey Finn on me. I can't stand for it. If I stand for it I'm licked, my nerve's gone. I'm not going to stand for it. I'm going after him. I'm going regardless, but you can smooth the way a lot by fixing me up."

Madvig put out a big open hand and roughly pushed Ned Beaumont's drawn face. "Oh, hell, Ned!" he said, "sure I'll fix you up. The only thing is I don't like you getting mixed up in things, but—hell!—if it's like that—I guess the best shot would be to make you a special investigator in the District Attorney's office. That way you'll be under Farr and he won't be poking his nose in."

Mrs. Madvig stood up with a plate in each bony hand. "If I didn't make a rule of not ever meddling in men's affairs," she said severely, "I certainly would have something to say to the pair of you, running around with the good Lord only knows what kind of monkey-business afoot that's likely as not to get you into the Lord only knows what kind of trouble."

Ned Beaumont grinned until she had left the room with the plates. Then he stopped grinning and said: "Will you fix it up now so everything'll be ready this afternoon?"

"Sure," Madvig agreed, rising. "I'll phone Farr. And if there's anything else I can do, you know."

Ned Beaumont said, "Sure," and Madvig went out.

Brown June came in and began to clear the table.

"Is Miss Opal sleeping now, do you think?" Ned Beaumont asked.

"No, sir, I just now took her up some tea and toast."

"Run up and ask her if I can pop in for a minute?"

"Yes, sir, I sure will."

After the Negress had gone out, Ned Beaumont got up from the table and began to walk up and down the room. Spots of color made his lean cheeks warm just beneath his cheek-bones. He stopped walking when Madvig came in.

"Oke," Madvig said. "If Farr's not in see Barbero. He'll fix you up and you don't have to tell him anything."

Ned Beaumont said, "Thanks," and looked at the brown girl in the doorway.

She said: "She says to come right up."

9

Opal Madvig's room was chiefly blue. She, in a blue and silver wrapper, was propped up on pillows in her bed when Ned Beaumont came in. She was blue-eyed as her father and grandmother, long-boned as they and firm-featured, with fair pink skin still childish in texture. Her eyes were reddened now.

She dropped a piece of toast on the tray in her lap, held her hand out to Ned Beaumont, showed him strong white teeth in a smile, and said: "Hello, Ned." Her voice was not steady.

He did not take her hand. He slapped the back of it lightly, said, " 'Lo, snip," and sat on the foot of her bed. He crossed his long legs and took a cigar from his pocket. "Smoke hurt the head?"

"Oh, no," she said.

He nodded as if to himself, returned the cigar to his pocket, and dropped his careless air. He twisted himself around on the bed to look more directly at her. His eyes were humid with sympathy. His voice was husky. "I know, youngster, it's tough."

She stared baby-eyed at him. "No, really, most of the headache's gone and it wasn't so awfully wretched anyway." Her voice was no longer unsteady.

He smiled at her with thinned lips and asked: "So I'm an outsider now?"

She put a small frown between her brows. "I don't know what you mean, Ned."

Hard of mouth and eye, he replied: "I mean Taylor."

Though the tray moved a little on her knees, nothing in her face changed. She said: "Yes, but—you know—I hadn't seen him for months, since Dad made—"

Ned Beaumont stood up abruptly. He said, "All right," over his shoulder as he moved towards the door.

The girl in the bed did not say anything.

He went out of the room and down the stairs.

Paul Madvig, putting on his coat in the lower hall, said: "I've got to go down to the office to see about those sewer-contracts. I'll drop you at Farr's office if you want."

Ned Beaumont had said, "Fine," when Opal's voice came to them from upstairs: "Ned, oh, Ned!"

"Righto," he called back and then to Madvig: "Don't wait if you're in a hurry."

Madvig looked at his watch. "I ought to run along. See you at the Club tonight?"

Ned Beaumont said, "Uh-huh," and went upstairs again.

Opal had pushed the tray down to the foot of the bed. She said: "Close the door." When he had shut the door she moved over in bed to make a place for him to sit beside her. Then she asked: "What makes you act like that?"

"You oughtn't to lie to me," he said gravely as he sat down.

"But, Ned!" Her blue eyes tried to probe his brown ones.

He asked: "How long since you saw Taylor?"

"You mean to talk to?" Her face and voice were candid. "It's been weeks and—"

He stood up abruptly. He said, "All right," over his shoulder while walking towards the door.

She let him get within a step of the door before she called: "Oh, Ned, don't make it so hard for me."

He turned around slowly, his face blank.

"Aren't we friends?" she asked.

"Sure," he replied readily without eagerness, "but it's hard to remember it when we're lying to each other."

She turned sidewise in bed, laying her cheek against the topmost pillow, and began to cry. She made no sound. Her tears fell down on the pillow and made a greyish spot there.

He returned to the bed, sat down beside her again, and moved her head from the pillow to his shoulder.

She cried there silently for several minutes. Then muffled words came from where her mouth was pressed against his coat: "Did—did you know I had been meeting him?"

"Yes."

She sat up straight, alarmed. "Did Dad know it?"

"I don't think so. I don't know."

She lowered her head to his shoulder so that her next words were muffled. "Oh, Ned, I was with him only yesterday afternoon, all afternoon!"

He tightened his arm around her, but did not say anything.

After another pause she asked: "Who—who do you think could have done it to him?"

He winced.

She raised her head suddenly. There was no weakness in her now. "Do you know, Ned?"

He hesitated, wet his lips, mumbled: "I think I do."

"Who?" she asked fiercely.

He hesitated again, evading her eyes, then put a slow question to her: "Will you promise to keep it to yourself till the time comes?"

"Yes," she replied quickly, but when he would have spoken she stopped him by grabbing his nearer shoulder with both hands. "Wait. I won't promise unless you'll promise me that they won't get off, that they'll be caught and punished."

"I can't promise that. Nobody can."

She stared at him, biting her lip, then said: "All right, then, I'll promise anyway. Who?"

"Did he ever tell you that he owed a gambler named Bernie Despain more money than he could pay?"

"Did—did this Despain—?"

"I think so, but did he ever say anything to you about owing—?"

"I knew he was in trouble. He told me that, but he didn't say what it was except that he and his father had had a row about some money and that he was—'desperate' is what he said."

"Didn't mention Despain?"

"No. What was it? Why do you think this Despain did it?"

"He had over a thousand dollars' worth of Taylor's I O Us and couldn't collect. He left town last night in a hurry. The police are looking for him now." He lowered his voice, looking a little sidewise at her. "Would you do something to help them catch and convict him?"

"Yes. What?"

"I mean something a bit off-color. You see, it's going to be hard to convict him, but, if he's guilty, would you do something that might be a little bit—well—off-color to make sure of nailing him?"

"Anything," she replied.

He sighed and rubbed his lips together.

"What is it you want done?" she asked eagerly.

"I want you to get me one of his hats."

"What?"

"I want one of Taylor's hats," Ned Beaumont said. His face had flushed. "Can you get me one?"

She was bewildered. "But what for, Ned?"

"To make sure of nailing Despain. That's all I can tell you now. Can you get it for me or can't you?"

"I—I think I can, but I wish you'd—"

"How soon?"

"This afternoon, I think," she said, "but I wish—"

He interrupted her again. "You don't want to know anything about it. The fewer know about it the better, and the same thing goes for your getting the hat." He put his arm around her and drew her to him. "Did you really love him, snip, or was it just because your father—"

"I did really love him," she sobbed. "I'm pretty sure—I'm sure I did."

II · *The Hat Trick*

1

NED BEAUMONT, wearing a hat that did not quite fit him, followed the porter carrying his bags through Grand Central Terminal to a Forty-second Street exit, and thence to a maroon taxicab. He tipped the porter, climbed into the taxicab, gave its driver the name of a hotel off Broadway in the Forties, and settled back lighting a cigar. He chewed the cigar more than he smoked it as the taxicab crawled through theater-bound traffic towards Broadway.

At Madison Avenue a green taxicab, turning against the light, ran full tilt into Ned Beaumont's maroon one, driving it over against a car that was parked by the curb, hurling him into a corner in a shower of broken glass.

He pulled himself upright and climbed out into the gathering crowd. He was not hurt, he said. He answered a policeman's questions. He found the hat that did not quite fit him and put it on his head. He had his bags transferred to another taxicab, gave the hotel's name to the second driver, and huddled back in a corner, white-faced and shivering, while the ride lasted.

When he had registered at the hotel he asked for his mail and was given two telephone-memorandum-slips and two sealed envelopes without postage stamps.

He asked the bellboy who took him to his room to get him a pint of rye whisky. When the boy had gone he turned the key in the door and read the telephone-memoranda. Both slips were dated that day, one marked 4:50 P. M., the other 8:05 P. M. He looked at his wrist-watch. It was 8:45 P. M.

The earlier slip read: *At the Gargoyle.* The later read: *At Tom & Jerry's. Will phone later.* Both were signed: *Jack.*

He opened one of the envelopes. It contained two sheets of paper covered by bold masculine handwriting, dated the previous day.

She is staying at the Matin, room 1211, registered as Eileen Dale, Chicago. She did some phoning from the depot and connected with a man and girl who live E. 30th. They went to a lot of places, mostly speakies, probably hunting him, but don't seem to have much luck. My room is 734. Man and girl named Brook.

The sheet of paper in the other envelope, covered by the same handwriting, was dated that day.

I saw Deward this morning, but he says he did not know Bernie was in town. Will phone later.

Both of these messages were signed: *Jack.*

Ned Beaumont washed, put on fresh linen from his bags, and was lighting a cigar when the bellboy brought him his pint of whisky. He paid the boy, got a tumbler from the bathroom, and drew a chair up to the bedroom-window. He sat there smoking, drinking, and staring down at the other side of the street until his telephone-bell rang.

"Hello," he said into the telephone. "Yes, Jack. . . . Just now. . . . Where? . . . Sure. . . . Sure, on my way."

He took another drink of whisky, put on the hat that did not quite fit him, picked up the overcoat he had dropped across a chair-back, put it on, patted one of its pockets, switched off the lights, and went out.

It was then ten minutes past nine o'clock.

2

Through double swinging glazed doors under an electric sign that said *Tom & Jerry's* down the front of a building within sight of Broadway, Ned Beaumont passed into a narrow corridor. A single swinging door in the corridor's left wall let him into a small restaurant.

A man at a corner-table stood up and raised a forefinger at him. The man was of medium height, young and dapper, with a sleek dark rather good-looking face.

Ned Beaumont went over to him. " 'Lo, Jack," he said as they shook hands.

"They're upstairs, the girl and those Brook people," Jack told him. "You ought to be all right sitting here with your back to the stairs. I can spot them if they go out, or him coming in, and there's enough people in the way to keep him from making you."

Ned Beaumont sat down at Jack's table. "They waiting for him?"

Jack moved his shoulders. "I don't know, but they're doing some stalling about something. Want something to eat? You can't get anything to drink downstairs here."

Ned Beaumont said: "I want a drink. Can't we find a place upstairs where they won't see us?"

"It's not a very big joint," Jack protested. "There's a couple of booths up there where we might be hidden from them, but if he comes in he's likely to spot us."

"Let's risk it. I want a drink and I might as well talk to him right here if he does show up."

Jack looked curiously at Ned Beaumont, then turned his eyes away and said: "You're the boss. I'll see if one of the booths is empty." He hesitated, moved his shoulders again, and left the table.

Ned Beaumont twisted himself around in his chair to watch the dapper young man go back to the stairs and mount them. He watched the foot of the stairs until the young man came down again. From the second step Jack beckoned. He said, when Ned Beaumont had joined him there: "The best of them's empty and her back's this way, so you can get a slant at the Brooks as you go over."

They went upstairs. The booths—tables and benches set within breast-high wooden stalls—were to the right of the stair-head. They had to turn and look through a wide arch and down past the bar to see into the second-floor dining-room.

Ned Beaumont's eyes focused on the back of Lee Wilshire in sleeve-less fawn gown and brown hat. Her brown fur coat was hanging over the back of her chair. He looked at her companions. At her left was a hawk-nosed long-chinned pale man, a predatory animal of forty or so. Facing her sat a softly fleshed red-haired girl with eyes set far apart. She was laughing.

Ned Beaumont followed Jack to their stall. They sat down with the table between them. Ned Beaumont sat with his back to the dining-room, close to the end of his bench to take full advantage of the wooden wing's shelter. He took off his hat, but not his overcoat.

A waiter came. Ned Beaumont said: "Rye." Jack said: "Rickey."

Jack opened a package of cigarettes, took one out, and, staring at it, said: "It's your game and I'm working for you, but this isn't a hell of a good spot to go up against him if he's got friends here."

"Has he?"

Jack put the cigarette in a corner of his mouth so it moved batonwise with his words. "If they're waiting here for him, it might be one of his hang-outs."

The waiter came with their drinks. Ned Beaumont drained his glass immediately and complained: "Cut to nothing."

"Yes, I guess it is," Jack said and took a sip from his glass. He set fire to the end of his cigarette and took another sip.

"Well," Ned Beaumont said, "I'm going up against him as soon as he shows."

"Fair enough." Jack's good-looking dark face was inscrutable. "What do I do?"

Ned Beaumont said, "Leave it to me," and caught their waiter's attention.

He ordered a double Scotch, Jack another rickey. Ned Beaumont emptied his glass as soon as it arrived. Jack let his first drink be carried away no more than half consumed and sipped at his second. Presently Ned Beaumont had another double Scotch and another while Jack had time to finish none of his drinks.

Then Bernie Despain came upstairs.

Jack, watching the head of the stairs, saw the gambler and put a foot on Ned Beaumont's under the table. Ned Beaumont, looking up from his empty glass, became suddenly hard and cold of eye. He put his hands flat on the table and stood up. He stepped out of the stall and faced Despain. He said: "I want my money, Bernie."

The man who had come upstairs behind Despain now walked around him and struck Ned Beaumont very hard in the body with his left fist. He was not a tall man, but his shoulders were heavy and his fists were large globes.

Ned Beaumont was knocked back against a stall-partition. He bent forward and his knees gave, but he did not fall. He hung there for a moment. His eyes were glassy and his skin had taken on a greenish tinge. He said something nobody could have understood and went to the head of the stairs.

He went down the stairs, loose-jointed, pallid, and bare-headed. He
went through the downstairs dining-room to the street and out to the
curb, where he vomited. When he had vomited, he went to a taxicab that
stood a dozen feet away, climbed into it, and gave the driver an address
in Greenwich Village.

3

Ned Beaumont left the taxicab in front of a house whose open basement-
door, under brown stone steps, let noise and light out into a dark street.
He went through the basement-doorway into a narrow room where two
white-coated bar-tenders served a dozen men and women at a twenty-foot
bar and two waiters moved among tables at which other people sat.

The balder bar-tender said, "For Christ's sake, Ned!" put down the
pink mixture he was shaking in a tall glass, and stuck a wet hand out
across the bar.

Ned Beaumont said, " 'Lo, Mack," and shook the wet hand.

One of the waiters came up to shake Ned Beaumont's hand and
then a round and florid Italian whom Ned Beaumont called Tony. When
these greetings were over Ned Beaumont said he would buy a drink.

"Like hell you will," Tony said. He turned to the bar and rapped on
it with an empty cocktail-glass. "This guy can't buy so much as a glass of
water tonight," he said when he had the bar-tenders' attention. "What he
wants is on the house."

Ned Beaumont said: "That's all right for me, so I get it. Double
Scotch."

Two girls at a table in the other end of the room stood up and called
together: "Yoo-hoo, Ned!"

He told Tony, "Be back in a minute," and went to the girls' table.
They embraced him, asked him questions, introduced him to the men
with them, and made a place for him at their table.

He sat down and replied to their questions that he was back in New
York only for a short visit and not to stay and that his was double Scotch.

At a little before three o'clock they rose from their table, left Tony's
establishment, and went to another almost exactly like it three blocks
away, where they sat at a table that could hardly have been told from
the first and drank the same sort of liquor they had been drinking.

One of the men went away at half past three. He did not say good-by
to the others, nor they to him. Ten minutes later Ned Beaumont, the
other man, and the two girls left. They got into a taxicab at the corner
and went to a hotel near Washington Square, where the other man and
one of the girls got out.

The remaining girl took Ned Beaumont, who called her Fedink, to
an apartment in Seventy-third Street. The apartment was very warm.

When she opened the door warm air came out to meet them. When she was three steps inside the living-room she sighed and fell down on the floor.

Ned Beaumont shut the door and tried to awaken her, but she would not wake. He carried and dragged her difficultly into the next room and put her on a chintz-covered day-bed. He took off part of her clothing, found some blankets to spread over her, and opened a window. Then he went into the bathroom and was sick. After that he returned to the living-room, lay down on the sofa in all his clothes, and went to sleep.

4

A telephone-bell, ringing close to Ned Beaumont's head, awakened him. He opened his eyes, put his feet down on the floor, turned on his side, and looked around the room. When he saw the telephone he shut his eyes and relaxed.

The bell continued to ring. He groaned, opened his eyes again, and squirmed until he had freed his left arm from beneath his body. He put his wrist close to his eyes and looked at his watch, squinting. The watch's crystal was gone and its hands had stopped at twelve minutes to twelve.

Ned Beaumont squirmed again on the sofa until he was leaning on his left elbow, holding his head up on his left hand. The telephone-bell was still ringing. He looked around the room with miserably dull eyes. The lights were burning. Through an open doorway he could see Fedink's blanket-covered feet on an end of the day-bed.

He groaned again and sat up, running fingers through his tousled dark hair, squeezing his temples between the heels of his palms. His lips were dry and brownly encrusted. He ran his tongue over them and made a distasteful face. Then he rose, coughing a little, took off his gloves and overcoat, dropped them on the sofa, and went into the bathroom.

When he came out he went to the day-bed and looked down at Fedink. She was sleeping heavily, face down, one blue-sleeved arm crooked above her head. The telephone-bell had stopped ringing. He pulled his tie straight and returned to the living-room.

Three Murad cigarettes were in an open box on the table between two chairs. He picked up one of the cigarettes, muttered, "Nonchalant," without humor, found a paper of matches, lit the cigarette, and went into the kitchen. He squeezed the juice of four oranges into a tall glass and drank it. He made and drank two cups of coffee.

As he came out of the kitchen Fedink asked in a woefully flat voice: "Where's Ted?" Her one visible eye was partially open.

Ned Beaumont went over to her. "Who's Ted?" he asked.

"That fellow I was with."

"Were you with somebody? How do I know?"

She opened her mouth and made an unpleasant clucking sound shutting it. "What time is it?"

"I don't know that either. Somewhere around daylight."

She rubbed her face into the chintz cushion under it and said: "A swell guy I turned out to be, promising to marry him yesterday and then leaving him to take the first tramp I run into home with me." She opened and shut the hand that was above her head. "Or am I home?"

"You had a key to the place, anyway," Ned Beaumont told her. "Want some orange-juice and coffee?"

"I don't want a damned thing except to die. Will you go away, Ned, and not ever come back?"

"It's going to be hard on me," he said ill-naturedly, "but I'll try."

He put on his overcoat and gloves, took a dark wrinkled cap from one overcoat-pocket, put the cap on, and left the house.

5

Half an hour later Ned Beaumont was knocking on the door of room 734 at his hotel. Presently Jack's voice, drowsy, came through the door: "Who's that?"

"Beaumont."

"Oh," without enthusiasm, "all right."

Jack opened the door and turned on the lights. He was in green-spotted pajamas. His feet were bare. His eyes were dull, his face flushed, with sleepiness. He yawned, nodded, and went back to bed, where he stretched himself out on his back and stared at the ceiling. Then he asked, with not much interest: "How are you this morning?"

Ned Beaumont had shut the door. He stood between door and bed looking sullenly at the man in the bed. He asked: "What happened after I left?"

"Nothing happened." Jack yawned again. "Or do you mean what did I do?" He did not wait for a reply. "I went out and took a plant across the street till they came out. Despain and the girl and the guy that slugged you came out. They went to the Buckman, Forty-eighth Street. That's where Despain's holing up—apartment 938—name of Barton Dewey. I hung around there till after three and then knocked off. They were all still in there unless they were fooling me." He jerked his head slightly in the direction of a corner of the room. "Your hat's on the chair there. I thought I might as well save it for you."

Ned Beaumont went over to the chair and picked up the hat that did not quite fit him. He stuffed the wrinkled dark cap in his overcoat-pocket and put the hat on his head.

Jack said: "There's some gin on the table if you want a shot."

Ned Beaumont said: "No, thanks. Have you got a gun?"

Jack stopped staring at the ceiling. He sat up in bed, stretched his arms out wide, yawned for the third time, and asked: "What are you figuring on doing?" His voice held nothing beyond polite curiosity.

"I'm going to see Despain."

Jack had drawn his knees up, had clasped his hands around them, and was sitting hunched forward a little staring at the foot of the bed. He said slowly: "I don't think you ought to, not right now."

"I've got to, right now," Ned Beaumont said.

His voice made Jack look at him. Ned Beaumont's face was an unhealthy yellowish grey. His eyes were muddy, red-rimmed, not sufficiently open to show any of the whites. His lips were dry and somewhat thicker than usual.

"Been up all night?" Jack asked.

"I got some sleep."

"Unkdray?"

"Yes, but how about the gun?"

Jack swung his legs out from beneath the covers and down over the side of the bed. "Why don't you get some sleep first? Then we can go after them. You're in no shape now."

Ned Beaumont said: "I'm going now."

Jack said: "All right, but you're wrong. You know they're no babies to go up against shaky. They mean it."

"Where's the gun?" Ned Beaumont asked.

Jack stood up and began to unbutton his pajama-coat.

Ned Beaumont said: "Give me the gun and get back in bed. I'm going."

Jack fastened the button he had just unfastened and got into bed. "The gun's in the top bureau-drawer," he said. "There are extra cartridges in there too if you want them." He turned over on his side and shut his eyes.

Ned Beaumont found the pistol, put it in a hip-pocket, said, "See you later," switched off the lights, and went out.

6

The Buckman was a square-built yellow apartment-building that filled most of the block it stood in. Inside, Ned Beaumont said he wanted to see Mr. Dewey. When asked for his name he said: "Ned Beaumont."

Five minutes later he was walking away from an elevator down a long corridor towards an open door where Bernie Despain stood.

Despain was a small man, short and stringy, with a head too large for his body. The size of his head was exaggerated until it seemed a deformity by long thick fluffy waved hair. His face was swarthy, large-featured except for the eyes, and strongly lined across the forehead and down from nostrils past the mouth. He had a faintly reddish scar on one cheek. His blue suit was carefully pressed and he wore no jewelry.

He stood in the doorway, smiling sardonically, and said: "Good morning, Ned."

Ned Beaumont said: "I want to talk to you, Bernie."

"I guessed you did. As soon as they phoned your name up I said to myself: 'I bet you he wants to talk to me.'"

Ned Beaumont said nothing. His yellow face was tight-lipped.

Despain's smile became looser. He said: "Well, my boy, you don't have to stand here. Come on in." He stepped aside.

The door opened into a small vestibule. Through an opposite door that stood open Lee Wilshire and the man who had struck Ned Beaumont could be seen. They had stopped packing two traveling-bags to look at Ned Beaumont.

He went into the vestibule.

Despain followed him in, shut the corridor-door, and said: "The Kid's kind of hasty and when you come up to me like that he thought maybe you were looking for trouble, see? I give him hell about it and maybe if you ask him he'll apologize."

The Kid said something in an undertone to Lee Wilshire, who was glaring at Ned Beaumont. She laughed a vicious little laugh and replied: "Yes, a sportsman to the last."

Bernie Despain said: "Go right in, Mr. Beaumont. You've already met the folks, haven't you?"

Ned Beaumont advanced into the room where Lee and the Kid were.

The Kid asked: "How's the belly?"

Ned Beaumont did not say anything.

Bernie Despain exclaimed: "Jesus! For a guy that says he came up here to talk you've done less of it than anybody I ever heard of."

"I want to talk to you," Ned Beaumont said. "Do we have to have all these people around?"

"I do," Despain replied. "You don't. You can get away from them just by walking out and going about your own business."

"I've got business here."

"That's right, there was something about money." Despain grinned at the Kid. "Wasn't there something about money, Kid?"

The Kid had moved to stand in the doorway through which Ned Beaumont had come into the room. "Something," he said in a rasping voice, "but I forget what."

Ned Beaumont took off his overcoat and hung it on the back of a brown easy-chair. He sat down in the chair and put his hat behind him. He said: "That's not my business this time. I'm—let's see." He took a paper from his inner coat-pocket, unfolded it, glanced at it, and said: "I'm here as special investigator for the District Attorney's office."

For a small fraction of a second the twinkle in Despain's eyes was blurred, but he said immediately: "Ain't you getting up in the world! The last time I saw you you were just punking around for Paul."

Ned Beaumont refolded the paper and returned it to his pocket.

Despain said: "Well, go ahead, investigate something for us—anything—just to show us how it's done." He sat down facing Ned Beaumont, wagging his too-large head. "You ain't going to tell me you came all the way to New York to ask me about killing Taylor Henry?"

"Yes."

"That's too bad. I could've saved you the trip." He flourished a hand at the traveling-bags on the floor. "As soon as Lee told me what it was all about I started packing up to go back and laugh at your frame-up."

Ned Beaumont lounged back comfortably in his chair. One of his hands was behind him. He said: "If it's a frame-up it's Lee's. The police got their dope from her."

"Yes," she said angrily, "when I had to because you sent them there, you bastard."

Despain said: "Uh-huh, Lee's a dumb cluck, all right, but those markers don't mean anything. They—"

"I'm a dumb cluck, am I?" Lee cried indignantly. "Didn't I come all the way here to warn you after you'd run off with every stinking piece of—"

"Yes." Despain agreed pleasantly, "and coming here shows just what a dumb cluck you are, because you led this guy right to me."

"If that's the way you feel about it I'm damned glad I did give the police those I O Us, and what do you think of that?"

Despain said: "I'll tell you just exactly what I think of it after our company's gone." He turned to Ned Beaumont. "So honest Paul Madvig's letting you drop the shuck on me, huh?"

Ned Beaumont smiled. "You're not being framed, Bernie, and you know it. Lee gave us the lead-in and the rest that we got clicked with it."

"There's some more besides what she gave you?"

"Plenty."

"What?"

Ned Beaumont smiled again. "There are lots of things I could say to you, Bernie, that I wouldn't want to say in front of a crowd."

Despain said: "Nuts!"

The Kid spoke from the doorway to Despain in his rasping voice: "Let's chuck this sap out on his can and get going."

"Wait," Despain said. Then he frowned and put a question to Ned Beaumont: "Is there a warrant out for me?"

"Well, I don't—"

"Yes or no?" Despain's bantering humor was gone.

Ned Beaumont said slowly: "Not that I know of."

Despain stood up and pushed his chair back. "Then get the hell out of here and make it quick, or I'll let the Kid take another poke at you."

Ned Beaumont stood up. He picked up his overcoat. He took his cap out of his overcoat-pocket and, holding it in one hand, his overcoat over the other arm, said seriously: "You'll be sorry." Then he walked out in a dignified manner. The Kid's rasping laughter and Lee's shriller hooting followed him out.

7

Outside the Buckman Ned Beaumont started briskly down the street. His eyes were glowing in his tired face and his dark mustache twitched above a flickering smile.

At the first corner he came face to face with Jack. He asked: "What are you doing here?"

Jack said: "I'm still working for you, far as I know, so I came along to see if I could find anything to do."

"Swell. Find us a taxi quick. They're sliding out."

Jack said, "Ay, ay," and went down the street.

Ned Beaumont remained on the corner. The front and side entrances of the Buckman could be seen from there.

In a little while Jack returned in a taxicab. Ned Beaumont got into it and they told the driver where to park it.

"What did you do to them?" Jack asked when they were sitting still.

"Things."

"Oh."

Ten minutes passed and Jack, saying, "Look," was pointing a forefinger at a taxicab drawing up to the Buckman's side door.

The Kid, carrying two traveling-bags, left the building first, then, when he was in the taxicab, Despain and the girl ran out to join him. The taxicab ran away.

Jack leaned forward and told his driver what to do. They ran along in the other cab's wake. They wound through streets that were bright with morning sunlight, going by a devious route finally to a battered brown stone house in west Forty-ninth Street.

Despain's cab stopped in front of the house and, once more, the Kid was the first of the trio out on the sidewalk. He looked up and down the street. He went up to the front door of the house and unlocked it. Then he returned to the taxicab. Despain and the girl jumped out and went indoors hurriedly. The Kid followed with the bags.

"Stick here with the cab," Ned Beaumont told Jack.

"What are you going to do?"

"Try my luck."

Jack shook his head. "This is another wrong neighborhood to look for trouble in," he said.

Ned Beaumont said: "If I come out with Despain, you beat it. Get another taxi and go back to watch the Buckman. If I don't come out, use your own judgment."

He opened the cab-door and stepped out. He was shivering. His eyes were shiny. He ignored something that Jack leaned out to say and hurried across the street to the house into which the two men and the girl had gone.

He went straight up the front steps and put a hand on the door-knob. The knob turned in his hand. The door was not locked. He pushed it open and, after peering into the dim hallway, went in.

The door slammed shut behind him and one of the Kid's fists struck his head a glancing blow that carried his cap away and sent him crashing into the wall. He sank down a little, giddily, almost to one knee, and the Kid's other fist struck the wall over his head.

He pulled his lips back over his teeth and drove a fist into the Kid's groin, a short sharp blow that brought a snarl from the Kid and made him fall back so that Ned Beaumont could pull himself up straight before the Kid was upon him again.

Up the hallway a little, Bernie Despain was leaning against the wall, his mouth stretched wide and thin, his eyes narrowed to dark points, saying over and over in a low voice: "Sock him, Kid, sock him. . . ." Lee Wilshire was not in sight.

The Kid's next two blows landed on Ned Beaumont's chest, mashing him against the wall, making him cough. The third, aimed at his face, he avoided. Then he pushed the Kid away from him with a forearm against his throat and kicked the Kid in the belly. The Kid roared angrily and came in with both fists going, but forearm and foot had carried him away from Ned Beaumont and had given Ned Beaumont time to get his right hand to his hip-pocket and to get Jack's revolver out of his pocket. He had not time to level the revolver, but, holding it at a downward angle, he pulled the trigger and managed to shoot the Kid in the right thigh. The Kid yelped and fell down on the hallway floor. He lay there looking up at Ned Beaumont with frightened bloodshot eyes.

Ned Beaumont stepped back from him, put his left hand in his trousers-pocket, and addressed Bernie Despain: "Come on out with me. I want to talk to you." His face was sullenly determined.

Footsteps ran overhead, somewhere back in the building a door opened, and down the hallway excited voices were audible, but nobody came into sight.

Despain stared for a long moment at Ned Beaumont as if horribly fascinated. Then, without a word, he stepped over the man on the floor and went out of the building ahead of Ned Beaumont. Ned Beaumont put the revolver in his jacket-pocket before he went down the street-steps, but he kept his hand on it.

"Up to that taxi," he told Despain, indicating the car out of which Jack was getting. When they reached the taxicab he told the chauffeur to drive them anywhere, "just around till I tell you where to go."

They were in motion when Despain found his voice. He said: "This is a hold-up. I'll give you anything you want because I don't want to be killed, but it's just a hold-up."

Ned Beaumont laughed disagreeably and shook his head. "Don't forget I've risen in the world to be something or other in the District Attorney's office."

"But there's no charge against me. I'm not wanted. You said—"

"I was spoofing you, Bernie, for reasons. You're wanted."

"For what?"

"Killing Taylor Henry."

"That? Hell, I'll go back and face that. What've you got against me? I had some of his markers, sure. And I left the night he was killed, sure. And I gave him hell because he wouldn't make them good, sure. What kind of case is that for a first-class lawyer to beat? Jesus, if I left the markers behind in my safe at some time before nine-thirty—to go by Lee's story—don't that show I wasn't trying to collect that night?"

"No, and that isn't all the stuff we've got on you."

"That's all there could be," Despain said earnestly.

Ned Beaumont sneered. "Wrong, Bernie. Remember I had a hat on when I came to see you this morning?"

"Maybe. I think you did."

"Remember I took a cap out of my overcoat-pocket and put it on when I left?"

Bewilderment, fear, began to come into the swarthy man's small eyes. "By Jesus! Well? What are you getting at?"

"I'm getting at the evidence. Do you remember the hat didn't fit me very well?"

Bernie Despain's voice was hoarse: "I don't know, Ned. For Christ's sake, what do you mean?"

"I mean it didn't fit me because it wasn't my hat. Do you remember that the hat Taylor was wearing when he was murdered wasn't found?"

"I don't know. I don't know anything about him."

"Well, I'm trying to tell you the hat I had this morning was Taylor's hat and it's now planted down between the cushion-seat and the back of that brown easy-chair in the apartment you had at the Buckman. Do you think that, with the rest, would be enough to set you on the hot seat?"

Despain would have screamed in terror if Ned Beaumont had not clapped a hand over his mouth and growled, "Shut up," in his ear.

Sweat ran down the swarthy face. Despain fell over on Ned Beaumont, seizing the lapels of his coat with both hands, babbling: "Listen, don't you do that to me, Ned. You can have every cent I owe you, every cent with interest, if you won't do that. I never meant to rob you, Ned, honest to God. It was just that I was caught short and thought I'd treat it like a loan. Honest to God, Ned. I ain't got much now, but I'm fixed to get the money for Lee's rocks that I'm selling today and I'll give you your dough, every nickel of it, out of that. How much was it, Ned? I'll give you all of it right away, this morning."

Ned Beaumont pushed the swarthy man over to his own side of the taxicab and said: "It was thirty-two hundred and fifty dollars."

"Thirty-two hundred and fifty dollars. You'll get it, every cent of it, this morning, right away." Despain looked at his watch. "Yes, sir, right this minute as soon as we can get there. Old Stein will be at his place before this. Only say you'll let me go, Ned, for old times' sake."

Ned Beaumont rubbed his hands together thoughtfully. "I can't exactly let you go. Not right now, I mean. I've got to remember the District Attorney connection and that you're wanted for questioning. So all we can dicker about is the hat. Here's the proposition: give me my money and I'll see that I'm alone when I turn up the hat and nobody else will ever know about it. Otherwise I'll see that half the New York police are with me and— There you are. Take it or leave it."

"Oh, God!" Bernie Despain groaned. "Tell him to drive us to old Stein's place. It's on . . ."

III · *The Cyclone Shot*

1

NED BEAUMONT leaving the train that had brought him back from New York was a clear-eyed erect tall man. Only the flatness of his chest hinted at any constitutional weakness. In color and line his face was hale. His stride was long and elastic. He went nimbly up the concrete stairs that connected train-shed with street-level, crossed the waiting-room, waved a hand at an acquaintance behind the information counter, and passed out of the station through one of the street-doors.

While waiting on the sidewalk for the porter with his bags to come he bought a newspaper. He opened it when he was in a taxicab riding towards Randall Avenue with his luggage. He read a half-column on the front page:

SECOND BROTHER KILLED
FRANCIS F. WEST MURDERED
CLOSE TO SPOT WHERE
BROTHER MET DEATH

For the second time within two weeks tragedy came to the West family of 1342 N. Achland Avenue last night when Francis F. West, 31, was shot to death in the street less than a block from the corner where he had seen his brother Norman run down and killed by an alleged bootleg car last month.

Francis West, who was employed as waiter at the Rockaway Café, was returning from work at a little after midnight, when, according to those who witnessed the tragedy, he was overtaken by a black touring car that came down Achland Avenue at high speed. The car swung in to the curb as it reached West, and more than a score of shots are said to have been fired from it. West fell with eight bullets in his body, dying before anybody could reach him. The death car, which is said not to have stopped, immediately picked up speed again and vanished around the corner of Bowman Street. The police are hampered in their attempt to find the car by conflicting descriptions given by witnesses, none of whom claims to have seen any of the men in the automobile.

Boyd West, the surviving brother, who also witnessed Norman's death last month, could ascribe no reason for Francis's murder. He said he knew of no enemies his brother had made. Miss Marie Shepperd, 1917 Baker Avenue, to whom Francis West was to have been married next week, was likewise unable to name anyone who might have desired her fiancé's death.

Timothy Ivans, alleged driver of the car that accidentally ran down and killed Norman West last month, refused to talk to reporters in his cell at the City Prison, where he is held without bail, awaiting trial for manslaughter.

Ned Beaumont folded the newspaper with careful slowness and put it in one of his overcoat-pockets. His lips were drawn a little together and his eyes were bright with thinking. Otherwise his face was composed. He leaned back in a corner of the taxicab and played with an unlighted cigar.

In his rooms he went, without pausing to remove hat or coat, to the telephone and called four numbers, asking each time whether Paul Madvig was there and whether it was known where he could be found. After the fourth call he gave up trying to find Madvig.

He put the telephone down, picked his cigar up from where he had laid it on the table, lighted the cigar, laid it on the edge of the table again, picked up the telephone, and called the City Hall's number. He asked for the District Attorney's office. While he waited he dragged a chair, by means of a foot hooked under one of its rounds, over to the telephone, sat down, and put the cigar in his mouth.

Then he said into the telephone: "Hello. Is Mr. Farr in? . . . Ned Beaumont. . . . Yes, thanks." He inhaled and exhaled smoke slowly. "Hello, Farr? . . . Just got in a couple of minutes ago. . . . Yes. Can I see you now? . . . That's right. Has Paul said anything to you about the West killing? . . . Don't know where he is, do you? . . . Well, there's an angle I'd like to talk to you about. . . . Yes, say half an hour. . . . Right."

He put the telephone aside and went across the room to look at the mail on a table by the door. There were some magazines and nine letters. He looked rapidly at the envelopes, dropped them on the table again without having opened any, and went into his bedroom to undress, then into his bathroom to shave and bathe.

2

District Attorney Michael Joseph Farr was a stout man of forty. His hair was a florid stubble above a florid pugnacious face. His walnut desk-top was empty except for a telephone and a large desk-set of green onyx whereon a nude metal figure holding aloft an airplane stood on one foot between two black and white fountain-pens that slanted off to either side at rakish angles.

He shook Ned Beaumont's hand in both of his and pressed him down into a leather-covered chair before returning to his own seat. He rocked back in his chair and asked: "Have a nice trip?" Inquisitiveness gleamed through the friendliness in his eyes.

"It was all right," Ned Beaumont replied. "About this Francis West: with him out of the way how does the case against Tim Ivans stand?"

Farr started, then made that startled motion part of a deliberate squirming into a more comfortable position in his chair.

"Well, it won't make such a lot of difference there," he said, "that is, not a whole lot, since there's still the other brother to testify against Ivans." He very noticeably did not watch Ned Beaumont's face, but looked at a corner of the walnut desk. "Why? What'd you have on your mind?"

Ned Beaumont was looking gravely at the man who was not looking at him. "I was just wondering. I suppose it's all right, though, if the other brother can and will identify Tim."

Farr, still not looking up, said: "Sure." He rocked his chair back and forth gently, an inch or two each way half a dozen times. His fleshy cheeks moved in little ripples where they covered his jaw-muscles. He cleared his throat and stood up. He looked at Ned Beaumont now with friendly eyes. "Wait a minute," he said. "I've got to go see about something. They forget everything if I don't keep right on their tails. Don't go. I want to talk to you about Despain."

Ned Beaumont murmured, "Don't hurry," as the District Attorney left the office, and sat and smoked placidly all the fifteen minutes he was gone.

Farr returned frowning. "Sorry to leave you like that," he said as he sat down, "but we're fairly smothered under work. If it keeps up like this—" He completed the sentence by making a gesture of hopelessness with his hands.

"That's all right. Anything new on the Taylor Henry killing?"

"Nothing here. That's what I wanted to ask you about—Despain." Again Farr was definitely not watching Ned Beaumont's face.

A thin mocking smile that the other man could not see twitched for an instant the corners of Ned Beaumont's mouth. He said: "There's not much of a case against him when you come to look at it closely."

Farr nodded slowly at the corner of his desk. "Maybe, but his blowing town that same night don't look so damned good."

"He had another reason for that," Ned Beaumont said, "a pretty good one." The shadowy smile came and went.

Farr nodded again in the manner of one willing to be convinced. "You don't think there's a chance that he really killed him?"

Ned Beaumont's reply was given carelessly: "I don't think he did it, but there's always a chance and you've got plenty to hold him awhile on if you want to."

The District Attorney raised his head and looked at Ned Beaumont. He smiled with a mixture of diffidence and good-fellowship and said: "Tell me to go to hell if it's none of my business, but why in the name of God did Paul send you to New York after Bernie Despain?"

Ned Beaumont withheld his reply for a thoughtful moment. Then he moved his shoulders a little and said: "He didn't send me. He let me go."

Farr did not say anything.

Ned Beaumont filled his lungs with cigar-smoke, emptied them, and said: "Bernie welshed on a bet with me. That's why he took the run-out. It just happened that Taylor Henry was killed the night of the day Peggy O'Toole came in in front with fifteen hundred of my dollars on her."

The District Attorney said hastily: "That's all right, Ned. It's none of my business what you and Paul do. I'm—you see, it's just that I'm not so damned sure that maybe Despain didn't happen to run into young Henry on the street by luck and take a crack at him. I think maybe I'll hold him awhile to be safe." His blunt undershot mouth curved in a smile that was somewhat ingratiating. "Don't think I'm pushing my snoot into Paul's affairs, or yours, but—" His florid face was turgid and shiny. He suddenly bent over and yanked a desk-drawer open. Paper rattled under his fingers. His hand came out of the drawer and went across the desk towards Ned Beaumont. In his hand was a small white envelope with a slit edge. "Here." His voice was thick. "Look at this and see what you think of it, or is it only damned foolishness?"

Ned Beaumont took the envelope, but did not immediately look at it. He kept his eyes, now cold and bright, focused on the District Attorney's red face.

Farr's face became a darker red under the other man's stare and he raised a beefy hand in a placatory gesture. His voice was placatory: "I don't attach any importance to it, Ned, but—I mean we always get a lot of junk like that on every case that comes up and—well, read it and see."

After another considerable moment Ned Beaumont shifted his gaze from Farr to the envelope. The address was typewritten:

> *M. J. Farr, Esq.*
> *District Attorney*
> *City Hall*
> *City*

Personal

The postmark was dated the previous Saturday. Inside was a single sheet of white paper on which three sentences with neither salutation nor signature were typewritten:

Why did Paul Madvig steal one of Taylor Henry's hats after he was murdered?

What became of the hat that Taylor Henry was wearing when he was murdered?

Why was the man who claimed to have first found Taylor Henry's body made a member of your staff?

Ned Beaumont folded this communication, returned it to its envelope, dropped it down on the desk, and brushed his mustache with a thumb-nail from center to left and from center to right, looking at the District Attorney with level eyes, addressing him in a level tone: "Well?"

Farr's cheeks rippled again where they covered his jaw-muscles. He frowned over pleading eyes. "For God's sake, Ned," he said earnestly, "don't think I'm taking that seriously. We get bales of that kind of crap every time anything happens. I only wanted to show it to you."

Ned Beaumont said: "That's all right as long as you keep on feeling that way about it." He was still level of eye and voice. "Have you said anything to Paul about it?"

"About the letter? No. I haven't seen him since it came this morning."

Ned Beaumont picked the envelope up from the desk and put it in his inner coat-pocket. The District Attorney, watching the letter go into the pocket, seemed uncomfortable, but he did not say anything.

Ned Beaumont said, when he had stowed the letter away and had brought a thin dappled cigar out of another pocket: "I don't think I'd say anything to him about it if I were you. He's got enough on his mind."

Farr was saying, "Sure, whatever you say, Ned," before Ned Beaumont had finished his speech.

After that neither of them said anything for a while during which Farr resumed his staring at the desk-corner and Ned Beaumont stared thoughtfully at Farr. This period of silence was ended by a soft buzzing that came from under the District Attorney's desk.

Farr picked up his telephone and said: "Yes. . . . Yes." His undershot lip crept out over the edge of the upper lip and his florid face became mottled. "The hell he's not!" he snarled. "Bring the bastard in and put him up against him and then if he don't we'll do some work on him. . . . Yes. . . . Do it." He slammed the receiver on its prong and glared at Ned Beaumont.

Ned Beaumont had paused in the act of lighting his cigar. It was in one hand. His lighter, alight, was in the other. His face was thrust forward a little between them. His eyes glittered. He put the tip of his tongue between his lips, withdrew it, and moved his lips in a smile that had nothing to do with pleasure. "News?" he asked in a low persuasive voice.

The District Attorney's voice was savage: "Boyd West, the other brother that identified Ivans. I got to thinking about it when we were talking and sent out to see if he could still identify him. He says he's not sure, the bastard."

Ned Beaumont nodded as if this news was not unexpected. "How'll that fix things?"

"He can't get away with it," Farr snarled. "He identified him once and he'll stick to it when he gets in front of a jury. I'm having him brought in now and by the time I get through with him he'll be a good boy."

Ned Beaumont said: "Yes? And suppose he doesn't?"

The District Attorney's desk trembled under a blow from the District Attorney's fist. "He will."

Apparently Ned Beaumont was unimpressed. He lighted his cigar, extinguished and pocketed his lighter, blew smoke out, and asked in a mildly amused tone: "Sure he will, but suppose he doesn't? Suppose he looks at Tim and says: 'I'm not sure that's him'?"

Farr smote his desk again. "He won't—not when I'm through with him—he won't do anything but get up in front of the jury and say: 'That's him.'"

Amusement went out of Ned Beaumont's face and he spoke a bit wearily: "He's going to back down on the identification and you know he is. Well, what can you do about it? There's nothing you can do about it, is there? It means your case against Tim Ivans goes blooey. You found the carload of booze where he left it, but the only proof you've got that he was driving it when it ran down Norman West was the eyewitness testimony of his two brothers. Well, if Francis is dead and Boyd's afraid to talk you've got no case and you know it."

In a loud enraged voice Farr began: "If you think I'm going to sit on my—"

But with an impatient motion of the hand holding his cigar Ned Beaumont interrupted him. "Sitting, standing, or riding a bicycle," he said, "you're licked and you know it."

"Do I? I'm District Attorney of this city and county and I—" Abruptly Farr stopped blustering. He cleared his throat and swallowed. Belligerence went out of his eyes, to be replaced first by confusion and then by something akin to fear. He leaned across the desk, too worried to keep worry from showing in his florid face. He said: "Of course you know if you—if Paul—I mean if there's any reason why I shouldn't—you know—we can let it go at that."

The smile that had nothing to do with pleasure was lifting the ends of Ned Beaumont's lips again and his eyes glittered through cigar-smoke. He shook his head slowly and spoke slowly in an unpleasantly sweet tone: "No, Farr, there isn't any reason, or none of that kind. Paul promised to spring Ivans after election, but, believe it or not, Paul never had anybody killed and, even if he did, Ivans wasn't important enough to have anybody killed for. No, Farr, there isn't any reason and I wouldn't like to think you were going around thinking there was."

"For God's sake, Ned, get me right," Farr protested. "You know damned well there's nobody in the city any stronger for Paul and for you than me. You ought to know that. I didn't mean anything by what I said except that—well, that you can always count on me."

Ned Beaumont said, "That's fine," without much enthusiasm and stood up.

Farr rose and came around the desk with a red hand out. "What's your hurry?" he asked. "Why don't you stick around and see how this West acts when they bring him in? Or"—he looked at his watch—"what are you doing tonight? How about going to dinner with me?"

"Sorry I can't," Ned Beaumont replied. "I've got to run along."

He let Farr pump his hand up and down, murmured a "Yes, I will" in response to the District Attorney's insistence that he drop in often and that they get together some night, and went out.

3

Walter Ivans was standing beside one of a row of men operating nailing-machines in the box-factory where he was employed as foreman, when Ned Beaumont came in. He saw Ned Beaumont at once and, hailing him with an uplifted hand, came down the center aisle, but in Ivans's china-blue eyes and round fair face there was somewhat less pleasure than he seemed to be trying to put there.

Ned Beaumont said, " 'Lo, Walt," and by turning slightly towards the door escaped the necessity of either taking or pointedly ignoring the shorter man's proffered hand. "Let's get out of this racket."

Ivans said something that was blurred by the din of metal driving metal into wood and they went to the open door by which Ned Beaumont had entered. Outside was a wide platform of solid timber. A flight of wooden steps ran down twenty feet to the ground.

They stood on the wooden platform and Ned Beaumont asked: "You know one of the witnesses against your brother was knocked off last night?"

"Y-yes, I saw it in the p-p-paper."

Ned Beaumont asked: "You know the other one's not sure now he can identify Tim?"

"N-no, I didn't know that, N-ned."

Ned Beaumont said: "You know if he doesn't Tim'll get off."

"Y-yes."

Ned Beaumont said: "You don't look as happy about it as you ought to."

Ivans wiped his forehead with his shirt-sleeve. "B-b-but I am, N-ned, b-by God I am!"

"Did you know West? The one that was killed."

"N-no, except that I went to s-see him once, t-to ask him to g-go kind of easy on T-tim."

"What'd he say?"

"He wouldn't."

"When was that?"

Ivans shifted his feet and wiped his face with his sleeve again. "T-t-two or three d-days ago."

Ned Beaumont asked softly: "Any idea who could have killed him, Walt?"

Ivans shook his head violently from side to side.

"Any idea who could've had him killed, Walt?"

Ivans shook his head.

For a moment Ned Beaumont stared reflectively over Ivans's shoulder. The clatter of the nailing-machines came through the door ten feet away and from another story came the whirr of saws. Ivans drew in and expelled a long breath.

Ned Beaumont's mien had become sympathetic when he transferred his gaze to the shorter man's china-blue eyes again. He leaned down a little and asked: "Are you all right, Walt? I mean there are going to be people who'll think maybe you might have shot West to save your brother. Have you got—?"

"I-I-I was at the C-club all last night, from eight o'clock t-t-till after t-two this morning," Walter Ivans replied as rapidly as the impediment in his speech permitted. "Harry Sloss and B-ben Ferriss and Brager c-c-can tell you."

Ned Beaumont laughed. "That's a lucky break for you, Walt," he said gaily.

He turned his back on Walter Ivans and went down the wooden steps to the street. He paid no attention to Walter Ivans's very friendly "Good-by, Ned."

4

From the box-factory Ned Beaumont walked four blocks to a restaurant and used a telephone. He called the four numbers he had called earlier in the day, asking again for Paul Madvig and, not getting him on the wire, left instructions for Madvig to call him. Then he got a taxicab and went home.

Additional pieces of mail had been put with those already on the table by his door. He hung up his hat and overcoat, lighted a cigar, and sat down with his mail in the largest of the red-plush chairs. The fourth envelope he opened was similar to the one the District Attorney had shown him. It contained a single sheet of paper bearing three typewritten sentences without salutation or signature:

Did you find Taylor Henry's body after he was dead or were you present when he was murdered?

Why did you not report his death until after the police had found the body?

Do you think you can save the guilty by manufacturing evidence against the innocent?

Ned Beaumont screwed up his eyes and wrinkled his forehead over this message and drew much smoke from his cigar. He compared it with the one the District Attorney had received. Paper and typing were alike, as were the manner in which each paper's three sentences were arranged and the time of the postmarks.

Scowling, he returned each to its envelope and put them in his pocket, only to take them out again immediately to reread and re-examine them. Too rapid smoking made his cigar burn irregularly down one side. He put the cigar on the edge of the table beside him with a grimace of distaste and picked at his mustache with nervous fingers. He put the messages away once more and leaned back in his chair, staring at the ceiling and biting a finger-nail. He ran fingers through his hair. He put the end of a finger between his collar and his neck. He sat up and took the envelopes out of his pocket again, but put them back without having looked at them. He chewed his lower lip. Finally he shook himself impatiently and began to read the rest of his mail. He was reading it when the telephone-bell rang.

He went to the telephone. "Hello. . . . Oh, 'lo, Paul, where are you? . . . How long will you be there? . . . Yes, fine, drop in on your way. . . . Right, I'll be here."

He returned to his mail.

5

Paul Madvig arrived at Ned Beaumont's rooms as the bells in the grey church across the street were ringing the Angelus. He came in saying heartily: "Howdy, Ned. When'd you get back?" His big body was clothed in grey tweeds.

"Late this morning," Ned Beaumont replied as they shook hands.

"Make out all right?"

Ned Beaumont showed the edges of his teeth in a contented smile. "I got what I went after—all of it."

"That's great." Madvig threw his hat on a chair and sat on another beside the fireplace.

Ned Beaumont returned to his chair. "Anything happen while I was gone?" he asked as he picked up the half-filled cocktail-glass standing beside the silver shaker on the table at his elbow.

"We got the muddle on the sewer-contract straightened out."

Ned Beaumont sipped his cocktail and asked: "Have to make much of a cut?"

"Too much. There won't be anything like the profit there ought to be, but that's better than taking a chance on stirring things up this close to election. We'll make it up on the street-work next year when the Salem and Chestnut extensions go through."

Ned Beaumont nodded. He was looking at the blond man's outstretched crossed ankles. He said: "You oughtn't to wear silk socks with tweeds."

Madvig raised a leg straight out to look at the ankle. "No? I like the feel of silk."

"Then lay off tweeds. Taylor Henry buried?"

"Friday."

"Go to the funeral?"

"Yes," Madvig replied and added a little self-consciously: "The Senator suggested it."

Ned Beaumont put his glass on the table and touched his lips with a white handkerchief taken from the outer breast-pocket of his coat. "How is the Senator?" He looked obliquely at the blond man and did not conceal the amusement in his eyes.

Madvig replied, still somewhat self-consciously: "He's all right. I spent most of this afternoon up there with him."

"At his house?"

"Uh-huh."

"Was the blonde menace there?"

Madvig did not quite frown. He said: "Janet was there."

Ned Beaumont, putting his handkerchief away, made a choked gurgling sound in his throat and said: "M-m-m. It's Janet now. Getting anywhere with her?"

Composure came back to Madvig. He said evenly: "I still think I'm going to marry her."

"Does she know yet that—that your intentions are honorable?"

"For Christ's sake, Ned!" Madvig protested. "How long are you going to keep me on the witness-stand?"

Ned Beaumont laughed, picked up the silver shaker, shook it, and poured himself another drink. "How do you like the Francis West killing?" he asked when he was sitting back with the glass in his hand.

Madvig seemed puzzled for a moment. Then his face cleared and he said: "Oh, that's the fellow that got shot on Achland Avenue last night."

"That's the fellow."

A fainter shade of puzzlement returned to Madvig's blue eyes. He said: "Well, I didn't know him."

Ned Beaumont said: "He was one of the witnesses against Walter

Ivans's brother. Now the other witness, Boyd West, is afraid to testify, so the rap falls through."

"That's swell," Madvig said, but by the time the last word had issued from his mouth a doubtful look had come into his eyes. He drew his legs in and leaned forward. "Afraid?" he asked.

"Yes, unless you like scared better."

Madvig's face hardened into attentiveness and his eyes became stony blue disks. "What are you getting at, Ned?" he asked in a crisp voice.

Ned Beaumont emptied his glass and set it on the table. "After you told Walt Ivans you couldn't spring Tim till election was out of the way he took his troubles to Shad O'Rory," he said in a deliberate monotone, as if reciting a lesson. "Shad sent some of his gorillas around to scare the two Wests out of appearing against Tim. One of them wouldn't scare and they bumped him off."

Madvig, scowling, objected: "What the hell does Shad care about Tim Ivans's troubles?"

Ned Beaumont, reaching for the cocktail-shaker, said irritably: "All right, I'm just guessing. Forget it."

"Cut it out, Ned. You know your guesses are good enough for me. If you've got anything on your mind, spill it."

Ned Beaumont set the shaker down without having poured a drink and said: "It might be just a guess, at that, Paul, but this is the way it looks to me. Everybody knows Walt Ivans's been working for you down in the Third Ward and is a member of the Club and everything and that you'd do anything you could to get his brother out of a jam if he asked you. Well, everybody, or a lot of them, is going to start wondering whether you didn't have the witnesses against his brother shot and frightened into silence. That goes for the outsiders, the women's clubs you're getting so afraid of these days, and the respectable citizens. The insiders—the ones that mostly wouldn't care if you had done that—are going to get something like the real news. They're going to know that one of your boys had to go to Shad to get fixed up and that Shad fixed him up. Well, that's the hole Shad's put you in—or don't you think he'd go that far to put you in a hole?"

Madvig growled through his teeth: "I know damned well he would, the louse." He was lowering down at a green leaf worked in the rug at his feet.

Ned Beaumont, after looking intently at the blond man, went on: "And there's another angle to look for. Maybe it won't happen, but you're open to it if Shad wants to work it."

Madvig looked up to ask: "What?"

"Walt Ivans was at the Club all last night, till two this morning. That's about three hours later than he ever stayed there before except on election- or banquet-nights. Understand? He was making himself an alibi —in our Club. Suppose"—Ned Beaumont's voice sank to a lower key and his dark eyes were round and grave—"Shad jobs Walt by planting evidence that he killed West? Your women's clubs and all the people who like to squawk about things like that are going to think that Walt's alibi is phony —that we fixed it up to shield him."

Madvig said: "The louse." He stood up and thrust his hands into his trousers-pockets. "I wish to Christ the election was either over or further away."

"None of this would've happened then."

Madvig took two steps into the center of the room. He muttered, "God damn him," and stood frowning at the telephone on the stand beside the bedroom-door. His huge chest moved with his breathing. He said from the side of his mouth, without looking at Ned Beaumont: "Figure out a way of blocking that angle." He took a step towards the telephone and halted. "Never mind," he said and turned to face Ned Beaumont. "I think I'll knock Shad loose from our little city. I'm tired of having him around. I think I'll knock him loose right away, starting tonight."

Ned Beaumont asked: "For instance?"

Madvig grinned. "For instance," he replied, "I think I'll have Rainey close up the Dog House and Paradise Gardens and every dive that we know Shad or any of his friends are interested in. I think I'll have Rainey smack them over in one long row, one after the other, this very same night."

Ned Beaumont spoke hesitantly: "You're putting Rainey in a tough spot. Our coppers aren't used to bothering with Prohibition-enforcement. They're not going to like it very much."

"They can do it once for me," Madvig said, "without feeling that they've paid all their debts."

"Maybe." Ned Beaumont's face and voice were dubious still. "But this wholesale stuff is too much like using a cyclone shot to blow off a safe-door when you could get it off without any fuss by using a come-along."

"Have you got something up your sleeve, Ned?"

Ned Beaumont shook his head. "Nothing I'm sure of, but it wouldn't hurt to wait a couple of days till—"

Now Madvig shook his head. "No," he said. "I want action. I don't know a damned thing about opening safes, Ned, but I do know fighting— my kind—going in with both hands working. I never could learn to box and the only times I ever tried I got licked. We'll give Mr. O'Rory the cyclone shot."

6

The stringy man in horn-rimmed spectacles said: "So you don't have to worry none about that." He sat complacently back in his chair.

The man on his left—a raw-boned man with a bushy brown mustache and not much hair on his head—said to the man on his left: "It don't sound so God-damned swell to me."

"No?" The stringy man turned to glare through his spectacles at the raw-boned man. "Well, Paul don't never have to come down to my ward hisself to—"

The raw-boned man said: "Aw, nurts!"

Madvig addressed the raw-boned man: "Did you see Parker, Breen?"

Breen said: "Yes, I saw him and he says five, but I think we can get a couple more out of him."

The bespectacled man said contemptuously: "My God, I'd think so!"

Breen sneered sidewise at him. "Yes? And who'd you ever get that much out of?"

Three knocks sounded on the broad oaken door.

Ned Beaumont rose from the chair he was straddling and went to the door. He opened it less than a foot.

The man who had knocked was a small-browed dark man in blue clothes that needed pressing. He did not try to enter the room and he tried to speak in an undertone, but excitement made his words audible to everyone in the room. "Shad O'Rory's downstairs. He wants to see Paul."

Ned Beaumont shut the door and turned with his back against it to look at Paul Madvig. Only those two of the ten men in the room seemed undisturbed by the small-browed man's announcement. All the others did not show their excitement frankly—in some it could be seen in their suddenly acquired stoniness—but there was none whose respiration was exactly as it had been before.

Ned Beaumont, pretending he did not know repetition was unnecessary, said, in a tone that expressed suitable interest in his words: "O'Rory wants to see you. He's downstairs."

Madvig looked at his watch. "Tell him I'm tied up right now, but if he'll wait a little while I'll see him."

Ned Beaumont nodded and opened the door. "Tell him Paul's busy now," he instructed the man who had knocked, "but if he'll stick around awhile Paul'll see him." He shut the door.

Madvig was questioning a square-faced yellowish man about their chances of getting more votes on the other side of Chestnut Street. The square-faced man replied that he thought they would get more than last time "by a hell of a sight," but still not enough to make much of a dent in the opposition. While he talked his eyes kept crawling sidewise to the door.

Ned Beaumont sat astride his chair by the window again smoking a cigar.

Madvig addressed to another man a question having to do with the size of the campaign-contribution to be expected from a man named Hartwick. This other man kept his eyes from the door, but his reply lacked coherence.

Neither Madvig's and Ned Beaumont's calmness of mien nor their business-like concentration on campaign-problems could check the growth of tension in the room.

After fifteen minutes Madvig rose and said: "Well, we're not on Easy Street yet, but she's shaping up. Keep hard at it and we'll make the grade." He went to the door and shook each man's hand as they went out. They went out somewhat hurriedly.

Ned Beaumont, who had not left his chair, asked, when he and Madvig were the only ones in the room: "Do I stick around or beat it?"

"Stick around." Madvig crossed to the window and looked down into sunny China Street.

"Both hands working?" Ned Beaumont asked after a little pause.

Madvig turned from the window nodding. "I don't know anything else"—he grinned boyishly at the man straddling the chair—"except maybe the feet too."

Ned Beaumont started to say something, but was interrupted by the noise the turning door-knob made.

A man opened the door and came in. He was a man of little more than medium height, trimly built with a trimness that gave him a deceptively frail appearance. Though his hair was a sheer sleek white he was probably not much past his thirty-fifth year. His eyes were a notable clear grey-blue set in a rather long and narrow, but very finely sculptured, face. He wore a dark blue overcoat over a dark blue suit and carried a black derby hat in a black-gloved hand.

The man who came in behind him was a bow-legged ruffian of the same height, a swarthy man with something apish in the slope of his big shoulders, the length of his thick arms, and the flatness of his face. This one's hat—a grey fedora—was on his head. He shut the door and leaned against it, putting his hands in the pockets of his plaid overcoat.

The first man, having advanced by then some four or five steps into the room, put his hat on a chair and began to take off his gloves.

Madvig, hands in trousers-pockets, smiled amiably and said: "How are you, Shad?"

The white-haired man said: "Fine, Paul. How's yourself?" His voice was a musical barytone. The faintest of brogues colored his words.

Madvig indicated with a small jerk of his head the man on the chair and asked: "You know Beaumont?"

O'Rory said: "Yes."

Ned Beaumont said: "Yes."

Neither nodded to the other and Ned Beaumont did not get up from his chair.

Shad O'Rory had finished taking off his gloves. He put them in an overcoat-pocket and said: "Politics is politics and business is business. I've been paying my way and I'm willing to go on paying my way, but I want what I'm paying for." His modulated voice was no more than pleasantly earnest.

"What do you mean by that?" Madvig asked as if he did not greatly care.

"I mean that half the coppers in town are buying their cakes and ale with dough they're getting from me and some of my friends."

Madvig sat down by the table. "Well?" he asked, carelessly as before.

"I want what I'm paying for. I'm paying to be let alone. I want to be let alone."

Madvig chuckled. "You don't mean, Shad, that you're complaining to me because your coppers won't stay bought?"

"I mean that Doolan told me last night that the orders to shut up my places came straight from you."

Madvig chuckled again and turned his head to address Ned Beaumont: "What do you think of that, Ned?"

Ned Beaumont smiled thinly, but said nothing.

Madvig said: "You know what I think of it? I think Captain Doolan's been working too hard. I think somebody ought to give Captain Doolan a nice long leave of absence. Don't let me forget it."

O'Rory said: "I bought protection, Paul, and I want it. Business is business and politics is politics. Let's keep them apart."

Madvig said: "No."

Shad O'Rory's blue eyes looked dreamily at some distant thing. He smiled a little sadly and there was a note of sadness in his musical slightly Irish voice when he spoke. He said: "It's going to mean killing."

Madvig's blue eyes were opaque and his voice was as difficultly read as his eyes. He said. "If you make it mean killing."

The white-haired man nodded. "It'll have to mean killing," he said, still sadly. "I'm too big to take the boot from you now."

Madvig leaned back in his chair and crossed his legs. His tone attached little importance to his words. He said: "Maybe you're too big to take it laying down, but you'll take it." He pursed his lips and added as an afterthought: "You are taking it."

Dreaminess and sadness went swiftly out of Shad O'Rory's eyes. He put his black hat on his head. He adjusted his coat-collar to his neck. He pointed a long white finger at Madvig and said: "I'm opening the Dog House again tonight. I don't want to be bothered. Bother me and I'll bother you."

Madvig uncrossed his legs and reached for the telephone on the table. He called the Police Department's number, asked for the Chief, and said to him: "Hello, Rainey. . . . Yes, fine. How are the folks? . . . That's good. Say, Rainey, I hear Shad's thinking of opening up again tonight. . . . Yes. . . . Yes, slam it down so hard it bounces. . . . Right. . . . Sure. Good-by." He pushed the telephone back and addressed

O'Rory: "Now do you understand how you stand? You're through, Shad. You're through here for good."

O'Rory said softly, "I understand," turned, opened the door, and went out.

The bow-legged ruffian paused to spit—deliberately—on the rug in front of him and to stare with bold challenging eyes at Madvig and Ned Beaumont. Then he went out.

Ned Beaumont wiped the palms of his hands with a handkerchief. He said nothing to Madvig, who was looking at him with questioning eyes. Ned Beaumont's eyes were gloomy.

After a moment Madvig asked: "Well?"

Ned Beaumont said: "Wrong, Paul."

Madvig rose and went to the window. "Jesus Christ!" he complained over his shoulder, "don't anything ever suit you?"

Ned Beaumont got up from his chair and walked towards the door.

Madvig, turning from the window, asked angrily: "Some more of your God-damned foolishness?"

Ned Beaumont said, "Yes," and went out of the room. He went downstairs, got his hat, and left the Log Cabin Club. He walked seven blocks to the railroad station, bought a ticket for New York, and made reservations on a night train. Then he took a taxicab to his rooms.

7

A stout shapeless woman in grey clothes and a chubby half-grown boy were packing Ned Beaumont's trunk and three leather bags under his supervision when the door-bell rang.

The woman rose grunting from her knees and went to the door. She opened it wide. "My goodness, Mr. Madvig," she said. "Come right on in."

Madvig came in saying: "How are you, Mrs. Duveen? You get younger-looking every day." His gaze passed over the trunk and bags to the boy. "Hello, Charley. Ready for the job running the cement-mixer yet?"

The boy grinned bashfully and said: "How do you do, Mr. Madvig?"

Madvig's smile came around to Ned Beaumont. "Going places?"

Ned Beaumont smiled politely. "Yes," he said.

The blond man looked around the room, at the bags and trunk again, at the clothes piled on chairs and the drawers standing open. The woman and the boy went back to their work. Ned Beaumont found two somewhat faded shirts in a pile on a chair and put them aside.

Madvig asked: "Got half an hour to spare, Ned?"

"I've got plenty of time."

Madvig said: "Get your hat."

Ned Beaumont got his hat and overcoat. "Get as much of it in as you can," he told the woman as he and Madvig moved towards the door, "and what's left over can be sent on with the other stuff."

He and Madvig went downstairs to the street. They walked south a block. Then Madvig asked: "Where're you going, Ned?"

"New York."

They turned into an alley.

Madvig asked: "For good?"

Ned Beaumont shrugged. "I'm leaving here for good."

They opened a green wooden door set in the red brick rear wall of a building and went down a passageway and through another door into a bar-room where half a dozen men were drinking. They exchanged greetings with the bar-tender and three of the drinkers as they passed through to a small room where there were four tables. Nobody else was there. They sat at one of the tables.

The bar-tender put his head in and asked: "Beer as per usual, gents?"

Madvig said, "Yes," and then, when the bar-tender had withdrawn: "Why?"

Ned Beaumont said: "I'm tired of hick-town stuff."

"Meaning me?"

Ned Beaumont did not say anything.

Madvig did not say anything for a while. Then he sighed and said: "This is a hell of a time to be throwing me down."

The bar-tender came in with two seidels of pale beer and a bowl of pretzels. When he had gone out again, shutting the door behind him, Madvig exclaimed: "Christ, you're hard to get along with, Ned!"

Ned Beaumont moved his shoulders. "I never said I wasn't." He lifted his seidel and drank.

Madvig was breaking a pretzel into small bits. "Do you really want to go, Ned?" he asked.

"I'm going."

Madvig dropped the fragments of pretzel on the table and took a check-book from his pocket. He tore out a check, took a fountain-pen from another pocket, and filled in the check. Then he fanned it dry and dropped it on the table in front of Ned Beaumont.

Ned Beaumont, looking down at the check, shook his head and said: "I don't need money and you don't owe me anything."

"I do. I owe you more than that, Ned. I wish you'd take it."

Ned Beaumont said, "All right, thanks," and put the check in his pocket.

Madvig drank beer, ate a pretzel, started to drink again, set his seidel down on the table, and asked: "Was there anything on your mind —any kick—besides that back in the Club this afternoon?"

Ned Beaumont shook his head. "You don't talk to me like that. Nobody does."

"Hell, Ned, I didn't say anything."

Ned Beaumont did not say anything.

Madvig drank again. "Mind telling me why you think I handled O'Rory wrong?"

"It wouldn't do any good."

"Try."

Ned Beaumont said: "All right, but it won't do any good." He tilted his chair back, holding his seidel in one hand, some pretzels in the other. "Shad'll fight. He's got to. You've got him in a corner. You've told him he's through here for good. There's nothing he can do now but play the long shot. If he can upset you this election he'll be fixed to square anything he has to do to win. If you win the election he's got to drift anyhow. You're using the police on him. He'll have to fight back at the police and he will. That means you're going to have something that can be made to look like a crime-wave. You're trying to re-elect the whole city administration. Well, giving them a crime-wave—and one it's an even bet they're not going to be able to handle—just before election isn't going to make them look any too efficient. They—"

"You think I ought to've laid down to him?" Madvig demanded, scowling.

"I don't think that. I think you should have left him an out, a line of retreat. You shouldn't have got him with his back to the wall."

Madvig's scowl deepened. "I don't know anything about your kind of fighting. He started it. All I know is when you got somebody cornered you go in and finish them. That system's worked all right for me so far." He blushed a little. "I don't mean I think I'm Napoleon or something, Ned, but I came up from running errands for Packy Flood in the old Fifth to where I'm sitting kind of pretty today."

Ned Beaumont emptied his seidel and let the front legs of his chair come down on the floor. "I told you it wouldn't do any good," he said. "Have it your own way. Keep on thinking that what was good enough for the old Fifth is good enough anywhere."

In Madvig's voice there was something of resentment and something of humility when he asked: "You don't think much of me as a big-time politician, do you, Ned?"

Now Ned Beaumont's face flushed. He said: "I didn't say that, Paul."

"But that's what it amounts to, isn't it?" Madvig insisted.

"No, but I do think you've let yourself be outsmarted this time. First you let the Henrys wheedle you into backing the Senator. There was your chance to go in and finish an enemy who was cornered, but that enemy happened to have a daughter and social position and what not, so you—"

"Cut it out, Ned," Madvig grumbled.

Ned Beaumont's face became empty of expression. He stood up saying, "Well, I must be running along," and turned to the door.

Madvig was up behind him immediately, with a hand on his shoulder, saying: "Wait, Ned."

Ned Beaumont said: "Take your hand off me." He did not look around.

Madvig put his other hand on Ned Beaumont's arm and turned him around. "Look here, Ned," he began.

Ned Beaumont said: "Let go." His lips were pale and stiff.

Madvig shook him. He said: "Don't be a God-damned fool. You and I—"

Ned Beaumont struck Madvig's mouth with his left fist.

Madvig took his hands away from Ned Beaumont and fell back two steps. While his pulse had time to beat perhaps three times his mouth hung open and astonishment was in his face. Then his face darkened with anger and he shut his mouth tight, so his jaw was hard and lumpy. He made fists of his hands, hunched his shoulders, and swayed forward.

Ned Beaumont's hand swept out to the side to grasp one of the heavy glass seidels on the table, though he did not lift it from the table. His body leaned a little to that side as he had leaned to get the seidel. Otherwise he stood squarely confronting the blond man. His face was drawn thin and rigid, with white lines of strain around the mouth. His dark eyes glared fiercely into Madvig's blue ones.

They stood thus, less than a yard apart—one blond, tall and powerfully built, leaning far forward, big shoulders hunched, big fists ready; the other dark of hair and eye, tall and lean, body bent a little to one side with an arm slanting down from that side to hold a heavy glass seidel by its handle—and except for their breathing there was no sound in the room. No sound came in from the bar-room on the other side of the thin door, the rattling of glasses nor the hum of talk nor the splash of water.

When quite two minutes had passed Ned Beaumont took his hand away from the seidel and turned his back to Madvig. Nothing changed in Ned Beaumont's face except that his eyes, when no longer focused on Madvig's, became hard and cold instead of angrily glaring. He took an unhurried step towards the door.

Madvig spoke hoarsely from deep down in him. "Ned."

Ned Beaumont halted. His face became paler. He did not turn around.

Madvig said: "You crazy son of a bitch."

Then Ned Beaumont turned around, slowly.

Madvig put out an open hand and pushed Ned Beaumont's face sidewise, shoving him off balance so he had to put a foot out quickly to that side and put a hand on one of the chairs at the table.

Madvig said: "I ought to knock hell out of you."

Ned Beaumont grinned sheepishly and sat down on the chair he had staggered against. Madvig sat down facing him and knocked on the top of the table with his seidel.

The bar-tender opened the door and put his head in.

"More beer," Madvig said.

From the bar-room, through the open door, came the sound of men talking and the sound of glasses rattling against glasses and against wood.

IV · *The Dog House*

1

NED BEAUMONT, at breakfast in bed, called, "Come in," and then, when the outer door had opened and closed: "Yes?"

A low-pitched rasping voice in the living-room asked: "Where are you, Ned?" Before Ned Beaumont could reply the rasping voice's owner had come to the bedroom-door and was saying: "Pretty soft for you." He was a sturdy young man with a square-cut sallow face, a wide thick-lipped mouth, from a corner of which a cigarette dangled, and merry dark squinting eyes.

"'Lo, Whisky," Ned Beaumont said to him. "Treat yourself to a chair."

Whisky looked around the room. "Pretty good dump you've got here," he said. He removed the cigarette from his lips and, without turning his head, used the cigarette to point over his shoulder at the living-room behind him. "What's all the keysters for? Moving out?"

Ned Beaumont thoroughly chewed and swallowed the scrambled eggs in his mouth before replying: "Thinking of it."

Whisky said, "Yes?" while moving towards a chair that faced the bed. He sat down. "Where to?"

"New York maybe."

"What do you mean maybe?"

Ned Beaumont said: "Well, I've got a ducat that reads to there, anyway."

Whisky knocked cigarette-ash on the floor and returned the cigarette to the left side of his mouth. He snuffled. "How long you going to be gone?"

Ned Beaumont held a coffee-cup half-way between the tray and his mouth. He looked thoughtfully over it at the sallow young man. Finally he said, "It's a one-way ticket," and drank.

Whisky squinted at Ned Beaumont now until one of his dark eyes was entirely shut and the other was no more than a thin black gleam. He took the cigarette from his mouth and knocked more ash on the floor. His rasping voice held a persuasive note. "Why don't you see Shad before you go?" he suggested.

Ned Beaumont put his cup down and smiled. He said: "Shad and I aren't good enough friends that his feelings'll be hurt if I go away without saying good-by."

Whisky said: "That ain't the point."

Ned Beaumont moved the tray from his lap to the bedside-table. He turned on his side, propping himself up on an elbow on the pillows. He pulled the bed-clothes higher up over his chest. Then he asked: "What is the point?"

"The point is you and Shad ought to be able to do business together."

Ned Beaumont shook his head. "I don't think so."

"Can't you be wrong?" Whisky demanded.

"Sure," the man in bed confessed. "Once back in 1912 I was. I forget what it was about."

Whisky rose to mash his cigarette in one of the dishes on the tray. Standing beside the bed, close to the table, he said: "Why don't you try it, Ned?"

Ned Beaumont frowned. "Looks like a waste of time, Whisky. I don't think Shad and I could get along together."

Whisky sucked a tooth noisily. The downward curve of his thick lips gave the noise a scornful cast. "Shad thinks you could," he said.

Ned Beaumont opened his eyes. "Yes?" he asked. "He sent you here?"

"Hell, yes," Whisky said. "You don't think I'd be here talking like this if he hadn't."

Ned Beaumont narrowed his eyes again and asked: "Why?"

"Because he thought him and you could do business together."

"I mean," Ned Beaumont explained, "why did he think I'd want to do business with him?"

Whisky made a disgusted face. "Are you trying to kid me, Ned?" he asked.

"No."

"Well, for the love of Christ, don't you think everybody in town knows about you and Paul having it out at Pip Carson's yesterday?"

Ned Beaumont nodded. "So that's it," he said softly, as if to himself.

"That's it," the man with the rasping voice assured him, "and Shad happens to know you fell out over thinking Paul hadn't ought to've had Shad's joints smeared. So you're sitting pretty with Shad now if you use your head."

Ned Beaumont said thoughtfully: "I don't know. I'd like to get out of here, get back to the big city."

"Use your head," Whisky rasped. "The big city'll still be there after election. Stick around. You know Shad's dough-heavy and's putting it out in chunks to beat Madvig. Stick around and get yourself a slice of it."

"Well," Ned Beaumont said slowly, "it wouldn't hurt to talk it over with him."

"You're damned right it wouldn't," Whisky said heartily. "Pin your diapers on and we'll go now."

Ned Beaumont said, "Right," and got out of bed.

2

Shad O'Rory rose and bowed. "Glad to see you, Beaumont," he said. "Drop your hat and coat anywhere." He did not offer to shake hands.

Ned Beaumont said, "Good morning," and began to take off his overcoat.

Whisky, in the doorway, said: "Well, I'll be seeing you guys later."

O'Rory said, "Yes, do," and Whisky, drawing the door shut as he backed out, left them.

Ned Beaumont dropped his overcoat on the arm of a sofa, put his hat on the overcoat, and sat down beside them. He looked without curiosity at O'Rory.

O'Rory had returned to his chair, a deeply padded squat affair of dull wine and gold. He crossed his knees and put his hands together—tips of fingers and thumbs touching—atop his uppermost knee. He let his finely sculptured head sink down towards his chest so that his grey-blue eyes looked upward under his brows at Ned Beaumont. He said, in his pleasantly modulated Irish voice: "I owe you something for trying to talk Paul out of—"

"You don't," Ned Beaumont said.

O'Rory asked: "I don't?"

"No. I was with him then. What I told him was for his own good. I thought he was making a bad play."

O'Rory smiled gently. "And he'll know it before he's through," he said.

Silence was between them awhile then. O'Rory sat half-buried in his chair smiling at Ned Beaumont. Ned Beaumont sat on the sofa looking, with eyes that gave no indication of what he thought, at O'Rory.

The silence was broken by O'Rory asking: "How much did Whisky tell you?"

"Nothing. He said you wanted to see me."

"He was right enough as far as he went," O'Rory said. He took his finger-tips apart and patted the back of one slender hand with the palm of the other. "Is it so that you and Paul have broken for good and all?"

"I thought you knew it," Ned Beaumont replied. "I thought that's why you sent for me."

"I heard it," O'Rory said, "but that's not always the same thing. What were you thinking you might do now?"

"There's a ticket for New York in my pocket and my clothes are packed."

O'Rory raised a hand and smoothed his sleek white hair. "You came here from New York, didn't you?"

"I never told anybody where I came from."

O'Rory took his hand from his hair and made a small gesture of protestation. "You don't think I'm one to give a damn where any man comes from, do you?" he asked.

Ned Beaumont did not say anything.

The white-haired man said: "But I do care about where you go and if I have my way as much as I'd like you won't be going off to New York yet awhile. Did you never happen to think that maybe you could still do yourself a lot of good right here?"

"No," Ned Beaumont said, "that is, not till Whisky came."

"And what do you think now?"

"I don't know anything about it. I'm waiting to hear what you've got to say."

O'Rory put his hand to his hair again. His blue-grey eyes were friendly and shrewd. He asked: "How long have you been here?"

"Fifteen months."

"And you and Paul have been close as a couple of fingers how long?"

"Year."

O'Rory nodded. "And you ought to know a lot of things about him," he said.

"I do."

O'Rory said: "You ought to know a lot of things I could use."

Ned Beaumont said evenly: "Make your proposition."

O'Rory got up from the depths of his chair and went to a door opposite the one through which Ned Beaumont had come. When he opened the door a huge English bulldog waddled in. O'Rory went back to his chair. The dog lay on the rug in front of the wine and gold chair staring with morose eyes up at its master.

O'Rory said: "One thing I can offer you is a chance to pay Paul back plenty."

Ned Beaumont said: "That's nothing to me."

"It is not?"

"Far as I'm concerned we're quits."

O'Rory raised his head. He asked softly: "And you wouldn't want to do anything to hurt him?"

"I didn't say that," Ned Beaumont replied a bit irritably. "I don't mind hurting him, but I can do it any time I want to on my own account and I don't want you to think you're giving me anything when you give me a chance to."

O'Rory wagged his head up and down, pleasantly. "Suits me," he said, "so he's hurt. Why did he bump off young Henry?"

Ned Beaumont laughed. "Take it easy," he said. "You haven't made your proposition yet. That's a nice pooch. How old is he?"

"Just about the limit, seven." O'Rory put out a foot and rubbed the dog's nose with the tip of it. The dog moved its tail sluggishly. "How does this hit you? After election I'll stake you to the finest gambling-house this state's ever seen and let you run it to suit yourself with all the protection you ever heard of."

"That's an *if* offer," Ned Beaumont said in a somewhat bored manner, "*if* you win. Anyhow, I'm not sure I want to stay here after election, or even that long."

O'Rory stopped rubbing the dog's nose with his shoe-tip. He looked up at Ned Beaumont again, smiled dreamily, and asked: "Don't you think we're going to win the election?"

Ned Beaumont smiled. "You won't bet even money on it."

O'Rory, still smiling dreamily, asked another question: "You're not so God-damned hot for putting in with me, are you, Beaumont?"

"No." Ned Beaumont rose and picked up his hat. "It wasn't any idea of mine." His voice was casual, his face politely expressionless. "I told Whisky it'd just be wasting time." He reached for his overcoat.

The white-haired man said: "Sit down. We can still talk, can't we? And maybe we'll get somewhere before we're through."

Ned Beaumont hesitated, moved his shoulders slightly, took off his hat, put it and his overcoat on the sofa, and sat down beside them.

O'Rory said: "I'll give you ten grand in cash right now if you'll come in and ten more election-night if we beat Paul and I'll keep that house-offer open for you to take or leave."

Ned Beaumont pursed his lips and stared gloomily at O'Rory under brows drawn together. "You want me to rat on him, of course," he said.

"I want you to go into the *Observer* with the lowdown on everything you know about him being mixed up in—the sewer-contracts, the how and why of killing Taylor Henry, that Shoemaker junk last winter, the dirt on how he's running the city."

"There's nothing in the sewer-business now," Ned Beaumont said, speaking as if his mind was more fully occupied with other thoughts. "He let his profits go to keep from raising a stink."

"All right," O'Rory conceded, blandly confident, "but there is something in the Taylor Henry business."

"Yes, we'd have him there," Ned Beaumont said, frowning, "but I don't know whether we could use the Shoemaker stuff"—he hesitated—"without making trouble for me."

"Hell, we don't want that," O'Rory said quickly. "That's out. What else have we got?"

"Maybe we can do something with the street-car-franchise extension and with that trouble last year in the County Clerk's office. We'll have to do some digging first, though."

"It'll be worth it for both of us," O'Rory said. "I'll have Hinkle—he's the *Observer* guy—put the stuff in shape. You just give him the dope and let him write it. We can start off with the Taylor Henry thing. That's something that's right on tap."

Ned Beaumont brushed his mustache with a thumb-nail and murmured: "Maybe."

Shad O'Rory laughed. "You mean we ought to start off first with the ten thousand dollars?" he asked. "There's something in that." He got up and crossed the room to the door he had opened for the dog. He opened it and went out, shutting it behind him. The dog did not get up from in front of the wine and gold chair.

Ned Beaumont lit a cigar. The dog turned his head and watched him.

O'Rory came back with a thick sheaf of green hundred-dollar bills held together by a band of brown paper on which was written in blue ink: $10,000. He thumped the sheaf down on the hand not holding it and said: "Hinkle's out there now. I told him to come in."

Ned Beaumont frowned. "I ought to have a little time to straighten it out in my mind."

"Give it to Hinkle any way it comes to you. He'll put it in shape."

Ned Beaumont nodded. He blew cigar-smoke out and said: "Yes, I can do that."

O'Rory held out the sheaf of paper money.

Saying, "Thanks," Ned Beaumont took it and put it in his inside coat-pocket. It made a bulge there in the breast of his coat over his flat chest.

Shad O'Rory said, "The thanks go both ways," and went back to his chair.

Ned Beaumont took the cigar out of his mouth. "Here's something I want to tell you while I think of it," he said. "Framing Walt Ivans for the West killing won't bother Paul as much as leaving it as is."

O'Rory looked curiously at Ned Beaumont for a moment before asking: "Why?"

"Paul's not going to let him have the Club alibi."

"You mean he's going to give the boys orders to forget Ivans was there?"

"Yes."

O'Rory made a clucking noise with his tongue, asked: "How'd he get the idea I was going to play tricks on Ivans?"

"Oh, we figured it out."

O'Rory smiled. "You mean you did," he said. "Paul's not that shifty."

Ned Beaumont made a modest grimace and asked: "What kind of job did you put up on him?"

O'Rory chuckled. "We sent the clown over to Braywood to buy the guns that were used." His grey-blue eyes suddenly became hard and sharp. Then amusement came back into them and he said: "Oh, well, none of that's big stuff now, now that Paul's hell-bent on making a row of it. But that's what started him picking on me, isn't it?"

"Yes," Ned Beaumont told him, "though it was likely to come sooner or later anyhow. Paul thinks he gave you your start here and you ought to stay under his wing and not grow big enough to buck him."

O'Rory smiled gently. "And I'm the boy that'll make him sorry he ever gave me that start," he promised. "He can—"

A door opened and a man came in. He was a young man in baggy grey clothes. His ears and nose were very large. His indefinitely brown hair needed trimming and his rather grimy face was too deeply lined for his years.

"Come in, Hinkle," O'Rory said. "This is Beaumont. He'll give you the dope. Let me see it when you've shaped it up and we'll get the first shot in tomorrow's paper."

Hinkle smiled with bad teeth and muttered something unintelligibly polite to Ned Beaumont.

Ned Beaumont stood up saying: "Fine. We'll go over to my place now and get to work on it."

O'Rory shook his head. "It'll be better here," he said.

Ned Beaumont, picking up hat and overcoat, smiled and said: "Sorry, but I'm expecting some phone-calls and things. Get your hat, Hinkle."

Hinkle, looking frightened, stood still and dumb.

O'Rory said: "You'll have to stay here, Beaumont. We can't afford to have anything happen to you. Here you'll have plenty of protection."

Ned Beaumont smiled his nicest smile. "If it's the money you're worried about"—he put his hand inside his coat and brought it out holding the money—"you can hang on to it till I've turned in the stuff."

"I'm not worried about anything," O'Rory said calmly. "But you're in a tough spot if Paul gets the news you've come over to me and I don't want to take any chances on having you knocked off."

"You'll have to take them," Ned Beaumont said. "I'm going."

O'Rory said: "No."

Ned Beaumont said: "Yes."

Hinkle turned quickly and went out of the room.

Ned Beaumont turned around and started for the other door, the one through which he had come into the room, walking erectly without haste.

O'Rory spoke to the bulldog at his feet. The dog got up in cumbersome haste and waddled around Ned Beaumont to the door. He stood on wide-spread legs in front of the door and stared morosely at Ned Beaumont.

Ned Beaumont smiled with tight lips and turned to face O'Rory again. The package of hundred-dollar bills was in Ned Beaumont's hand. He raised the hand, said, "You know where you can stick it," and threw the package of bills at O'Rory.

As Ned Beaumont's arm came down the bulldog, leaping clumsily, came up to meet it. His jaws shut over Ned Beaumont's wrist. Ned Beaumont was spun to the left by the impact and he sank on one knee with his arm down close to the floor to take the dog's weight off his arm.

Shad O'Rory rose from his chair and went to the door through which Hinkle had retreated. He opened it and said: "Come in a minute." Then he approached Ned Beaumont who, still down on one knee, was trying to let his arm yield to the strain of the dog's pulling. The dog was almost flat on the floor, all four feet braced, holding the arm.

Whisky and two other men came into the room. One of the others was the apish bow-legged man who had accompanied Shad O'Rory to the Log Cabin Club. One was a sandy-haired boy of nineteen or twenty, stocky, rosy-cheeked, and sullen. The sullen boy went around behind Ned Beaumont, between him and the door. The bow-legged ruffian put his right hand on Ned Beaumont's left arm, the arm the dog was not holding. Whisky halted half-way between Ned Beaumont and the other door.

Then O'Rory said, "Patty," to the dog.

The dog released Ned Beaumont's wrist and waddled over to its master.

Ned Beaumont stood up. His face was pallid and damp with sweat. He looked at his torn coat-sleeve and wrist and at the blood running down his hand. His hand was trembling.

O'Rory said in his musical Irish voice: "You would have it."

Ned Beaumont looked up from his wrist at the white-haired man. "Yes," he said, "and it'll take some more of it to keep me from going out of here."

3

Ned Beaumont opened his eyes and groaned.

The rosy-cheeked boy with sandy hair turned his head over his shoulder to growl: "Shut up, you bastard."

The apish dark man said: "Let him alone, Rusty. Maybe he'll try to get out again and we'll have some more fun." He grinned down at his swollen knuckles. "Deal the cards."

Ned Beaumont mumbled something about Fedink and sat up. He was in a narrow bed without sheets or bed-clothes of any sort. The bare mattress was blood-stained. His face was swollen and bruised and blood-smeared. Dried blood glued his shirt-sleeve to the wrist the dog had bitten and that hand was caked with drying blood. He was in a small yellow and white bedroom furnished with two chairs, a table, a chest of drawers, a wall-mirror, and three white-framed French prints, besides the bed. Facing the foot of the bed was a door that stood open to show part of the interior of a white-tiled bathroom. There was another door, shut. There were no windows.

The apish dark man and the rosy-cheeked boy with sandy hair sat on the chairs playing cards on the table. There was about twenty dollars in paper and silver on the table.

Ned Beaumont looked, with brown eyes wherein hate was a dull glow that came from far beneath the surface, at the card-players and began to get out of bed. Getting out of bed was a difficult task for him. His right arm hung useless. He had to push his legs over the side of the bed one at a time with his left hand and twice he fell over on his side and had to push himself upright again in bed with his left arm.

Once the apish man leered up at him from his cards to ask humorously: "How're you making out, brother?" Otherwise the two at the table let him alone.

He stood finally, trembling, on his feet beside the bed. Steadying himself with his left hand on the bed he reached its end. There he drew himself erect and, staring fixedly at his goal, lurched towards the closed door. Near it he stumbled and went down on his knees, but his left hand, thrown desperately out, caught the knob and he pulled himself up on his feet again.

Then the apish man laid his cards carefully down on the table and said: "Now." His grin, showing remarkably beautiful white teeth, was wide enough to show that the teeth were not natural. He went over and stood beside Ned Beaumont.

Ned Beaumont was tugging at the door-knob.

The apish man said, "Now there, Houdini," and with all his weight behind the blow drove his right fist into Ned Beaumont's face.

Ned Beaumont was driven back against the wall. The back of his head struck the wall first, then his body crashed flat against the wall, and he slid down the wall to the floor.

Rosy-cheeked Rusty, still holding his cards at the table, said gloomily, but without emotion: "Jesus, Jeff, you'll croak him."

Jeff said: "Him?" He indicated the man at his feet by kicking him not especially hard on the thigh. "You can't croak him. He's tough. He's a tough baby. He likes this." He bent down, grasped one of the unconscious man's lapels in each hand, and dragged him to his knees. "Don't you like it, baby?" he asked and, holding Ned Beaumont up on his knees with one hand, struck his face with the other fist.

The door-knob was rattled from the outside.

Jeff called: "Who's that?"

Shad O'Rory's pleasant voice: "Me."

Jeff dragged Ned Beaumont far enough from the door to let it open, dropped him there, and unlocked the door with a key taken from his pocket.

O'Rory and Whisky came in. O'Rory looked at the man on the floor, then at Jeff, and finally at Rusty. His blue-grey eyes were clouded. When he spoke it was to ask Rusty: "Jeff been slapping him down for the fun of it?"

The rosy-cheeked boy shook his head. "This Beaumont is a son of a bitch," he said sullenly. "Every time he comes to he gets up and starts something."

"I don't want him killed, not yet," O'Rory said. He looked down at Ned Beaumont. "See if you can bring him around again. I want to talk to him."

Rusty got up from the table. "I don't know," he said. "He's pretty far gone."

Jeff was more optimistic. "Sure we can," he said. "I'll show you. Take his feet, Rusty." He put his hands under Ned Beaumont's armpits.

They carried the unconscious man into the bathroom and put him in the tub. Jeff put the stopper in and turned on cold water from both the faucet below and the shower above. "That'll have him up and singing in no time," he predicted.

Five minutes later, when they hauled him dripping from the tub and set him on his feet, Ned Beaumont could stand. They took him into the bedroom again. O'Rory was sitting on one of the chairs smoking a cigarette. Whisky had gone.

"Put him on the bed," O'Rory ordered.

Jeff and Rusty led their charge to the bed, turned him around, and pushed him down on it. When they took their hands away from him he fell straight back on the bed. They pulled him into a sitting position again and Jeff slapped his battered face with an open hand, saying: "Come on, Rip Van Winkle, come to life."

"A swell chance of him coming to life," the sullen Rusty grumbled.

"You think he won't?" Jeff asked cheerfully and slapped Ned Beaumont again.

Ned Beaumont opened the one eye not too swollen to be opened. O'Rory said: "Beaumont."

Ned Beaumont raised his head and tried to look around the room, but there was nothing to show he could see Shad O'Rory.

O'Rory got up from his chair and stood in front of Ned Beaumont, bending down until his face was a few inches from the other man's. He asked: "Can you hear me, Beaumont?"

Ned Beaumont's open eye looked dull hate into O'Rory's eyes.

O'Rory said: "This is O'Rory, Beaumont. Can you hear what I say?"

Moving his swollen lips with difficulty, Ned Beaumont uttered a thick "Yes."

O'Rory said: "Good. Now listen to what I tell you. You're going to give me the dope on Paul." He spoke very distinctly without raising his voice, without his voice losing any of its musical quality. "Maybe you think you won't, but you will. I'll have you worked on from now till you do. Do you understand me?"

Ned Beaumont smiled. The condition of his face made the smile horrible. He said: "I won't."

O'Rory stepped back and said: "Work on him."

While Rusty hesitated, the apish Jeff knocked aside Ned Beaumont's upraised hand and pushed him down on the bed. "I got something to try." He scooped up Ned Beaumont's legs and tumbled them on the bed. He leaned over Ned Beaumont, his hands busy on Ned Beaumont's body.

Ned Beaumont's body and arms and legs jerked convulsively and three times he groaned. After that he lay still.

Jeff straightened up and took his hands away from the man on the bed. He was breathing heavily through his ape's mouth. He growled, half in complaint, half in apology: "It ain't no good now. He's throwed another joe."

4

When Ned Beaumont recovered consciousness he was alone in the room. The lights were on. As laboriously as before he got himself out of bed and across the room to the door. The door was locked. He was fumbling with the knob when the door was thrown open, pushing him back against the wall.

Jeff in his underwear, barefoot, came in. "Ain't you a pip?" he said. "Always up to some kind of tricks. Don't you never get tired of being bounced on the floor?" He took Ned Beaumont by the throat with his left hand and struck him in the face with his right fist, twice, but not so hard as he had hit him before. Then he pushed him backwards over to the bed and threw him on it. "And stay put awhile this time," he growled.

Ned Beaumont lay still with closed eyes.

Jeff went out, locking the door behind him.

Painfully Ned Beaumont climbed out of bed and made his way to the door. He tried it. Then he withdrew two steps and tried to hurl himself against it, succeeding only in lurching against it. He kept trying until the door was flung open again by Jeff.

Jeff said: "I never seen a guy that liked being hit so much or that I liked hitting so much." He leaned far over to one side and swung his fist up from below his knee.

Ned Beaumont stood blindly in the fist's path. It struck his cheek and knocked him the full length of the room. He lay still where he fell. He was lying there two hours later when Whisky came into the room.

Whisky awakened him with water from the bathroom and helped him to the bed. "Use your head," Whisky begged him. "These mugs'll kill you. They've got no sense."

Ned Beaumont looked dully at Whisky through a dull and bloody eye. "Let 'em," he managed to say.

He slept then until he was awakened by O'Rory, Jeff, and Rusty. He refused to tell O'Rory anything about Paul Madvig's affairs. He was dragged out of bed, beaten into unconsciousness, and flung into bed again. This was repeated a few hours later. No food was brought to him.

Going on hands and knees into the bathroom when he had regained consciousness after the last of these beatings, he saw, on the floor behind the wash-stand's pedestal, a narrow safety-razor-blade red with the rust of months. Getting it out from behind the pedestal was a task that took him all of ten minutes and his nerveless fingers failed a dozen times before they succeeded in picking it up from the tiled floor. He tried to cut his throat with it, but it fell out of his hand after he had no more than scratched his chin in three places. He lay down on the bathroom-floor and sobbed himself to sleep.

When he awakened again he could stand, and did. He doused his head in cold water and drank four glasses of water. The water made him sick and after that he began to shake with a chill. He went into the bedroom and lay down on the bare blood-stained mattress, but got up almost immediately to go stumbling and staggering in haste back to the bathroom, where he got down on hands and knees and searched the floor until he had found the rusty razor-blade. He sat on the floor and put the razor-blade into his vest-pocket. Putting it in, his fingers touched his lighter. He took the lighter out and looked at it. A cunning gleam came into his one open eye as he looked at the lighter. The gleam was not sane.

Shaking so that his teeth rattled together, he got up from the bathroom-floor and went into the bedroom again. He laughed harshly when he saw the newspaper under the table where the apish dark man and the sullen rosy-cheeked boy had played cards. Tearing and rumpling and wadding the paper in his hands, he carried it to the door and put it on the floor there. In each of the drawers in the chest of drawers he found a piece of wrapping-paper folded to cover the bottom. He rumpled them and put them with the newspaper against the door. With the razor-blade he made a long gash in the mattress, pulled out big handfuls of the coarse grey cotton with which the mattress was stuffed, and carried them to the door. He was not shaking now, nor stumbling, and he used both hands dexterously, but presently he tired of gutting the mattress and dragged what was left of it—tick and all—to the door.

He giggled then and, after the third attempt, got his lighter ignited. He set fire to the bottom of the heap against the door. At first he stood close to the heap, crouching over it, but as the smoke increased it drove him back step by step, reluctantly, coughing as he retreated. Presently he went into the bathroom, soaked a towel with water, and wrapped it around his head, covering eyes, nose, and mouth. He came stumbling back into the bedroom, a dim figure in the smoky room, fell against the bed, and sat down on the floor beside it.

Jeff found him there when he came in.

Jeff came in cursing and coughing through the rag he held against nose and mouth. In opening the door he had pushed most of the burning heap back a little. He kicked some more out of the way and stamped through the rest to reach Ned Beaumont. He took Ned Beaumont by the back of the collar and dragged him out of the room.

Outside, still holding Ned Beaumont by the back of the collar, Jeff kicked him to his feet and ran him down to the far end of the corridor. There he pushed him through an open doorway, bawled, "I'm going to eat one of your ears when I come back, you bastard," at him, kicked him again, stepped back into the corridor, slammed the door, and turned the key in its lock.

Ned Beaumont, kicked into the room, saved himself from a fall by catching hold of a table. He pushed himself up a little nearer straight and looked around. The towel had fallen down muffler-fashion around his neck and shoulders. The room had two windows. He went to the nearer window and tried to raise it. It was locked. He unfastened the lock and raised the window. Outside was night. He put a leg over the sill, then the other, turned so that he was lying belly-down across the sill, lowered himself until he was hanging by his hands, felt with his feet for some support, found none, and let himself drop.

V · *The Hospital*

1

A nurse was doing something to Ned Beaumont's face.

"Where am I?" he asked.

"St. Luke's Hospital." She was a small nurse with very large bright hazel eyes, a breathless sort of hushed voice, and an odor of mimosa.

"What day?"

"It's Monday."

"What month and year?" he asked. When she frowned at him he said: "Oh, never mind. How long have I been here?"

"This is the third day."

"Where's the telephone?" He tried to sit up.

"Stop that," she said. "You can't use the telephone and you mustn't get yourself excited."

"You use it, then. Call Hartford six one one six and tell Mr. Madvig that I've got to see him right away."

"Mr. Madvig's here every afternoon," she said, "but I don't think Doctor Tait will let you talk to anybody yet. As a matter of fact you've done a whole lot more talking now than you ought to."

"What is it now? Morning or afternoon?"

"Morning."

"That's too long to wait," he said. "Call him now."

"Doctor Tait will be in in a little while."

"I don't want any Doctor Taits," he said irritably. "I want Paul Madvig."

"You'll do what you're told," she replied. "You'll lie there and be quiet till Doctor Tait comes."

He scowled at her. "What a swell nurse you are. Didn't anybody ever tell you it's not good for patients to be quarreled with?"

She ignored his question.

He said: "Besides, you're hurting my jaw."

She said: "If you'd keep it still it wouldn't get hurt."

He was quiet for a moment. Then he asked: "What's supposed to have happened to me? Or didn't you get far enough in your lessons to know?"

"Probably a drunken brawl," she told him, but she could not keep her face straight after that. She laughed and said: "But honestly you shouldn't talk so much and you can't see anybody till the doctor says so."

2

Paul Madvig arrived early in the afternoon. "Christ, I'm glad to see you alive again!" he said. He took the invalid's unbandaged left hand in both of his.

Ned Beaumont said: "I'm all right. But here's what we've got to do: grab Walt Ivans and have him taken over to Braywood and shown to the gun-dealers there. He—"

"You told me all that," Madvig said. "That's done."

Ned Beaumont frowned. "I told you?"

"Sure—the morning you were picked up. They took you to the Emergency Hospital and you wouldn't let them do anything to you till you'd seen me and I came down there and you told me about Ivans and Braywood and passed out cold."

"It's a blank to me," Ned Beaumont said. "Did you nail them?"

"We got the Ivanses, all right, and Walt Ivans talked after he was identified in Braywood and the Grand Jury indicted Jeff Gardner and two John Does, but we're not going to be able to nail Shad on it. Gardner's the man Ivans dickered with and anybody knows he wouldn't do anything without Shad's say-so, but proving it's another thing."

"Jeff's the monkey-looking guy, huh? Has he been picked up yet?"

"No. Shad took him into hiding with him after you got away, I guess. They had you, didn't they?"

"Uh-huh. In the Dog House, upstairs. I went there to lay a trap for the gent and he out-trapped me." He scowled. "I remember going there with Whisky Vassos and being bitten by the dog and knocked around by

Jeff and a blond kid. Then there was something about a fire and—that's about all. Who found me? and where?"

"A copper found you crawling on all fours up the middle of Colman Street at three in the morning leaving a trail of blood behind you."

"I think of funny things to do," Ned Beaumont said.

3

The small nurse with large eyes opened the door cautiously and put her head in.

Ned Beaumont addressed her in a tired voice: "All right—peekaboo! But don't you think you're a little old for that?"

The nurse opened the door wider and stood on the sill holding the edge of the door with one hand. "No wonder people beat you up," she said. "I wanted to see if you were awake. Mr. Madvig and"—the breathless quality became more pronounced in her voice and her eyes became brighter—"a lady are here."

Ned Beaumont looked at her curiously and a bit mockingly. "What kind of lady?"

"It's Miss Janet Henry," she replied in the manner of one revealing some unexpected pleasant thing.

Ned Beaumont turned on his side, his face away from the nurse. He shut his eyes. A corner of his mouth twitched, but his voice was empty of expression: "Tell them I'm still asleep."

"You can't do that," she said. "They know you're not asleep—even if they haven't heard you talking—or I'd've been back before this."

He groaned dramatically and propped himself up on his elbow. "She'd only come back again some other time," he grumbled. "I might as well get it over with."

The nurse, looking at him with contemptuous eyes, said sarcastically: "We've had to keep policemen in front of the hospital to fight off all the women that've been trying to see you."

"That's all right for you to say," he told her. "Maybe you're impressed by senators' daughters who are in the roto all the time, but you've never been hounded by them the way I have. I tell you they've made my life miserable, them and their brown roto-sections. Senators' daughters, always senators' daughters, never a representative's daughter or a cabinet minister's daughter or an alderman's daughter for the sake of variety—never anything but— Do you suppose senators are more prolific than—"

"You're not really funny," the nurse said. "It's the way you comb your hair. I'll bring them in." She left the room.

Ned Beaumont took a long breath. His eyes were shiny. He moistened his lips and then pressed them together in a tight secretive smile, but when Janet Henry came into the room his face was a mask of casual politeness.

She came straight to his bed and said: "Oh, Mr. Beaumont, I was so glad to hear that you were recovering so nicely that I simply had to come." She put a hand in his and smiled down at him. Though her eyes were not a dark brown her otherwise pure blondness made them seem dark. "So if you didn't want me to come you're not to blame Paul. I made him bring me."

Ned Beaumont smiled back at her and said: "I'm awfully glad you did. It's terribly kind of you."

Paul Madvig, following Janet Henry into the room, had gone around to the opposite side of the bed. He grinned affectionately from her to Ned Beaumont and said: "I knew you'd be, Ned. I told her so. How's it go to-day?"

"Nobly. Pull some chairs up."

"We can't stay," the blond man replied. "I've got to meet M'Laughlin at the Grandcourt."

"But I don't," Janet Henry said. She directed her smile at Ned Beaumont again. "Mayn't I stay—a little while?"

"I'd love that," Ned Beaumont assured her while Madvig, coming around the bed to place a chair for her, beamed delightedly upon each of them in turn and said: "That's fine." When the girl was sitting beside the bed and her black coat had been laid back over the back of the chair, Madvig looked at his watch and growled: "I've got to run." He shook Ned Beaumont's hand. "Anything I can get for you?"

"No, thanks, Paul."

"Well, be good." The blond man turned towards Janet Henry, stopped, and addressed Ned Beaumont again: "How far do you think I ought to go with M'Laughlin this first time?"

Ned Beaumont moved his shoulders a little. "As far as you want, so long as you don't put anything in plain words. They scare him. But you could hire him to commit murders if you put it to him in a long-winded way, like: 'If there was a man named Smith who lived in such and such a place and he got sick or something and didn't get well and you happened to drop in to see me some time and just by luck an envelope addressed to you had been sent there in care of me, how would I know it had five hundred dollars in it?'."

Madvig nodded. "I don't want any murders," he said, "but we do need that railroad vote." He frowned. "I wish you were up, Ned."

"I will be in a day or two. Did you see the *Observer* this morning?"

"No."

Ned Beaumont looked around the room. "Somebody's run off with it. The dirt was in an editorial in a box in the middle of the front page. *What are our city officials going to do about it?* A list of six weeks' crimes to show we're having a crime-wave. A lot smaller list of who's been caught to show the police aren't able to do much about it. Most of the squawking done about Taylor Henry's murder."

When her brother was named, Janet Henry winced and her lips parted in a little silent gasp. Madvig looked at her and then quickly at Ned Beaumont to move his head in a brief warning gesture.

Ned Beaumont, ignoring the effect of his words on the others, continued: "They were brutal about that. Accused the police of deliberately keeping their hands off the murder for a week so a gambler high in political circles could use it to square a grievance with another gambler—meaning my going after Despain to collect my money. Wondered what Senator Henry thought of his new political allies' use of his son's murder for this purpose."

Madvig, red of face, fumbling for his watch, said hastily: "I'll get a copy and read it. I've got to—"

"Also," Ned Beaumont went on serenely, "they accuse the police of raiding—after having protected them for years—those joints whose owners wouldn't come across with enormous campaign-contributions. That's what they make of your fight with Shad O'Rory. And they promise to print a list of the places that are still running because their owners did come across."

Madvig said, "Well, well," uncomfortably, said, "Good-by, have a nice visit," to Janet Henry, "See you later," to Ned Beaumont, and went out.

Janet Henry leaned forward in her chair. "Why don't you like me?" she asked Ned Beaumont.

"I think maybe I do," he said.

She shook her head. "You don't. I know it."

"You can't go by my manners," he told her. "They're always pretty bad."

"You don't like me," she insisted, not answering his smile, "and I want you to."

He was modest. "Why?"

"Because you are Paul's best friend," she replied.

"Paul," he said, looking obliquely at her, "has a lot of friends: he's a politician."

She moved her head impatiently. "You're his best friend." She paused, then added: "He thinks so."

"What do you think?" he asked with incomplete seriousness.

"I think you are," she said gravely, "or you would not be here now. You would not have gone through that for him."

His mouth twitched in a meager smile. He did not say anything.

When it became manifest that he was not going to speak she said earnestly: "I wish you would like me, if you can."

He repeated: "I think maybe I do."

She shook her head. "You don't."

He smiled at her. His smile was very young and engaging, his eyes shy, his voice youthfully diffident and confiding, as he said: "I'll tell you what makes you think that, Miss Henry. It's—you see, Paul picked me up out of the gutter, as you might say, just a year or so ago, and so I'm kind of awkward and clumsy when I'm around people like you who belong to another world altogether—society and roto-sections and all—and you mistake that—uh—*gaucherie* for enmity, which it isn't at all."

She rose and said, "You're ridiculing me," without resentment.

When she had gone Ned Beaumont lay back on his pillows and stared at the ceiling with glittering eyes until the nurse came in.

The nurse came in and asked: "What have you been up to now?"

Ned Beaumont raised his head to look sullenly at her, but he did not speak.

The nurse said: "She went out of here as near crying as anybody could without crying."

Ned Beaumont lowered his head to the pillow again. "I must be losing my grip," he said. "I usually make senators' daughters cry."

4

A man of medium size, young and dapper, with a sleek, dark, rather good-looking face, came in.

Ned Beaumont sat up in bed and said: "'Lo, Jack."

Jack said, "You don't look as bad as I thought you would," and advanced to the side of the bed.

"I'm still all in one piece. Grab a chair."

Jack sat down and took out a package of cigarettes.

Ned Beaumont said: "I've got another job for you." He put a hand under his pillows and brought out an envelope.

Jack lit his cigarette before he took the envelope from Ned Beaumont's hand. It was a plain white envelope addressed to Ned Beaumont at St. Luke's Hospital and bore the local postmark dated two days before. Inside was a single typewritten sheet of paper which Jack took out and read.

> What do you know about Paul Madvig that Shad O'Rory was so anxious to learn?
>
> Has it anything to do with the murder of Taylor Henry?
>
> If not, why should you have gone to such lengths to keep it secret?

Jack refolded the sheet of paper and returned it to the envelope before he raised his head. Then he asked: "Does it make sense?"

"Not that I know of. I want you to find out who wrote it."

Jack nodded. "Do I keep it?"

"Yes."

Jack put the envelope in his pocket. "Any ideas about who might have done it?"

"None at all."

Jack studied the lighted end of his cigarette. "It's a job, you know," he said presently.

"I know it," Ned Beaumont agreed, "and all I can tell you is that there's been a lot of them—or several of them—in the past week. That's my third. I know Farr got at least one. I don't know who else has been getting them."

"Can I see some of the others?"

Ned Beaumont said: "That's the only one I kept. They're all pretty much alike, though—same paper, same typewriting, three questions in each, all on the same subject."

Jack regarded Ned Beaumont with inquisitive eyes. "But not exactly the same questions?" he asked.

"Not exactly, but all getting to the same point."

Jack nodded and smoked his cigarette.

Ned Beaumont said: "You understand this is to be strictly on the qt."

"Sure." Jack took the cigarette from his mouth. "The 'same point' you mentioned is Madvig's connection with the murder?"

"Yes," Ned Beaumont replied, looking with level eyes at the sleek dark young man, "and there isn't any connection."

Jack's dark face was inscrutable. "I don't see how there could be," he said as he stood up.

5

The nurse came in carrying a large basket of fruit. "Isn't it lovely?" she said as she set it down.

Ned Beaumont nodded cautiously.

The nurse took a small stiff envelope from the basket. "I bet you it's from her," she said, giving Ned Beaumont the envelope.

"What'll you bet?"

"Anything you want."

Ned Beaumont nodded as if some dark suspicion had been confirmed. "You looked," he said.

"Why, you—" Her words stopped when he laughed, but indignation remained in her mien.

He took Janet Henry's card from the envelope. One word was written on it: *Please!* Frowning at the card, he told the nurse, "You win," and tapped the card on a thumb-nail. "Help yourself to that gunk and take enough of it so it'll look as if I'd been eating it."

Later that afternoon he wrote:

My dear Miss Henry—

You've quite overwhelmed me with your kindness—first your coming to see me, and then the fruit. I don't at all know how to thank you, but I hope I shall some day be able to more clearly show my gratitude.

Sincerely yours,
NED BEAUMONT

When he had finished he read what he had written, tore it up, and rewrote it on another sheet of paper, using the same words, but rearranging them to make the ending of the second sentence read: "be able some day to show my gratitude more clearly."

6

Ned Beaumont, in bathrobe and slippers this morning, was reading a copy of the *Observer* over his breakfast at a table by the window of his hospital-room when Opal Madvig came in. He folded the newspaper, put it face-down on the table beside his tray, and rose saying, " 'Lo, snip," cordially. He was pale.

"Why didn't you call me up when you got back from New York?" she demanded in an accusing tone. She too was pale. Pallor accentuated the childlike texture of her skin, yet made her face seem less young. Her blue eyes were wide open and dark with emotion, but not to be read easily. She held herself tall without stiffness, in the manner of one more sure of his balance than of stability underfoot. Ignoring the chair he moved out from the wall for her, she repeated, imperatively as before: "Why didn't you?"

He laughed at her, softly, indulgently, and said: "I like you in that shade of brown."

"Oh, Ned, please—"

"That's better," he said. "I intended coming out to the house, but—well—there were lots of things happening when I got back and a lot of loose ends of things that had happened while I was gone, and by the time I finished with those I ran into Shad O'Rory and got sent here." He waved an arm to indicate the hospital.

Her gravity was not affected by the lightness of his tone.

"Are they going to hang this Despain?" she asked curtly.

He laughed again and said: "We're not going to get very far talking like this."

She frowned, but said, "Are they, Ned?" with less haughtiness.

"I don't think so," he told her, shaking his head a little. "The chances are he didn't kill Taylor after all."

She did not seem surprised. "Did you know that when you asked me to—to help you get—or fix up—evidence against him?"

He smiled reproachfully. "Of course not, snip. What do you think I am?"

"You did know it." Her voice was cold and scornful as her blue eyes. "You only wanted to get the money he owed you and you made me help you use Taylor's murder for that."

"Have it your own way," he replied indifferently.

She came a step closer to him. The faintest of quivers disturbed her chin for an instant, then her young face was firm and bold again. "Do you know who killed him?" she asked, her eyes probing his.

He shook his head slowly from side to side.

"Did Dad?"

He blinked. "You mean did Paul know who killed him?"

She stamped a foot. "I mean did Dad kill him?" she cried.

He put a hand over her mouth. His eyes had jerked into focus on the closed door. "Shut up," he muttered.

She stepped back from his hand as one of her hands pushed it away from her face. "Did he?" she insisted.

In a low angry voice he said: "If you must be a nit-wit at least don't go around with a megaphone. Nobody cares what kind of idiotic notions you have as long as you keep them to yourself, but you've got to keep them to yourself."

Her eyes opened wide and dark. "Then he did kill him," she said in a small flat voice, but with utter certainty.

He thrust his face down towards hers. "No, my dear," he said in an enraged sugary voice, "he didn't kill him." He held his face near hers. A vicious smile distorted his features.

Firm of countenance and voice, not drawing back from him, she said: "If he didn't I can't understand what difference it makes what I say or how loud."

An end of his mouth twitched up in a sneer. "You'd be surprised how many things there are you can't understand," he said angrily, "and never will if you keep on like this." He stepped back from her, a long step, and put his fists in the pockets of his bathrobe. Both corners of his mouth were pulled down now and there were grooves in his forehead. His narrowed eyes stared at the floor in front of her feet. "Where'd you get this crazy idea?" he growled.

"It's not a crazy idea. You know it's not."

He moved his shoulders impatiently and demanded: "Where'd you get it?"

She too moved her shoulders. "I didn't get it anywhere. I—I suddenly saw it."

"Nonsense," he said sharply, looking up at her under his brows. "Did you see the *Observer* this morning?"

"No."

He stared at her with hard skeptical eyes.

Annoyance brought a little color into her face. "I did not," she said. "Why do you ask?"

"No?" he asked in a tone that said he did not believe her, but the skeptical gleam had gone out of his eyes. They were dull and thoughtful. Suddenly they brightened. He took his right hand from his bathrobe-pocket. He held it out towards her, palm up. "Let me see the letter," he said.

She stared at him with round eyes. "What?"

"The letter," he said, "the typewritten letter—three questions and no signature."

She lowered her eyes to avoid his and embarrassment disturbed, very slightly, her features. After a moment of hesitation she asked, "How did you know?" and opened her brown hand-bag.

"Everybody in town's had at least one," he said carelessly. "Is this your first?"

"Yes." She gave him a crumpled sheet of paper.

He straightened it out and read:

Are you really too stupid to know that your father murdered your lover?

If you do not know it, why did you help him and Ned Beaumont in their attempt to fasten the crime on an innocent man?

Do you know that by helping your father escape justice you are making yourself an accomplice in his crime?

Ned Beaumont nodded and smiled lightly. "They're all pretty much alike," he said. He wadded the paper in a loose ball and tossed it at the waste-basket beside the table. "You'll probably get some more of them now you're on the mailing-list."

Opal Madvig drew her lower lip in between her teeth. Her blue eyes were bright without warmth. They studied Ned Beaumont's composed face.

He said: "O'Rory's trying to make campaign-material out of it. You know about my trouble with him. That was because he thought I'd broken with your father and could be paid to help frame him for the murder—enough at least to beat him at the polls—and I wouldn't."

Her eyes did not change. "What did you and Dad fight about?" she asked.

"That's nobody's business but ours, snip," he said gently, "if we did fight."

"You did," she said, "in Carson's speakeasy." She put her teeth together with a click and said boldly: "You quarreled when you found out that he really had—had killed Taylor."

He laughed and asked in a mocking tone: "Hadn't I known that all along?"

Her expression was not affected by his humor. "Why did you ask if I had seen the *Observer?*" she demanded. "What was in it?"

"Some more of the same sort of nonsense," he told her evenly. "It's there on the table if you want to see it. There'll be plenty of it before the campaign's over: this is going to be that kind. And you'll be giving your father a swell break by swallowing—" He broke off with an impatient gesture because she was no longer listening to him.

She had gone to the table and was picking up the newspaper he had put down when she came in.

He smiled pleasantly at her back and said: "It's on the front page, *An Open Letter to the Mayor.*"

As she read she began to tremble—her knees, her hands, her mouth—so that Ned Beaumont frowned anxiously at her, but when she had finished and had dropped the newspaper on the table and had turned to face him directly her tall body and fair face were statue-like in their immobility. She addressed him in a low voice between lips that barely moved to let the words out: "They wouldn't dare say such things if they were not true."

"That's nothing to what'll be said before they're through," he drawled lazily. He seemed amused, though there was a suggestion of anger difficultly restrained in the glitter of his eyes.

She looked at him for a long moment, then, saying nothing, turned towards the door.

He said: "Wait."

She halted and confronted him again. His smile was friendly now, ingratiating. Her face was a tinted statue's.

He said: "Politics is a tough game, snip, the way it's being played here this time. The *Observer* is on the other side of the fence and they're not worrying much about the truth of anything that'll hurt Paul. They—"

"I don't believe that," she said. "I know Mr. Mathews—his wife was only a few years ahead of me at school and we were friends—and I don't believe he'd say anything like that about Dad unless it was true, or unless he had good reason for thinking it true."

Ned Beaumont chuckled. "You know a lot about it. Mathews is up to his ears in debt. The State Central Trust Company holds both mortgages on his plant—one on his house too, for that matter. The State Central belongs to Bill Roan. Bill Roan is running for the Senate against Henry. Mathews does what he's told to do and prints what he's told to print."

Opal Madvig did not say anything. There was nothing to indicate that she had been at all convinced by Ned Beaumont's argument.

He went on, speaking in an amiable, persuasive tone: "This"—he flicked a finger at the paper on the table—"is nothing to what'll come later. They're going to rattle Taylor Henry's bones till they think up something worse and we're going to have this sort of stuff to read till election's over. We might just as well get used to it now and you, of all people, oughtn't to let yourself be bothered by it. Paul doesn't mind it much. He's a politician and—"

"He's a murderer," she said in a low distinct voice.

"And his daughter's a chump," he exclaimed irritably. "Will you stop that foolishness?"

"My father is a murderer," she said.

"You're crazy. Listen to me, snip. Your father had absolutely nothing to do with Taylor's murder. He—"

"I don't believe you," she said gravely. "I'll never believe you again."

He scowled at her.

She turned and went to the door.

"Wait," he said. "Let me—"

She went out and shut the door behind her.

7

Ned Beaumont's face, after a grimace of rage at the closed door, became heavily thoughtful. Lines came into his forehead. His dark eyes grew narrow and introspective. His lips puckered up under his mustache. Presently he put a finger to his mouth and bit its nail. He breathed regularly, but with more depth than usual.

Footsteps sounded outside his door. He dropped his appearance of thoughtfulness and walked idly towards the window, humming *Little Lost Lady*. The footsteps went on past his door. He stopped humming and bent to pick up the sheet of paper holding the three questions that had been addressed to Opal Madvig. He did not smooth the paper, but thrust it, crumpled in a loose ball as it was, into one of his bathrobe-pockets.

He found and lit a cigar then and, with it between his teeth burning, stood by the table and squinted down through smoke at the front page of the *Observer* lying there.

AN OPEN LETTER TO THE MAYOR

SIR:

The *Observer* has come into possession of certain information which it believes to be of paramount importance in clearing up the mystery surrounding the recent murder of Taylor Henry.

This information is incorporated in several affidavits now in the *Observer's* safety-deposit box. The substance of these affidavits is as follows:

1. That Paul Madvig quarreled with Taylor Henry some months ago over the young man's attentions to his daughter and forbade his daughter to see Henry again.
2. That Paul Madvig's daughter nevertheless continued to meet Taylor Henry in a furnished room he had rented for that purpose.
3. That they were together in this furnished room the afternoon of the very day on which he was killed.
4. That Paul Madvig went to Taylor Henry's home that evening, supposedly to remonstrate with the young man, or his father, again.
5. That Paul Madvig appeared angry when he left the Henry residence a few minutes before Taylor Henry was murdered.
6. That Paul Madvig and Taylor Henry were seen within half a block of each other, less than a block from the spot where the young man's body was found, not more than fifteen minutes before his body was found.
7. That the Police Department has not at present a single detective engaged in trying to find Taylor Henry's murderer.

The *Observer* believes that you should know these things and that the voters and taxpayers should know them. The *Observer* has no ax to grind, no motive except the desire to see justice done. The *Observer* will welcome an opportunity to hand these affidavits, as well as all other information it has, to you or to any qualified city or state official and, if such a course can be shown an aid to justice, to refrain from publishing any or all of the details of these affidavits.

But the *Observer* will not permit the information incorporated in these affidavits to be ignored. If the officials elected and appointed to enforce law and order in this city and state do not consider these affidavits of sufficient importance to be acted upon, the *Observer* will carry the matter to that higher tribunal, the People of this City, by publishing them in full.

H. K. MATHEWS, Publisher

Ned Beaumont grunted derisively and blew cigar-smoke down at this declaration, but his eyes remained somber.

8

Early that afternoon Paul Madvig's mother came to see Ned Beaumont.

He put his arms around her and kissed her on both cheeks until she pushed him away with a mock-severe "Do stop it. You're worse than the Airedale Paul used to have."

"I'm part Airedale," he said, "on my father's side," and went behind her to help her out of her sealskin coat.

Smoothing her black dress, she went to the bed and sat on it.

He hung the coat on the back of a chair and stood—legs apart, hands in bathrobe-pockets—before her.

She studied him critically. "You don't look so bad," she said presently, "nor yet so good. How do you feel?"

"Swell. I'm only hanging around here on account of the nurses."

"That wouldn't surprise me much, neither," she told him. "But don't stand there ogling me like a Cheshire cat. You make me nervous. Sit down." She patted the bed beside her.

He sat down beside her.

She said: "Paul seems to think you did something very grand and noble by doing whatever it was you did, but you can't tell me that if you had behaved yourself you would ever have got into whatever scrape you got into at all."

"Aw, Mom," he began.

She cut him off. The gaze of her blue eyes that were young as her son's bored into Ned Beaumont's brown ones. "Look here, Ned, Paul didn't kill that whipper-snapper, did he?"

Surprise opened Ned Beaumont's eyes and mouth. "No."

"I didn't think so," the old woman said. "He's always been a good boy, but I've heard that there's some nasty hints going around and the Lord only knows what goes on in this politics. I'm sure I haven't any idea."

Amazement tinged with humor was in the eyes with which Ned Beaumont looked at her bony face.

She said: "Well, goggle at me, but I haven't got any way of knowing what you men are up to, or what you do without thinking anything of it. It was a long while before ever you were born that I gave up trying to find out."

He patted her shoulder. "You're a humdinger, Mom," he said admiringly.

She drew away from his hand and fixed him with severe penetrant eyes again. "Would you tell me if he had killed him?" she demanded.

He shook his head no.

"Then how do I know he didn't?"

He laughed. "Because," he explained, "if he had I'd still say, 'No,' but then, if you asked me if I'd tell you the truth if he had, I'd say, 'Yes.'" Merriment went out of his eyes and voice. "He didn't do it, Mom." He smiled at her. He smiled with his lips only and they were thin against his teeth. "It would be nice if somebody in town besides me thought he didn't do it and it would be especially nice if that other one was his mother."

9

An hour after Mrs. Madvig's departure Ned Beaumont received a package containing four books and Janet Henry's card. He was writing her a note of thanks when Jack arrived.

Jack, letting cigarette-smoke come out with his words, said: "I think I've got something, though I don't know how you're going to like it."

Ned Beaumont looked thoughtfully at the sleek young man and smoothed the left side of his mustache with a forefinger. "If it's what I hired you to get I'll like it well enough." His voice was matter-of-fact as Jack's. "Sit down and tell me about it."

Jack sat down carefully, crossed his legs, put his hat on the floor, and looked from his cigarette to Ned Beaumont. He said: "It looks like those things were written by Madvig's daughter."

Ned Beaumont's eyes widened a little, but only for a moment. His face lost some of its color and his breathing became irregular. There was no change in his voice. "What makes it look like that?"

From an inner pocket Jack brought two sheets of paper similar in size and make, folded alike. He gave them to Ned Beaumont who, when he had unfolded them, saw that on each were three typewritten questions, the same three questions on each sheet.

"One of them's the one you gave me yesterday," Jack said. "Could you tell which?"

Ned Beaumont shook his head slowly from side to side.

"There's no difference," Jack said. "I wrote the other one on Charter Street where Taylor Henry had a room that Madvig's daughter used to come to—with a Corona typewriter that was there and on paper that was there. So far as anybody seems to know there were only two keys to the place. He had one and she had one. She's been back there at least a couple of times since he was killed."

Ned Beaumont, scowling now at the sheets of paper in his hands, nodded without looking up.

Jack lit a fresh cigarette from the one he had been smoking, rose and went to the table to mash the old cigarette in the ash-tray there, and returned to his seat. There was nothing in his face or manner to show that he had any interest in Ned Beaumont's reaction to their discovery.

After another minute of silence Ned Beaumont raised his head a little and asked: "How'd you get this?"

Jack put his cigarette in a corner of his mouth where it wagged with his words. "The *Observer* tip on the place this morning gave me the lead. That's where the police got theirs too, but they got there first. I got a pretty good break, though: the copper left in charge was a friend of mine

—Fred Hurley—and for a ten-spot he let me do all the poking around I wanted."

Ned Beaumont rattled the papers in his hand. "Do the police know this?" he asked.

Jack shrugged. "I didn't tell them. I pumped Hurley, but he didn't know anything—just put there to watch things till they decide what they're going to do. Maybe they know, maybe they don't." He shook cigarette-ash on the floor. "I could find out."

"Never mind that. What else did you turn up?"

"I didn't look for anything else."

Ned Beaumont, after a quick glance at the dark young man's inscrutable face, looked down at the sheets of paper again. "What kind of dump is it?"

"Thirteen twenty-four. They had a room and bath under the name of French. The woman that runs the place claims she didn't know who they really were till the police came today. Maybe she didn't. It's the kind of joint where not much is asked. She says they used to be there a lot, mostly in the afternoons, and that the girl's been back a couple of times in the last week or so that she knows of, though she could pop in and out without being seen easily enough."

"Sure it's her?"

Jack made a noncommittal gesture with one hand. "The description's right." He paused, then added carelessly as he exhaled smoke: "She's the only one the woman saw since he was killed."

Ned Beaumont raised his head again. His eyes were hard. "Taylor had others coming there?" he asked.

Jack made the noncommittal gesture once more. "The woman wouldn't say so. She said she didn't know, but from the way she said it I'd say it was a safe bet she was lying."

"Couldn't tell by what's in the place?"

Jack shook his head. "No. There's not much woman stuff there—just a kimono and toilet things and pajamas and stuff like that."

"Much of his stuff there?"

"Oh, a suit and a pair of shoes and some underwear and pajamas and socks and so on."

"Any hats?"

Jack smiled. "No hats," he said.

Ned Beaumont got up and went to the window. Outside darkness was almost complete. A dozen raindrops clung to the glass and as many more struck it lightly while Ned Beaumont stood there. He turned to face Jack again. "Thanks a lot, Jack," he said slowly. His eyes were focused on Jack's face in a dully absent-minded stare. "I think maybe I'll have another job for you soon—maybe tonight. I'll give you a ring."

Jack said, "Right," and rose and went out.

Ned Beaumont went to the closet for his clothes, carried them into the bathroom, and put them on. When he came out a nurse was in his room, a tall full-bodied woman with a shiny pale face.

"Why, you're dressed!" she exclaimed.

"Yes, I've got to go out."

Alarm joined astonishment in her mien. "But you can't, Mr. Beaumont," she protested. "It's night and it's beginning to rain and Doctor Tait would—"

"I know, I know," he said impatiently, and went around her to the door.

VI · *The Observer*

1

MRS. MADVIG opened her front door. "Ned!" she cried, "are you crazy? Running around on a night like this, and you just out of the hospital."

"The taxi didn't leak," he said, but his grin lacked virility. "Paul in?"

"He went out not more than half an hour ago, I think to the Club. But come in, come in."

"Opal home?" he asked as he shut the door and followed her down the hall.

"No. She's been off somewhere since morning."

Ned Beaumont halted in the living-room doorway. "I can't stay," he said. "I'll run on down to the Club and see Paul there." His voice was not quite steady.

The old woman turned quickly towards him. "You'll do no such thing," she said in a scolding voice. "Look at you, you're just about to have a chill. You'll sit right down there by the fire and let me get you something hot to drink."

"Can't, Mom," he told her. "I've got to go places."

Her blue eyes wherein age did not show became bright and keen. "When did you leave the hospital?" she demanded.

"Just now."

She put her lips together hard, then opened them a little to say accusingly: "You walked out." A shadow disturbed the clear blueness of her eyes. She came close to Ned Beaumont and held her face close to his: she was nearly as tall as he. Her voice was harsh now as if coming from a parched throat. "Is it something about Paul?" The shadow in her eyes became recognizable as fear. "And Opal?"

His voice was barely audible. "It's something I've got to see them about."

She touched one of his cheeks somewhat timidly with bony fingers. "You're a good boy, Ned," she said.

He put an arm around her. "Don't worry, Mom. None of it's bad as it could be. Only—if Opal comes home make her stay—if you can."

"Is it anything you can tell me, Ned?" she asked.

"Not now and—well—it might be just as well not to let either of them know you think anything's wrong."

2

Ned Beaumont walked five blocks through the rain to a drug-store. He used a telephone there first to order a taxicab and then to call two numbers and ask for Mr. Mathews. He did not get Mr. Mathews on the wire.

He called another number and asked for Mr. Rumsen. A moment later he was saying: "'Lo, Jack, this is Ned Beaumont. Busy? . . . Fine. Here it is. I want to know if the girl we were talking about went to see Mathews of the *Observer* today and what she did afterwards, if she did. . . . That's right, Hal Mathews. I tried to get him by phone, there and home, but no luck. . . . Well, on the quiet if you can, but get it and get it quick. . . . No, I'm out of the hospital. I'll be home waiting. You know my number. . . . Yes, Jack. Fine, thanks, and ring me as often as you can. . . . 'By."

He went out to the waiting taxicab, got into it, and gave the driver his address, but after half a dozen blocks he tapped the front window with his fingers and gave the driver another address.

Presently the taxicab came to rest in front of a squat greyish house set in the center of a steeply sloping smooth lawn. "Wait," he told the driver as he got out.

The greyish house's front door was opened to his ring by a red-haired maid.

"Mr. Farr in?" he asked her.

"I'll see. Who shall I tell him?"

"Mr. Beaumont."

The District Attorney came into the reception-hall with both hands out. His florid pugnacious face was all smiling. "Well, well, Beaumont, this is a real pleasure," he said as he rushed up to his visitor. "Here, give me your coat and hat."

Ned Beaumont smiled and shook his head. "I can't stay," he said. "I just dropped in for a second on my way home from the hospital."

"All shipshape again? Splendid!"

"Feeling pretty good," Ned Beaumont said. "Anything new?"

"Nothing very important. The birds who manhandled you are still loose—in hiding somewhere—but we'll get them."

Ned Beaumont made a depreciatory mouth. "I didn't die and they weren't trying to kill me: you could only stick them with an assault-charge." He looked somewhat drowsily at Farr. "Had any more of those three-question epistles?"

The District Attorney cleared his throat. "Uh—yes, come to think of it, there were one or two more of them."

"How many?" Ned Beaumont asked. His voice was politely casual. The ends of his lips were raised a little in an idle smile. Amusement glinted in his eyes, but his eyes held Farr's.

The District Attorney cleared his throat. "Three," he said reluctantly. Then his eyes brightened. "Did you hear about the splendid meeting we had at—?"

Ned Beaumont interrupted him. "All along the same line?" he asked.

"Uh—more or less." The District Attorney licked his lips and a pleading expression began to enter his eyes.

"How much more—or less?"

Farr's eyes slid their gaze down from Ned Beaumont's eyes to his necktie and sidewise to his left shoulder. He moved his lips vaguely, but did not utter a sound.

Ned Beaumont's smile was openly malicious now. "All saying Paul killed Taylor Henry?" he asked in a sugary voice.

Farr jumped, his face faded to a light orange, and in his excitement he let his startled eyes focus on Ned Beaumont's eyes again. "Christ, Ned!" he gasped.

Ned Beaumont laughed. "You're getting nerves, Farr," he said, still sugary of voice. "Better watch yourself or you'll be going to pieces." He made his face grave. "Has Paul said anything to you about it? About your nerves, I mean."

"N-no."

Ned Beaumont smiled again. "Maybe he hasn't noticed it—yet." He raised an arm, glanced at his wrist-watch, then at Farr. "Found out who wrote them yet?" he asked sharply.

The District Attorney stammered: "Look here, Ned, I don't—you know—it's not—" floundered and stopped.

Ned Beaumont asked: "Well?"

The District Attorney gulped and said desperately: "We've got something, Ned, but it's too soon to say. Maybe there's nothing to it. You know how these things are."

Ned Beaumont nodded. There was nothing but friendliness in his face now. His voice was level and cool without chilliness saying: "You've learned where they were written and you've found the machine they were written on, but that's all you've got so far. You haven't got enough to even guess who wrote them."

"That's right, Ned," Farr blurted out with a great air of relief.

Ned Beaumont took Farr's hand and shook it cordially. "That's the stuff," he said. "Well, I've got to run along. You can't go wrong taking things slowly, being sure you're right before you go ahead. You can take my word for that."

The District Attorney's face and voice were warm with emotion. "Thanks, Ned, thanks!"

3

At ten minutes past nine o'clock that evening the telephone-bell in Ned Beaumont's living-room rang. He went quickly to the telephone. "Hello. . . . Yes, Jack. . . . Yes. . . . Yes. . . . Where? . . . Yes, that's fine. . . . That'll be all tonight. Thanks a lot."

When he rose from the telephone he was smiling with pale lips. His eyes were shiny and reckless. His hands shook a little.

The telephone-bell rang again before he had taken his third step. He hesitated, went back to the telephone. "Hello. . . . Oh, hello, Paul. . . . Yes, I got tired of playing invalid. . . . Nothing special—just thought I'd drop in and see you. . . . No, I'm afraid I can't. I'm not feeling as strong as I thought I was, so I think I'd better go to bed. . . . Yes, tomorrow, sure. . . . 'By."

He put on rain-coat and hat going downstairs. Wind drove rain in at him when he opened the street-door, drove it into his face as he walked half a block to the garage on the corner.

In the garage's glass-walled office a lanky brown-haired man in once-white overalls was tilted back on a wooden chair, his feet on a shelf above an electric heater, reading a newspaper. He lowered the newspaper when Ned Beaumont said: " 'Lo, Tommy."

The dirtiness of Tommy's face made his teeth seem whiter than they were. He showed many of them in a grin and said: "Kind of weatherish tonight."

"Yes. Got an iron I can have? One that'll carry me over country roads tonight?"

Tommy said: "Jesus! Lucky for you you could pick your night. You might've had to go on a bad one. Well, I got a Buick that I don't care what happens to."

"Will it get me there?"

"It's just as likely to as anything else," Tommy said, "tonight."

"All right. Fill it up for me. What's the best road up Lazy Creek way on a night like this?"

"How far up?"

Ned Beaumont looked thoughtfully at the garageman, then said: "Along about where it runs into the river."

Tommy nodded. "The Mathews place?" he asked.

Ned Beaumont did not say anything.

Tommy said: "It makes a difference which place you're going to."

"Yes? The Mathews place." Ned Beaumont frowned. "This is under the hat, Tommy."

"Did you come to me because you thought I'd talk or because you knew I wouldn't?" Tommy demanded argumentatively.

Ned Beaumont said: "I'm in a hurry."

"Then you take the New River Road as far as Barton's, take the dirt road over the bridge there—if you can make it at all—and then the first cross-road back east. That'll bring you in behind Mathews's place along about the top of the hill. If you can't make the dirt road in this weather you'll have to go on up the New River Road to where it crosses and then cut back along the old one."

"Thanks."

When Ned Beaumont was getting into the Buick Tommy said to him in a markedly casual tone: "There's an extra gun in the side-pocket."

Ned Beaumont stared at the lanky man. "Extra?" he asked blankly.

"Pleasant trip," Tommy said.

Ned Beaumont shut the door and drove away.

4

The clock in the dashboard said ten-thirty-two. Ned Beaumont switched off the lights and got somewhat stiffly out of the Buick. Wind-driven rain hammered tree, bush, ground, man, car with incessant wet blows. Downhill, through rain and foliage, irregular small patches of yellow light glowed faintly. Ned Beaumont shivered, tried to draw his rain-coat closer around him, and began to stumble downhill through drenched underbrush towards the patches of light.

Wind and rain on his back pushed him downhill towards the patches. As he went downhill stiffness gradually left him so that, though he stumbled often and staggered, and was tripped by obstacles underfoot, he kept his feet under him and moved nimbly enough, if erratically, towards his goal.

Presently a path came under his feet. He turned into it, holding it partly by its sliminess under his feet, partly by the feel of the bushes whipping his face on either side, and not at all by sight. The path led him off to the left for a little distance, but then, swinging in a broad curve, brought him to the brink of a small gorge through which water rushed noisily and from there, in another curve, to the front door of the building where the yellow light glowed.

Ned Beaumont went straight up to the door and knocked.

The door was opened by a grey-haired bespectacled man. His face was mild and greyish and the eyes that peered anxiously through the pale-tortoise-shell-encircled lenses of his spectacles were grey. His brown suit was neat and of good quality, but not fashionably cut. One side of his rather high stiff white collar had been blistered in four places by drops of water. He stood aside holding the door open and said, "Come in, sir, come in out of the rain," in a friendly if not hearty voice. "A wretched night to be out in."

Ned Beaumont lowered his head no more than two inches in the beginning of a bow and stepped indoors. He was in a large room that occupied all the building's ground-floor. The sparseness and simplicity of the room's furnishings gave it a primitive air that was pleasantly devoid of ostentation. It was a kitchen, a dining-room, and a living-room.

Opal Madvig rose from the footstool on which she had been sitting at one end of the fireplace and, holding herself tall and straight, stared with hostile bleak eyes at Ned Beaumont.

He took off his hat and began to unbutton his rain-coat. The others recognized him then.

The man who had opened the door said, "Why, it's Beaumont!" in an incredulous voice and looked wide-eyed at Shad O'Rory.

Shad O'Rory was sitting in a wooden chair in the center of the room facing the fireplace. He smiled dreamily at Ned Beaumont, saying, in his musical faintly Irish barytone, "And so it is," and, "How are you, Ned?"

Jeff Gardner's apish face broadened in a grin that showed his beautiful false teeth and almost completely hid his little red eyes. "By Jesus, Rusty!" he said to the sullen rosy-cheeked boy who lounged on the bench beside him, "little Rubber Ball has come back to us. I told you he liked the way we bounced him around."

Rusty lowered at Ned Beaumont and growled something that did not carry across the room.

The thin girl in red sitting not far from Opal Madvig looked at Ned Beaumont with bright interested dark eyes.

Ned Beaumont took off his coat. His lean face, still bearing the marks of Jeff's and Rusty's fists, was tranquil except for the recklessness aglitter in his eyes. He put his coat and hat on a long unpainted chest that was against one wall near the door. He smiled politely at the man who had admitted him and said: "My car broke down as I was passing. It's very kind of you to give me shelter, Mr. Mathews."

Mathews said, "Not at all—glad to," somewhat vaguely. Then his frightened eyes looked pleadingly at O'Rory again.

O'Rory stroked his smooth white hair with a slender pale hand and smiled pleasantly at Ned Beaumont, but did not say anything.

Ned Beaumont advanced to the fireplace. "'Lo, snip," he said to Opal Madvig.

She did not respond to his greeting. She stood there and looked at him with hostile bleak eyes.

He directed his smile at the thin girl in red. "This is Mrs. Mathews, isn't it?"

She said, "It is," in a soft, almost cooing, voice and held out her hand.

"Opal told me you were a schoolmate of hers," he said as he took her hand. He turned from her to face Rusty and Jeff. "'Lo, boys," he said carelessly. "I was hoping I'd see you some time soon."

Rusty said nothing.

Jeff's face became an ugly mask of grinning delight. "Me and you both," he said heartily, "now that my knuckles are all healed up again. What do you guess it is that makes me get such a hell of a big kick out of slugging you?"

Shad O'Rory gently addressed the apish man without turning to look at him: "You talk too much with your mouth, Jeff. Maybe if you didn't you'd still have your own teeth."

Mrs. Mathews spoke to Opal in an undertone. Opal shook her head and sat down on the stool by the fire again.

Mathews, indicating a wooden chair at the other end of the fireplace, said nervously: "Sit down, Mr. Beaumont, and dry your feet and —and get warm."

"Thanks." Ned Beaumont pulled the chair out more directly in the fire's glow and sat down.

Shad O'Rory was lighting a cigarette. When he had finished he took it from between his lips and asked: "How are you feeling, Ned?"

"Pretty good, Shad."

"That's fine." O'Rory turned his head a little to speak to the two men on the bench: "You boys can go back to town tomorrow." He turned back to Ned Beaumont, explaining blandly: "We were playing safe as long as we didn't know for sure you weren't going to die, but we don't mind standing an assault-rap."

Ned Beaumont nodded. "The chances are I won't go to the trouble of appearing against you, anyhow, on that, but don't forget our friend Jeff's wanted for West's murder." His voice was light, but into his eyes, fixed on the log burning in the fireplace, came a brief evil glint. There was nothing in his eyes but mockery when he moved them to the left to focus on Mathews. "Though of course I might so I could make trouble for Mathews for helping you hide out."

Mathews said hastily: "I didn't, Mr. Beaumont. I didn't even know they were here until we came up today and I was as surprised as—" He broke off, his face panicky, and addressed Shad O'Rory, whining: "You know you are welcome. You know that, but the point I'm trying to make" —his face was illuminated by a sudden glad smile—"is that by helping you without knowing it I didn't do anything I could be held legally responsible for."

O'Rory said softly: "Yes, you helped me without knowing it." His notable clear blue-grey eyes looked without interest at the newspaper-publisher.

Mathews's smile lost its gladness, flickered out entirely. He fidgeted with fingers at his necktie and presently evaded O'Rory's gaze.

Mrs. Mathews spoke to Ned Beaumont, sweetly: "Everybody's been so dull this evening. It was simply ghastly until you came."

He looked at her curiously. Her dark eyes were bright, soft, inviting. Under his appraising look she lowered her head a little and pursed her lips a little, coquettishly. Her lips were thin, too dark with rouge, but beautiful in form. He smiled at her and, rising, went over to her.

Opal Madvig stared at the floor before her. Mathews, O'Rory, and the two men on the bench watched Ned Beaumont and Mathews's wife.

He asked, "What makes them so dull?" and sat down on the floor in front of her, cross-legged, not facing her directly, his back to the fire, leaning on a hand on the floor behind him, his face turned up to one side towards her.

"I'm sure I don't know," she said, pouting. "I thought it was going to be fun when Hal asked me if I wanted to come up here with him and Opal. And then, when we got here, we found these—" she paused a moment—said, "friends of Hal's," with poorly concealed dubiety—and went on: "here and everybody's been sitting around hinting at some secret they've all got between them that I don't know anything about and it's been unbearably stupid. Opal's been as bad as the rest. She—"

Her husband said, "Now, Eloise," in an ineffectually authoritative tone and, when she raised her eyes to meet his, got more embarrassment than authority in his gaze.

"I don't care," she told him petulantly. "It's true and Opal is as bad as the rest of you. Why, you and she haven't even talked about whatever business it was you were coming up here to discuss in the first place. Don't think I'd've stayed here this long if it hadn't been for the storm. I wouldn't."

Opal Madvig's face had flushed, but she did not raise her eyes.

Eloise Mathews bent her head down towards Ned Beaumont again and the petulance in her face became playful. "That's what you've got to make up for," she assured him, "and that and not because you're beautiful is why I was so glad to see you."

He frowned at her in mock indignation.

She frowned at him. Her frown was genuine. "Did your car really break down?" she demanded, "or did you come here to see them on the same dull business that's making them so stupidly mysterious? You did. You're another one of them."

He laughed. He asked: "It wouldn't make any difference why I came if I changed my mind after seeing you, would it?"

"No—o—o"—she was suspicious—"but I'd have to be awfully sure you had changed it."

"And anyway," he promised lightly, "I won't be mysterious about anything. Haven't you really got an idea of what they're all eating their hearts out about?"

"Not the least," she replied spitefully, "except that I'm pretty sure it must be something very stupid and probably political."

He put his free hand up and patted one of hers. "Smart girl, right on both counts." He turned his head to look at O'Rory and Mathews. When his eyes came back to hers they were shiny with merriment. "Want me to tell you about it?"

"No."

"First," he said, "Opal thinks her father murdered Taylor Henry."

Opal Madvig made a horrible strangling noise in her throat and sprang up from the footstool. She put the back of one hand over her mouth. Her eyes were open so wide the whites showed all around the irises and they were glassy and dreadful.

Rusty lurched to his feet, his face florid with anger, but Jeff, leering, caught the boy's arm. "Let him alone," he rasped good-naturedly. "He's all right." The boy stood straining against the apish man's grip on his arm, but did not try to free himself.

Eloise Mathews sat frozen in her chair, staring without comprehension at Opal.

Mathews was trembling, a shrunken grey-faced sick man whose lower lip and lower eyelids sagged.

Shad O'Rory was sitting forward in his chair, finely modeled long face pale and hard, eyes like blue-grey ice, hands gripping chair-arms, feet flat on the floor.

"Second," Ned Beaumont said, his poise nowise disturbed by the agitation of the others, "she—"

"Ned, don't!" Opal Madvig cried.

He screwed himself around on the floor then to look up at her.

She had taken her hand from her mouth. Her hands were knotted together against her chest. Her stricken eyes, her whole haggard face, begged mercy of him.

He studied her gravely awhile. Through window and wall came the sound of rain dashing against the building in wild gusts and between gusts the bustling of the near-by river. His eyes, studying her, were cool, deliberate. Presently he spoke to her in a voice kind enough but aloof: "Isn't that why you're here?"

"Please don't," she said hoarsely.

He moved his lips in a thin smile that his eyes had nothing to do with and asked: "Nobody's supposed to go around talking about it except you and your father's other enemies?"

She put her hands—fists—down at her sides, raised her face angrily, and said in a hard ringing voice: "He did murder Taylor."

Ned Beaumont leaned back against his hand again and looked up at Eloise Mathews. "That's what I was telling you," he drawled. "Thinking that, she went to your husband after she saw the junk he printed this morning. Of course he didn't think Paul had done any killing: he's just in a tough spot—with his mortgages held by the State Central, which is owned by Shad's candidate for the Senate—and he has to do what he's told. What she—"

Mathews interrupted him. The publisher's voice was thin and desperate. "Now you stop that, Beaumont. You—"

O'Rory interrupted Mathews. O'Rory's voice was quiet, musical. "Let him talk, Mathews," he said. "Let him say his say."

"Thanks, Shad," Ned Beaumont said carelessly, not looking around, and went on: "She went to your husband to have him confirm her suspicion, but he couldn't give her anything that would do that unless he lied to her. He doesn't know anything. He's simply throwing mud wherever Shad tells him to throw it. But here's what he can do and does. He can print in tomorrow's paper the story about her coming in and telling him she believes her father killed her lover. That'll be a lovely wallop. 'Opal Madvig Accuses Father of Murder; Boss's Daughter Says He Killed Senator's Son!' Can't you see that in black ink all across the front of the *Observer?*"

Eloise Mathews, her eyes large, her face white, was listening breathlessly, bending forward, her face above his. Wind-flung rain beat walls and windows. Rusty filled and emptied his lungs with a long sighing breath.

Ned Beaumont put the tip of his tongue between smiling lips, withdrew it, and said: "That's why he brought her up here, to keep her under cover till the story breaks. Maybe he knew Shad and the boys were here, maybe not. It doesn't make any difference. He's getting her off where nobody can find out what she's done till the papers are out. I don't mean that he'd've brought her here, or would hold her here, against her will—that wouldn't be very bright of him the way things stack up now—but none of that's necessary. She's willing to go to any lengths to ruin her father."

Opal Madvig said, in a whisper, but distinctly: "He did kill him."

Ned Beaumont sat up straight and looked at her. He looked solemnly at her for a moment, then smiled, shook his head in a gesture of amused resignation, and leaned back on his elbows.

Eloise Mathews was staring with dark eyes wherein wonder was predominant at her husband. He had sat down. His head was bowed. His hands hid his face.

Shad O'Rory recrossed his legs and took out a cigarette. "Through?" he asked mildly.

Ned Beaumont's back was to O'Rory. He did not turn to reply: "You'd hardly believe how through I am." His voice was level, but his face was suddenly tired, spent.

O'Rory lit his cigarette. "Well," he said when he had done that, "what the hell does it all amount to? It's our turn to hang a big one on you and we're doing it. The girl came in with the story on her own hook. She came here because she wanted to. So did you. She and you and anybody else can go wherever they want to go whenever they want to." He stood up. "Personally, I'm wanting to go to bed. Where do I sleep, Mathews?"

Eloise Mathews spoke, to her husband: "This is not true, Hal." It was not a question.

He was slow taking his hands from his face. He achieved dignity saying: "Darling, there is a dozen times enough evidence against Madvig to justify us in insisting that the police at least question him. That is all we have done."

"I did not mean that," his wife said.

"Well, darling, when Miss Madvig came—" He faltered, stopped, a grey-faced man who shivered before the look in his wife's eyes and put his hands over his face again.

5

Eloise Mathews and Ned Beaumont were alone in the large ground-floor room, sitting, in chairs a few feet apart, with the fireplace in front of them. She was bent forward, looking with tragic eyes at the last burning log. His legs were crossed. One of his arms was hooked over the back of his chair. He smoked a cigar and watched her surreptitiously.

The stairs creaked and her husband came half-way down them. He was fully clothed except that he had taken off his collar. His necktie, partially loosened, hung outside his vest. He said: "Darling, won't you come to bed? It's midnight."

She did not move.

He said: "Mr. Beaumont, will you—?"

Ned Beaumont, when his name was spoken, turned his face towards the man on the stairs, a face cruelly placid. When Mathews's voice broke, Ned Beaumont returned his attention to his cigar and Mathews's wife.

After a little while Mathews went upstairs again.

Eloise Mathews spoke without taking her gaze from the fire. "There is some whisky in the chest. Will you get it?"

"Surely." He found the whisky and brought it to her, then found some glasses. "Straight?" he asked.

She nodded. Her round breasts were moving the red silk of her dress irregularly with her breathing.

He poured two large drinks.

She did not look up from the fire until he had put one glass in her hand. When she looked up she smiled, crookedly, twisting her heavily rouged exquisite thin lips sidewise. Her eyes, reflecting red light from the fire, were too bright.

He smiled down at her.

She lifted her glass and said, cooing: "To my husband!"

Ned Beaumont said, "No," casually and tossed the contents of his glass into the fireplace, where it spluttered and threw dancing flames up.

She laughed in delight and jumped to her feet. "Pour another," she ordered.

He picked the bottle up from the floor and refilled his glass.

She lifted hers high over her head. "To you!"

They drank. She shuddered.

"Better take something with it or after it," he suggested.

She shook her head. "I want it that way." She put a hand on his arm and turned her back to the fire, standing close beside him. "Let's bring that bench over here."

"That's an idea," he agreed.

They moved the chairs from in front of the fireplace and brought the bench there, he carrying one end, she the other. The bench was broad, low, backless.

"Now turn off the lights," she said.

He did so. When he returned to the bench she was sitting on it pouring whisky into their glasses.

"To you, this time," he said and they drank and she shuddered.

He sat beside her. They were rosy in the glow from the fireplace.

The stairs creaked and her husband came down them. He halted on the bottom step and said: "Please, darling!"

She whispered in Ned Beaumont's ear, savagely: "Throw something at him."

Ned Beaumont chuckled.

She picked up the whisky-bottle and said: "Where's your glass?"

While she was filling their glasses Mathews went upstairs.

She gave Ned Beaumont his glass and touched it with her own. Her eyes were wild in the red glow. A lock of dark hair had come loose and was down across her brow. She breathed through her mouth, panting softly. "To us!" she said.

They drank. She let her empty glass fall and came into his arms. Her mouth was to his when she shuddered. The fallen glass broke noisily on the wooden floor. Ned Beaumont's eyes were narrow, crafty. Hers were shut tight.

They had not moved when the stairs creaked. Ned Beaumont did not move then. She tightened her thin arms around him. He could not see the stairs. Both of them were breathing heavily now.

Then the stairs creaked again and, shortly afterwards, they drew their heads apart, though they kept their arms about one another. Ned Beaumont looked at the stairs. Nobody was there.

Eloise Mathews slid her hand up the back of his head, running her fingers through his hair, digging her nails into his scalp. Her eyes were not now altogether closed. They were laughing dark slits. "Life's like that," she said in a small bitter mocking voice, leaning back on the bench, drawing him with her, drawing his mouth to hers.

They were in that position when they heard the shot.

Ned Beaumont was out of her arms and on his feet immediately. "His room?" he asked sharply.

She blinked at him in dumb terror.

"His room?" he repeated.

She moved a feeble hand. "In front," she said thickly.

He ran to the stairs and went up in long leaps. At the head of the stairs he came face to face with the apish Jeff, dressed except for his shoes, blinking sleep out of his swollen eyes. Jeff put a hand to his hip, put the other hand out to stop Ned Beaumont, and growled: "Now what's all this?"

Ned avoided the outstretched hand, slid past it, and drove his left fist into the apish muzzle. Jeff staggered back snarling. Ned Beaumont sprang past him and ran towards the front of the building. O'Rory came out of another room and ran behind him.

From downstairs came Mrs. Mathews's scream.

Ned Beaumont flung a door open and stopped. Mathews lay on his back on the bedroom-floor under a lamp. His mouth was open and a little blood had trickled from it. One of his arms was thrown out across the floor. The other lay on his chest. Over against the wall, where the outstretched arm seemed to be pointing at it, was a dark revolver. On a table by the window was a bottle of ink—its stopper upside down beside it—a pen, and a sheet of paper. A chair stood close to the table, facing it.

Shad O'Rory pushed past Ned Beaumont and knelt beside the man on the floor. While he was there Ned Beaumont, behind him, swiftly glanced at the paper on the table, then thrust it into his pocket.

Jeff came in, followed by Rusty, naked.

O'Rory stood up and spread his hands apart in a little gesture of finality. "Shot himself through the roof of the mouth," he said. "Finis."

Ned Beaumont turned and went out of the room. In the hall he met Opal Madvig.

"What, Ned?" she asked in a frightened voice.

"Mathews has shot himself. I'll go down and stay with her till you get some clothes on. Don't go in there. There's nothing to see." He went downstairs.

Eloise Mathews was a dim shape lying on the floor beside the bench.

He took two quick steps towards her, halted, and looked around the room with shrewd cold eyes. Then he walked over to the woman, went down on a knee beside her, and felt her pulse. He looked at her as closely as he could in the dull light of the dying fire. She gave no sign of consciousness. He pulled the paper he had taken from her husband's table out of his pocket and moved on his knees to the fireplace, where, in the red embers' glow, he read:

> I, Howard Keith Mathews, being of sound mind and memory, declare this to be my last will and testament:
> I give and bequeath to my beloved wife, Eloise Braden Mathews, her heirs and assigns, all my real and personal property, of whatever nature or kind.
> I hereby appoint the State Central Trust Company the sole executor of this will.
> In witness whereof I have hereunto subscribed my name this . . .

Ned Beaumont, smiling grimly, stopped reading and tore the will three times across. He stood up, reached over the fire-screen, and dropped the torn pieces of paper into the glowing embers. The fragments blazed brightly a moment and were gone. With the wrought-iron shovel that stood beside the fire he mashed the paper-ash into the wood-coals.

Then he returned to Mrs. Mathews's side, poured a little whisky into the glass he had drunk from, raised her head, and forced some of the liquor between her lips. She was partly awake, coughing, when Opal Madvig came downstairs.

6

Shad O'Rory came down the stairs. Jeff and Rusty were behind him. All of them were dressed. Ned Beaumont was standing by the door, in raincoat and hat.

"Where are you going, Ned?" Shad asked.

"To find a phone."

O'Rory nodded. "That's a good enough idea," he said, "but there's something I want to ask you about." He came the rest of the way down the stairs, his followers close behind him.

Ned Beaumont said: "Yes?" He took his hand out of his pocket. The hand was visible to O'Rory and the men behind him, but Ned Beaumont's body concealed it from the bench where Opal sat with arms around Eloise Mathews. A square pistol was in the hand. "Just so there won't be any foolishness. I'm in a hurry."

O'Rory did not seem to see the pistol, though he came no nearer. He said, reflectively: "I was thinking that with an open ink-bottle and a pen on the table and a chair up to it it's kind of funny we didn't find any writing up there."

Ned Beaumont smiled in mock astonishment. "What, no writing?" He took a step backwards, towards the door. "That's a funny one, all right. I'll discuss it with you for hours when I come back from phoning."

"Now would be better," O'Rory said.

"Sorry." Ned Beaumont backed swiftly to the door, felt behind him for the knob, found it, and had the door open. "I won't be gone long." He jumped out and slammed the door.

The rain had stopped. He left the path and ran through tall grass around the other side of the house. From the house came the sound of another door slamming in the rear. The river was audible not far to Ned Beaumont's left. He worked his way through underbrush towards it.

A high-pitched sharp whistle, not loud, sounded somewhere behind him. He floundered through an area of soft mud to a clump of trees and turned away from the river among them. The whistle came again, on his right. Beyond the trees were shoulder-high bushes. He went among them, bending forward from the waist for concealment, though the night's blackness was all but complete.

His way was uphill, up a hill frequently slippery, always uneven, through brush that tore his face and hands, caught his clothing. Three times he fell. He stumbled many times. The whistle did not come again. He did not find the Buick. He did not find the road along which he had come.

He dragged his feet now and stumbled where there were no obstructions and when presently he had topped the hill and was going down its other slope he began to fall more often. At the bottom of the hill he found a road and turned to the right on it. Its clay stuck to his feet in increasing bulk so that he had to stop time after time to scrape it off. He used his pistol to scrape it off.

When he heard a dog bark behind him he stopped and turned drunkenly to look back. Close to the road, fifty feet behind him, was the vague outline of a house he had passed. He retraced his steps and came to a tall gate. The dog—a shapeless monster in the night—hurled itself at the other side of the gate and barked terrifically.

Ned Beaumont fumbled along an end of the gate, found the catch, unfastened it, and staggered in. The dog backed away, circling, feinting attacks it never made, filling the night with clamor.

A window screeched up and a heavy voice called: "What the hell are you doing to that dog?"

Ned Beaumont laughed weakly. Then he shook himself and replied in not too thin a voice: "This is Beaumont of the District Attorney's office. I want to use your phone. There's a dead man down there."

The heavy voice roared: "I don't know what you're talking about. Shut up, Jeanie!" The dog barked three times with increased energy and became silent. "Now what is it?"

"I want to phone. District Attorney's office. There's a dead man down there."

The heavy voice exclaimed: "The hell you say!" The window screeched shut.

The dog began its barking and circling and feinting again. Ned Beaumont threw his muddy pistol at it. It turned and ran out of sight behind the house.

The front door was opened by a red-faced barrel-bodied short man in a long blue night-shirt. "Holy Maria, you're a mess!" he gasped when Ned Beaumont came into the light from the doorway.

"Phone," Ned Beaumont said.

The red-faced man caught him as he swayed. "Here," he said gruffly, "tell me who to call and what to say. You can't do anything."

"Phone," Ned Beaumont said.

The red-faced man steadied him along a hallway, opened a door, said: "There she is and it's a damned good thing for you the old woman ain't home or you'd never get in with all that mud on you."

Ned Beaumont fell into the chair in front of the telephone, but he did not immediately reach for the telephone. He scowled at the man in the blue night-shirt and said thickly: "Go out and shut the door."

The red-faced man had not come into the room. He shut the door.

Ned Beaumont picked up the receiver, leaned forward so that he was propped against the table by his elbows on it, and called Paul Madvig's number. Half a dozen times while he waited his eyelids closed, but each time he forced them open again and when, at last, he spoke into the telephone it was clearly.

"'Lo, Paul—Ned. . . . Never mind that. Listen to me. Mathews's committed suicide at his place on the river and didn't leave a will. . . . Listen to me. This is important. With a lot of debts and no will naming an executor it'll be up to the courts to appoint somebody to administer the estate. Get that? . . . Yes. See that it comes up before the right judge—Phelps, say—and we can keep the *Observer* out of the fight—except on our side—till after election. Got that? . . . All right, all right, now listen. That's only part of it. This is what's got to be done now. The *Observer* is loaded with dynamite for the morning. You've got to stop it. I'd say get Phelps out of bed and get an injunction out of him—anything to stop it till you can show the *Observer's* hired men where they stand now that the paper's going to be bossed for a month or so by our friends. . . . I can't tell you now, Paul, but it's dynamite and you've got to keep it from going on sale. Get Phelps out of bed and go down and look at it yourselves. You've got maybe three hours before it's out on the streets. . . . That's right. . . . What? . . . Opal? Oh, she's all right. She's with me. . . . Yes, I'll bring her home. . . . And will you phone the county people about Mathews? I'm going back there now. Right."

He laid the receiver on the table and stood up, staggered to the door, got it open after the second attempt, and fell out into the hallway, where the wall kept him from tumbling down on the floor.

The red-faced man came hurrying to him. "Just lean on me, brother, and I'll make you comfortable. I got a blanket spread over the davenport so we won't have to worry about the mud and—"

Ned Beaumont said: "I want to borrow a car. I've got to go back to Mathews's."

"Is it him that's dead?"

"Yes."

The red-faced man raised his eyebrows and made a squeaky whistling sound.

"Will you lend me the car?" Ned Beaumont demanded.

"My God, brother, be reasonable! How could you drive a car?"

Ned Beaumont backed away from the other, unsteadily. "I'll walk," he said.

The red-faced man glared at him. "You won't neither. If you'll keep your hair on till I get my pants I'll drive you back, though likely enough you'll die on me on the way."

Opal Madvig and Eloise Mathews were together in the large ground-floor room when Ned Beaumont was carried rather than led into it by the red-faced man. The men had come in without knocking. The two girls were standing close together, wide-eyed, startled.

Ned Beaumont pulled himself out of his companion's arms and looked dully around the room. "Where's Shad?" he mumbled.

Opal answered him: "He's gone. All of them have gone."

"All right," he said, speaking difficultly. "I want to talk to you alone."

Eloise Mathews ran over to him. "You killed him!" she cried.

He giggled idiotically and tried to put his arms around her.

She screamed, struck him in the face with an open hand.

He fell straight back without bending. The red-faced man tried to catch him, but could not. He did not move at all after he struck the floor.

VII · *The Henchmen*

1

SENATOR HENRY put his napkin on the table and stood up. Rising, he seemed taller than he was and younger. His somewhat small head, under its thin covering of grey hair, was remarkably symmetrical. Aging muscles sagged in his patrician face, accentuating its vertical lines, but slackness had not yet reached his lips, nor was it apparent that the years had in any way touched his eyes: they were a greenish grey, deep-set, not large but brilliant, and their lids were firm. He spoke with studied grave courtesy: "You'll forgive me if I carry Paul off upstairs for a little while?"

His daughter replied: "Yes, if you'll leave me Mr. Beaumont and if you'll promise not to stay up there all evening."

Ned Beaumont smiled politely, inclining his head.

He and Janet Henry went into a white-walled room where coal burned sluggishly in a grate under a white mantelpiece and put somber red gleams on the mahogany furniture.

She turned on a lamp beside the piano and sat down there with her back to the keyboard, her head between Ned Beaumont and the lamp. Her blond hair caught lamplight and held it in a nimbus around her head. Her black gown was of some suèdelike material that reflected no light and she wore no jewelry.

Ned Beaumont leaned over to knock ash from his cigar down on the burning coal. A dark pearl in his shirt-bosom, twinkling in the fire's glow as he moved, was like a red eye winking. When he straightened, he asked: "You'll play something?"

"Yes, if you wish—though I don't play exceptionally well—but later. I'd like to talk to you now while I've an opportunity." Her hands were together in her lap. Her arms, held straight, forced her shoulders up and in towards her neck.

Ned Beaumont nodded politely, but did not say anything. He left the fireplace and sat not far from her on a sofa with lyre ends. Though he was attentive, there was no curiosity in his mien.

Turning on the piano-bench to face him directly, she asked: "How is Opal?" Her voice was low, intimate.

His voice was casual: "Perfectly all right as far as I know, though I haven't seen her since last week." He lifted his cigar half a foot towards his mouth, lowered it, and as if the question had just come to his mind asked: "Why?"

She opened her brown eyes wide. "Isn't she in bed with a nervous break-down?"

"Oh, that!" he said carelessly, smiling. "Didn't Paul tell you?"

"Yes, he told me she was in bed with a nervous break-down." She stared at him, perplexed. "He told me that."

Ned Beaumont's smile became gentle. "I suppose he's sensitive about it," he said slowly, looking at his cigar. Then he looked up at her and moved his shoulders a little. "There's nothing the matter with her that way. It's simply that she got the foolish idea that he had killed your brother and—still more foolishly—was going around talking about it. Well, Paul couldn't have his daughter running around accusing him of murder, so he had to keep her home till she gets the notion out of her head."

"You mean she's—" she hesitated: her eyes were bright "—she's—well—a prisoner?"

"You make it sound melodramatic," he protested carelessly. "She's only a child. Isn't making children stay in their rooms one of the usual ways of disciplining them?"

Janet Henry replied hastily: "Oh, yes! Only—" She looked at her hands in her lap, up at his face again. "But why did she think that?"

Ned Beaumont's voice was tepid as his smile. "Who doesn't?" he asked.

She put her hands on the edge of the piano-bench beside her and leaned forward. Her white face was earnestly set. "That's what I wanted to ask you, Mr. Beaumont. Do people think that?"

He nodded. His face was placid.

Her knuckles were white over the bench-edge. Her voice was parched asking: "Why?"

He rose from the sofa and crossed to the fireplace to drop the remainder of his cigar into the fire. When he returned to his seat he crossed his long legs and leaned back at ease. "The other side thinks it's good politics to make people think that," he said. There was nothing in his voice, his face, his manner to show that he had any personal interest in what he was talking about.

She frowned. "But, Mr. Beaumont, why should people think it unless there's some sort of evidence, or something that can be made to look like evidence?"

He looked curiously and amusedly at her. "There is, of course," he said. "I thought you knew that." He combed a side of his mustache with a thumb-nail. "Didn't you get any of the anonymous letters that've been going around?"

She stood up quickly. Excitement distorted her face. "Yes, today!" she exclaimed. "I wanted to show it to you, to—"

He laughed softly and raised a hand, palm out in an arresting gesture. "Don't bother. They all seem to be pretty much alike and I've seen plenty of them."

She sat down again, slowly, reluctantly.

He said: "Well, those letters, the stuff the *Observer* was printing till we pulled it out of the fight, the talk the others have been circulating"— he shrugged his thin shoulders—"they've taken what facts there are and made a pretty swell case against Paul."

She took her lower lip from between her teeth to ask: "Is—is he actually in danger?"

Ned Beaumont nodded and spoke with calm certainty: "If he loses the election, loses his hold on the city and state government, they'll electrocute him."

She shivered and asked in a voice that shook: "But he's safe if he wins?"

Ned Beaumont nodded again. "Sure."

She caught her breath. Her lips trembled so that her words came out jerkily: "Will he win?"

"I think so."

"And it won't make any difference then no matter how much evidence there is against him, he'll—" her voice broke "—he'll not be in danger?"

"He won't be tried," Ned Beaumont told her. Abruptly he sat up straight. He shut his eyes tight, opened them, and stared at her tense pale face. A glad light came into his eyes, gladness spread over his face. He laughed—not loud but in complete delight—and stood up exclaiming: "Judith herself!"

Janet Henry sat breathlessly still, looking at him with uncomprehending brown eyes in a blank white face.

He began to walk around the room in an irregular route, talking happily—not to her—though now and then he turned his head over his shoulder to smile at her. "That's the game, of course," he said. "She could put up with Paul—be polite to him—for the sake of the political backing her father needed, but that would have its limits. Or that's all that would be necessary, Paul being so much in love with her. But when she decided Paul had killed her brother and was going to escape punishment unless she— That's splendid! Paul's daughter and his sweetheart both trying to steer him to the electric chair. He certainly has a lot of luck with women." He had a slender pale-green-spotted cigar in one hand now. He halted in front of Janet Henry, clipped the end of the cigar, and said, not accusingly, but as if sharing a discovery with her: "You sent those anonymous letters around. Certainly you did. They were written on the typewriter in the room where your brother and Opal used to meet. He had a key and she had a key. She didn't write them because she was stirred up by them. You did. You took his key when it was turned over to you and your father with the rest of his stuff by the police, sneaked into the room, and wrote them. That's fine." He began to walk again. He said: "Well, we'll have to make the Senator get in a squad of good able-bodied nurses and lock you in your room with a nervous break-down. It's getting to be epidemic among our politicians' daughters, but we've got to make sure of the election even if every house in town has to have its patient." He turned his head over his shoulder to smile amiably at her.

She put a hand to her throat. Otherwise she did not move. She did not speak.

He said: "The Senator won't give us much trouble, luckily. He doesn't care about anything—not you or his dead son—as much as he does about being re-elected and he knows he can't do that without Paul." He laughed. "That's what drove you into the Judith rôle, huh? You knew your father wouldn't split with Paul—even if he thought him guilty—till the election was won. Well, that's a comforting thing to know—for us."

When he stopped talking to light his cigar she spoke. She had taken her hand down from her throat. Her hands were in her lap. She sat erect without stiffness. Her voice was cool and composed. She said: "I am not good at lying. I know Paul killed Taylor. I wrote the letters."

Ned Beaumont took the burning cigar from his mouth, came back to the lyre-end sofa, and sat down facing her. His face was grave, but without hostility. He said: "You hate Paul, don't you? Even if I proved to you that he didn't kill Taylor you'd still hate him, wouldn't you?"

"Yes," she replied, her light brown eyes steady on his darker ones, "I think I should."

"That's it," he said. "You don't hate him because you think he killed your brother. You think he killed your brother because you hate him."

She moved her head slowly from side to side. "No," she said.

He smiled skeptically. Then he asked: "Have you talked it over with your father?"

She bit her lip and her face flushed a little.

Ned Beaumont smiled again. "And he told you it was ridiculous," he said.

Pink deepened in her cheeks. She started to say something, but did not.

He said: "If Paul killed your brother your father knows it."

She looked down at her hands in her lap and said dully, miserably: "My father should know it, but he will not believe it."

Ned Beaumont said: "He ought to know." His eyes became narrower. "Did Paul say anything at all to him that night about Taylor and Opal?"

She raised her head, astonished. "Don't you know what happened that night?" she asked.

"No."

"It hadn't anything to do with Taylor and Opal," she said, word tumbling over word in her eagerness to get them spoken. "It—" She jerked her face towards the door and shut her mouth with a click. Deep-chested rumbling laughter had come through the door, and the sound of approaching steps. She faced Ned Beaumont again, hastily, lifting her hands in an appealing gesture. "I've got to tell you," she whispered, desperately earnest. "Can I see you tomorrow?"

"Yes."

"Where?"

"My place?" he suggested.

She nodded quickly. He had time to mutter his address, she to whisper, "After ten?" and he to nod before Senator Henry and Paul Madvig came into the room.

2

Paul Madvig and Ned Beaumont said good-night to the Henrys at half past ten o'clock and got into a brown sedan which Madvig drove down Charles Street. When they had ridden a block and a half Madvig blew his breath out in a satisfied gust and said: "Jesus, Ned, you don't know how tickled I am that you and Janet are hitting it off so nice."

Ned Beaumont, looking obliquely at the blond man's profile, said: "I can get along with anybody."

Madvig chuckled. "Yes you can," he said indulgently, "like hell."

Ned Beaumont's lips curved in a thin secretive smile. He said: "I've got something I want to talk to you about tomorrow. Where'll you be, say, in the middle of the afternoon?"

Madvig turned the sedan into China Street. "At the office," he said. "It's the first of the month. Why don't you do your talking now? There's a lot of night left yet."

"I don't know it all now. How's Opal?"

"She's all right," Madvig said gloomily, then exclaimed: "Christ! I wish I could be sore at the kid. It'd make it a lot easier." They passed a street-light. He blurted out: "She's not pregnant."

Ned Beaumont did not say anything. His face was expressionless.

Madvig reduced the sedan's speed as they approached the Log Cabin Club. His face was red. He asked huskily: "What do you think, Ned? Was she"—he cleared his throat noisily—"his mistress? Or was it just boy and girl stuff?"

Ned Beaumont said: "I don't know. I don't care. Don't ask her, Paul."

Madvig stopped the sedan and sat for a moment at the wheel staring straight ahead. Then he cleared his throat again and spoke in a low hoarse voice: "You're not the worst guy in the world, Ned."

"Uh-uh," Ned Beaumont agreed as they got out of the sedan.

They entered the Club, separating casually under the Governor's portrait at the head of the stairs on the second floor.

Ned Beaumont went into a rather small room in the rear where five men were playing stud poker and three were watching them play. The players made a place for him at the table and by three o'clock, when the game broke up, he had won some four hundred dollars.

3

It was nearly noon when Janet Henry arrived at Ned Beaumont's rooms. He had been pacing the floor, alternately biting his finger-nails and puffing at cigars, for more than an hour. He went without haste to the door when she rang, opened it, and, smiling with an air of slight but pleasant surprise, said: "Good morning."

"I'm awfully sorry to be late," she began, "but—"

"But you're not," he assured her. "It was to have been any time after ten."

He ushered her into his living-room.

"I like this," she said, turning around slowly, examining the old-fashioned room, the height of its ceiling, the width of its windows, the tremendous mirror over the fireplace, the red plush of the furniture. "It's delightful." She turned her brown eyes towards a half-open door. "Is that your bedroom?"

"Yes. Would you like to see it?"

"I'd love to."

He showed her the bedroom, then the kitchen and bathroom.

"It's perfect," she said as they returned to the living-room. "I didn't know there could be any more of these left in a city as horribly up to date as ours has become."

He made a little bow to acknowledge her approval. "I think it's rather nice and, as you can see, there's no one here to eavesdrop on us unless they're stowed away in a closet, which isn't likely."

She drew herself up and looked straight into his eyes. "I did not think of that. We may not agree, may even become—or now be—enemies, but I know you're a gentleman, or I shouldn't be here."

He asked in an amused tone: "You mean I've learned not to wear tan shoes with blue suits? Things like that?"

"I don't mean things like that."

He smiled. "Then you're wrong. I'm a gambler and a politician's hanger-on."

"I'm not wrong." A pleading expression came into her eyes. "Please don't let us quarrel, at least not until we must."

"I'm sorry." His smile was apologetic now. "Won't you sit down?"

She sat down. He sat in another wide red chair facing her. He said: "Now you were going to tell me what happened at your house the night your brother was killed."

"Yes," issuing from her mouth, was barely audible. Her face became pink and she transferred her gaze to the floor. When she raised her eyes again they were shy. Embarrassment clogged her voice: "I wanted you to know. You are Paul's friend and that—that may make you my enemy, but— I think when you know what happened—when you know the truth— you'll not be—at least not be my enemy. I don't know. Perhaps you'll— But you ought to know. Then you can decide. And he hasn't told you." She looked intently at him so that shyness went out of her eyes. "Has he?"

"I don't know what happened at your house that night," he said. "He didn't tell me."

She leaned towards him quickly to ask: "Doesn't that show it's something he wants to conceal, something he has to conceal?"

He moved his shoulders. "Suppose it does?" His voice was unexcited, uneager.

She frowned. "But you must see— Never mind that now. I'll tell you what happened and you can see it for yourself." She continued to lean far forward, staring at his face with intent brown eyes. "He came to dinner, the first time we'd had him to dinner."

"I knew that," Ned Beaumont said, "and your brother wasn't there."

"Taylor wasn't at the dinner-table," she corrected him earnestly, "but he was up in his room. Only Father, Paul, and I were at the table. Taylor was going out to dinner. He—he wouldn't eat with Paul because of the trouble they'd had about Opal."

Ned Beaumont nodded attentively without warmth.

"After dinner Paul and I were alone for a little while in—in the room where you and I talked last night and he suddenly put his arms around me and kissed me."

Ned Beaumont laughed, not loudly, but with abrupt irrepressible merriment.

Janet Henry looked at him in surprise.

He modified his laugh to a smile and said: "I'm sorry. Go on. I'll tell you later why I laughed." But when she would have gone on he said: "Wait. Did he say anything when he kissed you?"

"No. That is, he may have, but nothing I understood." Perplexity was deepening in her face. "Why?"

Ned Beaumont laughed again. "He ought to've said something about his pound of flesh. It was probably my fault. I had been trying to persuade him not to support your father in the election, had told him that your father was using you as bait to catch his support, and had advised him that if he was willing to be bought that way he ought to be sure and collect his pound of flesh ahead of the election or he'd never get it."

She opened her eyes wide and there was less perplexity in them.

He said: "That was that afternoon, though I didn't think I'd had much luck putting it over." He wrinkled his forehead. "What did you do to him? He was meaning to marry you and was chock-full of respect and what not for you and you must have rubbed him pretty thoroughly the wrong way to make him jump at you like that."

"I didn't do anything to him," she replied slowly, "though it had been a difficult evening. None of us was comfortable. I thought—I tried not to show that—well—that I resented having to entertain him. He wasn't at ease, I know, and I suppose that—his embarrassment—and perhaps a suspicion that you had been right made him—" She finished the sentence with a brief quick outward motion of both hands.

Ned Beaumont nodded. "What happened then?" he asked.

"I was furious, of course, and left him."

"Didn't you say anything to him?" Ned Beaumont's eyes twinkled with imperfectly hidden mirth.

"No, and he didn't say anything I could hear. I went upstairs and met Father coming down. While I was telling him what had happened— I was as angry with Father as with Paul, because it was Father's fault that Paul was there—we heard Paul going out the front door. And then Taylor came down from his room." Her face became white and tense, her voice husky with emotion. "He had heard me talking to Father and he asked me what had happened, but I left him there with Father and went on to my room, too angry to talk any more about it. And I didn't see either of them again until Father came to my room and told me Taylor had— had been killed." She stopped talking and looked white-faced at Ned Beaumont, twisting her fingers together, awaiting his response to her story.

His response was a cool question: "Well, what of it?"

"What of it?" she repeated in amazement. "Don't you see? How could I help knowing then that Taylor had run out after Paul and had caught up with him and had been killed by him? He was furious and—" Her face brightened. "You know his hat wasn't found. He was too much in a hurry—too angry—to stop for his hat. He—"

Ned Beaumont shook his head slowly from side to side and interrupted her. His voice held nothing but certainty. "No," he said. "That won't do. Paul wouldn't've had to kill Taylor and he wouldn't've done it. He could have managed him with one hand and he doesn't lose his head in a fight. I know that. I've seen Paul fight and I've fought with him. That won't do." He drew eyelids closer together around eyes that had become stony. "But suppose he did? I mean accidentally, though I can't believe even that. But could you make anything out of it except self-defense?"

She raised her head scornfully. "If it were self-defense, why should he hide it?"

Ned Beaumont seemed unimpressed. "He wants to marry you," he explained. "It wouldn't help him much to admit he'd killed your brother even—" He chuckled. "I'm getting as bad as you are. Paul didn't kill him, Miss Henry."

Her eyes were stony as his had been. She looked at him and did not speak.

His expression became thoughtful. He asked: "You've only"—he wriggled the fingers of one hand—"the two and two you think you've put together to tell you that your brother ran out after Paul that night?"

"That is enough," she insisted. "He did. He must've. Otherwise— why, otherwise what would he have been doing down there in China Street bare-headed?"

"Your father didn't see him go out?"

"No. He didn't know it either until we heard—"

He interrupted her. "Does he agree with you?"

"He must," she cried. "It's unmistakable. He must, no matter what he says, just as you must." Tears were in her eyes now. "You can't expect me to believe that you don't, Mr. Beaumont. I don't know what you knew before. You found Taylor dead. I don't know what else you found, but now you must know the truth."

Ned Beaumont's hands began to tremble. He slumped farther down in his chair so he could thrust his hands into his trousers-pockets. His face was tranquil except for hard lines of strain around his mouth. He said: "I found him dead. There was nobody else there. I didn't find anything else."

"You have now," she said.

His mouth twitched under his dark mustache. His eyes became hot with anger. He spoke in a low, harsh, deliberately bitter voice: "I know whoever killed your brother did the world a favor."

She shrank back in her chair with a hand thrown up to her throat, at first, but almost immediately the horror went out of her face and she sat upright and looked compassionately at him. She said softly: "I know. You're Paul's friend. It hurts."

He lowered his head a little and muttered: "It was a rotten thing to say. It was silly." He smiled wryly. "You see I was right about not being a gentleman." He stopped smiling and shame went out of his eyes leaving them clear and steady. He said in a quiet voice: "You're right about my being Paul's friend. I'm that no matter who he killed."

After a long moment of earnest staring at him she spoke in a small flat voice: "Then this is useless? I thought if I could show you the truth—" She broke off with a hopeless gesture in which hands, shoulders, and head took part.

He moved his head slowly from side to side.

She sighed and stood up holding out her hand. "I'm sorry and disappointed, but we needn't be enemies, need we?"

He rose facing her, but did not take her hand. He said: "The part of you that's tricked Paul and is trying to trick him is my enemy."

She held her hand there while asking: "And the other part of me, the part that hasn't anything to do with that?"

He took her hand and bowed over it.

4

When Janet Henry had gone Ned Beaumont went to his telephone, called a number, and said: "Hello, this is Mr. Beaumont. Has Mr. Madvig come in yet? . . . . When he comes will you tell him I called and will be in to see him? . . . Yes, thanks."

He looked at his wrist-watch. It was a little after one o'clock. He lit a cigar and sat down at a window, smoking and staring at the grey church across the street. Out-blown cigar-smoke recoiled from the window-panes in grey clouds over his head. His teeth crushed the end of his cigar. He sat there for ten minutes, until his telephone-bell rang.

He went to the telephone. "Hello. . . . Yes, Harry. . . . Sure. Where are you? . . . I'm coming downtown. Wait there for me. . . . Half an hour. . . . Right."

He threw his cigar into the fireplace, put on his hat and overcoat, and went out. He walked six blocks to a restaurant, ate a salad and rolls, drank a cup of coffee, walked four blocks to a small hotel named Majestic, and rode to the fourth floor in an elevator operated by an undersized youth who called him Ned and asked what he thought of the third race.

Ned Beaumont thought and said: "Lord Byron ought to do it."

The elevator-operator said: "I hope you're wrong. I got Pipe-organ."

Ned Beaumont shrugged. "Maybe, but he's carrying a lot of weight." He went to room 417 and knocked on the door.

Harry Sloss, in his shirt-sleeves, opened the door. He was a thickset pale man of thirty-five, broad-faced and partially bald. He said: "On the dot. Come on in."

When Sloss had shut the door Ned Beaumont asked: "What's the diffugalty?"

The thickset man went over to the bed and sat down. He scowled anxiously at Ned Beaumont. "It don't look so damned good to me, Ned."

"What don't?"

"This thing of Ben going to the Hall with it."

Ned Beaumont said irritably: "All right. Any time you're ready to tell me what you're talking about's soon enough for me."

Sloss raised a pale broad hand. "Wait, Ned, I'll tell you what it's about. Just listen." He felt in his pocket for cigarettes, bringing out a package mashed limp. "You remember the night the Henry kid was pooped?"

Ned Beaumont's "Uh-huh" was carelessly uttered.

"Remember me and Ben had just come in when you got there, at the Club?"

"Yes."

"Well, listen: we saw Paul and the kid arguing up there under the trees."

Ned Beaumont brushed a side of his mustache with a thumb-nail, once, and spoke slowly, looking puzzled: "But I saw you get out of the car in front of the Club—that was just after I found him—and you came up the other way." He moved a forefinger. "And Paul was already in the Club ahead of you."

Sloss nodded his broad head vigorously. "That's all right," he said, "but we'd drove on down China Street to Pinky Klein's place and he wasn't there and we turned around and drove back to the Club."

Ned Beaumont nodded. "Just what did you see?"

"We saw Paul and the kid standing there under the trees arguing."

"You could see that as you rode past?"

Sloss nodded vigorously again.

"It was a dark spot," Ned Beaumont reminded him. "I don't see how you could've made out their faces riding past like that, unless you slowed up or stopped."

"No, we didn't, but I'd know Paul anywhere," Sloss insisted.

"Maybe, but how'd you know it was the kid with him?"

"It was. Sure, it was. We could see enough of him to know that."

"And you could see they were arguing? What do you mean by that? Fighting?"

"No, but standing like they were having an argument. You know how you can tell when people are arguing sometimes by the way they stand."

Ned Beaumont smiled mirthlessly. "Yes, if one of them's standing on the other's face." His smile vanished. "And that's what Ben went to the Hall with?"

"Yes. I don't know whether he went in with it on his own account or whether Farr got hold of it somehow and sent for him, but anyhow he spilled it to Farr. That was yesterday."

"How'd you hear about it, Harry?"

"Farr's hunting for me," Sloss said. "That's the way I heard about it. Ben'd told him I was with him and Farr sent word for me to drop in and see him, but I don't want any part of it."

"I hope you don't, Harry," Ned Beaumont said. "What are you going to say if Farr catches you?"

"I'm not going to let him catch me if I can help it. That's what I wanted to see you about." He cleared his throat and moistened his lips. "I thought maybe I ought to get out of town for a week or two, till it kind of blows over, and that'd take a little money."

Ned Beaumont smiled and shook his head. "That's not the thing to do," he told the thickset man. "If you want to help Paul go tell Farr you couldn't recognize the two men under the trees and that you don't think anybody in your car could."

"All right, that's what I'll do," Sloss said readily, "but, listen, Ned, I ought to get something out of it. I'm taking a chance and—well—you know how it is."

Ned Beaumont nodded. "We'll pick you out a soft job after election, one you'll have to show up on maybe an hour a day."

"That'll be—" Sloss stood up. His green-flecked palish eyes were urgent. "I'll tell you, Ned, I'm broke as hell. Couldn't you make it a little dough now instead? It'd come in damned handy."

"Maybe. I'll talk it over with Paul."

"Do that, Ned, and give me a ring."

"Sure. So long."

5

From the Majestic Hotel Ned Beaumont went to the City Hall, to the District Attorney's office, and said he wanted to see Mr. Farr.

The round-faced youth to whom he said it left the outer office, returning a minute later apologetic of mien. "I'm sorry, Mr. Beaumont, but Mr. Farr is not in."

"When will he be back?"

"I don't know. His secretary says he didn't leave word."

"I'll take a chance. I'll wait awhile in his office."

The round-faced youth stood in his way. "Oh, you can't do—"

Ned Beaumont smiled his nicest smile at the youth and asked softly: "Don't you like this job, son?"

The youth hesitated, fidgeted, and stepped out of Ned Beaumont's way. Ned Beaumont walked down the inner corridor to the District Attorney's door and opened it.

Farr looked up from his desk, sprang to his feet. "Was that you?" he cried. "Damn that boy! He never gets anything right. A Mr. Bauman, he said."

"No harm done," Ned Beaumont said mildly. "I got in."

He let the District Attorney shake his hand up and down and lead him to a chair. When they were seated he asked idly: "Anything new?"

"Nothing." Farr rocked back in his chair, thumbs hooked in lower vest-pockets. "Just the same old grind, though God knows there's enough of that."

"How's the electioneering going?"

"It could be better"—a shadow passed over the District Attorney's pugnacious red face—"but I guess we'll manage all right."

Ned Beaumont kept idleness in his voice. "What's the matter?"

"This and that. Things always come up. That's politics, I guess."

"Anything I can do—or Paul—to help?" Ned Beaumont asked and then, when Farr had shaken his red-stubble-covered head: "This talk that Paul's got something to do with the Henry killing the worst thing you're up against?"

A frightened gleam came into Farr's eyes, disappeared as he blinked. He sat up straight in his chair. "Well," he said cautiously, "there's a lot of feeling that we ought to've cleared the murder up before this. That is one of the things—maybe one of the biggest."

"Made any progress since I saw you last? Turned up anything new on it?"

Farr shook his head. His eyes were wary.

Ned Beaumont smiled without warmth. "Still taking it slow on some of the angles?"

The District Attorney squirmed in his chair. "Well, yes, of course, Ned."

Ned Beaumont nodded approvingly. His eyes were shiny with malice. His voice was a taunt: "Is the Ben Ferriss angle one of them that you're taking it slow on?"

Farr's blunt undershot mouth opened and shut. He rubbed his lips together. His eyes, after their first startled widening, became devoid of expression. He said: "I don't know whether there's anything at all in Ferriss's story or not, Ned. I don't guess there is. I didn't even think enough of it to tell you about it."

Ned Beaumont laughed derisively.

Farr said: "You know I wouldn't hold out anything on you and Paul, anything that was important. You know me well enough for that."

"We knew you before you got nerves," Ned Beaumont replied. "But that's all right. If you want the fellow that was in the car with Ferriss you can pick him up right now in room 417 at the Majestic."

Farr was staring at his green desk-set, at the dancing nude figure holding an airplane aloft between two slanting pens. His face was lumpy. He said nothing.

Ned Beaumont rose from his chair smiling with thin lips. He said: "Paul's always glad to help the boys out of holes. Do you think it would help if he'd let himself be arrested and tried for the Henry murder?"

Farr did not move his eyes from the green desk-set. He said doggedly: "It's not for me to tell Paul what to do."

"There's a thought!" Ned Beaumont exclaimed. He leaned over the side of the desk until his face was near the District Attorney's ear and lowered his voice to a confidential key. "And here's another one that goes with it. It's not for you to do much Paul wouldn't tell you to do."

He went out grinning, but stopped grinning when he was outside.

VIII · *The Kiss-Off*

1

NED BEAUMONT opened a door marked *East State Construction & Contracting Company* and exchanged good-afternoons with the two young ladies at desks inside, then he passed through a larger room in which there were half a dozen men to whom he spoke and opened a door marked *Private*. He went into a square room where Paul Madvig sat at a battered desk looking at papers placed in front of him by a small man who hovered respectfully over his shoulder.

Madvig raised his head and said: "Hello, Ned." He pushed the papers aside and told the small man: "Bring this junk back after while."

The small man gathered up his papers and, saying, "Certainly, sir," and, "How do you do, Mr. Beaumont?" left the room.

Madvig said: "You look like you'd had a tough night, Ned. What'd you do? Sit down."

Ned Beaumont had taken off his overcoat. He put it on a chair, put his hat on it, and took out a cigar. "No, I'm all right. What's new in your life?" He sat on a corner of the battered desk.

"I wish you'd go see M'Laughlin," the blond man said. "You can handle him if anybody can."

"All right. What's the matter with him?"

Madvig grimaced. "Christ knows! I thought I had him lined up, but he's going shifty on us."

A somber gleam came into Ned Beaumont's dark eyes. He looked down at the blond man and said: "Him too, huh?"

Madvig asked slowly, after a moment's deliberation: "What do you mean by that, Ned?"

Ned Beaumont's reply was another question: "Is everything going along to suit you?"

Madvig moved his big shoulders impatiently, but his eyes did not lose their surveying stare. "Nor so damned bad either," he said. "We can get along without M'Laughlin's batch of votes if we have to."

"Maybe," Ned Beaumont's lips had become thin, "but we can't keep on losing them and come out all right." He put his cigar in a corner of his mouth and said around it: "You know we're not as well off as we were two weeks ago."

Madvig grinned indulgently at the man on his desk. "Jesus, you like to sing them, Ned! Don't anything ever look right to you?" He did not wait for a reply, but went on placidly: "I've never been through a campaign yet that didn't look like it was going to hell at some time or other. They don't, though."

Ned Beaumont was lighting his cigar. He blew smoke out and said: "That doesn't mean they never will." He pointed the cigar at Madvig's chest. "If Taylor Henry's killing isn't cleared up pronto you won't have to worry about the campaign. You'll be sunk whoever wins."

Madvig's blue eyes became opaque. There was no other change in his face. His voice was unchanged. "Just what do you mean by that, Ned?"

"Everybody in town thinks you killed him."

"Yes?" Madvig put a hand up to his chin, rubbed it thoughtfully. "Don't let that worry you. I've had things said about me before."

Ned Beaumont smiled tepidly and asked with mock admiration: "Is there anything you haven't been through before? Ever been given the electric cure?"

The blond man laughed. "And don't think I ever will," he said.

"You're not very far from it right now, Paul," Ned Beaumont said softly.

Madvig laughed again. "Jesus Christ!" he scoffed.

Ned Beaumont shrugged. "You're not busy?" he asked. "I'm not taking up your time with my nonsense?"

"I'm listening to you," Madvig told him quietly. "I never lost anything listening to you."

"Thank you, sir. Why do you suppose M'Laughlin's wiggling out from under?"

Madvig shook his head.

"He figures you're licked," Ned Beaumont said. "Everybody knows the police haven't tried to find Taylor's murderer and everybody thinks it's because you killed him. M'Laughlin figures that's enough to lick you at the polls this time."

"Yes? He figures they'd rather have Shad running the city than me? He figures being suspected of one murder makes my rep worse than Shad's?"

Ned Beaumont scowled at the blond man. "You're either kidding yourself or trying to kid me. What's Shad's reputation got to do with it? He's not out in the open behind his candidates. You are and it's your candidates who're responsible for nothing being done about the murder."

Madvig put his hand to his chin again and leaned his elbow on the desk. His handsome ruddy face was unlined. He said: "We've been talking a lot about what other people figure, Ned. Let's talk about what you figure. Figure I'm licked?"

"You probably are," Ned Beaumont said in a low sure voice. "It's a cinch you are if you sit still." He smiled. "But your candidates ought to come out all right."

"That," Madvig said phlegmatically, "ought to be explained."

Ned Beaumont leaned over and carefully knocked cigar-ash into the brass spittoon beside the desk. Then he said, unemotionally: "They're going to cross you up."

"Yes?"

"Why not? You've let Shad take most of the riffraff from behind you. You're counting on the respectable people, the better element, to carry the election. They're getting leery. Well, your candidates make a grandstand-play, arrest you for murder, and the respectable citizens—delighted with these noble officials who are brave enough to jail their own acknowledged boss when he breaks the law—trample each other to death in their hurry to get to the polls and elect the heroes to four more years of city-administering. You can't blame the boys much. They know they're sitting pretty if they do it and out of work if they don't."

Madvig took his hand from his chin to ask: "You don't count much on their loyalty, do you, Ned?"

Ned Beaumont smiled. "Just as much as you do," he replied. His smile went away. "I'm not guessing, Paul. I went in to see Farr this afternoon. I had to walk in, crash the gate—he tried to dodge me. He pretended he hadn't been digging into the killing. He tried to stall me on what he'd found out. In the end he dummied up on me." He made a disdainful mouth. "Farr, the guy I could always make jump through hoops."

"Well, that's only Farr," Madvig began.

Ned Beaumont cut him short. "Only Farr, and that's the tip-off. Rutlege or Brody or even Rainey might clip you on their own, but if Farr's doing anything it's a pipe he knows the others are with him." He frowned at the blond man's stolid face. "You can stop believing me any time you want to, Paul."

Madvig made a careless gesture with the hand he had held to his chin. "I'll let you know when I stop," he said. "How'd you happen to drop in on Farr?"

"Harry Sloss called me up today. It seems he and Ben Ferriss saw you arguing with Taylor in China Street the night of the murder, or claim they did." Ned Beaumont was looking with eyes that held no particular expression at the blond man and his voice was matter-of-fact. "Ben had gone to Farr with it. Harry wanted to be paid for not going. There's a couple of your Club-members reading the signs. I've been watching Farr lose his nerve for some time, so I went in to check him up."

Madvig nodded. "And you're sure he's knifing me?"

"Yes."

Madvig got up from his chair and went to the window. He stood there, hands in trousers-pockets, looking through the glass for perhaps three minutes while Ned Beaumont, sitting on the desk, smoked and looked at the blond man's wide back. Then, not turning his head, Madvig asked: "What'd you say to Harry?"

"Stalled him."

Madvig left the window and came back to the desk, but he did not sit down. His ruddiness had deepened. Otherwise no change had come into his face. His voice was level. "What do you think we ought to do?"

"About Sloss? Nothing. The other monkey's already gone to Farr. It doesn't make much difference what Sloss does."

"I didn't mean that. I meant about the whole thing."

Ned Beaumont dropped his cigar into the spittoon. "I've told you. If Taylor Henry's murder isn't cleared up pronto you're sunk. That's the whole thing. That's the only thing worth doing anything about."

Madvig stopped looking at Ned Beaumont. He looked at a wide vacant space on the wall. He pressed his full lips together. Moisture appeared on his temples. He said from deep in his chest: "That won't do. Think up something else."

Ned Beaumont's nostrils moved with his breathing and the brown of his eyes seemed dark as the pupils. He said: "There isn't anything else, Paul. Any other way plays into the hands of either Shad or Farr and his crew and either of them will ruin you."

Madvig said somewhat hoarsely: "There must be an out, Ned. Think."

Ned Beaumont left the desk and stood close in front of the blond man. "There isn't. That's the only way. You're going to take it whether you like it or not, or I'm going to take it for you."

Madvig shook his head violently. "No. Lay off."

Ned Beaumont said: "That's one thing I won't do for you, Paul."

Then Madvig looked Ned Beaumont in the eyes and said in a harsh whisper: "I killed him, Ned."

Ned Beaumont drew a breath in and let it out in a long sigh.

Madvig put his hands on Ned Beaumont's shoulders and his words came out thick and blurred. "It was an accident, Ned. He ran down the street after me when I left, with a cane he'd picked up on the way out. We'd had—there'd been some trouble there and he caught up with me and tried to hit me with the stick. I don't know how it happened, but pulling it away from him I hit him on the head with it—not hard—it couldn't've been very hard—but he fell back and smashed his head on the curb."

Ned Beaumont nodded. His face had suddenly become empty of all expression except hard concentration on Madvig's words. He asked in a crisp voice that matched his face: "What happened to the cane?"

"I took it away under my overcoat and burned it. After I knew he was dead I found it in my hand, when I was walking down to the Club, so I put it under my overcoat and then burned it."

"What kind of cane was it?"

"A rough brown one, heavy."

"And his hat?"

"I don't know, Ned. I guess it was knocked off and somebody picked it up."

"He had one on?"

"Yes, sure."

Ned Beaumont brushed a side of his mustache with a thumb-nail. "You remember Sloss's and Ferriss's car passing you?"

Madvig shook his head. "No, though they may have."

Ned Beaumont frowned at the blond man. "You gummed things up plenty by running off with the stick and burning it and keeping quiet all this time," he grumbled. "You had a clear self-defense plea."

"I know, but I didn't want that, Ned," Madvig said hoarsely. "I want Janet Henry more than I ever wanted anything in my life and what chance would I have then, even if it was an accident?"

Ned Beaumont laughed in Madvig's face. It was a low laugh and bitter. He said: "You'd have more chance than you've got now."

Madvig, staring at him, said nothing.

Ned Beaumont said: "She's always thought you killed her brother. She hates you. She's been trying to play you into the electric chair. She's responsible for first throwing suspicion on you with anonymous letters sent around to everybody that might be interested. She's the one that turned Opal against you. She was in my rooms this morning telling me this, trying to turn me. She—"

Madvig said: "That's enough." He stood erect, a big blond man whose eyes were cold blue disks. "What is it, Ned? Do you want her yourself or is it—" He broke off contemptuously. "It doesn't make any difference." He jerked a thumb carelessly at the door. "Get out, you heel, this is the kiss-off."

Ned Beaumont said: "I'll get out when I've finished talking."

Madvig said: "You'll get out when you're told to. You can't say anything I'll believe. You haven't said anything I believe. You never will now."

Ned Beaumont said: "Oke." He picked up his hat and overcoat and went out.

2

Ned Beaumont went home. His face was pale and sullen. He slouched down in one of the big red chairs with a bottle of Bourbon whisky and a glass on the table beside him, but he did not drink. He stared gloomily at his black-shod feet and bit a finger-nail. His telephone-bell rang. He did not answer it. Twilight began to displace day in the room. The room was dusky when he rose and went to the telephone.

He called a number. Then: "Hello, I'd like to speak to Miss Henry, please." After a pause that he spent whistling tunelessly under his breath, he said: "Hello, Miss Henry? . . . Yes. . . . I've just come from telling Paul all about it, about you. . . . Yes, and you were right. He did what you counted on his doing. . . ." He laughed. "You did. You knew he'd call me a liar, refuse to listen to me, and throw me out, and he did all of it. . . . No, no, that's all right. It had to happen. . . . No, really. . . . Oh, it's probably permanent enough. Things were said that can't easily be unsaid. . . . Yes, all evening, I think. . . . That'll be fine. . . . All right. 'By."

He poured out a glass of whisky then and drank it. After that he went into his darkening bedroom, set his alarm-clock for eight o'clock, and lay down fully clothed on his back on the bed. For a while he looked at the ceiling. Then he slept, breathing irregularly, until the alarm rang.

He got up sluggishly from his bed and, switching on lights, went into the bathroom, washed his face and hands, put on a fresh collar, and started a fire in the living-room fireplace. He read a newspaper until Janet Henry arrived.

She was excited. Though she at once began to assure Ned Beaumont that she had not foreseen the result of his telling Paul about her visit, had not counted on it, elation danced frankly in her eyes and she could not keep smiles from curving her lips while they shaped the apologetic words.

He said: "It doesn't matter. I'd've had to do it if I'd known how it was going to turn out. I suppose I did know down underneath. It's one of those things. And if you'd told me it would happen I'd only've taken that for a challenge and would've jumped to it."

She held her hands out to him. "I'm glad," she said. "I won't pretend I'm not."

"I'm sorry," he told her as he took her hands, "but I wouldn't have gone a step out of my way to avoid it."

She said: "And now you know I'm right. He did kill Taylor." Her eyes were inquisitive.

He nodded. "He told me he did."

"And you'll help me now?" Her hands pressed his. She came closer to him.

He hesitated, frowning down at her eager face. "It was self-defense, or an accident," he said slowly. "I can't—"

"It was murder!" she cried. "Of course he'd say it was self-defense!" She shook her head impatiently. "And even if it was self-defense or an accident, shouldn't he be made to go into court and prove it like anybody else?"

"He's waited too long. This month he's kept quiet would be against him."

"Well, whose fault was that?" she demanded. "And do you think he would have kept quiet so long if it had been self-defense?"

He nodded with slow emphasis. "That was on your account. He's in love with you. He didn't want you to know he'd killed your brother."

"I do know it!" she cried fiercely. "And everybody's going to know it!"

He moved his shoulders a little. His face was gloomy.

"You won't help me?" she asked.

"No."

"Why? You've quarreled with him."

"I believe his story. I know it's too late for him to put it across in court. We're through, but I won't do that to him." He moistened his lips. "Let him alone. It's likely they'll do it to him without your help or mine."

"I won't," she said. "I won't let him alone until he's been punished as he deserves." She caught her breath and her eyes darkened. "Do you believe him enough to risk finding proof that he lied to you?"

"What do you mean?" he asked cautiously.

"Will you help me find proof of the truth, whether he's lying or not? There must be positive proof somewhere, some proof that we can find. If you really believe him you won't be afraid to help me find it."

He studied her face awhile before asking: "If I do and we find your positive proof, will you promise to accept it whichever way it stacks up?"

"Yes," she said readily, "if you will too."

"And you'll keep what we find to yourself till we've finished the job —found our positive proof—won't use what we find against him till we've got it all?"

"Yes."

"It's a bargain," he said.

She sobbed happily and tears came to her eyes.

He said: "Sit down." His face was lean and hard, his voice curt. "We've got to get schemes rigged. Have you heard from him this afternoon or evening, since he and I had our row?"

"No."

"Then we can't be sure how you stand with him. There's a chance he may have decided later that I was right. That won't make any difference between him and me now—we're done—but we've got to find out as soon as we can." He scowled at her feet and brushed his mustache with a thumb-nail. "You'll have to wait till he comes to you. You can't afford to call him up. If he's shaky about you that might decide him. How sure of him are you?"

She was sitting in the chair by the table. She said: "I'm as sure of him as a woman can be of a man." She uttered a little embarrassed laugh. "I know that sounds— But I am, Mr. Beaumont."

He nodded. "Then that's probably all right, but you ought to know definitely by tomorrow. Have you ever tried to pump him?"

"Not yet, not really. I was waiting—"

"Well, that's out for the time being. No matter how sure you are of him you'll have to be careful now. Have you picked up anything you haven't told me about?"

"No," she said, shaking her head. "I haven't known very well how to go about it. That's why I so wanted you to—"

He interrupted her again: "Didn't it occur to you to hire a private detective?"

"Yes, but I was afraid, afraid I'd go to one who'd tell Paul. I didn't know who to go to, who I could trust."

"I've got one we can use." He ran fingers through his dark hair. "Now there are two things I want you to find out, if you don't know them now. Are any of your brother's hats missing? Paul says he had a hat on. There was none there when I found him. See if you can find out how many he had and if they're all accounted for"—he smiled obliquely—"except the one I borrowed."

She paid no attention to his smile. She shook her head and raised her hands a little, dispiritedly. "I can't," she said. "We got rid of all his things some time ago and I doubt if anybody knew exactly what he had anyway."

Ned Beaumont shrugged. "I didn't think we'd get anywhere on that," he told her. "The other thing's a walking-stick, whether any of them —his or your father's—are missing, particularly a rough heavy brown one."

"It would be Father's," she said eagerly, "and I think it's there."

"Check it up." He bit his thumb-nail. "That'll be enough for you to do between now and tomorrow, that and maybe find out how you stand with Paul."

"What is it?" she asked. "I mean about the stick." She stood up, excited.

"Paul says your brother attacked him with it and was struck by it while Paul was taking it away from him. He says he carried the stick away and burned it."

"Oh, I'm sure Father's sticks are all there," she cried. Her face was white, her eyes wide.

"Didn't Taylor have any?"

"Only a silver-headed black one." She put a hand on his wrist. "If they're all there it will mean that—"

"It might mean something," he said and put a hand on her hand. "But no tricks," he warned her.

"I won't," she promised. "If you only knew how happy I am to have your help, how much I've wanted it, you'd know you could trust me."

"I hope so." He took his hand from hers.

3

Alone in his rooms Ned Beaumont walked the floor awhile, his face pinched, his eyes shiny. At twenty minutes to ten he looked at his wrist-watch. Then he put on his overcoat and went down to the Majestic Hotel, where he was told that Harry Sloss was not in. He left the hotel, found a taxicab, got into it, and said: "West Road Inn."

The West Road Inn was a square white building—grey in the night—set among trees back from the road some three miles beyond the city limits. Its ground-floor was brightly lighted and half a dozen automobiles stood in front of it. Others were in a long dark shed off to the left.

Ned Beaumont, nodding familiarly at the doorman, went into a large dining-room where a three-man orchestra was playing extravagantly and eight or ten people were dancing. He passed down an aisle between tables, skirted the dance-floor, and stopped in front of the bar that occupied one corner of the room. He was alone on the customers' side of the bar.

The bar-tender, a fat man with a spongy nose, said: "Evening, Ned. We ain't been seeing you much lately."

" 'Lo, Jimmy. Been behaving. Manhattan."

The bar-tender began to mix the cocktail. The orchestra finished its piece. A woman's voice rose thin and shrill: "I won't stay in the same place with that Beaumont bastard."

Ned Beaumont turned around, leaning back against the edge of the bar. The bar-tender became motionless with the cocktail-shaker in his hand.

Lee Wilshire was standing in the center of the dance-floor glaring at Ned Beaumont. One of her hands was on the forearm of a bulky youth in a blue suit a bit too tight for him. He too was looking at Ned Beaumont, rather stupidly. She said: "He's a no-good bastard and if you don't throw him out I'm going out."

Everyone else in the place was attentively silent.

The youth's face reddened. His attempt at a scowl increased his appearance of embarrassment.

The girl said: "I'll go over and slap him myself if you don't."

Ned Beaumont, smiling, said: " 'Lo, Lee. Seen Bernie since he got out?"

Lee cursed him and took an angry step forward.

The bulky youth put out a hand and stopped her. "I'll fix him," he said, "the bastard." He adjusted his coat-collar to his neck, pulled the front of his coat down, and stalked off the dance-floor to face Ned Beaumont. "What's the idea?" he demanded. "What's the idea of talking to the little lady like that?"

Ned Beaumont, staring soberly at the youth, stretched his right arm out to the side and laid his hand palm-up on the bar. "Give me something to tap him with, Jimmy," he said. "I don't feel like fist-fighting."

One of the bar-tender's hands was already out of sight beneath the bar. He brought it up holding a small bludgeon and put the bludgeon in Ned Beaumont's hand. Ned Beaumont let it lie there while he said: "She gets called a lot of things. The last guy I saw her with was calling her a dumb cluck."

The youth drew himself up straight, his eyes shifting from side to side. He said: "I won't forget you and some day me and you will meet when there's nobody around." He turned on his heel and addressed Lee Wilshire. "Come on, let's blow out of this dump."

"Go ahead and blow," she said spitefully. "I'll be God-damned if I'm going with you. I'm sick of you."

A thick-bodied man with nearly all gold teeth came up and said: "Yes you will, the both of you. Get."

Ned Beaumont laughed and said: "The—uh—little lady's with me, Corky."

Corky said, "Fair enough," and then to the youth: "Outside, bum." The youth went out.

Lee Wilshire had returned to her table. She sat there with her cheeks between her fists, staring at the cloth.

Ned Beaumont sat down facing her. He said to the waiter: "Jimmy's got a Manhattan that belongs to me. And I want some food. Eaten yet, Lee?"

"Yes," she said without looking up. "I want a silver fizz."

Ned Beaumont said: "Fine. I want a minute steak with mushrooms, whatever vegetable Tony's got that didn't come out of a can, some lettuce and tomatoes with Roquefort dressing, and coffee."

When the waiter had gone Lee said bitterly: "Men are no good, none of them. That big false alarm!" She began to cry silently.

"Maybe you pick the wrong kind," Ned Beaumont suggested.

"You should tell me that," she said, looking up angrily at him, "after the lousy trick you played me."

"I didn't play you any lousy trick," he protested. "If Bernie had to hock your pretties to pay back the money he'd gypped me out of it wasn't my fault."

The orchestra began to play.

"Nothing's ever a man's fault," she complained. "Come on and dance."

"Oh, all right," he said reluctantly.

When they returned to the table his cocktail and her fizz were there.

"What's Bernie doing these days?" he asked as they drank.

"I don't know. I haven't seen him since he got out and I don't want to see him. Another swell guy! What breaks I've been getting this year! Him and Taylor and this bastard!"

"Taylor Henry?" he asked.

"Yes, but I didn't have much to do with him," she explained quickly, "because that's while I was living with Bernie."

Ned Beaumont finished his cocktail before he said: "You were just one of the girls who used to meet him in his Charter Street place now and then."

"Yes," she said, looking warily at him.

He said: "I think we ought to have a drink."

She powdered her face while he caught their waiter's attention and ordered their drinks.

4

The door-bell awakened Ned Beaumont. He got drowsily out of bed, coughing a little, and put on kimono and slippers. It was a few minutes after nine by his alarm-clock. He went to the door.

Janet Henry came in apologizing. "I know it's horribly early, but I simply couldn't wait another minute. I tried and tried to get you on the phone last night and hardly slept a wink because I couldn't. All of Father's sticks are there. So, you see, he lied."

"Has he got a heavy rough brown one?"

"Yes, that's the one Major Sawbridge brought him from Scotland. He never uses it, but it's there." She smiled triumphantly at Ned Beaumont.

He blinked sleepily and ran fingers through his tousled hair. "Then he lied, right enough," he said.

"And," she said gaily, "he was there when I got home last night."

"Paul?"

"Yes. And he asked me to marry him."

Sleepiness went out of Ned Beaumont's eyes. "Did he say anything about our battle?"

"Not a word."

"What did you say?"

"I said it was too soon after Taylor's death for me even to engage myself to him, but I didn't say I wouldn't a little later, so we've got what I believe is called an understanding."

He looked curiously at her.

Gaiety went out of her face. She put a hand on his arm. Her voice broke a little. "Please don't think I'm altogether heartless," she said, "but —oh!—I do so want to—to do what we set out to do that everything else seems—well—not important at all."

He moistened his lips and said in a grave gentle voice: "What a spot he'd be in if you loved him as much as you hate him."

She stamped her foot and cried: "Don't say that! Don't ever say that again!"

Irritable lines appeared in his forehead and his lips tightened together.

She said, "Please," contritely, "but I can't bear that."

"Sorry," he said. "Had breakfast yet?"

"No. I was too anxious to bring my news to you."

"Fine. You'll eat with me. What do you like?" He went to the telephone.

After he had ordered breakfast he went into the bathroom to wash his teeth, face, and hands and brush his hair. When he returned to the living-room she had removed her hat and coat and was standing by the fireplace smoking a cigarette. She started to say something, but stopped when the telephone-bell rang.

He went to the telephone. "Hello. . . . Yes, Harry, I stopped in, but you were out. . . . I wanted to ask you about—you know—the chap you saw with Paul that night. Did he have a hat? . . . He did? Sure? . . . And did he have a stick in his hand? . . . Oke. . . . No, I couldn't do anything with Paul on that, Harry. Better see him yourself. . . . Yes. . . . 'By."

Janet Henry's eyes questioned him as he got up from the telephone.

He said: "That was one of a couple of fellows who claim they saw Paul talking to your brother in the street that night. He says he saw the hat, but not the stick. It was dark, though, and this pair were riding past in a car. I wouldn't bet they saw anything very clearly."

"Why are you so interested in the hat? Is it so important?"

He shrugged. "I don't know. I'm only an amateur detective, but it looks like a thing that might have some meaning, one way or another."

"Have you learned anything else since yesterday?"

"No. I spent part of the evening buying drinks for a girl Taylor used to play around with, but there wasn't anything there."

"Anyone I know?" she asked.

He shook his head, then looked sharply at her and said: "It wasn't Opal, if that's what you're getting at."

"Don't you think we might be able to—to get some information from her?"

"Opal? No. She thinks her father killed Taylor, but she thinks it was on her account. It wasn't anything she knew that sent her off—not any inside stuff—it was your letters and the *Observer* and things like that."

Janet Henry nodded, but seemed unconvinced.

Their breakfast arrived.

The telephone-bell rang while they were eating. Ned Beaumont went to the telephone and said: "Hello. . . . Yes, Mom. . . . What?" He listened, frowning, for several seconds, then said: "There isn't much you can do about it except let them and I don't think it'll do any harm. . . . No, I don't know where he is. . . . I don't think I will. . . . Well, don't worry about it, Mom, it'll be all right. . . . Sure, that's right. . . . 'By." He returned to the table smiling. "Farr's got the same idea you had," he said as he sat down. "That was Paul's mother. A man from the District Attorney's office is there to question Opal." A bright gleam awakened in his eyes. "She can't help them any, but they're closing in on him."

"Why did she call you?" Janet Henry asked.

"Paul had gone out and she didn't know where to find him."

"Doesn't she know that you and Paul have quarreled?"

"Apparently not." He put down his fork. "Look here. Are you sure you want to go through with this thing?"

"I want to go through with it more than I ever wanted to do anything in my life," she told him.

Ned Beaumont laughed bitterly, said: "They're practically the same words Paul used telling me how much he wanted you."

She shuddered, her face hardened, and she looked coldly at him.

He said: "I don't know about you. I'm not sure of you. I had a dream I don't much like."

She smiled then. "Surely you don't believe in dreams?"

He did not smile. "I don't believe in anything, but I'm too much of a gambler not to be affected by a lot of things."

Her smile became less mocking. She asked: "What was this dream that makes you mistrust me?" She held up a finger, pretending seriousness. "And then I'll tell you one I had about you."

"I was fishing," he said, "and I caught an enormous fish—a rainbow trout, but enormous—and you said you wanted to look at it and you picked it up and threw it back in the water before I could stop you."

She laughed merrily. "What did you do?"

"That was the end of the dream."

"It was a lie," she said. "I won't throw your trout back. Now I'll tell you mine. I was—" Her eyes widened. "When was yours? The night you came to dinner?"

"No. Last night."

"Oh, that's too bad. It would be nicer in an impressive way if we'd done our dreaming on the same night and the same hour and the same minute. Mine was the night you were there. We were—this is in the dream —we were lost in a forest, you and I, tired and starving. We walked and walked till we came to a little house and we knocked on the door, but nobody answered. We tried the door. It was locked. Then we peeped through a window and inside we could see a great big table piled high with all imaginable kinds of food, but we couldn't get in through either of the windows because they had iron bars over them. So we went back to the door and knocked and knocked again and still nobody answered. Then we thought that sometimes people left their keys under door-mats and we looked and there it was. But when we opened the door we saw hundreds and hundreds of snakes on the floor where we hadn't been able to see them through the window and they all came sliding and slithering towards us. We slammed the door shut and locked it and stood there frightened to death listening to them hissing and knocking their heads against the inside of the door. Then you said that perhaps if we opened the door and hid from the snakes they'd come out and go away, so we did. You helped me climb up on the roof—it was low in this part of the dream: I don't remember what it was like before—and you climbed up after me and leaned down and unlocked the door, and all the snakes came slithering out. We lay holding our breath on the roof until the last of the hundreds and hundreds of them had slithered out of sight into the forest. Then we jumped down and ran inside and locked the door and ate and ate and ate and I woke sitting up in bed clapping my hands and laughing."

"I think you made that up," Ned Beaumont said after a little pause. "Why?"

"It starts out to be a nightmare and winds up something else and all the dreams I ever had about food ended before I got a chance to do any actual eating."

Janet Henry laughed. "I didn't make all of it up," she said, "but you needn't ask which part is true. You've accused me of lying and I'll tell you nothing now."

"Oh, all right." He picked up his fork again, but did not eat. He asked, with an air of just having the thought: "Does your father know anything? Do you think we could get anything out of him if we went to him with what we know?"

"Yes," she said eagerly, "I do."

He scowled thoughtfully. "The only trouble is he might go up in the air and explode the works before we're ready. He's hot-headed, isn't he?"

Her answer was given reluctantly: "Yes, but"—her face brightened, pleadingly—"I'm sure if we showed him why it's important to wait until we've— But we are ready now, aren't we?"

He shook his head. "Not yet."

She pouted.

"Maybe tomorrow," he said.

"Really?"

"That's not a promise," he cautioned her, "but I think we will be."

She put a hand across the table to take one of his hands. "But you will promise to let me know the very minute we're ready, no matter what time of day or night it is?"

"Sure, I'll promise you that." He looked obliquely at her. "You're not very anxious to be in at the death, are you?"

His tone brought a flush to her face, but she did not lower her eyes. "I know you think I'm a monster," she said. "Perhaps I am."

He looked down at his plate and muttered: "I hope you like it when you get it."

IX · *The Heels*

1

AFTER Janet Henry had gone Ned Beaumont went to his telephone, called Jack Rumsen's number, and when he had that one on the wire said: "Can you drop in to see me, Jack? . . . Fine. 'By."

He was dressed by the time Jack arrived. They sat in facing chairs, each with a glass of Bourbon whisky and mineral water, Ned Beaumont smoking a cigar, Jack a cigarette.

Ned Beaumont asked: "Heard anything about the split between Paul and me?"

Jack said, "Yes," casually.

"What do you think of it?"

"Nothing. I remember the last time it was supposed to happen it turned out to be a trick on Shad O'Rory."

Ned Beaumont smiled as if he had expected that reply. "Is that what everybody thinks it is this time?"

The dapper young man said: "A lot of them do."

Ned Beaumont inhaled cigar-smoke slowly, asked: "Suppose I told you it was on the level this time?"

Jack said nothing. His face told nothing of his thoughts.

Ned Beaumont said: "It is." He drank from his glass. "How much do I owe you?"

"Thirty bucks for that job on the Madvig girl. You settled for the rest."

Ned Beaumont took a roll of paper money from a trousers-pocket, separated three ten-dollar bills from the roll, and gave them to Jack.

Jack said: "Thanks."

Ned Beaumont said: "Now we're quits." He inhaled smoke and blew it out while saying: "I've got another job I want done. I'm after Paul's scalp on the Taylor Henry killing. He told me he did it, but I need a little more proof. Want to work on it for me?"

Jack said: "No."

"Why not?"

The dark young man rose to put his empty glass on the table. "Fred and I are building up a nice little private-detective business here," he said. "A couple of years more and we'll be sitting pretty. I like you, Beaumont, but not enough to monkey with the man that runs the city."

Ned Beaumont said evenly: "He's on the chutes. The whole crew's getting ready to ditch him. Farr and Rainey are—"

"Let them do it. I don't want in on that racket and I'll believe they can do it when it's done. Maybe they'll give him a bump or two, but making it stick's another thing. You know him better than I do. You know he's got more guts than all the rest of them put together."

"He has and that's what's licking him. Well, if you won't, you won't." Jack said, "I won't," and picked up his hat. "Anything else I'll be glad to do, but—" He moved one hand in a brief gesture of finality.

Ned Beaumont stood up. There was no resentment in his manner, none in his voice when he said: "I thought you might feel that way about it." He brushed a side of his mustache with a thumb and stared thoughtfully past Jack. "Maybe you can tell me this: any idea where I can find Shad?"

Jack shook his head. "Since the third time they knocked his place over—when the two coppers were killed—he's been laying low, though they don't seem to have a hell of a lot on him personally." He took his cigarette from his mouth. "Know Whisky Vassos?"

"Yes."

"You might find out from him if you know him well enough. He's around town. You can usually find him some time during the night at Tim Walker's place on Smith Street."

"Thanks, Jack, I'll try that."

"That's all right," Jack said. He hesitated. "I'm sorry as hell you and Madvig split. I wish you—" He broke off and turned towards the door. "You know what you're doing."

2

Ned Beaumont went down to the District Attorney's office. This time there was no delay in ushering him into Farr's presence.

Farr did not get up from his desk, did not offer to shake hands. He said: "How do you do, Beaumont? Sit down." His voice was coldly polite. His pugnacious face was not so red as usual. His eyes were level and hard.

Ned Beaumont sat down, crossed his legs comfortably, and said: "I wanted to tell you about what happened when I went to see Paul after I left here yesterday."

Farr's "Yes?" was cold and polite.

"I told him how I'd found you—panicky." Ned Beaumont, smiling his nicest smile, went on in the manner of one telling a fairly amusing but unimportant anecdote: "I told him I thought you were trying to get up enough nerve to hang the Taylor Henry murder on him. He believed me at first, but when I told him the only way to save himself was by turning up the real murderer, he said that was no good. He said he was the real murderer, though he called it an accident or self-defense or something."

Farr's face had become paler and was stiff around the mouth, but he did not speak.

Ned Beaumont raised his eyebrows. "I'm not boring you, am I?" he asked.

"Go on, continue," the District Attorney said coldly.

Ned Beaumont tilted his chair back. His smile was mocking. "You think I'm kidding, don't you? You think it's a trick we're playing on you." He shook his head and murmured: "You're a timid soul, Farr."

Farr said: "I'm glad to listen to any information you can give me, but I'm very busy, so I'll have to ask you—"

Ned Beaumont laughed then and replied: "Oke. I thought maybe you'd like to have this information in an affidavit or something."

"Very well." Farr pressed one of the pearl buttons on his desk.

A grey-haired woman in green came in.

"Mr. Beaumont wants to dictate a statement," Farr told her.

She said, "Yes, sir," sat at the other side of Farr's desk, put her notebook on the desk, and, holding a silver pencil over the book, looked at Ned Beaumont with blank brown eyes.

He said: "Yesterday afternoon in his office in the Nebel Building, Paul Madvig told me that he had been to dinner at Senator Henry's house the night Taylor Henry was killed; that he and Taylor Henry had some sort of trouble there; that after he left the house Taylor Henry ran after him and caught up with him and tried to hit him with a rough heavy brown walking-stick; that in trying to take the stick from Taylor Henry he accidentally struck him on the forehead with it, knocking him down; and that he carried the stick away with him and burned it. He said his only reason for concealing his part in Taylor Henry's death was his desire to keep it from Janet Henry. That's all of it."

Farr addressed the stenographer: "Transcribe that right away."

She left the office.

Ned Beaumont said: "I thought I was bringing you news that would get you all excited." He sighed. "I thought you'd fairly tear your hair over it."

The District Attorney looked steadily at him.

Ned Beaumont, unabashed, said: "I thought at least you'd have Paul dragged in and confronted with this"—he waved a hand—" 'damaging disclosure' is a good phrase."

The District Attorney spoke in a restrained tone: "Please permit me to run my own office."

Ned Beaumont laughed again and relapsed into silence until the grey-haired stenographer returned with a typed copy of his statement. Then he asked: "Do I swear to it?"

"No," Farr said, "just sign it. That will be sufficient."

Ned Beaumont signed the paper. "This isn't nearly so much fun as I thought it was going to be," he complained cheerfully.

Farr's undershot jaw tightened. "No," he said with grim satisfaction, "I don't suppose it is."

"You're a timid soul, Farr," Ned Beaumont repeated. "Be careful about taxis when you cross streets." He bowed. "See you later."

Outside, he grimaced angrily.

3

That night Ned Beaumont rang the door-bell of a dark three-story house in Smith Street. A short man who had a small head and thick shoulders opened the door half a foot, said, "All right," and opened it the rest of the way.

Ned Beaumont, saying, " 'Lo," entered, walked twenty feet down a dim hallway past two closed doors on the right, opened a door on the left, and went down a wooden flight of steps into a basement where there was a bar and where a radio was playing softly.

Beyond the bar was a frosted glass door marked *Toilet*. This door opened and a man came out, a swarthy man with something apish in the slope of his big shoulders, the length of his thick arms, the flatness of his face, and the curve of his bowed legs—Jeff Gardner.

He saw Ned Beaumont and his reddish small eyes glistened. "Well, blind Christ, if it ain't Sock-me-again Beaumont!" he roared, showing his beautiful teeth in a huge grin.

Ned Beaumont said, " 'Lo, Jeff," while everyone in the place looked at them.

Jeff swaggered over to Ned Beaumont, threw his left arm roughly around his shoulders, seized Ned Beaumont's right hand with his right hand, and addressed the company jovially: "This is the swellest guy I ever skinned a knuckle on and I've skinned them on plenty." He dragged Ned Beaumont to the bar. "We're all going to have a little drink and then I'll show you how it's done. By Jesus, I will!" He leered into Ned Beaumont's face. "What do you say to that, my lad?"

Ned Beaumont, looking stolidly at the ugly dark face so close to, though lower than, his, said: "Scotch."

Jeff laughed delightedly and addressed the company again: "You see, he likes it. He's a—" he hesitated, frowning, wet his lips "—a God-damned massacrist, that's what he is." He leered at Ned Beaumont. "You know what a massacrist is?"

"Yes."

Jeff seemed disappointed. "Rye," he told the bar-tender. When their drinks were set before them he released Ned Beaumont's hand, though he kept his arm across his shoulders. They drank. Jeff set down his glass and put his hand on Ned Beaumont's wrist. "I got just the place for me and you upstairs," he said, "a room that's too little for you to fall down in. I can bounce you around off the walls. That way we won't be wasting a lot of time while you're getting up off the floor."

Ned Beaumont said: "I'll buy a drink."

"That ain't a dumb idea," Jeff agreed.

They drank again.

When Ned Beaumont had paid for the drinks Jeff turned him towards the stairs. "Excuse us, gents," he said to the others at the bar, "but we got to go up and rehearse our act." He patted Ned Beaumont's shoulder. "Me and my sweetheart."

They climbed two flights of steps and went into a small room in which a sofa, two tables, and half a dozen chairs were crowded. There were some empty glasses and plates holding the remains of sandwiches on one table.

Jeff peered near-sightedly around the room and demanded: "Now where in hell did she go?" He released Ned Beaumont's wrist, took the arm from around his shoulders, and asked: "You don't see no broad here, do you?"

"No."

Jeff wagged his head up and down emphatically. "She's gone," he said. He took an uncertain step backwards and jabbed the bell-button beside the door with a dirty finger. Then, flourishing his hand, he made a grotesque bow and said: "Set down."

Ned Beaumont sat down at the less disorderly of the two tables.

"Set in any God-damned chair you want to set in," Jeff said with another large gesture. "If you don't like that one, take another. I want you to consider yourself my guest and the hell with you if you don't like it."

"It's a swell chair," Ned Beaumont said.

"It's a hell of a chair," Jeff said. "There ain't a chair in the dump that's worth a damn. Look." He picked up a chair and tore one of its front legs out. "You call that a swell chair? Listen, Beaumont, you don't know a damned thing about chairs." He put the chair down, tossed the leg on the sofa. "You can't fool me. I know what you're up to. You think I'm drunk, don't you?"

Ned Beaumont grinned. "No, you're not drunk."

"The hell I'm not drunk. I'm drunker than you are. I'm drunker than anybody in this dump. I'm drunk as hell and don't think I'm not, but—" He held up a thick unclean forefinger.

A waiter came in the doorway asking: "What is it, gents?"

Jeff turned to confront him. "Where've you been? Sleeping? I rung for you one hour ago."

The waiter began to say something.

Jeff said: "I bring the best friend I got in the world up here for a drink and what the hell happens? We have to sit around a whole God-damned hour waiting for a lousy waiter. No wonder he's sore at me."

"What do you want?" the waiter asked indifferently.

"I want to know where in hell the girl that was in here went to."

"Oh, her? She's gone."

"Gone where?"

"I don't know."

Jeff scowled. "Well, you find out, and God-damned quick. What's the idea of not knowing where she went? If this ain't a swell joint where nobody—" A shrewd light came into his red eyes. "I'll tell you what to do. You go up to the ladies' toilet and see if she's there."

"She ain't there," the waiter said. "She went out."

"The dirty bastard!" Jeff said and turned to Ned Beaumont. "What'd you do to a dirty bastard like that? I bring you up here because I want you to meet her because I know you'll like her and she'll like you and she's too God-damned snotty to meet my friends and out she goes."

Ned Beaumont was lighting a cigar. He did not say anything.

Jeff scratched his head, growled, "Well, bring us something to drink, then," sat down across the table from Ned Beaumont, and said savagely: "Mine's rye."

Ned Beaumont said: "Scotch."

The waiter went away.

Jeff glared at Ned Beaumont. "Don't get the idea that I don't know what you're up to, either," he said angrily.

"I'm not up to anything," Ned Beaumont replied carelessly. "I'd like to see Shad and I thought maybe I'd find Whisky Vassos here and he'd send me to Shad."

"Don't you think I know where Shad is?"

"You ought to."

"Then why didn't you ask me?"

"All right. Where is he?"

Jeff slapped the table mightily with an open hand and bawled: "You're a liar. You don't give a God-damn where Shad is. It's me you're after."

Ned Beaumont smiled and shook his head.

"It is," the apish man insisted. "You know God-damned well that—"

A young-middle-aged man with plump red lips and round eyes came to the door. He said: "Cut it out, Jeff. You're making more noise than everybody else in the place."

Jeff screwed himself around in his chair. "It's this bastard," he told the man in the doorway, indicating Ned Beaumont with a jerk of his thumb. "He thinks I don't know what he's up to. I know what he's up to. He's a heel and that's what he is. And I'm going to beat hell out of him and that's what I'm going to do."

The man in the doorway said reasonably, "Well, you don't have to make so much noise about it," winked at Ned Beaumont, and went away.

Jeff said gloomily: "Tim's turning into a heel too." He spit on the floor.

The waiter came in with their drinks.

Ned Beaumont raised his glass, said, "Looking at you," and drank.

Jeff said: "I don't want to look at you. You're a heel." He stared somberly at Ned Beaumont.

"You're crazy."

"You're a liar. I'm drunk. But I ain't so drunk that I don't know what you're up to." He emptied his glass, wiped his mouth with the back of his hand. "And I say you're a heel."

Ned Beaumont, smiling amiably, said: "All right. Have it your way."

Jeff thrust his apish muzzle forward a little. "You think you're smart as hell, don't you?"

Ned Beaumont did not say anything.

"You think it's a damned smart trick coming in here and trying to get me plastered so you can turn me up."

"That's right," Ned Beaumont said carelessly, "there is a murder-charge against you for bumping off Francis West, isn't there?"

Jeff said: "Hell with Francis West."

Ned Beaumont shrugged. "I didn't know him."

Jeff said: "You're a heel."

Ned Beaumont said: "I'll buy a drink."

The apish man nodded solemnly and tilted his chair back to reach the bell-button. With his finger on the button he said: "But you're still a heel." His chair swayed back under him, turning. He got his feet flat on the floor and brought the chair down on all fours before it could spill him. "The bastard!" he snarled, pulling it around to the table again. He put his elbows on the table and propped his chin up on one fist. "What the hell do I care who turns me up? You don't think they'd ever fry me, do you?"

"Why not?"

"Why not? Jesus! I wouldn't have to stand the rap till after election and then it's all Shad's."

"Maybe."

"Maybe hell!"

The waiter came in and they ordered their drinks.

"Maybe Shad would let you take the fall anyhow," Ned Beaumont said idly when they were alone again. "Things like that have happened."

"A swell chance," Jeff scoffed, "with all I've got on him."

Ned Beaumont exhaled cigar-smoke. "What've you got on him?"

The apish man laughed, boisterously, scornfully, and pounded the table with an open hand. "Christ!" he roared, "he thinks I'm drunk enough to tell him."

From the doorway came a quiet voice, a musical slightly Irish bary-tone: "Go on, Jeff, tell him." Shad O'Rory stood in the doorway. His grey-blue eyes looked somewhat sadly at Jeff.

Jeff squinted his eyes merrily at the man in the doorway and said: "How are you, Shad? Come in and set down to a drink. Meet Mr. Beau-mont. He's a heel."

O'Rory said softly: "I told you to stay under cover."

"But, Jesus, Shad, I was getting so's I was afraid I'd bite myself! And this joint's under cover, ain't it? It's a speakeasy."

O'Rory looked a moment longer at Jeff, then at Ned Beaumont. "Good evening, Beaumont."

"'Lo, Shad."

O'Rory smiled gently and, indicating Jeff with a tiny nod, asked: "Get much out of him?"

"Not much I didn't already know," Ned Beaumont replied. "He makes a lot of noise, but all of it doesn't make sense."

Jeff said: "I think you're a pair of heels."

The waiter arrived with their drinks. O'Rory stopped him. "Never mind. They've had enough." The waiter carried their drinks away. Shad O'Rory came into the room and shut the door. He stood with his back against it. He said: "You talk too much, Jeff. I've told you that before."

Ned Beaumont deliberately winked at Jeff.

Jeff said angrily to him: "What the hell's the matter with you?"

Ned Beaumont laughed.

"I'm talking to you, Jeff," O'Rory said.

"Christ, don't I know it?"

O'Rory said: "We're coming to the place where I'm going to stop talking to you."

Jeff stood up. "Don't be a heel, Shad," he said. "What the hell?" He came around the table. "Me and you've been pals a long time. You always were my pal and I'll always be yours." He put his arms out to embrace O'Rory, lurching towards him. "Sure, I'm smoked, but—"

O'Rory put a white hand on the apish man's chest and thrust him back. "Sit down." He did not raise his voice.

Jeff's left fist whipped out at O'Rory's face.

O'Rory's head moved to the right, barely enough to let the fist whip past his cheek. O'Rory's long finely sculptured face was gravely composed. His right hand dropped down behind his hip.

Ned Beaumont flung from his chair at O'Rory's right arm, caught it with both hands, going down on his knees.

Jeff, thrown against the wall by the impetus behind his left fist, now turned and took Shad O'Rory's throat in both hands. The apish face was yellow, distorted, hideous. There was no longer any drunkenness in it.

"Got the roscoe?" Jeff panted.

"Yes." Ned Beaumont stood up, stepped back holding a black pistol leveled at O'Rory.

O'Rory's eyes were glassy, protuberant, his face mottled, turgid. He did not struggle against the man holding his throat.

Jeff turned his head over his shoulder to grin at Ned Beaumont. The grin was wide, genuine, idiotically bestial. Jeff's little red eyes glinted merrily. He said in a hoarse good-natured voice: "Now you see what we got to do. We got to give him the works."

Ned Beaumont said: "I don't want anything to do with it." His voice was steady. His nostrils quivered.

"No?" Jeff leered at him. "I expect you think Shad's a guy that'll forget what we done." He ran his tongue over his lips. "He'll forget. I'll fix that."

Grinning from ear to ear at Ned Beaumont, not looking at the man whose throat he held in his hands, Jeff began to take in and let out long slow breaths. His coat became lumpy over his shoulders and back and along his arms. Sweat appeared on his ugly dark face.

Ned Beaumont was pale. He too was breathing heavily and moisture filmed his temples. He looked over Jeff's lumpy shoulder at O'Rory's face.

O'Rory's face was liver-colored. His eyes stood far out, blind. His tongue came out blue between bluish lips. His slender body writhed. One of his hands began to beat the wall behind him, mechanically, without force.

Grinning at Ned Beaumont, not looking at the man whose throat he held, Jeff spread his legs a little wider and arched his back. O'Rory's hand stopped beating the wall. There was a muffled crack, then, almost immediately, a sharper one. O'Rory did not writhe now. He sagged in Jeff's hands.

Jeff laughed in his throat. "That's keno," he said. He kicked a chair out of the way and dropped O'Rory's body on the sofa. O'Rory's body fell there face down, one hand and his feet hanging down to the floor. Jeff rubbed his hands on his hips and faced Ned Beaumont. "I'm just a big good-natured slob," he said. "Anybody can kick me around all they want to and I never do nothing about it."

Ned Beaumont said: "You were afraid of him."

Jeff laughed. "I hope to tell you I was. So was anybody that was in their right mind. I suppose you wasn't?" He laughed again, looked around the room, said: "Let's screw before anybody pops in." He held out his hand. "Give me the roscoe. I'll ditch it."

Ned Beaumont said: "No." He moved his hand sidewise until the pistol was pointed at Jeff's belly. "We can say this was self-defense. I'm with you. We can beat it at the inquest."

"Jesus, that's a bright idea!" Jeff exclaimed. "Me with a murder-rap hanging over me for that West guy!" His small red eyes kept shifting their focus from Ned Beaumont's face to the pistol in his hand.

Ned Beaumont smiled with thin pale lips. "That's what I was thinking about," he said softly.

"Don't be a God-damned sap," Jeff blustered, taking a step forward. "You—"

Ned Beaumont backed away, around one of the tables. "I don't mind plugging you, Jeff," he said. "Remember I owe you something."

Jeff stood still and scratched the back of his head. "What kind of a heel are you?" he asked perplexedly.

"Just a pal." Ned Beaumont moved the pistol forward suddenly. "Sit down."

Jeff, after a moment's glowering hesitation, sat down.

Ned Beaumont put out his left hand and pressed the bell-button.

Jeff stood up.

Ned Beaumont said: "Sit down."

Jeff sat down.

Ned Beaumont said: "Keep your hands on the table."

Jeff shook his head lugubriously. "What a half-smart bastard you turned out to be," he said. "You don't think they're going to let you drag me out of here, do you?"

Ned Beaumont went around the table again and sat on a chair facing Jeff and facing the door.

Jeff said: "The best thing for you to do is give me that gun and hope I'll forget you made the break. Jesus, Ned, this is one of my hang-outs! You ain't got a chance in the world of pulling a fast one here."

Ned Beaumont said: "Keep your hand away from the catchup-bottle."

The waiter opened the door, goggled at them.

"Tell Tim to come up," Ned Beaumont said, and then, to the apish man when he would have spoken: "Shut up."

The waiter shut the door and hurried away.

Jeff said: "Don't be a sap, Neddy. This can't get you anything but a rub-out. What good's it going to do you to try to turn me up? None." He wet his lips with his tongue. "I know you're kind of sore about the time we were rough with you, but—hell!—that wasn't my fault. I was just doing what Shad told me, and ain't I evened that up now by knocking him off for you?"

Ned Beaumont said: "If you don't keep your hand away from that catchup-bottle I'm going to shoot a hole in it."

Jeff said: "You're a heel."

The young-middle-aged man with plump lips and round eyes opened the door, came in quickly, and shut it behind him.

Ned Beaumont said: "Jeff's killed O'Rory. Phone the police. You'll have time to clear the place before they get here. Better get a doctor, too, in case he's not dead."

Jeff laughed scornfully. "If he ain't dead I'm the Pope." He stopped laughing and addressed the plump-mouthed man with careless familiarity: "What do you think of this guy thinking you're going to let him get away with that? Tell him what a fat chance he has of getting away with it, Tim."

Tim looked at the dead man on the sofa, at Jeff, and at Ned Beaumont. His round eyes were sober. He spoke to Ned Beaumont, slowly: "This is a tough break for the house. Can't we drag him out in the street and let him be found there?"

Ned Beaumont shook his head. "Get your place cleaned up before the coppers get here and you'll be all right. I'll do what I can for you."

While Tim hesitated Jeff said: "Listen, Tim, you know me. You know—"

Tim said without especial warmth: "For Christ's sake pipe down."

Ned Beaumont smiled. "Nobody knows you, Jeff, now Shad's dead."

"No?" The apish man sat back more comfortably in his chair and his face cleared. "Well, turn me up. Now I know what kind of sons of bitches you are I'd rather take the fall than ask a God-damned thing of either of you."

Tim, ignoring Jeff, asked: "Have to play it that way?"

Ned Beaumont nodded.

"I guess I can stand it," Tim said and put his hand on the door-knob.

"Mind seeing if Jeff's got a gun on him?" Ned Beaumont asked.

Tim shook his head. "It happened here, but I've got nothing to do with it and I'm going to have nothing to do with it," he said and went out.

Jeff, slouching back comfortably in his chair, his hands idle on the edge of the table before him, talked to Ned Beaumont until the police came. He talked cheerfully, calling Ned Beaumont numerous profane and obscene and merely insulting names, accusing him of a long and varied list of vices.

Ned Beaumont listened with polite interest.

A raw-boned white-haired man in a lieutenant's uniform was the first policeman to come in. Half a dozen police detectives were behind him.

Ned Beaumont said: "'Lo, Brett. I think he's got a gun on him."

"What's it all about?" Brett asked, looking at the body on the sofa while two of the detectives, squeezing past him, took hold of Jeff Gardner.

Ned Beaumont told Brett what had happened. His story was truthful except in giving the impression that O'Rory had been killed in the heat of their struggle and not after he had been disarmed.

While Ned Beaumont was talking a doctor came in, turned Shad O'Rory's body over on the sofa, examined him briefly, and stood up. The Lieutenant looked at the doctor. The doctor said, "Gone," and went out of the small crowded room.

Jeff was jovially cursing the two detectives who held him. Every time he cursed, one of the detectives struck him in the face with his fist. Jeff laughed and kept on cursing them. His false teeth had been knocked out. His mouth bled.

Ned Beaumont gave the dead man's pistol to Brett and stood up. "Want me to come along to headquarters now? Or will tomorrow do?"

"Better come along now," Brett replied.

4

It was long past midnight when Ned Beaumont left police headquarters. He said good-night to the two reporters who had come out with him and got into a taxicab. The address he gave the driver was Paul Madvig's.

Lights were on in the ground-floor of Madvig's house and as Ned Beaumont climbed the front steps the door was opened by Mrs. Madvig. She was dressed in black and had a shawl over her shoulders.

He said: "'Lo, Mom. What are you doing up so late?"

She said, "I thought it was Paul," though she looked at him without disappointment.

"Isn't he home? I wanted to see him." He looked sharply at her. "What's the matter?"

The old woman stepped back, pulling the door back with her. "Come in, Ned."

He went in.

She shut the door and said: "Opal tried to commit suicide."

He lowered his eyes and mumbled: "What? What do you mean?"

"She had cut one of her wrists before the nurse could stop her. She didn't lose much blood, though, and she's all right if she doesn't try it again." There was as little of weakness in her voice as in her mien.

Ned Beaumont's voice was not steady. "Where's Paul?"

"I don't know. We haven't been able to find him. He ought to be home before this. I don't know where he is." She put a bony hand on Ned Beaumont's upper arm and now her voice shook a little. "Are you—are you and Paul—?" She stopped, squeezing his arm.

He shook his head. "That's done for good."

"Oh, Ned, boy, isn't there anything you can do to patch it up? You and he—" Again she broke off.

He raised his head and looked at her. His eyes were wet. He said gently: "No, Mom, that's done for good. Did he tell you about it?"

"He only told me, when I said I'd phoned you about that man from the District Attorney's office being here, that I wasn't ever to do anything like that again, that you—that you were not friends now."

Ned Beaumont cleared his throat. "Listen, Mom, tell him I came to see him. Tell him I'm going home and will wait there for him, will be waiting all night." He cleared his throat again and added lamely: "Tell him that."

Mrs. Madvig put her bony hands on his shoulders. "You're a good boy, Ned. I don't want you and Paul to quarrel. You're the best friend he ever had, no matter what's come between you. What is it? Is it that Janet—?"

"Ask Paul," he said in a low bitter voice. He moved his head impatiently. "I'm going to run along, Mom, unless there's something I can do for you or Opal. Is there?"

"Not unless you'd go up to see her. She's not sleeping yet and maybe it would do some good to talk to her. She used to listen to you."

He shook his head. "No," he said, "she wouldn't want to see me"—he swallowed—"either."

X · *The Shattered Key*

1

NED BEAUMONT went home. He drank coffee, smoked, read a newspaper, a magazine, and half a book. Now and then he stopped reading to walk, fidgeting, around his rooms. His door-bell did not ring. His telephone-bell did not ring.

At eight o'clock in the morning he bathed, shaved, and put on fresh clothes. Then he had breakfast sent in and ate it.

At nine o'clock he went to the telephone, called Janet Henry's number, asked for her, and said: "Good morning. . . . Yes, fine, thanks. . . . Well, we're ready for the fireworks. . . . Yes. . . . If your father's there suppose we let him in on the whole thing first. . . . Fine, but not a word till I get there. . . . As soon as I can make it. I'm leaving now. . . . Right. See you in minutes."

He got up from the telephone staring into space, clapped his hands together noisily, and rubbed their palms together. His mouth was a sullen line under his mustache, his eyes hot brown points. He went to the closet and briskly put on his overcoat and hat. He left his room whistling *Little Lost Lady* between his teeth and took long steps through the streets.

"Miss Henry's expecting me," he said to the maid who opened the Henrys' door.

She said, "Yes, sir," and guided him to a sunny bright-papered room where the Senator and his daughter were at breakfast.

Janet Henry jumped up immediately and came to him with both hands out, crying excitedly: "Good morning!"

The Senator rose in more leisurely manner, looking with polite surprise at his daughter, then holding his hand out to Ned Beaumont, saying: "Good morning, Mr. Beaumont. I'm very glad to see you. Won't you—?"

"Thanks, no, I've had breakfast."

Janet Henry was trembling. Excitement had drained her skin of color, had darkened her eyes, giving her the appearance of one drugged. "We have something to tell you, Father," she said in a strained uneven voice, "something that—" She turned abruptly to Ned Beaumont. "Tell him! Tell him!"

Ned Beaumont glanced obliquely at her, drawing his brows together, then looked directly at her father. The Senator had remained standing by his place at the table. Ned Beaumont said: "What we've got is pretty strong evidence—including a confession—that Paul Madvig killed your son."

The Senator's eyes became narrower and he put a hand flat on the table in front of him. "What is this pretty strong evidence?" he asked.

"Well, sir, the chief thing is the confession, of course. He says your son ran out after him that night and tried to hit him with a rough brown walking-stick and that in taking the stick away from your son he accidentally struck him with it. He says he took the stick away and burned it, but your daughter"—he made a little bow at Janet Henry—"says it's still here."

"It is," she said. "It's the one Major Sawbridge brought you."

The Senator's face was pale as marble and as firm. "Proceed," he said.

Ned Beaumont made a small gesture with one hand. "Well, sir, that would blow up his story about its being an accident or self-defense—your son's not having the stick." He moved his shoulders a little. "I told Farr this yesterday. He's apparently afraid to take many chances—you know what he is—but I don't see how he can keep from picking Paul up today."

Janet Henry frowned at Ned Beaumont, obviously perplexed by something, started to speak, but pressed her lips together instead.

Senator Henry touched his lips with the napkin he held in his left hand, dropped the napkin on the table, and asked: "Is there—ah—any other evidence?"

Ned Beaumont's reply was another question carelessly uttered: "Isn't that enough?"

"But there is still more, isn't there?" Janet demanded.

"Stuff to back this up," Ned Beaumont said depreciatively. He addressed the Senator: "I can give you more details, but you've got the main story now. That's enough, isn't it?"

"Quite enough," the Senator said. He put a hand to his forehead. "I cannot believe it, yet it is so. If you'll excuse me for a moment and"—to his daughter—"you too, my dear, I should like to be alone, to think, to adjust myself to— No, no, stay here. I should like to go to my room." He bowed gracefully. "Please remain, Mr. Beaumont. I shall not be long—merely a moment to—to adjust myself to the knowledge that this man with whom I've worked shoulder to shoulder is my son's murderer."

He bowed again and went out, carrying himself rigidly erect.

Ned Beaumont put a hand on Janet Henry's wrist and asked in a low tense voice: "Look here, is he likely to fly off the handle?"

She looked at him, startled.

"Is he likely to go dashing off hunting for Paul?" he explained. "We don't want that. There's no telling what would happen."

"I don't know," she said.

He grimaced impatiently. "We can't let him do it. Can't we go somewhere near the front door so we can stop him if he tries it?"

"Yes." She was frightened.

She led him to the front of the house, into a small room that was dim behind heavily curtained windows. Its door was within a few feet of the street-door. They stood close together in the dim room, close to the door that stood some six inches ajar. Both of them were trembling. Janet Henry tried to whisper to Ned Beaumont, but he sh-h-hed her into silence.

They were not there long before soft footfalls sounded on the hall-carpet and Senator Henry, wearing hat and overcoat, hurried towards the street-door.

Ned Beaumont stepped out and said: "Wait, Senator Henry."

The Senator turned. His face was hard and cold, his eyes imperious. "You will please excuse me," he said. "I must go out."

"That's no good," Ned Beaumont said. He went up close to the Senator. "Just more trouble."

Janet Henry went to her father's side. "Don't go, Father," she begged. "Listen to Mr. Beaumont."

"I have listened to Mr. Beaumont," the Senator said. "I'm perfectly willing to listen to him again if he has any more information to give me. Otherwise I must ask you to excuse me." He smiled at Ned Beaumont. "It is on what you told me that I'm acting now."

Ned Beaumont regarded him with level eyes. "I don't think you ought to go to see him," he said.

The Senator looked haughtily at Ned Beaumont.

Janet said, "But, Father," before the look in his eyes stopped her.

Ned Beaumont cleared his throat. Spots of color were in his cheeks. He put his left hand out quickly and touched Senator Henry's right-hand overcoat-pocket.

Senator Henry stepped back indignantly.

Ned Beaumont nodded as if to himself. "That's no good at all," he said earnestly. He looked at Janet Henry. "He's got a gun in his pocket."

"Father!" she cried and put a hand to her mouth.

Ned Beaumont pursed his lips. "Well," he told the Senator, "it's a cinch we can't let you go out of here with a gun in your pocket."

Janet Henry said: "Don't let him, Ned."

The Senator's eyes burned scornfully at them. "I think both of you have quite forgotten yourselves," he said. "Janet, you will please go to your room."

She took two reluctant steps away, then halted and cried: "I won't! I won't let you do it. Don't let him, Ned."

Ned Beaumont moistened his lips. "I won't," he promised.

The Senator, staring coldly at him, put his right hand on the street-door's knob.

Ned Beaumont leaned forward and put a hand over the Senator's. "Look here, sir," he said respectfully, "I can't let you do this. I'm not just interfering." He took his hand off the Senator's, felt in the inside pocket of his coat, and brought out a torn, creased, and soiled piece of folded paper. "Here's my appointment as special investigator for the District Attorney's office last month." He held it out to the Senator. "It's never been cancelled as far as I know, so"—he shrugged—"I can't let you go off to shoot somebody."

The Senator did not look at the paper. He said contemptuously: "You are trying to save your murderous friend's life."

"You know that isn't so."

The Senator drew himself up. "Enough of this," he said and turned the door-knob.

Ned Beaumont said: "Step on the sidewalk with that gun in your pocket and I'll arrest you."

Janet Henry wailed: "Oh, Father!"

The Senator and Ned Beaumont stood staring into each other's eyes, both breathing audibly.

The Senator was the first to speak. He addressed his daughter: "Will you leave us for a few minutes, my dear? There are things I should like to say to Mr. Beaumont."

She looked questioningly at Ned Beaumont. He nodded. "Yes," she told her father, "if you won't go out before I've seen you again."

He smiled and said: "You shall see me."

The two men watched her walk away down the hall, turn to the left with a glance thrown back at them, and vanish through a doorway.

The Senator said ruefully: "I'm afraid you've not had so good an influence on my daughter as you should. She isn't usually so—ah—head-strong."

Ned Beaumont smiled apologetically, but did not speak.

The Senator asked: "How long has this been going on?"

"You mean our digging into the murder? Only a day or two for me. Your daughter's been at it from the beginning. She's always thought Paul did it."

"What?" The Senator's mouth remained open.

"She's always thought he did it. Didn't you know? She hates him like poison—always has."

"Hates him?" the Senator gasped. "My God, no!"

Ned Beaumont nodded and smiled curiously at the man against the door. "Didn't you know that?"

The Senator blew his breath out sharply. "Come in here," he said and led the way into the dim room where Ned Beaumont and Janet Henry had hidden. The Senator switched on the lights while Ned Beaumont was shutting the door. Then they faced one another, both standing.

"I want to talk to you as man to man, Mr. Beaumont," the Senator began. "We can forget your"—he smiled—"official connections, can't we?"

Ned Beaumont nodded. "Yes. Farr's probably forgotten them too."

"Exactly. Now, Mr. Beaumont, I am not a blood-thirsty man, but I'm damned if I can bear the thought of my son's murderer walking around free and unpunished when—"

"I told you they'll have to pick him up. They can't get out of it. The evidence is too strong and everybody knows it."

The Senator smiled again, icily. "You are surely not trying to tell me, as one practicing politician to another, that Paul Madvig is in any danger of being punished for anything he might do in this city?"

"I am. Paul's sunk. They're double-crossing him. The only thing that's holding them up is that they're used to jumping when he cracks the whip and they need a little time to gather courage."

Senator Henry smiled and shook his head. "You'll allow me to disagree with you? And to point out the fact that I've been in politics more years than you've lived?"

"Sure."

"Then I can assure you that they never will get the necessary amount of courage, no matter how much time they're given. Paul is their boss and, despite possible temporary rebellions, he will remain their boss."

"It doesn't look like we'll agree on that," Ned Beaumont said. "Paul's sunk." He frowned. "Now about this gun business. That's no good. You'd better give it to me." He held out his hand.

The Senator put his right hand in his overcoat-pocket.

Ned Beaumont stepped close to the Senator and put his left hand on the Senator's wrist. "Give me it."

The Senator glared angrily at him.

"All right," Ned Beaumont said, "if I've got to do that," and, after a brief struggle in which a chair was upset, took the weapon—an old-fashioned nickeled revolver—away from the Senator. He was thrusting the revolver into one of his hip-pockets when Janet Henry, wild of eye, white of face, came in.

"What is it?" she cried.

"He won't listen to reason," Ned Beaumont grumbled. "I had to take the gun away from him."

The Senator's face was twitching and he panted hoarsely. He took a step towards Ned Beaumont. "Get out of my house," he ordered.

"I won't," Ned Beaumont said. The ends of his lips jerked. Anger began to burn in his eyes. He put a hand out and touched Janet Henry's arm roughly. "Sit down and listen to this. You asked for it and you're going to get it." He spoke to the Senator: "I've got a lot to say, so maybe you'd better sit down too."

Neither Janet Henry nor her father sat down. She looked at Ned Beaumont with wide panic-stricken eyes, he with hard wary ones. Their faces were similarly white.

Ned Beaumont said to the Senator: "You killed your son."

Nothing changed in the Senator's face. He did not move.

For a long moment Janet Henry was still as her father. Then a look of utter horror came into her face and she sat down slowly on the floor. She did not fall. She slowly bent her knees and sank down on the floor in a sitting position, leaning to the right, her right hand on the floor for support, her horrified face turned up to her father and Ned Beaumont.

Neither of the men looked at her.

Ned Beaumont said to the Senator: "You want to kill Paul now so he can't say you killed your son. You know you can kill him and get away with it—dashing gentleman of the old school stuff—if you can put over on the world the attitude you tried to put over on us." He stopped.

The Senator said nothing.

Ned Beaumont went on: "You know he's going to stop covering you up if he's arrested, because he's not going to have Janet thinking he killed her brother if he can help it." He laughed bitterly. "And what a swell joke on him that is!" He ran fingers through his hair. "What happened is something like this: when Taylor heard about Paul kissing Janet he ran after him, taking the stick with him and wearing a hat, though that's not as important. When you thought of what might happen to your chances of being re-elected—"

The Senator interrupted him in a hoarse angry tone: "This is nonsense! I will not have my daughter subjected—"

Ned Beaumont laughed brutally. "Sure it's nonsense," he said. "And your bringing the stick you killed him with back home, and wearing his hat because you'd run out bare-headed after him, is nonsense too, but it's nonsense that'll nail you to the cross."

Senator Henry said in a low scornful voice: "And what of Paul's confession?"

Ned Beaumont grinned. "Plenty of it," he said. "I tell you what let's do. Janet, you phone him and ask him to come over right away. Then we'll tell him about your father starting after him with a gun and see what he says."

Janet stirred, but did not rise from the floor. Her face was blank.

Her father said: "That is ridiculous. We will do nothing of the sort."

Ned Beaumont said peremptorily: "Phone him, Janet."

She got up on her feet, still blank of face, and, paying no attention to the Senator's sharp "Janet!" went to the door.

The Senator changed his tone then and said, "Wait, dear," to her and, "I should like to speak to you alone again," to Ned Beaumont.

"All right," Ned Beaumont said, turning to the girl hesitating in the doorway.

Before he could speak to her she was saying stubbornly: "I want to hear it. I've a right to hear it."

He nodded, looked at her father again, and said: "She has."

"Janet, dear," the Senator said, "I'm trying to spare you. I—"

"I don't want to be spared," she said in a small flat voice. "I want to know."

The Senator turned his palms out in a defeated gesture. "Then I shall say nothing."

Ned Beaumont said: "Phone Paul, Janet."

Before she could move the Senator spoke: "No. This is more difficult than it should be made for me, but—" He took out a handkerchief and wiped his hands. "I am going to tell you exactly what happened and then I am going to ask a favor of you, one I think you cannot refuse. However—" He broke off to look at his daughter. "Come in, my dear, and close the door, if you must hear it."

She shut the door and sat on a chair near it, leaning forward, her body stiff, her face tense.

The Senator put his hands behind him, the handkerchief still in them, and, looking without enmity at Ned Beaumont, said: "I ran out after Taylor that night because I did not care to lose Paul's friendship through my son's hot-headedness. I caught up with them in China Street. Paul had taken the stick from him. They were, or at least Taylor was, quarreling hotly. I asked Paul to leave us, to leave me to deal with my son, and he did so, giving me the stick. Taylor spoke to me as no son should speak to a father and tried to thrust me out of his way so he could pursue Paul again. I don't know exactly how it happened—the blow—but it happened and he fell and struck his head on the curb. Paul came back then—he hadn't gone far—and we found that Taylor had died instantly. Paul insisted that we leave him there and not admit our part in his death. He said no matter how unavoidable it was a nasty scandal could be made of it in the coming campaign and—well—I let him persuade me. It was he who picked up Taylor's hat and gave it to me to wear home—I had run out bareheaded. He assured me that the police investigation would be stopped if it threatened to come too near us. Later—last week, in fact— when I had become alarmed by the rumors that he had killed Taylor, I went to him and asked him if we hadn't better make a clean breast of it. He laughed at my fears and assured me he was quite able to take care of himself." He brought his hands from behind him, wiped his face with the handkerchief, and said: "That is what happened."

His daughter cried out in a choking voice: "You let him lie there, like that, in the street!"

He winced, but did not say anything.

Ned Beaumont, after a moment's frowning silence, said: "A campaign-speech—some truth gaudied up." He grimaced. "You had a favor to ask."

The Senator looked down at the floor, then up at Ned Beaumont again. "But that is for your ear alone."

Ned Beaumont said: "No."

"Forgive me, dear," the Senator said to his daughter, then to Ned Beaumont: "I have told you the truth, but I realize fully the position I have put myself in. The favor I ask is the return of my revolver and five minutes—a minute—alone in this room."

Ned Beaumont said: "No."

The Senator swayed with a hand to his breast, the handkerchief hanging down from his hand.

Ned Beaumont said: "You'll take what's coming to you."

2

Ned Beaumont went to the street-door with Farr, his grey-haired stenographer, two police-detectives, and the Senator.

"Not going along?" Farr asked.

"No, but I'll be seeing you."

Farr pumped his hand up and down with enthusiasm. "Make it sooner and oftener, Ned," he said. "You play tricks on me, but I don't hold that against you when I see what comes of them."

Ned Beaumont grinned at him, exchanged nods with the detectives, bowed to the stenographer, and shut the door. He walked upstairs to the white-walled room where the piano was. Janet Henry rose from the lyre-end sofa when he came in.

"They've gone," he said in a consciously matter-of-fact voice.

"Did—did they—?"

"They got a pretty complete statement out of him—more details than he told us."

"Will you tell me the truth about it?"

"Yes," he promised.

"What—" She broke off. "What will they do to him, Ned?"

"Probably not a great deal. His age and prominence and so on will help him. The chances are they'll convict him of manslaughter and then set the sentence aside or suspend it."

"Do you think it was an accident?"

Ned Beaumont shook his head. His eyes were cold. He said bluntly: "I think he got mad at the thought of his son interfering with his chances of being re-elected and hit him."

She did not protest. She was twining her fingers together. When she asked her next question it was with difficulty. "Was—was he going to—to shoot Paul?"

"He was. He could get away with the grand-old-man-avenging-the-death-the-law-couldn't-avenge line. He knew Paul wasn't going to stay dummied up if he was arrested. Paul was doing it, just as he was supporting your father for re-election, because he wanted you. He couldn't get you by pretending he'd killed your brother. He didn't care what anybody else thought, but he didn't know you thought he had and he would have cleared himself in a second if he had."

She nodded miserably. "I hated him," she said, "and I wronged him and I still hate him." She sobbed. "Why is that, Ned?"

He made an impatient gesture with one hand. "Don't ask me riddles."

"And you," she said, "tricked me and made a fool of me and brought this on me and I don't hate you."

"More riddles," he said.

"How long, Ned," she asked, "how long have you known—known about Father?"

"I don't know. It's been in the back of my head for a long time. That was about the only thing that'd fit in with Paul's foolishness. If he'd killed Taylor he'd've let me know before this. There was no reason why he should hide that from me. There was a reason why he'd hide your father's crimes from me. He knew I didn't like your father. I'd made that plain enough. He didn't think he could trust me not to knife your father. He knew I wouldn't knife *him*. So, when I'd told him I was going to clear up the killing regardless of what he said, he gave me that phony confession to stop me."

She asked: "Why didn't you like Father?"

"Because," he said hotly, "I don't like pimps."

Her face became red, her eyes abashed. She asked in a dry constricted voice: "And you don't like me because—?"

He did not say anything.

She bit her lip and cried: "Answer me!"

"You're all right," he said, "only you're not all right for Paul, not the way you've been playing him. Neither of you were anything but poison for him. I tried to tell him that. I tried to tell him you both considered him a lower form of animal life and fair game for any kind of treatment. I tried to tell him your father was a man all his life used to winning without much trouble and that in a hole he'd either lose his head or turn wolf. Well, he was in love with you, so—" He snapped his teeth together and walked over to the piano.

"You despise me," she said in a low hard voice. "You think I'm a whore."

"I don't despise you," he said irritably, not turning to face her. "Whatever you've done you've paid for and been paid for and that goes for all of us."

There was silence between them then until she said: "Now you and Paul will be friends again."

He turned from the piano with a movement as if he were about to shake himself and looked at the watch on his wrist. "I'll have to say good-by now."

A startled light came into her eyes. "You're not going away?"

He nodded. "I can catch the four-thirty."

"You're not going away for good?"

"If I can dodge being brought back for some of these trials and I don't think that'll be so hard."

She held her hands out impulsively. "Take me with you."

He blinked at her. "Do you really want to go or are you just being hysterical?" he asked. Her face was crimson by then. Before she could speak he said: "It doesn't make any difference. I'll take you if you want to go." He frowned. "But all this"—he waved a hand to indicate the house—"who'll take care of that?"

She said bitterly: "I don't care—our creditors."

"There's another thing you ought to think about," he said slowly. "Everybody's going to say you deserted your father as soon as he got in trouble."

"I am deserting him," she said, "and I want people to say that. I don't care what they say—if you'll take me away." She sobbed. "If—I wouldn't if only he hadn't gone away and left him lying there alone in that dark street."

Ned Beaumont said brusquely: "Never mind that now. If you're going get packed. Only what you can get in a couple of bags. We can send for the other stuff later, maybe."

She uttered a high-pitched unnatural laugh and ran out of the room. He lit a cigar, sat down at the piano, and played softly until she returned. She had put on a black hat and black coat and was carrying two traveling-bags.

3

They rode in a taxicab to his rooms. For most of the ride they were silent. Once she said suddenly: "In that dream—I didn't tell you—the key was glass and shattered in our hands just as we got the door open, because the lock was stiff and we had to force it."

He looked sidewise at her and asked: "Well?"

She shivered. "We couldn't lock the snakes in and they came out all over us and I woke up screaming."

"That was only a dream," he said. "Forget it." He smiled without merriment. "You threw my trout back—in the dream."

The taxicab stopped in front of his house. They went up to his rooms. She offered to help him pack, but he said: "No, I can do it. Sit down and rest. We've got an hour before the train leaves."

She sat in one of the red chairs. "Where are you—we going?" she asked timidly.

"New York, first anyhow."

He had one bag packed when the door-bell rang. "You'd better go into the bedroom," he told her and carried her bags in there. He shut the connecting door when he came out.

He went to the outer door and opened it.

Paul Madvig said: "I came to tell you you were right and I know it now."

"You didn't come last night."

"No, I didn't know it then. I got home right after you left."

Ned Beaumont nodded. "Come in," he said, stepping out of the doorway.

Madvig went into the living-room. He looked immediately at the bags, but let his glance roam around the room for a while before asking: "Going away?"

"Yes."

Madvig sat in the chair Janet Henry had occupied. His age showed in his face and he sat down wearily.

"How's Opal?" Ned Beaumont asked.

"She's all right, poor kid. She'll be all right now."

"You did it to her."

"I know, Ned. Jesus, I know it!" Madvig stretched his legs out and looked at his shoes. "I hope you don't think I'm feeling proud of myself." After a pause Madvig added: "I think—I know Opal'd like to see you before you go."

"You'll have to say good-by to her for me and to Mom too. I'm leaving on the four-thirty."

Madvig raised blue eyes clouded by anguish. "You're right, of course, Ned," he said huskily, "but—well—Christ knows you're right!" He looked down at his shoes again.

Ned Beaumont asked: "What are you going to do with your not quite faithful henchmen? Kick them back in line? Or have they kicked themselves back?"

"Farr and the rest of those rats?"

"Uh-huh."

"I'm going to teach them something." Madvig spoke with determination, but there was no enthusiasm in his voice and he did not look up from his shoes. "It'll cost me four years, but I can use those four years cleaning house and putting together an organization that will stay put."

Ned Beaumont raised his eyebrows. "Going to knife them at the polls?"

"Knife them, hell, dynamite them! Shad's dead. I'm going to let his crew run things for the next four years. There's none of them that can build anything solid enough for me to worry about. I'll get the city back next time and by then I'll have done my housecleaning."

"You could win now," Ned Beaumont said.

"Sure, but I don't want to win with those bastards."

Ned Beaumont nodded. "It takes patience and guts, but it's the best way to play it, I reckon."

"They're all I've got," Madvig said miserably. "I'll never have any brains." He shifted the focus of his eyes from his feet to the fireplace. "Have you got to go, Ned?" he asked almost inaudibly.

"Got to."

Madvig cleared his throat violently. "I don't want to be a God-damned fool," he said, "but I'd like to think that whether you went or stayed you weren't holding anything against me, Ned."

"I'm not holding anything against you, Paul."

Madvig raised his head quickly. "Shake hands with me?"

"Certainly."

Madvig jumped up. His hand caught Ned Beaumont's, crushed it. "Don't go, Ned. Stick it out with me. Christ knows I need you now. Even if I didn't—I'll do my damndest to make up for all that."

Ned Beaumont shook his head. "You haven't got anything to make up for with me."

"And you'll—?"

Ned Beaumont shook his head again. "I can't. I've got to go."

Madvig released the other's hand and sat down again, morosely, saying: "Well, it serves me right."

Ned Beaumont made an impatient gesture. "That's got nothing to do with it." He stopped and bit his lip. Then he said bluntly: "Janet's here."

Madvig stared at him.

Janet Henry opened the bedroom-door and came into the living-room. Her face was pale and drawn, but she held it high. She went straight up to Paul Madvig and said: "I've done you a lot of harm, Paul. I've—"

His face had become pale as hers. Now blood rushed into it. "Don't, Janet," he said hoarsely. "Nothing you could do . . ." The rest of his speech was unintelligibly mumbled.

She stepped back, flinching.

Ned Beaumont said: "Janet is going away with me."

Madvig's lips parted. He looked dumbly at Ned Beaumont and as he looked the blood went out of his face again. When his face was quite bloodless he mumbled something of which only the word "luck" could be understood, turned clumsily around, went to the door, opened it, and went out, leaving it open behind him.

Janet Henry looked at Ned Beaumont. He stared fixedly at the door.

THE
THIN MAN

TO LILLIAN

THE THIN MAN

1

I was leaning against the bar in a speakeasy on Fifty-second Street, waiting for Nora to finish her Christmas shopping, when a girl got up from the table where she had been sitting with three other people and came over to me. She was small and blonde, and whether you looked at her face or at her body in powder-blue sports clothes the result was satisfactory. "Aren't you Nick Charles?" she asked.

I said: "Yes."

She held out her hand. "I'm Dorothy Wynant. You don't remember me, but you ought to remember my father, Clyde Wynant. You—"

"Sure," I said, "and I remember you now, but you were only a kid of eleven or twelve then, weren't you?"

"Yes, that was eight years ago. Listen: remember those stories you told me? Were they true?"

"Probably not. How is your father?"

She laughed. "I was going to ask you. Mamma divorced him, you know, and we never hear from him—except when he gets in the newspapers now and then with some of his carryings on. Don't you ever see him?"

My glass was empty. I asked her what she would have to drink, she said Scotch and soda, I ordered two of them and said: "No, I've been living in San Francisco."

She said slowly: "I'd like to see him. Mamma would raise hell if she found it out, but I'd like to see him."

"Well?"

"He's not where we used to live, on Riverside Drive, and he's not in the phone book or city directory."

"Try his lawyer," I suggested.

Her face brightened. "Who is he?"

"It used to be a fellow named Mac-something-or-other—Macaulay, that's it, Herbert Macaulay. He was in the Singer Building."

"Lend me a nickel," she said, and went out to the telephone. She came back smiling. "I found him. He's just round the corner on Fifth Avenue."

"Your father?"

"The lawyer. He says my father's out of town. I'm going round to see him." She raised her glass to me. "Family reunions. Look, why don't—"

Asta jumped up and punched me in the belly with her front feet. Nora, at the other end of the leash, said: "She's had a swell afternoon—knocked over a table of toys at Lord & Taylor's, scared a fat woman silly by licking her leg in Saks', and's been patted by three policemen."

I made introductions. "My wife, Dorothy Wynant. Her father was once a client of mine, when she was only so high. A good guy, but screwy."

"I was fascinated by him," Dorothy said, meaning me, "a real live detective, and used to follow him around making him tell me about his experiences. He told me awful lies, but I believed every word."

I said: "You look tired, Nora."

"I am. Let's sit down."

Dorothy Wynant said she had to go back to her table. She shook hands with Nora; we must drop in for cocktails, they were living at the Courtland, her mother's name was Jorgensen now. We would be glad to and she must come see us some time, we were at the Normandie and would be in New York for another week or two. Dorothy patted the dog's head and left us.

We found a table. Nora said: "She's pretty."

"If you like them like that."

She grinned at me. "You got types?"

"Only you, darling—lanky brunettes with wicked jaws."

"And how about the red-head you wandered off with at the Quinns' last night?"

"That's silly," I said. "She just wanted to show me some French etchings."

2

THE next day Herbert Macaulay telephoned me. "Hello. I didn't know you were back in town till Dorothy Wynant told me. How about lunch?"

"What time is it?"

"Half past eleven. Did I wake you up?"

"Yes," I said, "but that's all right. Suppose you come up here for lunch: I've got a hangover and don't feel like running around much. . . . O. K., say one o'clock."

I had a drink with Nora, who was going out to have her hair washed, then another after a shower, and was feeling better by the time the telephone rang again.

A female voice asked: "Is Mr. Macaulay there?"

"Not yet."

"Sorry to trouble you, but would you mind asking him to call his office as soon as he gets there? It's important."

I promised to do that.

Macaulay arrived about ten minutes later. He was a big curly-haired, rosy-cheeked, rather good-looking chap of about my age—forty-one— though he looked younger. He was supposed to be a pretty good lawyer. I had worked on several jobs for him when I was living in New York and we had always got along nicely.

Now we shook hands and patted each other's backs, and he asked me how the world was treating me, and I said, "Fine," and asked him and he said, "Fine," and I told him to call his office.

He came away from the telephone frowning. "Wynant's back in town," he said, "and wants me to meet him."

I turned around with the drinks I had poured. "Well, the lunch can—"

"Let him wait," he said, and took one of the glasses from me.

"Still as screwy as ever?"

"That's no joke," Macaulay said solemnly. "You heard they had him in a sanatorium for nearly a year back in '29?"

"No."

He nodded. He sat down, put his glass on a table beside his chair, and leaned towards me a little. "What's Mimi up to, Charles?"

"Mimi? Oh, the wife—the ex-wife. I don't know. Does she have to be up to something?"

"She usually is," he said dryly, and then very slowly, "and I thought you'd know."

So that was it. I said: "Listen, Mac, I haven't been a detective for six years, since 1927."

He stared at me.

"On the level," I assured him, "a year after I got married, my wife's father died and left her a lumber mill and a narrow-gauge railroad and some other things and I quit the Agency to look after them. Anyway I wouldn't be working for Mimi Wynant, or Jorgensen, or whatever her name is—she never liked me and I never liked her."

"Oh, I didn't think you—" Macaulay broke off with a vague gesture and picked up his glass. When he took it away from his mouth, he said: "I was just wondering. Here Mimi phones me three days ago—Tuesday— trying to find Wynant; then yesterday Dorothy phones, saying you told her to, and comes around, and—I thought you were still sleuthing, so I was wondering what it was all about."

"Didn't they tell you?"

"Sure—they wanted to see him for old times' sake. That means a lot."

"You lawyers are a suspicious crew," I said. "Maybe they did—that and money. But what's the fuss about? Is he in hiding?"

Macaulay shrugged. "You know as much about it as I do. I haven't seen him since October." He drank again. "How long are you going to be in town?"

"Till after New Year's," I told him and went to the telephone to ask room service for menus.

3

NORA and I went to the opening of *Honeymoon* at the Little Theatre that night and then to a party given by some people named Freeman or Fielding or something. I felt pretty low when she called me the next morning. She gave me a newspaper and a cup of coffee and said: "Read that."

I patiently read a paragraph or two, then put the paper down and took a sip of coffee. "Fun's fun," I said, "but right now I'd swap you all the interviews with Mayor-elect O'Brien ever printed—and throw in the Indian picture—for a slug of whis—"

"Not that, stupid." She put a finger on the paper. "That."

INVENTOR'S SECRETARY MURDERED IN APARTMENT

JULIA WOLF'S BULLET-RIDDLED BODY FOUND; POLICE SEEK HER EM-PLOYER, CLYDE WYNANT

The bullet-riddled body of Julia Wolf, thirty-two-year-old confidential secretary to Clyde Miller Wynant, well-known inventor, was discovered late yesterday afternoon in the dead woman's apartment at 411 East Fifty-fourth St. by Mrs. Christian Jorgensen, divorced wife of the inventor, who had gone there in an attempt to learn her former husband's present address.

Mrs. Jorgensen, who returned Monday after a six-year stay in Europe, told police that she heard feeble groans when she rang the murdered woman's doorbell, whereupon she notified an elevator boy, Mervin Holly, who called Walter Meany, apartment-house superintendent. Miss Wolf was lying on the bed-room floor with four .32-calibre bullet-wounds in her chest when they entered the apartment, and died without having recovered consciousness before police and medical aid arrived.

Herbert Macaulay, Wynant's attorney, told the police that he had not seen the inventor since October. He stated that Wynant called him on the telephone yesterday and made an appointment, but failed to keep it; and disclaimed any knowledge of his client's whereabouts. Miss Wolf, Macaulay stated, had been in the inventor's employ for the past eight years. The attorney said he knew nothing about the dead woman's family or private affairs and could throw no light on her murder.

The bullet-wounds could not have been self-inflicted, according to . . .

The rest of it was the usual police department hand-out.

"Do you suppose he killed her?" Nora asked when I put the paper down again.

"Wynant? I wouldn't be surprised. He's batty as hell."

"Did you know her?"

"Yes. How about a drop of something to cut the phlegm?"

"What was she like?"

"Not bad," I said. "She wasn't bad-looking and she had a lot of sense and a lot of nerve—and it took both to live with that guy."

"She lived with him?"

"Yes. I want a drink, please. That is, it was like that when I knew them."

"Why don't you have some breakfast first? Was she in love with him or was it just business?"

"I don't know. It's too early for breakfast."

When Nora opened the door to go out, the dog came in and put her front feet on the bed, her face in my face. I rubbed her head and tried to remember something Wynant had once said to me, something about women and dogs. It was not the woman-spaniel-walnut-tree line. I could not remember what it was, but there seemed to be some point in trying to remember.

Nora returned with two drinks and another question: "What's he like?"

"Tall—over six feet—and one of the thinnest men I've ever seen. He must be about fifty now, and his hair was almost white when I knew him. Usually needs a haircut, ragged brindle mustache, bites his fingernails." I pushed the dog away to reach for my drink.

"Sounds lovely. What were you doing with him?"

"A fellow who'd worked for him accused him of stealing some kind of idea or invention from him. Kelterman was his name. He tried to shake Wynant down by threatening to shoot him, bomb his house, kidnap his children, cut his wife's throat—I don't know what all—if he didn't come across. We never caught him—must've scared him off. Anyway, the threats stopped and nothing happened."

Nora stopped drinking to ask: "Did Wynant really steal it?"

"Tch, tch, tch," I said. "This is Christmas Eve: try to think good of your fellow man."

4

THAT afternoon I took Asta for a walk, explained to two people that she was a Schnauzer and not a cross between a Scottie and an Irish terrier, stopped at Jim's for a couple of drinks, ran into Larry Crowley, and brought him back to the Normandie with me. Nora was pouring cocktails for the Quinns, Margot Innes, a man whose name I did not catch, and Dorothy Wynant.

Dorothy said she wanted to talk to me, so we carried our cocktails into the bedroom.

She came to the point right away. "Do you think my father killed her, Nick?"

"No," I said. "Why should I?"

"Well, the police have— Listen, she was his mistress, wasn't she?"

I nodded. "When I knew them."

She stared at her glass while saying, "He's my father. I never liked him. I never liked Mamma." She looked up at me. "I don't like Gilbert." Gilbert was her brother.

"Don't let that worry you. Lots of people don't like their relatives."

"Do you like them?"

"My relatives?"

"Mine." She scowled at me. "And stop talking to me as if I was still twelve."

"It's not that," I explained. "I'm getting tight."

"Well, do you?"

I shook my head. "You were all right, just a spoiled kid. I could get along without the rest of them."

"What's the matter with us?" she asked, not argumentatively, but as if she really wanted to know.

"Different things. Your—"

Harrison Quinn opened the door and said: "Come on over and play some ping-pong, Nick."

"In a little while."

"Bring beautiful along." He leered at Dorothy and went away.

She said: "I don't suppose you know Jorgensen."

"I know a Nels Jorgensen."

"Some people have all the luck. This one's named Christian. He's a honey. That's Mamma—divorces a lunatic and marries a gigolo." Her eyes became wet. She caught her breath in a sob and asked: "What am I going to do, Nick?" Her voice was a frightened child's.

I put an arm around her and made what I hoped were comforting sounds. She cried on my lapel. The telephone beside the bed began to ring. In the next room *Rise and Shine* was coming through the radio. My glass was empty. I said: "Walk out on them."

She sobbed again. "You can't walk out on yourself."

"Maybe I don't know what you're talking about."

"Please don't tease me," she said humbly.

Nora, coming in to answer the telephone, looked questioningly at me. I made a face at her over the girl's head.

When Nora said "Hello" into the telephone, the girl stepped quickly back away from me and blushed. "I—I'm sorry," she stammered, "I didn't—"

Nora smiled sympathetically at her. I said: "Don't be a dope." The girl found her handkerchief and dabbed at her eyes with it.

Nora spoke into the telephone: "Yes. . . . I'll see if he's in. Who's calling, please?" She put a hand over the mouthpiece and addressed me: "It's a man named Norman. Do you want to talk to him?"

I said I didn't know and took the telephone. "Hello."

A somewhat harsh voice said: "Mr. Charles? . . . Mr. Charles, I understand that you were formerly connected with the Trans-American Detective Agency."

"Who is this?" I asked.

"My name is Albert Norman, Mr. Charles, which probably means nothing to you, but I would like to lay a proposition before you. I am sure you will—"

"What kind of a proposition?"

"I can't discuss it over the phone, Mr. Charles, but if you will give me half an hour of your time, I can promise—"

"Sorry," I said. "I'm pretty busy and—"

"But, Mr. Charles, this is—" Then there was a loud noise: it could have been a shot or something falling or anything else that would make a loud noise. I said, "Hello," a couple of times, got no answer, and hung up.

Nora had Dorothy over in front of a looking-glass soothing her with powder and rouge. I said, "A guy selling insurance," and went into the living-room for a drink.

Some more people had come in. I spoke to them. Harrison Quinn left the sofa where he had been sitting with Margot Innes and said: "Now ping-pong." Asta jumped up and punched me in the belly with her front feet. I shut off the radio and poured myself a cocktail. The man whose name I had not caught was saying: "Comes the revolution and we'll all be lined up against the wall—first thing." He seemed to think it was a good idea.

Quinn came over to refill his glass. He looked towards the bedroom door. "Where'd you find the little blonde?"

"Used to bounce it on my knee."

"Which knee?" he asked. "Could I touch it?"

Nora and Dorothy came out of the bedroom. I saw an afternoon paper on the radio and picked it up. Headlines said:

JULIA WOLF ONCE RACKETEER'S GIRL; ARTHUR NUNHEIM IDEN- TIFIES BODY; WYNANT STILL MISSING

Nora, at my elbow, spoke in a low voice: "I asked her to have dinner with us. Be nice to the child"—Nora was twenty-six—"she's all upset."

"Whatever you say." I turned around. Dorothy, across the room, was laughing at something Quinn was telling her. "But if you get mixed up in people's troubles, don't expect me to kiss you where you're hurt."

"I won't. You're a sweet old fool. Don't read that here now." She took the newspaper away from me and stuck it out of sight behind the radio.

5

NORA could not sleep that night. She read Chaliapin's mem- oirs until I began to doze and then woke me up by asking: "Are you asleep?"

I said I was.

She lit a cigarette for me, one for herself. "Don't you ever think you'd like to go back to detecting once in a while just for the fun of it? You know, when something special comes up, like the Lindb—"

"Darling," I said, "my guess is that Wynant killed her, and the po- lice'll catch him without my help. Anyway, it's nothing in my life."

"I didn't mean just that, but—"

"But besides I haven't the time: I'm too busy trying to see that you don't lose any of the money I married you for." I kissed her. "Don't you think maybe a drink would help you to sleep?"

"No, thanks."

"Maybe it would if I took one." When I brought my Scotch and soda back to bed, she was frowning into space. I said: "She's cute, but she's cuckoo. She wouldn't be his daughter if she wasn't. You can't tell how much of what she says is what she thinks and you can't tell how much of what she thinks ever really happened. I like her, but I think you're letting—"

"I'm not sure I like her," Nora said thoughtfully, "she's probably a little bastard, but if a quarter of what she told us is true, she's in a tough spot."

"There's nothing I can do to help her."

"She thinks you can."

"And so do you, which shows that no matter what you think, you can always get somebody else to go along with you."

Nora sighed. "I wish you were sober enough to talk to." She leaned over to take a sip of my drink. "I'll give you your Christmas present now if you'll give me mine."

I shook my head. "At breakfast."

"But it's Christmas now."

"Breakfast."

"Whatever you're giving me," she said, "I hope I don't like it."

"You'll have to keep them anyway, because the man at the Aquarium said he positively wouldn't take them back. He said they'd already bitten the tails off the—"

"It wouldn't hurt you any to find out if you can help her, would it? She's got so much confidence in you, Nicky."

"Everybody trusts Greeks."

"Please."

"You just want to poke your nose into things that—"

"I meant to ask you: did his wife know the Wolf girl was his mistress?"

"I don't know. She didn't like her."

"What's the wife like?"

"I don't know—a woman."

"Good-looking?"

"Used to be very."

"She old?"

"Forty, forty-two. Cut it out, Nora. You don't want any part of it. Let the Charleses stick to the Charleses' troubles and the Wynants stick to the Wynants'."

She pouted. "Maybe that drink would help me."

I got out of bed and mixed her a drink. As I brought it into the bedroom, the telephone began to ring. I looked at my watch on the table. It was nearly five o'clock.

Nora was talking into the telephone: "Hello. . . . Yes, speaking." She looked sidewise at me. I shook my head no. "Yes. . . . Why, certainly. . . . Yes, certainly." She put the telephone down and grinned at me.

"You're wonderful," I said. "Now what?"

"Dorothy's coming up. I think she's tight."

"That's great." I picked up my bathrobe. "I was afraid I was going to have to go to sleep."

She was bending over looking for her slippers. "Don't be such an old fuff. You can sleep all day." She found her slippers and stood up in them. "Is she really as afraid of her mother as she says?"

"If she's got any sense. Mimi's poison."

Nora screwed up her dark eyes at me and asked slowly: "What are you holding out on me?"

"Oh, dear," I said, "I was hoping I wouldn't have to tell you. Dorothy is really my daughter. I didn't know what I was doing, Nora. It was spring in Venice and I was so young and there was a moon over the—"

"Be funny. Don't you want something to eat?"

"If you do. What do you want?"

"Raw chopped beef sandwich with a lot of onion and some coffee."

Dorothy arrived while I was telephoning an all-night delicatessen. When I went into the living-room, she stood up with some difficulty and said: "I'm awfully sorry, Nick, to keep bothering you and Nora like this, but I can't go home this way tonight. I can't. I'm afraid to. I don't know what'd happen to me, what I'd do. Please don't make me." She was very drunk. Asta sniffed at her ankles.

I said: "Sh-h-h. You're all right here. Sit down. There'll be some coffee in a little while. Where'd you get the snoutful?"

She sat down and shook her head stupidly. "I don't know. I've been everywhere since I left you. I've been everywhere except home because I can't go home this way. Look what I got." She stood up again and took a battered automatic pistol out of her coat pocket. "Look at that." She waved it at me while Asta, wagging her tail, jumped happily at it.

Nora made a noise with her breathing. The back of my neck was cold. I pushed the dog aside and took the pistol away from Dorothy. "What kind of clowning is this? Sit down." I dropped the pistol into a bathrobe pocket and pushed Dorothy down in her chair.

"Don't be mad at me, Nick," she whined. "You can keep it. I don't want to make a nuisance of myself."

"Where'd you get it?" I asked.

"In a speakeasy on Tenth Avenue. I gave a man my bracelet—the one with the emeralds and diamonds—for it."

"And then won it back from him in a crap game," I said. "You've still got it on."

She stared at her bracelet. "I thought I did."

I looked at Nora and shook my head. Nora said: "Aw, don't bully her, Nick. She's—"

"He's not bullying me, Nora, he's really not," Dorothy said quickly. "He—he's the only person I got in the world to turn to."

I remembered Nora had not touched her Scotch and soda, so I went into the bedroom and drank it. When I came back, Nora was sitting on the arm of Dorothy's chair with an arm around the girl. Dorothy was sniffling; Nora was saying: "But Nick's not mad, dear. He likes you." She looked up at me. "You're not mad, are you, Nicky?"

"No, I'm just hurt." I sat on the sofa. "Where'd you get the gun, Dorothy?"

"From a man—I told you."

"What man?"

"I told you—a man in a speakeasy."

"And you gave him a bracelet for it."

"I thought I did, but—look—I've still got my bracelet."

"I noticed that."

Nora patted the girl's shoulder. "Of course you've still got your bracelet."

I said: "When the boy comes with that coffee and stuff, I'm going to bribe him to stick around. I'm not going to stay alone with a couple of—"

Nora scowled at me, told the girl: "Don't mind him. He's been like that all night."

The girl said: "He thinks I'm a silly little drunken fool."

Nora patted her shoulder some more.

I asked: "But what'd you want a gun for?"

Dorothy sat up straight and stared at me with wide drunken eyes. "Him," she whispered excitedly, "if he bothered me. I was afraid because I was drunk. That's what it was. And then I was afraid of that, too, so I came here."

"You mean your father?" Nora asked, trying to keep excitement out of her voice.

The girl shook her head. "Clyde Wynant's my father. My stepfather." She leaned against Nora's breast.

Nora said, "Oh," in a tone of very complete understanding. Then she said, "You poor child," and looked significantly at me.

I said: "Let's all have a drink."

"Not me." Nora was scowling at me again. "And I don't think Dorothy wants one."

"Yes, she does. It'll help her sleep." I poured her a terrific dose of Scotch and saw that she drank it. It worked nicely: she was sound asleep by the time our coffee and sandwiches came.

Nora said: "Now you're satisfied."

"Now I'm satisfied. Shall we tuck her in before we eat?"

I carried her into the bedroom and helped Nora undress her. She had a beautiful little body.

We went back to our food. I took the pistol out of my pocket and examined it. It had been kicked around a lot. There were two cartridges in it, one in the chamber, one in the magazine.

"What are you going to do with it?" Nora asked.

"Nothing till I find out if it's the one Julia Wolf was killed with. It's a .32."

"But she said—"

"She got it in a speakeasy—from a man—for a bracelet. I heard her."

Nora leaned over her sandwich at me. Her eyes were very shiny and almost black. "Do you suppose she got it from her stepfather?"

"I do," I said, but I said it too earnestly.

Nora said: "You're a Greek louse. But maybe she did; you don't know. And you don't believe her story."

"Listen, darling, tomorrow I'll buy you a whole lot of detective stories, but don't worry your pretty little head over mysteries tonight. All she was trying to tell you was that she was afraid Jorgensen was waiting to try to make her when she got home and she was afraid she was drunk enough to give in."

"But her mother!"

"This family's a family. You can—"

Dorothy Wynant, standing unsteadily in the doorway in a night-gown much too long for her, blinked at the light and said: "Please, can I come in for a little while? I'm afraid in there alone."

"Sure."

She came over and curled up beside me on the sofa while Nora went to get something to put around her.

6

The three of us were at breakfast early that afternoon when the Jorgensens arrived. Nora answered the telephone and came away from it trying to pretend she was not tickled. "It's your mother," she told Dorothy. "She's downstairs. I told her to come up."

Dorothy said: "Damn it. I wish I hadn't phoned her."

I said: "We might just as well be living in the lobby."

Nora said: "He doesn't mean that." She patted Dorothy's shoulder. The doorbell rang. I went to the door.

Eight years had done no damage to Mimi's looks. She was a little riper, showier, that was all. She was larger than her daughter, and her blondness was more vivid. She laughed and held her hands out to me. "Merry Christmas. It's awfully good to see you after all these years. This is my husband. Mr. Charles. Chris."

I said, "I'm glad to see you, Mimi," and shook hands with Jorgensen. He was probably five years younger than his wife, a tall thin erect dark man, carefully dressed and sleek, with smooth hair and a waxed mustache.

He bowed from the waist. "How do you do, Mr. Charles?" His accent was heavy, Teutonic, his hand was lean and muscular.

We went inside.

Mimi, when the introductions were over, apologized to Nora for popping in on us. "But I did want to see your husband again, and then I know the only way to get this brat of mine anywhere on time is to carry her off bodily." She turned her smile on Dorothy. "Better get dressed, honey."

Honey grumbled through a mouthful of toast that she didn't see why she had to waste an afternoon at Aunt Alice's even if it was Christmas. "I bet Gilbert's not going."

Mimi said Asta was a lovely dog and asked me if I had *any* idea where that ex-husband of hers might be.

"No."

She went on playing with the dog. "He's crazy, absolutely crazy, to disappear at a time like this. No wonder the police at first thought he had something to do with it."

"What do they think now?" I asked.

She looked up at me. "Haven't you seen the papers?"

"No."

"It's a man named Morelli—a gangster. He killed her. He was her lover."

"They caught him?"

"Not yet, but he did it. I wish I could find Clyde. Macaulay won't help me at all. He says he doesn't know where he is, but that's ridiculous. He has powers of attorney from him and everything and I know very well he's in touch with Clyde. Do you think Macaulay's trustworthy?"

"He's Wynant's lawyer," I said. "There's no reason why you should trust him."

"Just what I thought." She moved over a little on the sofa. "Sit down. I've got millions of things to ask you."

"How about a drink first?"

"Anything but egg-nog," she said. "It makes me bilious."

When I came out of the pantry, Nora and Jorgensen were trying their French on each other, Dorothy was still pretending to eat, and Mimi was playing with the dog again. I distributed the drinks and sat down beside Mimi.

She said: "Your wife's lovely."

"I like her."

"Tell me the truth, Nick: do you think Clyde's really crazy? I mean crazy enough that something ought to be done about it."

"How do I know?"

"I'm worried about the children," she said. "I've no claim on him any more—the settlement he made when I divorced him took care of all that—but the children have. We're absolutely penniless now and I'm worried about them. If he is crazy he's just as likely as not to throw away everything and leave them without a cent. What do you think I ought to do?"

"Thinking about putting him in the booby-hatch?"

"No—o," she said slowly, "but I would like to talk to him." She put a hand on my arm. "You could find him."

I shook my head.

"Won't you help me, Nick? We used to be friends." Her big blue eyes were soft and appealing.

Dorothy, at the table, was watching us suspiciously.

"For Christ's sake, Mimi," I said, "there's a thousand detectives in New York. Hire one of them. I'm not working at it any more."

"I know, but— Was Dorry very drunk last night?"

"Maybe I was. She seemed all right to me."

"Don't you think she's gotten to be a pretty little thing?"

"I always thought she was."

She thought that over for a moment, then said: "She's only a child, Nick."

"What's that got to do with what?" I asked.

She smiled. "How about getting some clothes on, Dorry?"

Dorothy sulkily repeated that she didn't see why she had to waste an afternoon at Aunt Alice's.

Jorgensen turned to address his wife: "Mrs. Charles has the great kindness to suggest that we do not—"

"Yes," Nora said, "why don't you stay awhile? There'll be some people coming in. It won't be very exciting, but—" She waved her glass a little to finish the sentence.

"I'd love to," Mimi replied slowly, "but I'm afraid Alice—"

"Make our apologies to her by telephone," Jorgensen suggested.

"I'll do it," Dorothy said.

Mimi nodded. "Be nice to her."

Dorothy went into the bedroom. Everybody seemed much brighter. Nora caught my eye and winked merrily and I had to take it and like it because Mimi was looking at me then.

Mimi asked me: "You really didn't want us to stay, did you?"

"Of course."

"Chances are you're lying. Weren't you sort of fond of poor Julia?"

" 'Poor Julia' sounds swell from you. I liked her all right."

Mimi put her hand on my arm again. "She broke up my life with Clyde. Naturally I hated her—then—but that's a long time ago. I had no feeling against her when I went to see her Friday. And, Nick, I saw her die. She didn't deserve to die. It was horrible. No matter what I'd felt, there'd be nothing left but pity now. I meant 'poor Julia' when I said it."

"I don't know what you're up to," I said. "I don't know what any of you are up to."

"Any of us," she repeated. "Has Dorry been—"

Dorothy came in from the bedroom. "I squared it." She kissed her mother on the mouth and sat down beside her.

Mimi, looking in her compact-mirror to see her mouth had not been smeared, asked: "She wasn't peevish about it?"

"No, I squared it. What do you have to do to get a drink?"

I said: "You have to walk over to that table where the ice and bottles are and pour it."

Mimi said: "You drink too much."

"I don't drink as much as Nick." She went over to the table.

Mimi shook her head. "These children! I mean you were pretty fond of Julia Wolf, weren't you?"

Dorothy called: "You want one, Nick?"

"Thanks," I said; then to Mimi, "I liked her well enough."

"You're the damnedest evasive man," she complained. "Did you like her as much as you used to like me, for instance?"

"You mean those couple of afternoons we killed?"

Her laugh was genuine. "That's certainly an answer." She turned to Dorothy, carrying glasses towards us. "You'll have to get a robe that shade of blue, darling. It's very becoming to you."

I took one of the glasses from Dorothy and said I thought I had better get dressed.

7

WHEN I came out of the bathroom, Nora and Dorothy were in the bedroom, Nora combing her hair, Dorothy sitting on the side of the bed dangling a stocking.

Nora made a kiss at me in the dressing-table mirror. She looked very happy.

"You like Nick a lot, don't you, Nora?" Dorothy asked.

"He's an old Greek fool, but I'm used to him."

"Charles isn't a Greek name."

"It's Charalambides," I explained. "When the old man came over, the mugg that put him through Ellis Island said Charalambides was too long—too much trouble to write—and whittled it down to Charles. It was all right with the old man; they could have called him X so they let him in."

Dorothy stared at me. "I never know when you're lying." She started to put on the stocking, stopped. "What's Mamma trying to do to you?"

"Nothing. Pump me. She'd like to know what you did and said last night."

"I thought so. What'd you tell her?"

"What could I tell her? You didn't do or say anything."

She wrinkled her forehead over that, but when she spoke again it was about something else: "I never knew there was anything between you and Mamma. Of course I was only a kid then and wouldn't have known what it was all about even if I'd noticed anything, but I didn't even know you called each other by your first names."

Nora turned from the mirror laughing. "Now we're getting somewhere." She waved the comb at Dorothy. "Go on, dear."

Dorothy said earnestly: "Well, I didn't know."

I was taking laundry pins out of a shirt. "What do you know now?" I asked.

"Nothing," she said slowly, and her face began to grow pink, "but I can guess." She bent over her stocking.

"Can and do," I growled. "You're a dope, but don't look so embarrassed. You can't help it if you've got a dirty mind."

She raised her head and laughed, but when she asked, "Do you think I take after Mamma much?" she was serious.

"I wouldn't be surprised."

"But do you?"

"You want me to say no. No."

"That's what I have to live with," Nora said cheerfully. "You can't do anything with him."

I finished dressing first and went out to the living-room. Mimi was sitting on Jorgensen's knees. She stood up and asked: "What'd you get for Christmas?"

"Nora gave me a watch." I showed it to her.

She said it was lovely, and it was. "What'd you give her?"

"Necklace."

Jorgensen said, "May I?" and rose to mix himself a drink.

The doorbell rang. I let the Quinns and Margot Innes in, introduced them to the Jorgensens. Presently Nora and Dorothy finished dressing and came out of the bedroom, and Quinn attached himself to Dorothy. Larry Crowley arrived, with a girl named Denis, and a few minutes later the Edges. I won thirty-two dollars—on the cuff—from Margot at backgammon. The Denis girl had to go into the bedroom and lie down awhile. Alice Quinn, with Margot's help, tore her husband away from Dorothy at a little after six and carried him off to keep a date they had. The Edges left. Mimi put on her coat, got her husband and daughter into their coats.

"It's awful short notice," she said, "but can't you come to dinner tomorrow night?"

Nora said: "Certainly."

We shook hands and made polite speeches all around and they went away.

Nora shut the door after them and leaned her back against it. "Jesus, he's a handsome guy," she said.

8

So far I had known just where I stood on the Wolf-Wynant-Jorgensen troubles and what I was doing—the answers were, respectively, nowhere and nothing—but when we stopped at Reuben's for coffee on our way home at four the next morning, Nora opened a newspaper and found a line in one of the gossip columns: "Nick Charles, former Trans-American Detective Agency ace, on from Coast to sift the Julia Wolf murder mystery"; and when I opened my eyes and sat up in bed some six hours later Nora was shaking me and a man with a gun in his hand was standing in the bedroom doorway.

He was a plump dark youngish man of medium height, broad through the jaws, narrow between the eyes. He wore a black derby hat, a black overcoat that fitted him very snugly, a dark suit, and black shoes, all looking as if he had bought them within the past fifteen minutes. The gun, a blunt black .38-calibre automatic, lay comfortably in his hand, not pointing at anything.

Nora was saying: "He made me let him in, Nick. He said he had to—"

"I got to talk to you," the man with the gun said. "That's all, but I got to do that." His voice was low, rasping.

I had blinked myself awake by then. I looked at Nora. She was excited, but apparently not frightened: she might have been watching a horse she had a bet on coming down the stretch with a nose lead.

I said: "All right, talk, but do you mind putting the gun away? My wife doesn't care, but I'm pregnant and I don't want the child to be born with—"

He smiled with his lower lip. "You don't have to tell me you're tough. I heard about you." He put the pistol in his overcoat pocket. "I'm Shep Morelli."

"I never heard about you," I said.

He took a step into the room and began to shake his head from side to side. "I didn't knock Julia off."

"Maybe you didn't, but you're bringing the news to the wrong place. I got nothing to do with it."

"I haven't seen her in three months," he said. "We were washed up."

"Tell the police."

"I wouldn't have any reason to hurt her: she was always on the up and up with me."

"That's all swell," I said, "only you're peddling your fish in the wrong market."

"Listen." He took another step towards the bed. "Studsy Burke tells me you used to be O. K. That's why I'm here. Do the—"

"How is Studsy?" I asked. "I haven't seen him since the time he went up the river in '23 or '24."

"He's all right. He'd like to see you. He's got a joint on West Forty-ninth, the Pigiron Club. But listen, what's the law doing to me? Do they think I did it? Or is it just something else to pin on me?"

I shook my head. "I'd tell you if I knew. Don't let newspapers fool you: I'm not in this. Ask the police."

"That'd be very smart." He smiled with his lower lip again. "That'd be the smartest thing I ever did. Me that a police captain's been in a hospital three weeks on account we had an argument. The boys would like me to come in and ask 'em questions. They'd like it right down to the end of their blackjacks." He turned a hand over, palm up. "I come to you on the level. Studsy says you're on the level. Be on the level."

"I'm being on the level," I assured him. "If I knew anything I'd—"

Knuckles drummed on the corridor door, three times, sharply. Morelli's gun was in his hand before the noise stopped. His eyes seemed to move in all directions at once. His voice was a metallic snarl deep in his chest: "Well?"

"I don't know." I sat up a little higher in bed and nodded at the gun in his hand. "That makes it your party." The gun pointed very accurately at my chest. I could hear the blood in my ears, and my lips felt swollen. I said: "There's no fire-escape." I put my left hand out towards Nora, who was sitting on the far side of the bed.

The knuckles hit the door again, and a deep voice called: "Open up. Police."

Morelli's lower lip crawled up to lap the upper, and the whites of his eyes began to show under the irises. "You son of a bitch," he said slowly, almost as if he were sorry for me. He moved his feet the least bit, flattening them against the floor.

A key touched the outer lock.

I hit Nora with my left hand, knocking her down across the room. The pillow I chucked with my right hand at Morelli's gun seemed to have no weight; it drifted slow as a piece of tissue paper. No noise in the world, before or after, was ever as loud as Morelli's gun going off. Something pushed my left side as I sprawled across the floor. I caught one of his ankles and rolled over with it, bringing him down on me, and he clubbed my back with the gun until I got a hand free and began to hit him as low in the body as I could.

Men came in and dragged us apart.

It took us five minutes to bring Nora to.

She sat up holding her cheek and looked around the room until she saw Morelli, nippers on one wrist, standing between two detectives. Morelli's face was a mess: the coppers had worked him over a little just for the fun of it. Nora glared at me. "You damned fool," she said, "you didn't have to knock me cold. I knew you'd take him, but I wanted to see it."

One of the coppers laughed. "Jesus," he said admiringly, "there's a woman with hair on her chest."

She smiled at him and stood up. When she looked at me she stopped smiling. "Nick, you're—"

I said I didn't think it was much and opened what was left of my pyjama-coat. Morelli's bullet had scooped out a gutter perhaps four inches long under my left nipple. A lot of blood was running out of it, but it was not very deep.

Morelli said: "Tough luck. A couple of inches over would make a lot of difference the right way."

The copper who had admired Nora—he was a big sandy man of forty-eight or fifty in a gray suit that did not fit him very well—slapped Morelli's mouth.

Keyser, the Normandie's manager, said he would get a doctor and went to the telephone. Nora ran to the bathroom for towels.

I put a towel over the wound and lay down on the bed. "I'm all right. Don't let's fuss over it till the doctor comes. How'd you people happen to pop in?"

The copper who had slapped Morelli said: "We happen to hear this is getting to be kind of a meeting-place for Wynant's family and his lawyer and everybody, so we think we'll kind of keep an eye on it in case he happens to show up, and this morning when Mack here, who was the eye we were kind of keeping on it at the time, sees this bird duck in, he gives us a ring and we get hold of Mr. Keyser and come on up, and pretty lucky for you."

"Yes, pretty lucky for me, or maybe I wouldn't've got shot."

He eyed me suspiciously. His eyes were pale gray and watery. "This bird a friend of yours?"

"I never saw him before."

"What'd he want of you?"

"Wanted to tell me he didn't kill the Wolf girl."

"What's that to you?"

"Nothing."

"What'd he think it was to you?"

"Ask him. I don't know."

"I'm asking you."

"Keep on asking."

"I'll ask you another one: you're going to swear to the complaint on him shooting you?"

"That's another one I can't answer right now. Maybe it was an accident."

"Oke. There's plenty of time. I guess we got to ask you a lot more things than we'd figured on." He turned to one of his companions: there were four of them. "We'll frisk the joint."

"Not without a warrant," I told him.

"So you say. Come on, Andy." They began to search the place.

The doctor—a colorless whisp of a man with the snuffles—came in, clucked and sniffed over my side, got the bleeding stopped and a bandage on, and told me I would have nothing to worry about if I lay still for a couple of days. Nobody would tell the doctor anything. The police would not let him touch Morelli. He went away looking even more colorless and vague.

The big sandy man had returned from the living-room holding one hand behind him. He waited until the doctor had gone, then asked: "Have you got a pistol permit?"

"No."

"Then what are you doing with this?" He brought from behind him the gun I had taken from Dorothy Wynant.

There was nothing I could say.

"You've heard about the Sullivan Act?" he asked.

"Yes."

"Then you know where you stand. This gun yours?"

"No."

"Whose is it?"

"I'll have to try to remember."

He put the pistol in his pocket and sat down on a chair beside the bed. "Listen, Mr. Charles," he said. "I guess we're both of us doing this wrong. I don't want to get tough with you and I don't guess you really want to get tough with me. That hole in your side can't be making you feel any too good, so I ain't going to bother you any more till you've had a little rest. Then maybe we can get together the way we ought to."

"Thanks," I said and meant it. "We'll buy a drink."

Nora said, "Sure," and got up from the edge of the bed.

The big sandy man watched her go out of the room. He shook his head solemnly. His voice was solemn: "By God, sir, you're a lucky man." He suddenly held out his hand. "My name's Guild, John Guild."

"You know mine." We shook hands.

Nora came back with a siphon, a bottle of Scotch, and some glasses on a tray. She tried to give Morelli a drink, but Guild stopped her. "It's mighty kind of you, Mrs. Charles, but it's against the law to give a prisoner drinks or drugs except on a doctor's say-so." He looked at me. "Ain't that right?"

I said it was. The rest of us drank.

Presently Guild set down his empty glass and stood up. "I got to take this gun along with me, but don't you worry about that. We got plenty of time to talk when you're feeling better." He took Nora's hand and made an awkward bow over it. "I hope you didn't mind what I said back there awhile ago, but I meant it in a—"

Nora can smile very nicely. She gave him one of her nicest smiles. "Mind? I liked it."

She let the policemen and their prisoner out. Keyser had gone a few minutes before.

"He's sweet," she said when she came back from the door. "Hurt much?"

"No."

"It's pretty much my fault, isn't it?"

"Nonsense. How about another drink?"

She poured me one. "I wouldn't take too many of these today."

"I won't," I promised. "I could do with some kippers for breakfast. And, now our troubles seem to be over for a while, you might have them send up our absentee watchdog. And tell the operator not to give us any calls; there'll probably be reporters."

"What are you going to tell the police about Dorothy's pistol? You'll have to tell them something, won't you?"

"I don't know yet."

"Tell me the truth, Nick: have I been too silly?"

I shook my head. "Just silly enough."

She laughed, said, "You're a Greek louse," and went around to the telephone.

NORA said: "You're just showing off, that's all it is. And what for? I know bullets bounce off you. You don't have to prove it to me."

"It's not going to hurt me to get up."

"And it's not going to hurt you to stay in bed at least one day. The doctor said—"

"If he knew anything he'd cure his own snuffles." I sat up and put my feet on the floor. Asta tickled them with her tongue.

Nora brought me slippers and robe. "All right, hard guy, get up and bleed on the rugs."

I stood up cautiously and seemed to be all right as long as I went easy with my left arm and kept out of the way of Asta's front feet.

"Be reasonable," I said. "I didn't want to get mixed up with these people—still don't—but a fat lot of good that's doing me. Well, I can't just blunder out of it. I've got to see."

"Let's go away," she suggested. "Let's go to Bermuda or Havana for a week or two, or back to the Coast."

"I'd still have to tell the police some kind of story about that gun. And suppose it turns out to be the gun she was killed with? If they don't know already they're finding out."

"Do you really think it is?"

"That's guessing. We'll go there for dinner tonight and—"

"We'll do nothing of the kind. Have you gone completely nuts? If you want to see anybody have them come here."

"It's not the same thing." I put my arms around her. "Stop worrying about this scratch. I'm all right."

"You're showing off," she said. "You want to let people see you're a hero who can't be stopped by bullets."

"Don't be nasty."

"I will be nasty. I'm not going to have you—"

I shut her mouth with a hand over it. "I want to see the Jorgensens together at home, I want to see Macaulay, and I want to see Studsy Burke. I've been pushed around too much. I've got to see about things."

"You're so damned pig-headed," she complained. "Well, it's only five o'clock. Lie down till it's time to dress."

I made myself comfortable on the living-room sofa. We had the afternoon papers sent up. Morelli, it seemed, had shot me—twice for one of the papers and three times for another—when I tried to arrest him for Julia Wolf's murder, and I was too near death to see anybody or to be moved to a hospital. There were pictures of Morelli and a thirteen-year-old one of me in a pretty funny-looking hat, taken, I remembered, when I was working on the Wall Street explosion. Most of the follow-up stories on the murder of Julia Wolf were rather vague. We were reading them when our little constant visitor, Dorothy Wynant, arrived.

I could hear her at the door when Nora opened it: "They wouldn't send my name up, so I sneaked up. Please don't send me away. I can help you nurse Nick. I'll do anything. Please, Nora."

Nora had a chance then to say: "Come on in."

Dorothy came in. She goggled at me. "B-but the papers said you—"

"Do I look like I'm dying? What's happened to you?" Her lower lip was swollen and cut near one corner, there was a bruise on one cheek-bone and two fingernail scratches down the other cheek, and her eyes were red and swollen.

"Mamma beat me," she said. "Look." She dropped her coat on the floor, tore off a button unbuttoning her dress, took an arm out of its sleeve, and pushed the dress down to show her back. There were dark bruises on her arm, and her back was criss-crossed by long red welts. She was crying now. "See?"

Nora put an arm around her. "You poor kid."

"What'd she beat you for?" I asked.

She turned from Nora and knelt on the floor beside my sofa. Asta came over and nuzzled her. "She thought I came—came to see you about Father and Julia Wolf." Sobs broke up her sentences. "That's why she came over here—to find out—and you made her think I didn't. You—you made her think you didn't care anything about what happened—just like you made me—and she was all right till she saw the papers this afternoon. Then she knew—she knew you'd been lying about not having anything to do with it. She beat me to try to make me tell her what I'd told you."

"What'd you tell her?"

"I couldn't tell her anything. I—I couldn't tell her about Chris. I couldn't tell her anything."

"Was he there?"

"Yes."

"And he let her beat you like this?"

"But he—he never makes her stop."

I said to Nora: "For God's sake, let's have a drink."

Nora said, "Sure," picked up Dorothy's coat, laid it across the back of a chair, and went into the pantry.

Dorothy said: "Please let me stay here, Nick. I won't be any trouble, honestly, and you told me yourself I ought to walk out on them. You know you did, and I've got nowhere else to go. Please."

"Take it easy. This thing needs a little figuring out. I'm as much afraid of Mimi as you are, you know. What did she think you'd told me?"

"She must know something—something about the murder that she thinks I know—but I don't, Nick. Honest to God, I don't."

"That helps a lot," I complained. "But listen, sister: there are things you know and we're going to start with those. You come clean at and from the beginning—or we don't play."

She made a movement as if she were about to cross her heart. "I swear I will," she said.

"That'll be swell. Now let's drink." We took a glass apiece from Nora. "Tell her you were leaving for good?"

"No, I didn't say anything. Maybe she doesn't know yet I'm not in my room."

"That helps some."

"You're not going to make me go back?" she cried.

Nora said over her glass: "The child can't stay and be beaten like that, Nick."

I said: "Sh-h-h. I don't know. I was just thinking that if we're going there for dinner maybe it's better for Mimi not to know—"

Dorothy stared at me with horrified eyes while Nora said: "Don't think you're going to take me there now."

Then Dorothy spoke rapidly: "But Mamma doesn't expect you. I don't even know whether she'll be there. The papers said you were dying. She doesn't think you're coming."

"So much the better," I said. "We'll surprise them."

She put her face, white now, close to mine, spilling some of her drink on my sleeve in her excitement. "Don't go. You can't go there now. Listen to me. Listen to Nora. You can't go." She turned her white face around to look up at Nora. "Can he? Tell him he can't."

Nora, not shifting the focus of her dark eyes from my face, said: "Wait, Dorothy. He ought to know what's best. What is it, Nick?"

I made a face at her. "I'm just fumbling around. If you say Dorothy stays here, she stays. I guess she can sleep with Asta. But you've got to leave me alone on the rest of it. I don't know what I'm going to do because I don't know what's being done to me. I've got to find out. I've got to find out in my own way."

"We won't interfere," Dorothy said. "Will we, Nora?"

Nora continued to look at me, saying nothing.

I asked Dorothy: "Where'd you get that gun? And nothing out of books this time."

She moistened her lower lip and her face became pinker. She cleared her throat.

"Careful," I said. "If it's another piece of chewing-gum, I'll phone Mimi to come get you."

"Give her a chance," Nora said.

Dorothy cleared her throat again. "Can—can I tell you something that happened to me when I was a little child?"

"Has it got anything to do with the gun?"

"Not exactly, but it'll help you understand why I—"

"Not now. Some other time. Where'd you get the gun?"

"I wish you'd let me." She hung her head.

"Where'd you get the gun?"

Her voice was barely audible. "From a man in a speakeasy."

I said: "I knew we'd get the truth at last." Nora frowned and shook her head at me. "All right, say you did. What speakeasy?"

Dorothy raised her head. "I don't know. It was on Tenth Avenue, I think. Your friend Mr. Quinn would know. He took me there."

"You met him after you left us that night?"

"Yes."

"By accident, I suppose."

She looked reproachfully at me. "I'm trying to tell you the truth, Nick. I'd promised to meet him at a place called the Palma Club. He wrote the address down for me. So after I said good-night to you and Nora, I met him there and we went to a lot of places, winding up in this place where I got the gun. It was an awful tough place. You can ask him if I'm not telling the truth."

"Quinn get the gun for you?"

"No. He'd passed out then. He was sleeping with his head on the table. I left him there. They said they'd get him home all right."

"And the gun?"

"I'm coming to it." She began to blush. "He told me it was a gunman's hang-out. That's why I'd said let's go there. And after he went to sleep I got to talking to a man there, an awful tough-looking man. I was fascinated. And all the time I didn't want to go home, I wanted to come back here, but I didn't know if you'd let me." Her face was quite red now and in her embarrassment she blurred her words. "So I thought perhaps if I—if you thought I was in a terrible fix—and, besides, that way I wouldn't feel so silly. Anyhow, I asked this awful tough-looking gangster, or whatever he was, if he would sell me a pistol or tell me where I could buy one. He thought I was kidding and laughed at first, but I told him I wasn't, and then he kept on grinning, but he said he'd see, and when he came back he said yes, he could get me one and asked how much I would pay for it. I didn't have much money, but I offered him my bracelet, but I guess he didn't think it was any good, because he said no, he'd have to have cash, so finally I gave him twelve dollars—all I had but a dollar for the taxi—and he gave me the pistol and I came over here and made up that about being afraid to go home because of Chris." She finished so rapidly her words ran together, and she sighed as if very glad to have finished.

"Then Chris hasn't been making passes at you?"

She bit her lip. "Yes, but not—not that bad." She put both hands on my arm, and her face almost touched mine. "You've got to believe me. I couldn't tell you all that, couldn't make myself out such a cheap little lying fool, if it wasn't the truth."

"It makes more sense if I don't believe you," I said. "Twelve bucks isn't enough money. We'll let that rest for a minute, though. Did you know Mimi was going to see Julia Wolf that afternoon?"

"No. I didn't even know she was trying to find my father then. They didn't say where they were going that afternoon."

"They?"

"Yes, Chris left the apartment with her."

"What time was that?"

She wrinkled her forehead. "It must've been pretty close to three o'clock—after two thirty, anyway—because I remember I was late for a date to go shopping with Elsie Hamilton and was hurrying into my clothes."

"They come back together?"

"I don't know. They were both home before I came."

"What time was that?"

"Some time after six. Nick, you don't think they— Oh, I remember something she said while she was dressing. I don't know what Chris said, but she said: 'When I ask her she'll tell me,' in that Queen-of-France way she talks sometimes. You know. I didn't hear anything else. Does that mean anything?"

"What'd she tell you about the murder when you came home?"

"Oh, just about finding her and how upset she was and about the police and everything."

"She seem very shocked?"

Dorothy shook her head. "No, just excited. You know Mamma." She stared at me for a moment, asked slowly: "You don't think she had anything to do with it?"

"What do you think?"

"I hadn't thought. I just thought about my father." A little later she said gravely: "If he did it, it's because he's crazy, but she'd kill somebody if she wanted to."

"It doesn't have to be either of them," I reminded her. "The police seem to have picked Morelli. What'd she want to find your father for?"

"For money. We're broke: Chris spent it all." She pulled down the corners of her mouth. "I suppose we all helped, but he spent most of it. Mamma's afraid he'll leave her if she hasn't any money."

"How do you know that?"

"I've heard them talk."

"Do you think he will?"

She nodded with certainty. "Unless she has money."

I looked at my watch and said: "The rest of it'll have to wait till we get back. You can stay here tonight, anyhow. Make yourself comfortable and have the restaurant send up your dinner. It's probably better if you don't go out."

She stared miserably at me and said nothing.

Nora patted her shoulder. "I don't know what he's doing, Dorothy, but if he says we ought to go there for dinner he probably knows what he's talking about. He wouldn't—"

Dorothy smiled and jumped up from the floor. "I believe you. I won't be silly any more."

I called the desk on the telephone and asked them to send up our mail. There were a couple of letters for Nora, one for me, some belated Christmas cards (including one from Larry Crowley, which was a copy of Haldeman-Julius Little Blue Book Number 1534, with "and a Merry Christmas," followed by Larry's name enclosed in a holly wreath, all printed in red under the book's title, *How to Test Your Urine at Home*), a number of telephone-call memoranda slips, and a telegram from Philadelphia:

NICK CHARLES
THE NORMANDIE NEW YORK N Y
WILL YOU COMMUNICATE WITH HERBERT MACAULAY TO DISCUSS
TAKING CHARGE OF INVESTIGATION OF WOLF MURDER STOP AM
GIVING HIM FULL INSTRUCTIONS STOP BEST REGARDS
                    CLYDE MILLER WYNANT

I put the telegram in an envelope with a note saying it had just reached me and sent it by messenger to the Police Department Homicide Bureau.

10

In the taxicab Nora asked: "You're sure you feel all right?"

"Sure."

"And this isn't going to be too much for you?"

"I'm all right. What'd you think of the girl's story?"

She hesitated. "You don't believe her, do you?"

"God forbid—at least till I've checked it up."

"You know more about this kind of thing than I do," she said, "but I think she was at least trying to tell the truth."

"A lot of the fancier yarns come from people who are trying to do that. It's not easy once you're out of the habit."

She said: "I bet you know a lot about human nature, Mr. Charles. Now don't you? Some time you must tell me about your experiences as a detective."

I said: "Buying a gun for twelve bucks in a speakeasy. Well, maybe, but . . ."

We rode a couple of blocks in silence. Then Nora asked: "What's really the matter with her?"

"Her old man's crazy: she thinks she is."

"How do you know?"

"You asked me. I'm telling you."

"You mean you're guessing?"

"I mean that's what's wrong with her; I don't know whether Wynant's actually nuts and I don't know whether she inherited any of it if he is, but she thinks both answers are yes, and it's got her doing figure eights."

When we stopped in front of the Courtland she said: "That's horrible, Nick. Somebody ought to—"

I said I didn't know: maybe Dorothy was right. "Likely as not she's making doll clothes for Asta right now."

We sent our names up to the Jorgensens and, after some delay, were told to go up. Mimi met us in the corridor when we stepped out of the elevator, met us with open arms and many words. "Those wretched newspapers. They had me frantic with their nonsense about your being at death's door. I phoned twice, but they wouldn't give me your apartment, wouldn't tell me how you were." She had both of my hands. "I'm so glad, Nick, that it was just a pack of lies, even if you will have to take pot luck with us tonight. Naturally I didn't expect you and— But you're pale. You really have been hurt."

"Not much," I said. "A bullet scraped my side, but it doesn't amount to anything."

"And you came to dinner in spite of that! That is flattering, but I'm afraid it's foolish too." She turned to Nora. "Are you sure it was wise to let him—"

"I'm not sure," Nora said, "but he wanted to come."

"Men are such idiots," Mimi said. She put an arm around me. "They either make mountains out of nothing or utterly neglect things that may— But come in. Here, let me help you."

"It's not that bad," I assured her, but she insisted on leading me to a chair and packing me in with half a dozen cushions.

Jorgensen came in, shook hands with me, and said he was glad to find me more alive than the newspapers had said. He bowed over Nora's

hand. "If I may be excused one little minute more I will finish the cocktails." He went out.

Mimi said: "I don't know where Dorry is. Off sulking somewhere, I
suppose. You haven't any children, have you?"

Nora said: "No."

"You're missing a lot, though they can be a great trial sometimes."
Mimi sighed. "I suppose I'm not strict enough. When I do have to scold
Dorry she seems to think I'm a complete monster." Her face brightened.
"Here's my other tot. You remember Mr. Charles, Gilbert. And this is
Mrs. Charles."

Gilbert Wynant was two years younger than his sister, a gangling
pale blond boy of eighteen with not too much chin under a somewhat
slack mouth. The size of his remarkably clear blue eyes, and the length of
the lashes, gave him a slightly effeminate look. I hoped he had stopped
being the whining little nuisance he was as a kid.

Jorgensen brought in his cocktails, and Mimi insisted on being told
about the shooting. I told her, making it even more meaningless than it
had been.

"But why should he have come to you?" she asked.

"God knows. I'd like to know. The police'd like to know."

Gilbert said: "I read somewhere that when habitual criminals are
accused of things they didn't do—even little things—they're much more
upset by it than other people would be. Do you think that's so, Mr.
Charles?"

"It's likely."

"Except," Gilbert added, "when it's something big, you know, something they would like to've done."

I said again it was likely.

Mimi said: "Don't be polite to Gil if he starts talking nonsense, Nick.
His head's so cluttered up with reading. Get us another cocktail, darling."

He went over to get the shaker. Nora and Jorgensen were in a corner
sorting phonograph records.

I said: "I had a wire from Wynant today."

Mimi looked warily around the room, then leaned forward, and her
voice was almost a whisper: "What did he say?"

"Wanted me to find out who killed her. It was sent from Philadelphia this afternoon."

She was breathing heavily. "Are you going to do it?"

I shrugged. "I turned it over to the police."

Gilbert came back with the shaker. Jorgensen and Nora had put
Bach's *Little Fugue* on the phonograph. Mimi quickly drank her cocktail
and had Gilbert pour her another.

He sat down and said: "I want to ask you: can you tell dope-addicts
by looking at them?" He was trembling.

"Very seldom. Why?"

"I was wondering. Even if they're confirmed addicts?"

"The further along they are, the better the chances of noticing that something's wrong, but you can't often be sure it's dope."

"Another thing," he said, "Gross says when you're stabbed you only feel a sort of push at the time and it's not until afterwards that it begins to hurt. Is that so?"

"Yes, if you're stabbed reasonably hard with a reasonably sharp knife. A bullet's the same way: you only feel the blow—and with a small-calibre steel-jacketed bullet not much of that—at first. The rest comes when the air gets to it."

Mimi drank her third cocktail and said: "I think you're both being indecently gruesome, especially after what happened to Nick today. Do try to find Dorry, Gil. You must know some of her friends. Phone them. I suppose she'll be along presently, but I worry about her."

"She's over at our place," I said.

"At your place?" Her surprise may have been genuine.

"She came over this afternoon and asked if she could stay with us awhile."

She smiled tolerantly and shook her head. "These youngsters!" She stopped smiling. "Awhile?"

I nodded.

Gilbert, apparently waiting to ask me another question, showed no interest in this conversation between his mother and me.

Mimi smiled again and said: "I'm sorry she's bothering you and your wife, but it's a relief to know she's there instead of off the Lord only knows where. She'll have finished her pouting by the time you get back. Send her along home, will you?" She poured me a cocktail. "You've been awfully nice to her."

I did not say anything.

Gilbert began: "Mr. Charles, do criminals—I mean professional criminals—usually—"

"Don't interrupt, Gil," Mimi said. "You will send her along home, won't you?" She was pleasant, but she was Dorothy's Queen of France.

"She can stay if she wants. Nora likes her."

She shook a crooked finger at me. "But I won't have you spoiling her like that. I suppose she told you all sorts of nonsense about me."

"She did say something about a beating."

"There you are," Mimi said complacently, as if that proved her point. "No, you'll have to send her home, Nick."

I finished my cocktail.

"Well?" she asked.

"She can stay with us if she wants, Mimi. We like having her."

"That's ridiculous. Her place is at home. I want her here." Her voice was a little sharp. "She's only a baby. You shouldn't encourage her foolish notions."

"I'm not doing anything. If she wants to stay, she stays."

Anger was a very pretty thing in Mimi's blue eyes. "She's my child and she's a minor. You've been very kind to her, but this isn't being kind to her or to me, and I won't have it. If you won't send her home, I'll take steps to bring her home. I'd rather not be disagreeable about it, but"—she leaned forward and deliberately spaced her words—"she's coming home."

I said: "You don't want to pick a fight with me, Mimi."

She looked at me as if she were going to say "I love you," and asked: "Is that a threat?"

"All right," I said, "have me arrested for kidnapping, contributing to the delinquency of a minor, and mopery."

She said suddenly in a harsh enraged voice: "And tell your wife to stop pawing my husband."

Nora, looking for another phonograph record with Jorgensen, had a hand on his sleeve. They turned to look at Mimi in surprise.

I said: "Nora, Mrs. Jorgensen wants you to keep your hands off Mr. Jorgensen."

"I'm awfully sorry." Nora smiled at Mimi, then looked at me, put a very artificial expression of concern on her face, and in a somewhat sing-song voice, as if she were a schoolchild reciting a piece, said: "Oh, Nick, you're pale. I'm sure you have exceeded your strength and will have a relapse. I'm sorry, Mrs. Jorgensen, but I think I should get him home and to bed right away. You will forgive us, won't you?"

Mimi said she would. Everybody was the soul of politeness to everybody else. We went downstairs and got a taxicab.

"Well," Nora said, "so you talked yourself out of a dinner. What do you want to do now? Go home and eat with Dorothy?"

I shook my head. "I can do without Wynants for a little while. Let's go to Max's: I'd like some snails."

"Right. Did you find out anything?"

"Nothing."

She said meditatively: "It's a shame that guy's so handsome."

"What's he like?"

"Just a big doll. It's a shame."

We had dinner and went back to the Normandie. Dorothy was not there. I felt as if I had expected that.

Nora went through the rooms, called up the desk. No note, no message had been left for us.

"So what?" she asked.

It was not quite ten o'clock. "Maybe nothing," I said. "Maybe anything. My guess is she'll show up about three in the morning, tight, with a machine-gun she bought in Childs'."

Nora said: "To hell with her. Get into pyjamas and lie down."

11

My side felt a lot better when Nora called me at noon the next day. "My nice policeman wants to see you," she said. "How do you feel?"

"Terrible. I must've gone to bed sober." I pushed Asta out of the way and got up.

Guild rose with a drink in his hand when I entered the living-room, and smiled all across his broad sandy face. "Well, well, Mr. Charles, you look spry enough this morning."

I shook hands with him and said yes I felt pretty good, and we sat down.

He frowned good-naturedly. "Just the same, you oughtn't've played that trick on me."

"Trick?"

"Sure, running off to see people when I'd put off asking you questions to give you a chance to rest up. I kind of figured that ought to give me first call on you, as you might say."

"I didn't think," I said. "I'm sorry. See that wire I got from Wynant?"

"Uh-huh. We're running it out in Philly."

"Now about that gun," I began, "I—"

He stopped me. "What gun? That ain't a gun any more. The firing pin's busted off, the guts are rusted and jammed. If anybody's fired it in six months—or could—I'm the Pope of Rome. Don't let's waste any time talking about that piece of junk."

I laughed. "That explains a lot. I took it away from a drunk who said he'd bought it in a speakeasy for twelve bucks. I believe him now."

"Somebody'll sell him the City Hall one of these days. Man to man, Mr. Charles, are you working on the Wolf job or ain't you?"

"You saw the wire from Wynant."

"I did. Then you ain't working for him. I'm still asking you."

"I'm not a private detective any more. I'm not any kind of a detective."

"I heard that. I'm still asking you."

"All right. No."

He thought for a moment, said: "Then let me put it another way: are you interested in the job?"

"I know the people, naturally I'm interested."

"And that's all?"

"Yes."

"And you don't expect to be working on it?"

The telephone rang and Nora went to answer it.

"To be honest with you, I don't know. If people keep on pushing me into it, I don't know how far they'll carry me."

Guild wagged his head up and down. "I can see that. I don't mind telling you I'd like to have you in on it—on the right side."

"You mean not on Wynant's side. Did he do it?"

"That I couldn't say, Mr. Charles, but I don't have to tell you he ain't helping us any to find out who did it."

Nora appeared in the doorway. "Telephone, Nick."

Herbert Macaulay was on the wire. "Hello, Charles. How's the wounded?"

"I'm all right, thanks."

"Did you hear from Wynant?"

"Yes."

"I got a letter from him saying he had wired you. Are you too sick to—"

"No, I'm up and around. If you'll be in your office late this afternoon I'll drop in."

"Swell," he said. "I'll be here till six."

I returned to the living-room. Nora was inviting Guild to have lunch while we had breakfast. He said it was mighty kind of her. I said I ought to have a drink before breakfast. Nora went to order meals and pour drinks.

Guild shook his head and said: "She's a mighty fine woman, Mr. Charles."

I nodded solemnly.

He said: "Suppose you should get pushed into this thing, as you say, I'd like it a lot more to feel you were working with us than against us."

"So would I."

"That's a bargain then," he said. He hunched his chair around a little. "I don't guess you remember me, but back when you were working this town I was walking beat on Forty-third Street."

"Of course," I said, lying politely. "I knew there was something familiar about— Being out of uniform makes a difference."

"I guess it does. I'd like to be able to take it as a fact that you're not holding out anything we don't already know."

"I don't mean to. I don't know what you know. I don't know very much. I haven't seen Macaulay since the murder and I haven't even been following it in the newspapers."

The telephone was ringing again. Nora gave us our drinks and went to answer it.

"What we know ain't much of a secret," Guild said, "and if you want to take the time to listen I don't mind giving it to you." He tasted his drink and nodded approvingly. "Only there's a thing I'd like to ask first. When you went to Mrs. Jorgensen's last night, did you tell her about getting the telegram from him?"

"Yes, and I told her I'd turned it over to you."

"What'd she say?"

"Nothing. She asked questions. She's trying to find him."

He put his head a little to one side and partly closed one eye. "You don't think there's any chance of them being in cahoots, do you?" He held up a hand. "Understand I don't know why they would be or what it'd be all about if they were, but I'm just asking."

"Anything's possible," I said, "but I'd say it was pretty safe they aren't working together. Why?"

"I guess you're right." Then he added vaguely: "But there's a couple of points." He sighed. "There always is. Well, Mr. Charles, here's just about all we know for certain and if you can give us a little something more here and there as we go along I'll be mighty thankful to you."

I said something about doing my best.

"Well, along about the 3rd of last October Wynant tells Macaulay he's got to leave town for a while. He don't tell Macaulay where he's going or what for, but Macaulay gets the idea that he's off to work on some invention or other that he wants to keep quiet—and he gets it out of Julia Wolf later that he's right—and he guesses Wynant's gone off to hide somewhere in the Adirondacks, but when he asks her about that later she says she don't know any more about it than he does."

"She know what the invention was?"

Guild shook his head. "Not according to Macaulay, only that it was probably something that he needed room for and machinery or things that cost money, because that's what he was fixing up with Macaulay. He was fixing it so Macaulay could get hold of his stocks and bonds and other things he owned and turn 'em into money when he wanted it and take care of his banking and everything just like Wynant himself."

"Power of attorney covering everything, huh?"

"Exactly. And listen, when he wanted money, he wanted it in cash."

"He was always full of screwy notions," I said.

"That's what everybody says. The idea seems to be he don't want to take any chances on anybody tracing him through checks, or anybody up there knowing he's Wynant. That's why he didn't take the girl along with him—didn't even let her know where he was, if she was telling the truth—and let his whiskers grow." With his left hand he stroked an imaginary beard.

" 'Up there,' " I quoted. "So he was in the Adirondacks?"

Guild moved one shoulder. "I just said that because that and Philadelphia are the only ideas anybody's given us. We're trying the mountains, but we don't know. Maybe Australia."

"And how much of this money in cash did Wynant want?"

"I can tell you that exactly." He took a wad of soiled, bent and dog-eared papers out of his pocket, selected an envelope that was a shade dirtier than most of the others, and stuffed the others back in his pocket. "The day after he talked to Macaulay he drew five thousand out of the bank himself, in cash. On the 28th—this is October, you understand—he had Macaulay get another five for him, and twenty-five hundred on the 6th of November, and a thousand on the 15th, and seventy-five hundred on the 30th, and fifteen hundred on the 6th—that would be December—and a thousand on the 18th, and five thousand on the 22nd, which was the day before she was killed."

"Nearly thirty thou," I said. "A nice bank balance he had."

"Twenty-eight thousand five hundred, to be exact." Guild returned the envelope to his pocket. "But you understand it wasn't all in there. After the first call Macaulay would sell something every time to raise the dough." He felt in his pocket again. "I got a list of the stuff he sold, if you want to see it."

I said I didn't. "How'd he turn the money over to Wynant?"

"Wynant would write the girl when he wanted it, and she'd get it from Macaulay. He's got her receipts."

"And how'd she get it to Wynant?"

Guild shook his head. "She told Macaulay she used to meet him places he told her, but he thinks she knew where he was, though she always said she didn't."

"And maybe she still had that last five thousand on her when she was killed, huh?"

"Which might make it robbery, unless"—Guild's watery gray eyes were almost shut—"he killed her when he came there to get it."

"Or unless," I suggested, "somebody else who killed her for some other reason found the money there and thought they might as well take it along."

"Sure," he agreed. "Things like that happen all the time. It even happens sometimes that the first people that find a body like that pick up a little something before they turn in the alarm." He held up a big hand. "Of course, with Mrs. Jorgensen—a lady like that—I hope you don't think I'm—"

"Besides," I said, "she wasn't alone, was she?"

"For a little while. The phone in the apartment was out of whack, and the elevator boy rode the superintendent down to phone from the office. But get me right on this, I'm not saying Mrs. Jorgensen did anything funny. A lady like that wouldn't be likely—"

"What was the matter with the phone?" I asked.

The doorbell rang.

"Well," Guild said, "I don't know just what to make of it. The phone had—"

He broke off as a waiter came in and began to set a table.

"About the phone," Guild said when we were sitting at the table, "I don't know just what to make of it, as I said. It had a bullet right smack through the mouthpiece of it."

"Accidental or—?"

"I'd just as lief ask you. It was from the same gun as the four that hit her, of course, but whether he missed her with that one or did it on purpose I don't know. It seems like a kind of noisy way to put a phone on the bum."

"That reminds me," I said, "didn't anybody hear all this shooting? A .32's not a shotgun, but somebody ought to've heard it."

"Sure," he said disgustedly. "The place is lousy with people that think they heard things now, but nobody did anything about it then, and God knows they don't get together much on what they think they heard."

"It's always like that," I said sympathetically.

"Don't I know it." He put a forkful of food in his mouth. "Where was I? Oh, yes, about Wynant. He gave up his apartment when he went away, and put his stuff in storage. We been looking through it—the stuff —but ain't found anything yet to show where he went or even what he was working on, which we thought maybe might help. We didn't have any better luck in his shop on First Avenue. It's been locked up too since he went away, except that she used to go down there for an hour or two once or twice a week to take care of his mail and things. There's nothing to tell us anything in the mail that's come since she got knocked off. We didn't find anything in her place to help." He smiled at Nora. "I guess this must be pretty dull to you, Mrs. Charles."

"Dull?" She was surprised. "I'm sitting on the edge of my chair."

"Ladies usually like more color," he said, and coughed, "kind of glamour. Anyways, we got nothing to show where he's been, only he phones Macaulay last Friday and says to meet him at two o'clock in the Plaza lobby. Macaulay wasn't in, so he just left the message."

"Macaulay was here," I said, "for lunch."

"He told me. Well, Macaulay don't get to the Plaza till nearly three and he don't find any Wynant there and Wynant ain't registered there. He tries describing him, with and without a beard, but nobody at the Plaza remembers seeing him. He phones his office, but Wynant ain't called up again. And when he phones Julia Wolf and she tells him she don't even know Wynant's in town, which he figures is a lie, because he had just give her five thousand dollars for Wynant yesterday and figures Wynant's come for it, but he just says all right and hangs up and goes on about his business."

"His business such as what?" I asked.

Guild stopped chewing the piece of roll he had just bitten off. "I guess it wouldn't hurt to know, at that. I'll find out. There didn't seem to be anything pointing at him, so we didn't bother with that, but it don't ever hurt any to know who's got an alibi and who ain't."

I shook my head no at the question he had decided not to ask. "I don't see anything pointing at him, except that he's Wynant's lawyer and probably knows more than he's telling."

"Sure. I understand. Well, that's what people have lawyers for, I guess. Now about the girl: maybe Julia Wolf wasn't her real name at all. We ain't been able to find out for sure yet, but we have found out she wasn't the kind of dame you'd expect him to be trusting to handle all that dough—I mean if he knew about her."

"Had a record?"

He wagged his head up and down. "This is elegant stew. A couple of years before she went to work for him she did six months on a badger-game charge out West, in Cleveland, under the name of Rhoda Stewart."

"You suppose Wynant knew that?"

"Search me. Don't look like he'd turned her loose with that dough if he did, but you can't tell. They tell me he was kind of nuts about her, and you know how guys can go. She was running around off and on with this Shep Morelli and his boys too."

"Have you really got anything on him?" I asked.

"Not on this," he said regretfully, "but we wanted him for a couple of other things." He drew his sandy brows together a little. "I wish I knew what sent him here to see you. Of course these junkies are likely to do anything, but I wish I knew."

"I told you all I knew."

"I'm not doubting that," he assured me. He turned to Nora. "I hope you don't think we were too rough with him, but you see you got to—"

Nora smiled and said she understood perfectly and filled his cup with coffee.

"Thank you, ma'am."

"What's a junkie?" she asked.

"Hop-head."

She looked at me. "Was Morelli—?"

"Primed to the ears," I said.

"Why didn't you tell me?" she complained. "I miss everything." She left the table to answer the telephone.

Guild asked: "You going to prosecute him for shooting you?"

"Not unless you need it."

He shook his head. His voice was casual, though there was some curiosity in his eyes. "I guess we got enough on him for a while."

"You were telling me about the girl."

"Yes," he said. "Well, we found out she's been spending a lot of nights away from her apartment—two or three days at a stretch sometimes. Maybe that's when she was meeting Wynant. I don't know. We ain't been able to knock any holes in Morelli's story of not seeing her for three months. What do you make of that?"

"The same thing you do," I replied. "It's just about three months since Wynant went off. Maybe it means something, maybe not."

Nora came in and said Harrison Quinn was on the telephone. He told me he had sold some bonds I was writing off losses on and gave me the prices.

"Have you seen Dorothy Wynant?" I asked.

"Not since I left her in your place, but I'm meeting her at the Palma for cocktails this afternoon. Come to think of it, she told me not to tell you. How about that gold, Nick? You're missing something if you don't get in on it. Those wild men from the West are going to give us some kind of inflation as soon as Congress meets, that's certain, and even if they don't, everybody expects them to. As I told you last week, there's already talk of a pool being—"

"All right," I said and gave him an order to buy some Dome Mines at 12½.

He remembered then that he had seen something in the newspapers about my having been shot. He was pretty vague about it and paid very little attention to my assurances that I was all right. "I suppose that means no ping-pong for a couple of days," he said with what seemed genuine regret. "Listen: you've got tickets for the opening tonight. If you can't use them I'll be—"

"We're going to use them. Thanks just the same."

He laughed and said good-by.

A waiter was carrying away the table when I returned to the living-room. Guild had made himself comfortable on the sofa. Nora was telling him: ". . . have to go away over the Christmas holidays every year because what's left of my family make a fuss over them and if we're home they come to visit us or we have to visit them, and Nick doesn't like it." Asta was licking her paws in a corner.

Guild looked at his watch. "I'm taking up a lot of you folks' time. I didn't mean to impose—"

I sat down and said: "We were just about up to the murder, weren't we?"

"Just about." He relaxed on the sofa again. "That was on Friday the 23rd at some time before twenty minutes after three in the afternoon, which was the time Mrs. Jorgensen got there and found her. It's kind of hard to say how long she'd been laying there dying before she was found. The only thing we know is that she was all right and answered the phone —and the phone was all right—at about half past two, when Mrs. Jorgensen called her up and was still all right around three, when Macaulay phoned."

"I didn't know Mrs. Jorgensen phoned."

"It's a fact." Guild cleared his throat. "We didn't suspect anything there, you understand, but we checked it up just as a matter of course and found out from the girl at the switchboard at the Courtland that she put the call through for Mrs. J. about two thirty."

"What did Mrs. J. say?"

"She said she called up to ask where she could find Wynant, but this Julia Wolf said she didn't know, so Mrs. J., thinking she's lying and maybe she can get her to tell the truth if she sees her, asks if she can drop in for a minute, and she says sure." He frowned at my right knee. "Well, she went there and found her. The apartment-house people don't remember seeing anybody going in or out of the Wolf apartment, but that's easy. A dozen people could do it without being seen. The gun wasn't there. There wasn't any signs of anybody busting in, and things in the place hadn't been disturbed any more than I've told you. I mean the place didn't look like it had been frisked. She had on a diamond ring that must've been worth a few hundred and there was thirty-some bucks in her bag. The people there know Wynant and Morelli—both of 'em have been in and out enough—but claim they ain't seen either for some time. The fire-escape window was locked and the fire-escape didn't look like it had been walked on recently." He turned his hands over, palms up. "I guess that's the crop."

"No fingerprints?"

"Hers, some belonging to the people that clean up the place, near as we can figure. Nothing any good to us."

"Nothing out of her friends?"

"She didn't seem to have any—not any close ones."

"How about the—what was his name?—Nunheim who identified her as a friend of Morelli's?"

"He just knew her by sight through seeing her around with Morelli and recognized her picture when he saw it in the paper."

"Who is he?"

"He's all right. We know all about him."

"You wouldn't hold out on me, would you," I asked, "after getting me to promise not to hold out on you?"

Guild said: "Well, if it don't go any further, he's a fellow that does some work for the department now and then."

"Oh."

He stood up. "I hate to say it, but that's just about as far as we've got. You got anything you can help with?"

"No."

He looked at me steadily for a moment. "What do you think of it?"

"That diamond ring, was it an engagement ring?"

"She had it on that finger." After a pause he asked: "Why?"

"It might help to know who bought it for her. I'm going to see Macaulay this afternoon. If anything turns up I'll give you a ring. It looks like Wynant, all right, but—"

He growled good-naturedly, "Uh-huh, but," shook hands with Nora and me, thanked us for our whisky, our lunch, our hospitality, and our kindness in general, and went away.

I told Nora: "I'm not one to suggest that your charm wouldn't make any man turn himself inside out for you, but don't be too sure that guy isn't kidding us."

"So it's come to that," she said. "You're jealous of policemen."

12

MACAULAY'S letter from Clyde Wynant was quite a document. It was very badly typewritten on plain white paper and dated Philadelphia, Pa., December 26, 1932. It read:

Dear Herbert:

I am telegraphing Nick Charles who worked for me you will remember some years ago and who is in New York to get in touch with you about the terrible death of poor Julia. I want you to do everything in your power to [a line had been x'd and m'd out here so that it was impossible to make anything at all of it] *persuade him to find her murderer. I don't care what it costs—pay him!*

Here are some facts I want you to give him outside of all you know about it yourself. I don't think he should tell these facts to the police, but he will know what is best and I want him to have a completely free hand as I have got the utmost confidence in him. Perhaps you had better just show him this letter, after which I must ask you to carefully destroy it.

Here are the facts.

When I met Julia Thursday night to get that $1000 from her she told me she wanted to quit her job. She said she hadn't been at all well for some time and her doctor had told her she ought to go away and rest and now that her uncle's estate had been settled she could afford to and wanted to do it. She had never said anything about bad health before and I thought she was hiding her real reason and tried to get it out of her, but she stuck to what she had said. I didn't know anything about her uncle dying either. She said it was her Uncle John in Chicago. I suppose that could be looked up if it's important. I couldn't *persuade her to change her mind, so she was to leave the last day of the month. She seemed worried or frightened, but she said she wasn't. I was sorry at first that she was going, but then I wasn't, because I had always been able to trust her and now I wouldn't be if she was lying, as I thought she was.*

The next fact I want Charles to know is that whatever anybody may think or whatever was true some time ago Julia and I ["are now" was x'd out lightly] *were at the time of her murder* and had been for more than a year *not anything more to each other than employee and employer. This relationship was the result of mutual agreement.*

Next, I believe some attempt should be made to learn the present whereabouts of the Sidney Kelterman with whom we had trouble some years ago inasmuch as the experiments I am now engaged in are in line with those he claimed I cheated him out of and I consider him quite insane enough to have killed Julia in a rage at her refusal to tell him where I could be found.

Fourth, and most important, *has my divorced wife been in communication with Kelterman? How did she learn I was carrying out the experiments with which he once assisted me?*

Fifth, the police must be convinced at once that I can tell them nothing about the murder so that they will take no steps to find me—steps that might lead to a discovery of and a premature exposure of my experiments, which I would consider very dangerous *at this time. This can best be avoided by clearing up the mystery of her murder immediately, and that is what I wish to have done.*

I will communicate with you from time to time and if in the meanwhile anything should arise to make communication with me imperative *insert the following advertisement in the Times:*

Abner. Yes. Bunny.

I will thereupon arrange to get in touch with you.

I hope you sufficiently understand the necessity of persuading Charles to act for me, since he is already acquainted with the Kelterman trouble and knows most of the people concerned.

Yours truly,
Clyde Miller Wynant

I put the letter down on Macaulay's desk and said: "It makes a lot of sense. Do you remember what his row with Kelterman was about?"

"Something about changes in the structure of crystals. I can look it up." Macaulay picked up the first sheet of the letter and frowned at it.

"He says he got a thousand dollars from her that night. I gave her five thousand for him; she told me that's what he wanted."

"Four thousand from Uncle John's estate?" I suggested.

"Looks like it. That's funny: I never thought she'd gyp him. I'll have to find out about the other money I turned over to her."

"Did you know she'd done a jail sentence in Cleveland on a badger-game charge?"

"No. Had she really?"

"According to the police—under the name of Rhoda Stewart. Where'd Wynant find her?"

He shook his head. "I've no idea."

"Know anything about where she came from originally, relatives, things like that?"

He shook his head again.

"Who was she engaged to?" I asked.

"I didn't know she was engaged."

"She was wearing a diamond ring on that finger."

"That's news to me," he said. He shut his eyes and thought. "No, I can't remember ever noticing an engagement ring." He put his forearms on his desk and grinned over them at me. "Well, what are the chances of getting you to do what he wants?"

"Slim."

"I thought so." He moved a hand to touch the letter. "You know as much about how he feels as I do. What would make you change your mind?"

"I don't—"

"Would it help any if I could persuade him to meet you? Maybe if I told him that was the only way you'd take it—"

"I'm willing to talk to him," I said, "but he'd have to talk a lot straighter than he's writing."

Macaulay asked slowly: "You mean you think he may have killed her?"

"I don't know anything about that," I said. "I don't know as much as the police do, and it's a cinch they haven't got enough on him to make the pinch even if they could find him."

Macaulay sighed. "Being a goof's lawyer is not much fun. I'll try to make him listen to reason, but I know he won't."

"I meant to ask, how are his finances these days? Is he as well fixed as he used to be?"

"Almost. The depression's hurt him some, along with the rest of us, and the royalties from his smelting process have gone pretty much to hell now that the metals are dead, but he can still count on fifty or sixty thousand a year from his glassine and soundproofing patents, with a little more coming in from odds and ends like—" He broke off to ask: "You're not worrying about his ability to pay whatever you'd ask?"

"No, I was just wondering." I thought of something else: "Has he any relatives outside of his ex-wife and children?"

"A sister, Alice Wynant, that hasn't been on speaking terms with him for—it must be four or five years now."

I supposed that was the Aunt Alice the Jorgensens had not gone to see Christmas afternoon. "What'd they fall out about?" I asked.

"He gave an interview to one of the papers saying he didn't think the Russian Five Year Plan was necessarily doomed to failure. Actually he didn't make it much stronger than that."

I laughed. "They're a—"

"She's even better than he is. She can't remember things. The time her brother had his appendix out, she and Mimi were in a taxi going to see him the first afternoon and they passed a hearse coming from the direction of the hospital. Miss Alice turned pale and grabbed Mimi by the arm and said: 'Oh, dear! If that should be what's-his-name!'"

"Where does she live?"

"On Madison Avenue. It's in the phone book." He hesitated. "I don't think—"

"I'm not going to bother her." Before I could say anything else his telephone began to ring.

He put the receiver to his ear and said: "Hello. . . . Yes, speaking. . . . Who? . . . Oh, yes. . . ." Muscles tightened around his mouth, and his eyes opened a little wider. "Where?" He listened some more. "Yes, surely. Can I make it?" He looked at the watch on his left wrist. "Right. See you on the train." He put the telephone down. "That was Lieutenant Guild," he told me. "Wynant's tried to commit suicide in Allentown, Pennsylvania."

13

DOROTHY and Quinn were at the bar when I went into the Palma Club. They did not see me until I came up beside Dorothy and said: "Hello, folks." Dorothy had on the same clothes I had last seen her in.

She looked at me and at Quinn and her face flushed. "You had to tell him."

"The girl's in a pet," Quinn said cheerfully. "I got that stock for you. You ought to pick up some more and what are you drinking?"

"Old-fashioned. You're a swell guest—ducking out without leaving a word behind you."

Dorothy looked at me again. The scratches on her face were pale, the bruise barely showed, and her mouth was no longer swollen. "I trusted you," she said. She seemed about to cry.

"What do you mean by that?"

"You know what I mean. Even when you went to dinner at Mamma's I trusted you."

"And why not?"

Quinn said: "She's been in a pet all afternoon. Don't bait her." He put a hand on one of hers. "There, there, darling, don't you—"

"Please shut up." She took her hand away from him. "You know very well what I mean," she told me. "You and Nora both made fun of me to Mamma and—"

I began to see what had happened. "She told you that and you believed it?" I laughed. "After twenty years you're still a sucker for her lies? I suppose she phoned you after we left: we had a row and didn't stay long."

She hung her head and said, "Oh, I am a fool," in a low miserable voice. Then she grabbed me by both arms and said: "Listen, let's go over and see Nora now. I've got to square myself with her. I'm such an ass. It'd serve me right if she never—"

"Sure. There's plenty of time. Let's have this drink first."

Quinn said: "Brother Charles, I'd like to shake your hand. You've brought sunshine back into the life of our little tot and joy to—" He emptied his glass. "Let's go over and see Nora. The booze there is just as good and costs us less."

"Why don't you stay here?" she asked him.

He laughed and shook his head. "Not me. Maybe you can get Nick to stay here, but I'm going with you. I've put up with your snottiness all afternoon: now I'm going to bask in the sunshine."

Gilbert Wynant was with Nora when we reached the Normandie. He kissed his sister and shook hands with me and, when he had been introduced, Harrison Quinn.

Dorothy immediately began to make long and earnest and none too coherent apologies to Nora.

Nora said: "Stop it. There's nothing to forgive. If Nick's told you I was sore or hurt or anything of the sort he's just a Greek liar. Let me take your coat."

Quinn turned on the radio. At the stroke of the gong it was five thirty-one and one quarter, Eastern Standard Time.

Nora told Quinn, "Play bar-tender: you know where the stuff is," and followed me into the bathroom. "Where'd you find her?"

"In a speak. What's Gilbert doing here?"

"He came over to see her, so he said. She didn't go home last night and he thought she was still here." She laughed. "He wasn't surprised at not finding her, though. He said she was always wandering off somewhere, she has dromomania, which comes from a mother fixation and is very interesting. He said Stekel claims people who have it usually show kleptomaniac impulses too, and he's left things around to see if she'd steal them, but she never has yet that he knows of."

"He's quite a lad. Did he say anything about his father?"

"No."

"Maybe he hadn't heard. Wynant tried to commit suicide down in Allentown. Guild and Macaulay have gone down to see him. I don't know whether to tell the youngsters or not. I wonder if Mimi had a hand in his coming over here."

"I wouldn't think so, but if you do—"

"I'm just wondering," I said. "Has he been here long?"

"About an hour. He's a funny kid. He's studying Chinese and writing a book on Knowledge and Belief—not in Chinese—and thinks Jack Oakie's very good."

"So do I. Are you tight?"

"Not very."

When we returned to the living-room, Dorothy and Quinn were dancing to *Eadie Was a Lady*.

Gilbert put down the magazine he was looking at and politely said he hoped I was recovering from my injury.

I said I was.

"I've never been hurt, really hurt," he went on, "that I can remember. I've tried hurting myself, of course, but that's not the same thing. It just made me uncomfortable and irritable and sweat a lot."

"That's pretty much the same thing," I said.

"Really? I thought there'd be more—well, more to it." He moved a little closer to me. "It's things like that I don't know. I'm so horribly young I haven't had a chance to— Mr. Charles, if you're too busy or don't want to, I hope you'll say so, but I'd appreciate it very much if you'd let me talk to you some time when there aren't a lot of people around to interrupt us. There are so many things I'd like to ask you, things I don't know anybody else could tell me and—"

"I'm not so sure about that," I said, "but I'll be glad to try any time you want."

"You really don't mind? You're not just being polite?"

"No, I mean it, only I'm not sure you'll get as much help as you expect. It depends on what you want to know."

"Well, things like cannibalism," he said. "I don't mean in places like Africa and New Guinea—in the United States, say. Is there much of it?"

"Not nowadays. Not that I know of."

"Then there was once?"

"I don't know how much, but it happened now and then before the country was completely settled. Wait a minute: I'll give you a sample." I went over to the bookcase and got the copy of Duke's *Celebrated Criminal Cases of America* that Nora had picked up in a second-hand-book store, found the place I wanted, and gave it to him. "It's only three or four pages."

ALFRED G. PACKER, THE "MANEATER," WHO MURDERED HIS FIVE COMPANIONS IN THE MOUNTAINS OF COLORADO, ATE THEIR BODIES AND STOLE THEIR MONEY.

In the fall of 1873 a party of twenty daring men left Salt Lake City, Utah, to prospect in the San Juan country. Having heard glowing accounts of the fortunes to be made, they were light-hearted and full of hope as they started on their journey, but as the weeks rolled by and they beheld nothing but barren wastes and snowy mountains, they grew despondent. The further they proceeded, the less inviting appeared the country, and they finally became desperate when it appeared that their only reward would be starvation and death.

Just as the prospectors were about to give up in despair, they saw an Indian camp in the distance, and while they had no assurance as to what treatment they would receive at the hands of the "Reds," they decided that any death was preferable to starvation, so they agreed to take a chance.

When they approached the camp they were met by an Indian who appeared to be friendly and escorted them to Chief Ouray. To their great surprise, the Indians treated them with every consideration and insisted upon their remaining in the camp until they had fully recuperated from their hardships.

Finally the party decided to make another start, with the Los Pinos Agency as their goal. Ouray attempted to dissuade them from continuing the journey, and did succeed in influencing ten of the party to abandon the trip and return to Salt Lake. The other ten determined to continue, so Ouray supplied them with provisions and admonished them to follow the Gunnison River, which was named after Lieutenant Gunnison, who was murdered in 1852. (See life of Joe Smith, the Mormon.)

Alfred G. Packer, who appeared as the leader of the party which continued the journey, boasted of his knowledge of the topography of the country and expressed confidence in his ability to find his way without difficulty. When his party had traveled a short distance, Packer told them that rich mines had recently been discovered near the headwaters of the Rio Grande River, and he offered to guide the party to the mines.

Four of the party insisted that they follow Ouray's instructions, but Packer persuaded five men, named Swan, Miller, Noon, Bell and Humphreys, to accompany him to the mines, while the other four proceeded along the river.

Of the party of four, two died from starvation and exposure, but the other two finally reached the Los Pinos Agency in February, 1874, after enduring indescribable hardships. General Adams was in command of this agency, and the unfortunate men were treated with every consideration. When they regained their strength they started back to civilization.

In March, 1874, General Adams was called to Denver on business, and one cold, blizzardy morning, while he was still away, the employees of the Agency, who were seated at the breakfast table, were startled by the appearance at the door of a wild-looking man who begged piteously for food and shelter. His face was frightfully bloated but otherwise he appeared to be in fairly good condition, although his stomach would not retain the food given him. He stated that his name was Packer and claimed that his five companions had deserted him while he was ill, but had left a rifle with him which he brought into the Agency.

After partaking of the hospitality of the employees at the Agency for ten days, Packer proceeded to a place called Saquache, claiming that he intended to work his way to Pennsylvania, where he had a brother. At Saquache, Packer drank heavily and appeared to be well supplied with money. While intoxicated, he told many conflicting stories regarding the fate of his companions, and it was suspected that he had disposed of his erstwhile associates by foul means.

At this time General Adams stopped at Saquache on his return from Denver to the Agency, and while at the home of Otto Mears he was advised to arrest Packer and investigate his movements. The General decided to take him back to the Agency, and while en route they stopped at the cabin of Major Downey, where they met the ten men who listened to the Indian chief and abandoned the trip. It was then proven that a great part of Packer's statement was false, so the General decided that the matter required a complete investigation, and Packer was bound and taken to the Agency, where he was held in close confinement.

On April 2, 1874, two wildly excited Indians ran into the Agency, holding strips of flesh in their hands which they called "white man's meat," and which they stated they found just outside the Agency. As it had been lying on the snow and the weather had been extremely cold, it was still in good condition.

When Packer caught sight of the exhibits, his face became livid, and with a low moan he sank to the floor. Restoratives were administered and after pleading for mercy, he made a statement substantially as follows:

"When I and five others left Ouray's camp, we estimated that we had sufficient provisions for the long and arduous journey before us, but our food rapidly disappeared and we were soon on the verge of starvation. We dug roots from the ground upon which we subsisted for some days, but as they were not nutritious and as the extreme cold had driven all animals and birds to shelter, the situation became desperate. Strange looks came into the eyes of each of the party and they all became suspicious of each other. One day I went out to gather wood for the fire and when I returned I found that Mr. Swan, the oldest man in the party, had been struck on the head and killed, and the remainder of the party were in the act of cutting up the body preparatory to eating it. His money, amounting to $2000.00, was divided among the remainder of the party.

"This food only lasted a few days, and I suggested that Miller be the next victim because of the large amount of flesh he carried. His skull was split open with a hatchet as he was in the act of picking up a piece of wood. Humphreys and Noon were the next victims. Bell and I then entered into a solemn compact that as we were the only ones left we would stand by each other whatever befell, and rather than harm each other we would die of starvation. One day Bell said, 'I can stand it no longer,' and he rushed at me like a famished tiger, at the same time attempting to strike me with his gun. I parried the blow and killed him with a hatchet. I then cut his flesh into strips which I carried with me as I pursued my journey. When I espied the Agency from the top of the hill, I threw away the strips I had left, and I confess I did so reluctantly as I had grown fond of human flesh, especially that portion around the breast."

After relating this grewsome story, Packer agreed to guide a party in charge of H. Lauter to the remains of the murdered men. He led them to some high, inaccessible mountains, and as he claimed to be bewildered, it was decided to abandon the search and start back the next day.

That night Packer and Lauter slept side by side, and during the night Packer assaulted him with the intent to commit murder and escape, but he was overpowered, bound, and after the party reached the Agency, he was turned over to the Sheriff.

Early in June of that year, an artist named Reynolds, from Peoria, Ill., while sketching along the shores of Lake Christoval, discovered the remains of the five men lying in a grove of hemlocks. Four of the bodies were lying together in a row, and the fifth, minus the head, was found a short distance away. The bodies of Bell, Swan, Humphreys and Noon had rifle bullet wounds in the back of the head, and when Miller's head was found it was crushed in, evidently by a blow from a rifle which was lying near by, the stock being broken from the barrel.

The appearance of the bodies clearly indicated that Packer had been guilty of cannibalism as well as murder. He probably spoke the truth when he stated his preference for the breast of man, as in each instance the entire breast was cut away to the ribs.

A beaten path was found leading from the bodies to a near-by cabin, where blankets and other articles belonging to the murdered men were discovered, and everything indicated that Packer lived in this cabin for many days after the murders, and that he made frequent trips to the bodies for his supply of human meat.

After these discoveries the Sheriff procured warrants charging Packer with five murders, but during his absence the prisoner escaped.

Nothing was heard of him again until January 29, 1883, nine years later, when General Adams received a letter from Cheyenne, Wyoming, in which a Salt Lake prospector stated that he had met Packer face to face in that locality. The informant stated that the fugitive was known as John Schwartze, and was suspected of being engaged in operations with a gang of outlaws.

Detectives began an investigation, and on March 12, 1883, Sheriff Sharpless of Laramie County arrested Packer, and on the 17th inst. Sheriff Smith of Hinsdale County brought the prisoner back to Lake City, Col.

His trial on the charge of murdering Israel Swan in Hinsdale County on March 1, 1874, was begun on April 3, 1883. It was proven that each member of the party except Packer possessed considerable money. The defendant repeated his former statement, wherein he claimed that he had only killed Bell, and had done so in self-defense.

On April 13, the jury found the defendant guilty with the death penalty attached. A stay of execution was granted to Packer, who immediately appealed to the Supreme Court. In the meantime he was transferred to the Gunnison jail to save him from mob violence.

In October, 1885, the Supreme Court granted a new trial and it was then decided to bring him to trial on five charges of manslaughter. He was found guilty on each charge and was sentenced to serve eight years for each offense, making a total of forty years.

He was pardoned on January 1, 1901, and died on a ranch near Denver on April 24, 1907.

While Gilbert was reading this, I got myself a drink. Dorothy stopped dancing to join me. "Do you like him?" she asked, jerking her head to indicate Quinn.

"He's all right."

"Maybe, but he can be terribly silly. You didn't ask me where I stayed last night. Don't you care?"

"It's none of my business."

"But I found out something for you."

"What?"

"I stayed at Aunt Alice's. She's not exactly right in the head, but she's awfully sweet. She told me she had a letter from my father today warning her against Mamma."

"Warning her how? Just what did he say?"

"I didn't see it. Aunt Alice has been mad with him for several years and she tore it up. She says he's become a Communist and she's sure the Communists killed Julia Wolf and will kill him in the end. She thinks it's all over some secret they betrayed."

I said: "Oh my God!"

"Well, don't blame me. I'm just telling you what she told me. I told you she wasn't exactly right in the head."

"Did she tell you that junk was in the letter?"

Dorothy shook her head. "No. She only said the warning was. As near as I remember she said he wrote her not to trust Mamma under any circumstances and not to trust anybody connected with her, which I suppose means all of us."

"Try to remember more."

"But there wasn't any more. That's all she told me."

"Where was the letter from?" I asked.

"She didn't know—except that it had come air-mail. She said she wasn't interested."

"What did she think of it? I mean, did she take the warning seriously?"

"She said he was a dangerous radical—they're her very words—and she wasn't interested in anything he had to say."

"How seriously do you take it?"

She stared at me for a long moment and she moistened her lips before she spoke. "I think he—"

Gilbert, book in hand, came over to us. He seemed disappointed in the story I had given him. "It's very interesting," he said, "but, if you know what I mean, it's not a pathological case." He put an arm around his sister's waist. "It was more a matter of that or starving."

"Not unless you want to believe him," I said.

Dorothy asked: "What is it?"

"A thing in the book," Gilbert replied.

"Tell him about the letter your aunt got," I said to Dorothy.

She told him.

When she had finished, he grimaced impatiently. "That's silly. Mamma's not really dangerous. She's just a case of arrested development. Most of us have outgrown ethics and morals and so on. Mamma's just not grown up to them yet." He frowned and corrected himself thoughtfully: "She might be dangerous, but it would be like a child playing with matches."

Nora and Quinn were dancing.

"And what do you think of your father?" I asked.

Gilbert shrugged. "I haven't seen him since I was a child. I've got a theory about him, but a lot of it's guess-work. I'd like—the chief thing I'd like to know is if he's impotent."

I said: "He tried to kill himself today, down in Allentown."

Dorothy cried, "He didn't," so sharply that Quinn and Nora stopped dancing, and she turned and thrust her face up at her brother's. "Where's Chris?" she demanded.

Gilbert looked from her face to mine and quickly back to hers. "Don't be an ass," he said coldly. "He's off with that girl of his, that Fenton girl."

Dorothy did not look as if she believed him.

"She's jealous of him," he explained to me. "It's that mother fixation."

I asked: "Did either of you ever see the Sidney Kelterman your father had trouble with back when I first knew you?"

Dorothy shook her head. Gilbert said: "No. Why?"

"Just an idea I had. I never saw him either, but the description they gave me, with some easy changes, could be made to fit your Chris Jorgensen."

14

THAT night Nora and I went to the opening of the Radio City Music Hall, decided we had had enough of the performance after an hour, and left. "Where to?" Nora asked.

"I don't care. Want to hunt up that Pigiron Club that Morelli told us about? You'll like Studsy Burke. He used to be a safe-burglar. He claims to've cracked the safe in the Hagerstown jail while he was doing thirty days there for disorderly conduct."

"Let's," she said.

We went down to Forty-ninth Street and, after asking two taxi-drivers, two newsboys, and a policeman, found the place. The doorman said he didn't know about any Burkes, but he'd see. Studsy came to the door. "How are you, Nick?" he said. "Come on in."

He was a powerfully built man of medium height, a little fat now, but not soft. He must have been at least fifty, but looked ten years younger than that. He had a broad, pleasantly ugly, pockmarked face under not much hair of no particular color, and even his baldness could not make his forehead seem large. His voice was a deep bass growl.

I shook hands with him and introduced him to Nora.

"A wife," he said. "Think of that. By God, you'll drink champagne or you'll fight me."

I said we wouldn't fight and we went inside. His place had a comfortably shabby look. It was between hours: there were only three customers in the place. We sat at a table in a corner and Studsy told the waiter exactly which bottle of wine to bring. Then he examined me carefully and nodded. "Marriage done you good." He scratched his chin. "It's a long time I don't see you."

"A long time," I agreed.

"He sent me up the river," he told Nora.

She clucked sympathetically. "Was he a good detective?"

Studsy wrinkled what forehead he had. "Folks say, but I don't know. The once he caught me was a accident: I led with my right."

"How come you sicked this wild man Morelli on me?" I asked.

"You know how foreigners are," he said; "they're hysterical. I don't know he's going to do nothing like that. He's worrying about the coppers trying to hang that Wolf dame's killing on him and we see in the paper you got something to do with it and I say to him, 'Nick might not maybe sell his own mother out and you feel like you got to talk to somebody,' so he says he will. What'd you do, make faces at him?"

"He let himself be spotted sneaking in and then blamed me for it. How'd he find me?"

"He's got friends and you wasn't hiding, was you?"

"I'd only been in town a week and there was nothing in the paper saying where I was staying."

"Is that so?" Studsy asked with interest. "Where you been?"

"I live in San Francisco now. How'd he find me?"

"That's a swell town. I ain't been there in years, but it's one swell town. I oughtn't tell you, Nick. Ask him. It's his business."

"Except that you sent him to me."

"Well, yes," he said, "except that, of course; but then, see, I was putting in a boost for you." He said it seriously.

I said: "My pal."

"How did I know he was going to blow his top? Anyways, he didn't hurt you much, did he?"

"Maybe not, but it didn't do me any good and I—" I stopped as the waiter arrived with the champagne. We tasted it and said it was swell. It was pretty bad. "Think he killed the girl?" I asked.

Studsy shook his head sidewise with certainty. "No chance."

"He's a fellow you can persuade to shoot," I said.

"I know—these foreigners are hysterical—but he was around here all that afternoon."

"All?"

"All. I'll take my oath to it. Some of the boys and girls were celebrating upstairs and I know for a fact he wasn't off his hip, let alone out of here, all afternoon. No kidding, that's a thing he can prove."

"Then what was he worried about?"

"Do I know? Ain't that what I been asking him myself? But you know how these foreigners are."

I said: "Uh-huh. They're hysterical. He wouldn't've sent a friend around to see her, would he?"

"I think you got the boy wrong," Studsy said. "I knew the dame. She used to come in here with him sometimes. They was just playing. He wasn't nuts enough about her that he'd have any reason for weighting her down like that. On the level."

"Was she on the stuff too?"

"I don't know. I seen her take it sometimes, but maybe she was just being sociable, taking a shot because he did."

"Who else did she play around with?"

"Nobody I know," Studsy replied indifferently. "There was a rat named Nunheim used to come in here that was on the make for her, but he didn't get nowhere that I could see."

"So that's where Morelli got my address."

"Don't be silly. All Morelli'd want of him would be a crack at him. What's it to him telling the police Morelli knew the dame? A friend of yours?"

I thought it over and said: "I don't know him. I hear he does chores for the police now and then."

"M-m-m. Thanks."

"Thanks for what? I haven't said anything."

"Fair enough. Now you tell me something: what's all this fiddlede-dee about, huh? That guy Wynant killed her, didn't he?"

"A lot of people think so," I said, "but fifty bucks'll get you a hundred he didn't."

He shook his head. "I don't bet with you in your own racket"—his face brightened—"but I tell you what I will do and we can put some dough on it if you want. You know that time you copped me, I did lead with my right like I said, and I always wondered if you could do it again. Some time when you're feeling well I'd like—"

I laughed and said: "No, I'm all out of condition."

"I'm hog-fat myself," he insisted.

"Besides, that was a fluke: you were off balance and I was set."

"You're just trying to let me down easy," he said, and then more thoughtfully, "though I guess you did get the breaks at that. Well, if you won't— Here, let me fill your glasses."

Nora decided that she wanted to go home early and sober, so we left Studsy and his Pigiron Club at a little after eleven o'clock. He escorted us to a taxicab and shook our hands vigorously. "This has been a fine pleasure," he told us.

We said equally polite things and rode away.

Nora thought Studsy was marvelous. "Half his sentences I can't understand at all."

"He's all right."

"You didn't tell him you'd quit gum-shoeing."

"He'd've thought I was trying to put something over on him," I explained. "To a mugg like him, once a sleuth always a sleuth, and I'd rather lie to him than have him think I'm lying. Have you got a cigarette? He really trusts me, in a way."

"Were you telling the truth when you said Wynant didn't kill her?"

"I don't know. My guess is I was."

At the Normandie there was a telegram for me from Macaulay in Allentown:

MAN HERE IS NOT WYNANT AND DID NOT TRY TO COMMIT SUICIDE

15

I had a stenographer in the next morning and got rid of most of the mail that had been accumulating; had a telephone conversation with our lawyer in San Francisco—we were trying to keep one of the mill's customers from being thrown into bankruptcy; spent an hour going over a plan we had for lowering our state taxes; was altogether the busy business man, and felt pretty virtuous by two o'clock, when I knocked off work for the day and went out to lunch with Nora.

She had a date to play bridge after lunch. I went down to see Guild: I had talked to him on the telephone earlier in the day.

"So it was a false alarm?" I said after we had shaken hands and made ourselves comfortable in chairs.

"That's what it was. He wasn't any more Wynant than I am. You know how it is: we told the Philly police he'd sent a wire from there and broadcasted his description, and for the next week anybody that's skinny and maybe got whiskers is Wynant to half of the State of Pennsylvania. This was a fellow named Barlow, a carpenter out of work as near as we can figure out, that got shot by a nigger trying to stick him up. He can't talk much yet."

"He couldn't've been shot by somebody who made the same mistake the Allentown police did?" I asked.

"You mean thought he was Wynant? I guess that could be—if it helps any. Does it?"

I said I didn't know. "Did Macaulay tell you about the letter he got from Wynant?"

"He didn't tell me what was in it."

I told him. I told him what I knew about Kelterman.

He said: "Now, that's interesting."

I told him about the letter Wynant had sent his sister.

He said: "He writes a lot of people, don't he?"

"I thought of that." I told him Sidney Kelterman's description with a few easy changes would fit Christian Jorgensen.

He said: "It don't hurt any to listen to a man like you. Don't let me stop you."

I told him that was the crop.

He rocked back in his chair and screwed his pale gray eyes up at the ceiling. "There's some work to be done there," he said presently.

"Was this fellow in Allentown shot with a .32?" I asked.

Guild stared curiously at me for a moment, then shook his head. "A .44. You got something on your mind?"

"No. Just chasing the set-up around in my head."

He said, "I know what that is," and leaned back to look at the ceiling some more. When he spoke again it was as if he was thinking of something else. "That alibi of Macaulay's you was asking about is all right. He was late for a date then and we know for a fact he was in a fellow's office named Hermann on Fifty-seventh Street from five minutes after three till twenty after, the time that counts."

"What's the five minutes after three?"

"That's right, you don't know about that. Well, we found a fellow named Caress with a cleaning and dyeing place on First Avenue that called her up at five minutes after three to ask her if she had any work for him, and she said no and told him she was liable to go away. So that narrows the time down to from three five to three twenty. You ain't really suspicious of Macaulay?"

"I'm suspicious of everybody," I said. "Where were you between three five and three twenty?"

He laughed. "As a matter of fact," he said, "I'm just about the only one of the lot that ain't got an alibi. I was at the moving pictures."

"The rest of them have?"

He wagged his head up and down. "Jorgensen left his place with Mrs. Jorgensen—that was about five minutes to three—and sneaked over on West Seventy-third Street to see a girl named Olga Fenton—we promised not to tell his wife—and stayed there till about five. We know what Mrs. Jorgensen did. The daughter was dressing when they left and she took a taxi at a quarter past and went straight to Bergdorf-Goodman's. The son was in the Public Library all afternoon—Jesus, he reads funny books. Morelli was in a joint over in the Forties." He laughed. "And where was you?"

"I'm saving mine till I really need it. None of those look too airtight, but legitimate alibis seldom do. How about Nunheim?"

Guild seemed surprised. "What makes you think of him?"

"I hear he had a yen for the girl."

"And where'd you hear it?"

"I heard it."

He scowled. "Would you say it was reliable?"

"Yes."

"Well," he said slowly, "he's one guy we can check up on. But look here, what do you care about these people? Don't you think Wynant done it?"

I gave him the same odds I had given Studsy: "Twenty-five'll get you fifty he didn't."

He scowled at me over that for a long silent moment, then said: "That's an idea, anyways. Who's your candidate?"

"I haven't got that far yet. Understand, I don't know anything. I'm not saying Wynant didn't do it. I'm just saying everything doesn't point at him."

"And saying it two to one. What don't point at him?"

"Call it a hunch, if you want," I said, "but—"

"I don't want to call it anything," he said. "I think you're a smart detective. I want to listen to what you got to say."

"Mostly I've got questions to say. For instance, how long was it from the time the elevator boy let Mrs. Jorgensen off at the Wolf girl's floor until she rang for him and said she heard groans?"

Guild pursed his lips, opened them to ask, "You think she might've—?" and left the rest of the question hanging in the air.

"I think she might've. I'd like to know where Nunheim was. I'd like to know the answers to the questions in Wynant's letter. I'd like to know where the four-thousand-dollar difference between what Macaulay gave the girl and what she seems to have given Wynant went. I'd like to know where her engagement ring came from."

"We're doing the best we can," Guild said. "Me—just now I'd like to know why, if he didn't do it, Wynant don't come in and answer questions for us."

"One reason might be that Mrs. Jorgensen'd like to slam him in the squirrel cage again." I thought of something. "Herbert Macaulay's working for Wynant: you didn't just take Macaulay's word for it that the man in Allentown wasn't him?"

"No. He was a younger man than Wynant, with damned little gray in his hair and no dye, and he didn't look like the pictures we got." He seemed positive. "You got anything to do the next hour or so?"

"No."

"That's fine." He stood up. "I'll get some of the boys working on these things we been discussing and then maybe me and you will pay some visits."

"Swell," I said, and he went out of the office.

There was a copy of the *Times* in his wastebasket. I fished it out and turned to the Public Notices columns. Macaulay's advertisement was there:

"*Abner. Yes. Bunny.*"

When Guild returned I asked: "How about Wynant's help, whoever he had working in the shop? Have they been looked up?"

"Uh-huh, but they don't know anything. They was laid off at the end of the week that he went away—there's two of them—and haven't seen him since."

"What were they working on when the shop was closed?"

"Some kind of paint or something—something about a permanent green. I don't know. I'll find out if you want."

"I don't suppose it matters. Is it much of a shop?"

"Looks like a pretty good lay-out, far as I can tell. You think the shop might have something to do with it?"

"Anything might."

"Uh-huh. Well, let's run along."

16

"FIRST thing," Guild said as we left his office, "we'll go see Mr. Nunheim. He ought to be home: I told him to stick around till I phoned him."

Mr. Nunheim's home was on the fourth floor of a dark, damp, and smelly building made noisy by the Sixth Avenue elevated. Guild knocked on the door.

There were sounds of hurried movement inside, then a voice asked: "Who is it?" The voice was a man's, nasal, somewhat irritable.

Guild said: "John."

The door was hastily opened by a small sallow man of thirty-five or -six whose visible clothes were an undershirt, blue pants, and black silk stockings. "I wasn't expecting you, Lieutenant," he whined. "You said you'd phone." He seemed frightened. His dark eyes were small and set close together; his mouth was wide, thin, and loose; and his nose was peculiarly limber, a long, drooping nose, apparently boneless.

Guild touched my elbow with his hand and we went in. Through an open door to the left an unmade bed could be seen. The room we entered was a living-room, shabby and dirty, with clothing, newspapers, and dirty dishes sitting around. In an alcove to the right there was a sink and a stove. A woman stood between them holding a sizzling skillet in her hand. She was a big-boned, full-fleshed, red-haired woman of perhaps twenty-eight, handsome in a rather brutal, sloppy way. She wore a rumpled pink kimono and frayed pink mules with lopsided bows on them. She stared sullenly at us.

Guild did not introduce me to Nunheim and he paid no attention to the woman. "Sit down," he said, and pushed some clothing out of the way to make a place for himself on an end of the sofa.

I removed part of a newspaper from a rocking-chair and sat down. Since Guild kept his hat on I did the same with mine.

Nunheim went over to the table, where there was about two inches of whisky in a pint bottle and a couple of tumblers, and said: "Have a shot?"

Guild made a face. "Not that vomit. What's the idea of telling me you just knew the Wolf girl by sight?"

"That's all I did, Lieutenant, that's the Christ's truth." Twice his eyes slid sidewise towards me and he jerked them back. "Maybe I said hello to her or how are you or something like that when I saw her, but that's all I knew her. That's the Christ's truth."

The woman in the alcove laughed, once, derisively, and there was no merriment in her face.

Nunheim twisted himself around to face her. "All right," he told her, his voice shrill with rage, "put your mouth in and I'll pop a tooth out of it."

She swung her arm and let the skillet go at his head. It missed, crashing into the wall. Grease and egg-yolks made fresher stains on wall, floor, and furniture.

He started for her. I did not have to rise to put out a foot and trip him. He tumbled down on the floor. The woman had picked up a paring knife.

"Cut it out," Guild growled. He had not stood up either. "We come here to talk to you, not to watch this rough-house comedy. Get up and behave yourself."

Nunheim got slowly to his feet. "She drives me nuts when she's drinking," he said. "She been ragging me all day." He moved his right hand back and forth. "I think I sprained my wrist."

The woman walked past us without looking at any of us, went into the bedroom, and shut the door.

Guild said: "Maybe if you'd quit sucking around after other women you wouldn't have so much trouble with this one."

"What do you mean, Lieutenant?" Nunheim was surprised and innocent and perhaps pained.

"Julia Wolf."

The little sallow man was indignant now. "That's a lie, Lieutenant. Anybody that say I ever—"

Guild interrupted him by addressing me: "If you want to take a poke at him, I wouldn't stop on account of his bum wrist: he couldn't ever hit hard anyhow."

Nunheim turned to me with both hands out. "I didn't mean you were a liar. I meant maybe somebody made a mistake if they—"

Guild interrupted him again: "You wouldn't've taken her if you could've gotten her?"

Nunheim moistened his lower lip and looked warily at the bedroom door. "Well," he said slowly in a cautiously low voice, "of course she was a classy number. I guess I wouldn't've turned it down."

"But you never tried to make her?"

Nunheim hesitated, then moved his shoulders and said: "You know how it is. A fellow knocking around tries most everything he runs into."

Guild looked sourly at him. "You'd done better to tell me that in the beginning. Where were you the afternoon she was knocked off?"

The little man jumped as if he had been stuck with a pin. "For Christ's sake, Lieutenant, you don't think I had anything to do with that. What would I want to hurt her for?"

"Where were you?"

Nunheim's loose lips twitched nervously. "What day was she—" He broke off as the bedroom door opened.

The big woman came out carrying a suitcase. She had put on street clothes.

"Miriam," Nunheim said.

She stared at him dully and said: "I don't like crooks, and even if I did, I wouldn't like crooks that are stool-pigeons, and if I liked crooks that are stool-pigeons, I still wouldn't like you." She turned to the outer door.

Guild, catching Nunheim's arm to keep him from following the woman, repeated: "Where were you?"

Nunheim called: "Miriam. Don't go. I'll behave, I'll do anything. Don't go, Miriam."

She went out and shut the door.

"Let me go," he begged Guild. "Let me bring her back. I can't get along without her. I'll bring her right back and tell you anything you want to know. Let me go. I've got to have her."

Guild said: "Nuts. Sit down." He pushed the little man down in a chair. "We didn't come here to watch you and that broad dance around a maypole. Where were you the afternoon the girl was killed?"

Nunheim put his hands over his face and began to cry.

"Keep on stalling," Guild said, "and I'm going to slap you silly."

I poured some whisky in a tumbler and gave it to Nunheim.

"Thank you, sir, thank you." He drank it, coughed, and brought out a dirty handkerchief to wipe his face with. "I can't remember offhand, Lieutenant," he whined. "Maybe I was over at Charlie's shooting pool, maybe I was here. Miriam would remember if you'll let me go bring her back."

Guild said: "The hell with Miriam. How'd you like to be thrown in the can on account of not remembering?"

"Just give me a minute. I'll remember. I'm not stalling, Lieutenant. You know I always come clean with you. I'm just upset now. Look at my wrist." He held up his right wrist to let us see it was swelling. "Just one minute." He put his hands over his face again.

Guild winked at me and we waited for the little man's memory to work.

Suddenly he took his hands down from his face and laughed. "Holy hell! It would serve me right if you had pinched me. That's the afternoon I was— Wait, I'll show you." He went into the bedroom.

After a few minutes Guild called: "Hey, we haven't got all night. Shake it up."

There was no answer.

The bedroom was empty when we went into it and when we opened the bathroom door the bathroom was empty. There was an open window and a fire-escape.

I said nothing, tried to look nothing.

Guild pushed his hat back a little from his forehead and said: "I wish he hadn't done that." He went to the telephone in the living-room.

While he was telephoning, I poked around in drawers and closets, but found nothing. My search was not very thorough and I gave it up as soon as he had finished putting the police machinery in action.

"I guess we'll find him, all right," he said. "I got some news. We've identified Jorgensen as Kelterman."

"Who made the identification?"

"I sent a man over to talk to the girl that gave him his alibi, this Olga Fenton, and he finally got it out of her. He says he couldn't shake her on the alibi, though. I'm going over and have a try at her. Want to come along?"

I looked at my watch and said: "I'd like to, but it's too late. Picked him up yet?"

"The order's out." He looked thoughtfully at me. "And will that baby have to do some talking!"

I grinned at him. "Now who do you think killed her?"

"I'm not worrying," he said. "Just let me have things to squeeze enough people with and I'll turn up the right one before the whistle blows."

In the street he promised to let me know what happened, and we shook hands and separated. He ran after me a couple of seconds later to send his very best regards to Nora.

17

HOME, I delivered Guild's message to Nora and told her the day's news.

"I've got a message for you, too," she said. "Gilbert Wynant dropped in and was quite disappointed at missing you. He asked me to tell you he has something of the 'utmost importance' to tell you."

"He's probably discovered that Jorgensen has a mother fixation."

"Do you think Jorgensen killed her?" she asked.

"I thought I knew who did it," I said, "but it's too mixed up right now for anything but guesses."

"And what's your guess?"

"Mimi, Jorgensen, Wynant, Nunheim, Gilbert, Dorothy, Aunt Alice, Morelli, you, me, or Guild. Maybe Studsy did it. How about shaking up a drink?"

She mixed some cocktails. I was on my second or third when she came back from answering the telephone and said: "Your friend Mimi wants to talk to you."

I went to the telephone. "Hello, Mimi."

"I'm awfully sorry I was so rude the other night, Nick, but I was so upset and I just simply lost my temper and made a show of myself. Please forgive me." She ran through this very rapidly, as if anxious to get it over with.

"That's all right," I said.

She hardly let me get my three words out before she was speaking again, but slower and more earnestly now: "Can I see you, Nick? Something horrible has happened, something—I don't know what to do, which way to turn."

"What is it?"

"I can't tell you over the phone, but you've got to tell me what to do. I've got to have somebody's advice. Can't you come over?"

"You mean now?"

"Yes. Please."

I said, "All right," and went back to the living-room. "I'm going to run over and see Mimi. She says she's in a jam and needs help."

Nora laughed. "Keep your legs crossed. She apologize to you? She did to me."

"Yes, all in one breath. Is Dorothy home or still at Aunt Alice's?"

"Still at Auntie's, according to Gilbert. How long will you be?"

"No longer than I have to. The chances are they've copped Jorgensen and she wants to know if it can be fixed."

"Can they do anything to him? I mean if he didn't kill the Wolf girl."

"I suppose the old charges against him—threats by mail, attempted extortion—could be raked up." I stopped drinking to ask Nora and myself a question: "I wonder if he and Nunheim know each other." I thought that over, but could make nothing more than a possibility of it. "Well, I'm on my way."

18

MIMI received me with both hands. "It's awfully, awfully nice of you to forgive me, Nick, but then you've always been awfully nice. I don't know what got into me Monday night."

I said: "Forget it."

Her face was somewhat pinker than usual and the firmness of its muscles made it seem younger. Her blue eyes were very bright. Her hands had been cold on mine. She was tense with excitement, but I could not figure out what kind of excitement it was.

She said: "It was awfully sweet of your wife, too, to—"

"Forget it."

"Nick, what can they do to you for concealing evidence that somebody's guilty of a murder?"

"Make you an accomplice—accomplice after the fact is the technical term—if they want."

"Even if you voluntarily change your mind and give them the evidence?"

"They can. Usually they don't."

She looked around the room as if to make sure there was nobody else there and said: "Clyde killed Julia. I found the proof and hid it. What'll they do to me?"

"Probably nothing except give you hell—if you turn it in. He was once your husband: you and he are close enough together that no jury'd be likely to blame you for trying to cover him up—unless, of course, they had reason to think you had some other motive."

She asked coolly, deliberately: "Do you?"

"I don't know," I said. "My guess would be that you had intended to use this proof of his guilt to shake him down for some dough as soon as you could get in touch with him, and that now something else has come up to make you change your mind."

She made a claw of her right hand and struck at my face with her pointed nails. Her teeth were together, her lips drawn far back over them.

I caught her wrist. "Women are getting tough," I said, trying to sound wistful. "I just left one that heaved a skillet at a guy."

She laughed, though her eyes did not change. "You're such a bastard. You always think the worst of me, don't you?"

I took my hand away from her wrist and she rubbed the marks my fingers had left on it.

"Who was the woman who threw the skillet?" she asked. "Anyone I know?"

"It wasn't Nora, if that's what you mean. Have they arrested Sidney-Christian Kelterman-Jorgensen yet?"

"What?"

I believed in her bewilderment, though both it and my belief in it surprised me. "Jorgensen is Kelterman," I said. "You remember him. I thought you knew."

"You mean that horrible man who—?"

"Yes."

"I won't believe it." She stood up working her fingers together. "I won't. I won't." Her face was sick with fear, her voice strained, unreal as a ventriloquist's. "I won't believe it."

"That'll help a lot," I said.

She was not listening to me. She turned her back to me and went to a window, where she stood with her back to me.

I said: "There's a couple of men in a car out front who look like they might be coppers waiting to pick him up when he—"

She turned around and asked sharply: "Are you sure he's Kelterman?" Most of the fear had already gone out of her face and her voice was at least human again.

"The police are."

We stared at each other, both of us busy thinking. I was thinking she had not been afraid that Jorgensen killed Julia Wolf, or even that he might be arrested: she was afraid his only reason for marrying her had been as a move in some plot against Wynant.

When I laughed—not because the idea was funny, but because it had come to me so suddenly—she started and smiled uncertainly. "I won't believe it," she said, and her voice was very soft now, "until he tells me himself."

"And when he does—then what?"

She moved her shoulders a little, and her lower lip quivered. "He is my husband."

That should have been funny, but it annoyed me. I said: "Mimi, this is Nick. You remember me, N-i-c-k."

"I know you never think any good of me," she said gravely. "You think I'm—"

"All right. All right. Let it pass. Let's get back to the dope on Wynant you found."

"Yes, that," she said, and turned away from me. When she turned back her lip was quivering again. "That was a lie, Nick. I didn't find anything." She came close to me. "Clyde had no right to send those letters to Alice and Macaulay trying to make everybody suspicious of me and I thought it would serve him right if I made up something against him, because I really did think—I mean, I do think—he killed her and it was only—"

"What'd you make up?" I asked.

"I—I hadn't made it up yet. I wanted to find out about what they could do—you know, the things I asked you—first. I might've pretended she came to a little when I was alone with her, while the others were phoning, and told me he did it."

"You didn't say you heard something and kept quiet, you said you found something and hid it."

"But I hadn't really made up my mind what I—"

"When'd you hear about Wynant's letter to Macaulay?"

"This afternoon," she said, "there was a man here from the police."

"Didn't he ask you anything about Kelterman?"

"He asked me if I knew him or had ever known him, and I thought I was telling the truth when I said no."

"Maybe you did," I said, "and for the first time I now believe you were telling the truth when you said you found some sort of evidence against Wynant."

She opened her eyes wider. "I don't understand."

"Neither do I, but it could be like this: you could've found something and decided to hold it out, probably with the idea of selling it to Wynant; then when his letters started people looking you over, you decided to give up the money idea and both pay him back and protect yourself by turning it over to the police; and, finally, when you learn that Jorgensen is Kelterman, you make another about-face and hold it out, not for money this time, but to leave Jorgensen in as bad a spot as possible as punishment for having married you as a trick in his game against Wynant and not for love."

She smiled calmly and asked: "You really think me capable of anything, don't you?"

"That doesn't matter," I said. "What ought to matter to you is that you'll probably wind up your life in prison somewhere."

Her scream was not loud, but it was horrible, and the fear that had been in her face before was as nothing to that there now. She caught my lapels and clung to them, babbling: "Don't say that, please don't. Say you don't think it." She was trembling so I put an arm around her to keep her from falling.

We did not hear Gilbert until he coughed and asked: "Aren't you well, Mamma?"

She slowly took her hands down from my lapels and moved back a step and said: "Your mother's a silly woman." She was still trembling, but she smiled at me and she made her voice playful: "You're a brute to frighten me like that."

I said I was sorry.

Gilbert put his coat and hat on a chair and looked from one to the other of us with polite interest. When it became obvious that neither of us was going to tell him anything he coughed again, said, "I'm awfully glad to see you," and came over to shake hands with me.

I said I was glad to see him.

Mimi said: "Your eyes look tired. I bet you've been reading all afternoon without your glasses again." She shook her head and told me: "He's as unreasonable as his father."

"Is there any news of Father?" he asked.

"Not since that false alarm about his suicide," I said. "I suppose you heard it was a false alarm."

"Yes." He hesitated. "I'd like to see you for a few minutes before you go."

"Sure."

"But you're seeing him now, darling," Mimi said. "Are there secrets between you that I'm not supposed to know about?" Her tone was light enough. She had stopped trembling.

"It would bore you." He picked up his hat and coat, nodded at me, and left the room.

Mimi shook her head again and said: "I don't understand that child at all. I wonder what he made of our tableau." She did not seem especially worried. Then, more seriously: "What made you say that, Nick?"

"About you winding up in—?"

"No, never mind." She shuddered. "I don't want to hear it. Can't you stay for dinner? I'll probably be all alone."

"I'm sorry I can't. Now how about this evidence you found?"

"I didn't really find anything. That was a lie." She frowned earnestly. "Don't look at me like that. It really was a lie."

"So you sent for me just to lie to me?" I asked. "Then why'd you change your mind?"

She chuckled. "You must really like me, Nick, or you wouldn't always be so disagreeable."

I could not follow that line of reasoning. I said: "Well, I'll see what Gilbert wants and run along."

"I wish you could stay."

"I'm sorry I can't," I said again. "Where'll I find him?"

"The second door to the— Will they really arrest Chris?"

"That depends," I told her, "on what kind of answers he gives them. He'll have to talk pretty straight to stay out."

"Oh, he'll—" she broke off, looked sharply at me, asked, "You're not playing a trick on me? He's really that Kelterman?"

"The police are sure enough of it."

"But the man who was here this afternoon didn't ask a single question about Chris," she objected. "He only asked me if I knew—"

"They weren't sure then," I explained. "It was just a half-idea."

"But they're sure now?"

I nodded.

"How'd they find out?"

"From a girl he knows," I said.

"Who?" Her eyes darkened a little, but her voice was under control.

"I can't remember her name." Then I went back to the truth: "The one that gave him his alibi for the afternoon of the murder."

"Alibi?" she asked indignantly. "Do you mean to tell me the police would take the word of a girl like that?"

"Like what?"

"You know what I mean."

"I don't. Do you know the girl?"

"No," she said as if I had insulted her. She narrowed her eyes and lowered her voice until it was not much more than a whisper: "Nick, do you suppose he killed Julia?"

"What would he do that for?"

"Suppose he married me to get revenge on Clyde," she said, "and— You know he did urge me to come over here and try to get some money from Clyde. Maybe I suggested it—I don't know—but he did urge me. And then suppose he happened to run into Julia. She knew him, of course, because they worked for Clyde at the same time. And he knew I was going over to see her that afternoon and was afraid if I made her mad she might expose him to me and so— Couldn't that be?"

"That doesn't make any sense at all. Besides, you and he left here together that afternoon. He wouldn't't've had time to—"

"But my taxicab was awfully slow," she said, "and then I may have stopped somewhere on— I think I did. I think I stopped at a drug store to get some aspirin." She nodded energetically. "I remember I did."

"And he knew you were going to stop, because you had told him," I suggested. "You can't go on like this, Mimi. Murder's serious. It's nothing to frame people for just because they played tricks on you."

"Tricks?" she asked, glaring at me. "Why, that . . ." She called Jorgensen all the usual profane, obscene, and otherwise insulting names, her voice gradually rising until towards the end she was screaming into my face.

When she stopped for breath I said: "That's pretty cursing, but it—"

"He even had the nerve to hint that I might've killed her," she told me. "He didn't have nerve enough to ask me, but he kept leading up to it until I told him positively that—well, that I didn't do it."

"That's not what you started to say. You told him positively what?" She stamped her foot. "Stop heckling me."

"All right and to hell with you," I said. "Coming here wasn't my idea." I started towards my hat and coat.

She ran after me, caught my arm. "Please, Nick, I'm sorry. It's this rotten temper of mine. I don't know what I—"

Gilbert came in and said: "I'll go along part of the way with you."

Mimi scowled at him. "You were listening."

"How could I help it, the way you screamed?" he asked. "Can I have some moncy?"

"And we haven't finished talking," she said.

I looked at my watch. "I've got to run, Mimi. It's late."

"Will you come back after you get through with your date?"

"If it's not too late. Don't wait for me."

"I'll be here," she said. "It doesn't matter how late it is."

I said I would try to make it. She gave Gilbert his money. He and I went downstairs.

19

"I was listening," Gilbert told me as we left the building. "I think it's silly not to listen whenever you get a chance if you're interested in studying people, because they're never exactly the same as when you're with them. People don't like it when they know about it, of course, but"—he smiled—"I don't suppose birds and animals like having naturalists spying on them either."

"Hear much of it?" I asked.

"Oh, enough to know I didn't miss any of the important part."

"And what'd you think of it?"

He pursed his lips, wrinkled his forehead, said judicially: "It's hard to say exactly. Mamma's good at hiding things sometimes, but she's never much good at making them up. It's a funny thing—I suppose you've noticed it—the people who lie the most are nearly always the clumsiest at it, and they're easier to fool with lies than most people, too. You'd think they'd be on the look-out for lies, but they seem to be the very ones that will believe almost anything at all. I suppose you've noticed that, haven't you?"

"Yes."

He said: "What I wanted to tell you: Chris didn't come home last night. That's why Mamma's more upset than usual, and when I got the mail this morning there was a letter for him that I thought might have something in it, so I steamed it open." He took a letter from his pocket and held it out to me. "You'd better read it and then I'll seal it again and put it with tomorrow's mail in case he comes back, though I don't think he will."

"Why don't you?" I asked as I took the letter.

"Well, he's really Kelterman. . . ."

"You say anything to him about it?"

"I didn't have a chance. I haven't seen him since you told me."

I looked at the letter in my hand. The envelope was postmarked Boston, Massachusetts, December 27, 1932, and addressed in a slightly childish feminine hand to Mr. Christian Jorgensen, Courtland Apts., New York, N. Y. "How'd you happen to open it?" I asked, taking the letter out of the envelope.

"I don't believe in intuition," he said, "but there are probably odors, sounds, maybe something about the handwriting, that you can't analyze, maybe aren't even conscious of, that influence you sometimes. I don't know what it was: I just felt there might be something important in it."

"You often feel that way about the family's mail?"

He glanced quickly at me as if to see whether I was spoofing, then said: "Not often, but I have opened their mail before. I told you I was interested in studying people."

I read the letter:

Dear Sid—

Olga wrote me about you being back in the U. S. married to another woman and using the name of Christian Jorgensen. That is not right Sid as you very well know the same as leaving me without word of any kind all these years. And no money. I know that you had to go away on account of that trouble you had with Mr. Wynant but am sure he has long since forgot all

*about that and I do think you might have written to me as you
know very well I have always been your friend and am willing to
do anything within my power for you at any time. I do not want
to scold you Sid but I have to see you. I will be off from the
store Sunday and Monday on account of New Years and will
come down to N. Y. Saturday night and must have a talk with
you. Write me where you will meet me and what time as I do
not want to make any trouble for you. Be sure and write me
right away so I will get it in time.*

Your true wife,
Georgia

There was a street address.

I said, "Well, well, well," and put the letter back in its envelope.
"And you resisted the temptation to tell your mother about this?"

"Oh, I knew what her reaction would be. You saw how she carried on
with just what you told her. What do you think I ought to do about it?"

"You ought to let me tell the police."

He nodded immediately. "If you think that's the best thing. You can
show it to them if you want."

I said, "Thanks," and put the letter in my pocket.

He said: "Now there's another thing: I had some morphine I was experimenting with and somebody stole it, about twenty grains."

"Experimenting how?"

"Taking it. I wanted to study the effects."

"And how'd you like them?" I asked.

"Oh, I didn't expect to like it. I just wanted to know about it. I don't
like things that dull my mind. That's why I don't very often drink, or
even smoke. I want to try cocaine, though, because that's supposed to
sharpen the brain, isn't it?"

"It's supposed to. Who do you think copped the stuff?"

"I suspect Dorothy, because I have a theory about her. That's why
I'm going over to Aunt Alice's for dinner: Dorry's still there and I want
to find out. I can make her tell me anything."

"Well, if she's been over there," I asked, "how could she—"

"She was home for a little while last night," he said, "and, besides,
I don't know exactly when it was taken. Today was the first time I opened
the box it was in for three or four days."

"Did she know you had it?"

"Yes. That's one of the reasons I suspect her. I don't think anybody
else did. I experimented on her too."

"How'd she like it?"

"Oh, she liked it all right, but she'd have taken it anyhow. But what
I want to ask you is could she have become an addict in a little time
like that?"

"Like what?"

"A week—no—ten days."

"Hardly, unless she thought herself into it. Did you give her much?"

"No."

"Let me know if you find out," I said. "I'm going to grab a taxi here. Be seeing you."

"You're coming over later tonight, aren't you?"

"If I can make it. Maybe I'll see you then."

"Yes," he said, "and thanks awfully."

At the first drug store I stopped to telephone Guild, not expecting to catch him in his office, but hoping to learn how to reach him at his home. He was still there, though.

"Working late," I said.

His "That's what" sounded very cheerful.

I read Georgia's letter to him, gave him her address.

"Good pickings," he said.

I told him Jorgensen had not been home since the day before.

"Think we'll find him in Boston?" he asked.

"Either there," I guessed, "or as far south as he could manage to get by this time."

"We'll try 'em both," he said, still cheerful. "Now I got a bit of news for you. Our friend Nunheim was filled full of .32s just about an hour after he copped the sneak on us—deader'n hell. The pills look like they come from the same gun that cut down the Wolf dame. The experts are matching 'em up now. I guess he wishes he'd stayed and talked to us."

20

Nora was eating a piece of cold duck with one hand and working on a jig-saw puzzle with the other when I got home.

"I thought you'd gone to live with her," she said. "You used to be a detective: find me a brownish piece shaped something like a snail with a long neck."

"Piece of duck or puzzle? Don't let's go to the Edges' tonight: they're dull folk."

"All right, but they'll be sore."

"We wouldn't be that lucky," I complained. "They'd get sore at the Quinns and—"

"Harrison called you up. He told me to tell you now's the time to buy some McIntyre Porcupine—I think that's right—to go with your Dome stock. He said it closed at twenty and a quarter." She put a finger on her puzzle. "The piece I want goes in there."

I found the piece she wanted and told her, almost word for word, what had been done and said at Mimi's.

"I don't believe it," she said. "You made it up. There aren't any people like that. What's the matter with them? Are they the first of a new race of monsters?"

"I just tell you what happens; I don't explain it."

"How would you explain it? There doesn't seem to be a single one in the family—now that Mimi's turned against her Chris—who has even the slightest reasonably friendly feeling for any of the others, and yet there's something very alike in all of them."

"Maybe that explains it," I suggested.

"I'd like to see Aunt Alice," she said. "Are you going to turn that letter over to the police?"

"I've already phoned Guild," I replied, and told her about Nunheim.

"What does that mean?" she asked.

"For one thing, if Jorgensen's out of town, as I think he is, and the bullets are from the same gun that was used on Julia Wolf, and they probably are, then the police'll have to find his accomplice if they want to hang anything on him."

"I'm sure if you were a good detective you'd be able to make it much clearer to me than it is." She went to work on her puzzle again. "Are you going back to see Mimi?"

"I doubt it. How about letting that dido rest while we get some dinner?"

The telephone rang and I said I would get it. It was Dorothy Wynant. "Hello. Nick?"

"The same. How are you, Dorothy?"

"Gil just got here and asked me about that you-know, and I wanted to tell you I did take it, but I only took it to try to keep him from becoming a dope-fiend."

"What'd you do with it?" I asked.

"He made me give it back to him and he doesn't believe me, but, honestly, that's the only reason I took it."

"I believe you."

"Will you tell Gil, then? If you believe me, he will, because he thinks you know all about things like that."

"I'll tell him as soon as I see him," I promised.

There was a pause, then she asked: "How's Nora?"

"Looks all right to me. Want to talk to her?"

"Well, yes, but there's something I want to ask you. Did—did Mamma say anything about me when you were over there today?"

"Not that I remember. Why?"

"And did Gil?"

"Only about the morphine."

"Are you sure?"

"Pretty sure," I said. "Why?"

"It's nothing, really—if you're sure. It's just silly."

"Right. I'll call Nora." I went into the living-room. "Dorothy wants to talk to you. Don't ask her to eat with us."

When Nora returned from the telephone she had a look in her eye.

"Now what's up?" I asked.

"Nothing. Just 'How are you' and all that."

I said: "If you're lying to the old man, God'll punish you."

We went over to a Japanese place on Fifty-eighth Street for dinner and then I let Nora talk me into going to the Edges' after all.

Halsey Edge was a tall scrawny man of fifty-something with a pinched yellow face and no hair at all. He called himself "a ghoul by profession and inclination"—his only joke, if that is what it was—by which he meant he was an archæologist, and he was very proud of his collection of battle-axes. He was not so bad once you had resigned yourself to the fact that you were in for occasional cataloguings of his armory—stone axes, copper axes, bronze axes, double-bladed axes, faceted axes, polygonal axes, scalloped axes, hammer axes, adze axes, Mesopotamian axes, Hungarian axes, Nordic axes, and all of them looking pretty moth-eaten. It was his wife we objected to. Her name was Leda, but he called her Tip. She was very small and her hair, eyes, and skin, though naturally of different shades, were all muddy. She seldom sat—she perched on things—and liked to cock her head a little to one side. Nora had a theory that once when Edge opened an antique grave, Tip ran out of it, and Margot Innes always spoke of her as the gnome, pronouncing all the letters. She once told me that she did not think any literature of twenty years ago would live, because it had no psychiatry in it. They lived in a pleasant old three-story house on the edge of Greenwich Village and their liquor was excellent.

A dozen or more people were there when we arrived. Tip introduced us to the ones we did not know and then backed me into a corner. "Why didn't you tell me that those people I met at your place Christmas were mixed up in a murder mystery?" she asked, tilting her head to the left until her ear was practically resting on her shoulder.

"I don't know that they are. Besides, what's one murder mystery nowadays?"

She tilted her head to the right. "You didn't even tell me you had taken the case."

"I had done what? Oh, I see what you mean. Well, I hadn't and haven't. My getting shot ought to prove I was an innocent bystander."

"Does it hurt much?"

"It itches. I forgot to have the dressing changed this afternoon."

"Wasn't Nora utterly terrified?"

"So was I and so was the guy that shot me. There's Halsey. I haven't spoken to him yet."

As I slid around her to escape she said: "Harrison promised to bring the daughter tonight."

I talked to Edge for a few minutes—chiefly about a place in Pennsylvania he was buying—then found myself a drink and listened to Larry Crowley and Phil Thames swap dirty stories until some woman came over and asked Phil—he taught at Columbia—one of the questions about technocracy that people were asking that week. Larry and I moved away.

We went over to where Nora was sitting. "Watch yourself," she told me. "The gnome's hell-bent on getting the inside story of Julia Wolf's murder out of you."

"Let her get it out of Dorothy," I said. "She's coming with Quinn."

"I know."

Larry said: "He's nuts over that girl, isn't he? He told me he was going to divorce Alice and marry her."

Nora said, "Poor Alice," sympathetically. She did not like Alice.

Larry said: "That's according to how you look at it." He liked Alice. "I saw that fellow who's married to the girl's mother yesterday. You know, the tall fellow I met at your house."

"Jorgensen?"

"That's it. He was coming out of a pawnshop on Sixth Avenue near Forty-sixth."

"Talk to him?"

"I was in a taxi. It's probably polite to pretend you don't see people coming out of pawnshops, anyhow."

Tip said, "Sh-h-h," in all directions, and Levi Oscant began to play the piano. Quinn and Dorothy arrived while he was playing. Quinn was drunk as a lord and Dorothy seemed to have something better than a glow.

She came over to me and whispered: "I want to leave when you and Nora do."

I said: "You won't be here for breakfast."

Tip said, "Sh-h-h," in my direction.

We listened to some more music.

Dorothy fidgeted beside me for a minute and whispered again: "Gil says you're going over to see Mamma later. Are you?"

"I doubt it."

Quinn came unsteadily around to us. "How're you, boy? How're you, Nora? Give him my message?" (Tip said, "Sh-h-h," at him. He paid no attention to her. Other people looked relieved and began to talk.) "Listen, boy, you bank at the Golden Gate Trust in San Francisco, don't you?"

"Got a little money there."

"Get it out, boy. I heard tonight they're plenty shaky."

"All right. I haven't got much there, though."

"No? What do you do with all your money?"

"Me and the French hoard gold."

He shook his head solemnly. "It's fellows like you that put the country on the bum."

"And it's fellows like me that don't go on the bum with it," I said. "Where'd you get the skinful?"

"It's Alice. She's been sulking for a week. If I didn't drink I'd go crazy."

"What's she sulking about?"

"About my drinking. She thinks—" He leaned forward and lowered his voice confidentially. "Listen. You're all my friends and I'm going to tell you what I'm going to do. I'm going to get a divorce and marry—"

He had tried to put an arm around Dorothy. She pushed it away and said: "You're silly and you're tiresome. I wish you'd leave me alone."

"She thinks I'm silly and tiresome," he told me. "You know why she don't want to marry me? I bet you don't. It's because she's in—"

"Shut up! Shut up, you drunken fool!" Dorothy began to beat his face with both hands. Her face was red, her voice shrill. "If you say that again I'll kill you!"

I pulled Dorothy away from Quinn; Larry caught him, kept him from falling. He whimpered: "She hit me, Nick." Tears ran down his cheeks.

Dorothy had her face against my coat and seemed to be crying.

We had what audience there was. Tip came running, her face bright with curiosity. "What is it, Nick?"

I said: "Just a couple of playful drunks. They're all right. I'll see that they get home all right."

Tip was not for that: she wanted them to stay at least until she had a chance to discover what had happened. She urged Dorothy to lie down awhile, offered to get something—whatever she meant by that—for Quinn, who was having trouble standing up now.

Nora and I took them out. Larry offered to go along, but we decided that was not necessary. Quinn slept in a corner of the taxicab during the ride to his apartment, and Dorothy sat stiff and silent in the other corner, with Nora between them. I clung to a folding seat and thought that anyway we had not stayed long at the Edges'.

Nora and Dorothy remained in the taxicab while I took Quinn upstairs. He was pretty limp.

Alice opened the door when I rang. She had on green pyjamas and held a hairbrush in one hand. She looked wearily at Quinn and spoke wearily: "Bring it in."

I took it in and spread it on a bed. It mumbled something I could not make out and moved one hand feebly back and forth, but its eyes stayed shut.

"I'll tuck him in," I said and loosened his tie.

Alice leaned on the foot of the bed. "If you want to. I've given up doing it."

I took off his coat, vest, and shirts.

"Where'd he pass out this time?" she asked with not much interest. She was still standing at the foot of the bed, brushing her hair now.

"The Edges'." I unbuttoned his pants.

"With that little Wynant bitch?" The question was casual.

"There were a lot of people there."

"Yes," she said. "He wouldn't pick a secluded spot." She brushed her hair a couple of times. "So you don't think it's clubby to tell me anything."

Her husband stirred a little and mumbled: "Dorry."

I took off his shoes.

Alice sighed. "I can remember when he had muscles." She stared at her husband until I took off the last of his clothes and rolled him under the covers. Then she sighed again and said: "I'll get you a drink."

"You'll have to make it short: Nora's waiting in the cab."

She opened her mouth as if to speak, shut it, opened it again to say: "Righto."

I went into the kitchen with her.

Presently she said: "It's none of my business, Nick, but what do people think of me?"

"You're like everybody else: some people like you, some people don't, and some have no feeling about it one way or the other."

She frowned. "That's not exactly what I meant. What do people think about my staying with Harrison with him chasing everything that's hot and hollow?"

"I don't know, Alice."

"What do you think?"

"I think you probably know what you're doing and whatever you do is your own business."

She looked at me with dissatisfaction. "You'll never talk yourself into any trouble, will you?" She smiled bitterly. "You know I'm only staying with him for his money, don't you? It may not be a lot to you, but it is to me—the way I was raised."

"There's always divorce and alimony. You ought to have—"

"Drink your drink and get to hell out of here," she said wearily.

21

NORA made a place for me between her and Dorothy in the taxicab. "I want some coffee," she said. "Reuben's?"

I said, "All right," and gave the driver the address.

Dorothy asked timidly: "Did his wife say anything?"

"She sent her love to you."

Nora said: "Stop being nasty."

Dorothy said: "I don't really like him, Nick. I won't ever see him again—honestly." She seemed pretty sober now. "It was—well, I was lonesome and he was somebody to run around with."

I started to say something, but stopped when Nora poked me in the side.

Nora said: "Don't worry about it. Harrison's always been a simpleton."

"I don't want to stir things up," I said, "but I think he's really in love with the girl."

Nora poked me in the side again.

Dorothy peered at my face in the dim light. "You're—you're not—You're not making fun of me, Nick?"

"I ought to be."

"I heard a new story about the gnome tonight," Nora said in the manner of one who did not mean to be interrupted, and explained to Dorothy, "That's Mrs. Edge. Levi says . . ." The story was funny enough if you knew Tip. Nora went on talking about her until we got out of the taxicab at Reuben's.

Herbert Macaulay was in the restaurant, sitting at a table with a plump dark-haired girl in red. I waved at him and, after we had ordered some food, went over to speak to him.

"Nick Charles, Louise Jacobs," he said. "Sit down. What's news?"

"Jorgensen's Kelterman," I told him.

"The hell he is!"

I nodded. "And he seems to have a wife in Boston."

"I'd like to see him," he said slowly. "I knew Kelterman. I'd like to make sure."

"The police seem sure enough. I don't know whether they've found him yet. Think he killed Julia?"

Macaulay shook his head with emphasis. "I can't see Kelterman killing anybody—not as I knew him—in spite of those threats he made. You remember I didn't take them very seriously at the time. What else has happened?" When I hesitated, he said: "Louise is all right. You can talk."

"It's not that. I've got to go back to my folks and food. I came over to ask if you'd got an answer to your ad in this morning's *Times*."

"Not yet. Sit down, Nick, there's a lot I want to ask you. You told the police about Wynant's letter, didn't—"

"Come up to lunch tomorrow and we'll bat it around. I've got to get back to my folks."

"Who is the little blonde girl?" Louise Jacobs asked. "I've seen her places with Harrison Quinn."

"Dorothy Wynant."

"You know Quinn?" Macaulay asked me.

"Ten minutes ago I was putting him to bed."

Macaulay grinned. "I hope you keep his acquaintance like that—social."

"Meaning what?"

Macaulay's grin became rueful. "He used to be my broker, and his advice led me right up to the poor-house steps."

"That's sweet," I said. "He's my broker now and I'm following his advice."

Macaulay and the girl laughed. I pretended I was laughing and returned to my table.

Dorothy said: "It's not midnight yet and Mamma said she'd be expecting you. Why don't we all go to see her?"

Nora was very carefully pouring coffee into her cup.

"What for?" I asked. "What are you two up to now?"

It would have been hard to find two more innocent faces than theirs.

"Nothing, Nick," Dorothy said. "We thought it would be nice. It's early and—"

"And we all love Mimi."

"No—o, but—"

"It's too early to go home," Nora said.

"There are speakeasies," I suggested, "and nightclubs and Harlem."

Nora made a face. "All your ideas are alike."

"Want to go over to Barry's and try our luck at faro?"

Dorothy started to say yes, but stopped when Nora made another face.

"That's the way I feel about seeing Mimi again," I said. "I've had enough of her for one day."

Nora sighed to show she was being patient. "Well, if we're going to wind up in a speakeasy as usual, I'd rather go to your friend Studsy's, if you won't let him give us any more of that awful champagne. He's cute."

"I'll do my best," I promised and asked Dorothy, "Did Gilbert tell you he caught Mimi and me in a compromising position?"

She tried to exchange glances with Nora, but Nora's glance was occupied with a cheese blintz on her plate. "He—he didn't exactly say that."

"Did he tell you about the letter?"

"From Chris's wife? Yes." Her blue eyes glittered. "Won't Mamma be furious!"

"You like it, though."

"Suppose I do? What of it? What did she ever do to make me—"

Nora said: "Nick, stop bullying the child."

I stopped.

22

BUSINESS was good at the Pigiron Club. The place was full of people, noise, and smoke. Studsy came from behind the cash register to greet us. "I was hoping you'd come in." He shook my hand and Nora's and grinned broadly at Dorothy.

"Anything special?" I asked.

He made a bow. "Everything's special with ladies like these."

I introduced him to Dorothy.

He bowed to her and said something elaborate about any friend of Nick's and stopped a waiter. "Pete, put a table up here for Mr. Charles."

"Pack them in like this every night?" I asked.

"I got no kick," he said. "They come once, they come back again. Maybe I ain't got no black marble cuspidors, but you don't have to spit out what you buy here. Want to lean against the bar whilst they're putting up that table?"

We said we did and ordered drinks.

"Hear about Nunheim?" I asked.

He looked at me for a moment before making up his mind to say: "Uh-huh, I heard. His girl's down there"—he moved his head to indicate the other end of the room—"celebrating, I guess."

I looked past Studsy down the room and presently picked out big red-haired Miriam sitting at a table with half a dozen men and women. "Hear who did it?" I asked.

"She says the police done it—he knew too much."

"That's a laugh," I said.

"That's a laugh," he agreed. "There's your table. Set right down. I'll be back in a minute."

We carried our glasses over to a table that had been squeezed in between two tables which had occupied a space large enough for one and made ourselves as nearly comfortable as we could.

Nora tasted her drink and shuddered. "Do you suppose this could be the 'bitter vetch' they used to put in cross-word puzzles?"

Dorothy said: "Oh, look."

We looked and saw Shep Morelli coming towards us. His face had attracted Dorothy's attention. Where it was not dented it was swollen and its coloring ranged from deep purple around one eye to the pale pink of a piece of court-plaster on his chin.

He came to our table and leaned over a little to put both fists on it. "Listen," he said, "Studsy says I ought to apologize."

Nora murmured, "Old Emily Post Studsy," while I asked, "Well?"

Morelli shook his battered head. "I don't apologize for what I do—people've got to take it or leave it—but I don't mind telling you I'm sorry I lost my noodle and cracked down on you and I hope it ain't bothering you much and if there's anything I can do to square it I—"

"Forget it. Sit down and have a drink. This is Mr. Morelli, Miss Wynant."

Dorothy's eyes became wide and interested.

Morelli found a chair and sat down. "I hope you won't hold it against me, neither," he told Nora.

She said: "It was fun."

He looked at her suspiciously.

"Out on bail?" I asked.

"Uh-huh, this afternoon." He felt his face gingerly with one hand. "That's where the new ones come from. They had me resisting some more arrest just for good measure before they turned me loose."

Nora said indignantly: "That's horrible. You mean they really—"

I patted her hand.

Morelli said: "You got to expect it." His swollen lower lip moved in what was meant for a scornful smile. "It's all right as long as it takes two or three of 'em to do it."

Nora turned to me. "Did you do things like that?"

"Who? Me?"

Studsy came over to us carrying a chair. "They lifted his face, huh?" he said, nodding at Morelli. We made room for him and he sat down. He grinned complacently at Nora's drink and at Nora. "I guess you don't get no better than that in your fancy Park Avenue joints—and you pay four bits a slug for it here."

Nora's smile was weak, but it was a smile. She put her foot on mine under the table.

I asked Morelli: "Did you know Julia Wolf in Cleveland?"

He looked sidewise at Studsy, who was leaning back in his chair, gazing around the room, watching his profits mount.

"When she was Rhoda Stewart," I added.

He looked at Dorothy.

I said: "You don't have to be cagey. She's Clyde Wynant's daughter."

Studsy stopped gazing around the room and beamed on Dorothy. "So you are? And how is your pappy?"

"But I haven't seen him since I was a little girl," she said.

Morelli wet the end of a cigarette and put it between his swollen lips. "I come from Cleveland." He struck a match. His eyes were dull—he was trying to keep them dull. "She wasn't Rhoda Stewart except once—Nancy Kane." He looked at Dorothy again. "Your father knows it."

"Do you know my father?"

"We had some words once."

"What about?" I asked.

"Her." The match in his hand had burned down to his fingers. He dropped it, struck another, and lit his cigarette. He raised his eyebrows at me, wrinkling his forehead. "Is this O. K.?"

"Sure. There's nobody here you can't talk in front of."

"O. K. He was jealous as hell. I wanted to take a poke at him, but she wouldn't let me. That was all right: he was her bank-roll."

"How long ago was this?"

"Six months, eight months."

"Have you seen him since she got knocked off?"

He shook his head. "I never seen him but a couple of times, and this time I'm telling you about is the last."

"Was she gypping him?"

"She don't say she is. I figure she is."

"Why?"

"She's a wise head—plenty smart. She was getting dough somewheres. Once I wanted five grand." He snapped his fingers. "Cash."

I decided against asking if he had paid her back. "Maybe he gave it to her."

"Sure—maybe."

"Did you tell any of this to the police?" I asked.

He laughed once, contemptuously. "They thought they could smack it out of me. Ask 'em what they think now. You're a right guy, I don't—" He broke off, took the cigarette from between his lips. "The earysipelas kid," he said and put out a hand to touch the ear of a man who, sitting at one of the tables we had been squeezed in between, had been leaning further and further back towards us.

The man jumped and turned a startled pale pinched face around over his shoulder at Morelli.

Morelli said: "Pull in that lug—it's getting in our drinks."

The man stammered, "I d-didn't mean nothing, Shep," and rammed his belly into his table trying to get as far as possible from us, which still did not take him out of ear-shot.

Morelli said, "You won't ever mean nothing, but that don't keep you from trying," and returned his attention to me. "I'm willing to go all the way with you—the kid's dead, it's not going to hurt her any—but Mulrooney ain't got a wrecking crew that can get it out of me."

"Swell," I said. "Tell me about her, where you first ran into her, what she did before she tied up with Wynant, where he found her."

"I ought to have a drink." He twisted himself around in his chair and called: "Hey, garsong—you with the boy on your back!"

The somewhat hunchbacked waiter Studsy had called Pete pushed through people to our table and grinned affectionately down at Morelli. "What'll it be?" He sucked a tooth noisily.

We gave our orders and the waiter went away.

Morelli said: "Me and Nancy lived in the same block. Old man Kane had a candy store on the corner. She used to pinch cigarettes for me." He laughed. "Her old man kicked hell out of me once for showing her how to get nickels out of the telephone with a piece of wire. You know, the old style ones. Jesus, we couldn't've been more than in the third grade." He laughed again, low in his throat. "I wanted to glaum some fixtures from a row of houses they were building around the corner and plant 'em in his cellar and tell Schultz, the cop on the beat, to pay him back, but she wouldn't let me."

Nora said: "You must've been a little darling."

"I was that," he said fondly. "Listen. Once when I was no more'n five or—"

A feminine voice said: "I thought that was you."

I looked up and saw it was red-haired Miriam speaking to me. I said: "Hello."

She put her hands on her hips and stared somberly at me. "So he knew too much for you."

"Maybe, but he took it on the lam down the fire-escape with his shoes in his hand before he told us any of it."

"Balls!"

"All right. What do you think he knew that was too much for us?"

"Where Wynant is," she said.

"So? Where is he?"

"I don't know. Art knew."

"I wish he'd told us. We—"

"Balls!" she said again. "You know and the police know. Who do you think you're kidding?"

"I'm not kidding. I don't know where Wynant is."

"You're working for him and the police are working with you. Don't kid me. Art thought knowing was going to get him a lot of money, poor sap. He didn't know what it was going to get him."

"Did he tell you he knew?" I asked.

"I'm not as dumb as you think. He told me he knew something that was going to get him big dough and I've seen how it worked out. I guess I can put two and two together."

"Sometimes the answer's four," I said, "and sometimes it's twenty-two. I'm not working for Wynant. Now don't say, 'Balls,' again. Do you want to help—"

"No. He was a rat and he held out on the people he was ratting for. He asked for what he got, only don't expect me to forget that I left him with you and Guild, and the next time anybody saw him he was dead."

"I don't want you to forget anything. I'd like you to remember whether—"

"I've got to go to the can," she said and walked away. Her carriage was remarkably graceful.

"I don't know as I'd want to be mixed up with that dame," Studsy said thoughtfully. "She's mean medicine."

Morelli winked at me.

Dorothy touched my arm. "I don't understand, Nick."

I told her that was all right and addressed Morelli: "You were telling us about Julia Wolf."

"Uh-huh. Well, old man Kane booted her out when she was fifteen or sixteen and got in some kind of a jam with a high-school teacher and she took up with a guy called Face Peppler, a smart kid if he didn't talk too much. I remember once me and Face were—" He broke off and cleared his throat. "Anyways, Face and her stuck together—what the hell —it must be five, six years, thowing out the time he was in the army and she was living with some guy that I can't remember his name—a cousin of Dick O'Brien's, a skinny dark-headed guy that liked his liquor. But she went back to Face when he come out of the army, and they stuck together till they got nailed trying to shake down some bird from Toronto. Face took it and got her off with six months—they give him the business. Last I heard he was still in. I saw her when she came out—she touched me for a couple hundred to blow town. I hear from her once, when she sends it back to me and tells me Julia Wolf's her name now and she likes the big city fine, but I know Face is hearing from her right along. So when I move here in '28, I look her up. She's—"

Miriam came back and stood with her hands on her hips as before. "I've been thinking over what you said. You must think I'm pretty dumb."

"No," I said, not very truthfully.

"It's a cinch I'm not dumb enough to fall for that song and dance you tried to give me. I can see things when they're right in front of me."

"All right."

"It's not all right. You killed Art and—"

"Not so loud, girlie." Studsy rose and took her arm. His voice was soothing. "Come along. I want to talk to you." He led her towards the bar.

Morelli winked again. "He likes that. Well, I was saying I looked her up when I moved here, and she told me she had this job with Wynant and he was nuts about her and she was sitting pretty. It seems they learned her shorthand in Ohio when she was doing her six months and she figures maybe it'll be an in to something—you know, maybe she can get a job somewheres where they'll go out and leave the safe open. A agency had sent her over to do a couple days' work for Wynant and she figured maybe he'd be worth more for a long pull than for a quick tap and a get-away, so she give him the business and wound up with a steady connection. She was smart enough to tell him she had a record and was trying to go straight now and all that, so's not to have the racket spoiled if he found out anyhow, because she said his lawyer was a little leery of her and might have her looked up. I don't know just what she was doing, you understand, because it's her game and she don't need my help, and even if we are pals in a way, there's no sense in telling me anything I might want to go to her boss with. Understand, she wasn't my girl or anything —we was just a couple old friends, been kids playing together. Well, I used to see her ever once in a while—we used to come here a lot—till he kicked up too much of a fuss and then she said she was going to cut it out, she wasn't going to lose a soft bed over a few drinks with me. So that was that. That was October, I guess, and she stuck to it. I haven't seen her since."

"Who else did she run around with?" I asked.

Morelli shook his head. "I don't know. She don't do much talking about people."

"She was wearing a diamond engagement ring. Know anything about it?"

"Nothing except she didn't get it from me. She wasn't wearing it when I see her."

"Do you think she meant to throw in with Peppler again when he got out?"

"Maybe. She didn't seem to worry much about him being in, but she liked to work with him all right and I guess they'd've teamed up again."

"And how about the cousin of Dick O'Brien, the skinny dark-headed lush? What became of him?"

Morelli looked at me in surprise. "Search me."

Studsy returned alone. "Maybe I'm wrong," he said as he sat down, "but I think somebody could do something with that cluck if they took hold of her right."

Morelli said: "By the throat."

Studsy grinned good-naturedly. "No. She's trying to get somewhere. She works hard at her singing lessons and—"

Morelli looked at his empty glass and said: "This tiger milk of yours must be doing her pipes a lot of good." He turned his head to yell at Pete: "Hey, you with the knapsack, some more of the same. We got to sing in the choir tomorrow."

Pete said: "Coming up, Sheppy." His lined gray face lost its dull apathy when Morelli spoke to him.

An immensely fat blond man—so blond he was nearly albino—who had been sitting at Miriam's table came over and said to me in a thin, tremulous, effeminate voice: "So you're the party who put it to little Art Nunhei—"

Morelli hit the fat man in his fat belly, as hard as he could without getting up. Studsy, suddenly on his feet, leaned over Morelli and smashed a big fist into the fat man's face. I noticed, foolishly, that he still led with his right. Hunchbacked Pete came up behind the fat man and banged his empty tray down with full force on the fat man's head. The fat man fell back, upsetting three people and a table. Both bar-tenders were with us by then. One of them hit the fat man with a blackjack as he tried to get up, knocking him forward on hands and knees, the other put a hand down inside the fat man's collar in back, twisting the collar to choke him. With Morelli's help they got the fat man to his feet and hustled him out.

Pete looked after them and sucked a tooth. "That God-damned Sparrow," he explained to me, "you can't take no chances on him when he's drinking."

Studsy was at the next table, the one that had been upset, helping people pick up themselves and their possessions. "That's bad," he was saying, "bad for business, but where you going to draw the line? I ain't running a dive, but I ain't trying to run a young ladies' seminary neither."

Dorothy was pale, frightened; Nora wide-eyed and amazed. "It's a madhouse," she said. "What'd they do that for?"

"You know as much about it as I do," I told her.

Morelli and the bar-tenders came in again, looking pretty pleased with themselves. Morelli and Studsy returned to their seats at our table.

"You boys are impulsive," I said.

Studsy repeated, "Impulsive," and laughed, "Ha-ha-ha."

Morelli was serious. "Any time that guy starts anything, you got to start it first. It's too late when he gets going. We seen him like that before, ain't we, Studsy?"

"Like what?" I asked. "He hadn't done anything."

"He hadn't, all right," Morelli said slowly, "but it's a kind of feeling you get about him sometimes. Ain't that right, Studsy?"

Studsy said: "Uh-huh, he's hysterical."

23

It was about two o'clock when we said good-night to Studsy and Morelli and left the Pigiron Club.

Dorothy slumped down in her corner of the taxicab and said: "I'm going to be sick. I know I am." She sounded as if she was telling the truth.

Nora said: "That booze." She put her head on my shoulder. "Your wife is drunk, Nicky. Listen, you've got to tell me what happened—everything. Not now, tomorrow. I don't understand a thing that was said or a thing that was done. They're marvelous."

Dorothy said: "Listen, I can't go to Aunt Alice's like this. She'd have a fit."

Nora said: "They oughtn't've hit that fat man like that, though it must've been funny in a cruel way."

Dorothy said: "I suppose I'd better go to Mamma's."

Nora said: "Erysipelas hasn't got anything to do with ears. What's a lug, Nicky?"

"An ear."

Dorothy said: "Aunt Alice would have to see me because I forgot the key and I'd have to wake her up."

Nora said: "I love you, Nicky, because you smell nice and know such fascinating people."

Dorothy said: "It's not much out of your way to drop me at Mamma's, is it?"

I said, "No," and gave the driver Mimi's address.

Nora said: "Come home with us."

Dorothy said: "No—o, I'd better not."

Nora asked, "Why not?" and Dorothy said, "Well, I don't think I ought to," and that kind of thing went on until the taxicab stopped at the Courtland.

I got out and helped Dorothy out. She leaned heavily on my arm. "Please come up, just for a minute."

Nora said, "Just for a minute," and got out of the taxicab.

I told the driver to wait. We went upstairs. Dorothy rang the bell. Gilbert, in pyjamas and bathrobe, opened the door. He raised one hand in a warning gesture and said in a low voice: "The police are here."

Mimi's voice came from the living-room: "Who is it, Gil?"

"Mr. and Mrs. Charles and Dorothy."

Mimi came to meet us as we went in. "I never was so glad to see anybody. I just didn't know which way to turn." She had on a pinkish satin robe over a pinkish silk nightgown, and her face was pink and by no means unhappy. She ignored Dorothy, squeezed one of Nora's hands, one of mine. "Now I'm going to stop worrying and leave it all up to you, Nick. You'll have to tell the foolish little woman what to do."

Dorothy, behind me, said, "Balls!" under her breath, but with a lot of feeling.

Mimi did not show that she had heard her daughter. Still holding our hands, she drew us back towards the living-room, chattering: "You know Lieutenant Guild. He's been very nice, but I'm sure I must have tried his patience. I've been so—well—I mean I've been so bewildered. But now you're here and—"

We went into the living-room.

Guild said, "Hello," to me and, "Good evening, ma'am," to Nora. The man with him, the one he had called Andy and who had helped him search our rooms the morning of Morelli's visit, nodded and grunted at us.

"What's up?" I asked.

Guild looked at Mimi out the corners of his eyes, then at me, and said: "The Boston police found Jorgensen or Kelterman or whatever you want to call him at his first wife's place and asked him some questions for us. The chief answer seems to be he don't have anything to do with Julia Wolf getting killed or not getting killed and Mrs. Jorgensen can prove it because she's been holding out what amounts to the goods on Wynant." His eyes slid sidewise in their sockets to focus on Mimi again. "The lady kind of don't want to say yes and kind of don't want to say no. To tell you the truth, Mr. Charles, I don't know what to make of her in a lot of ways."

I could understand that. I said, "She's probably frightened," and Mimi tried to look frightened. "Has he been divorced from the first wife?"

"Not according to the first wife."

Mimi said: "She's lying, I bet."

I said: "Sh-h-h. Is he coming back to New York?"

"It looks like he's going to make us extradite him if we want him. Boston says he's squawking his head off for a lawyer."

"Do you want him that bad?"

Guild moved his big shoulders. "If bringing him back'll help us on this murder. I don't care much about any of the old charges or the bigamy. I never believe in hounding a man over things that are none of my business."

I asked Mimi: "Well?"

"Can I talk to you alone?"

I looked at Guild, who said: "Anything that'll help."

Dorothy touched my arm. "Nick, listen to me first. I—" She broke off. Everybody was staring at her.

"What?" I asked.

"I—I want to talk to you first."

"Go ahead."

"I mean alone," she said.

I patted her hand. "Afterwards."

Mimi led me into her bedroom and carefully shut the door. I sat on the bed and lit a cigarette. Mimi leaned back against the door and smiled at me very gently and trustingly. Half a minute passed that way.

Then she said, "You do like me, Nick," and when I said nothing she asked, "Don't you?"

"No."

She laughed and came away from the door. "You mean you don't approve of me." She sat on the bed beside me. "But you do like me well enough to help me?"

"That depends."

"Depends on wha—"

The door opened and Dorothy came in. "Nick, I've got to—"

Mimi jumped up and confronted her daughter. "Get out of here," she said through her teeth.

Dorothy flinched, but she said: "I won't. You're not going to make a—"

Mimi slashed Dorothy across the mouth with the back of her right hand. "Get out of here."

Dorothy screamed and put a hand to her mouth. Holding it there, holding her wide frightened eyes on Mimi's face, she backed out of the room.

Mimi shut the door again.

I said: "You must come over to our place some time and bring your little white whips."

She did not seem to hear me. Her eyes were heavy, brooding, and her lips were thrust out a little in a half-smile, and when she spoke, her voice seemed heavier, throatier, than usual. "My daughter's in love with you."

"Nonsense."

"She is and she's jealous of me. She has absolute spasms whenever I get within ten feet of you." She spoke as if thinking of something else.

"Nonsense. Maybe she's got a little hangover from that crush she had on me when she was twelve, but that's all it is."

Mimi shook her head. "You're wrong, but never mind." She sat down on the bed beside me again. "You've got to help me out of this. I—"

"Sure," I said. "You're a delicate *fleur* that needs a great big man's protection."

"Oh, that?" She waved a hand at the door through which Dorothy had gone. "You're surely not getting— Why, it's nothing you haven't heard about before—and seen and done, for that matter. It's nothing to worry you." She smiled as before, with heavy, brooding eyes, and lips thrust out a little. "If you want Dorry, take her, but don't get sentimental about it.

But never mind that. Of course I'm not a delicate *fleur*. You never thought I was."

"No," I agreed.

"Well, then," she said with an air of finality.

"Well then what?"

"Stop being so damned coquettish," she said. "You know what I mean. You understand me as well as I understand you."

"Just about, but you've been doing the coquetting ever since—"

"I know. That was a game. I'm not playing now. That son of a bitch made a fool of me, Nick, an out and out fool, and now he's in trouble and expects me to help him. I'll help him." She put a hand on my knee and her pointed nails dug into my flesh. "The police, they don't believe me. How can I make them believe that he's lying, that I know nothing more than I've told them about the murder?"

"You probably can't," I said slowly, "especially since Jorgensen's only repeating what you told me a few hours ago."

She caught her breath, and her nails dug into me again. "Did you tell them that?"

"Not yet." I took her hand off my knee.

She sighed with relief. "And of course you won't tell them now, will you?"

"Why not?"

"Because it's a lie. He lied and I lied. I didn't find anything, anything at all."

I said: "We're back where we were earlier, and I believe you just as much now as I did then. What happened to those new terms we were on? You understanding me, me understanding you, no coquetting, no games, no playing."

She slapped my hand lightly. "All right. I did find something—not much, but something—and I'm not going to give it up to help that son of a bitch. You can understand how I feel about it, Nick. You'd feel the same—"

"Maybe," I said, "but the way it stands, I've got no reason for putting in with you. Your Chris is no enemy of mine. I've got nothing to gain by helping you frame him."

She sighed. "I've been thinking about that a lot. I don't suppose what money I could give you would mean much to you now"—she smiled crookedly—"nor my beautiful white body. But aren't you interested in saving Clyde?"

"Not necessarily."

She laughed at that. "I don't know what that means."

"It might mean I don't think he needs saving. The police haven't got much on him. He's screwy, he was in town the day Julia was killed, and she had been gypping him. That's not enough to arrest him on."

She laughed again. "But with my contribution?"

"I don't know. What is it?" I asked, and went on without waiting for the answer I did not expect. "Whatever it is, you're being a sap, Mimi. You've got Chris cold on bigamy. Sock that to him. There's no—"

She smiled sweetly and said: "But I am holding that in reserve to use after this if he—"

"If he gets past the murder charge, huh? Well, it won't work out that way, lady. You can get him about three days in jail. By that time the District Attorney will have questioned him and checked up on him enough to know that he didn't kill Julia and that you've been making a chump of the D. A., and when you spring your little bigamy charge the D. A. will tell you to go jump in the lake, and he'll refuse to prosecute."

"But he can't do that, Nick."

"Can and will," I assured her, "and if he can dig up proof that you're holding out something he'll make it as tough for you as he can."

She chewed her lower lip, asked: "You're being honest with me?"

"I'm telling you exactly what'll happen, unless district attorneys have changed a lot since my day."

She chewed her lip some more. "I don't want him to get off," she said presently, "and I don't want to get into any trouble myself." She looked up at me. "If you're lying to me, Nick . . ."

"There's nothing you can do about it except believe me or disbelieve me."

She smiled and put a hand on my cheek and kissed me on the mouth and stood up. "You're such a bastard. Well, I'm going to believe you." She walked down to the other end of the room and back again. Her eyes were shiny, her face pleasantly excited.

"I'll call Guild," I said.

"No, wait. I'd rather—I'd rather see what you think of it first."

"All right, but no clowning."

"You're certainly afraid of your shadow," she said, "but don't worry, I'm not going to play any tricks on you."

I said that would be swell and how about showing me whatever she had to show me. "The others will be getting restless."

She went around the bed to a closet, opened the door, pushed some clothes aside, and put a hand among other clothes behind them. "That's funny," she said.

"Funny?" I stood up. "It's a panic. It'll have Guild rolling on the floor." I started towards the door.

"Don't be so bad-tempered," she said. "I've got it." She turned to me holding a wadded handkerchief in her hand. As I approached, she opened the handkerchief to show me a three-inch length of watch-chain, broken at one end, attached at the other to a small gold knife. The handkerchief was a woman's and there were brown stains on it.

"Well?" I asked.

"It was in her hand and I saw it when they left me with her and I knew it was Clyde's, so I took it."

"You're sure it's his?"

"Yes," she said impatiently. "See, they're gold, silver, and copper links. He had it made out of the first batches of metal that came through that smelting process he invented. Anybody who knows him at all well can identify it—there can't be another like it." She turned the knife over to let me see the C M W engraved in it. "They're his initials. I never saw the knife before, but I'd know the chain anywhere. Clyde's worn it for years."

"Did you remember it well enough that you could've described it without seeing it again?"

"Of course."

"Is that your handkerchief?"

"Yes."

"And the stain on it's blood?"

"Yes. The chain was in her hand—I told you—and there was some blood on them." She frowned at me. "Don't you— You act as if you don't believe me."

"Not exactly," I said, "but I think you ought to be sure you're telling your story straight this time."

She stamped her foot. "You're—" She laughed and anger went out of her face. "You can be the most annoying man. I'm telling the truth now, Nick. I've told you everything that happened exactly as it happened."

"I hope so. It's about time. You're sure Julia didn't come to enough to say anything while you were alone with her?"

"You're trying to make me mad again. Of course I'm sure."

"All right," I said. "Wait here. I'll get Guild, but if you tell him the chain was in Julia's hand and she wasn't dead yet he's going to wonder whether you didn't have to rough her up a little to get it away from her."

She opened her eyes wide. "What should I tell him?"

I went out and shut the door.

24

Nora, looking a little sleepy, was entertaining Guild and Andy in the living-room. The Wynant offspring were not in sight.

"Go ahead," I told Guild. "First door to the left. I think she's readied up for you."

"Crack her?" he asked.

I nodded.

"What'd you get?"

"See what you get and we'll put them together and see how they add up," I suggested.

"O. K. Come on, Andy." They went out.

"Where's Dorothy?" I asked.

Nora yawned. "I thought she was with you and her mother. Gilbert's around somewhere. He was here till a few minutes ago. Do we have to hang around long?"

"Not long." I went back down the passageway past Mimi's door to another bedroom door, which was open, and looked in. Nobody was there. A door facing it was shut. I knocked on it.

Dorothy's voice: "What is it?"

"Nick," I said and went in.

She was lying on her side on a bed, dressed except for her slippers. Gilbert was sitting on the bed beside her. Her mouth seemed a little puffy, but it may have been from crying: her eyes were red. She raised her head to stare sullenly at me.

"Still want to talk to me?" I asked.

Gilbert got up from the bed. "Where's Mamma?"

"Talking to the police."

He said something I did not catch and left the room.

Dorothy shuddered. "He gives me the creeps," she said, and then remembered to stare sullenly at me again.

"Still want to talk to me?"

"What made you turn against me like that?"

"You're being silly." I sat down where Gilbert had been sitting. "Do you know anything about this knife and chain your mother's supposed to have found?"

"No. Where?"

"What'd you want to tell me?"

"Nothing—now," she said disagreeably, "except you might at least wipe her lipstick off your mouth."

I wiped it off. She snatched the handkerchief from my hand and rolled over to pick up a package of matches from the table on that side of the bed. She struck a match.

"That's going to stink like hell," I said.

She said, "I don't care," but she blew out the match. I took the handkerchief, went to a window, opened it, dropped the handkerchief out, shut the window, and went back to my seat on the bed. "If that makes you feel any better."

"What did Mamma say—about me?"

"She said you're in love with me."

She sat up abruptly. "What did you say?"

"I said you just liked me from when you were a kid."

Her lower lip twitched. "Do—do you think that's what it is?"

"What else could it be?"

"I don't know." She began to cry. "Everybody's made so much fun of me about it—Mamma and Gilbert and Harrison— I—"

I put my arms around her. "To hell with them."

After a while she asked: "Is Mamma in love with you?"

"Good God, no! She hates men more than any woman I've ever known who wasn't a Lesbian."

"But she's always having some sort of—"

"That's the body. Don't let it fool you. Mimi hates men—all of us—bitterly."

She had stopped crying. She wrinkled her forehead and said: "I don't understand. Do you hate her?"

"Not as a rule."

"Now?"

"I don't think so. She's being stupid and she's sure she's being very clever, and that's a nuisance, but I don't think I hate her."

"I do," Dorothy said.

"So you told me last week. Something I meant to ask you: did you know or did you ever see the Arthur Nunheim we were talking about in the speakeasy tonight?"

She looked sharply at me. "You're just trying to change the subject."

"I want to know. Did you?"

"No."

"He was mentioned in the newspapers," I reminded her. "He was the one who told the police about Morelli knowing Julia Wolf."

"I didn't remember his name," she said. "I don't remember ever having heard it until tonight."

I described him. "Ever see him?"

"No."

"He may have been known as Albert Norman sometimes. Does that sound familiar?"

"No."

"Know any of the people we saw at Studsy's tonight? Or anything about them?"

"No. Honestly, Nick, I'd tell you if I knew anything at all that might help you."

"No matter who it hurt?"

"Yes," she said immediately, then, "What do you mean?"

"You know damned well what I mean."

She put her hands over her face, and her words were barely audible: "I'm afraid, Nick. I—" She jerked her hands down as someone knocked on the door.

"All right," I called.

Andy opened the door far enough to stick his head in. He tried to keep curiosity from showing in his face while saying: "The Lieutenant wants to see you."

"Be right out," I promised.

He opened the door wider. "He's waiting." He gave me what was probably meant to be a significant wink, but a corner of his mouth moved more than his eye did and the result was a fairly startling face.

"I'll be back," I told Dorothy, and followed him out.

He shut the door behind me and put his mouth close to my ear. "The kid was at the keyhole," he muttered.

"Gilbert?"

"Yep. He had time to get away from it when he heard me coming, but he was there, right enough."

"That's mild for him," I said. "How'd you all make out with Mrs. J.?"

He puckered his thick lips up in an o and blew breath out noisily. "What a dame!"

25

We went into Mimi's bedroom. She was sitting in a deep chair by a window looking very pleased with herself. She smiled gayly at me and said: "My soul is spotless now. I've confessed everything."

Guild stood by a table wiping his face with a handkerchief. There were still some drops of sweat on his temples, and his face seemed old and tired. The knife and chain, and the handkerchief they had been wrapped in, were on the table.

"Finished?" I asked.

"I don't know, and that's a fact," he said. He turned his head to address Mimi: "Would you say we were finished?"

Mimi laughed. "I can't imagine what more there would be."

"Well," Guild said slowly, somewhat reluctantly, "in that case I guess I'd like to talk to Mr. Charles, if you'll excuse us for a couple of minutes." He folded his handkerchief carefully and put it in his pocket.

"You can talk here." She got up from the chair. "I'll go out and talk to Mrs. Charles till you're through." She tapped my cheek playfully with the tip of a forefinger as she passed me. "Don't let them say too horrid things about me, Nick."

Andy opened the door for her, shut it behind her, and made the o and the blowing noise again.

I lay down on the bed. "Well," I asked, "what's what?"

Guild cleared his throat. "She told us about finding this here chain and knife on the floor where the Wolf dame had most likely broke it off fighting with Wynant, and she told us the reasons why she'd hid it till now. Between me and you, that don't make any too much sense, looking at it reasonably, but maybe that ain't the way to look at it in this case. To tell you the plain truth, I don't know what to make of her in a lot of ways, I don't for a fact."

"The chief thing," I advised them, "is not to let her tire you out. When you catch her in a lie, she admits it and gives you another lie to take its place and, when you catch her in that one, admits it and gives you still another, and so on. Most people—even women—get discouraged after you've caught them in the third or fourth straight lie and fall back on either the truth or silence, but not Mimi. She keeps trying and you've got to be careful or you'll find yourself believing her, not because she seems to be telling the truth, but simply because you're tired of disbelieving her."

Guild said: "Hm-m-m. Maybe." He put a finger inside his collar. He seemed very uncomfortable. "Look here, do you think she killed that dame?"

I discovered that Andy was staring at me so intently that his eyes bulged. I sat up and put my feet on the floor. "I wish I knew. That chain business looks like a plant, all right, but . . . We can find out whether he had a chain like that, maybe whether he still has it. If she remembered the chain as well as she said she did, there's no reason why she couldn't have told a jeweler how to make one, and anybody can buy a knife and have any initials they want engraved on it. There's plenty to be said against the probability of her having gone that far. If she did plant it, it's more likely she had the original chain—maybe she's had it for years—but all that's something for you folks to check up."

"We're doing the best we can," Guild said patiently. "So you do think she did it?"

"The murder?" I shook my head. "I haven't got that far yet. How about Nunheim? Did the bullets match up?"

"They did—from the same gun as was used on the dame—all five of them."

"He was shot five times?"

"He was, and close enough to burn his clothes."

"I saw his girl, the big red-head, tonight in a speak," I told him. "She's saying you and I killed him because he knew too much."

He said: "Hm-m-m. What speak was that? I might want to talk to her."

"Studsy Burke's Pigiron Club," I said, and gave him the address. "Morelli hangs out there too. He tells me Julia Wolf's real name is Nancy Kane and she has a boy friend doing time in Ohio—Face Peppler."

From the tone of Guild's "Yes?" I imagined he had already found out about Peppler and about Julia's past. "And what else did you pick up in your travels?"

"A friend of mine—Larry Crowley, a press agent—saw Jorgensen coming out of a hock-shop on Sixth near Forty-sixth yesterday afternoon."

"Yes?"

"You don't seem to get excited about my news. I'm—"

Mimi opened the door and came in with glasses, whisky, and mineral water on a tray. "I thought you'd like a drink," she said cheerfully.

We thanked her.

She put the tray on the table, said, "I don't mean to interrupt," smiled at us with that air of amused tolerance which women like to affect towards male gatherings, and went out.

"You were saying something," Guild reminded me.

"Just that if you people think I'm not coming clean with you, you ought to say so. We've been playing along together so far and I wouldn't want—"

"No, no," Guild said hastily, "it's nothing like that, Mr. Charles." His face had reddened a little. "I been— The fact is the Commissioner's been riding us for action and I guess I been kind of passing it on. This second murder's made things tough." He turned to the tray on the table. "How'll you have yours?"

"Straight, thanks. No leads on it?"

"Well, the same gun and a lot of bullets, same as with her, but that's about all. It was a rooming-house hallway in between a couple stores. Nobody there claims they know Nunheim or Wynant or anybody else we can connect. The door's left unlocked, anybody could walk in, but that don't make too much sense when you come to think of it."

"Nobody saw or heard anything?"

"Sure, they heard the shooting, but they didn't see anybody doing it." He gave me a glass of whisky.

"Find any empty shells?" I asked.

He shook his head. "Neither time. Probably a revolver."

"And he emptied it both times—counting the shot that hit her telephone—if, like a lot of people, he carried an empty chamber under the hammer."

Guild lowered the glass he was raising towards his mouth. "You're not trying to find a Chinese angle on it, are you?" he complained, "just because they shoot like that."

"No, but any kind of angle would help some. Find out where Nunheim was the afternoon the girl was killed?"

"Uh-huh. Hanging around the girl's building—part of the time anyhow. He was seen in front and he was seen in back, if you're going to believe people that didn't think much of it at the time and haven't got any reason for lying about it. And the day before the killing he had been up to her apartment, according to an elevator boy. The boy says he came down right away and he don't know whether he got in or not."

I said: "So. Maybe Miriam's right, maybe he did know too much. Find out anything about the four thousand difference between what Macaulay gave her and what Clyde Wynant says he got from her?"

"No."

"Morelli says she always had plenty of money. He says she once lent him five thousand in cash."

Guild raised his eyebrows. "Yes?"

"Yes. He also says Wynant knew about her record."

"Seems to me," Guild said slowly, "Morelli did a lot of talking to you."

"He likes to talk. Find out anything more about what Wynant was working on when he left, or what he was going away to work on?"

"No. You're kind of interested in that shop of his."

"Why not? He's an inventor, the shop's his place. I'd like to have a look at it some time."

"Help yourself. Tell me some more about Morelli, and how you go about getting him to open up."

"He likes to talk. Do you know a fellow called Sparrow? A big fat pale fellow with a pansy voice?"

Guild frowned. "No. Why?"

"He was there—with Miriam—and wanted to take a crack at me, but they wouldn't let him."

"And what'd he want to do that for?"

"I don't know. Maybe because she told him I helped knock Nunheim off—helped you."

Guild said: "Oh." He scratched his chin with a thumb-nail, looked at his watch. "It's getting kind of late. Suppose you drop in and see me some time tomorrow—today."

I said, "Sure," instead of the things I was thinking, nodded at him and Andy, and went out to the living-room.

Nora was sleeping on the sofa. Mimi put down the book she was reading and asked: "Is the secret session over?"

"Yes." I moved towards the sofa.

Mimi said: "Let her sleep awhile, Nick. You're going to stay till after your police friends have gone, aren't you?"

"All right. I want to see Dorothy again."

"But she's asleep."

"That's all right. I'll wake her up."

"But—"

Guild and Andy came in, said their good nights, Guild looked regretfully at the sleeping Nora, and they left.

Mimi sighed. "I'm tired of policemen," she said. "You remember that story?"

"Yes."

Gilbert came in. "Do they really think Chris did it?"

"No," I said.

"Who do they think?"

"I could've told you yesterday. I can't today."

"That's ridiculous," Mimi protested. "They know very well and you know very well that Clyde did it." When I said nothing she repeated more sharply: "You know very well that Clyde did it."

"He didn't," I said.

An expression of triumph brightened Mimi's face. "You *are* working for him, now aren't you?"

My "No" bounced off her with no effect whatever.

Gilbert asked, not argumentatively, but as if he wanted to know: "Why couldn't he?"

"He could've, but he didn't. Would he have written those letters throwing suspicion on Mimi, the one person who's helping him by hiding the chief evidence against him?"

"But maybe he didn't know that. Maybe he thought the police were simply not telling all they knew. They often do that, don't they? Or maybe he thought he could discredit her, so they wouldn't believe her if—"

"That's it," Mimi said. "That's exactly what he did, Nick."

I said to Gilbert: "You don't think he killed her."

"No, I don't think he did, but I'd like to know why you don't think so—you know—your method."

"And I'd like to know yours."

His face flushed a little and there was some embarrassment in his smile. "Oh, but I—it's different."

"He *knows* who killed her," Dorothy said from the doorway. She was still dressed. She stared at me fixedly, as if afraid to look at anybody else. Her face was pale and she held her small body stiffly erect.

Nora opened her eyes, pushed herself up on an elbow, and asked, "What?" sleepily. Nobody answered her.

Mimi said: "Now, Dorry, don't let's have one of those idiotic dramatic performances."

Dorothy said: "You can beat me after they've gone. You will." She said it without taking her eyes off mine.

Mimi tried to look as if she did not know what her daughter was talking about.

"Who does he know killed her?" I asked.

Gilbert said: "You're making an ass of yourself, Dorry, you're—"

I interrupted him: "Let her. Let her say what she's got to say. Who killed her, Dorothy?"

She looked at her brother and lowered her eyes and no longer held herself erect. Looking at the floor, she said indistinctly: "I don't know. He knows." She raised her eyes to mine and began to tremble. "Can't you see I'm afraid?" she cried. "I'm afraid of them. Take me away and I'll tell you, but I'm afraid of them."

Mimi laughed at me. "You asked for it. It serves you right."

Gilbert was blushing. "It's so silly," he mumbled.

I said: "Sure, I'll take you away, but I'd like to have it out now while we're all together."

Dorothy shook her head. "I'm afraid."

Mimi said: "I wish you wouldn't baby her so, Nick. It only makes her worse. She—"

I asked Nora: "What do you say?"

She stood up and stretched without lifting her arms. Her face was pink and lovely as it always is when she has been sleeping. She smiled drowsily at me and said: "Let's go home. I don't like these people. Come on, get your hat and coat, Dorothy."

Mimi said to Dorothy: "Go to bed."

Dorothy put the tips of the fingers of her left hand to her mouth and whimpered through them: "Don't let her beat me, Nick."

I was watching Mimi, whose face wore a placid half-smile, but her nostrils moved with her breathing and I could hear her breathing.

Nora went around to Dorothy. "Come on, we'll wash your face and—"

Mimi made an animal noise in her throat, muscles thickened on the back of her neck, and she put her weight on the balls of her feet.

Nora stepped between Mimi and Dorothy. I caught Mimi by a shoulder as she started forward, put my other arm around her waist from behind, and lifted her off her feet. She screamed and hit back at me with her fists and her hard sharp high heels made dents in my shins.

Nora pushed Dorothy out of the room and stood in the doorway watching us. Her face was very live. I saw it clearly, sharply: everything else was blurred. When clumsy, ineffectual blows on my back and shoulder brought me around to find Gilbert pommeling me, I could see him but dimly and I hardly felt the contact when I shoved him aside. "Cut it out. I don't want to hurt you, Gilbert." I carried Mimi over to the sofa and dumped her on her back on it, sat on her knees, got a wrist in each hand.

Gilbert was at me again. I tried to pop his kneecap, but kicked him too low, kicked his leg from under him. He went down on the floor in a tangle. I kicked at him again, missed, and said: "We can fight afterwards. Get some water."

Mimi's face was becoming purple. Her eyes protruded, glassy, senseless, enormous. Saliva bubbled and hissed between clenched teeth with her breathing, and her red throat—her whole body—was a squirming mass of veins and muscles swollen until it seemed they must burst. Her wrists were hot in my hands and sweat made them hard to hold.

Nora beside me with a glass of water was a welcome sight. "Chuck it in her face," I said.

Nora chucked it. Mimi separated her teeth to gasp and she shut her eyes. She moved her head violently from side to side, but there was less violence in the squirming of her body.

"Do it again," I said.

The second glass of water brought a spluttering protest from Mimi and the fight went out of her body. She lay still, limp, panting.

I took my hands away from her wrists and stood up. Gilbert, standing on one foot, was leaning against a table nursing the leg I had kicked. Dorothy, big-eyed and pale, was in the doorway, undecided whether to come in or run off and hide. Nora, beside me, holding the empty glass in her hand, asked: "Think she's all right?"

"Sure."

Presently Mimi opened her eyes, tried to blink the water out of them. I put a handkerchief in her hand. She wiped her face, gave a long shivering sigh, and sat up on the sofa. She looked around the room, still blinking a little. When she saw me she smiled feebly. There was guilt in her smile, but nothing you could call remorse. She touched her hair with an unsteady hand and said: "I've certainly been drowned."

I said: "Some day you're going into one of those things and not come out of it."

She looked past me at her son. "Gil. What's happened to you?" she asked.

He hastily took his hand off his leg and put his foot down on the floor. "I—uh—nothing," he stammered. "I'm perfectly all right." He smoothed his hair, straightened his necktie.

She began to laugh. "Oh, Gil, did you really try to protect me? And from Nick?" Her laughter increased. "It was awfully sweet of you, but awfully silly. Why, he's a monster, Gil. Nobody could—" She put my handkerchief over her mouth and rocked back and forth.

I looked sidewise at Nora. Her mouth was set and her eyes were almost black with anger. I touched her arm. "Let's blow. Give your mother a drink, Gilbert. She'll be all right in a minute or two."

Dorothy, hat and coat in her hands, tiptoed to the outer door. Nora and I found our hats and coats and followed her out, leaving Mimi laughing into my handkerchief on the sofa.

None of the three of us had much to say in the taxicab that carried us over to the Normandie. Nora was brooding, Dorothy seemed still pretty frightened, and I was tired—it had been a full day.

It was nearly five o'clock when we got home. Asta greeted us boisterously. I lay down on the floor to play with her while Nora went into the pantry to make coffee. Dorothy wanted to tell me something that happened to her when she was a little child.

I said: "No. You tried that Monday. What is it? a gag? It's late. What was it you were afraid to tell me over there?"

"But you'd understand better if you'd let me—"

"You said *that* Monday. I'm not a psychoanalyst. I don't know anything about early influences. I don't give a damn about them. And I'm tired—I been ironing all day."

She pouted at me. "You seem to be trying to make it as hard for me as you can."

"Listen, Dorothy," I said, "you either know something you were afraid to say in front of Mimi and Gilbert or you don't. If you do, spit it out. I'll ask you about any of it I find myself not understanding."

She twisted a fold of her skirt and looked sulkily at it, but when she raised her eyes they became bright and excited. She spoke in a whisper loud enough for anybody in the room to hear: "Gil's been seeing my father and he saw him today and my father told him who killed Miss Wolf."

"Who?"

She shook her head. "He wouldn't tell me. He'd just tell me that."

"And that's what you were afraid to say in front of Gil and Mimi?"

"Yes. You'd understand that if you'd let me tell you—"

"Something that happened when you were a little child. Well, I won't. Stop it. What else did he tell you?"

"Nothing."

"Nothing about Nunheim?"

"No, nothing."

"Where is your father?"

"Gil didn't tell me."

"When did he meet him?"

"He didn't tell me. Please don't be mad, Nick. I've told you everything he told me."

"And a fat lot it is," I growled. "When'd he tell you this?"

"Tonight. He was telling me when you came in my room, and, honest, that's all he told me."

I said: "It'd be swell if just once one of you people would make a clear and complete statement about something—it wouldn't matter what."

Nora came in with the coffee. "What's worrying you now, son?" she asked.

"Things," I said, "riddles, lies, and I'm too old and too tired for them to be any fun. Let's go back to San Francisco."

"Before New Year's?"

"Tomorrow, today."

"I'm willing." She gave me a cup. "We can fly back, if you want, and be there for New Year's Eve."

Dorothy said tremulously: "I didn't lie to you, Nick. I told you everything I— Please, please don't be mad with me. I'm so—" She stopped talking to sob.

I rubbed Asta's head and groaned.

Nora said: "We're all worn out and jumpy. Let's send the pup downstairs for the night and turn in and do our talking after we've had some rest. Come on, Dorothy, I'll bring your coffee into the bedroom and give you some night-clothes."

Dorothy got up, said, "Good-night," to me, "I'm sorry I'm so silly," and followed Nora out.

When Nora returned she sat down on the floor beside me. "Our Dorry does her share of weeping and whining," she said. "Admitting life's not too pleasant for her just now, still . . ." She yawned. "What was her fearsome secret?"

I told her what Dorothy had told me. "It sounds like a lot of hooey."

"Why?"

"Why not? Everything else we've got from them has been hooey."

Nora yawned again. "That may be good enough for a detective, but it's not convincing enough for me. Listen, why don't we make a list of all the suspects and all the motives and clues, and check them off against—"

"You do it. I'm going to bed. What's a clue, Mamma?"

"It's like when Gilbert tiptoed over to the phone tonight when I was alone in the living-room, and he thought I was asleep, and told the operator not to put through any in-coming calls until morning."

"Well, well."

"And," she said, "it's like Dorothy discovering that she had Aunt Alice's key all the time."

"Well, well."

"And it's like Studsy nudging Morelli under the table when he started to tell you about the drunken cousin of—what was it?—Dick O'Brien's that Julia Wolf knew."

I got up and put our cups on a table. "I don't see how any detective can hope to get along without being married to you, but, just the same, you're overdoing it. Studsy nudging Morelli is my idea of something to spend a lot of time not worrying about. I'd rather worry about whether they pushed Sparrow around to keep me from being hurt or to keep me from being told something. I'm sleepy."

"So am I. Tell me something, Nick. Tell me the truth: when you were wrestling with Mimi, didn't you have an erection?"

"Oh, a little."

She laughed and got up from the floor. "If you aren't a disgusting old lecher," she said. "Look, it's daylight."

26

NORA shook me awake at quarter past ten. "The telephone," she said. "It's Herbert Macaulay and he says it's important."

I went into the bedroom—I had slept in the living-room—to the telephone. Dorothy was sleeping soundly. I mumbled, "Hello," into the telephone.

Macaulay said: "It's too early for that lunch, but I've got to see you right away. Can I come up now?"

"Sure. Come up for breakfast."

"I've had it. Get yours and I'll be up in fifteen minutes."

"Right."

Dorothy opened her eyes less than half-way, said, "It must be late," sleepily, turned over, and returned to unconsciousness.

I put cold water on my face and hands, brushed my teeth and hair, and went back to the living-room. "He's coming up," I told Nora. "He's had breakfast, but you'd better order some coffee for him. I want chicken livers."

"Am I invited to your party or do I—"

"Sure. You've never met Macaulay, have you? He's a pretty good guy. I was attached to his outfit for a few days once, up around Vaux, and we looked each other up after the war. He threw a couple of jobs my way, including the Wynant one. How about a drop of something to cut the phlegm?"

"Why don't you stay sober today?"

"We didn't come to New York to stay sober. Want to see a hockey game tonight?"

"I'd like to." She poured me a drink and went to order breakfast.

I looked through the morning papers. They had the news of Jorgensen's being picked up by the Boston police and of Nunheim's murder, but further developments of what the tabloids called "The Hell's Kitchen Gang War," the arrest of "Prince Mike" Gerguson, and an interview with the "Jafsie" of the Lindbergh kidnapping negotiations got more space.

Macaulay and the bellboy who brought Asta up arrived together. Asta liked Macaulay because when he patted her he gave her something to set her weight against: she was never very fond of gentleness.

He had lines around his mouth this morning and some of the rosiness was gone from his cheeks. "Where'd the police get this new line?" he asked. "Do they think—" He broke off as Nora came in. She had dressed.

"Nora, this is Herbert Macaulay," I said. "My wife."

They shook hands and Nora said: "Nick would only let me order some coffee for you. Can't I—"

"No, thanks, I've just finished breakfast."

I said: "Now what's this about the police?"

He hesitated.

"Nora knows practically everything I know," I assured him, "so unless it's something you'd rather not—"

"No, no, nothing like that," he said. "It's—well—for Mrs. Charles's sake. I don't want to cause her anxiety."

"Then out with it. She only worries about things she doesn't know. What's the new police line?"

"Lieutenant Guild came to see me this morning," he said. "First he showed me a piece of watch-chain with a knife attached to it and asked me if I'd ever seen them before. I had: they were Wynant's. I told him I thought I had: I thought they looked like Wynant's. Then he asked me if I knew of any way in which they could have come into anybody else's possession and, after some beating about the bush, I discovered that by anybody else he meant you or Mimi. I told him certainly—Wynant could have given them to either of you, you could have stolen them or found them on the street or have been given them by somebody who stole them or found them on the street, or you could have got them from somebody Wynant gave them to. There were other ways, too, for you to have got them, I told him, but he knew I was kidding him, so he wouldn't let me tell him about them."

There were spots of color in Nora's cheeks and her eyes were dark. "The idiot!"

"Now, now," I said. "Maybe I should have warned you—he was heading in that direction last night. I think it's likely my old pal Mimi gave him a prod or two. What else did he turn the searchlight on?"

"He wanted to know about—what he asked was: 'Do you figure Charles and the Wolf dame was still playing around together? Or was that all washed up?'"

"That's the Mimi touch, all right," I said. "What'd you tell him?"

"I told him I didn't know whether you were 'still' playing around together because I didn't know that you had ever played around together, and reminded him that you hadn't been living in New York for a long time anyway."

Nora asked me: "Did you?"

I said: "Don't try to make a liar out of Mac. What'd he say to that?"

"Nothing. He asked me if I thought Jorgensen knew about you and

Mimi and, when I asked him what about you and Mimi, he accused me of acting the innocent—they were his words—so we didn't get very far. He was interested in the times I had seen you, also, where and when to the exact inch and second."

"That's nice," I said. "I've got lousy alibis."

A waiter came in with our breakfast. We talked about this and that until he had set the table and gone away.

Then Macaulay said: "You've nothing to be afraid of. I'm going to turn Wynant over to the police." His voice was unsteady and a little choked.

"Are you sure he did it?" I asked. "I'm not."

He said simply: "I know." He cleared his throat. "Even if there was a chance in a thousand of my being wrong—and there isn't—he's a madman, Charles. He shouldn't be loose."

"That's probably right enough," I began, "and if you know—"

"I know," he repeated. "I saw him the afternoon he killed her; it couldn't've been half an hour after he'd killed her, though I didn't know that, didn't even know she'd been killed. I—well—I know it now."

"You met him in Hermann's office?"

"What?"

"You were supposed to have been in the office of a man named Hermann, on Fifty-seventh Street, from around three o'clock till around four that afternoon. At least, that's what the police told me."

"That's right," he said. "I mean that's the story they got. What really happened: after I failed to find Wynant or any news of him at the Plaza and phoned my office and Julia with no better results, I gave him up and started walking down to Hermann's. He's a mining engineer, a client of mine; I had just finished drawing up some articles of incorporation for him, and there were some minor changes to be made in them. When I got to Fifty-seventh Street I suddenly got a feeling that I was being followed—you know the feeling. I couldn't think of any reason for anybody shadowing me, but, still, I'm a lawyer and there might be. Anyhow, I wanted to find out, so I turned east on Fifty-seventh and walked over to Madison and still wasn't sure. There was a small sallow man I thought I'd seen around the Plaza, but— The quickest way to find out seemed to be by taking a taxi, so I did that and told the driver to drive east. There was too much traffic there for me to see whether this small man or anybody else took a taxi after me, so I had my driver turn south at Third, east again on Fifty-sixth, and south again on Second Avenue, and by that time I was pretty sure a yellow taxi was following me. I couldn't see whether my small man was in it, of course; it wasn't close enough for that. And at the next corner, when a red light stopped us, I saw Wynant. He was in a taxicab going west on Fifty-fifth Street. Naturally, that didn't surprise me very much: we were only two blocks from

Julia's and I took it for granted she hadn't wanted me to know he was there when I phoned and that he was now on his way over to meet me at the Plaza. He was never very punctual. So I told my driver to turn west, but at Lexington Avenue—we were half a block behind him—Wynant's taxicab turned south. That wasn't the way to the Plaza and wasn't even the way to my office, so I said to hell with him and turned my attention back to the taxi following me—and it wasn't there any more. I kept a look-out behind all the way over to Hermann's and saw no sign at all of anybody following me."

"What time was it when you saw Wynant?" I asked.

"It must've been fifteen or twenty minutes past three. It was twenty minutes to four when I got to Hermann's and I imagine that was twenty or twenty-five minutes later. Well, Hermann's secretary—Louise Jacobs, the girl I was with when I saw you last night—told me he had been locked up in a conference all afternoon, but would probably be through in a few minutes, and he was, and I got through with him in ten or fifteen minutes and went back to my office."

"I take it you weren't close enough to Wynant to see whether he looked excited, was wearing his watch-chain, smelled of gunpowder—things like that."

"That's right. All I saw was his profile going past, but don't think I'm not sure it was Wynant."

"I won't. Go ahead," I said.

"He didn't phone again. I'd been back about an hour when the police phoned—Julia was dead. Now you must understand that I didn't think Wynant had killed her—not for a minute. You can understand that —you still don't think he did. So when I went over there and the police began to ask me questions about him and I could see they suspected him, I did what ninety-nine out of a hundred lawyers would've done for their clients—I said nothing about having seen him in that neighborhood at about the time that the murder must have been committed. I told them what I told you—about having the date with him and him not showing up—and let them understand that I had gone over to Hermann's straight from the Plaza."

"That's understandable enough," I agreed. "There was no sense in your saying anything until you had heard his side of the story."

"Exactly and, well, the catch is I never heard his side of the story. I'd expected him to show up, phone me, something, but he didn't—until Tuesday, when I got that letter from him from Philadelphia, and there was not a word in it about his failure to meet me Friday, nothing about —but you saw the letter. What'd you think of it?"

"You mean did it sound guilty?"

"Yes."

"Not particularly," I said. "It's about what could be expected from him if he didn't kill her—no great alarm over the police suspecting him except as it might interfere with his work, a desire to have it all cleaned up with no inconvenience to him—not too bright a letter to have come from anybody else, but in line with his particular form of goofiness. I can see him sending it off without the faintest notion that the best thing he could do would be to account for his own actions on the day of the murder. How sure are you he was coming from Julia's when you saw him?"

"I'm sure now. I thought it likely at first. Then I thought he may have been to his shop. It's on First Avenue, just a few blocks from where I saw him, and, though it's been closed since he went away, we renewed the lease last month and everything's there waiting for him to come back to it, and he could have been there that afternoon. The police couldn't find anything there to show whether he had or hadn't."

"I meant to ask you: there was some talk about his having grown whiskers. Was he—"

"No—the same long bony face with the same ragged near-white mustache."

"Another thing: there was a fellow named Nunheim killed yesterday, a small—"

"I'm coming to that," he said.

"I was thinking about the little fellow you thought might be shadowing you."

Macaulay stared at me. "You mean that might've been Nunheim?"

"I don't know. I was wondering."

"And I don't know," he said. "I never saw Nunheim, far as I—"

"He was a little fellow, not more than five feet three, and would weigh maybe a hundred and twenty. I'd say he was thirty-five or -six. Sallow, dark hair and eyes, with the eyes set pretty close together, big mouth, long limp nose, bat-wing ears—shifty-looking."

"That could easily be him," he said, "though I didn't get too close a view of my man. I suppose the police would let me see him"—he shrugged—"not that it matters now. Where was I? Oh, yes, about not being able to get in touch with Wynant. That put me in an uncomfortable position, since the police clearly thought I was in touch with him and lying about it. So did you, didn't you?"

"Yes," I admitted.

"And you also, like the police, probably suspected that I *had* met him, either at the Plaza or later, on the day of the murder."

"It seemed possible."

"Yes. And of course you were partly right. I had at least seen him, and seen him at a place and time that would've spelled Guilty with a capital G to the police, so, having lied instinctively and by inference, I now lied directly and deliberately. Hermann had been tied up in a conference all that afternoon and didn't know how long I had been waiting to see him. Louise Jacobs is a good friend of mine. Without going into details, I told her she could help me help a client by saying I had arrived there at a minute or two after three o'clock and she agreed readily enough. To protect her in case of trouble, I told her that if anything went wrong she could always say that she hadn't remembered what time I arrived, but that I, the next day, had casually mentioned my arrival at that time and she had no reason for doubting me—throwing the whole thing on me." Macaulay took a deep breath. "None of that's important now. What's important is that I heard from Wynant this morning."

"Another one of those screwy letters?" I asked.

"No, he phoned. I made a date with him for tonight—for you and me. I told him you wouldn't do anything for him unless you could see him, so he promised to meet us tonight. I'm going to take the police, of course. I can't go on justifying my shielding him like this. I can get him an acquittal on grounds of insanity and have him put away. That's all I can do, all I want to do."

"Have you told the police yet?"

"No. He didn't phone till just after they'd left. Anyway, I wanted to see you first. I wanted to tell you I hadn't forgotten what I owed you and—"

"Nonsense," I said.

"It's not." He turned to Nora. "I don't suppose he ever told you he saved my life once in a shell-hole in—"

"He's nuts," I told her. "He fired at a fellow and missed and I fired at him and didn't and that's all there was to it." I addressed him again: "Why don't you let the police wait awhile? Suppose you and I keep this date tonight and hear what he's got to say. We can sit on him and blow whistles when the meeting's about to break up if we're convinced he's the murderer."

Macaulay smiled wearily. "You're still doubtful, aren't you? Well, I'm willing to do it that way if you want, though it seems like a— But perhaps you'll change your mind when I tell you about our telephone conversation."

Dorothy, wearing a nightgown and a robe of Nora's, both much too long for her, came in yawning. "Oh!" she exclaimed when she saw Macaulay, and then, when she had recognized him, "Oh, hello, Mr. Macaulay. I didn't know you were here. Is there any news of my father?"

He looked at me. I shook my head. He told her: "Not yet, but perhaps we'll have some today."

I said: "Dorothy's had some, indirectly. Tell Macaulay about Gilbert."

"You mean about—about my father?" she asked hesitantly, staring at the floor.

"Oh, dear me, no," I said.

Her face flushed and she glanced reproachfully at me; then, hastily, she told Macaulay: "Gil saw my father yesterday and he told Gil who killed Miss Wolf."

"What?"

She nodded four or five times, earnestly.

Macaulay looked at me with puzzled eyes.

"This doesn't have to've happened," I reminded him. "It's what Gil says happened."

"I see. Then you think he might be—?"

"You haven't done much talking to that family since hell broke loose, have you?" I asked.

"No."

"It's an experience. They're all sex-crazy, I think, and it backs up into their heads. They start off—"

Dorothy said angrily: "I think you're horrid. I've done my best to—"

"What are you kicking about?" I demanded. "I'm giving you the break this time: I'm willing to believe Gil did tell you that. Don't expect too much of me."

Macaulay asked: "And who killed her?"

"I don't know. Gil wouldn't tell me."

"Had your brother seen him often?"

"I don't know how often. He said he had been seeing him."

"And was anything said—well—about the man Nunheim?"

"No. Nick asked me that. He didn't tell me anything else at all."

I caught Nora's eye and made signals. She stood up saying: "Let's go in the other room, Dorothy, and give these lads a chance to do whatever it is they think they're doing."

Dorothy went reluctantly, but she went out with Nora.

Macaulay said: "She's grown up to be something to look at." He cleared his throat. "I hope your wife won't—"

"Forget it. Nora's all right. You started to tell me about your conversation with Wynant."

"He phoned right after the police left and said he'd seen the ad in the *Times* and wanted to know what I wanted. I told him you weren't anxious to get yourself mixed up in his troubles and had said you wouldn't touch it at all without talking it over with him first, and we made the date for tonight. Then he asked if I'd seen Mimi and I told him I'd seen her once or twice since her return from Europe and had also seen his daughter. And then he said this: 'If my wife should ask for money, give her any sum in reason.'"

"I'll be damned," I said.

Macaulay nodded. "That's the way I felt about it. I asked him why and he said what he'd read in the morning papers had convinced him that she was Rosewater's dupe, not his confederate, and he had reason to believe she was 'kindly disposed' towards him, Wynant. I began to see what he was up to, then, and I told him she had already turned the knife and chain over to the police. And try to guess what he said to that."

"I give up."

"He hemmed and hawed a bit—not much, mind you—and then as smooth as you like asked: 'You mean the chain and knife on the watch I left with Julia to be repaired?' "

I laughed. "What'd you say?"

"That stumped me. Before I could think up an answer he was saying: 'However, we can discuss that more fully when we meet tonight.' I asked him where and when we'd meet him and he said he'd have to phone me, he didn't know where he'd be. He's to phone me at my house at ten o'clock. He was in a hurry now, though he had seemed leisurely enough before, and hadn't time to answer any of the things I wanted to ask, so he hung up and I phoned you. What do you think of his innocence now?"

"Not as much as I did," I replied slowly. "How sure are you of hearing from him at ten tonight?"

Macaulay shrugged. "You know as much about that as I do."

"Then if I were you I wouldn't bother the police till we've grabbed our wild man and can turn him over to them. This story of yours isn't going to make them exactly love you and, even if they don't throw you in the can right away, they'll make things pretty disagreeable for you if Wynant gives us a run-around tonight."

"I know, but I'd like to get the load off my shoulders."

"A few hours more oughtn't to matter much," I said. "Did either of you say anything about his not keeping the date at the Plaza?"

"No. I didn't get a chance to ask him. Well, if you say wait, I'll wait, but—"

"Let's wait till tonight, anyhow, till he phones you—if he does—and then we can make up our minds whether to take the police along."

"You don't think he'll phone?"

"I'm not too sure," I said. "He didn't keep his last date with you, and he seems to have gone pretty vague on you as soon as he learned that Mimi had turned in the watch-chain and knife. I wouldn't be too optimistic about it. We'll see, though. I'd better get out to your house at about nine o'clock, hadn't I?"

"Come for dinner."

"I can't, but I'll make it as early as I can, in case he's ahead of time. We'll want to move fast. Where do you live?"

Macaulay gave me his address, in Scarsdale, and stood up. "Will you say good-by to Mrs. Charles for me and thank— Oh, by the way, I hope you didn't misunderstand me about Harrison Quinn last night. I meant only just what I said, that I'd had bad luck taking his advice on the market. I didn't mean to insinuate that there was anything—you know—or that he might not've made money for his other customers."

"I understand," I said, and called Nora.

She and Macaulay shook hands and made polite speeches to each other and he pushed Asta around a little and said, "Make it as early as you can," to me and went away.

"There goes the hockey game," I said, "unless you find somebody else to go with."

"Did I miss anything?" Nora asked.

"Not much." I told her what Macaulay had told me. "And don't ask me what I think of it. I don't know. I know Wynant's crazy, but he's not acting like a crazy man and he's not acting like a murderer. He's acting like a man playing some kind of game. God only knows what the game is."

"I think," she said, "that he's shielding somebody else."

"Why don't you think he did it?"

She looked surprised. "Because you don't."

I said that was a swell reason. "Who is the somebody else?"

"I don't know yet. Now don't make fun of me: I've thought about it a lot. It wouldn't be Macaulay, because he's using him to help shield whoever it is and—"

"And it wouldn't be me," I suggested, "because he wants to use me."

"That's right," she said, "and you're going to feel very silly if you make fun of me and then I guess who it is before you do. And it wouldn't be either Mimi or Jorgensen, because he tried to throw suspicion on them. And it wouldn't be Nunheim, because he was most likely killed by the same person and, furthermore, wouldn't have to be shielded now. And it wouldn't be Morelli, because Wynant was jealous of him and they'd had a row." She frowned at me. "I wish you'd found out more about that big fat man they called Sparrow and that big red-haired woman."

"But how about Dorothy and Gilbert?"

"I wanted to ask you about them. Do you think he's got any very strong paternal feeling for them?"

"No."

"You're probably just trying to discourage me," she said. "Well, knowing them, it's hard to think either of them might've been guilty, but I tried to throw out my personal feelings and stick to logic. Before I went to sleep last night I made a list of all the—"

"There's nothing like a little logic-sticking to ward off insomnia. It's like—"

"Don't be so damned patronizing. Your performance so far has been a little less than dazzling."

"I didn't mean no harm," I said and kissed her. "That a new dress?"

"Ah! Changing the subject, you coward."

27

I went to see Guild early in the afternoon and went to work on him as soon as we had shaken hands. "I didn't bring my lawyer along. I thought it looked better if I came by myself."

He wrinkled his forehead and shook his head as if I had hurt him. "Now it was nothing like that," he said patiently.

"It was too much like that."

He sighed. "I wouldn't've thought you'd make the mistake that a lot of people make thinking just because we— You know we got to look at every angle, Mr. Charles."

"That sounds familiar. Well, what do you want to know?"

"All I want to know is who killed her—and him."

"Try asking Gilbert," I suggested.

Guild pursed his lips. "Why him exactly?"

"He told his sister he knew who did it, told her he got it from Wynant."

"You mean he's been seeing the old man?"

"So she says he said. I haven't had a chance to ask him about it."

He squinted his watery eyes at me. "Just what is that lay-out over there, Mr. Charles?"

"The Jorgensen family? You probably know as much about it as I do."

"I don't," he said, "and that's a fact. I just can't size them up at all. This Mrs. Jorgensen, now, what is she?"

"A blonde."

He nodded gloomily. "Uh-huh, and that's all I know. But look, you've known them a long time and from what she says you and her—"

"And me and her daughter," I said, "and me and Julia Wolf and me and Mrs. Astor. I'm hell with the women."

He held up a hand. "I'm not saying I believe everything she says, and there's nothing to get sore about. You're taking the wrong attitude, if you don't mind me saying it. You're acting like you thought we were out to get you, and that's all wrong, absolutely all wrong."

"Maybe, but you've been talking double to me ever since last—"

He looked at me with steady pale eyes and said calmly: "I'm a copper and I got my work to do."

"That's reasonable enough. You told me to come in today. What do you want?"

"I didn't tell you to come in, I asked you."

"All right. What do you want?"

"I don't want this," he said. "I don't want anything like this. We've been talking man to man up to this time and I'd kind of like to go on thataway."

"You made the change."

"I don't think that's a fact. Look here, Mr. Charles, would you take your oath, or even just tell me straight out, that you've been emptying your pockets to me right along?"

There was no use saying yes—he would not have believed me. I said: "Practically."

"Practically, yes," he grumbled. "Everybody's been telling me practically the whole truth. What I want's some impractical son of a gun that'll shoot the works."

I could sympathize with him: I knew how he felt. I said: "Maybe nobody you've found knows the whole truth."

He made an unpleasant face. "That's very likely, ain't it? Listen, Mr. Charles, I've talked to everybody I could find. If you can find any more for me, I'll talk to them too. You mean Wynant? Don't you suppose we got every facility the department's got working night and day trying to turn him up?"

"There's his son," I suggested.

"There's his son," he agreed. He called in Andy and a swarthy bow-legged man named Kline. "Get me that Wynant kid—the punk—I want to talk to him." They went out. He said: "See, I want people to talk to."

I said: "Your nerves are in pretty bad shape this afternoon, aren't they? Are you bringing Jorgensen down from Boston?"

He shrugged his big shoulders. "His story listens all right to me. I don't know. Want to tell me what you think of it?"

"Sure."

"I'm kind of jumpy this afternoon, for a fact," he said. "I didn't get a single solitary wink of sleep last night. It's a hell of a life. I don't know why I stick at it. A fellow can get a piece of land and some wire fencing and a few head of silver fox and— Well, anyways, when you people scared Jorgensen off back in '25, he says he lit out for Germany, leaving his wife in the lurch—though he don't say much about that—and changing his name to give you more trouble finding him, and on the same account he's afraid to work at his regular job—he calls himself some kind of a technician or something—so pickings are kind of slim. He says he worked at one thing and another, whatever he could get, but near as I can figure out he was mostly gigoloing, if you know what I mean, and not finding too many heavy-money dames. Well, along about '27 or '28 he's in Milan—that's a city in Italy—and he sees in the Paris *Herald* where this Mimi, recently divorced wife of Clyde Miller Wynant, has arrived in Paris. He don't know her personally and she don't know him, but he knows she's a dizzy blonde that likes men and fun and hasn't got much sense. He figures a bunch of Wynant's dough must've come to her with the divorce and, the way he looks at it, any of it he could take away from her wouldn't be any more than what Wynant had gypped him out of—he'd only be getting some of what belonged to him. So he scrapes up the fare to Paris and goes up there. All right so far?"

"Sounds all right."

"That's what I thought. Well, he don't have any trouble getting to know her in Paris—either picking her up or getting somebody to introduce him or whatever happened—and the rest of it's just as easy. She goes for him in a big way—bing, according to him—right off the bat, and the first thing you know she's one jump ahead of him, she's thinking about marrying him. Naturally he don't try to talk her out of that. She'd gotten a lump sum—two hundred thousand berries, by God!—out of Wynant instead of alimony, so her marrying again wasn't stopping any payments, and it'll put him right in the middle of the cash-drawer. So they do it. According to him, it was a trick marriage up in some mountains he says are between Spain and France and was done by a Spanish priest on what was really French soil, which don't make it legal, but I figure he's just trying to discourage a bigamy rap. Personally, I don't care one way or the other. The point is he got his hands on the dough and kept them on it till there wasn't any more dough. And all this time, understand, he says she didn't know he was anybody but Christian Jorgensen, a fellow she met in Paris, and still didn't know it up to the time we grabbed him in Boston. Still sound all right?"

"Still sounds all right," I said, "except, as you say, about the marriage, and even that could be all right."

"Uh-huh, and what difference does it make anyways? So comes the winter and the bank-roll's getting skinny and he's getting ready to take a run-out on her with the last of it, and then she says maybe they could come back to America and tap Wynant for some more. He thinks that's fair enough if it can be done, and she thinks it can be done, so they get on a boat and—"

"The story cracks a little there," I said.

"What makes you think so? He's not figuring on going to Boston, where he knows his first wife is, and he's figuring on keeping out of the way of the few people that know him, including especially Wynant, and somebody's told him there's a statute of limitation making everything just lovely after seven years. He don't figure he's running much risk. They ain't going to stay here long."

"I still don't like that part of his story," I insisted, "but go ahead."

"Well, the second day he's here—while they're still trying to find Wynant—he gets a bad break. He runs into a friend of his first wife's—

this Olga Fenton—on the street and she recognizes him. He tries to talk her out of tipping off the first wife and does manage to stall her along a couple days with a moving-picture story he makes up—what an imagination that guy's got!—but he don't fool her long, and she goes to her parson and tells him about it and asks him what she ought to do and he says she ought to tell the first wife, and so she does, and the next time she sees Jorgensen she tells him what she'd done, and he lights out for Boston to try to keep his wife from kicking up trouble and we pick him up there."

"How about his visit to the hock-shop?" I asked.

"That was part of it. He says there was a train for Boston leaving in a few minutes and he didn't have any dough with him and didn't have time to go home for some—besides not being anxious to face the second wife till he had the first one quieted down—and the banks were closed, so he soaked his watch. It checks up."

"Did you see the watch?"

"I can. Why?"

"I was wondering. You don't think it was once on the other end of that piece of chain Mimi turned over to you?"

He sat up straight. "By God!" Then he squinted at me suspiciously and asked: "Do you know anything about it or are you—"

"No. I was just wondering. What does he say about the murders now? Who does he think did them?"

"Wynant. He admits for a while he thought Mimi might've, but he says she convinced him different. He claims she wouldn't tell him what she had on Wynant. He might be just trying to cover himself up on that. I don't guess there's any doubt about them meaning to use it to shake him down for that money they wanted."

"Then you don't think she planted the knife and chain?"

Guild pulled down the ends of his mouth. "She could've planted them to shake him down with. What's wrong with that?"

"It's a little complicated for a fellow like me," I said. "Find out if Face Peppler's still in the Ohio pen?"

"Uh-huh. He gets out next week. That accounts for the diamond ring. He had a pal of his on the outside send it to her for him. Seems they were planning to get married and go straight together after he got out, or some such. Anyways, the warden says he saw letters passing between them reading like that. This Peppler won't tell the warden that he knows anything that'll help us, and the warden don't call to mind anything that was in their letters that's any good to us. Of course, even this much helps some, with the motive. Say Wynant's jealous and she's wearing this other guy's ring and getting ready to go away with him. That'll—" he broke off to answer his telephone. "Yes," he said into it. "Yes. . . . What? . . . Sure. . . . Sure, but leave somebody there. . . . That's right." He pushed the telephone aside. "Another bum steer on that West Twenty-ninth Street killing yesterday."

"Oh," I said. "I thought I heard Wynant's name. You know how some telephone voices carry."

He blushed, cleared his throat. "Maybe something sounded like it —*why not*, I guess. Uh-huh, that could sound like it—*why not*. I almost forgot: we looked up that fellow Sparrow for you."

"What'd you find out?"

"It looks like there's nothing there for us. His name's Jim Brophy. It figures out that he was making a play for that girl of Nunheim's and she was sore at you and he was just drunk enough to think he could put himself in solid with her by taking a poke at you."

"A nice idea," I said. "I hope you didn't make any trouble for Studsy."

"A friend of yours? He's an ex-con, you know, with a record as long as your arm."

"Sure. I sent him over once." I started to gather up my hat and overcoat. "You're busy. I'll run along and—"

"No, no," he said. "Stick around if you got the time. I got a couple things coming in that'll maybe interest you, and you can give me a hand with that Wynant kid, too, maybe."

I sat down again.

"Maybe you'd like a drink," he suggested, opening a drawer of his desk, but I had never had much luck with policemen's liquor, so I said: "No, thanks."

His telephone rang again and he said into it: "Yes. . . . Yes. . . . That's all right. Come on in." This time no words leaked out to me.

He rocked back in his chair and put his feet on his desk. "Listen, I'm on the level about that silver fox farming and I want to ask you what you think of California for a place."

I was trying to decide whether to tell him about the lion and ostrich farms in the lower part of the state when the door opened and a fat red-haired man brought Gilbert Wynant in. One of Gilbert's eyes was completely shut by swollen flesh around it and his left knee showed through a tear in his pants-leg.

28

I said to Guild: "When you say bring 'em in, they bring 'em in, don't they?"

"Wait," he told me. "This is more'n you think." He addressed the fat red-haired man: "Go ahead, Flint, let's have it."

Flint wiped his mouth with the back of a hand. "He's a wildcat for fair, the young fellow. He don't look tough, but, man, he didn't want to come along, I can tell you that. And can he run!"

Guild growled: "You're a hero and I'll see the Commissioner about your medal right away, but never mind that now. Talk turkey."

"I wasn't saying I did anything great," Flint protested. "I was just—"

"I don't give a damn what you did," Guild said. "I want to know what he did."

"Yes, sir, I was getting to that. I relieved Morgan at eight o'clock this morning and everything went along smooth and quiet as per usual, with not a creature was stirring, as the fellow says, till along about ten minutes after two, and then what do I hear but a key in the lock." He sucked in his lips and gave us a chance to express our amazement.

"The Wolf dame's apartment," Guild explained to me. "I had a hunch."

"And what a hunch!" Flint exclaimed, practically top-heavy with admiration. "Man, what a hunch!" Guild glared at him and he went on hastily: "Yes, sir, a key, and then the door opens and this young fellow comes in." He grinned proudly, affectionately, at Gilbert. "Scared stiff, he looked, and when I went for him he was out and away like a streak and it wasn't till the first floor that I caught him, and then, by golly, he put up a tussle and I had to bat him in the eye to tone him down. He don't look tough, but—"

"What'd he do in the apartment?" Guild asked.

"He didn't have a chance to do nothing. I—"

"You mean you jumped him without waiting to see what he was up to?" Guild's neck bulged over the edge of his collar, and his face was as red as Flint's hair.

"I thought it was best not to take no chances."

Guild stared at me with angry incredulous eyes. I did my best to keep my face blank. He said in a choking voice: "That'll do, Flint. Wait outside."

The red-haired man seemed puzzled. He said, "Yes, sir," slowly. "Here's his key." He put the key on Guild's desk and went to the door. There he twisted his head over a shoulder to say: "He claims he's Clyde Wynant's son." He laughed merrily.

Guild, still having trouble with his voice, said: "Oh, he does, does he?"

"Yeah. I seen him somewhere before. I got an idea he used to belong to Big Shorty Dolan's mob. Seems to me I used to see him around—"

"Get out!" Guild snarled, and Flint got out. Guild groaned from deep down in his big body. "That mugg gets me. Big Shorty Dolan's mob. Christ." He shook his head hopelessly and addressed Gilbert: "Well, son?"

Gilbert said: "I know I shouldn't've done it."

"That's a fair start," Guild said genially. His face was becoming normal again. "We all make mistakes. Pull yourself up a chair and let's see what we can do about getting you out of the soup. Want anything for that eye?"

"No, thank you, it's quite all right." Gilbert moved a chair two or three inches towards Guild and sat down.

"Did that bum smack you just to be doing something?"

"No, no, it was my fault. I—I did resist."

"Oh, well," Guild said, "nobody likes to be arrested, I guess. Now what's the trouble?"

Gilbert looked at me with his one good eye.

"You're in as bad a hole as Lieutenant Guild wants to put you," I told him. "You'll make it easy for yourself by making it easy for him."

Guild nodded earnestly. "And that's a fact." He settled himself comfortably in his chair and asked, in a friendly tone: "Where'd you get the key?"

"My father sent it to me in his letter." He took a white envelope from his pocket and gave it to Guild.

I went around behind Guild and looked at the envelope over his shoulder. The address was typewritten, *Mr. Gilbert Wynant, The Courtland*, and there was no postage stamp stuck on it.

"When'd you get it?" I asked.

"It was at the desk when I got in last night, around ten o'clock. I didn't ask the clerk how long it had been there, but I don't suppose it was there when I went out with you, or they'd have given it to me."

Inside the envelope were two sheets of paper covered with the familiar unskillful typewriting. Guild and I read together:

Dear Gilbert:

If all these years have gone by without my having communicated with you, it is only because your mother wished it so and if now I break this silence with a request for your assistance it is because only great need could make me go against your mother's wishes. Also you are a man now and I feel that you yourself are the one to decide whether or not we should go on being strangers or whether we should act in accordance with our ties of blood. That I am in an embarrassing situation now in connection with Julia Wolf's so-called murder I think you know and I trust that you still have remaining enough affection for me to at least hope that I am in all ways guiltless of any complicity therein, which is indeed the case. I turn to you now for help in demonstrating my innocence once and for all to the police and to the world with every confidence that even could I not count on your affection for me I nevertheless could count on your natural desire to do anything within your power to keep

*unblemished the name that is yours and your sister's as well as
your Father's. I turn to you also because while I have a lawyer
who is able and who believes in my innocence and who is leaving no stone unturned to prove it and have hopes of engaging
Mr. Nick Charles to assist him I cannot ask either of them to
undertake what is after all a patently illegal act nor do I know
anybody else except you that I dare confide in. What I wish you
to do is this, tomorrow go to Julia Wolf's apartment at 411 East
54th St. to which the enclosed key will admit you and between
the pages of a book called* The Grand Manner *you will find a
certain paper or statement which you are to read and destroy
immediately. You are to be sure you destroy it completely leaving not so much as an ash and when you have read it you will
know why this must be done and will understand why I have
entrusted this task to you. In the event that something should
develop to make a change in our plans advisable I will call you
on the telephone late tonight. If you do not hear from me I will
telephone you tomorrow evening to learn if you have carried out
my instructions and to make arrangements for a meeting. I
have every confidence that you will realize the tremendous responsibility I am placing on your shoulders and that my confidence is not misplaced.*

Affectionately,
    Your Father

Wynant's sprawling signature was written in ink beneath "Your
Father."

Guild waited for me to say something. I waited for him. After a
little of that he asked Gilbert: "And did he phone?"

"No, sir."

"How do you know?" I asked. "Didn't you tell the operator not to
put any calls through?"

"I—yes, I did. I was afraid you'd find out who it was if he called up
while you were there, but he'd've left some kind of message with the
operator, I think, and he didn't."

"Then you haven't been seeing him?"

"No."

"And he didn't tell you who killed Julia Wolf?"

"No."

"You were lying to Dorothy?"

He lowered his head and nodded at the floor. "I was—it was—I suppose it was jealousy really." He looked up at me now and his face was
pink. "You see, Dorry used to look up to me and think I knew more than
anybody else about almost everything and—you know—she'd come to me
if there was anything she wanted to know and she always did what I told

her, and then, when she got to seeing you, it was different. She looked up to you and respected you more— She naturally would, I mean, she'd've been silly if she hadn't, because there's no comparison, of course, but I —I suppose I was jealous and resented—well, not exactly resented it, because I looked up to you too—but I wanted to do something to impress her again—show off, I guess you'd call it—and when I got that letter I pretended I'd been seeing my father and he'd told me who committed those murders, so she'd think I knew things even you didn't." He stopped, out of breath, and wiped his face with a handkerchief.

I outwaited Guild again until presently he said: "Well, I guess there ain't been a great deal of harm done, sonny, if you're sure you ain't doing harm by holding back some other things we ought to know."

The boy shook his head. "No, sir, I'm not holding back anything."

"You don't know anything about that knife and chain your mother give us?"

"No, sir, and I didn't know a thing about it till after she had given it to you."

"How is she?" I asked.

"Oh, she's all right, I think, though she said she was going to stay in bed today."

Guild narrowed his eyes. "What's the matter with her?"

"Hysteria," I told him. "She and the daughter had a row last night and she blew up."

"A row about what?"

"God knows—one of those feminine brain-storms."

Guild said, "Hm-m-m," and scratched his chin.

"Was Flint right in saying you didn't get a chance to hunt for your paper?" I asked the boy.

"Yes. I hadn't even had time to shut the door when he ran at me."

"They're grand detectives I got working for me," Guild growled. "Didn't he yell, 'Boo!' when he jumped out at you? Never mind. Well, son, I can do one of two things, and the which depends on you. I can hold you for a while or I can let you go in exchange for a promise that you'll let me know as soon as your father gets in touch with you and let me know what he tells you and where he wants you to meet him, if any."

I spoke before Gilbert could speak: "You can't ask that of him, Guild. It's his own father."

"I can't, huh?" He scowled at me. "Ain't it for his father's good if he's innocent?"

I said nothing.

Guild's face cleared slowly. "All right, then, son, suppose I put you on a kind of parole. If your father or anybody else asks you to do anything, will you promise to tell them you can't because you give me your word of honor you wouldn't?"

The boy looked at me.

I said: "That sounds reasonable."

Gilbert said: "Yes, sir, I'll give you my word."

Guild made a large gesture with one hand. "Oke. Run along."

The boy stood up saying: "Thank you very much, sir." He turned to me. "Are you going to be—"

"Wait for me outside," I told him, "if you're not in a hurry."

"I will. Good-by, Lieutenant Guild, and thank you." He went out.

Guild grabbed his telephone and ordered *The Grand Manner* and its contents found and brought to him. That done, he clasped his hands behind his head and rocked back in his chair. "So what?"

"It's anybody's guess," I said.

"Look here, you don't still think Wynant didn't do it?"

"What difference does it make what I think? You've got plenty on him now with what Mimi gave you."

"It makes a lot of difference," he assured me. "I'd like a lot to know what you think and why."

"My wife thinks he's trying to cover up somebody else."

"Is that so? Hm-m-m. I was never one to belittle women's intuition and, if you don't mind me saying so, Mrs. Charles is a mighty smart woman. Who does she think it is?"

"She hadn't decided, the last I heard."

He sighed. "Well, maybe that paper he sent the kid for will tell us something."

But the paper told us nothing that afternoon: Guild's men could not find it, could not find a copy of *The Grand Manner* in the dead woman's rooms.

29

GUILD had red-haired Flint in again and put the thumbscrews on him. The red-haired man sweat away ten pounds, but he stuck to it that Gilbert had had no opportunity to disturb anything in the apartment and throughout Flint's guardianship nobody hadn't touched nothing. He did not remember having seen a book called *The Grand Manner*, but he was not a man you would expect to memorize book titles. He tried to be helpful and made idiotic suggestions until Guild chased him out.

"The kid's probably waiting for me outside," I said, "if you think talking to him again will do any good."

"Do you?"

"No."

"Well, then. But, by God, somebody took that book and I'm going to—"

"Why?" I asked.

"Why what?"

"Why'd it have to be there for somebody to take?"

Guild scratched his chin. "Just what do you mean by that?"

"He didn't meet Macaulay at the Plaza the day of the murder, he didn't commit suicide in Allentown, he says he only got a thousand from Julia Wolf when we thought he was getting five thousand, he says they were just friends when we think they were lovers, he disappoints us too much for me to have much confidence in what he says."

"It's a fact," Guild said, "that I'd understand it better if he'd either come in or run away. Him hanging around like this, just messing things up, don't fit in anywheres that I can see."

"Are you watching his shop?"

"We're kind of keeping an eye on it. Why?"

"I don't know," I said truthfully, "except that he's pointed his finger at a lot of things that got us nowhere. Maybe we ought to pay some attention to the things he hasn't pointed at, and the shop's one of them."

Guild said: "Hm-m-m."

I said, "I'll leave you with that bright thought," and put on my hat and coat. "Suppose I wanted to get hold of you late at night, how would I reach you?"

He gave me his telephone number, we shook hands, and I left.

Gilbert Wynant was waiting for me in the corridor. Neither of us said anything until we were in a taxicab. Then he asked: "He thinks I was telling the truth, doesn't he?"

"Sure. Weren't you?"

"Oh, yes, but people don't always believe you. You won't say anything to Mamma about this, will you?"

"Not if you don't want me to."

"Thank you," he said. "In your opinion, is there more opportunity for a young man out West than here in the East?"

I thought of him working on Guild's fox farm while I replied: "Not now. Thinking of going west?"

"I don't know. I want to do something." He fidgeted with his necktie. "You'll think it's a funny question: is there much incest?"

"There's some," I told him; "that's why they've got a name for it." His face flushed.

I said: "I'm not making fun of you. It's one of the things nobody knows. There's no way of finding out."

We had a couple of blocks of silence after that. Then he said: "There's another funny question I'd like to ask you: what do you think of me?" He was more self-conscious about it than Alice Quinn had been.

"You're all right," I told him, "and you're all wrong."

He looked away, out the window. "I'm so awfully young."

We had some more silence. Then he coughed and a little blood trickled from one corner of his mouth.

"That guy did hurt you," I said.

He nodded shamefacedly and put his handkerchief to his mouth. "I'm not very strong."

At the Courtland he would not let me help him out of the taxicab and he insisted he could manage alone, but I went upstairs with him, suspecting that otherwise he would say nothing to anybody about his condition.

I rang the apartment bell before he could get his key out, and Mimi opened the door. She goggled at his black eye.

I said: "He's hurt. Get him to bed and get him a doctor."

"What happened?"

"Wynant sent him into something."

"Into what?"

"Never mind that until we get him fixed up."

"But Clyde was here," she said. "That's why I phoned you."

"What?"

"He was." She nodded vigorously. "And he asked where Gil was. He was here for an hour or more. He hasn't been gone ten minutes."

"All right, let's get him to bed."

Gilbert stubbornly insisted that he needed no help, so I left him in the bedroom with his mother and went out to the telephone.

"Any calls?" I asked Nora when I had her on the line.

"Yes, sir. Messrs. Macaulay and Guild want you to phone them, and Mesdames Jorgensen and Quinn want you to phone them. No children so far."

"When did Guild call?"

"About five minutes ago. Mind eating alone? Larry asked me to go see the new Osgood Perkins show with him."

"Go ahead. See you later."

I called up Herbert Macaulay.

"The date's off," he told me. "I heard from our friend and he's up to God knows what. Listen, Charles, I'm going to the police. I've had enough of it."

"I guess there's nothing else to do now," I said. "I was thinking about telephoning some policemen myself. I'm at Mimi's. He was here a few minutes ago. I just missed him."

"What was he doing there?"

"I'm going to try to find out now."

"Were you serious about phoning the police?"

"Sure."

"Then suppose you do that and I'll come on over."

"Right. Be seeing you."

I called up Guild.

"A little news came in right after you left," he said. "Are you where I can give it to you?"

"I'm at Mrs. Jorgensen's. I had to bring the kid home. That red-head lad of yours has got him bleeding somewhere inside."

"I'll kill that mugg," he snarled. "Then I better not talk."

"I've got some news, too. Wynant was here for about an hour this afternoon, according to Mrs. Jorgensen, and left only a few minutes before I got here."

There was a moment of silence, then he said: "Hold everything. I'll be right up."

Mimi came into the living-room while I was looking up the Quinns' telephone number. "Do you think he's seriously hurt?" she asked.

"I don't know, but you ought to get your doctor right away." I pushed the telephone towards her. When she was through with it, I said: "I told the police Wynant had been here."

She nodded. "That's what I phoned you for, to ask if I ought to tell them."

"I phoned Macaulay, too. He's coming over."

"He can't do anything," she said indignantly. "Clyde gave them to me of his own free will—they're mine."

"What's yours?"

"Those bonds, the money."

"What bonds? what money?"

She went to the table and pulled the drawer out. "See?"

Inside were three packages of bonds held together by thick rubber bands. Across the top of them lay a pink check on the Park Avenue Trust Company to the order of Mimi Jorgensen for ten thousand dollars, signed Clyde Miller Wynant, and dated January 3, 1933.

"Dated five days ahead," I said. "What kind of nonsense is that?"

"He said he hadn't that much in his account and might not be able to make a deposit for a couple of days."

"There's going to be hell about this," I warned her. "I hope you're ready for it."

"I don't see why," she protested. "I don't see why my husband—my former husband—can't provide for me and his children if he wants to."

"Cut it out. What'd you sell him?"

"Sell him?"

"Uh-huh. What'd you promise to do in the next few days or he fixes it so the check's no good?"

She made an impatient face. "Really, Nick, I think you're a half-wit sometimes with your silly suspicions."

"I'm studying to be one. Three more lessons and I get my diploma. But remember I warned you yesterday that you'll probably wind up in—"

"Stop it," she cried. She put a hand over my mouth. "Do you have to keep saying that? You know it terrifies me and—" Her voice became soft and wheedling. "You must know what I'm going through these days, Nick. Can't you be a little kinder?"

"Don't worry about me," I said. "Worry about the police." I went back to the telephone and called up Alice Quinn. "This is Nick. Nora said you—"

"Yes. Have you seen Harrison?"

"Not since I left him with you."

"Well, if you do, you won't say anything about what I said last night, will you? I didn't mean it, really I didn't mean a word of it."

"I didn't think you did," I assured her, "and I wouldn't say anything about it anyway. How's he feeling today?"

"He's gone," she said.

"What?"

"He's gone. He's left me."

"He's done that before. He'll be back."

"I know, but I'm afraid this time. He didn't go to his office. I hope he's just drunk somewhere and—but this time I'm afraid. Nick, do you think he's really in love with that girl?"

"He seems to think he is."

"Did he tell you he was?"

"That wouldn't mean anything."

"Do you think it would do any good to have a talk with her?"

"No."

"Why don't you? Do you think she's in love with him?"

"No."

"What's the matter with you?" she asked irritably.

"No, I'm not home."

"What? Oh, you mean you're some place where you can't talk?"

"That's it."

"Are you—are you at her house?"

"Yes."

"Is she there?"

"No."

"Do you think she's with him?"

"I don't know. I don't think so."

"Will you call me when you can talk, or, better still, will you come up to see me?"

"Sure," I promised, and we hung up.

Mimi was looking at me with amusement in her blue eyes. "Somebody's taking my brat's affairs seriously?" When I did not answer her, she laughed and asked: "Is Dorry still being the maiden in distress?"

"I suppose so."

"She will be, too, as long as she can get anybody to believe in it. And you, of all people, to be fooled, you who are afraid to believe that —well—that I, for instance, am ever telling the truth."

"That's a thought," I said. The doorbell rang before I could go on.

Mimi let the doctor in—he was a roly-poly elderly man with a stoop and a waddle—and took him in to Gilbert.

I opened the table-drawer again and looked at the bonds, Postal Telegraph & Cable 5s, Sao Paulo City 6½s, American Type Founders 6s, Certain-teed Products 5½s, Upper Austria 6½s, United Drugs 5s, Philippine Railway 4s, Tokio Electric Lighting 6s, about sixty thousand dollars at face value, I judged, and—guessing—between a quarter and a third of that at the market.

When the doorbell rang I shut the drawer and let Macaulay in.

He looked tired. He sat down without taking off his overcoat and said: "Well, tell me the worst. What was he up to here?"

"I don't know yet, except that he gave Mimi some bonds and a check."

"I know that." He fumbled in his pocket and gave me a letter:

Dear Herbert:

I am today giving Mrs. Mimi Jorgensen the securities listed below and a ten thousand dollar check on the Park Ave. Trust dated Jan. 3. Please arrange to have sufficient money there on that date to cover it. I would suggest that you sell some more of the public utility bonds, but use your own judgment. I find that I cannot spend any more time in New York at present and probably will not be able to get back here for several months, but will communicate with you from time to time. I am sorry I will not be able to wait over to see you and Charles tonight.

Yours truly,
Clyde Miller Wynant

Under the sprawling signature was a list of the bonds.

"How'd it come to you?" I asked.

"By messenger. What do you suppose he was paying her for?"

I shook my head. "I tried to find out. She said he was 'providing for her and his children.'"

"That's likely, as likely as that she'd tell the truth."

"About these bonds?" I asked. "I thought you had all his property in your hands."

"I thought so too, but I didn't have these, didn't know he had them." He put his elbows on his knees, his head in his hands. "If all the things I don't know were laid end to end. . . ."

30

Mimi came in with the doctor, said, "Oh, how do you do," a little stiffly to Macaulay, and shook hands with him. "This is Doctor Grant, Mr. Macaulay, Mr. Charles."

"How's the patient?" I asked.

Doctor Grant cleared his throat and said he didn't think there was anything seriously the matter with Gilbert, effects of a beating, slight hemorrhage of course, should rest, though. He cleared his throat again and said he was happy to have met us, and Mimi showed him out.

"What happened to the boy?" Macaulay asked me.

"Wynant sent him on a wild-goose chase over to Julia's apartment and he ran into a tough copper."

Mimi returned from the door. "Has Mr. Charles told you about the bonds and the check?" she asked.

"I had a note from Mr. Wynant saying he was giving them to you," Macaulay said.

"Then there will be no—"

"Difficulty? Not that I know of."

She relaxed a little and her eyes lost some of their coldness. "I didn't see why there should be, but he"—pointing at me—"likes to frighten me."

Macaulay smiled politely. "May I ask whether Mr. Wynant said anything about his plans?"

"He said something about going away, but I don't suppose I was listening very attentively. I don't remember whether he told me when he was going or where."

I grunted to show skepticism; Macaulay pretended he believed her. "Did he say anything that you could repeat to me about Julia Wolf, or about his difficulties, or about anything connected with the murder and all?" he asked.

She shook her head emphatically. "Not a word I could either repeat or couldn't, not a word at all. I asked him about it, but you know how unsatisfactory he can be when he wants. I couldn't get as much as a grunt out of him about it."

I asked the question Macaulay seemed too polite to ask: "What did he talk about?"

"Nothing, really, except ourselves and the children, particularly Gil. He was very anxious to see him and waited nearly an hour, hoping he'd come home. He asked about Dorry, but didn't seem very interested."

"Did he say anything about having written Gilbert?"

"Not a word. I can repeat our whole conversation, if you want me to. I didn't know he was coming, he didn't even phone from downstairs. The doorbell just rang and when I went to the door there he was, looking a lot older than when I'd seen him last and even thinner, and I said, 'Why Clyde!' or something like that, and he said: 'Are you alone?' I told him I was and he came in. Then he—"

The doorbell rang and she went to answer it.

"What do you think of it?" Macaulay asked in a low voice.

"When I start believing Mimi," I said, "I hope I have sense enough not to admit it."

She returned from the door with Guild and Andy. Guild nodded to me and shook hands with Macaulay, then turned to Mimi and said: "Well, ma'am, I'll have to ask you to tell—"

Macaulay interrupted him: "Suppose you let me tell what I have to tell first, Lieutenant. It belongs ahead of Mrs. Jorgensen's story and—"

Guild waved a big hand at the lawyer. "Go ahead." He sat down on an end of the sofa.

Macaulay told him what he had told me that morning. When he mentioned having told it to me that morning Guild glanced bitterly at me, once, and thereafter ignored me completely. Guild did not interrupt Macaulay, who told his story clearly and concisely. Twice Mimi started to say something, but each time broke off to listen. When Macaulay had finished, he handed Guild the note about the bonds and check. "That came by messenger this afternoon."

Guild read the note very carefully and addressed Mimi: "Now then, Mrs. Jorgensen."

She told him what she had told us about Wynant's visit, elaborating the details as he patiently questioned her, but sticking to her story that he had refused to say a word about anything connected with Julia Wolf or her murder, that in giving her the bonds and check he had simply said that he wished to provide for her and the children, and that though he had said he was going away she did not know where or when. She seemed not at all disturbed by everybody's obvious disbelief. She wound up smiling, saying: "He's a sweet man in a lot of ways, but quite mad."

"You mean he's really insane, do you?" Guild asked; "not just nutty?"

"Yes."

"What makes you think that?"

"Oh, you'd have to live with him to really know how mad he is," she replied airily.

Guild seemed dissatisfied. "What kind of clothes was he wearing?"

"A brown suit and brown overcoat and hat and I think brown shoes and a white shirt and a grayish necktie with either red or reddish brown figures in it."

Guild jerked his head at Andy. "Tell 'em."

Andy went out.

Guild scratched his jaw and frowned thoughtfully. The rest of us watched him. When he stopped scratching, he looked at Mimi and Macaulay, but not at me, and asked: "Any of you know anybody that's got the initials of D. W. Q.?"

Macaulay shook his head from side to side slowly.

Mimi said: "No. Why?"

Guild looked at me now. "Well?"

"I don't know them."

"Why?" Mimi repeated.

Guild said: "Try to remember back. He'd most likely've had dealings with Wynant."

"How far back?" Macaulay asked.

"That's hard to say right now. Maybe a few months, maybe a few years. He'd be a pretty large man, big bones, big belly, and maybe lame."

Macaulay shook his head again. "I don't remember anybody like that."

"Neither do I," Mimi said, "but I'm bursting with curiosity. I wish you'd tell us what it's all about."

"Sure, I'll tell you." Guild took a cigar from his vest pocket, looked at it, and returned it to the pocket. "A dead man like that's buried under the floor of Wynant's shop."

I said: "Ah."

Mimi put both hands to her mouth and said nothing. Her eyes were round and glassy.

Macaulay, frowning, asked: "Are you sure?"

Guild sighed. "Now you know that ain't something anybody would guess at," he said wearily.

Macaulay's face flushed and he smiled sheepishly. "That was a silly question. How did you happen to find him—it?"

"Well, Mr. Charles here kept hinting that we ought to pay more attention to that shop, so, figuring that Mr. Charles here is a man that's liable to know a lot more things than he tells anybody right out, I sent some men around this morning to see what they could find. We'd give it the once over before and hadn't turned up nothing, but this time I told 'em to take the dump apart, because Mr. Charles here had said we ought to pay more attention to it. And Mr. Charles here was right." He looked at me with cool unfriendliness. "By and by they found a corner of the cement floor looking a little newer maybe than the rest and they cracked it and there was the mortal remains of Mr. D. W. Q. What do you think of that?"

Macaulay said: "I think it was a damned good guess of Charles's." He turned to me. "How did you—"

Guild interrupted him. "I don't think you ought to say that. When you call it just a guess, you ain't giving Mr. Charles here the proper credit for being as smart as he is."

Macaulay was puzzled by Guild's tone. He looked questioningly at me.

"I'm being stood in the corner for not telling Lieutenant Guild about our conversation this morning," I explained.

"There's that," Guild agreed calmly, "among other things."

Mimi laughed, and smiled apologetically at Guild when he stared at her.

"How was Mr. D. W. Q. killed?" I asked.

Guild hesitated, as if making up his mind whether to reply, then moved his big shoulders slightly and said: "I don't know yet, or how long ago. I haven't seen the remains yet, what there is of them, and the Medical Examiner wasn't through the last I heard."

"What there is of them?" Macaulay repeated.

"Uh-huh. He'd been sawed up in pieces and buried in lime or something so there wasn't much flesh left on him, according to the report I got, but his clothes had been stuck in with him rolled up in a bundle, and enough was left of the inside ones to tell us something. There was part of a cane, too, with a rubber tip. That's why we thought he might be lame, and we—" He broke off as Andy came in. "Well?"

Andy shook his head gloomily. "Nobody sees him come, nobody sees him go. What was that joke about a guy being so thin he had to stand in the same place twice to throw a shadow?"

I laughed—not at the joke—and said: "Wynant's not that thin, but he's thin enough, say as thin as the paper in that check and in those letters people have been getting."

"What's that?" Guild demanded, his face reddening, his eyes angry and suspicious.

"He's dead. He's been dead a long time except on paper. I'll give you even money they're his bones in the grave with the fat lame man's clothes."

Macaulay leaned towards me. "Are you sure of that, Charles?"

Guild snarled at me: "What are you trying to pull?"

"There's the bet if you want it. Who'd go to all that trouble with a corpse and then leave the easiest thing of all to get rid of—the clothes—untouched unless they—"

"But they weren't untouched. They—"

"Of course not. That wouldn't look right. They'd have to be partly destroyed, only enough left to tell you what they were supposed to tell. I bet the initials were plenty conspicuous."

"I don't know," Guild said with less heat. "They were on a belt buckle."

I laughed.

Mimi said angrily: "That's ridiculous, Nick. How could that be Clyde? You know he was here this afternoon. You know he—"

"Sh-h-h. It's very silly of you to play along with him," I told her. "Wynant's dead, your children are probably his heirs, that's more money than you've got over there in the drawer. What do you want to take part of the loot for when you can get it all?"

"I don't know what you mean," she said. She was very pale.

Macaulay said: "Charles thinks Wynant wasn't here this afternoon and that you were given those securities and the check by somebody else, or perhaps stole them yourself. Is that it?" he asked me.

"Practically."

"But that's ridiculous," she insisted.

"Be sensible, Mimi," I said. "Suppose Wynant was killed three months ago and his corpse disguised as somebody else. He's supposed to have gone away leaving powers of attorney with Macaulay. All right, then, the estate's completely in Macaulay's hands for ever and ever, or at least until he finishes plundering it, because you can't even—"

Macaulay stood up saying: "I don't know what you're getting at, Charles, but I'm—"

"Take it easy," Guild told him. "Let him have his say out."

"He killed Wynant and he killed Julia and he killed Nunheim," I assured Mimi. "What do you want to do? Be next on the list? You ought to know damned well that once you've come to his aid by saying you've seen Wynant alive—because that's his weak spot, being the only person up to now who claims to have seen Wynant since October—he's not going to take any chances on having you change your mind—not when it's only a matter of knocking you off with the same gun and putting the blame on Wynant. And what are you doing it for? For those few crummy bonds in the drawer, a fraction of what you get your hands on through your children if we prove Wynant's dead."

Mimi turned to Macaulay and said: "You son of a bitch."

Guild gaped at her, more surprised by that than by anything else that had been said.

Macaulay started to move. I did not wait to see what he meant to do, but slammed his chin with my left fist. The punch was all right, it landed solidly and dropped him, but I felt a burning sensation on my left side and knew I had torn the bullet-wound open.

"What do you want me to do?" I growled at Guild. "Put him in Cellophane for you?"

31

IT was nearly three in the morning when I let myself into our apartment at the Normandie. Nora, Dorothy, and Larry Crowley were in the living-room, Nora and Larry playing backgammon, Dorothy reading a newspaper.

"Did Macaulay really kill them?" Nora asked immediately.

"Yes. Did the morning papers have anything about Wynant?"

Dorothy said: "No, just about Macaulay being arrested. Why?"

"Macaulay killed him too."

Nora said, "Really?" Larry said, "I'll be damned." Dorothy began to cry. Nora looked at Dorothy in surprise.

Dorothy sobbed: "I want to go home to Mamma."

Larry said not very eagerly: ' I'll be glad to take you home if . . .''

Dorothy said she wanted to go. Nora fussed over her, but did not try to talk her out of going. Larry, trying not to look too unwilling, found his hat and coat. He and Dorothy left.

Nora shut the door behind them and leaned against it. "Explain that to me, Mr. Charalambides," she said.

I shook my head.

She sat on the sofa beside me. "Now out with it. If you skip a single word, I'll—"

"I'd have to have a drink before I could do any talking."

She cursed me and brought me a drink. "Has he confessed?"

"Why should he? You can't plead guilty of murder in the first degree. There were too many murders—and at least two of them were too obviously done in cold blood—for the District Attorney to let him plead guilty of second-degree murder. There's nothing for him to do but fight it out."

"But he did commit them?"

"Sure."

She pushed my glass down from my mouth. "Stop stalling and tell me about it."

"Well, it figures out that he and Julia had been gypping Wynant for some time. He'd dropped a lot of money in the market and he'd found out about her past—as Morelli hinted—and the pair of them teamed up on the old man. We're sicking accountants on Macaulay's books and Wynant's and shouldn't have much trouble tracing some of the loot from one to the other."

"Then you don't know positively that he was robbing Wynant?"

"Sure we know. It doesn't click any other way. The chances are Wynant was going away on a trip the 3rd of October, because he did draw five thousand dollars out of the bank in cash, but he didn't close up his shop and give up his apartment. That was done by Macaulay a few days later. Wynant was killed at Macaulay's in Scarsdale on the night of the 3rd. We know that because on the morning of the 4th, when Macaulay's cook, who slept at home, came to work, Macaulay met her at the door with some kind of trumped-up complaint and two weeks' wages and fired her on the spot, not letting her in the house to find any corpses or bloodstains."

"How did you find that out? Don't skip details."

"Ordinary routine. Naturally after we grabbed him we went to his office and house to see what we could find out—you know, where-were-you-on-the-night-of-June-6, 1894-stuff—and the present cook said she'd only been working for him since the 8th of October, and that led to that. We also found a table with a very faint trace of what we hope is human blood not quite scrubbed out. The scientific boys are making shavings of it now to see if they can soak out any results for us." (It turned out to be beef blood.)

"Then you're not sure he—"

"Stop saying that. Of course we're sure. That's the only way it clicks. Wynant had found out that Julia and Macaulay were gypping him and also thought, rightly or wrongly, that Julia and Macaulay were cheating on him—and we know he was jealous—so he went up there to confront him with whatever proof he had, and Macaulay, with prison looking him in the face, killed the old man. Now don't say we're not sure. It doesn't make any sense otherwise. Well, there he is with a corpse, one of the harder things to get rid of. Can I stop to take a swallow of whisky?"

"Just one," Nora said. "But this is just a theory, isn't it?"

"Call it any name you like. It's good enough for me."

"But I thought everybody was supposed to be considered innocent until they were proved guilty and if there was any reasonable doubt, they—"

"That's for juries, not detectives. You find the guy you think did the murder and you slam him in the can and let everybody know you think he's guilty and put his picture all over newspapers, and the District Attorney builds up the best theory he can on what information you've got and meanwhile you pick up additional details here and there, and people who recognize his picture in the paper—as well as people who'd think he was innocent if you hadn't arrested him—come in and tell you things about him and presently you've got him sitting on the electric chair." (Two days later a woman in Brooklyn identified Macaulay as a George Foley who for the past three months had been renting an apartment from her.)

"But that seems so loose."

"When murders are committed by mathematics," I said, "you can solve them by mathematics. Most of them aren't and this one wasn't. I don't want to go against your idea of what's right and wrong, but when I say he probably dissected the body so he could carry it into town in bags I'm only saying what seems most probable. That would be on the 6th of October or later, because it wasn't until then that he laid off the two mechanics Wynant had working in the shop—Prentice and McNaughton—and shut it up. So he buried Wynant under the floor, buried him with a fat man's clothes and a lame man's stick and a belt marked D. W. Q., all arranged so they wouldn't get too much of the lime—or whatever he used to eat off the dead man's features and flesh—on them, and he re-cemented the floor over the grave. Between police routine and publicity we've got more than a fair chance of finding out where he bought or otherwise got the clothes and stick and the cement." (We traced the cement to him later—he had bought it from a coal and wood dealer uptown—but had no luck with the other things.)

"I hope so," she said, not too hopefully.

"So now that's taken care of. By renewing the lease on the shop and keeping it vacant—supposedly waiting for Wynant to return—he can make sure—reasonably sure—that nobody will discover the grave, and if it is accidentally discovered, then fat Mr. D. W. Q.—by that time Wynant's bones would be pretty bare and you can't tell whether a man was thin or fat by his skeleton—was murdered by Wynant, which explains why Wynant has made himself scarce. That taken care of, Macaulay forges the power of attorney and, with Julia's help, settles down to the business of gradually transferring the late Clyde's money to themselves. Now I'm going theoretical again. Julia doesn't like murder, and she's frightened, and he's not too sure she won't weaken on him. That's why he makes her break with Morelli—giving Wynant's jealousy as an excuse. He's afraid she might confide to Morelli in a weak moment and, as the time draws near for her still closer friend, Face Peppler, to get out of prison, he gets more and more worried. He's been safe there as long as Face stayed in, because she's not likely to put anything dangerous in a letter that has to pass through the warden's hands, but now . . . Well, he starts to plan, and then all hell breaks loose. Mimi and her children arrive and start hunting for Wynant and I come to town and am in touch with them and he thinks I'm helping them. He decides to play safe on Julia by putting her out of the way. Like it so far?"

"Yes, but . . ."

"It gets worse as it goes along," I assured her. "On his way here for lunch that day he stops and phones his office, pretending he's Wynant, and making that appointment at the Plaza, the idea being to establish Wynant's presence in town. When he leaves here he goes to the Plaza and asks people if they've seen Wynant, to make that plausible, and for the same reason phones his office to ask if any further word has come from Wynant, and phones Julia. She tells him she's expecting Mimi and she tells him Mimi thought she was lying when she said she didn't know where Wynant was, and Julia probably sounds pretty frightened. So he decides he's got to beat Mimi to the interview and he does. He beats it over there and kills her. He's a terrible shot. I saw him shoot during the war. It's likely he missed her with the first shot, the one that hit the telephone, and didn't succeed in killing her right away with the other four, but he probably thought she was dead, and, anyhow, he had to get out before Mimi arrived, so he dropped the piece of Wynant's chain that he had brought along as a clincher—and his having saved that for three months makes it look as if he'd intended killing her from the beginning—and scoots over to the engineer Hermann's office, where he takes advantage of the breaks and fixes himself up with an alibi. The two things he doesn't expect—couldn't very well have foreseen—are that Nunheim, hanging around trying to get at the girl, had seen him leave her apartment —may even have heard the shots—and that Mimi, with blackmail in her heart, was going to conceal the chain for use in shaking down her ex-husband. That's why he had to go down to Philadelphia and send me that wire and the letter to himself and one to Aunt Alice later—if Mimi thinks Wynant's throwing suspicion on her she'll get mad enough to give the police the evidence she's got against him. Her desire to hurt Jorgensen nearly gummed that up, though. Macaulay, by the way, knew Jorgensen was Kelterman. Right after he killed Wynant he had detectives look Mimi and her family up in Europe—their interest in the estate made them potentially dangerous—and the detectives found out who Jorgensen was. We found the reports in Macaulay's files. He pretended he was getting the information for Wynant, of course. Then he started worrying about me, about my not thinking Wynant guilty and—"

"And why didn't you?"

"Why should he write letters antagonizing Mimi, the one who was helping him by holding back incriminating evidence? That's why I thought the chain had been planted when she did turn it in, only I was a little bit too willing to believe she had done the planting. Morelli worried Macaulay, too, because he didn't want suspicion thrown on anybody who might, in clearing themselves, throw it in the wrong direction. Mimi was all right, because she'd throw it back on Wynant, but everybody else was out. Suspicion thrown on Wynant was the one thing that was guaranteed to keep anybody from suspecting that Wynant was dead, and if Macaulay hadn't killed Wynant, then there was no reason for his having killed either of the others. The most obvious thing in the whole lay-out and the key to the whole lay-out was that Wynant had to be dead."

"You mean you thought that from the beginning?" Nora demanded, fixing me with a stern eye.

"No, darling, though I ought to be ashamed of myself for not seeing it, but once I heard there was a corpse under the floor, I wouldn't have cared if doctors swore it was a woman's, I'd have insisted it was Wynant's. It had to be. It was the one right thing."

"I guess you're awfully tired. That must be what makes you talk like this."

"Then he had Nunheim to worry about too. After pointing the finger at Morelli, just to show the police he was being useful, he went to see Macaulay. I'm guessing again, sweetheart. I had a phone-call from a man who called himself Albert Norman, and the conversation ended with a noise on his end of the wire. My guess is that Nunheim went to see Macaulay and demanded some dough to keep quiet and, when Macaulay tried to bluff him, Nunheim said he'd show him and called me up to make a date with me to see if I'd buy his information—and Macaulay grabbed the phone and gave Nunheim something, if only a promise, but when Guild and I had our little talk with Nunheim, and he ran out on us, then he phoned Macaulay and demanded real action, probably a lump sum, with a promise to beat it out of town, away from us meddling sleuths. We do know he called up that afternoon—Macaulay's telephone-operator remembers a Mr. Albert Norman calling up, and she remembers that Macaulay went out right after talking to him, so don't get snooty about this—uh—reconstruction of mine. Macaulay wasn't silly enough to think Nunheim was to be trusted even if he paid him, so he lured him down to this spot he had probably picked out ahead of time and let him have it —and that took care of that."

"Probably," Nora said.

"It's a word you've got to use a lot in this business. The letter to Gilbert was only for the purpose of showing that Wynant had a key to the girl's apartment, and sending Gilbert there was only a way of making sure that he'd fall into the hands of the police, who'd squeeze him and not let him keep the information about the letter and the key to himself. Then Mimi finally comes through with the watch-chain, but meanwhile another worry comes up. She's persuaded Guild to suspect me a little. I've an idea that when Macaulay came to me this morning with that hooey he intended to get me up to Scarsdale and knock me off, making me number three on the list of Wynant's victims. Maybe he just changed his mind, maybe he thought I was suspicious, too willing to go up there without policemen. Anyhow, Gilbert's lie about having seen Wynant gave him another idea. If he could get somebody to say they had seen Wynant and stick to it . . . Now this part we know definitely."

"Thank God."

"He went to see Mimi this afternoon—riding up two floors above hers and walking down so the elevator boys wouldn't remember having carried him to her floor—and made her a proposition. He told her there was no question about Wynant's guilt, but that it was doubtful if the police would ever catch him. Meanwhile he, Macaulay, had the whole estate in his hands. He couldn't take a chance on appropriating any of it, but he'd fix it so she could—if she would split with him. He'd give her these bonds he had in his pocket and this check, but she'd have to say that Wynant had given them to her and she'd have to send this note, which he also had, over to Macaulay as if from Wynant. He assured her that Wynant, a fugitive, could not show up to deny his gift, and, except for herself and her children, there was no one else who had any interest in the estate, any reason for questioning the deal. Mimi's not very sensible where she sees a chance to make a profit, so it was all O. K. with her, and he had what he wanted—somebody who'd seen Wynant alive. He warned her that everybody would think Wynant was paying her for some service, but if she simply denied it there would be nothing anybody could prove."

"Then what he told you this morning about Wynant instructing him to give her any amount she asked for was simply in preparation?"

"Maybe, maybe it was an earlier fumbling towards that idea. Now are you satisfied with what we've got on him?"

"Yes, in a way. There seems to be enough of it, but it's not very neat."

"It's neat enough to send him to the chair," I said, "and that's all that counts. It takes care of all the angles and I can't think of any other theory that would. Naturally it wouldn't hurt to find the pistol, and the typewriter he used for the Wynant letters, and they must be somewhere around where he can get at them when he needs them." (We found them in the Brooklyn apartment he had rented as George Foley.)

"Have it your own way," she said, "but I always thought detectives waited until they had every little detail fixed in—"

"And then wonder why the suspect's had time to get to the farthest country that has no extradition treaty."

She laughed. "All right, all right. Still want to leave for San Francisco tomorrow?"

"Not unless you're in a hurry. Let's stick around awhile. This excitement has put us behind in our drinking."

"It's all right by me. What do you think will happen to Mimi and Dorothy and Gilbert now?"

"Nothing new. They'll go on being Mimi and Dorothy and Gilbert just as you and I will go on being us and the Quinns will go on being the Quinns. Murder doesn't round out anybody's life except the murdered's and sometimes the murderer's."

"That may be," Nora said, "but it's all pretty unsatisfactory."

The text of this book is set in Electra, a typeface designed by W(illiam) A(ddison) Dwiggins for the Mergenthaler Linotype Company and first made available in 1935. Electra cannot be classified as either "modern" or "old style." It is not based on any historical model, and hence does not echo any particular period or style of type design. It avoids the extreme contrast between "thick" and "thin" elements that marks most modern faces, and is without eccentricities which catch the eye and interfere with reading. In general, Electra is a simple, readable typeface which attempts to give a feeling of fluidity, power, and speed.

W. A. Dwiggins (1880–1956) was born in Martinsville, Ohio, and studied art in Chicago. In 1904 he moved to Hingham, Massachusetts, where he built a solid reputation as a designer of advertisements and as a calligrapher. He began an association with the Mergenthaler Linotype Company in 1929, and over the next twenty-seven years designed a number of book types, of which Metro, Electra, and Caledonia have been used very widely In 1930 Dwiggins became interested in marionettes, and through the years made many important contributions to the art of puppetry and the design of marionettes.